THE EDINBURGH EDITION OF
THE WAVERLEY NOVELS

EDITOR-IN-CHIEF
Professor David Hewitt

VOLUME NINE

THE MONASTERY

EDINBURGH EDITION OF THE
WAVERLEY NOVELS

to be complete in thirty volumes

Each volume will be published separately but original conjoint publication of certain works is indicated in the EEWN volume numbering [4a, b; 7a, b, etc.]. Where EEWN editors have been appointed, their names are listed

WALTER SCOTT

THE MONASTERY

Edited by
Penny Fielding

EDINBURGH
University
Press

© The University Court of the University of Edinburgh 2000
Edinburgh University Press
22 George Square, Edinburgh

Typeset in Linotronic Ehrhardt
by Speedspools, Edinburgh
and printed and bound in Great Britain
on acid-free paper at the University Press, Cambridge

ISBN 0 7486 0574 6

A CIP record for this book is available from the British Library

FOREWORD

THE PUBLICATION of *Waverley* in 1814 marked the emergence of the modern novel in the western world. It is difficult now to recapture the impact of this and the following novels of Scott on a readership accustomed to prose fiction either as picturesque romance, 'Gothic' quaintness, or presentation of contemporary manners. For Scott not only invented the historical novel, but gave it a dimension and a relevance that made it available for a great variety of new kinds of writing. Balzac in France, Manzoni in Italy, Gogol and Tolstoy in Russia, were among the many writers of fiction influenced by the man Stendhal called 'notre père, Walter Scott'.

What Scott did was to show history and society in motion: old ways of life being challenged by new; traditions being assailed by counter-statements; loyalties, habits, prejudices clashing with the needs of new social and economic developments. The attraction of tradition and its ability to arouse passionate defence, and simultaneously the challenge of progress and 'improvement', produce a pattern that Scott saw as the living fabric of history. And this history was rooted in *place*; events happened in localities still recognisable after the disappearance of the original actors and the establishment of new patterns of belief and behaviour.

Scott explored and presented all this by means of stories, entertainments, which were read and enjoyed as such. At the same time his passionate interest in history led him increasingly to see these stories as illustrations of historical truths, so that when he produced his final *Magnum Opus* edition of the novels he surrounded them with historical notes and illustrations, and in this almost suffocating guise they have been reprinted in edition after edition ever since. The time has now come to restore these novels to the form in which they were presented to their first readers, so that today's readers can once again capture their original power and freshness. At the same time, serious errors of transcription, omission, and interpretation, resulting from the haste of their transmission from manuscript to print can now be corrected.

DAVID DAICHES

EDINBURGH
University
Press

CONTENTS

ACKNOWLEDGEMENTS

The Scott Advisory Board and the editors of the Edinburgh Edition of the Waverley Novels wish to express their gratitude to The University Court of the University of Edinburgh *for its vision in initiating and supporting the preparation of the first critical edition of Walter Scott's fiction. Those Universities which employ the editors have also contributed greatly in paying the editors' salaries, and awarding research leave and grants for travel and materials. In the case of* The Monastery *particular thanks are due to the* Universities of Aberdeen *and* Edinburgh.

Although the edition is the work of scholars employed by universities, the project could not have prospered without the help of the sponsors cited below. Their generosity has met the direct costs of the initial research and of the preparation of the text of the novels appearing in this edition.

BANK OF SCOTLAND
The collapse of the great Edinburgh publisher Archibald Constable in January 1826 entailed the ruin of Sir Walter Scott who found himself responsible for his own private debts, for the debts of the printing business of James Ballantyne and Co. in which he was co-partner, and for the bank advances to Archibald Constable which had been guaranteed by the printing business. Scott's largest creditors were Sir William Forbes and Co., bankers, and the Bank of Scotland. On the advice of Sir William Forbes himself, the creditors did not sequester his property, but agreed to the creation of a trust to which he committed his future literary earnings, and which ultimately repaid the debts of over £120,000 for which he was legally liable.

In the same year the Government proposed to curtail the rights of the Scottish banks to issue their own notes; Scott wrote the 'Letters of Malachi Malagrowther' in their defence, arguing that the measure was neither in the interests of the banks nor of Scotland. The 'Letters' were so successful that the Government was forced to withdraw its proposal and to this day the Scottish Banks issue their own notes.

A portrait of Sir Walter appears on all current bank notes of the Bank of Scotland because Scott was a champion of Scottish banking, and because he was an illustrious and honourable customer not just of the Bank of Scotland itself, but also of three other banks now incorporated within it—the British Linen Bank which continues today as the merchant banking arm of the Bank of Scotland, Sir William Forbes and Co., and Ramsays, Bonars and Company.

Bank of Scotland's *support of the EEWN continues its long and fruitful involvement with the affairs of Walter Scott.*

THE BRITISH ACADEMY AND THE ARTS AND HUMANITIES RESEARCH BOARD

Major research grants have been awarded by the British Academy, the Humanities Research Board, and the Arts and Humanities Research Board, and have been used to employ a research fellow to work full-time on the EEWN. This help is acknowledged with great gratitude; it has assured the process of establishing reliable texts, and facilitated the rapid progress of the edition.

OTHER BENEFACTORS

The Advisory Board and editors also wish to acknowledge with gratitude the generous grants, gifts and assistance to the EEWN from the P. F. Charitable Trust, the main charitable trust of the Fleming family which founded the City firm of Robert Fleming Holdings Limited; *the Edinburgh University General Council Trust, now incorporated within the* Edinburgh University Development Trust, *and the alumni who contributed to the Trust;* Sir Gerald Elliott; *the* Carnegie Trust for the Universities of Scotland; *and particularly the* Robertson Trust *whose help has been especially important in the production of this volume.*

LIBRARIES

Without the generous assistance of the two great repositories of Scott manuscripts, the National Library of Scotland *and the* Pierpont Morgan Library, *New York, it would not have been possible to have undertaken the editing of Scott's novels, and the Board and editors cannot overstate the extent to which they are indebted to their Trustees and staffs.*

THE MONASTERY

A project such as this is necessarily collaborative in many ways, and many institutions and individuals have helped to make this volume possible. The manuscript of The Monastery *belongs to the Pierpont Morgan Library which generously lent it to the National Library of Scotland for the duration of the editing process. Staff at the National Library of Scotland helped in providing access to books during a difficult period of renovation, and assisted the preparation of this edition in many ways. Particular thanks are due to Frances Abercromby who secured copies and microfilms of early editions. Microfilms of American editions were supplied by the Beinecke Library, Brown University Library, and the library of Hobart and William Smith Colleges, Queensland. Dan Blewett, librarian at the Loyola University of Chicago, very kindly permitted an interlibrary loan of a rare early edition.*

David Hewitt made valuable comments on all aspects of the edition, and Christopher Johnson, editor of The Abbot *in the EEWN, generously shared his editorial discoveries as the two editions progressed. Alistair Rennie's help with a number of tasks made preparation of the typescript much easier. Many people answered questions and sent information and I would like to thank Ian*

Duncan, Michael Dobson, Aileen Douglas, Susanne Kries, Magarette Lincoln, Jane Millgate, and Ian Ross. Special thanks are due to Graham Tulloch who patiently addressed queries both directly, and through his EEWN edition of Ivanhoe from which I learned much. The EEWN's special subject advisers were of great help and much information was found by John Cairns (Law), Thomas Craik (Shakespeare), Caroline Jackson-Houlston (Popular Song), David Stevenson (History), and Roy Pinkerton (Classics). Ann Jones, archivist at Heriot-Watt University Library, produced a treasury of information about James Watt. Mark Dilworth contributed invaluable information about Benedictine Monasticism, and Edith Philip, librarian at the Scottish United Services Museum, supplied military details. My colleagues in the University of Edinburgh deftly fielded questions from all directions, and I thank Ronnie Jack, Roger Savage, and Karina Williamson for their help with specific queries. The reliability of the text is due in no small way to the work of proofreaders, and to Ian Clark, Gillian Hughes, and Sheena Sutherland the editor expresses her thanks, as well as to Audrey Inglis, and Harry McIntosh who were responsible for the production of the text.

Two people have above all made this volume possible, and I would like to extend my warmest thanks to them. It has been a great privilege and a pleasure to work with J. H. Alexander whose extensive knowledge of Scott editing and whose considerable and precise help with all aspects of the edition have enriched this volume enormously. Alison Lumsden undertook a number of the collations. provided a meticulous glossary, and tracked down many recalcitrant notes. Her friendship and support, together with her many skills and scholarly acumen, kept this volume going and saw it through to its end.

The general editor for this volume was J. H. Alexander. The glossary was prepared by Alison Lumsden.

GENERAL INTRODUCTION

What has the Edinburgh Edition of the Waverley Novels achieved? The original version of this General Introduction said that many hundreds of readings were being recovered from the manuscripts, and commented that although the individual differences were often minor, they were 'cumulatively telling'. Such an assessment now looks tentative and tepid, for the textual strategy pursued by the editors has been justified by spectacular results.

In each novel up to 2000 readings never before printed are being recovered from the manuscripts. Some of these are major changes although they are not always verbally extensive. The restoration of the pen-portraits of the Edinburgh literati in *Guy Mannering*, the reconstruction of the way in which Amy Robsart was murdered in *Kenilworth*, the recovery of the description of Clara Mowbray's previous relationship with Tyrrel in *Saint Ronan's Well*—each of these fills out what was incomplete, or corrects what was obscure. A surprising amount of what was once thought loose or unidiomatic has turned out to be textual corruption. Many words which were changed as the holograph texts were converted into print have been recognised as dialectal, period or technical terms wholly appropriate to their literary context. The mistakes in foreign languages, in Latin, and in Gaelic found in the early printed texts are usually not in the manuscripts, and so clear is this manuscript evidence that one may safely conclude that Friar Tuck's Latin in *Ivanhoe* is deliberately full of errors. The restoration of Scott's own shaping and punctuating of speech has often enhanced the rhetorical effectiveness of dialogue. Furthermore, the detailed examination of the text and supporting documents such as notes and letters has revealed that however quickly his novels were penned they mostly evolved over long periods; that although he claimed not to plan his work yet the shape of his narratives seems to have been established before he committed his ideas to paper; and that each of the novels edited to date has a precise time-scheme which implies formidable control of his stories. The Historical and Explanatory Notes reveal an intellectual command of enormously diverse materials, and an equal imaginative capacity to synthesise them. Editing the texts has revolutionised the editors' understanding and appreciation of Scott, and will ultimately generate a much wider recognition of his quite extraordinary achievement.

The text of the novels in the Edinburgh Edition is normally based on the first editions, but incorporates all those manuscript readings which were lost through accident, error, or misunderstanding in the process of converting holograph manuscripts into printed books. The Edition is the first to investigate all Scott's manuscripts and proofs, and all the printed editions to have appeared in his lifetime, and it has adopted the textual strategy which best makes sense of the textual problems.

It is clear from the systematic investigation of all the different states of Scott's texts that the author was fully engaged only in the early stages (manuscripts and proofs, culminating in the first edition), and when preparing the last edition to be published in his lifetime, familiarly known as the Magnum Opus (1829–33). There may be authorial readings in some of the many intermediate editions, and there certainly are in the third edition of *Waverley*, but not a single intermediate edition of any of the nineteen novels so far investigated shows evidence of sustained authorial involvement. There are thus only two stages in the textual development of the Waverley Novels which might provide a sound basis for a critical edition.

Scott's holograph manuscripts constitute the only purely authorial state of the texts of his novels, for they alone proceed wholly from the author. They are for the most part remarkably coherent, although a close examination shows countless minor revisions made in the process of writing, and usually at least one layer of later revising. But the heaviest revising was usually done by Scott when correcting his proofs, and thus the manuscripts could not constitute the textual basis of a new edition; despite their coherence they are drafts. Furthermore, the holograph does not constitute a public form of the text: Scott's manuscript punctuation is light (in later novels there are only dashes, full-stops, and speech marks), and his spelling system though generally consistent is personal and idiosyncratic.

Scott's novels were, in theory, anonymous publications—no title page ever carried his name. To maintain the pretence of secrecy, the original manuscripts were copied so that his handwriting should not be seen in the printing house, a practice which prevailed until 1827, when Scott acknowledged his authorship. Until 1827 it was these copies, not Scott's original manuscripts, which were used by the printers. Not a single leaf of these copies is known to survive but the copyists probably began the tidying and regularising. As with Dickens and Thackeray in a later era, copy was sent to the printers in batches, as Scott wrote and as it was transcribed; the batches were set in type, proof-read, and ultimately printed, while later parts of the novel were still being written. When typesetting, the compositors did not just follow what was before them, but supplied punctuation, normalised spelling, and corrected minor errors. Proofs were first read in-house against the transcripts, and, in addition to the normal checking for mistakes, these proofs were used to improve the punctuation and the spelling.

When the initial corrections had been made, a new set of proofs went to James Ballantyne, Scott's friend and partner in the printing firm which bore his name. He acted as editor, not just as proof-reader. He drew Scott's attention to gaps in the text and pointed out inconsistencies in detail; he asked Scott to standardise names; he substituted nouns for pronouns when they occurred in the first sentence of a paragraph, and inserted the names of speakers in dialogue; he changed incorrect punctuation, and added punctuation he thought desirable; he corrected grammatical errors; he removed close verbal repetitions; and in a cryptic correspondence in the margins of the proofs he told Scott when he could not follow what was happening, or when he particularly enjoyed something.

These annotated proofs were sent to the author. Scott usually accepted Ballantyne's suggestions, but sometimes rejected them. He made many more changes; he cut out redundant words, and substituted the vivid for the pedestrian; he refined the punctuation; he sometimes reworked and revised passages extensively, and in so doing made the proofs a stage in the creative composition of the novels.

When Ballantyne received Scott's corrections and revisions, he transcribed all the changes on to a clean set of proofs so that the author's hand would not be seen by the compositors. Further revises were prepared. Some of these were seen and read by Scott, but he usually seems to have trusted Ballantyne to make sure that the earlier corrections and revisions had been executed. When doing this Ballantyne did not just read for typesetting errors, but continued the process of punctuating and tidying the text. A final proof allowed the corrections to be inspected and the imposition of the type to be checked prior to printing.

Scott expected his novels to be printed; he expected that the printers would correct minor errors, would remove words repeated in close proximity to each other, would normalise spelling, and would insert a printed-book style of punctuation, amplifying or replacing the marks he had provided in manuscript. There are no written instructions to the printers to this effect, but in the proofs he was sent he saw what Ballantyne and his staff had done and were doing, and by and large he accepted it. This assumption of authorial approval is better founded for Scott than for any other writer, for Scott was the dominant partner in the business which printed his work, and no doubt could have changed the practices of his printers had he so desired.

It is this history of the initial creation of Scott's novels that led the editors of the Edinburgh Edition to propose the first editions as base texts. That such a textual policy has been persuasively theorised by Jerome J. McGann in his *A Critique of Modern Textual Criticism* (1983) is a bonus: he argues that an authoritative work is usually found not in the artist's manuscript, but in the printed book, and that there is a collective responsibility in converting an author's manuscript into print, exercised by author, printer and publisher, and governed by the nature of the understanding between the author and the other parties. In Scott's case the exercise of such a collective responsibility produced the first editions of the Waverley Novels. On the whole Scott's printers fulfilled his expectations. There are normally in excess of 50,000 variants in the first edition of a three-volume novel when compared with the manuscript, and the great majority are in accordance with Scott's general wishes as described above.

But the intermediaries, as the copyist, compositors, proof-readers, and James Ballantyne are collectively described, made mistakes; from time to time they misread the manuscripts, and they did not always understand what Scott had written. This would not have mattered had there not also been procedural failures: the transcripts were not thoroughly checked against the original manuscripts; Scott himself does not seem to have read the proofs against the manuscripts and thus did not notice transcription errors which made sense in their context; Ballantyne continued his editing in post-authorial proofs. Furthermore, it has become increasingly evident that, although in theory Scott as partner in the printing firm could get what he wanted, he also succumbed to the pressure of printer and publisher. He often had to accept mistakes both in names and the spelling of names because they were enshrined in print before he realised what had happened. He was obliged to accept the movement of chapters between volumes, or the deletion or addition of material, in the interests of equalising the size of volumes. His work was subject to bowdlerisation, and to a persistent attempt to have him show a 'high example' even in the words put in the mouths of his characters; he regularly objected, but conformed nonetheless. From time to time he inserted, under protest, explanations of what was happening in the narrative because the literal-minded Ballantyne required them.

The editors of modern texts have a basic working assumption that what is written by the author is more valuable than what is generated by compositors and proof-readers. Even McGann accepts such a position, and argues that while the changes made in the course of translating the manuscript text into print are a feature of the acceptable 'socialisation' of the authorial text, they have authority only to the extent that they fulfil the author's expectations about the public form of the text. The editors of the Edinburgh Edition normally choose the first edition of a novel as base-text, for the first edition usually represents the culmination of the initial creative process, and usually seems closest to the form of his work Scott wished his public to have. But they also recognise the failings of the first editions, and thus after the careful collation of all pre-publication materials, and in the light of their investigation into the factors governing the writing and printing of the Waverley Novels, they incorporate into the base-text those manuscript readings which were lost in the production process through accident, error, misunderstanding, or a misguided attempt to 'improve'. In certain cases they also introduce into the base-texts revisions found in editions published almost immediately after the first, which they believe to be Scott's, or which complete the intermediaries' preparation of the text. In addition, the editors correct various kinds of error, such as typographical and copy-editing mistakes including the misnumbering of chapters, inconsistencies in the naming of characters, egregious errors of fact that are not part of the fiction, and failures of sense which a simple emendation can restore. In doing all this the editors follow the model for editing the Waverley Novels which was provided by Claire Lamont in her edition of *Waverley* (Oxford, 1981): her base-text is the first edition emended in the light of the manuscript. But they have also developed that model because working on the Waverley Novels as a whole has greatly increased knowledge of the practices and procedures followed by Scott, his printers and his publishers in translating holograph manuscripts into printed books. The result is an 'ideal' text, such as his first readers might have read had the production process been less pressurised and more considered.

The Magnum Opus could have provided an alternative basis for a new edition. In the Advertisement to the Magnum Scott wrote that his insolvency in 1826 and the public admission of authorship in 1827 restored to him 'a sort of parental control', which enabled him to re-issue his novels 'in a corrected and . . . an improved form'. His assertion of authority in word and deed gives the Magnum a status which no editor can ignore. His introductions are fascinating autobiographical essays which write the life of the Author of Waverley. In addition, the Magnum has a considerable significance in the history of culture. This was the first time all Scott's works of fiction had been gathered together, published in a single uniform edition, and given an official general title, in the process converting diverse narratives into a literary monument, the Waverley Novels.

There were, however, two objections to the use of the Magnum as the base-text for the new edition. Firstly, this has been the form of Scott's work which has been generally available for most of the nineteenth and twentieth centuries; a Magnum-based text is readily accessible to any-one who wishes to read it. Secondly, a proper recognition of the Mag-num does not extend to approving its text. When Scott corrected his novels for the Magnum, he marked up printed books (specially pre-pared by the binder with interleaves, hence the title the 'Interleaved Set'), but did not perceive the extent to which these had slipped from the text of the first editions. He had no means of recognising that, for example, over 2000 differences had accumulated between the first edi-tion of *Guy Mannering* and the text which he corrected, in the 1822 octavo edition of the *Novels and Tales of the Author of Waverley*. The printed text of *Redgauntlet* which he corrected, in the octavo *Tales and Romances of the Author of Waverley* (1827), has about 900 divergences from the first edition, none of which was authorially sanctioned. He himself made about 750 corrections to the text of *Guy Mannering* and

200 to *Redgauntlet* in the Interleaved Set, but those who assisted in the production of the Magnum were probably responsible for a further 1600 changes to *Guy Mannering*, and 1200 to *Redgauntlet*. Scott marked up a corrupt text, and his assistants generated a systematically cleaned-up version of the Waverley Novels.

The Magnum constitutes the author's final version of his novels and thus has its own value, and as the version read by the great Victorians has its own significance and influence. To produce a new edition based on the Magnum would be an entirely legitimate project, but for the reasons given above the Edinburgh editors have chosen the other valid option. What is certain, however, is that any compromise edition, that drew upon both the first and the last editions published in Scott's lifetime, would be a mistake. In the past editors, following the example of W. W. Greg and Fredson Bowers, would have incorporated into the first-edition text the introductions, notes, revisions and corrections Scott wrote for the Magnum Opus. This would no longer be considered acceptable editorial practice, as it would confound versions of the text produced at different stages of the author's career. To fuse the two would be to confuse them. Instead, Scott's own material in the Interleaved Set is so interesting and important that it will be published separately, and in full, in the two parts of Volume 25 of the Edinburgh Edition. For the first time in print the new matter written by Scott for the Magnum Opus will be wholly visible.

The Edinburgh Edition of the Waverley Novels aims to provide the first reliable text of Scott's fiction. It aims to recover the lost Scott, the Scott which was misunderstood as the printers struggled to set and print novels at high speed in often difficult circumstances. It aims in the Historical and Explanatory Notes and in the Glossaries to illuminate the extraordinary range of materials that Scott weaves together in creating his stories. All engaged in fulfilling these aims have found their enquiries fundamentally changing their appreciation of Scott. They hope that readers will continue to be equally excited and astonished, and to have their understanding of these remarkable novels transformed by reading them in their new guise.

DAVID HEWITT
January 1999

THE

MONASTERY.

A ROMANCE.

BY THE AUTHOR OF " WAVERLEY."

═══

IN THREE VOLUMES.

VOL. I.

═══

EDINBURGH:

PRINTED FOR LONGMAN, HURST, REES, ORME, AND BROWN,
LONDON;
AND FOR ARCHIBALD CONSTABLE AND CO.,
AND JOHN BALLANTYNE, BOOKSELLER TO THE KING,
EDINBURGH.

───

1820.

INTRODUCTORY EPISTLE

FROM

CAPTAIN CLUTTERBUCK,

OF HIS MAJESTY'S —— REGIMENT OF INFANTRY,

TO

THE AUTHOR OF "WAVERLEY."

SIR,

ALTHOUGH I DO NOT PRETEND to the pleasure of your personal acquaintance, like many who I believe to be equally strangers to you, I am nevertheless interested in your publications, and desire their continuance. Not that I pretend to much taste in fictitious composition, or that I am apt to be interested in your grave scenes, or amused by those which are meant to be lively. I will not disguise from you, that I have yawned over the last interview of MacIvor and his sister, and fell fairly asleep while the school-master was reading the humours of Dandie Dinmont. You see, sir, that I scorn to solicit your favour in a way to which you are no stranger. If the papers I enclose you are worth nothing, I will not endeavour to recommend them by personal flattery, as a bad cook pours rancid butter upon her stale fish. No, sir! What I respect in you, is the lights you have occasionally thrown on national antiquities, a study which I have commenced rather late in life, but to which I am attached with the devotion of a first love, because it is the only study I ever cared a farthing for.

You shall have my history, sir, (it will not reach to three volumes,) before that of my manuscript; and as you usually throw out a few lines of verse (by way of skirmishers, I suppose,) at the head of each division of prose, I have had the luck to light upon a stanza in the schoolmaster's copy of Burns which describes me exactly. I love it the better, because it was originally designed for Captain Grose, an excellent antiquary, though, like yourself, somewhat too apt to treat with levity his own pursuits:

> 'Tis said he was a soldier bred,
> And ane wad rather fa'an than fled;
> But now he has quit the spurtle blade,

3

And dog-skin wallet,
And ta'en the—antiquarian trade,
I think they call it.

I never could conceive what influenced me, when a boy, in the choice of a profession. Military zeal and ardour it was not, which made me stand out for a commission in the Scots Fuzileers, when my tutors and curators wished to bind me apprentice to old David Stiles, Clerk to his Majesty's Signet. I say, military zeal it was *not*; for I was no fighting boy in my own person, and cared not a penny to read the history of the heroes who turned the world upside down in former ages. As for courage, I had, as I have since discovered, just as much of it as served my turn, and not one grain of surplus. I soon found out, indeed, that in action there was more danger in running away than in standing; and besides, I could not afford to lose my commission, which was my chief means of support. But, as for that over-boiling valour, which I have heard many of *Ours* talk of, though I seldom observed that it influenced them in the actual affair—that exuberant zeal, which courts Danger as a bride, truly my courage was of a complexion much less ecstatical.

Again, the love of a red coat, which, in default of all other aptitudes to the profession, has made many a bad soldier and some good ones, was an utter stranger to my disposition. I cared not a "bodle" for the company of the misses: Nay, though there was a boarding-school in the village, and though we used to meet with its fair inmates at Simon Lightfoot's Weekly Practising, I cannot recollect any strong emotions being excited on these occasions, excepting the infinite regret with which I went through the polite ceremonial of presenting my partner with an orange, thrust into my pocket by my aunt for this special purpose, but which, had I dared, I would certainly have secreted for my own use. As for personal vanity, or love of finery for itself, I was such a stranger to it, that the difficulty was great to make me brush my coat, and appear in proper trim upon parade. I shall never forget the rebuke of my old Colonel, on a morning when the King reviewed a brigade of which we made part. "I am no friend to extravagance, Ensign Clutterbuck," said he; "but, on the day when we are to pass before the Sovereign of the Kingdom, in the name of God I would have at least shewn him an inch of clean linen."

Thus, a stranger to all the ordinary motives which lead young men to make the army their choice, and without the least desire to become either a hero or a dandy, I really do not know what determined my thoughts that way, unless it were the happy state of half-pay indolence enjoyed by Captain Doolittle, who had set up his staff of rest in my native village. Every other person had, or seemed to have, something

to do, less or more. They did not indeed precisely go to school and
learn tasks, that last of evils in my estimation; but it did not escape my
boyish observation, that they were all "bothered" with something or
other like duty or labour—all but the happy Captain Doolittle. The
minister had his parish to visit, and his "preaching" to prepare, though
perhaps he made more fuss than he needed about both. The laird had
his farming and improving operations to superintend, and, besides
that he had to attend trustee-meetings, and lieutenancy-meetings, and
head-courts, and meetings of justices, and what not, was as early up,
(that I always detested,) and as much in the open air, wet and dry, as
his own grieve. The shop-keeper (the village boasted but one of
eminence) stood indeed pretty much at his ease behind his counter,
for his custom was by no means over-burthensome; but still he
enjoyed his *status*, as the Bailie calls it, upon condition of tumbling all
the wares in his booth over and over, when any one chose to want a
yard of muslin, a mouse-trap, an ounce of carraway, a paper of pins,
the Sermons of Mr Peden, or the Life of Jack the Giant-Queller, (not
Killer, as usually erroneously written and pronounced.—See my
essay on the true history of this worthy, where real feats have in a
peculiar degree been obscured by fable.) In short, all in the village
were under the necessity of doing something which they would rather
have left undone, excepting Captain Doolittle, who walked every
morning in the open street, which formed the high-mall of our village,
in a blue coat with a red neck, and played at whist the whole evening,
when he could make up a party. This happy vacuity of all employment
appeared to me so delicious, that it became the primary hint, which,
according to the system of Helvetius, as the minister says, determined
my infant talents towards the profession I was destined to illustrate.

But who, alas, can form a just estimate of future prospects in this
deceitful world! I was not long engaged in my new profession, before I
discovered, that if the independent indolence of half-pay was a paradise, the officer must pass through the purgatory of duty and service in
order to gain admission to it. Captain Doolittle might brush his blue
coat with the red neck, or leave it unbrushed, at his pleasure; but
Ensign Clutterbuck had no such option. Captain Doolittle might go to
bed at ten o'clock, if he had a mind; but the Ensign must make the
rounds in his turn. What was worse, the Captain might repose under
the tester of his tent-bed until noon, if he was so pleased; but the
Ensign, God help him, had to appear upon parade at peep of day. As
for duty, I made that as easy as I could, had the sergeant to whisper to
me the words of command, and hustled through as other folks did. Of
service, I saw enough for an indolent man—was buffetted up and
down the world, and visited both the East and West Indies, Egypt, and

other distant places, which my youth had scarce dreamed of. The French I saw, and felt too; witness two fingers of my right hand, which one of their cursed hussars took off with his sabre as neatly as an hospital surgeon. At length the death of an old aunt, who left me some fifteen hundred pounds, snugly vested in the three per cents., gave me the long-wished-for opportunity of retiring, with the prospect of enjoying a clean shirt and a guinea four times a-week.

For the purpose of commencing my new way of life, I selected for my residence the village of Kennaquhair, in the south of Scotland, celebrated for the ruins of its magnificent Monastery, intending there to lead my future life in the *otium cum dignitate* of half-pay and annuity. I was not long, however, in making the grand discovery, that in order to enjoy leisure, it is absolutely necessary it should be preceded by occupation. For some time, it was delightful to wake at day-break, dreaming of the reveillée—then to recollect my happy emancipation from the slavery that doomed me to start at a piece of clattering parchment, turn on my other side, damn the parade, and go to sleep again. But even this enjoyment had its termination; and time, when it became a stock entirely at my own disposal, began to hang heavy on my hands.

I tried field sports, but they would not do. I angled for two days, during which time I lost twenty hooks, and several scores of yards of gut-and-line, and caught not even a minnow. Hunting was out of the question, for the stomach of a horse by no means agrees with the half-pay establishment. When I shot, the shepherds and ploughmen, and my very dog, quizzed me every time that I missed, which was, generally speaking, every time that I fired. Besides, the country gentlemen in this quarter like their game, and began to talk of prosecutions and interdicts. I did not give up fighting the French to commence a domestic war with the "pleasant men of Teviotdale," as the song calls them; so I e'en spent three days (very pleasantly) in cleaning my gun, and disposing it upon two hooks over my chimney-piece.

The success of this accidental experiment set me on trying my skill in the mechanical arts. Accordingly, I took down and cleaned my landlady's cuckoo-clock, and in so doing, silenced that companion of the spring for ever and a day. I mounted a turning lathe, and, in attempting to use it, I very nearly cribbed off, with an inch-and-half former, one of the fingers which the hussar had left me.

Books I tried, both those of the little circulating library, and of the more rational subscription-collection maintained by this intellectual people. But neither the light reading of the one, or the heavy artillery of the other, suited my purpose. I always fell asleep at the fourth or fifth page of history or disquisition; and it took me a month's hard reading to wade through a half-bound trashy novel, during which I was pestered with applications to return the volumes, by every half-bred milliner's miss about town. In short, during the hours when all the town besides had something to do, I had nothing for it, but to walk in the church-yard, and whistle till it was dinner-time.

During these promenades, the ruins necessarily forced themselves on my attention, and, by degrees, I found myself engaged in studying the more minute ornaments, and at length the general plan, of this noble structure. The old sexton aided my labours, and gave me his portion of traditional lore. Every day added something to my stock of knowledge respecting the ancient state of the building; and at length I made discoveries concerning the purpose of several detached and very ruinous portions of the building, the use of which had hitherto been either unknown altogether, or erroneously explained.

The knowledge which I thus acquired I had frequent opportunities of retailing to those visitors whom the progress of a Scottish tour brought to visit this celebrated spot. Without encroaching on the privilege of my friend the sexton, I became gradually an assistant Cicerone in the task of description and explanation, and oft (seeing a fresh party of visitors arrive) has he turned over to me those to whom he has told half his story, with the flattering observation, "What needs I say ony mair about it? There's the Captain kens mair anent it than I do, or ony man in the town." Then would I salute the strangers courteously, and expatiate to their astonished minds upon crypts and chancels, and naves, arches, Gothic or Saxon architraves, mullions and flying buttresses. It not unfrequently happened, that an acquaintance which commenced in the abbey concluded in the inn, which served to relieve the solitude as well as the monotony of my landlady's shoulder of mutton, whether hot, cold, or hashed.

By degrees my mind became enlarged. I found a book or two which enlightened me on the subject of Gothic architecture, and I read now with pleasure, because I was interested in what I read about. Even my character began to dilate and expand. I spoke with more authority at the club, and was listened to with deference, because on one subject, at least, I possessed more information than any of its members. Indeed, I found that even my stories about Egypt, which, to say truth, were somewhat thread-bare, were now listened to with more respect than formerly. "The Captain," they said, "had something in him after a',—few folk ken'd sae mickle about the Abbey."

With this general approbation waxed my own sense of self-importance, and my feeling of general comfort. I eat with more appetite, I digested with more ease, I lay down at night with joy, and slept sound till morning, when I arose with a sense of busy importance, and hied me to measure, to examine, and to compare the various parts of this interesting structure. I lost all sense and consciousness of certain unpleasant sensations of a non-descript nature, about my head and stomach, to which I had been in the habit of attending, more for the benefit of the village apothecary than my own, for the pure want of something else to think about. I had found out an occupation unwittingly, and was happy because I had something to do. In a word, I had commenced local antiquary, and was not unworthy of the name.

Whilst I was in this pleasing career of busy idleness, for so it might best be called, it happened that I was one night sitting in my little parlour, adjacent to the closet which my landlady calls my bedroom, in the act of preparing for an early retreat to the realms of Morpheus. Dugdale's Monasticon, borrowed from the library at A——, was lying on the table before me, flanked by some excellent Cheshire cheese, (a present by the way from an honest London citizen, to whom I had explained the difference betwixt a Gothic and a Saxon arch,) and a glass of Vanderhagen's best ale. Thus armed at all points against my old enemy Time, I was leisurely and deliciously preparing for bed— now reading a line of old Dugdale—now sipping my ale, or munching my bread and cheese—now undoing the strings at my breeches' knees, or a button or two of my waistcoat, until the village clock should strike ten, before which time I make it a rule never to go to bed. A loud knocking, however, interrupted my ordinary process on this occasion, and the voice of mine honest landlord of the George was heard vociferating, "What the deevil, Mrs Grimslees, the Captain is no in his bed? and a gentleman at our house has ordered a fowl and minced collops, and a bottle of sherry, and has sent to ask him to supper, to tell him all about the Abbey."

"Na," answered Luckie Grimslees, in the true sleepy tone of a Scotch matron when ten o'clock is going to strike, "he's no in his bed, but I'se warrant him no gae out at this time o' night to keep folks sitting up waiting for him—the Captain's a decent man."

I plainly perceived this last compliment was made for my hearing, by way both of indicating and of recommending the course of conduct which Mrs Grimslees desired I should pursue. But I had not been knocked about the world for thirty years and odd, and lived a bluff bachelor all the while, to come home and be put under petticoat government by my landlady. Accordingly I opened my chamber-door, and desired my old friend David to walk up stairs.

"Captain," said he, as he entered, "I am as glad to find you up as if I had hooked a twenty pound saumon. There's a gentleman up yonder that will not sleep sound in his bed this blessed night, unless he has the pleasure to drink a glass of wine with you."

"You know, David," I replied, with becoming dignity, "that I cannot with propriety go out to visit strangers at this time of night, or accept of invitations from people of whom I know nothing."

David swore a round oath, and added, "Was ever the like heard of? He has ordered a fool and egg-sauce, a pancake and minced collops, and a bottle of sherry—D'ye think I wad come and ask ye to go to keep company with ony bit English rider, that sups on toasted cheese and a cheerer of rum-toddy? This is a gentleman every inch of him—and a virtuoso, a clean virtuoso—A sad-coloured stand of claiths, and a wig like the curled back of a mug-ewe. The very first question he speered was about the auld draw-brig that has been at the bottom of the waeter these twalscore years—I have seen the fundations when we were sticking saumon—and how the deevil suld he ken ony thing about the auld brig, unless he were a virtuoso?"

David being a virtuoso in his own way, and moreover a landholder and heritor, was a qualified judge of all who frequented his house, and therefore I could not avoid again tying the strings of my knees.

"That's right, Captain," vociferated David; "you twa will be as thick as three in a bed an' ance ye foregather. I haena seen the like o' him my very sell since I saw the great Doctor Samuel Johnson on his tower through Scotland, whilk tower is lying in my back-parlour for the amusement of my guests, wi' the twa boards torn aff."

"Then the gentleman is a scholar, David?"

"I'se uphaud him a scholar," answered David; "he has a black coat on, or a brown ane at ony rate."

"Is he a clergyman?"

"I am thinking no, for he looked after his horse's supper before he spoke o' his ain," replied mine host.

"Has he a servant?" demanded I.

"Nae servant," answered David; "but a grand face he has o' his ain, that wad gar ony body be willing to serve him that looks upon him."

"And what makes him think of disturbing me? Ah, David, this has been some of your chattering. You are perpetually bringing your guests on my shoulders, as if it were my business to entertain every man who comes to the George."

"What the de'il wad ye hae me do, Captain?" answered mine host; "a gentleman lights down, and asks me in a maist earnest manner, what man of sense and learning there is about our town, that can tell him about the antiquities of the place, and specially about the auld Abbey—Ye wadna hae me tell the gentleman a lee, and ye ken weel eneugh there is naebody in the town can say a reasonable word about it, be it no yoursel', except the bedral, and he is as fou as a piper be this time. So, says I, there's Captain

Clutterbuck, that's a very civil gentleman, and has little to do forbye telling a' the auld cracks about the Abbey, and dwells just hard bye. Then says the gentleman to me, 'Sir,' says he, very civilly, 'have the goodness to step to Captain Clutterbuck with my compliments, and say I am a stranger, who have been led to these parts chiefly by the fame of these ruins, and that I would call upon him, but the hour is late'—and mair he said that I have forgotten, but I weel remember it ended—'And, landlord, get a bottle of your best sherry, and supper for two'—Ye wadna have had me refuse to do the gentleman's bidding, and me a publican?"

"Well, David," said I, "I wish your virtuoso had taken a fitter hour —but as you say he is a gentleman"——

"I'se uphaud him that—the order speaks for itsel'—a bottle of sherry—minced collops and a fool—that's speaking like a gentleman, I trow?—That's right, Captain, button weel up—the night's raw—but the water's clearing for a' that, we'll be on't neist night wi' my Lord's boats, and we'll hae ill luck if I dinna send you a kipper to relish your ale at e'en."

In five minutes after this dialogue, I found myself in the parlour of the George, and in the presence of the stranger.

He was a grave personage, about my own age, (which we shall call about fifty), and really had, as my friend David expressed it, something in his face that inclined men to oblige and to serve him. Yet this expression of authority was not at all of the cast which I have seen in the countenance of a general of brigade, neither was the stranger's dress at all martial. It consisted of an uniform suit of raven-grey clothes, cut in rather an old-fashioned form. His legs were defended with strong leathern gambadoes, which, according to an antiquated contrivance, opened at the sides, and were secured by steel clasps. His countenance was worn as much by toil and sorrow as by age, for it intimated that he had seen and endured much. His address was singularly pleasing and gentleman-like, and the apology which he made for disturbing me at such an hour, and in such a manner, was so well and handsomely expressed, that I could not reply otherwise than by expressing my willingness to be of service to him.

"I have been a traveller to-day, sir," said he, "and I would willingly defer the little I have to say till after our supper, for which I feel rather more appetized than usual."

We sate down to table, and notwithstanding the stranger's alleged appetite, as well as the gentle preparative of cheese and ale which I had already laid aboard, I really believe that I of the two did the greatest honour to my friend David's fool and minced collops.

When the cloth was removed, and we had each made a tumbler of negus of that liquor which hosts call Sherry, and guests Lisbon, I perceived that the stranger seemed pensive, silent, and somewhat embarrassed, as if he had something to communicate which he knew not well how to introduce. To pave the way for him, I spoke of the ancient ruins of the Monastery, and of their history. But, to my great surprise, I found I had met my match with a witness. The stranger not only knew all that I could tell him, but a great deal more; and, what was still more mortifying, he was able, by reference to dates, charters, and other evidence of facts, that, as Burns says, "downa be confuted," to correct many of the vague tales which I had adopted on loose and vulgar tradition, as well as to confute more than one of my favourite theories on the subject of the old monks and their dwellings, which I had sported freely in all the presumption of superior information. And here I cannot but remark, that much of the stranger's arguments and inductions rested upon the authority of Mr Deputy Register of Scotland, and his lucubrations; a gentleman whose indefatigable research into the national records is like to destroy my trade, and that of all such local antiquaries, by substituting truth instead of legend and romance. Alas, I would the learned gentleman did but know how difficult it is for us dealers in petty wares of antiquity to—

> Pluck from our memories a rooted "legend,"
> Raze out the written records of our brain,
> Or cleanse our bosoms of that perilous stuff——

And so forth. It would, I think, move his pity to think how many old dogs he has set to learn new tricks, how many venerable parrots he hath taught to sing a new song, how many grey heads he has addled by vain attempts to exchange their own old *Mumpsimus* for his new *Sumpsimus*. But let it pass—*Humana perpessi sumus*—All changes round us, past, present, and to come; that which was history yesterday becomes fable to-day, and the truth of to-day is hatched into a lie by to-morrow.

Finding myself like to be overpowered in the Monastery, which I had hitherto regarded as my citadel, I began, like a skilful general, to evacuate that place of defence, and fight my way through the adjacent country. I had recourse to my acquaintance with the families and antiquities of the neighbourhood, ground on which I thought I might skirmish at large without its being possible for the stranger to meet me with advantage. But I was mistaken.

The man in the iron-grey suit shewed a much more minute knowledge of these particulars than I had the least pretension to. He could tell the very year in which the family of De Haga first settled on their ancient barony. Not a Thane within reach but he knew his family and connections, how many of his ancestors had fallen by the sword of the

English, how many in domestic brawl, and how many by the hands of the executioner for march-treason. Their castles he was acquainted with from turret to foundation-stone; and as for the miscellaneous antiquities scattered about the country, he knew every one of them, from a *cromlech* to a *cairn*, and could give as good an account of each as if he had lived in the time of the Danes or Druids.

I was now in the mortifying predicament of one who suddenly finds himself a scholar where he came to teach, and nothing was left for me but to pick up as much of his conversation as I could, for the benefit of the next company. I told, indeed, Allan Ramsay's story of the Monk and Miller's Wife, in order to retreat with some honour under cover of a parting volley. Here, however, my flank was again turned by the eternal stranger.

"You are pleased to be facetious, sir," said he, "but you cannot be ignorant, that the ludicrous incident you have mentioned is the subject of a tale much older than that of Allan Ramsay."

I nodded, unwilling to acknowledge my ignorance, though, in fact, I knew no more what he meant than did one of my friend David's posthorses.

"I do not allude," continued my omniscient companion, "to the curious poem published by the learned Pinkerton from the Maitland Manuscript, called the Fryars of Berwick, although it presents a very minute and curious picture of Scottish manners during the reign of James V.; but rather to the Italian novelist, by whom, so far as I know, the story was first printed, although unquestionably he first took his original from some ancient *fabliau*."

"It is not to be doubted," answered I, not very well understanding, however, the proposition to which I gave such unqualified assent.

"Yet," continued my companion, "I question much, had you known my situation and profession, whether you would have pitched upon this precise anecdote for my amusement."

This observation he made in a tone of perfect good humour. I pricked up my ears at the hint, and answered as politely as I could, that my ignorance of his condition and rank could be the only cause of my having stumbled on any thing disagreeable; and that I was most willing to apologize for my unintentional offence, so soon as I should know wherein it consisted.

"Nay, no offence, sir," he replied; "offence can only exist where it is taken. I have been too long accustomed to more severe and cruel misconstructions, to be offended at a popular jest, though directed at my profession."

"Am I to understand then," I answered, "that I am speaking with a Catholic clergyman?"

"An unworthy Monk of the order of Saint Benedict," said the stranger, "belonging to a community of your own countrymen, long established in France, and scattered unhappily by the events of the Revolution."

"Then," said I, "you are a native Scotsman, and from this neighbourhood?"

"Not so," answered the Monk; "I am a Scotsman by extraction only, and never was in this neighbourhood during my whole life."

"Never in this neighbourhood, and yet so minutely acquainted with its history, its traditions, and even its external scenery! You surprise me, sir," I replied.

"It is not surprising," said he, "that I should have that sort of local information, when it is considered, that my uncle, an excellent man, as well as a good Scotsman, the head also of our religious community, employed much of his leisure in making me acquainted with these particulars; and that I myself, disgusted with what has been passing around me, have for many years amused myself, by digesting and arranging the various scraps of information which I derived from my worthy relative, and other aged brethren of our order."

"I presume, sir," said I, "though I would by no means intrude the question, that you are now returned to Scotland with a view to settle amongst your countrymen, since the grand political catastrophe of our time has reduced your corps?"

"No, sir," replied the Benedictine, "such is not my intention. A European potentate, who still cherishes the Catholic faith, has offered us a retreat within his dominions, where a few of my scattered brethren are already assembled, to pray to God for blessings on their protector, and pardon to their enemies. No one, I believe, will be able to object to us under our new establishment, that the extent of our revenues will be inconsistent with our vows of poverty and abstinence: let us strive to be thankful to God, that the snare of temporal abundance is removed from us."

"Many of your convents abroad, sir," said I, "enjoyed very handsome incomes—and yet, allowing for times, I question if any were better provided for than the Monastery of this village. It is said to have enjoyed nearly two thousand pounds in yearly money-rent, fourteen chalders and nine bolls of wheat, fifty-six chalders five bolls barley, forty-four chalders and ten bolls oats, capons and poultry, butter, salt, carriage and arriage, peats and hams, wool and ale."

"Even too much of all these temporal goods, sir," said my companion, "which, though well intended by the pious donors, served only to make the establishment the envy and the prey of those by whom it was finally devoured."

"In the meanwhile, however," I observed, "the Monks had an easy life of it, and, as the old song goes,

——made gude kale
On Fridays when they fasted."

"I understand you, sir," said the Benedictine; "it is difficult, saith the proverb, to carry a full cup without spilling. Unquestionably the wealth of the community, as it endangered the safety of the establishment by exciting the cupidity of others, was also in frequent instances a snare to the brethren themselves. And yet we have seen the revenues of convents expended, not only in acts of beneficence and hospitality to individuals, but in works of general and permanent advantage to the world at large. The noble folio collection of French historians commenced in 1737, under the inspection and at the expense of the community of Saint Maur, will long shew that the revenues of the Benedictines were not always spent in self-indulgence, and that the members of that order did not uniformly slumber in sloth and indolence, when they had discharged the formal duties of their rule."

As I knew nothing earthly at the time about the community of Saint Maur and their learned labours, I could only return a mumbling assent to this proposition. I have since seen this noble work in the library of a distinguished family, and I must own I am ashamed to reflect, that in so wealthy a country as ours, a similar digest of our historians should not be undertaken, under the patronage of the noble and the learned, in rivalry of that which the Benedictines of Paris executed at the expence of their own conventual funds.

"I perceive," said the ex-Benedictine smiling, "that your heretical prejudices are too strong to allow us poor brethren any merit, whether literary or spiritual."

"Far from it, sir," said I; "I assure you I have been much obliged to Monks in my time. When I was quartered in a Monastery in Flanders, in the campaign of 1793, I never lived more comfortably in my life. They were jolly dogs the Flemish Canons, and right sorry was I to leave my good quarters, and to know that my honest hosts were to be at the mercy of the Sans-Culottes. But *fortune de la guerre!*"

The poor Benedictine looked down and was silent. I had unwittingly awakened a train of bitter reflections, or rather I had touched somewhat rudely upon a chord which seldom ceased to vibrate of itself. But he was too much accustomed to this sorrowful train of ideas to suffer it to overcome him. On my part, I hastened to atone for my blunder. "If there were any object of his journey to this country in which I could, with propriety, assist him, I begged to offer him my best services." I own I laid some little emphasis on the words "with propriety," as I felt it would ill become me, a sound protestant, and a servant of government so far as my half-pay was concerned, to implicate myself in any recruiting which my companion might have undertaken in behalf of foreign seminaries, or in any similar design for the advancement of popery, which, whether the Pope be actually the Old Lady of Babylon or no, it did not become me in any manner to advance or countenance.

My new friend hastened to relieve my indecision. "I was about to request your assistance, sir," he said, "in a matter which cannot but interest you as an antiquary, and a person of research. But I assure you it relates entirely to events and persons removed to the distance of two centuries and a half. I have experienced too much evil from the violent unsettlement of the country in which I was born, to be a rash labourer in the work of innovation in that of my ancestors."

I again assured him of my willingness to assist him in any thing that was not contrary to my allegiance or religion.

"My proposal," he replied, "affects neither.—May God bless the reigning family of Britain! They are not, indeed, of that dynasty, to restore which my ancestors struggled and suffered in vain; but the Providence who has conducted his present Majesty to the throne, has given him the virtues necessary to his time—firmness and intrepidity—a true love of his country, and an enlightened view of the dangers by which she is surrounded.—For the religion of these realms, I am contented to hope that the Great Power, whose mysterious dispensation has rent them from the bosom of the church, will, in his own good time and manner restore them to its holy pale. The efforts of an individual obscure and humble as myself, might well retard, but could never advance a work so mighty."

"May I then enquire, sir," said I, "with what purpose you seek this country?"

Ere my companion replied, he took from his pocket a clasped paper book, about the size of a regimental orderly-book, full, as it seemed, of memoranda; and drawing one of the candles close to him, (for David, in strong proof of his respect for the stranger, had indulged us with two,) he seemed to peruse the contents very earnestly.

"There is among the ruins of the western end of the Abbey church," said he, looking up to me, yet keeping the memorandum-book half open, and occasionally glancing at it, as if to refresh his memory, "a sort of recess or chapel beneath a broken arch, and in the immediate vicinity of one of those shattered Gothic columns which once supported the magnificent roof, whose fall has now encumbered that part of the building with its ruins."

"I think," said I, "that I know whereabouts you are. Is there not in the side wall of the chapel, or recess which you mention, a large carved stone, bearing a coat of arms, which no one hitherto has been able to decypher?"

"You are right," answered the Benedictine, and again consulting his memoranda, he added, "the arms on the dexter side are those of Glendinning, being a cross parted by a cross indented and counter-charged of the same: and on the sinister three spurrowels for those of Avenel: they are two ancient families, now almost extinct in this country—the arms party *per pale.*"

"I think," said I, "there is no part of this ancient structure with which you are not as well acquainted as was the mason who built it. But if your information be correct, he who made out these bearings must have had better eyes than mine."

"His eyes," said the Benedictine, "have been long closed in death; probably when he inspected the monument it was in a more perfect state, or he may have derived his information from the tradition of the place."

"I assure you," said I, "that no such tradition now exists. I have made several reconnoissances among the old people, in hopes to learn something of the armorial bearings, but I never heard of such a circumstance. It seems odd that you should have acquired it in a foreign land."

"These trifling particulars," he replied, "were formerly looked upon as more important, and they were sanctified to the exiles who retained recollection of them, because they related to a place dear indeed to memory, but which their eyes could never again behold. It is possible, in like manner, that on the Potowmack or Susquehana, you may find traditions current concerning places in England, which are utterly forgotten in the neighbourhood where they originated. But to my purpose. In this recess, marked by the armorial bearings, lies buried a treasure, and it is in order to remove it that I have undertaken my present journey."

"A treasure!" echoed I, in astonishment.

"Yes," replied the Monk, "an inestimable treasure, for those who know how to use it rightly."

I own my ears did tingle a little at the word treasure, and that a handsome tilbury, with a neat groom in blue and scarlet livery, having a smart cockade on his glazed hat, seemed as it were to glide across the room before my eyes, while a voice, as of a crier, pronounced in my ears, "Captain Clutterbuck's tilbury—drive up." But I resisted the devil, and he fled from me.

"I believe," said I, "all hidden treasure belongs either to the king or the lord of the soil; and as I have served his Majesty, I cannot concern myself in any adventure which may have an end in the Court of Exchequer."

"The treasure I seek," said the stranger smiling, "will not be envied by princes or nobles,—it is simply the heart of an upright man."

"Ah! I understand you," I answered, "some relique, forgotten in the confusion of the Reformation. I know the value men of your persuasion put upon the bodies and limbs of saints. I have seen the three Kings of Cologne."

"The reliques which I seek, however," said the Benedictine, "are not precisely of that nature. The excellent relative whom I have already mentioned, amused his leisure hours with putting into form the traditions of his family, particularly some remarkable occurrences which took place about the first breaking out of the schism of the Church in Scotland. He became so much interested in his own labours, that at length he resolved that the heart of one individual, the hero of his tale, should rest no longer in a land of heresy, now deserted by all his kindred. As he knew where it was deposited, he formed the resolution to revisit his native country for the purpose of recovering this valued relique. But age, and at length disease, interfered with his resolution, and it was on his death-bed that he charged me to undertake the task in his stead. The various important events which have crowded upon each other, our ruin and our exile, have for many years obliged me to postpone this delegated duty. Why, indeed, transfer the reliques of a holy and worthy man to a country, where religion and virtue are become the mockery of the scorner! I have now a home, which I trust may be permanent, if any thing in this earth can be termed so. Thither will I transport the heart of the good father, and beside the shrine which it shall occupy, I will construct my own grave."

"He must have been indeed an excellent man," replied I, "whose memory, at so distant a period, calls forth such strong marks of regard."

"He was, as you justly term him," said the ecclesiastic, "indeed excellent—excellent in his life and doctrine—excellent, above all, in his self-denied and disinterested sacrifice of all that life holds dear, to principle and to friendship. But you shall read his history. I will be happy at once to gratify your curiosity, and to shew my sense of your kindness, if you will have the goodness to procure me the means of accomplishing my object."

I replied to the Benedictine, that, as the rubbish amongst which he proposed to search was no part of the ordinary burial-ground, and as I was on the best terms with the sexton, I had little doubt that I could procure him the means of executing his pious purpose.

With this promise, we parted for the night; and on the ensuing

morning I made it my business to see the sexton, who, for a small
gratuity, readily granted permission of search, on condition, however,
that he should be present himself, to see that the stranger removed
nothing of intrinsic value.

"To banes, and sculls, and hearts, if he can find ony, he shall be
welcome," said this guardian of the ruined Monastery, "there's
plenty o' them a' about, an' he's curious that way; but if there be
ony picts (meaning perhaps *pyx*) or chalishes, or the like of such
Popish veshells of gold and silver, de'il hae me an I conneeve at
their being removed."

The sexton also stipulated, that our researches should take place at
night, being unwilling to excite observation, or give rise to scandal.

My new acquaintance and I spent the day as became lovers of hoar
antiquity. We visited every corner of these magnificent ruins again
and again during the forenoon; and, having made a comfortable dinner at David's, we walked in the afternoon to such places in the
neighbourhood as ancient tradition or modern conjecture had rendered mark-worthy. Night found us in the interior of the ruins,
attended by the sexton, who carried a dark lantern, and stumbling
alternately over the graves of the dead, and the fragments of that
architecture, which they doubtless trusted would have "canopied their
bones till doomsday."

I am by no means particularly superstitious, and yet there was
something in the present service which I did not very much like.
There was something awful in the resolution of disturbing, at such an
hour and in such a place, the still, mute sanctity of the grave. My
companions were free from this impression—the stranger from his
energetic desire to execute the purpose for which he came—and
the sexton, from habitual indifference. They soon stood in the aisle,
which, by the account of the stranger, contained the bones of the
family of Glendinning, and were busily employed in removing the
rubbish from a corner which the stranger pointed out. If a half-pay
Captain could have represented an ancient Border-knight, or an ex-
Benedictine of the nineteenth century a wizard monk of the sixteenth,
we might have aptly enough personified the search after Michael
Scott's lamp and book of magic power. But the sexton would have
been *de trop* in the groupe.

Ere the stranger, assisted by the sexton in his task, had been long at
work, they came to some hewn stones, which seemed to have made
part of a small shrine, though now displaced and destroyed.

"Let us remove these with caution, my friend," said the stranger,
"lest we injure that which I come to seek."

"They are prime stanes," said the sexton, "picked free every ane of them;—warse than the best wad never serve the Monks, I'se warrant."

A minute after he had made this observation, he exclaimed, "I hae fund something now that stands again the spade, as if it were neither earth nor stane."

The stranger stooped eagerly to assist him.

"Na, na, hail o' my ain," said the sexton; "nae halves or quarters;" —and he lifted from amongst the ruins a small leaden box.

"You will be disappointed, my friend," said the Benedictine, "if you expect any thing there but the mouldering dust of a human heart, closed in an inner case of porphyry."

I interposed as a neutral party, and taking the box from the sexton, reminded him that if there were treasure concealed in it, still it could not become the property of the finder. I then proposed, that as the place was too dark to examine the contents of the leaden casket, we should adjourn to David's, where we might have the advantage of light and fire while carrying on our investigation. The stranger requested us to go before, assuring us that he would follow in a few minutes.

I fancy that old Mattocks suspected these few minutes might be employed in effecting further discoveries amongst the tombs, for he glided back through a side-aisle to watch the Benedictine's motions, but presently returned, and told me in a whisper, that "the gentleman was on his knees amang the cauld stanes, praying like ony saunt."

I stole back, and beheld the old man actually employed as Mattocks had informed me. The language seemed to be Latin; and as the whispered yet solemn accents glided away through the ruined aisles, I could not help reflecting how long it was since they had heard the forms of that religion, for the exercise of which they had been reared at such cost of time, taste, labour, and expence. "Come away—Come away," said I; "let us leave him to himself, Mattocks, this is no business of ours."

"My certes, no, Captain," said Mattocks; "ne'ertheless, it winna be amiss to keep e'e on him. My father, rest his saul, was a horse-couper, and used to say he never was cheated in a naig in his life, saving by a west-country whig frae Kilmarnock, that said a grace ower a dram o' whisky. But this gentleman will be a Roman, I'se warrant."

"You are perfectly right in that, Saunders," said I.

"Ay, I hae seen twa or three of their priests that were chaced ower here some score o' years syne—they just danced like mad when they looked on the friars' heads, and the nuns' heads, in the cloister yonder; they took to them like auld acquaintance like. Od, he is not stirring yet, mair than he were a through-stane!* I never kenn'd a

* A tombstone.

Roman, to say kenn'd him, but ane—mair by token, he was the only ane in the town to ken—and that was auld Jock of the Pend. It wad hae been lang or ye fand Jock praying in the Abbey in a thick night, wi' his knees on a cauld stane. Jock liket a kirk wi' a chimley in it. Mony a merry ploy I hae had wi' him down at the inn yonder; and when he died, decent I wad hae earded him; but, or I gat his grave weel howkit, some of the quality, that were o' his ain unhappy persuasion, had the corpse whirried away up the water, and buried him after their ain pleasure doubtless—they kenn'd best. I wad hae made nae great charge. I wadna hae excised Johnie, dead or alive.—Stay, see the strange gentleman is coming."

"Hold the lantern, to assist him, Mattocks," said I.—"This is rough walking, sir."

"Yes," replied the Benedictine; "I may say with a poet, who is doubtless familiar to you"——

"I should be surprised if he were," thought I internally.

The stranger continued:

"Saint Francis be my speed! how oft to-night
Have my old feet stumbled at graves."

"We are now clear of the churchyard," said I, "and have but a short walk to mine honest friend David's, where I hope we shall find a cheerful fire to enliven us after our night's work."

We entered, accordingly, the little parlour, into which Mattocks was also about to push himself with sufficient effrontery, when David, with a most astounding oath, expelled him by head and shoulders, d——ning his curiosity, that would not let gentlemen be private in their own inn. Apparently mine host considered his own presence as no intrusion, for he crowded up to the table on which I had laid down the leaden box. It was frail and wasted, as might be guessed, from having lain so many years in the ground. On opening it, we found deposited within, a case made of porphyry, as the stranger had announced to us.

"I fancy," he said, "gentlemen, your curiosity will not be satisfied, perhaps I should say that your suspicions will not be removed, unless I undo this casket; yet it only contains the mouldering remains of a heart once the seat of the noblest thoughts."

He undid the box with great caution; but the shrivelled substance which it contained bore now no resemblance to what it might once have been, the means used to preserve it having been apparently unequal to preserve its shape and colour, although they were adequate to prevent its total decay. We were quite satisfied, notwithstanding, that it was, what the stranger asserted, the remains of a human heart; and David readily promised his influence in the village, which was almost co-ordinate with that of the Baillie himself, to silence all idle rumours. He was, moreover, pleased to favour us with his company to supper; and having taken the lion's share of two bottles of sherry, he not only sanctioned with his plenary authority the stranger's removal of the heart, but, I believe, would have authorized the removal of the Abbey itself, but that it happens considerably to advantage the worthy publican's own custom.

The object of the Benedictine's visit to the land of his forefathers being now accomplished, he announced his intention of departing early in the ensuing day, but requested my company to breakfast with him before his departure. I came accordingly, and when we had finished our morning's meal, the priest took me apart, and, pulling from his pocket a large bundle of papers, he put them into my hands. "These," said he, "Captain Clutterbuck, are genuine Memoirs of the sixteenth century, and exhibit in a singular, and, as I think, an interesting point of view, the manners of that period. I am induced to believe that their publication will not be an unacceptable present to the British public; and I willingly make over to you any profit that may accrue from such a transaction."

I stared a little at this annunciation, and observed, that the hand seemed too modern for the date he assigned to the manuscript.

"Do not mistake me, sir," said the Benedictine; "I did not mean to say the Memoirs were written in the sixteenth century, but only, that they were compiled from authentic materials of that period, but written in the taste and language of the present day. My uncle commenced this task; and I, partly to improve my habit of English composition, partly to divert melancholy thoughts, amused my leisure hours with continuing and concluding it. You will see the period of the story where my uncle leaves off his narrative, and I commence mine. In fact, they relate in a great measure to different persons, as well as to a different period."

Retaining the papers in my hand, I proceeded to state to him my doubts, whether, as a good Protestant, I could undertake to superintend a publication written probably in the spirit of Popery.

"You will find," he said, "no matter of controversy, sir, in these sheets, nor any sentiments stated, with which, I trust, the good in all persuasions will not be willing to join. I remembered I was writing for a land unhappily divided from the Catholic faith; and I have taken care to say nothing which, justly interpreted, could give ground for accusing me of partiality. But if, upon collating my narrative with the proofs to which I refer you—for you will find copies of many of the original papers in that parcel—you are of opinion that I have been partial to my own faith, I freely give you leave to correct my errors in that respect. I own, however, I am not conscious of this defect, and have rather to fear that the Catholics may be of opinion, that I have mentioned circumstances respecting the decay of discipline which preceded, and partly occasioned, the great schism, called by you the Reformation, over which I ought to have drawn a veil. And indeed, this is one reason why I chuse the papers should appear in a foreign land, and pass to the press through the hands of a stranger."

To this I had nothing to reply, unless to object my own incompetence to the task the good father was desirous to impose on me. On this subject he was pleased to say more, I fear, than his knowledge of me fully warranted—more, at any rate, than my modesty will permit me to record. At length he ended with advising me, if I continued to feel the diffidence which I stated, to apply to some veteran of literature, whose experience might supply my deficiencies. Upon these terms we parted, with mutual expressions of regard, and I have never since heard of him.

After several attempts to peruse the quires of paper thus singularly conferred on me, in which I was interrupted by the most inexplicable fits of yawning, I at length, in a sort of despair, communicated them to our village club, from whom they found a more favourable reception than the unlucky conformation of my nerves had been able to afford them. They unanimously pronounced the work to be exceedingly good, and assured me that I would be guilty of the greatest possible injury to our flourishing village, if I should suppress what threw such an interesting and radiant light upon the history of the ancient Monastery of Saint Mary.

At length, by dint of listening to their opinion, I became dubious of my own; and indeed, when I heard passages read forth by the sonorous voice of our worthy pastor, I was scarce more tired than I have felt myself at some of his own sermons. Such, and so great is the difference betwixt reading a thing one's self, making toilsome way through all the difficulties of manuscript, and, as the man says in the play, "having the same read to you,"—it is positively like being wafted over a creek in a boat, or wading through it on your feet, with the mud up to your knees. Still, however, there remained the great difficulty of finding some one who could act as editor, corrector at once of the press and of the language, which, according to the schoolmaster, was absolutely necessary.

Since the trees walked forth to chuse themselves a king, never was an honour so bandied about. The parson would not leave the quiet of his chimney-corner—the baillie pleaded the dignity of his situation, and the approach of the great annual fair, as reasons against going to Edinburgh to make arrangements for printing the Benedictine's Manuscript. The schoolmaster alone seemed of malleable stuff; and, desirous perhaps of emulating the fame of Jedidiah Cleishbotham, evinced a wish to undertake this momentous commission. But a remonstrance from three opulent farmers, whose sons he had at bed, board, and schooling, for twenty pounds per annum a-head, came like a frost over the blossoms of his literary ambition, and he was compelled to decline the service.

In these circumstances, sir, I apply to you, by the advice of our little council of war, nothing doubting you will not be disinclined to take the duty upon you, as it is much connected with that in which you have distinguished yourself. What I request is, that you will review, or rather revise and correct the enclosed packet, and prepare it for the press, by such alterations, additions, and curtailments, as you think necessary. Forgive my hinting to you, that the deepest well may be exhausted,—the best corps of grenadiers, as our old general of brigade expressed himself, may be *used up*. A few hints can do you no harm; and, for the prize-money, let the battle be first won, and it shall be parted at the drum head. I hope you will take nothing amiss that I have said. I am a plain soldier, and little accustomed to compliments. I may add, that I should be well contented to march in the front with you —that is, to put my name with your's on the title-page. I have the honour to be,

SIR,

Your unknown humble Servt,

CUTHBERT CLUTTERBUCK.

VILLAGE OF KENNAQUHAIR,
On the 1st day of April 18—

For the Author of "Waverley," &c.
care of Mr John Ballantyne,
Hanover Street, Edinburgh.

ANSWER

BY

"THE AUTHOR OF WAVERLEY,"

TO THE

FOREGOING LETTER

FROM

CAPTAIN CLUTTERBUCK.

DEAR CAPTAIN,

DO NOT ADMIRE, that, notwithstanding the distance and ceremony of your address, I return an answer in the terms of familiarity. The truth is, your origin and native country is better known to me than even to yourself. You derive your respectable parentage, if I am not greatly mistaken, from a land which has afforded much pleasure, as well as profit, to those who have traded to it successfully. I mean that part of the *terra incognita* which is called the province of Utopia. Its productions, though censured by many (and some who use tea and tobacco without scruple) as idle and unsubstantial luxuries, have nevertheless, like many other luxuries, a general acceptation, and are curiously and secretly enjoyed even by those who express the greatest scorn and dislike of them in public. The dram-drinker is often the first to be shocked at the smell of spirits—it is usual to hear old maiden-ladies declaim against scandal—the private book-cases of some grave-seeming men would not brook decent eyes—and many, I say not of the wise and learned, but of those most anxious to seem such, when the spring-lock of their library is drawn, their velvet cap pulled over their ears, their steps insinuated into their turkey slippers, are to be found, were their retreats suddenly intruded upon, busily engaged with the last new novel.

I have said, the truly wise and learned disdain these shifts, and will open the said novel as openly as they would the lid of their snuff-box. I will quote only one instance, though I know a hundred. Did you know the celebrated Watt of Birmingham, Captain Clutterbuck? I believe not, though, from what I am about to state, he would not have failed to

24

have sought an acquaintance with you. It was only once my fortune to meet him, whether in body or in spirit it matters not. There were assembled about half a score of our Northern Lights, who had got amongst them, Heaven knows how, a well-known character of your country, Jedidiah Cleishbotham. This worthy person, having come to Edinburgh during the Christmas vacation, had become a sort of lion in the place, and was led in leash from house to house along with the guissards, the stone-eater, and other amusements of the season, which "exhibit their unparalleled feats to private family-parties, if required." Amidst this company stood Mr Watt, the man whose genius discovered the means of multiplying our national resources to a degree beyond perhaps even his own stupendous powers of calculation and combination; bringing the treasures of the abyss to the summit of the earth—giving the feeble arm of man the momentum of an Afrite—commanding manufactures to arise where he listed, as the rod of the prophet produced water in the desert, affording the means of dispensing with that time and tide which wait for no man, and of sailing without that wind which defied the commands and threats of Xerxes himself.* This potent commander of the elements—this abridger of time and space—this magician, whose cloudy machinery has produced a change on the world, the effects of which, extraordinary as they are, are perhaps only now beginning to be felt—was not only the most profound man of science, the most successful combiner of powers and calculator of numbers, as adapted to practical purposes,—was not only one of the most generally well-informed, but one of the best and kindest of human beings.

There he stood, surrounded by the little band I have mentioned of Northern literati, men not less tenacious, generally speaking, of their own fame and their own opinions, than the national regiments are supposed to be jealous of the high character which they have won upon service. Methinks I yet see and hear what I shall never see or hear again. In his eighty-fifth year, the alert, kind, benevolent old man, had his attention ready at every one's question, his information at every one's command. His talent and fancy overflowed on every subject. One gentleman was a deep philologist,—he talked with him on the origin of the alphabet as if he had been coeval with Cadmus; another a celebrated critic,—you would have said the old man had studied political economy and belles-lettres all his life,—of science it

* Note by Captain Clutterbuck.
Probably the ingenious author alludes to the national adage:
  The king said sail,
  But the wind said no.
Our schoolmaster (who is also a land-surveyor) thinks this whole passage refers to Mr Watt's improvements on the steam-engine.

is unnecessary to speak, it was his own distinguished walk. And yet, Captain Clutterbuck, when he spoke with your countryman Jedidiah Cleishbotham, you would have sworn he had been coeval with Claverse and Burley, with the persecutors and the persecuted, and could number every shot the dragoons had fired at the fugitive covenanters. In fact, we discovered that no novel of the least celebrity escaped his perusal, and that the gifted man of science was as much addicted to the productions of your native country, (the land of Utopia aforesaid;) in other words, as shameless and obstinate a peruser of novels as if he had been a very milliner's apprentice of eighteen. I know little apology for troubling you with these things, excepting the desire to commemorate a delightful evening, and the wish to encourage you to shake off that modest diffidence which makes you afraid of being supposed connected with the fairy-land of delusive fiction. I will requite your tag of verse, from Horace himself, with a paraphrase for your own use, my dear Captain, and for that of your country club, excepting in reverence the clergyman and schoolmaster:—

> *Ne sit ancillæ tibi amor pudori, &c.*
> Take thou no scorn,
> Of fiction born,
> Fair fiction's muse to woo;
> Old Homer's theme
> Was but a dream,
> Himself a fiction too.

Having told you your country, I must next, my dear Captain Clutterbuck, make free to mention to you your own immediate descent. You are not to suppose your land of prodigies so little known to us as your careful concealment of your origin would seem to imply. But you have it in common with many of your country, studiously and anxiously to hide your connection with it. There is this difference, indeed, betwixt your countrymen and those of our more material world, that many of the most estimable of yours, such as an old Highland gentleman called Ossian, a monk of Bristol named Rowley, and others, are inclined to pass themselves as denizens of the land of reality, whereas most of our fellow-citizens who deny their country are such as that country would be very willing to disclaim. The special circumstances you mention relating to your life and services, impose not upon us. We know the versatility of the unsubstantial species to which you belong permits them to assume all manner of disguises; we have seen them apparelled in the caftan of a Persian, and the silken robe of a Chinese,* and are prepared to suspect their real character under every disguise. But how can we be ignorant of your country and manners, or deceived by the evasions of its inhabitants, when the

---

* See "The Persian Letters," and "The Citizen of the World."

voyages of discovery which have been made to it rival in number those recorded by Purchas or by Hackluyt?* And to shew the skill and perseverance of your navigators and travellers, we have only to name Sindbad, Aboulfouaris, and Robinson Crusoe. These were the men for discoveries. Could we have sent Captain Greenland to look out for the north-west passage, or Peter Wilkins to examine Baffin's Bay, what discoveries might we not have expected! But there are feats, and these both numerous and extraordinary, performed by the inhabitants of your country, which we read without once attempting to emulate.

I wander from my purpose, which was to assure you, that I know you as well as the mother who did *not* bear you, for MacDuff's peculiarity sticks to your whole race. You are not born of woman, unless, indeed, in that figurative sense, in which the celebrated Maria Edgeworth may be termed mother of the finest family in England. You belong, sir, to the Editors of the land of Utopia, a sort of persons for whom I have the highest esteem. How is it possible it should be otherwise, when you reckon among your corporation the sage Cid Hamet Benengeli, the short-faced president of the Spectator's club, poor Ben Silton, and many others, who have acted as gentlemen ushers to works which have chased our heaviest, and added wings to our lightest hours.

What I have remarked as peculiar to Editors of the class in which I venture to enrol you, is the happy combination of fortuitous circumstances which usually put you in possession of the works which you have the goodness to bring into public notice. One walks on the seashore, and a wave casts on land a small cylindrical trunk or casket, containing a manuscript much damaged with sea-water, which is with difficulty decyphered, and so forth.† Another steps into a chandler's shop to purchase a pound of butter, and behold! the waste-paper on which it is laid is the manuscript of a cabalist.‡ A third is so fortunate as to obtain from a woman who lets lodgings, the curious contents of an antique bureau, the property of a deceased lodger.§ All these are certainly possible occurrences; but I know not how it is, they seldom occur to any Editors save those of your country. At least I can answer for myself, that in my solitary walks by the sea, I never saw it cast ashore any thing but dulse and tangle, and now and then a deceased star-fish; my landlady never presented me with any manuscript save her cursed bill; and the most interesting of my discoveries in the way of waste-paper, was finding a favourite passage of one of my own novels wrapt round an ounce of snuff. No, Captain, the funds from which I have drawn any power of amusing the public, have been bought otherwise than by fortuitous adventure. I have buried myself in

---

* See "Les Voyages Imaginaires." † See the History of Automathes.
‡ Adventures of a Guinea. § Adventures of an Atom.

libraries, to extract from the nonsense of ancient days new nonsense of mine own. I have turned over volumes, which, from the pot-hooks I was obliged to decypher, might have been the cabalistic manuscripts of Cornelius Agrippa, although I never saw "the door open and the devil come in."* But all the domestic inhabitants of the recesses of the libraries were disturbed by the vehemence of my studies;—

> From my research the boldest spiders fled,
> And moths, retreating, trembled as I read.

From this learned sepulchre I emerged like the Magician in the Persian Tales from his twelvemonth's residence in the mountain, not like him to soar over the heads of the multitude, but to mingle in their crowd, and to elbow amongst the throng, making my way from the highest society to the lowest, undergoing the scorn, or, what is harder to brook, the patronizing condescension of the one, and enduring the vulgar familiarity of the other,—and all, you will say, for what?—why, to collect materials for one of those manuscripts with which mere chance so often accommodates your countrymen; in other words, to write a successful novel.—"O, Athenians, how hard we labour to deserve your praise!"

I might stop here, my dear Clutterbuck; it would have a touching effect, and the air of proper deference to our dear Public. But I will not be false with you,—(though falsehood is—excuse the observation—the current coin of your country)—the truth is, that I have studied and lived for the purpose of gratifying my own curiosity, and passing away my own time; and although the result has been, that, in one shape or other, I have been frequently before the Public, perhaps more frequently than prudence warranted, yet I cannot claim from them the favour due to those who have dedicated their ease or leisure to the improvement and entertainment of others.

Having communicated thus freely with you, my dear Captain, it follows, of course, that I will gratefully accept of your communication, which, as your Benedictine observed, divides itself both by subject, manner, and age, into two parts. But I am sorry I cannot gratify your literary ambition, by suffering your name to appear upon the title-page; and I will candidly tell you the reason.

The Editors of your country are of such a soft and passive disposition, that they have frequently done themselves great disgrace by giving up the coadjutors who first brought them into public notice and public favour, and suffering their names to be used by those quacks and impostors who live upon the ideas of others. Thus I shame to tell how the sage Cid Hamet Benengeli was induced by one Juan Avellaneda to play the Turk with the ingenious Miguel Cervantes, and to

* See Southey's Ballad on the young Man that read in a Conjuror's Books.

publish a second part of the adventures of his hero the renowned
Don Quixote, without the knowledge or co-operation of his principal
aforesaid. It is true, the Arabian sage returned to his allegiance, and
thereafter composed a genuine continuation of the Knight of La
Mancha, in which the said Avellaneda of Tordesillas is severely chas-
tised. For in this you gentlemen, who may be termed Knights of the
Straw, resemble the juggler's disciplined ape, to which a sly old Scotsman likened James I., "if you have Jackoo in your hand, you can make
him bite me; if I have Jackoo in my hand, I can make him bite you."
Yet, notwithstanding the *amende honorable* thus made by Cid Hamet
Benengeli, his temporary defection did not the less occasion the
decease of the ingenious Hidalgo Don Quixote, if he can be said to
die, whose memory is immortal. Cervantes put him to death, lest he
should again fall into bad hands. Awful, yet just consequence of Cid
Hamet's defection!

To quote a more modern and much less important instance. I am
sorry to observe my old acquaintance Jedidiah Cleishbotham has
misbehaved himself so far as to desert his original patron, and set up
for himself. I am afraid the poor pedagogue will take little by his new
allies, unless the pleasure of entertaining the public, and, for ought I
know, the gentlemen of the long robe, with disputes about his identity.* Observe, therefore, Captain Clutterbuck, that, wise by these
great examples, I receive you as a partner, but a sleeping partner only.
As I give you no title to employ or use the firm of the copartnery we are
about to form, I will announce my property in my title-page, and put
my own buist† on my own cattle, which the attorney tells me will be a
crime to counterfeit, as much as it would to imitate the autograph of
any other empiric—amounting, as advertisements upon little vials
assure us, to nothing short of felony. If, therefore, my dear friend,
your name should hereafter appear on any title page without mine,
readers will know what to think of you. I scorn to use either arguments
or threats; but you cannot but be sensible, that, as you owe your
literary existence to me on the one hand, so, on the other, your very all
is at my disposal. I can at pleasure cut off your annuity, strike your
name from the half-pay establishment, nay actually put you to death,
without being answerable to any one. These are plain words to a

* I am since more correctly informed, that Mr Cleishbotham died some months since at
Gandercleugh, and that the person assuming his name is an impostor. The real Jedidiah
made a most christian and edifying end; and, as I am credibly informed, having sent for a
Cameronian clergyman when he was *in extremis*, was so fortunate as to convince the good
man, that, after all, he had no wish to bring down on the scattered remnants of Mountain-
folks, "the bonnets of Bonny Dundee." Hard! that the speculators in print and paper will
not allow a good man to rest quiet in his grave!!!

† *Buist*—The brand or mark set upon sheep or cattle by their owners.

gentleman who has served through the whole war; but, I am aware, you will take nothing amiss at my hand.

And now, my good sir, let us address ourselves to our task, and arrange as we best can the manuscript of your Benedictine, so as to suit the taste of this critical age. You will find I have made very liberal use of his permission, to alter whatever seemed too favourable to the Church of Rome, which I abominate, were it but for her fasts and penance.

Our reader is doubtless impatient, and we must own, with John Bunyan,

> We have too long detained him in the porch,
> And kept him from the sunshine with a torch.

Adieu, therefore, my dear Captain—Remember me respectfully to the parson, the schoolmaster, and the baillie, and all friends of the happy club in the village of Kennaquhair. I have never seen, and never will see, one of their faces; and notwithstanding, I believe that as yet I am better acquainted with them than any man who lives.—I will soon introduce you to my jocund friend Mr John Ballantyne of Trinity-Grove, whom you will find warm from his match at single-stick with a brother publisher. Peace to their differences! it is a wrathful trade, and the *irritable genus* comprehends the bookselling as well as the book-writing species.—Once more adieu!

THE AUTHOR OF WAVERLEY.

THE MONASTERY

VOLUME I

Chapter One

O aye! the Monks, the Monks! they did the mischief,
Theirs all the grossness, all the superstition
Of a most gross and superstitious age—
May *he* be praised that sent the healthful tempest,
And scattered all these pestilential vapours!
But that we owed them *all* to yonder Harlot
Throned on the seven hills with her cup of gold,
I will as soon believe, with kind Sir Roger,
That old Moll White took wing with cat and broomstick,
And raised the last night's thunder.

Old Play

THE VILLAGE described in the Benedictine's manuscript by the
name of Kennaquhair, bears the same Celtic termination which
occurs in Traquhair, Caquhair, and other compounds. The learned
Chalmers derives this word Quhair, from the winding course of the
stream; a definition which coincides in a remarkable degree with the
serpentine turns of the river Tweed near the village of which we
speak. It has been long famous for the splendid Monastery of Saint
Mary, founded by the first David of Scotland, in whose reign and in
the same country were formed the no less splendid establishments of
Melrose, Jedburgh, and Kelso. The donations of land with which
the King endowed these wealthy fraternities procured him from the
Monkish historians the epithet of Saint, and from one of his impoverished descendants the splenetic censure, "that he had been a sore
saint for the Crown."

It seems probable notwithstanding, that David, who was a wise as
well as a pious monarch, was not moved solely by religious motives to
those great acts of munificence to the church, but annexed political
views to his pious generosity. His possessions in Northumberland and

Cumberland became precarious after the loss of the Battle of the Standard; and since the comparatively fertile valley of Teviotdale was likely to become the frontier of his kingdom, it is probable he wished to secure at least a part of these valuable possessions by placing them in the hands of the Monks, whose property was for a long time respected, even amidst the rage of a frontier war. In this manner alone had the King some chance of insuring protection and security to the cultivators of the soil; and, in fact, for several ages the possessions of these Abbies were each a sort of Goshen, enjoying the calm light of peace and immunity, while the rest of the country, occupied by wild clans and marauding barons, was one dark scene of confusion, blood, and unremitted outrage.

But these immunities did not continue down to the union of the crowns. Long before that period the wars betwixt England and Scotland had lost their original character of international hostilities, and had become on the part of the English a war of subjugation, on that of the Scots a desperate and infuriated defence of their liberties. This introduced on both sides a degree of fury and animosity unknown to the earlier period of their history; and as religious scruples soon gave way to national hatred spurred by the love of plunder, the patrimony of the Church was no longer sacred from incursions on either side. Still, however, the tenants and vassals of the great Abbies had many advantages over those of the lay barons, who were harassed by constant military duty, until they became desperate, and lost all relish for the arts of peace. The vassals of the church, on the other hand, were only liable to be called to arms on general occasions, and at other times were permitted in comparative quiet to possess their farms and *feus*.* They of course exhibited superior skill in every thing that related to the cultivation of the soil, and were therefore both wealthier and better informed than the military retainers of the restless chiefs and nobles in their neighbourhood.

The residence of these church vassals was usually in a small village or hamlet, where, for the sake of mutual aid and protection, some thirty or forty families dwelt together. This was called the Town, and the land belonging to the various families by whom the Town was inhabited, was called the Township. They usually possessed the land in common, though in various proportions, according to their several grants. The part of the Township properly arable, and kept as such

---

* Small possessions conferred upon vassals and their heirs, held for a small quit-rent, or a moderate proportion of the produce. This was a favourite manner, by which the churchmen peopled the patrimony of their convents; and many descendants of such *feuars*, as they are called, are still to be found in possession of their family inheritances in the neighbourhood of the great Monasteries of Scotland.

continually under the plough, was called *in-field*. Here the use of quantities of manure supplied in some degree the exhaustion of the soil, and the feuars raised tolerable oats and bear,* usually sowed on alternate ridges, on which the labour of the whole community was bestowed without distinction, the produce being divided after harvest, agreeable to their respective interests.

There was, besides, *out-field* land, from which it was thought possible to extract a crop now and then, after which it was abandoned to the "skiey influences," until the exhausted powers of vegetation were restored. These out-field spots were selected by any feuar at his own choice, amongst the heaths and hills which were always annexed to the Township, to serve as pasturage to the community. The trouble of cultivating these patches of out-field, and the precarious chance that the crop would pay the labour, were considered as giving a right to any feuar, who chose to undertake the adventure, to the produce which might result from it.

There remained the pasturage of extensive moors, where the vallies often afforded good grass, and upon which the whole cattle belonging to the community fed indiscriminately during the summer, under the charge of the Town-herd, who regularly drove them out to pasture in the morning, and brought them back at night, without which precaution they would have fallen a speedy prey to some of the Snatchers in the neighbourhood. These are things to make modern agriculturists hold up their hands and stare; but the same mode of cultivation is not yet entirely in desuetude in some distant parts of North Britain, and may be witnessed in full force and exercise in the Zetland Archipelago.

The habitations of the church-feuars were not less primitive than their agriculture. In each small village or Town were several small towers, having battlements projecting over the side-walls, and usually an advanced angle or two with shot-holes for flanking the door-way, which was always defended by a strong door of oak, studded with nails, and often by an exterior grated door of iron. These small peel-houses were ordinarily inhabited by the principal feuars and their families; but, upon the alarm of approaching danger, the whole inhabitants thronged from their own miserable cottages, which were situated around, to garrison these points of defence. It was then no easy matter for a hostile party to penetrate into the village, for the men were habituated to the use of bows and fire-arms, and the towers being generally so placed, that the discharge from one crossed that of another, it was impossible to assail any of them individually.

The interior of these houses were usually sufficiently wretched, for

* Or bigg, a coarse kind of barley.

it would have been folly to have furnished them in a manner which could excite the avarice of their loose neighbours. Yet the families themselves exhibited in their appearance a degree of comfort, information, and independence, which could hardly have been expected. Their in-field supplied them with bread and home-brewed ale, their herds and flocks with beef and mutton, (the extravagance of killing lambs or calves was never thought of.) Each family killed a mart, or fat bullock, in November, which was salted up for winter use, to which the good-wife could, upon great occasions, add a dish of pigeons or a fat capon—the ill-cultivated garden gave "lang-cale,"—and the river gave salmon to relish them during the season of Lent.

Of fuel they had plenty, for the bogs afforded turf, and the remains of the abused woods continued to give them logs for burning, as well as timber for the usual domestic purposes. In addition to these comforts, the good-man would now and then sally forth to the greenwood, and mark down a buck of season with his gun or his cross-bow; and the Father Confessor seldom refused him absolution for the trespass, if duly invited to take his share of the smoking haunch. Some, yet bolder, made, either with their own domestics, or by associating themselves with the moss-troopers, in the language of shepherds, "a start and owerloup" into England; and the golden ornaments and silken head-gear worn by the females of one or two families of note, were invidiously traced by their neighbours to such successful excursions. This, however, was a more inexpiable crime in the eyes of the Abbot and Community of Saint Mary's, than the borrowing one of the "gude king's deer;" and they failed not to discountenance and punish, by every means in their power, offences which were sure to lead to severe retaliation on the property of the church, and which tended to alter the character of their peaceful vassalage.

As to the information possessed by those dependants of the Abbacies, they might have been truly said to be better fed than taught, even though their feeding had been worse than it was. Still, however, they enjoyed opportunities of knowledge from which others were secluded. The Monks were in general well acquainted with their vassals and tenants, and familiar in the families of the better class among them, where they were sure to be received with the respect due to their double character of spiritual father and secular landlord. Thus it often happened, when a boy displayed talents and inclination for study, one of the brethren, with a view to his being bred to the church, or out of good nature, or in order to pass away his own idle time if he had no better motive, initiated him into the mysteries of reading and writing, and imparted to him such other knowledge as he himself possessed. And the heads of these allied families, having more time for reflection, and more skill, as well as stronger motives for improving their small properties, bore amongst their neighbours the character of shrewd, intelligent men, who claimed respect on account of their comparative wealth, even while they were despised for a less warlike and enterprizing turn than the other Borderers. They lived as much as they well could amongst themselves, avoiding the company of others, and dreading nothing more than to be involved in the deadly feuds and ceaseless contentions of the secular landholders.

Such was the general picture of these communities. During the fatal wars in the commencement of Queen Mary's reign, they had suffered dreadfully by the hostile incursions; for the English, now a Protestant people, were so far from sparing the church-lands, that they forayed them with more unrelenting severity than even the possessions of the laity. But the peace of 1550 had restored some degree of tranquillity to those distracted and harassed regions, and matters began again gradually to settle upon the former footing. The Monks repaired their ravaged shrines—the feuar again roofed his small fortalice which the enemy had ruined—the poor labourer rebuilt his cottage,—an easy task, where a few sods, stones, and some pieces of wood from the next copse, furnished all the materials necessary. The cattle, lastly, were driven out of the wastes and thickets in which the remnant of them had been secreted; and the mighty bull moved at the head of his seraglio and their followers, to take possession of their wonted pastures. There ensued peace and quiet, the state of the age and nation considered, to the Monastery of Saint Mary, and its dependencies, for several tranquil years.

Chapter Two

In yon lone vale his early youth was bred,
Not solitary then—the bugle-horn
Of fell Alecto often waked its windings,
From where the brook joins the majestic river,
To the wild northern bog, the curlieu's haunt,
Where oozes forth its first and feeble streamlet.
                    Old Play

WE HAVE SAID, that most of the feuars dwelt in the village belonging to their townships. This was not, however, universally the case. A lonely tower, to which the reader must now be introduced, was at least one exception to the general rule.

It was of small dimensions, yet larger than those which occurred in the village, as intimating that, in case of assault, the proprietor would have to rely upon his own unassisted strength. Two or three miserable huts, at the foot of the fortalice, held the bondsmen and tenants of the feuar. The site was a beautiful green knoll, which started up suddenly in the very throat of a wild and narrow glen, and which, being surrounded, save on one side, by the winding of a small stream, afforded a position of considerable vantage.

But the great security of Glendearg, for so the place was called, lay in its secluded and hidden situation. To come at the Tower, it was necessary to travel three miles up the glen, crossing about twenty times the little stream which, twining through the narrow valley, encountered at every hundred yards the opposition of a rock or precipitous bank on the one side, which altered its direction, and caused it to shoot off in an oblique direction to the other. The hills which ascend on each side of this glen are very steep, and rise boldly over the stream, which is thus imprisoned within their barriers. The sides of the glen are impracticable for horse, and are only to be traversed by means of the sheep-paths which lie along their sides. It would be difficult to suppose that a road so hopeless and so difficult could lead to any habitation more important than the summer shealing of a shepherd.

Yet the glen, though lonely and difficult of access and sterile, was not then absolutely void of beauty. The turf which occupied the little plain ground on the sides of the stream, was as close and verdant as if it had occupied the scythes of a hundred gardeners once a-fortnight; and it was garnished with an embroidery of daisies and wild flowers, which the scythes would certainly have destroyed. The little brook, now confined betwixt closer limits, now left at large to chuse its course through the narrow valley, danced carelessly on from stream to pool, light and unturbid, as that better class of spirits who pass their way through life, yielding to insurmountable obstacles, but as far from being subdued by them as the sailor who meets by chance with an unfavourable wind, and shapes his course so as to be driven back as little as possible.

The mountains, as they would have been called in England, *Scotticé* the deep *braes*, rose abruptly over the little glen, here presenting the grey face of a rock, from which the turf had been peeled by the torrents, and there displaying little patches of wood and copse, which had escaped the waste of the cattle and the sheep and the feuars, and which, feathering naturally up the beds of empty torrents, or occupying the concave recesses of the bank, gave at once beauty and variety to the landscape. Above these scattered woods rose the hill, in barren, but purple majesty; the dark rich hue, particularly in autumn, contrasting beautifully with the thickets of oak and birch, the mountain-ashes and thorns, the alders and quivering aspens, which chequered and varied the descent, and not less with the dark-green and velvet turf, which composed the level part of the narrow glen.

Yet, though thus embellished, the scene could neither be strictly termed sublime or beautiful, and scarcely even picturesque or striking. But its extreme solitude pressed on the heart; the traveller felt that uncertainty whither he was going, or in what so wild a path was to terminate, which, at times, strikes more on the imagination than the grand features of a show-scene, when you know the exact distance of the inn where your dinner is bespoken, and at the moment preparing. These are ideas, however, of a far later age; for at the time we treat of, the picturesque, the beautiful, the sublime, and all their intermediate shades, were ideas absolutely unknown to the inhabitants and occasional visitors of Glendearg.

They had, however, attached to the scene feelings fitting the time. Its name, signifying the Red Valley, seems to have been derived, not only from the purple colour of the heath, with which the upper part of the rising banks was profusely cloathed, but also from the dark red colour of the rocks, and of the precipitous earthen banks, which in that country are called *scaurs*. Another glen, about the head of Ettrick, has acquired the same name from similar circumstances; and there are probably more in Scotland to which it has been given.

As our Glendearg did not abound in mortal visitants, superstition, that it might not be absolutely destitute of inhabitants, had peopled its recesses with beings belonging to another world. The savage and capricious Brown Man of the Moors, a being which seems the genuine descendant of the northern dwarfs, was supposed to be seen here frequently, especially after the autumnal equinox, when the fogs were thick, and objects not easily distinguished. The Scottish fairies, too, a whimsical, irritable, and mischievous tribe, who, though at times capriciously benevolent, were more frequently adverse to mortals, were also supposed to have formed a residence in a particularly wild recess of the glen, of which the real name was, in allusion to that circumstance, *Corri-nan-shian*, which, in corrupted Celtic, signifies the Hollow of the Fairies. But the neighbours were more cautious in speaking about this place, and avoided giving it a name, from an idea common then through all the British and Celtic provinces of Scotland, and still retained in many places, that to speak either good or ill of this capricious race of supernatural beings, is to provoke their resentment, and that secrecy and silence is what they chiefly desire from those who may intrude upon their revels, or discover their haunts.

A mysterious terror was thus attached to the little dale, which

afforded access from the broad valley of the Tweed, up the little glen
we have described, to the fortalice called the Tower of Glendearg.
Beyond the knoll, where, as we have said, the little tower was situated,
the hills grew more steep, and narrowed on the slender brook, so as
scarce to leave a foot-path; and there the glen terminated in a wild
water-fall, where a slender thread of water dashed in a precipitous
line of foam over two or three precipices. Yet farther in the same
direction, and above these successive cataracts, lay a wild and extensive morass, frequented only by water-fowl, wide, waste, apparently
almost interminable, and serving in a great measure to separate the
inhabitants of the little glen from those who lived to the northward.

To restless and indefatigable moss-troopers, indeed, these morasses were well known, and sometimes afforded a retreat. They often
rode down the glen—called at this tower—asked and received hospitality—but still with a sort of reserve on the part of its more
peaceful inhabitants, who entertained them as a party of North-Am-
erican Indians might be received by a new European settler, as much
out of fear as from hospitality, while the uppermost wish is the speedy
departure of these savage guests.

This had not always been the current of feeling in the little valley
and its tower. Simon Glendinning, its former inhabitant, boasted his
connection by blood with that ancient family of Glendonwyne, on
the western border. He was used to narrate, at his fire-side, in the
autumn evenings, the feats of the family to which he belonged, one
of whom fell by the side of the brave Earl of Douglas at Otterbourne.
On these occasions Simon usually had upon his knee an ancient
broad-sword, which had belonged to his ancestors before any of the
family had consented to accept a fief under the peaceful dominion of
the Monks of Saint Mary's. In modern days, Simon might have lived
at ease on his own estate, and quietly murmured against the fate that
had doomed him to dwell there, and cut off his access to martial
renown. But so many opportunities, nay, so many calls there were for
him, who in those days spoke big, to make good his words by his
actions, that Simon Glendinning was soon under the necessity of
marching with the men of the Halidome, as it was called, of Saint
Mary's, on that disastrous campaign which was concluded by the
Battle of Pinkie.

The Catholic clergy were deeply interested in that national quarrel,
the principal object of which was, to prevent the union of the infant
Queen Mary with the son of the heretical Henry VIII. The Monks had
called out all their vassals, under an experienced leader. Many of
themselves had taken arms, and marched to the field, under a banner
representing a female, supposed to personify the Scottish Church,

kneeling in the attitude of prayer, with the legend, *Afflictæ Sponsæ ne obliviscaris.**

The Scots, however, in all their wars, had more occasion for good and cautious generals than for excitation, whether political or enthusiastic. Their headlong and impatient courage uniformly induced them to rush to the action without duly weighing either their own situation, or that of their enemies, and the inevitable consequence was frequent defeat. With the dolorous slaughter of Pinkie we have nothing to do, excepting that, among ten thousand men of low and high degree, Simon Glendinning, of the Tower of Glendearg, bit the dust, no way disparaging in his death that ancient race from which he claimed his descent.

When the doleful news, which spread terror and mourning through the whole of Scotland, reached the Tower of Glendearg, the widow of Simon, Elspet Brydone by her family name, was alone in that desolate habitation, excepting a hind or two, alike past martial and agricultural labour, and the helpless widows and families of those who had fallen with their master. The feeling of desolation was universal;—but what availed it? The Monks, their patrons and protectors, were driven from their Abbey by the English forces, who now overrun the country, and compelled at least an appearance of submission on the part of the inhabitants. The Protector, Somerset, formed a strong camp among the ruins of the ancient Castle of Roxburgh, and compelled the neighbouring country to come in, pay tribute, and take assurance from him, as the phrase then went. Indeed, there was no power of resistance remaining, and the few barons, whose high spirit disdained even the appearance of surrender, could only retreat into the wildest fastnesses of the country, leaving their houses and properties to the wrath of the English, who detached parties through the country to distress, by military exaction, those whose chiefs had not made their submission. The Abbot and his community having retreated beyond Forth, their lands were severely forayed, as their sentiments were held peculiarly inimical to the alliance with England.

Amongst the troops detached on this service was a small party, commanded by Stawarth Bolton, a captain in the English army, and full of the blunt and unpretending gallantry and generosity which has so often distinguished the nation. Resistance was in vain. Elspet Brydone, when she discerned a dozen of horsemen threading their way up the glen, with a man at their head, whose scarlet cloak, bright armour, and dancing plume, proclaimed him a leader, saw no better protection for herself than to issue from the iron grate, covered with a long mourning veil, and holding one of her two sons in each hand, to meet

* Forget not the afflicted Spouse.

the Englishman—state her deserted condition,—place the little tower at his command—and beg for his mercy. She stated her intention in a few brief words, and added, "I submit only because I have nae means of resistance."

"And I do not ask your submission, mistress, for the same reason," replied the Englishman. "To be satisfied of your peaceful intentions is all I ask; and, from what you tell me, there is no reason to doubt them."

"At least, sir," said Elspet Brydone, "take share of what our spence and our garners afford—your horses are tired—your folk want refreshment."

"Not a whit—not a whit," answered the honest Englishman; "it shall never be said that we disturbed by carousal the widow of a brave soldier, while she was mourning for her husband.—Comrades—faces about.—Yet, stay," he added, checking his war-horse, "my parties are out in every direction; they must have some token that your family are under my assurance of safety.—Here, my little fellow," he said, speaking to the eldest boy, who might be about nine or ten years old, "lend me thy bonnet."

The child reddened, looked sulky, and hesitated, while the mother, with many a *fye* and *nay pshaw*, and such sarsenet chidings as tender mothers give to spoiled children, at length succeeded in snatching the bonnet from him, and handing it to the English leader.

Stawarth Bolton took his embroidered red cross from his barret-cap, and putting it into the loop of the boy's bonnet, said to the mistress, (for the title of lady was not given to dames of her degree,) "By this token, which all my people will respect, you will be freed from any importunity on the part of our foragers." He placed it on the boy's head; but it was no sooner there, than the little fellow, his veins swelling, and his eyes shooting fire through tears, snatched the bonnet from his head, and, ere his mother could interfere, skimmed it into the brook. The other boy ran instantly to fish it out again, threw his brother's bonnet back to him, first taking out the cross, which, with great veneration, he kissed, and put into his bosom. The Englishman was half diverted, half surprised, with the scene.

"What mean ye by throwing away Saint George's red cross?" said he to the elder boy, in a tone betwixt jest and earnest.

"Because Saint George is a southern saint," said the child sulkily.

"Good—" said Stawarth Bolton. "And what did you mean by taking it out of the brook again, my little fellow?" he demanded of the younger.

"Because the priest says it is the common sign of salvation to all good Christians."

"Why, good again!" said the honest soldier. "I protest unto you, mistress, I envy you these boys—are they both yours?"

Stawarth Bolton had reason to put the question, for Halbert Glendinning, the elder of the boys, had hair as dark as the raven's plumage, black eyes, large, bold, and sparkling, that glittered under eyebrows of the same complexion; a skin deep embrowned, though it could not be termed swarthy, and an air of activity, frankness, and determination far beyond his age. On the other hand, Edward, the younger brother, was light-haired, blue-eyed, and of fairer complexion, in countenance rather pale, and not exhibiting that rosy hue which colours the sanguine cheek of robust health. Yet the boy had nothing sickly or ill conditioned in his look, but was, on the contrary, a fair and handsome child, with a smiling face, and mild, yet cheerful eye.

The mother glanced a proud motherly glance, first at the one, and then at the other, ere she answered the Englishman, "Surely, sir, they are both my children."

"And by the same father, mistress?" said Stawarth; but, seeing a blush of displeasure arise on her brow, he instantly added, "Nay, I meant no offence; I would have asked the same question at any of my gossips in Merry Lincoln.—Well, dame, you have two fair boys; I would I could borrow one, for Dame Bolton and I live childless in our old hall.—Come, little fellows, which of you will go with me?"

The trembling mother, half-fearing as he spoke, drew the children towards her, one with either hand, while they both answered the stranger. "I will not go with you," said Halbert boldly, "for you are a false-hearted Southron; and the Southron killed my father; and I will war on you to the death, when I can draw my father's sword."

"God-a-mercy, my little levin-bolt," said Stawarth, "the goodly custom of deadly feud will never go down in thy day, I presume.—And you, my fine white-head, will you not go with me, to ride a cockhorse?"

"No," said Edward, demurely, "for you are a heretic."

"Why, God-a-mercy still," said Stawarth Bolton. "Well, dame, I see I shall find no recruits to my troop from you; and yet I do envy you these two little chubby knaves." He sighed a moment, as was visible, in spite of gorget and corslet, and then added, "And yet, my dame and I would but quarrel which of the knaves we should like best, for I should wish for the black-eyed rogue—and she, I warrant me, for that blue-eyed, fair-haired darling. Natheless, we must brook our solitary wedlock, and wish joy to those that are more fortunate.—Serjeant Brittson, do thou remain here till recalled—protect this family, as under assurance—do them no wrong, and suffer no wrong to be done to them, as thou wilt answer it.—Dame, Brittson is a married man, old and steady; feed him on what you will, but give him not over-much liquor."

Dame Glendinning again offered refreshments, but with a faulter-ing voice, and an obvious desire her invitation should not be accepted. The fact was, that, supposing her boys as precious in the eyes of the Englishman as in her own, (the most ordinary of parental errors,) she was half afraid, that the admiration he expressed of them in his blunt manner might end in his actually carrying off one or other of the little darlings which he appeared to covet so much. She kept hold of their hands, therefore, as if her feeble strength could have been of service, had any violence been intended, and saw, with joy she could not disguise, the little party of horse countermarch, in order to descend the glen. Her feelings did not escape Stawarth Bolton. "I forgive you, dame," he said, "for being suspicious that an English falcon was hovering over your Scottish moor-brood. But fear not—those who have fewest children have fewest cares; nor does a wise man covet those of another household. Adieu, dame; when the black-eyed rogue is able to 'drive a prey' from England, teach him to spare women and children, for the sake of Stawarth Bolton."

"God be with you, gallant Southron," said Elspet Glendinning, but not till he was out of hearing, spurring on his good horse to regain the head of his party, whose plumage and armour was now glancing and gradually disappearing in the distance, as they winded down the glen.

"Mother," said the elder boy, "I will not say amen to a prayer for a Southron."

"Mother," said the younger, more reverentially, "is it right to pray for a heretic?"

"The God to whom I pray only knows," answered poor Elspet; "but these two words, Southron and heretic, have already cost Scotland ten thousand of her best and bravest, and me a husband, and you a father; and, whether blessing or banning, I never wish to hear them more.— Follow us to the Place, sir," she said to Brittson, "and such as we have to offer you shall be at your disposal."

Chapter Three

They lighted down on Tweed water,
And blew their coals sae het,
And fired the March and Teviotdale,
All in an evening late.
Auld Maitland

THE REPORT soon spread through the patrimony of Saint Mary's and its vicinity, that the Mistress of Glendearg had received assurance from the English Captain, and that her cattle were not to be driven off, or her corns burned. Among others who heard this report, it reached the ears of a lady, who, once much higher in rank than Elspet Glendinning, was now by the same calamity reduced to even greater misfortune.

She was the widow of a brave soldier, Walter Avenel, descended of a very ancient Border family, who once possessed immense estates in Eskdale. These had long since passed from them into other hands, but they still enjoyed an ancient Barony of considerable extent, not very far from the patrimony of Saint Mary's, and lying upon the same side of the river with the narrow vale of Glendearg, at the head of which was the little tower of the Glendinnings. Here they had lived, bearing a respectable rank amongst the gentry of their province, though neither wealthy nor powerful. This general regard had been much augmented by the skill, courage, and enterprize which had been displayed by Walter Avenel, the last Baron.

When Scotland began to recover from the dreadful shock she had sustained after the battle of Pinkie Cleuch, Avenel was one of the first who, assembling a small force, set an example in these bloody and unsparing skirmishes, which shewed that a nation, though conquered and overrun by invaders, may yet wage against them such a war of detail as shall in the end become fatal to the foreigners. In one of these, however, Walter Avenel fell, and the news which came to the house of his fathers was followed by the distracting intelligence, that a party of Englishmen were coming to plunder the house and lands of his widow, in order by this act of terror to prevent others from following the example of the deceased.

The unfortunate lady had no better refuge than the miserable cottage of a shepherd among the hills, to which she was hastily removed, scarce conscious where or for what purpose her terrified attendants were removing her and her infant daughter from her own house. Here she was tended with all the duteous service of ancient times by the shepherd's wife, Tibb Tacket, who in better days had been her own bower-woman. For a time the lady was unconscious of the extent of her misery; but when the first stunning effect of grief was so far passed away that she could form an estimate of her own situation, the widow of Avenel had cause to envy the lot of her husband in his dark and silent asylum. The domestics who had guided her to her place of refuge, were presently obliged to disperse to consult for their own safety, or to seek for necessary subsistence, and the shepherd and his wife, whose poor cottage she shared, were soon after deprived of the means of affording their late mistress even that coarse sustenance which they had gladly shared with her. Some of the English foragers had discovered and driven off the few sheep which had escaped the first researches of their avarice. Two cows shared the fate of the remnant of their stock; they had afforded the family almost their sole support, and now famine appeared to stare them in the face.

"We are broken and beggared now, out and out," said old Martin the Shepherd—and he wrung his hands in the bitterness of agony, "the thieves, the harrying thieves! not a cloot left of the hail hirsel!"

"And to see poor Grizzy and Crombie," said his wife, "turning back their necks to the byre, and routing while the stony-hearted villains were brogging them on wi' their lances!"

"There were but four of them," said Martin, "and I have seen the day forty wad not have ventured this length. But our strength and manhood is gane with our puir maister."

"For the sake of the holy-rood, whisht man," said the goodwife, "our leddy is half gane already, as ye may see by that flighering of the ee-lid—a word mair and she is gane outright."

"I could almost wish," said Martin, "we were a' then gane, for what to do passes my puir wit. I care little for mysel, or you, Tibb,—we can make a fend—work and want—we can do baith, but she can do neither."

They canvassed their situation thus openly before the lady, convinced by the paleness of her looks, her quivering lip and dead-set eye, that she neither heard nor understood what they were saying.

"There is a way," said the shepherd, "but I kenna if she could bring her heart to it,—there's Simon Glendinning's widow of the glen yonder, has had assurance from the Southron loons, and nae soldier to steer them for one cause or other. Now, if the leddie could bow her mind to take quarters wi' Elspet Glendinning till better days cast up, nae doubt it wad be doing an honour to the like of her, but"——

"An honour?" answered Tibb, "ay, by my word, sic an honour as wad be pride to her kin mony a lang year after her banes were in the mould. Oh! gudeman, to hear ye even the Lady of Avenel, to seeking quarters wi' a Kirk-vassal's widow!"

"Loth should I be to wish her to it," said Martin; "but what may we do?—to stay here is mere starvation; and where to go, I'm sure I ken nae mair than ony tup I ever herded."

"Speak no more of it," said the widow of Avenel, suddenly joining in the conversation, "I will go to the Tower.—Dame Elspet is of good folk, a widow, and the mother of orphans,—she will give us house-room until something be thought upon. These evil showers make the worst bush better than no beild."

"See there, see there," said Martin, "you see the leddy has twice our sense."

"And natural it is," said Tibb, "seeing that she is convent-bred, and can lay silk broidery, forbye white seam and shell-work."

"Do you not think," said the lady to Martin, still clasping her child to her bosom, and making it clear from what motives she desired the refuge, "that Dame Glendinning will make us welcome."

"Blythely welcome, blythely welcome, my leddy," answered Martin cheerily, "and we will deserve a welcome at her hand. Men are scarce now, my leddy, with these wars, and gie me a thought of time to it, I can do as gude a day's darg as ever I did in my life—And Tibb can sort cows with ony living woman."

"And muckle mair could I do," said Tibb, "were it in ony feasible house; but there will be neither pearlins to mend, nor pinners to busk up in Elspet Glendinning's."

"Whisht wi' your pride, woman," said the shepherd; "eneugh ye can do, baith outside and inside, an ye set your mind to it; and hard it is if we twa canna work for threefolks' meat, forbye my dainty wee leddy there. Come awa—come awa—nae use in staying here langer; we have five Scots mile over moss and ling, and that is nae easy walk for a leddy born and bred."

Household stuff there was little or none to remove or care for; an old poney which had escaped the plunderers, owing partly to its pitiful appearance, partly from the reluctance which it shewed to be caught by strangers, was employed to carry the few blankets, and other trifles which they possessed. When Shagram came to his master's well-known whistle, he was surprised to find the poor thing had been wounded, though slightly, by an arrow, which one of the forayers had shot off in anger after he had long chased it in vain.

"Ay, Shagram," said the old man as he applied something to the wound, "must you rue the lang-bow as weel as all of us?"

"What corner in Scotland rues it not?" said the Lady of Avenel.

"Ay, ay, madam," said Martin, "God keep the kindly Scot from the cloth-yard shaft, and he will keep himself from the handy stroke. But let us go our way—the trash that is left I can come back for—there is nae ane to stir it but the good neighbours, and they"——

"For the love of God, goodman," said his wife in a remonstrating tone, "haud your peace! Think what ye're saying, and we hae sae muckle wild land to go over before we win to the girth-gate."

The husband nodded acquiescence; for it was deemed highly imprudent to speak of the fairies either by their title of *good neighbours* or by any other, especially when about to pass the places which they were supposed to haunt.

They set forward on their pilgrimage on the last day of October. "This is thy birthday, my sweet Mary," said the mother, as a sting of bitter recollection crossed her mind. "Oh, who could have believed that the head, which, few years since, was cradled amongst so many rejoicing friends, may perhaps this night seek a cover in vain!"

The exiled family then set forward. Mary Avenel, a lovely little girl now just six years old, riding gipsey-fashion upon Shagram, betwixt two bundles of bedding, the Lady of Avenel walking by the animal's side, Tibb leading the bridle, and old Martin a few paces before, looking anxiously round him to explore the way.

Martin's task as guide, after two or three miles walking, became more difficult than he himself had expected, or than he was willing to avow. It happened that the extensive range of pasturage, with which he was conversant, lay to the west, and to get into the little valley of Glendearg he was to proceed easterly. In the wilder districts of Scotland, the passage from one vale to another, otherwise than by descending that which you leave, and reascending the other, is often very difficult. Heights and hollows, mosses and rocks intervene, and all those local impediments which throw a traveller out of his course. So that Martin, however sure of his general direction, became conscious, and at length was forced reluctantly to admit, that he had missed the direct road to Glendearg, though he insisted they must be very near it. "If we can but win across this wide bog," he said, "I shall warrant ye are on the tap of the tower."

But to get across the bog was a point of no small difficulty—the farther they ventured into it, though proceeding with all the caution which Martin's experience recommended, the more unsound the ground became, until, after they had passed some places of great peril, their best argument for going forward came to be, that they had to encounter equal danger in returning.

The Lady of Avenel had been tenderly nurtured, but what will not a woman endure when her child is in danger? Complaining less of the dangers of the road than her attendants, who had been inured to such from their infancy, she kept herself close by the side of the poney, watching its every footstep, and ready, when it was about to flounder in the morass, to snatch her little Mary from its back.

At length they came to a place where the guide greatly hesitated, for all around him was now broken lumps of heath, divided from each other by deep sloughs of black tenacious mire. After some consideration, Martin, selecting what he thought the safest path, began himself to lead forward Shagram, in order to afford greater security to the child. But Shagram snorted, laid his ears back, stretched his two feet forwards, and drew his hind feet under him, so as to adopt the best possible posture for obstinate resistance, and refused to move one yard in the direction indicated. Old Martin, much puzzled, now hesitated whether to exert his absolute authority, or to defer to the contumacious obstinacy of Shagram, and was not greatly comforted by his wife's observation, who, seeing Shagram stare with his eyes, distend his nostrils, and tremble with terror, hinted that "he surely saw more than they could see."

In this dilemma, the child suddenly exclaimed—"Bonny ladie signs to us to come yon gate." They all looked in the direction where the child pointed, but saw nothing, save a wreath of rising mist, which fancy might form into a human figure, but which afforded to Martin only the sorrowful conviction, that the danger of their situation was about to be increased by a heavy fog. He once more assayed Shagram; but the animal was inflexible in its determination not to move in the direction Martin recommended. "Take your awn way for it then," said Martin, "and let us see what you can do for us."

Shagram, abandoned to the discretion of his own free will, set off boldly in the direction the little girl had pointed. There was nothing wonderful in this, nor in its bringing them safe to the other side of the dangerous morass; for the instinct of these animals in traversing bogs is one of the most curious parts of their nature, and is a fact generally established. But it was remarkable, that the child more than once mentioned the beautiful lady and her signals, and that Shagram seemed to be in the secret, always moving in the same direction which she indicated. The lady took little notice at the time, her mind being probably occupied by the instant danger; but her faithful attendants changed expressive looks with each other more than once.

"All-Hallow Eve!" said Tibby, in a whisper to Martin.

"For the mercy of Our Lady, not a word of that now," said Martin in reply. "Tell your beads, woman, if you cannot be silent."

When they got once more on firm ground, Martin recognized certain land-marks, or cairns, on the tops of neighbouring hills, by which he was enabled to guide his course, and ere long they arrived at the Tower of Glendearg.

It was at the first sight of this little fortalice that the misery of her lot pressed hard on the poor Lady of Avenel. When by any accident they had met at church, market, or other place of public resort, she remembered the distant and respectful air with which the wife of the warlike baron was addressed by the spouse of the more humble feuar. And now, so much was her pride humbled, that she was to ask to share the precarious safety of the same feuar's widow, and her pittance of food, which might perhaps be yet more precarious. Martin probably guessed what was passing in her mind, for he looked at her with a wistful glance, as if to deprecate any change of resolution; and answering to his looks, rather than his words, she said, while the sparkle of subdued pride once more glanced from her eye, "If it were for myself alone, I could but die—but for this infant—the last pledge of Avenel"——

"True, my lady, true," said Martin hastily; and, as if to prevent the possibility of her retracting, he added, "I will step in and see Dame Elspet—I kenn'd her husband weel, and have bought and sold with him, for as great a man as he was."

Martin's tale was soon told, and met all acceptance from her companion in misfortune. The Lady of Avenel had been meek and courteous in her prosperity; in adversity, therefore, she met with the greater sympathy. Besides, there was a point of pride in sheltering and supporting a woman of such superior birth and rank. And not to do Elspet Glendinning injustice, she felt sympathy for a woman whose fate resembled her own in so many parts, yet was so much more severe. Every species of hospitality was gladly and respectfully extended to the distressed travellers, and they were kindly requested to stay as long at Glendearg as their circumstances rendered necessary, or their inclination prompted.

Chapter Four

Ne'er be I found by thee o'er awed,
On that thrice hallow'd eve abroad,
When goblins haunt from flood and fen,
The steps of men.
COLLINS'S *Ode to Fear*

As THE COUNTRY became more settled, the lady would have willingly returned to her husband's mansion. But that was no longer in her power. It was a reign of minority, when the strongest had the best right, and when acts of usurpation were frequent amongst those who had much power and little conscience.

Julian Avenel, the younger brother of the deceased Walter, was a person of this description. He hesitated not to seize upon his brother's house and lands, so soon as the retreat of the English permitted him. At first, he occupied the property in the name of his niece, but when the lady proposed to return with her child to the mansion of its fathers, he gave her to understand that Avenel, being a male fief, descended to the brother, instead of the daughter, of the last possessor. The ancient philosopher declined a dispute with the emperor who commanded twenty legions, and the widow of Walter Avenel was in no condition to maintain a contest with the leader of twenty moss-troopers. Julian was also a man of service, who could back a friend in case of need, and was sure, therefore, to find protectors among the ruling powers. In short, however clear the little Mary's right to the possessions of her fathers, her mother saw the necessity of giving way, at least for the time, to the usurpation of her uncle.

Her patience and forbearance was so far attended with advantage, that Julian, for very shame's sake, could no longer suffer her to be absolutely dependent on the charity of Elspet Glendinning. A drove of cattle and a bull, (which were probably missed by some English farmer,) were sent to the pastures of Glendearg; presents of raiment and household stuff were sent liberally, and some little money, though with a more sparing hand; for those in the situation of Julian Avenel could come more easily by the goods represented, than the representing medium of value, and made their payments chiefly in kind.

In the meantime, the widows of Walter Avenel and Simon Glendinning had become habituated to each other's society, and were unwilling to part. The lady could hope no more secret or secure residence than in the Tower of Glendearg, and she was now in a condition to support her share of the mutual house-keeping. Elspet, on the other hand, felt pride, as well as pleasure, in the society of a guest of such distinction, and was at all times willing to pay much greater deference than the Lady of Walter Avenel could be prevailed on to accept.

Martin and his wife diligently served the united family in their several vocations, and yielded obedience to both mistresses, though always considering themselves as the especial servants of the Lady of Avenel. This distinction sometimes occasioned a slight degree of difference between Dame Elspet and Tibb; the former being jealous of her own consequence, and the latter apt to lay rather too much stress upon the rank and family of her mistress. But both were alike desirous to conceal such petty squabbles from the lady, her hostess scarce yielding to her old domestic in respect for her person. Neither did the difference exist in such a degree as to interrupt the general harmony of the family, for the one wisely gave way as she saw the other become warm; and Tibb, though she often gave the first provocation, had generally the sense to be the first in relinquishing the argument.

The world which lay beyond was gradually forgotten by the inhabitants of the sequestered glen, and unless when she attended mass at the Monastery Church upon some high holiday, Alice of Avenel almost forgot that she once held an equal rank with the proud wives of the neighbouring barons and nobles who on such occasions crowded to the solemnity. The recollection gave her little pain. She had loved her husband for himself, and in his inestimable loss all lesser subjects of regret had lost the power of interesting her. At times, indeed, she thought of claiming the protection of the Queen Regent (Mary of

Guise) for her little orphan, but the fear of Julian Avenel always came between. She was sensible that he would have neither scruple nor difficulty in spiriting away the child, (if he did not proceed further,) should he once consider its existence as formidable to his interest. Besides, he was a wild liver, mingling in all feuds and forays, wherever there was a spear to be broken; he evinced no purpose of marrying, and the fate which he continually was braving might at length remove him from his usurped inheritance. Alice of Avenel, therefore, judged it wise to check all ambitious thoughts for the present, and remain quiet in the rude, but peaceable retreat, to which Providence had conducted her.

It was upon an All-Hallow's Eve, when the family had resided together for nearly three years, that the domestic circle was assembled around the blazing turf-fire, in the old narrow hall of the Tower of Glendearg. The idea of the master and mistress of the mansion feeding or living apart from their domestics, was at this period never entertained. The highest end of the board, the most commodious settle by the fire,—these were their only marks of distinction; and the servants mingled with deference indeed, but unreproved and with freedom, in whatever conversation was going forward. But the two or three domestics, kept merely for agricultural purposes, had retired to their own cottages without, and with them a couple of wenches, usually employed within doors, the daughters of one of the hinds.

After their departure, Martin locked, first, the iron grate; and, secondly, the inner door of the tower, when the domestic circle was thus arranged. Dame Elspet sate pulling the thread from her distaff; Tibb watched the progress of scalding the whey, which hung in a large pot upon the *crook*, a chain terminated by a hook, which was suspended in the chimney to serve the purpose of the modern crane. Martin, while busied in repairing some of the household articles, (for every man in these days was his own carpenter and smith, as well as his own tailor and shoemaker,) kept from time to time a watchful eye upon the three children.

They were allowed, however, to exercise their juvenile restlessness by running up and down the hall, behind the seats of the elder members of the family, with the privilege of occasionally making excursions into one or two small apartments which opened from it, and gave excellent opportunity to play at hide-and-seek. This night, however, the children seemed not disposed to avail themselves of their privilege of visiting these dark regions, but preferred carrying on their gambols in the vicinity of the light.

In the mean while, Alice of Avenel, sitting close to an iron candle-stick, which supported a mis-shapen torch of domestic manufacture, read small detached passages from a thick clasped volume, which she preserved with the greatest care. The art of reading, the lady had acquired by her residence in a nunnery during her youth, but she seldom, of late years, put it to any other use than perusing this little volume, which formed her whole library. The family listened to the portions which she selected, as to some good thing which there was a merit in hearing with respect, whether it was fully understood or no. To her daughter, Alice of Avenel had determined to impart their mystery more fully, but the knowledge was at that period attended with great personal danger, and was not rashly to be trusted to a child.

The noise of the romping children interrupted, from time to time, the voice of the lady, and drew on the noisy culprits the rebuke of Elspet.

"Could they not go farther a-field, if they behoved needs to make such a din, and disturb the lady's good words?" And this command was backed with the threat of sending the whole party to bed if it was not attended to punctually. Acting under the injunction, the children first played at a greater distance from the party, and more quietly, and then began to stray into the adjacent apartments, as they became impatient of the restraint to which they were subject. But, all at once, the two boys came open-mouthed into the hall, to tell that there was an armed man in the spence.

"It must be Christie of Clinthill," said Martin, rising; "what can have brought him here at this time?"

"Or how came he in?" said Elspet.

"Alas, what can he seek?" said the Lady of Avenel, to whom this man, a retainer of her husband's brother, and who sometimes executed his commissions at Glendearg, was an object of secret apprehension and suspicion. "Gracious heaven!" she added, starting up, "where is my child?" All rushed to the spence, Halbert Glendinning first arming himself with a rusty sword, and the younger seizing upon the lady's book. They hastened to the spence, and were relieved of a part of their anxiety by meeting Mary at the door of the apartment. She did not seem in the slightest degree alarmed, or disturbed. They rushed into the spence, (a sort of interior apartment in which the family eat their victuals in the summer season), but there was no one there.

"Where is Christie of Clinthill?" said Martin.

"I do not know," said little Mary; "I never saw him."

"And what made you, ye misleard loons," said Dame Elspet to her two boys, "come tumbling yon gate into the ha', roaring like bull-segs, to frighten the leddy, and her far frae strong?" The boys looked at each other in silence and confusion, and their mother proceeded with her lecture. "Could ye find nae night for daffin but Hallowe'en, and nae time but when the leddy was reading to us about the holy Saints? May ne'er be in my fingers, if I dinna sort ye baith for it!" The eldest boy bent his eyes on the ground, the youngest began to weep, but neither spoke; and their mother would have proceeded to extremities, but for the interposition of the little maiden.

"Dame Elspet, it was *my* fault—I did cry to them, that I saw a man in the spence."

"And what made you do so, child," said her mother, "to startle us all thus?"

"Because," said Mary, lowering her voice, "I could not help it."

"Not help it, Mary!—you occasioned all this idle noise, and you could not help it? How mean you by that, minion?"

"There really was a man, an armed man, in this spence," said Mary; "and because I was surprised to see him, I cried out to Halbert and Edward"——

"She has told it herself," said Halbert Glendinning; "or it had never been told by me."

"Nor by me either," said Edward emulously.

"Mistress Mary," said Elspet, "you never told us any thing before that was not true; tell us if this was a Hallowe'en cantrip, and make an end of it." The Lady of Avenel looked as if she would have interfered, but knew not how; and Elspet, who was too eagerly curious to regard any distant hint, persevered in her enquiries. "Was it Christie of the Clinthill?—I would not for a mark that he were about the house, and a body no ken whare."

"It was not Christie," said Mary; "it was—it was a gentleman—a gentleman with a bright breast-plate, like what I hae seen langsyne, when we dwelt at Avenel"——

"What like was he?" continued Tibbie, who now took share in the investigation.

"Black-haired, black-eyed, with a peaked black beard," said the child, "and many a fold of pearling round his neck, and hanging down ower his breast-plate; and he had a beautiful hawk, with silver bells, standing on his left hand, with a crimson silk hood upon its head"——

"Ask her no more questions, for the love of God," said the anxious menial to Elspet, "but look to my leddy!" But the Lady of Avenel, taking Mary in her hand, turning hastily away, and walking into the hall, gave them no opportunity of remarking in what manner she received the child's communication, which she thus cut short. What Tibb thought of it appeared from her crossing herself repeatedly, and whispering into Elspet's ear, "Saint Mary preserve us!—the lassie has seen her father!"

When they reached the hall, they found the lady holding her daughter on her knee, and kissing her repeatedly. When they entered, she again arose, as to shun observation, and retired to the little apartment where her child and she occupied the same bed.

The boys were also sent to their cabin, and no one remained by the hall fire save the faithful Tibb and Dame Elspet, excellent persons both, but as thorough gossips as ever wagged a tongue.

It was but natural that they should instantly resume the subject of the supernatural appearance, for such they deemed it, which had this night alarmed the family.

"I could hae wished it had been the de'il himsel—Be good to and preserve us!—rather than Christie o' the Clinthill," said the matron of the mansion, "for the word runs rife in the country, that he is ane of the maist masterfu' thieves ever lap on horse."

"Hout-tout, Dame Elspet," said Tibb, "fear ye naething frae Christie—tods keep their ain holes clean. You kirk-folk make sic a fasherie about men shifting a wee bit for their living! Our Border-lairds wad ride with few men at their back, if a' the light-handed lads were out o' gate."

"Better they rade wi' nane than distress the country-side the gate they do," said Dame Elspet.

"But wha is to haud back the Southron then," said Tibb, "if ye take away the lances and broad-swords? I trow we auld wives couldna do that wi' rock and wheel, and as little the monks wi' bell and book."

"And sae weel as the lances and broad-swords hae kept them back, I trow!—I was mair beholden to ae Southron, and that was Stawarth Bolton, than to a' the Border-riders ever wore Saint Andrew's cross—I reckon their skelping back and forward, and lifting honest men's gear, hae been a main cause of a' the breach between us and England, and I am sure that cost me a kind goodman. They speak about the wedding of the Prince and our Queen, but it's as like to been the driving of the Cumberland folk's stocking that brought them down on us like dragons." Tibb would not in other circumstances have failed to answer what she thought reflections disparaging to her country-folks; but she recollected that Dame Elspet was mistress of the family, curbed her own zealous patriotism, and hastened to change the subject.

"And is it not strange," she said, "that the heiress of Avenel should hae seen her father this blessed night?"

"And ye think it was her father then," said Elspet Glendinning.

"What else can I think?" said Tibb.

"It may have been something waur, in his likeness," answered Dame Glendinning.

"I ken naething about that," said Tibb,—"but his likeness it was, that I will be sworn to, just as he used to ride out a hawking; for having enemies in the country, he seldom laid off the breast-plate—And, for my part," added Tibb, "I dinna think a man looks like a man unless he has steel on his breast and by his side too."

"I have no skill of your harness on breast or side either," said Dame Glendinning; "but I ken there is little luck in Hallowe'en sights, for I have had ane mysell."

"Indeed, Dame Elspet?" said old Tibb, edging her stool closer to the huge elbow-chair occupied by her friend, "I should like to hear about that."

"Ye maun ken then, Tibb," said Dame Glendinning, "that when I was a hempie of nineteen or twenty, it wasna my fault if I wasna at a' the merry-makings time about."

"That was very natural," said Tibb; "but ye hae sobered since that, or ye wadna haud our braw gallants sae lightly."

"I have had that wad sober me or ony ane," said the matron. "Aweel, Tibb, a lass like me wasna to lack wooers, for I wasna sae ill favoured that the tikes wad bark after me."

"How should that be," said Tibb, "and you sic a weel-favoured woman at this day?"

"Fie, fie! cummer," said the matron of Glendearg, hitching her seat of honour, in her turn, a little nearer to the cuttie-stool on which Tibb was seated; "weel-favoured is past my time of day. But I might pass then, for I wasna sae tocherless but what I had a bit land at my breast-lace.—My father was portioner of Littledearg."

"Ye hae tell'd me that before," said Tibb; "but anent the Hallowe'en."

"Aweel, aweel, I had mair joes than ane, but I favoured nane o' them; and sae, at Hallowe'en, Father Nicolas the cellarer—he was cellarer before this father, Father Clement, that now is—was cracking his nuts and drinking his brown beer with us, and as blythe as might be, and they would have me try a cantrip to ken wha suld wed me— And the Monk said there was nae ill in it, and if there was, he wad assoil me for it—and whae but I into the barn to winnow my three weights o' naething—Sair, sair my min' misgave me for fear of wrang-doing and wrang-suffering baith. But I had aye a bauld spirit. I had not winnowed the last weight clean out, and the moon was shining bright upon the floor, when in stalked the presence of my dear Simon Glendinning, that is now happy. I never saw him plainer in my life than I did that moment—he held up an arrow as he passed me, and I swarf'd awa' wi' fright. Muckle wark there was to bring me to mysel again, and sair they tried to make me believe that it was a trick of Father Nicolas and Simon between them, and that the arrow was to signify Cupid's shaft, as the Father called it; and mony a time Simon wad threep it to me after I was married—gude man, he liked not it should be said that he was seen out o' the body!—But mark the end o' it, Tibb; we were married, and the grey-goose wing was the death o' him, after a'.'"

"As it has been of ower mony brave men," said Tibb; "I could wish there wasna sic a bird as a goose in the wide warld, forbye the clecking that we hae at the burn-side."

"But tell me, Tibb," said Dame Glendinning, "what does your leddy aye do wi' that book in her hand?—It's nae wonder that her bairn sees bogles if she is aye reading on that thick black book wi' the silver clasps—there are ower mony gude words in it to come frae ony body but a priest—An' it were about Robin Hood, or some o' David Lindsay's ballats, ane wad ken better what to say to it. I am no misdoubting your mistress nae way, but I wad like ill to hae a decent house haunted wi' ghaists and gyre carlines."

"Ye hae nae reason to doubt my leddy, or ony thing she says or does, Dame Glendinning," said the faithful Tibb, something offended; "and touching the bairn, it's weel ken'd she was born on Hallowe'en, was nine years gane, and they that are born on Hallowe'en whiles see mair than ither folk."

"And that wad be the cause, then, that the bairn didna mak muckle din about what it saw—if it had been my Halbert himsel, forbye Edward, who is of safter nature, he wad hae yammered the hail night of a constancy. But it's like Mistress Mary has sic sights come mair natural to her."

"That may weel be," said Tibb; "for on Hallowe'en she was born, as I tell ye, and our auld parish priest wad fain hae had the night ower, and All-Hallow day begun. But for a' that, the sweet bairn is just like ither bairns, as ye may see yoursel; and except this blessed night, and ance before when we were in that weary bog on the road here, I kenna that it saw mair than ither folk."

"But what saw she in the bog, then," said Dame Glendinning, "forbye moor-cocks and heather-blutters?"

"The wean saw something like a white leddy that weised us the gate," said Tibb, "when we were like to hae perished in the mire cleughs—Certain it was that Shagram resisted, and I ken Martin thinks he saw something."

"And what might the white leddy be?" said Elspet; "have ye ony guess o' that?"

"It's weel ken'd that, Dame Elspet," said Tibb; "if ye had lived under grit folk, as I hae dune, ye wadna be to seek in that matter."

"I hae aye keepit my ain ha' house abune my head," said Elspet not without emphasis, "and if I havena lived wi' grit folk, grit folk have lived wi' me."

"Weel, weel, dame," said Tibb, "your pardon's prayed, there was nae offence meant. But ye maun ken the great ancient families canna be just served wi' the ordinary saunts, (praise to them) like Saunt Anthony, Saunt Cuthbert, and the like, that come and gang at every sinner's bidding, but they hae a sort of saunts or angels, or what not, to themsels; and as for the White Maiden of Avenel, she is ken'd ower the haill country. And she is aye seen to yammer and wail before ony o' them dies, as was weel ken'd by twenty folk before the death of Walter Avenel, haly be his cast!"

"If she can do nae mair than that," said Elspet somewhat scornfully, "they needna make mony vows to her I trow—can she make nae better fend for them than that, and has naething better to do than wait on them?"

"Mony braw services can the White Maiden do for them to the boot of that, and has dune in the auld histories," said Tibb, "but I mind o' naething in my day, except it was her that the bairn saw in the bog."

"Aweel, aweel, Tibbie," quoth Dame Glendinning, rising and lighting the iron lamp, "these are grand privileges of your grand folks. But Our Lady and Saint Paul are good enough saunts for me, and I'se warrant them never leave me in a bog that they can help me out o', seeing I send four waxen candles to their chapels every Candlemas; and if they are not seen to weep for my death, I'se warrant them smile at my joyful arising again—whilk Heaven send to all of us, Amen."

"Amen," answered Tibbie devoutly; "and now it's time I should hap up the wee bit gathering turf, or the fire is ower low."

Busily she set herself to perform this duty. The relict of Simon Glendinning did but pause a moment and cast a heedful and cautious glance all around the hall, to see that nothing was out of its proper place; then wishing Tibbie good-night, she retired to her repose.

"The de'il's in the carline," said Tibb to herself, "because she was the wife of a cock-laird, she thinks hersel grander, I trow, than the bower-woman of a lady of that ilk." Having given vent to her suppressed spleen in this little ejaculation, Tibb also betook herself to slumber.

Chapter Five

A priest, ye cry, a priest!—lame shepherds they,
How shall they gather in the straggling flock?
Dumb dogs which bark not—how shall they compel
The loitering vagrants to the Master's fold?
Fitter to bask before the blazing fire,
And snuff the mess neat-handed Phillis dresses,
Than on the snow-wreath battle with the wolf.
                                        Reformation

THE HEALTH of the Lady of Avenel had been gradually decaying ever since her disaster. It seemed, as if the few years which followed her husband's death had done on her the work of half a century. She lost the fresh elasticity of form, the colour and the mien of health, and became wasted, wan, and feeble. She appeared to have no formed complaint; yet it was evident to those who looked on her, that her strength waned daily. Her lip at length became blanched and her eye dim. Yet she spoke not of any desire to see a priest, until Elspet Glendinning in her zeal could not refrain from touching upon a point which she deemed essential to salvation. Alice of Avenel received her hint kindly, and thanked her for it.

"If any good priest would take the trouble of such a journey," she said, "he should be welcome; for the prayers and lessons of the good must be at all times advantageous."

This quiet acquiescence was not quite what Elspet Glendinning wished or expected. She made up, however, by her own enthusiasm for the lady's want of eagerness to avail herself of ghostly counsel, and Martin was dispatched with such haste as Shagram could make, to pray one of the religious men of Saint Mary's to come up to administer the last consolations to the widow of Walter de Avenel.

When the Sacristan had announced to the Lord Abbot, that the Lady of the umquhile Walter de Avenel was in very weak health in the Tower of Glendearg, and desired the assistance of a father confessor, the lordly monk paused on the request.

"We do remember Walter de Avenel," he said; "a good knight and a valiant—he was dispossessed of his lands, and slain by the Southron —May not the lady come hither to the sacrament of confession? the road is distant and painful to travel."

"The lady is unwell, holy father," answered the Sacristan, "and unable to bear the journey."

"True—ay—yes—then must one of our brethren go to her— Knowst thou if she hath aught of a jointure from this Walter de Avenel?"

"Very little, holy father," said the Sacristan; "she has resided at Glendearg since her husband's death, well nigh on the charity of a poor widow, called Elspet Glendinning."

"Why, thou knowst all the widows in the country-side?" said the Abbot. "Ho! ho! ho!" and he shook his portly sides at his own jest.

"Ho! Ho! Ho!" echoed the Sacristan, in the tone and tune in which an inferior applauds the jest of his superior.—Then added, with a hypocritical snuffle, and a sly twinkle of his eye, "It is our duty, most holy father, to comfort the widow—he! he! he!"

This last laugh was more moderate, until the Abbot should put his sanction on the jest.

"Ho! ho!" said the Abbot; "then, to leave jesting, Father Philip, take thou thy riding gear, and go to confess this Dame Avenel."

"But," said the Sacristan——

"But me no *Buts*—neither But nor If pass between monk and abbot —Father Philip, the bands of discipline must not be relaxed—heresy gathers force like a snow-ball—the multitude expect confessions and preachings from the Benedictines, as they would from so many beggarly friars—And we may not desert the vine-yard, though the toil be grievous unto us—what would all Christendom—what would our brother Eustace think of us!"

"And with so little advantage to the holy Monastery," said the Sacristan.

"True, Father Philip; but wot you not that that which preventeth harm doth good? This Julian de Avenel lives a light and evil life, and should we neglect the widow of his brother, he might foray our lands, and we never able to show who hurt us—Moreover there is our duty to an ancient family, who have in their day been benefactors to the Abbey. Away with thee instantly, brother; ride night and day, an it be necessary, and let men see how diligent Abbot Boniface and his faithful children are in the execution of their spiritual duty—toil not deterring them—for the glen is five miles in length—fear not withholding them—for it is said to be haunted of spectres—nothing moving them from pursuit of their spiritual calling; to the confusion of calumnious heretics, and the comfort and edification of all true and faithful sons of the Catholic Church. I wonder what our brother Eustace will say to this?"

Breathless with his own picture of the dangers and toil which he was to encounter, and the fame which he was to acquire, both by proxy, the Abbot moved slowly to finish his luncheon in the refectory, and the Sacristan, with no very good will, accompanied old Martin on his return to Glendearg; the greatest impediment in the journey being the trouble of restraining his pampered mule, that she might tread in something like an equal pace with poor jaded Shagram.

After remaining an hour in private with his penitent, the Monk returned moody and full of thought. Dame Elspet, who had placed for the honoured guest some refreshment in the hall, was struck with the embarrassment which appeared in his countenance. Elspet watched him with great anxiety. She observed there was that in his brow which rather resembled a person come from hearing the confession of some enormous crime, than the look of a confessor who resigns a reconciled penitent, not to earth, but to heaven. After long hesitating, she could not at length refrain from hazarding a question. She was sure, she said, the dear leddy had made an easy shrift. Five years had they resided together, and she could safely say, no woman lived better.

"Woman," said the Sacristan sternly, "thou speakest thou knowst not what—what avails cleansing the outside of the platter, if the inside be foul with heresy?"

"Our dishes and trenchers are not so clean as they could be wished, holy father," said Elspet, but half understanding what he said, and beginning with her apron to wipe the dust from the plates, of which she supposed him to complain.

"Forbear, Dame Elspet," said the Monk; "your plates are clean as wooden trenchers and pewter flagons can well be; the foulness of which I speak is of that pestilential heresy which is daily becoming ingrained in this our Holy Church of Scotland, and as a canker-worm in the rose-garland of the Spouse."

"Holy Mother of Heaven!" said Dame Elspet, crossing herself, "have I kept house with a heretic?"

"No, Elspet, no," replied the Monk; "it were too strong a speech for me to make of this unhappy lady, but I would I could say she is free from heretical opinions. Alas, they fly about like the pestilence by noon-day, and infect ever the first and fairest of the flock. For it is easy to see of this dame, that she hath been high in judgment as in rank."

"And she can write and read, I had almost said, as weel as your reverence," said Elspet.

"Whom doth she write to, and what doth she read?" said the Monk eagerly.

"Nay," replied Elspet, "I cannot say I ever saw her write at all, but her maiden that was—she now serves the family—says she can write —And for reading, she has often read to us good things out of a thick black volume with silver clasps."

"Let me see it," said the Monk, hastily, "on your allegiance as a true vassal—on your faith as a Catholic Christian—instantly—instantly let me see it."

The good woman hesitated, alarmed at the tone in which the confessor took up her information; and being moreover of opinion, that what so good a woman as the Lady of Avenel studied so devoutly, could not be of tendency actually evil. But borne down by the clamour, exclamation, and something like threats used by Father Philip, she at length brought him the fatal volume. It was easy to do this without suspicion on the part of the owner, as she lay on her bed exhausted with the fatigue of a long conference with her confessor, and as the small *round*, or turret closet, in which was the book and her other trifling property, was accessible by another door. Of all her effects the book was the last she would have thought of securing, for of what use or interest could it be in a family who neither read themselves, nor were in the habit of seeing any who did? So that Dame Elspet had no difficulty in possessing herself of the volume, although her heart all the while accused her of an ungenerous and an inhospitable part towards her friend and inmate. The double power of a landlord and a feudal superior were before her eyes; and to say truth, the boldness, with which she might otherwise have resisted this double authority, was, I grieve to say it, much qualified by the curiosity she entertained, as a daughter of Eve, to have some explanation respecting the mysterious volume which the lady cherished with so much care, yet whose contents she imparted with such caution. For never had the lady read them any passage from the book in question until the iron door of the tower was locked, and all possibility of intrusion prevented. Even then she had shewn, by the selection of particular passages, that she was more anxious to impress on their minds the precepts which the volume contained, than to introduce them to it as a new rule of faith.

When Elspet, half curious, half remorseful, had placed the book in the Monk's hands, he exclaimed, after turning over the leaves, "Now, by mine order, it is as I suspected!—My mule, my mule!—I abide no longer here—Well hast thou done, dame, in placing in my hands this perilous volume."

"Is it then witchcraft or devil's work?" said Dame Elspet, in great agitation.

"Nay, God forbid," said the Monk, signing himself with the cross, "it is the Holy Scripture. But it is rendered into the vulgar tongue, and therefore, by the order of the Holy Catholic Church, unfit to be in the hands of any lay person."

"And yet is the Holy Scripture communicated for our common salvation," said Elspet; "good father, you must instruct mine ignorance better; but lack of wit cannot be a deadly sin, and truly, to my poor thinking, I should be glad to read the Holy Scripture."

"I dare say thou wouldst," said the Monk; "and even thus did our mother Eve seek to have knowledge of good and evil, and thus Sin came into the world, and Death by Sin."

"I am sure, and it is true," said Elspet; "O, if she had but dealt by the counsel of Saint Peter and Saint Paul!"

"If she had reverenced the command of Heaven," said the Monk, "which, as it gave her birth, life, and happiness, fixed upon the grant such conditions as best corresponded with its holy pleasure. I tell thee, Elspet, *the Word slayeth*—that is, the text alone, read with unskilled eye and unhallowed lips, is like those strong medicines which sick men take by the advice of the learned. Such patients recover and thrive; while those dealing in them at their own hand, shall perish by their own deed."

"Nae doubt, nae doubt," said the poor woman, "your reverence knows best."

"Not I," said Father Philip, in a tone as deferential as he thought could possibly become the Sacristan of Saint Mary's,—"Not I, but the Holy Father of Christendom, and our own holy father the Lord Abbot, know best. I, the poor Sacristan of Saint Mary's, can but repeat what I hear from others my superiors. Yet of this, good woman, be assured,—the Word—the mere Word slayeth. But the church hath her ministers to gloze and to expound the same unto her faithful congregation—And this I say, not so much, my beloved brethren—I mean, my beloved sister,"—(for the Sacristan had got into the end of one of his old sermons)—"This I speak not so much of the rectors, curates, and secular clergy—so called because they live after the fashion of the *seculum* or age—unbound by those ties which sequestrate us from the world; neither do I speak this of the mendicant friars— whether black or grey, whether crossed or uncrossed; but of the Monks—and especially of the Monks Benedictine, reformed on the rule of Saint Bernard of Clairvaux, thence called Cistercian—Of which Monks, Christian brethren—sister I would say—great is the happiness and glory of the country in possessing the holy Monastery of Saint Mary's, whereof I, though an unworthy brother, may say it hath produced more saints, more bishops, more popes—may our patrons make us thankful!—than any holy foundation in Scotland. Wherefore——But I see Martin hath my mule in readiness, and so I will but salute you with the kiss of sisterhood, which maketh not ashamed, and so betake me to my toilsome return, for the glen is of bad reputation for the evil spirits which haunt it—moreover, I may arrive too late at the bridge, whereby I may be obliged to take the river, which I observed to be somewhat woxen."

Accordingly he took his leave of Dame Elspet, confounded by the rapidity of his utterance, and the doctrine he gave forth, and by no means easy on the subject of the book, which her conscience told her she should not have communicated to any one, without the knowledge of its owner.

Notwithstanding the haste which the Monk as well as his mule made to return to better quarters than they had left at the head of Glendearg; notwithstanding the eager desire Father Philip had to be the very first who should acquaint the Abbot that a copy of the book they most dreaded had been found within the Halidome, or patrimony of the Abbey; notwithstanding, moreover, certain feelings which induced him to hurry as fast as possible through the gloomy and evil-reputed glen, still the difficulties of the road, and the rider's want of habitude to quick motion were such, that twilight came upon him ere he had nearly cleared the narrow valley.

It was indeed a gloomy ride. The two sides of the valley were so near, that at every double of the river the shadows from the western sky fell upon, and totally obscured, the eastern bank; the thickets of copsewood seemed to wave with a portentous agitation of boughs and leaves, and the very crags and scaurs seemed higher and grimmer than they had appeared to the Monk while he was travelling in day-light, and in company. Father Philip was heartily rejoiced when, emerging from the narrow glen, he gained the open valley of the Tweed, which held on its majestic course from current to pool, and from pool stretched away to other currents, with a dignity peculiar to itself amongst the Scottish rivers; for whatever may have been the drought of the season, the Tweed usually fills up the space between its banks, seldom leaving these extensive sheets of shingle which deform the margin of many of the celebrated Scottish streams.

The Monk, insensible to beauties which the age had not regarded as deserving of notice, was nevertheless, like a prudent general, pleased to find himself out of the narrow glen in which the Enemy might have stolen upon him unperceived. He drew up his bridle, reduced his mule to her natural and luxurious amble, instead of the agitating and broken trot at which she had hitherto proceeded, to his no small inconvenience, and, wiping his brow, gazed forth at leisure on the broad moon, which, now mingling with the lights of evening, was rising over field and forest, village and fortalice, and, above all, over the stately Monastery, seen far and dim amid the yellow light.

The worst part of this magnificent view, in the Monk's apprehension, was that the Monastery stood on the opposite side of the river, and that of the many fair bridges which have since been built across that classical stream, not one then existed. There was, however, in recompense, a bridge then standing which has since disappeared, although its ruins may be still traced by the curious.

It was of a very peculiar form. Two strong abutments were built on either side of the river, at a part where the stream was peculiarly contracted. Upon a rock in the centre of the current was built a solid piece of masonry, constructed like the pier of a bridge, and presenting like a pier an angle to the current of the stream. The masonry continued solid until the pier rose to a level with the two abutments upon either side, and from thence the building arose in the form of a tower. The lower storey of this tower consisted only of an arch-way or passage through the building, over either entrance to which hung a draw-bridge with counter-poises, either of which, when dropped, connected the archway with the opposite abutment, where the further end of the draw-bridge rested. When both bridges were thus lowered, the passage over the river was complete.

The bridge-keeper, who was the dependent of a neighbouring baron, resided with his family in the second and third stories of the tower, which, when both draw-bridges were raised, formed an insulated fortalice in the midst of the river. He was entitled to a small toll or custom for the passage, concerning the amount of which disputes sometimes arose betwixt him and the passengers. It is needless to say, that the bridge-ward had usually the better of these disputes, since he could at pleasure detain the traveller on the opposite side, or, suffering him to pass half the way, keep him prisoner in his tower until they were agreed on the rate of pontage.

But it was most frequently with the Monks of Saint Mary's that the warder had to dispute his perquisites. These holy men insisted for, and at length obtained a right of gratuitous passage to themselves, greatly to the discontent of the bridge-keeper. But when they demanded the same immunity for the numerous pilgrims who visited the shrine, the bridge-keeper waxed restive, and was supported by his lord in his resistance. The controversy grew animated on both sides; the Abbot menaced excommunication, and the keeper of the bridge, though unable to retaliate in kind, yet made each individual Monk who had to cross and re-cross the river, endure a sort of purgatory, ere he would accommodate them with a passage. This was a great inconvenience, and would have proved a more serious one, but that the river was fordable for man and horse in ordinary weather.

It was a fine moonlight night, as we have already said, when Father Philip approached this passage, the singular construction of which gives a curious idea of the insecurity of the times. The river was not in flood, but it was above its ordinary level—a *heavy water*, as it is called in that country, through which the Monk had no particular inclination to ride, if he could manage the matter better.

"Peter, my good friend," cried the Sacristan, raising his voice; "my very excellent friend, Peter, be so kind as to lower the bridge. Peter, I say, does thou not hear?—it is thy gossip, Father Philip, who calls thee."

Peter heard him perfectly well, and saw him into the bargain; but, as he had considered the Sacristan as peculiarly his enemy in his dispute with the convent, he went quietly to bed, after reconnoitring through his loop-hole, observing to his wife, that "a riding the water in a moonlight night would do the Sacristan no harm, and would teach him the value of a brigg the neist time, on whilk a man might pass high and dry, winter and summer, flood and ebb."

After exhausting his voice in entreaties and threats, which were equally unattended by Peter of the Brigg, as he was called, Father Philip at length moved down the river to take the ordinary ford at the end of the next stream. Cursing the rustic obstinacy of Peter, he began, nevertheless, to persuade himself that the passage of the river by the ford was not only safe, but pleasant. The banks and scattered trees were so beautifully reflected from the bosom of the dark stream, the whole cool and delicious picture formed so pleasing a contrast to his late agitation, to the warmth occasioned by his vain endeavours to move the relentless porter of the bridge, that the result was rather agreeable than otherwise.

As Father Philip came close to the water's edge, at the spot where he was to enter it there sat a female under a large broken scathed oak tree, or rather the remains of such a tree, weeping, wringing her hands, and looking earnestly on the current of the river. The Monk was struck with astonishment to see a female here at this time of night. But he was, in all honest service,—and if a step farther, I put it upon his own conscience,—a devoted squire of dames. After observing the maiden for a moment, although she seemed to take no notice of his presence, he was moved by her distress and willing to offer his assistance. "Damsel," said he, "thou seemest in no ordinary distress; peradventure, like myself, thou hast been refused passage at the bridge by the churlish keeper, and thy crossing may concern thee either for performance of a vow, or for some other weighty charge."

The maiden uttered some inarticulate sounds, looked on the river, and then looked up in the face of the Sacristan. It struck Father Philip at that instant, that a Highland Chief of distinction had been for some time expected to pay his vows at the shrine of Saint Mary's; and that possibly this fair maiden might be one of his family, travelling alone for accomplishment of a vow, or left behind by some accident, to whom, therefore, it would be but right and courteous to use every civility in his power, especially as she seemed unacquainted with the Lowland tongue. Such at least was the only motive the Sacristan was ever known to assign for his courtesy; if there was any other, I once more refer it to his own conscience.

To express himself by signs, the common language of all nations, the courteous Sacristan first pointed to the river, then to his mule's crupper, and then made, as gracefully as he could, a sign to induce the fair solitary to mount behind him. She seemed to understand his meaning, for she rose up as if to accept his offer, and while the good Monk, who, as we have hinted, was no great cavalier, laboured, with the pressure of the right leg and the use of the left rein, to place his mule with her side to the bank in such a position that the lady might mount with ease, she rose from the ground with rather portentous activity, and at one bound sate behind the Monk upon the animal, much the firmer rider of the two. The mule by no means seemed to approve of this double burthen; she bounded, bolted, and would soon have thrown Father Philip over her head, had not the maiden with a firm hand detained him in the saddle.

At length the restive brute changed her humour; and, from refusing to budge off the spot, suddenly stretched her nose homeward, and dashed into the ford as fast as she could scamper. A new terror now invaded the Monk's mind—the ford seemed unusually deep, the water eddied off in strong ripple from the counter of the mule, and began to rise upon her side. Philip lost his presence of mind, which was at no time his most ready attribute, the mule yielded to the weight of the current, and as the rider was not attentive to keep her head turned up the river, she drifted downward, lost the ford and her footing at once, and began to swim with her head down the stream. And what was sufficiently strange, at the same moment, notwithstanding the extreme peril, the damsel began to sing—thereby increasing, if any thing could increase, the bodily fear of the worthy Sacristan.

I.

Merrily swim we, the moon shines bright,
Both current and ripple are dancing in light.
We have roused the night raven, I heard him croak,
As we plashed along beneath the oak
That flings its broad branches so far and so wide,
Their shadows are dancing in midst of the tide.
"Who wakens my nestlings," the raven he said,
"My beak shall ere morn in his blood be red,
For a blue swollen corpse is a dainty meal,
And I'll have my share with the pike and the eel."

II.

Merrily swim we, the moon shines bright,
There's a golden gleam on the distant height;
There's a silver shower on the alders dank,
And the drooping willows that wave on the bank.

I see the Abbey, both turret and tower,
It is all astir for the vesper hour;
The Monks for the chapel are leaving each cell,
But where's Father Philip, should toll the bell?

III.

Merrily swim we, the moon shines bright,
Downward we drift through shadow and light.
Under yon rock the eddies sleep,
Calm and silent, dark and deep.
The Kelpy has risen from the fathomless pool,
He has lighted his candle of death and of dool:
Look, Father, look, and you'll laugh to see
How he gapes and glares with his eyes on thee!

IV.

Good luck to your fishing—whom watch ye tonight?
A man of mean or a man of might?
Is it layman or priest that must float in your cove,
Or lover who crosses to visit his love?
Hark! heard ye the Kelpy reply as we passed,—
"God's blessing on the warder, he lock'd the bridge fast!
All that come to my cove are sunk,
Priest or layman, lover or monk."

How long the damsel might have continued to sing, or where the terrified Monk's journey might have ended, is uncertain. As she sung the last stanza, they arrived at, or rather in, a broad tranquil sheet of water, caused by a strong wier or dam-head, running across the river, which dashed in a broad cataract over the barrier. The mule, whether from choice, or influenced by the suction of the current, made towards the cut intended to supply the convent mills, and entered it half swimming half wading, and pitching the unlucky Monk to and fro in the saddle at a fearful rate.

As his person flew hither and thither, his garment became loose, and in an effort to retain it, his hand lighted on the volume of the Lady of Avenel which was in his bosom. No sooner had he grasped it, than his companion pitched him out of the saddle into the stream, where, still keeping her hand on his collar, she gave him two or three good souses in the watery fluid, so as to ensure that every part of him had its share of wetting, and then quitted her hold when he was so near the side that by a slight effort (of a great one he was incapable), he might scramble on shore. This accordingly he accomplished, and turning his eyes to see what had become of his extraordinary companion, she was no where to be seen, but still he heard as if from the surface of the river, and mixing with the noise of the water breaking over the dam-head, a fragment of her wild song, which seemed to run thus:

Landed—landed! the black book hath won,
Else had you seen Berwick with morning sun!

Sain ye, and save ye, and blythe mot ye be,
For seldom they land that go swimming with me.

The ecstacy of the Monk's terror could be endured no longer; his
head grew dizzy, and, after staggering a few steps onward and running
himself against a wall, he sunk down in a state of insensibility.

Chapter Six

Here let us sit in conclave. That these weeds
Be rooted from the vineyard of the church,
That these foul tares be severed from the wheat,
We are, I trust, agreed.—Yet how to do this,
Nor hurt the wholesome crop and tender vine-plants,
Craves good avisement.

The Reformation

THE VESPER SERVICE in the Monastery Church of Saint Mary's
was now over. The Abbot had disrobed himself of his magnificent
vestures of ceremony, and resumed his ordinary habit, which was a
black gown, worn over a white cassock, with a narrow scapulary; a
decent and venerable dress, which was well calculated to set off to
advantage the portly mien of Abbot Boniface.

In quiet times no one could have filled the state of a mitred Abbot,
for such was his dignity, more decently than this worthy prelate. He
had, no doubt, many of those habits of self-indulgence which men are
apt to acquire who live for themselves alone. He was vain, moreover;
and when boldly confronted, had sometimes shewn symptoms of timidity, not very consistent with the high claims which he preferred as an
eminent member of the church, or with the punctual deference which
he exacted from his religious brethren, and all who were placed
under his command. But he was hospitable, charitable, perfectly good
natured, and by no means of himself disposed to proceed with severity
against any one. In short, he would in other times have slumbered out
his term of preferment with as much credit as any other "purple
Abbot," who lived easily, but at the same time decorously—slept
soundly, and disquieted himself with no dreams.

But the wide alarm spread through the whole Church of Rome by
the progress of the reformed doctrines, sorely disturbed the repose of
Abbot Boniface, and opened to him a wide field of duties and cares
which he had never so much as dreamed of. There were opinions to be
combatted and refuted, practices to be enquired into, heretics to be
detected and punished, the fallen off to be reclaimed, the wavering to
be confirmed, scandal to be removed from the clergy, and the vigour
of discipline to be re-established. Post upon post arrived at the

Monastery of Saint Mary's—horses reeking, and riders exhausted—this from the Privy Council, that from the Primate of Scotland, and this other again from the Queen Mother, exhorting, approving, condemning, requesting advice upon this subject, and requiring information upon that.

These missives Abbot Boniface received with an important air of helplessness, or a helpless air of importance, whichever the reader may please to term it, evincing at once gratified vanity, and profound trouble of mind.

The sharp-witted Primate of Saint Andrews had foreseen the deficiencies of the Prior of Saint Mary's, and endeavoured to provide for them by getting admitted into his Monastery as Sub-Prior a brother Cistercian, a man of parts and knowledge, devoted to the service of the Catholic church, and very capable not only to advise the Abbot upon occasions of difficulty, but to make him sensible of his duty in case he should be, from good nature or timidity, disposed to shrink from it. In short, Father Eustace played the same part in the Monastery as the old general who, in foreign armies, is placed at the elbow of the Prince of the Blood, who nominally commands in chief, on condition of attempting nothing without the advice of his dry-nurse; and he shared the fate of all such dry-nurses, being heartily disliked as well as feared by his principal. Still, however, the Primate's intention was fully answered. Father Eustace became the constant theme and often the bug-bear of the worthy Abbot, who at length hardly dared to turn himself in his bed without considering what Father Eustace would think of it. In every case of difficulty, Father Eustace was summoned, and his opinion asked; and no sooner was the embarrassment removed, than the Abbot's next thought was how to get rid of his adviser. In every letter which he wrote to those in the government, he recommended Father Eustace to some high church preferment, a bishopric or an abbey; and as they dropped one after another, and were otherwise conferred, he began to think, as he confessed to the Sacristan in the bitterness of his spirit, that the Monastery of Saint Mary's had got a life-rent lease of their Sub-Prior.

Yet more indignant he would have been, had he suspected that Father Eustace's ambition was fixed upon his own mitre, which, from some attacks of an apoplectic nature, which the Abbot's friends deemed more serious than he himself, it was supposed might be shortly vacant. But the confidence which, like other dignitaries, he reposed in his own health, prevented Abbot Boniface from imagining that his own health held any concatenation with the motions of Father Eustace.

The necessity under which he found himself of consulting with his grand adviser, in cases of real difficulty, rendered the worthy Abbot particularly desirous of doing without him in all ordinary cases of administration, though not without considering what Father Eustace would have said of the matter. He scorned, therefore, to give a hint to the Sub-Prior of the bold stroke by which he had detached Brother Philip to Glendearg; but when the vespers came without his re-appearance he became a little uneasy, the more as other matters weighed upon his mind. The feud with the warder or keeper of the bridge threatened to be attended with bad consequences, as the man's quarrel was taken up by the martial Baron under whom he served. And pressing letters of an unpleasant tendency had just arrived from the Primate. Like a gouty man, who catches hold of his crutch while he curses the infirmity which reduces him to use it, the Abbot, however reluctant, found himself obliged to require Eustace's presence, after the service was over, in his house, or rather palace, which was attached to, and made part of, the Monastery.

Abbot Boniface was seated in his high-backed chair, the grotesque carving of which terminated in a mitre, before a fire where two or three large logs were reduced to one red glowing mass of charcoal. At his elbow, on an oaken stand, stood the remains of a roasted capon, on which his reverence had made his evening meal, flanked by a goodly stoup of Bourdeaux of excellent flavour. He was gazing indolently on the fire, partly engaged in meditation on his past and present fortunes, partly occupied by endeavouring to trace towers and steeples in the red embers.

"Yes," thought the Abbot to himself, "in that red perspective I could fancy to myself the peaceful towers of Dundrennan, where I passed my life ere I was called to pomp and to trouble—a quiet brotherhood we were, regular in our monastic duties; and when frail-ties of humanity prevailed over us, we confessed, and were absolved by each other, and the most formidable part of the penance was the jest of the convent on the culprit. I can almost fancy that I see the cloister-garden, and the pear-trees which I grafted with my own hands. And for what have I changed all this, but to be overwhelmed with business which concerns me not, to be called My Lord Abbot, and to be tutored by Father Eustace? I would these towers were the Abbey of Aberbrothock, and Father Eustace were the Abbot,—or I would he was in the fire on any terms, so I were rid of him. The Primate says our Holy Father the Pope hath an adviser—I am sure he could not live a week with such an adviser as mine—And then there is no learning what Father Eustace thinks till you confess your own difficulties—No hint will bring forth his opinion—he is like a miser, who will not unbuckle his purse to bestow a farthing, until the wretch who needs it has owned his excess of poverty, and wrung out the boon by importunity. And thus am I dishonoured in the eyes of my religious brethren, who behold me treated like a child which hath no sense of its own—I will bear it no longer!—Brother Bennet,—(a lay brother answered to his call)—tell Father Eustace that I need not his presence."

"I came to say to your reverence, that the holy father is entering even now from the cloisters."

"Be it so," said the Abbot, "he is welcome—remove those things—or rather, place a trencher, the holy father may be a hungry—yet, no—remove them, for there is no good fellowship in him—Let the stoup of wine remain howsoever, and place another cup."

The lay brother obeyed these contradictory commands in the way he judged most seemly—he removed the carcase of the half-sacked capon, and placed two goblets beside the stoup of Bourdeaux. At the same instant entered Father Eustace.

He was a thin, sharp-faced, slight-made, little man, whose keen grey eyes seemed almost to look through the person to whom he addressed himself. His body was emaciated not only with the fasts which he observed with rigid punctuality, but also by the active and unwearied exercise of his sharp and piercing intellect.

> A fiery soul, which, working out its way,
> Fretted the puny body to decay,
> And o'er-informed the tenement of clay.

He bowed with conventual reverence to the Lord Abbot; and as they stood together, it was scarce possible to see a more complete difference of form and expression. The good-natured rosy face and laughing eye of the Abbot, which even his present anxiety could not greatly ruffle, was a wonderful contrast to the thin pallid cheek and quick penetrating glance of the Monk, in which an eager and keen spirit glanced through eyes to which it seemed to give supernatural lustre.

The Abbot opened the conversation by motioning to his Monk to take a stool, and inviting him to a cup of wine. The courtesy was declined with respect, yet not without a remark, that the vesper-service was past.

"For the stomach's sake, brother," said the Abbot, colouring a little —"you know the text."

"It is a dangerous one," answered the Monk, "to handle alone, or at late hours. Cut off from human society, the juice of the grape becomes a perilous companion of solitude, and therefore I shun it."

Abbot Boniface had poured himself out a goblet which might hold about half an English pint; but, either struck with the truth of the

observation, or ashamed to act in direct opposition to it, he suffered it
to remain untasted before him and immediately changed the subject.

"The Primate hath written to us," said he, "to make strict search
within our bounds after the heretical persons denounced in this list,
who have withdrawn themselves from the justice which their opinions
deserve. It is deemed probable that they will attempt to retire to
England by our Borders, and the Primate requireth me to watch with
vigilance, and what not."

"Assuredly," said the Monk, "the magistrate should not bear the
sword in vain—those be they that turn the world upside down—and
doubtless your reverent wisdom will with due diligence second the
exertions of the Right Reverend Father in God, being in the peremptory defence of the Holy Church."

"Ay, but how is this to be done?" answered the Abbot; "Saint Mary
aid us! The Primate writes to me as if I were a temporal Baron—a man
under command, having soldiers under him! He says—send forth—
scour the country—guard the passes—Truly these men do not travel
as those who would give their lives for nothing—the last who went
south passed the dry-march at the Riding-burn with an escort of thirty
spears, as our reverend brother the Abbot of Kelso did write unto us.
How are cowls and scapularies to stop the way?"

"Your Bailiff is accounted a good man-at-arms, holy father," said
Eustace; "your vassals are obliged to rise for the defence of Holy Kirk
—it is the tenure on which they hold their lands—if they will not come
forth for the Church which gives them bread, let their possessions be
given to others."

"We shall not be wanting," said the Abbot, collecting himself with
importance, "to whatever may advantage Holy Kirk—thyself shall
hear the charge to our Bailiff and our officials—but here again is our
controversy with the warden of the bridge and the Baron of Meigallot
—Saint Mary! vexations do so multiply upon the House, and upon the
generation, that a man wots not where to turn to! Thou didst say,
Father Eustace, thou wouldst look into our evidents touching this free
passage for the pilgrims."

"I have looked into the Chartulary of the House, holy father," said
Eustace, "and therein I find a written and formal grant of all duties
and customs payable at the draw-bridge of Brigton, not only by ecclesiastics of this foundation, but by every pilgrim truly designed to
accomplish his vows at this House, to the Abbot Ailford, and the
Monks of the House of Saint Mary in Kennaquhair, from that time
and for ever. The deed is dated on Saint Bridget's Even, in the year of
Redemption, 1137, and bears the sign and seal of the granter, Charles
of Meigallot, great-great-grandfather of this Baron, and purports to

be granted for the safety of his own soul, and for the weal of the souls of his father and mother, and of all his precessors and all successors, being Barons of Meigallot."

"But he alleges," said the Abbot, "that the bridge-wards have been in possession of these dues, and have rendered them available for more than fifty years—and the Baron threatens violence—meanwhile, the journey of the pilgrims is interrupted, to the prejudice of their own souls, and the diminution of the revenues of Saint Mary. The Sacristan advised us to put on a boat; but the warden, whom thou knowest to be a godless man, has sworn the devil tear him, but that if we put on a boat on the laird's stream, he will rive her board from board—And then some say we should compound the claim for a small sum in silver." Here the Abbot paused a moment for a reply, but receiving none, he added, "But what thinkest thou, Father Eustace? why art thou silent?"

"Because I am surprised at the question which the Lord Abbot of Saint Mary's asks at the youngest of his brethren."

"Youngest in time of your abode with us, Brother Eustace," said the Abbot, "not youngest in years, or I think in experience—Sub-Prior also of this convent."

"I am astonished," continued Eustace, "that the Abbot of this venerable house should ask of any one, whether he can alienate the patrimony of our holy and divine patroness, or give up to an unconscientious, and perhaps a heretic baron, the rights conferred on this church by his devout progenitor. Popes and councils alike prohibit it —the honour of the living, and the weal of departed souls, alike forbid it—It may not be. To force, if he dare use it, we must surrender; but never by our consent should we see the goods of the church plundered, with as little scruple as he would drive off a herd of English beeves. Rouse yourself, reverend father, and doubt nothing but that the Good Cause shall prevail. Whet the spiritual sword, and direct it against the wicked who would usurp on our holy rights. Whet the temporal sword if it be necessary, and stir up the courage and zeal of your loyal vassals."

The Abbot sighed deeply. "All this," he said, "is soon spoken by him who hath to act it not; but"——He was interrupted by the entrance of Bennet rather hastily. "The mule on which the Sacristan had set out in the morning had returned," he said, "to the convent stable all over wet, and with the saddle turned round beneath her belly."

"Sancta Maria!" said the Abbot, crossing himself, "our dear brother hath perished from the way."

"It may be not," said Eustace hastily—"let the bell be tolled—cause the brethren to get torches—alarm the village—hurry down to the river—I myself will be the foremost."

The real Abbot stood astonished and agape, when at once he beheld his office filled, and all which he ought to have ordered, going forward at the dictates of the youngest Monk in the convent. But ere the orders of Eustace, which nobody dreamed of disputing, were carried into execution, the necessity was prevented by the sudden apparition of the Sacristan, whose supposed danger excited all the alarm.

Chapter Seben

Raze out the written troubles of the brain,
Cleanse the foul bosom of the perilous stuff
That weighs upon the heart.
                              Macbeth

WHAT BETWIXT cold and fright the afflicted Sacristan stood before his Superior, propped on the friendly arm of the convent miller, drenched with water, and scarce able to utter a syllable.

After various attempts to speak, the first words he uttered were,

"Swim we merrily—the moon shines bright."

"Swim we merrily!" retorted the Abbot indignantly, "a merry night have ye chosen for swimming, and a becoming salutation to your Superior!"

"Our brother is bewildered," said Eustace; "Speak, Father Philip, how is it with you?"

"Good luck to your fishing,"—

continued the Sacristan, with a most dolorous attempt at the tune of his strange companion.

"Good luck to your fishing!" repeated the Abbot, still more surprised and displeased; "by my halidome he is drunken with wine, and comes to our presence with his jolly catches in his throat; if bread and water can cure this folly"——

"With your pardon, venerable father," said the Sub-Prior, "of water our brother has had enough; and methinks, the confusion of his eye is rather that of terror, than of aught unbeseeming his profession. Where didst thou find him, Hob Miller?"

"An it please your reverence, I did but go to shut the sluice of my mill—and as I was going to shut the sluice, I heard something groan near to me—but judging it was one of Giles Fletcher's hogs, for so please you, he never sparreth his gate, I caught up my lever, and was about—Saint Mary forgive me!—to strike where I heard the sound, when, as the saints would have it, I heard the second groan just like that of a living man—so I called up my knaves, and found the Father Sacristan lying wet and senseless under the wall of our kiln. So soon as we brought him to himself a bit, he prayed to be brought to your reverence, but I doubt me, his wits have gone a bell-wavering by the road. It was but now that he spoke in somewhat better form."

"Well!" said Brother Eustace, "thou has done well Hob Miller; only begone now, and remember a second time, to pause, ere you strike in the dark."

"Please your reverence, it shall be a lesson to me," said the miller, "not to mistake a holy man for a hog again, so long as I live." And making a bow with profound humility, the miller withdrew.

"And now that this churl is gone, Father Philip," said Eustace, "wilt thou tell our venerable Superior what ails thee? Art thou *vino gravatus*, man? if so, we will have thee to thy cell."

"Water! water! not wine," muttered the exhausted Sacristan.

"Nay," said the Monk, "if that be thy complaint, wine may perhaps cure thee;" and he reached him a cup, which the patient drank off to his great benefit.

"And now," said the Abbot, "let his garments be changed, or rather let him be carried to the infirmary; for it will prejudice our health, should we hear his narrative while he stands there, steaming like a rising hoar-frost."

"I will hear his adventure," said Eustace, "and report it to your reverence." And, accordingly, he attended the Sacristan to his cell. In about half an hour he returned to the Abbot.

"How is it with Father Philip?" said the Abbot; "and through what came he into such a state?"

"He comes from Glendearg, reverend sir," said Eustace; "and for the rest, he telleth such a legend, as has not been heard in this Monastery for many a long day." He then gave the Abbot the outlines of the Sacristan's adventures in the homeward journey, and added, that for some time he was inclined to think his brain was infirm, seeing he had sung, laughed, and wept, all in the same breath.

"A wondrous thing it is to us," said the Abbot; "that Satan is permitted to put forward his hand thus far on one of our sacred brethren."

"True," said Father Eustace; "but for every text there is a paraphrase; and I have my suspicions, that if the drenching of Father Philip cometh of the Evil One, yet it may not have been by his own personal intervention."

"How!" said the Father Abbot; "I will not believe that thou makest doubt that Satan, in former days, hath been permitted to afflict saints and holy men, even as he afflicted the pious Job?"

"God forbid I should make question of it," said the Monk, crossing himself; "yet, where there is an exposition of the Sacristan's tale, which is less than miraculous, I hold it safe to consider it at least, if not to abide by it. Now, this Hob the Miller hath a buxom daughter. Suppose, I say only suppose, that our Sacristan met her at the ford on her return from her uncle's on the other side, for there she hath this evening been—suppose, that, in courtesy, and to save her stripping hose and shoon, the Sacristan brought her across behind him—suppose he carried his familiarities farther than the maiden was willing to admit—and we may easily suppose, farther, that this wetting was the result of it."

"And this legend invented to deceive us," said the Superior, reddening with wrath; "but most strictly shall it be sifted and enquired into—it is not upon us that Father Philip must hope to pass the result of his own evil practices for doings of Satan. To-morrow cite the wench to appear before us—we will examine, and we will punish."

"Under your Reverence's favour," said Eustace, "that were but poor policy. As things now stand with us, the heretics catch hold of each flying report which tends to the scandal of our clergy. We must abate the evil, not only by strengthening discipline, but also by suppressing and stifling the voice of scandal. If my conjectures are true, the miller's daughter will be silent for her own sake; and your Reverence's authority may also impose silence on her father, and on the Sacristan. If he is again found to afford room for throwing dishonour on his order, he can be punished with severity, but at the same time with secrecy. For what say the Decretals? *Facinora ostendi dum punientur, flagitia autem abscondi debent.*"

A sentence of Latin, as Eustace had before observed, had often much influence on the Abbot, because he understood it not fluently, and was ashamed to acknowledge his ignorance. On these terms they parted for the night.

The next day, Abbot Boniface strictly interrogated Philip on the real cause of his disaster of the previous night. But the Sacristan stood firm to his story; nor was he found to vary from any point of it, although the answers he returned were in some degree incoherent, owing to his intermingling with them ever and anon snatches of the strange damsel's song, which had made such deep impression on his imagination, that he could not prevent himself from imitating it repeatedly in the course of his examination. The Abbot had compassion with the Sacristan's involuntary frailty, to which something supernatural seemed annexed, and finally became of opinion, that Father Eustace's more natural explanation was rather plausible than just. And indeed, although we have recorded the adventure as we find it written down, we cannot forbear to add that there was a schism on the subject in the Convent, and that several of the brethren pretended to have good reason for thinking that the black-eyed miller's daughter was at the bottom of the affair after all. Whichever way it might be interpreted, all agreed that it had too ludicrous a sound to be permitted to get abroad, and therefore the Sacristan was charged on his vow of obedience to say no more of his ducking; an injunction which, having once eased his mind by telling his story, it may be well conjectured that he joyfully obeyed.

The attention of Father Eustace was much less forcibly arrested by the marvellous tale of the Sacristan's danger, and his escape, than by the mention of the volume which he had brought with him from the Tower of Glendearg. A copy of the Scriptures, translated into the vulgar tongue, had found its way even into the proper territory of the church, and had been found in one of the most hidden and sequestered recesses of the Halidome of Saint Mary's.

He anxiously requested to see the volume. In this the Sacristan was unable to gratify him, for he had lost it, as far as he recollected, when the supernatural being, as he conceived her to be, took her departure from him. Father Eustace went down to the spot in person, and searched all around it, in hopes of recovering the volume in question; but his labour was in vain. He returned to the Abbot, and reported that it must have fallen into the river or the mill-stream; "for I will hardly believe," he said, "that Father Philip's musical fiend would fly off with a copy of the Holy Scriptures."

"Being," said the Abbot, "as it is, a heretical translation, it is our thought that Satan may have power over it."

"Ay!" said Father Eustace, "it is indeed his chiefest magazine of artillery, when he inspireth presumptuous and daring men to set forth their own opinions and expositions of Holy Writ. But though thus abused, the Scriptures are the source of our salvation, and are no more to be reckoned unholy, because of these rash men's proceedings, than a powerful medicine is to be contemned, or held poisonous, because bold and evil leeches have employed it to the prejudice of their patients. With the permission of your reverence, I would that this matter were looked into more closely. I will myself visit the Tower of Glendearg ere I am many hours older, and we will see if any spectre or white woman of the wild will venture to interrupt my journey or return. Have I your reverend permission and your blessing?" he added, but in a tone that appeared to set no great store by either.

"Thou hast both, my brother," said the Abbot; but no sooner had Eustace left the apartment, than Boniface could not help breathing in the willing ear of the Sacristan his sincere wish, that any spirit, black, white, or grey, would read the adviser such a lesson, as to cure him of his presumption in esteeming himself wiser than the whole community.

"I wish him no worse lesson," said the Sacristan, "than to go swimming merrily down the river with a ghost behind, and Kelpie's night-crows and mud-eels all waiting to have a snatch at him.

> Merrily swim we, the moon shines bright!
> Good luck to your fishing, whom watch you to-night?"

"Brother Philip," said the Abbot, "we exhort thee to say thy prayers, compose thyself, and banish that foolish chaunt from thy mind;—it is but a deception of the devil's."

"I will essay, reverend father," said the Sacristan, "but the tune hangs by my memory like a burr in a beggar's rags—it mingles with the Psalter—the very bells of the convent seem to repeat the words, and jangle to the tune; and were you to put me to death at this very moment, it is my belief I should die singing it—'Now swim we merrily'—it is as it were a spell upon me."

He then again began to warble

> "Good luck to your fishing."

And checking himself in the strain with difficulty, he exclaimed, "It is too certain—I am but a lost priest! Swim we merrily—I will sing it at the very mass—Woe is me! I shall sing all the remainder of my life, and yet never be able to change the tune!"

The honest Abbot replied, "he knew many a good fellow in the same condition;" and concluded the remark with "ho! ho! ho!" for his reverence, as the reader may partly have observed, was one of those dull folks who love a quiet joke.

The Sacristan, well acquainted with his Superior's humour, endeavoured to join in the laugh, but his unfortunate canticle came again across his imagination, and interrupted the hilarity of his customary echo.

"By the rood, Brother Philip," said the Abbot much moved, "you become altogether intolerable! and I am convinced that such a spell could not subsist over a person of religion, and in a religious house, unless he were under mortal sin. Wherefore, say the seven penitentiary psalms—make diligent use of thy scourge and hair-cloth—refrain for three days from all save bread and water—I myself will shrive thee, and we will see if this singing devil may be driven out of thee; at least I think Father Eustace himself could devise no better exorcism."

The Sacristan sighed deeply, but knew remonstrance was vain. He retired therefore to his cell, to try how far psalmody might be able to drive off the sounds of the syren tune which haunted his memory.

Meanwhile, Father Eustace proceeded to the draw-bridge, in his way to the lonely valley of Glendearg. In a brief conversation with the churlish warder, he had the address to render him more tractable in the controversy betwixt him and the convent. He reminded him that his father had been a vassal under the community; that his brother was childless; and that their possession would revert to the church on his death, and might be either granted to himself the warder, or to some greater favourite of the Abbot, as matters chanced to stand betwixt them at the time. The Sub-Prior suggested to him also, the necessary connection of interests betwixt the Monastery and the office which this man enjoyed. He listened with temper to his rude and churlish answers; and by keeping his own interest firm pitched in his view, he had the satisfaction to find that Peter gradually softened his tone, and consented to let every pilgrim who travelled upon foot pass free of exaction until Pentecost next; they who travelled on horseback or otherwise, consenting to pay the ordinary custom. Having thus accommodated a matter in which the weal of the convent was so deeply interested, Father Eustace proceeded on his journey.

Chapter Eight

Nay, dally not with time, the wise man's treasure,
Though fools are lavish on't—the fatal Fisher
Hooks souls, while we waste moments.
Old Play

A NOVEMBER MIST overspread the little valley, up which slowly but steadily rode the Monk Eustace. He was not insensible to the feeling of melancholy inspired by the scene and by the season. The stream seemed to murmur with a deep and oppressed note, as if bewailing the departure of Autumn. Amongst the scattered copses which here and there fringed its banks, the oak-trees only retained that pallid green that precedes their russet hue. The leaves of the willows were most of them stripped from the branches, and lay rustling at each breath, and disturbed by every step of the mule; while the foliage of other trees, totally withered, kept still precarious possession of the boughs, waiting the first wind to strew them.

The Monk dropped into the natural train of pensive thought which these autumnal emblems of mortal hopes are peculiarly calculated to inspire. "There," said he, looking at the leaves which lay strewed around, "lie the hopes of early youth, first formed that they may soonest wither, and loveliest in spring to become most contemptible in winter—But you, ye lingerers," added he, looking to a knot of beeches which still bore their withered leaves, "you are the proud plans of adventurous manhood, formed later, and still clinging to the mind of age, although it acknowledges their inanity! None lasts—none endures, save the foliage of the hardy oak, which only begins to shew itself when that of the rest of the forest has enjoyed half its existence. A pale and decayed hue is all it possesses, but still it retains that symptom of vitality to the last.—So be it with Father Eustace! The fairy hopes of my youth I have trodden under foot like those neglected rustlers—to the prouder dreams of my manhood I look back as to lofty chimeras, of which the pith and essence has long since faded —but my religious vows, the faithful profession which I have made in my maturer age, shall retain life while aught of Eustace lives. Dangerous it may be—feeble it must be—yet live it shall, the proud determination to serve the church of which I am a member, and to combat the heresies by which she is assailed." Thus spoke, at least thus thought, a man zealous according to his imperfect knowledge, confounding the vital interests of Christianity with the extravagant and usurped claims of the Church of Rome, and defending his cause with ardour worthy of a better.

While moving onwards in this contemplative mood, he could not help thinking more than once, that he saw in his path the form of a female dressed in white, who appeared in the attitude of lamentation. But the impression was only momentary, and whenever he looked steadily to the point where he conceived the figure appeared, it always proved that he had mistaken some natural object, a white crag, or the trunk of a decayed birch tree with its silver bark, for the appearance in question.

Father Eustace had dwelt too long in Rome to partake the superstitious feelings of the more ignorant Scottish clergy; yet he certainly thought it extraordinary, that so strong an impression should have been made on his mind by the legend of the Sacristan. "It is strange," said he to himself, "that this story, which doubtless was the invention of Brother Philip to cover his own impropriety of conduct, should run so much in my head and disturb my more serious thoughts. I am wont, I think, to have more command upon my senses—I will repeat my prayers, and banish such folly from my recollection."

The Monk accordingly began with devotion to tell his beads, according to the prescribed rule of his order, and was not again disturbed by any wanderings of the imagination, until he found himself beneath the little fortalice of Glendearg.

Dame Glendinning, who stood at the gate, set up a shout of surprise and joy at seeing the good father. "Martin," she said, "Jasper, where be a' the folk?—help the right reverend Sub-Prior to dismount, and take his mule from him—O father! God has sent you in our need—I was just going to send man and horse to the Convent—though I ought to be ashamed to give so much trouble to your reverences."

"Our trouble matters not, good dame," said Father Eustace; "in what can I pleasure you? I came hither to visit the Lady of Avenel."

"Well-a-day!" said Dame Alice, "and it was on her part that I had the boldness to think of summoning you—for the good lady will never be able to wear over the day!—would it please you to go to her chamber?"

"Hath she not been shriven by Father Philip?" said the Monk.

"Shriven she was," said the Dame of Glendearg, "and by Father Philip, as your reverence truly says—but—but I wish it may have been a clean shrift—Methought Father Philip looked but moody upon it—and there was a book which he took away with him, that"——She paused as if unwilling to proceed.

"Speak out, Dame Glendinning," said the Father; "with us it is your duty to have no secrets."

"Nay, if it please your reverence—it is not that I would keep any thing from your reverence's knowledge, but I fear I should prejudice the lady in your opinion; for it is an excellent lady—months and years has she dwelt in this tower, and none more exemplary than she; but this matter, doubtless, she will explain it herself to your reverence."

"I desire first to know it from you, Dame Glendinning," said the Monk; "and I again repeat, it is your duty to explain it to me. This book, which Father Philip removed from Glendearg"——

"Was this morning returned to us in strange manner," said the good widow.

"Returned?" said the Monk; "How mean you?"

"I mean," answered Dame Glendinning, "that it was brought back to this tower of Glendearg, the saints best know how—that same book which Father Philip carried with him but yesterday. Old Martin, that is my tasker and the lady's servant, was driving out the cows to the pasture—for we have three good milk cows, reverend father, blessed be Saint Waldave, and thanks to the holy Monastery"——

The Monk groaned with impatience; but he remembered that a woman of the good dame's condition was like a top—if you let it spin on untouched, it will at last come to a pause; but, if you interrupt it by flogging, there is no end to its gyrations. "But to speak no more of the cows, your reverence, though they are likely cattle as ever were tied to a stake, the tasker was driving them out, and the lads, that is my Halbert and my Edward, that your reverence has seen at church on holidays, and especially Halbert,—for you patted him on the head and gave him a broach of Saint Cuthbert, which he wears in his bonnet,— and little Mary Avenel, that is the lady's daughter, they ran all after the cattle, and began to play up and down the pasture as young folk will, your reverence. And at length they lost sight of Martin and the cows; and they began to run up a little cleuch which we call *Corinan shian*, where there is a wee bit stripe of a burn, and they saw there—Gude guide us!—a white woman sitting on the burn-side wringing her hands—So the bairns were frighted to see a strange woman there— all but Halbert—who will be sixteen come Whitsuntide; and, besides, he never feared onything—and when they went up to her—behold she was passed away!"

"For shame, good woman!" said Father Eustace; "a woman of your sense and listen to a tale so idle!—the young folks told you a lie, and that was all."

"Nay, sir, it was more than that," said the old dame; "for, besides that they never told me a lie in their lives, I must warn you that on the very ground where the White Woman was sitting, they found the Lady of Avenel's book, and brought it back with them to the tower."

"That is worthy of mark at least," said the Monk. "Know you no other copy of this volume within these bounds?"

"None, your reverence," returned Elspet; "why should there?—no one could read it were there twenty."

"Then you are sure it is the very same volume which you gave to Father Philip?" said the Monk.

"As sure as that I now speak with your reverence."

"It is most singular!" said the Monk; and he walked across the room in a musing posture.

"I have been upon nettles to hear what your reverence would say," continued Dame Glendinning, "respecting this matter—There is nothing I would not do for the Lady of Avenel and her family, and that has been proved, and for her servants to boot, both Martin and Tibb, although Tibb is not so civil sometimes as altogether I have a right to expect; but I cannot think it beseeming to have angels, or ghosts, or fairies, or the like, waiting upon a leddy when she is in another woman's house, in respect it is no ways creditable. Onything she had to do was always done to her hand, without costing her either pains or pence, as a country body says; and besides the discredit, I cannot but think that there is no safety in having such unchancy creatures about ane. But I have tied red thread round the bairns's throats, (so her fondness still called them,) and given ilk ane of them a riding wand of rowan tree, forbye sewing up a slip of witch-elm into their doublets; and I wish to know of your reverence if there be ony thing mair that a lone woman can do in the matter of ghosts and fairies?—Be here! that I should have named their unlucky names twice ower!"

"Dame Glendinning," answered the Monk, somewhat abruptly,

when the good woman had finished her narrative, "I pray you, do you know the miller's daughter?"

"Did I know Kate Happer?" replied the widow; "that I did, as weel as the beggar knows his dish—A canty quean was Kate, and a special cummer of my ain may be twenty years syne."

"She cannot be the wench I mean," said Father Eustace; "she after whom I enquire is scarce fifteen, a black-eyed girl—you may have seen her at the kirk."

"Your reverence must be in the right; and she is my cummer's niece, doubtless, that you are pleased to speak of: But I thank God I have always been too duteous in attention to the mass, to know whether young wenches have black eyes or green ones."

The good father had so much of the world about him, that he was unable to avoid smiling, when the dame boasted her absolute resistance to a temptation, which was not quite so liable to beset her as those of the other sex.

"Perhaps, then," he said, "you know her usual dress, Dame Glendinning?"

"Ay, ay, Father," answered the dame readily enough, "a white kirtle the wench wears—for the dust of the mill no doubt—and a blue hood, that might weel be spared, for pridefulness."

"Then may it not be she," said the Father, "who has brought back this book, and stepped out of the way when the children came near her?"

The dame paused—was unwilling to combat the solution suggested by the Monk—but was at a loss to conceive why the lass of the mill should come so far from home into so wild a corner, merely to leave an old book with three children, from whose observation she wished to conceal herself. Above all, she could not understand why, since she had acquaintance of the family, and since the Dame Glendinning had always paid her multures and knaveship duly, the said lass of the mill had not come in to rest herself and eat a morsel, and tell her the current news of the water.

These very objections satisfied the Monk that his conjectures were right. "Dame," he said, "you will be cautious in what you say. This is an instance—I would it were the sole one—of the power of the Enemy in these days. The matter must be sifted with a curious and careful hand."

"Indeed," said Elspet, trying to catch and chime in with the ideas of the Sub-Prior, "I have often thought the miller's folks at the Monastery-mill were far over careless in sifting our melder, and in bolting it too—some folks say they will not stick at whiles to put in a handful of ashes amongst Christian folk's corn-meal."

"That shall be looked after also, dame," said the Sub-Prior, not displeased to see that the good old woman went off on a false scent; "and now, by your leave, I will see this lady—do you go before, and prepare her to see me."

Dame Glendinning left the lower apartment accordingly, which the Monk paced in anxious reflection how he might best discharge, with humanity as well as with effect, the important duty incumbent on him. He resolved to approach the bed-side of the sick person with reprimands, mitigated only by a feeling for her weak condition—he determined, in case of her reply, to which late examples of hardened heretics might encourage her, to be prepared with answers to their customary scruples. High fraught, also, with zeal against her unauthorized intrusion into the priestly function, by study of the Sacred Scriptures, he imagined to himself the answers which one of the modern school of heresy might return to him—the victorious refutation which should lay the disputant prostrate at the Confessor's mercy—and the healing, yet awful exhortation, which, under pain of refusing the last consolations of religion, he designed to make to the penitent, conjuring her, as she loved her own soul's welfare, to disclose to him what she knew of the dark mystery of iniquity, by which heresies were introduced into the most secluded spots of the very patrimony of the church herself—what agents they had who could thus glide, as it were unseen, from place to place, bring back the volumes which the church had interdicted to the spots from which they had been removed under her express auspices; and who, by encouraging the daring and profane thirst after knowledge forbidden and useless to the laity, had encouraged the fisher of souls to use with effect his old bait of ambition and vain glory.

Much of this premeditated disputation escaped the good father, when Elspet returned, her tears flowing faster than her apron could dry them, and made him a signal to follow her. "How," said the Monk, "is she then so near her end?—nay, the church must not break or bruise, when comfort is yet possible;" and, forgetting his polemics, the good Sub-Prior hastened to the little apartment, where, on the wretched bed which she had occupied since her misfortunes had driven her to the Tower of Glendearg, the widow of Walter Avenel had rendered up her spirit to her Creator. "My God!" said the Sub-Prior, "and has my unfortunate dallying suffered her to depart without the Church's consolation? Look to her, dame," he exclaimed with eager impatience; "is there not yet a sparkle of life left?—may she not be recalled—recalled but for a moment?—Oh! would that she could express, but by the most imperfect word—but by the most feeble motion, her acquiescence in the needful task of penitential prayer!

Does she not breathe?—art thou sure she doth not?"

"She will never breathe more," said the matron. "O! the poor fatherless girl—now motherless also—O! the kind companion I have had these many years, that I shall never see again! But she is in Heaven for certain, if ever woman went there—for a woman of better life"——

"Woe to me," said the good Monk, "if indeed she went not hence in good assurance—woe to the reckless shepherd, who suffered the wolf to carry a choice one from the flock, while he busied himself with trimming his sling and his staff to give the monster battle! O! if, in the long Hereafter, ought but weal should that poor spirit share, what has my delay cost?—the value of an immortal soul!"

He then approached the body, full of the deep remorse natural to a good man of his persuasion, who devoutly believed the doctrines of the Catholic Church. "Ay," said he, gazing on the pallid corpse, from which the spirit had parted so placidly as to leave a smile upon the thin blue lips, which had been so long wasted by decay that they had parted with the last breath of animation without the slightest convulsive tremor—"Ay," said Father Eustace, "there lies the faded tree, and, as it fell, so it lies—awful thought for me, should my neglect have left it to descend in an evil direction." He then again and again conjured Dame Glendinning to tell him what she knew of the demeanour and ordinary walk of the deceased.

All tended to the high honour of the deceased lady; for her companion, who admired her sufficiently while alive, notwithstanding some trifling points of jealousy, now idolized her after her death, and could think of no attribute of praise with which she did not adorn her memory.

Indeed, the Lady of Avenel, however she might privately doubt some of the doctrines announced by the Church of Rome, and although she had probably tacitly appealed from that corrupted system of Christianity to the volume on which Christianity itself is founded, had nevertheless been regular in her attendance on the worship of the church, not, perhaps, extending her scruples so far as to break off communion. Such indeed was the first sentiment of the earlier reformers, who seem to have studied, for a time at least, to avoid a schism, until the violence of the Pope rendered it unavoidable.

Father Eustace, on the present occasion, listened with eagerness to every thing which could lead to assure him of the lady's orthodoxy in the main points of belief; for his conscience reproached him sorely, that, instead of protracting conversation with the Dame of Glendearg, he ought instantly to have hastened where his presence was so necessary. "If," he said, addressing the dead body, "thou art yet free from the utmost penalty due to the followers of false doctrine—if thou doest but suffer for a time, to expiate faults done in the body, but partaking of mortal frailty more than deadly sin, fear not that thy abode shall be long in the penal regions to which thou mayst be doomed—if vigils—if masses—if penance—if maceration of my body, till it resembles that extenuated form which the soul hath abandoned, may assure thy deliverance. The Holy Church—the godly foundation—our blessed Patroness herself, shall intercede for one whose errors were counterbalanced by so many virtues.—Leave me, dame—here, and by her bed-side, will I perform those duties which this piteous case demands!"

Elspet left the Monk, who employed himself in fervent and sincere, though erroneous prayers, for the weal of the departed spirit. For an hour he remained in the apartment of death, and then returned to the hall, where he found the still weeping friend of the deceased.

But it would be injustice to Mrs Elspet Glendinning's hospitality, if we suppose her to have been weeping during this long interval, or rather, if we suppose her so entirely absorbed by the tribute of sorrow which she paid frankly and plentifully to her deceased friend, as to be incapable of attending to the rites of hospitality due to her holy visitor —confessor at once, and Sub-Prior—mighty in all religious and secular considerations, so far as the vassals of the Monastery were interested.

Her barley-bread had been toasted—her choicest cask of home-brewed ale had been broached—her best butter had been placed on the hall-table, along with her most savoury ham and her choicest cheese, ere she abandoned herself to the extremity of sorrow; and it was not till she had arranged her little repast neatly on the board, that she sat down in the chimney corner, threw her checked apron over her head, and gave way to the current of tears and sobs. In this there was no grimace or affectation. The good dame held the honours of her house to be as essential a duty, especially when a Monk was her visitant, as any other pressing call upon her conscience; nor until these were suitably attended to did she find herself at liberty to indulge her sorrow for her departed friend.

When she was conscious of the Sub-Prior's presence, she rose with the same attention to his reception; but he declined all the offers of hospitality with which she endeavoured to tempt him. Not her butter, as yellow as gold, and the best, she assured him, that was made in the patrimony of Saint Mary—not the barley-scones, which "the departed saint, God sain her! used to say were so good"—not the ale, nor any other cates which poor Elspet's stores afforded, could prevail on the Sub-Prior to break his fast.

"This day," he said, "I must not taste food until the sun go down, happy if, in so doing, I can expiate my own negligence—happier still, if my sufferings of this trifling nature, undertaken in pure faith and singleness of heart, may benefit the soul of the deceased. Yet, dame," he added, "I may not so far forget the living in my cares for the dead, as to leave behind me that book, which is to the ignorant what, to our first parents, the tree of Knowledge of Good and Evil unhappily proved— excellent indeed in itself, but fatal, because used by those to whom it is prohibited."

"O, blithely, reverend father," said the widow of Simon Glendinning, "will I give you the book, if so be I can wile it from the bairns; and indeed, poor things, as the case stands with them even now, you might take the heart out of their bodies, and they never find it out, they are sae begrutten."*

"Give them this missal instead, good dame," said the Father, drawing from his pocket one which was curiously illuminated with paintings, "and I will come myself, or send some one at a fitting time, and teach them the meaning of these pictures."

"The bonnie images," said Dame Glendinning, forgetting for an instant her grief in her admiration "and weel I wot," added she, "it is another sort of a book than the poor Lady of Avenel's—and blessed might we have been this day, if your reverence had found the way up the glen, instead of Father Philip—though the Sacristan is a powerful man too, and speaks as if he would gar the house fly abroad, save that the walls are gay thick—Simon's forebears (may he and they be blessed!) took care of that."

The Monk ordered his mule, and was about to take his leave; and the good dame was still delaying him with questions about the funeral, when a horseman, armed and accoutred, rode into the little courtyard which surrounded the Keep.

Chapter Nine

> For since they rode among our doors
> With splent on spauld and rusty spurs,
> There grows no fruit into our furs;
>   Thus said John Up-on-land.
>   *Bannatyne MS*

THE SCOTTISH LAWS, which were as wisely and judiciously made as they were carelessly and ineffectually executed, had in vain endeavoured to restrain the damage done to agriculture, by the chiefs and landed proprietors retaining in their service what were called Jack-

* Begrutten,—over-weeped.

men, from the *jack*, or doublet quilted with iron, which they wore as defensive armour. These military retainers conducted themselves with great insolence towards the industrious part of the community, lived in a great measure by plunder, and were ready to execute any commands of their master, however unlawful. In adopting this mode of life, men resigned the quiet hopes and regular labours of industry, for an unsettled, precarious, and dangerous trade, which yet had such charms for those who once became accustomed to it, that they became incapable of following any other. Hence the complaint of John Upland, a fictitious character, representing a countryman, into whose mouth the poets of the day put their general satires upon men and manners:

> They ride about in such a rage,
> By forest, frith and field,
> With buckler, bow, and brand.
> Lo! where they ride out through the rye!
> The Devil mot save the company,
> Quoth John Up-on-land.

Christie of Clinthill, the horseman who now arrived at the little tower of Glendearg, was one of the hopeful company of whom the poet complains, as was indicated by his "splent on spauld," (iron-plates on his shoulder,) his rusted spurs, and his long lance. An iron scull-cap, none of the brightest, bore for distinction a sprig of the holly, which was Avenel's badge. A long two-edged straight sword, having a handle made of polished oak, hung down by his side. The meagre condition of his horse, and the wild and emaciated look of the rider, shewed their occupation could not be accounted an easy or a thriving one. He saluted Dame Glendinning with little courtesy, and the Monk with less; for the growing disrespect to the religious orders had not failed to extend itself among a class of men of such disorderly habits, although it may be supposed they were altogether indifferent alike to the new or the ancient doctrines.

"So, our lady is dead, Dame Glendinning," said the jack-man; "my master sent you even now a fat bullock for her mart—it may serve for her funeral. I have left him in the upper cleuch, as he is somewhat ken-speckle,* and is marked both with cut and birn—the sooner the skin is off, and he is in saultfat, the less like you are to have trouble— you understand me. Let me have a peck of corn for my horse, and beef and beer for myself, for I must go on to the Monastery—though I think this Monk here might do mine errand."

"Thine errand, rude man," said the Sub-Prior, knitting his brows——

"For God's sake!" said poor Dame Glendinning, terrified at the

---

* *Ken-speckle*—that which is easily recognised by the eye.

idea of a quarrel betwixt them,—"O Christie! it is the Sub Prior—O reverend sir, it is Christie of Clinthill, the laird's chief jackman—ye know that little havings can be expected from the like o' them."

"Are you a retainer of the laird of Avenel?" said the Monk, addressing himself to the horseman; "and do you speak thus rude to a brother of Saint Mary's, to whom thy master is so much beholden?"

"He means to be yet more beholden to your house, Sir Monk," answered the fellow; "for hearing his sister-in-law, the widow of Walter of Avenel, was on her death-bed, he sent me to say to the Father Abbot and the brethren, that he will hold the funeral-feast at their convent, and invites himself thereto with a score of horse, and some friends, to abide there for three days and three nights,—having horse-meat and men's meat at the charge of the community; of which his intention he sends this due notice, that fitting preparation may be timeously made."

"Friend," said the Sub-Prior, "believe not that I will do to the Father Abbot the indignity of delivering such an errand—think'st thou the goods of the church were bestowed upon her by holy princes and pious nobles, now dead and gone, to be consumed in revelry by every profligate layman who numbers in his train more followers than he can support by honest means, or by his own incomings? Tell thy master, from the Sub-Prior of Saint Mary's, that the Primate hath issued his commands to us that we submit no longer to this compulsory exaction of hospitality on slight or false pretences. Our lands and goods were given to relieve pilgrims and pious persons, not to feast bands of rude soldiers."

"This to me!" said the rude spear-man, "this to me and to my master?—Look to yourself then, Sir Priest, and try if *Ave* and *Credo* will keep bullocks from wandering, and hay-stacks from burning."

"Doest thou menace the holy Church's patrimony with waste and fire-raising," said the Sub Prior, "and that in the face of the sun? I call on all who hear me to bear witness to the words this ruffian has spoken. Remember how the Lord James drowned such as you by scores in the black pool at Jeddart.—To him and to the Primate will I complain." The soldier shifted the position of his lance, and brought it down to a level with the Monk's body.

Dame Glendinning began to shriek for assistance. "Tibb Tacket! Martin! where be ye all?—Christie, for the love of God, consider—he is a man of holy kirk."

"I care not for his spear," said the Sub-Prior; "if I am slain in defending the rights and privileges of my community, the Primate will know how to take vengeance."

"Let him look to himself," said Christie, but at the same time depositing his lance against the wall of the tower; "if the Fife men spoke true who came hither with the Governor in the last raid, Norman Leslie has him at feud, and is like to set him hard. We know Norman—a true blood-hound, who will never quit the slot. But I had no design to offend the holy father," he added, thinking perhaps he had gone a little too far; "I am a rude man, bred to lance and stirrup, and not used to deal with book-learned men and priests—and I am willing to ask his forgiveness and blessing, if I have said aught amiss."

"For God's sake, your reverence," said the widow of Glendearg apart to the Sub-Prior, "bestow on him your forgiveness—how shall we poor folks sleep in security in the dark nights, if the Convent is at feud with such men as he is?"

"You are right, dame," said the Sub-Prior, "your safety should, and must be in the first instance consulted.—Soldier, I forgive thee, and may God bless thee and send thee honesty."

Christie of the Clinthill made an unwilling inclination with his head, and muttered apart, "that is as much as to say, God send thee starvation.—But now to my master's demand, Sir Priest? What answer am I to return?"

"That the body of the widow of Walter of Avenel," answered the Father, "shall be interred as becomes her rank, and in the tomb of her valiant husband. For your master's proffered visit of three days, with such a company and retinue, I have no authority to reply to it; you must intimate your Chief's purpose to the Reverend Lord Abbot."

"That will cost me a farther ride," said the man, "but it is all in the day's work.—How now, my lad," said he to Halbert, who was handling the long lance which he had laid aside; "how do you like such a play-thing?—will you go with me and be a moss-trooper?"

"The Saints in their mercy forbid!" said the poor mother; and then, afraid of having displeased Christie by the vivacity of her exclamation, she followed it up by explaining, that since Simon's death she could not look on a spear or a bow, or any implement of destruction, without trembling.

"Pshaw!" answered Christie, "thou should'st take another husband, dame, and drive such follies out of thy thoughts—What say'st thou to such a strapping lad as I? Why, this old tower of thine is fencible enough, and there is no want of cleughs, and craggs, and bogs, and thickets, if one was set hard; a man might bide here and keep his half-score of lads, and as many geldings, and live on what he could lay his hand on, and be kind to thee, old wench."

"Alas! Master Christie, that you would talk to a lone woman in such a fashion, and death in the house besides!"

"Lone woman!—why, that is the very reason thou should'st take a mate. Thy old friend is dead—why good—chuse thee another of somewhat tougher frame, and that will not die of the pip like a young chicken.—Better still—Come, dame, let me have something to eat, and we will talk more of this."

Dame Elspet, though she well knew the man's character, which in fact she both disliked and feared, could not help simpering at the personal address which he thought proper to make to her. She whispered to the Sub-Prior, "ony thing just to keep him quiet," and went into the tower to set before the soldier the food he desired, trusting, betwixt good cheer and the power of her own charms, to keep Christie of the Clinthill so well amused, that the altercation betwixt him and the holy father should not be renewed.

The Sub-Prior was equally unwilling to hazard any unnecessary rupture betwixt the community and such a person as Julian of Avenel. He was sensible that moderation, as well as firmness, was necessary to support the tottering cause of the Church of Rome; and that, contrary to the former ages, the quarrels betwixt the clergy and laity had, in the present, usually terminated to the advantage of the latter. He resolved, therefore, to avoid further strife by withdrawing, but failed not, in the first place, to possess himself of the volume which the Sacristan had carried off the evening before, and which had been returned to the glen in such a marvellous manner.

Edward, the younger of Dame Elspet's boys, made great objections to the book being removed, in which Mary would probably have joined, but that she was now in her little sleeping chamber with Tibb, who was exerting her simple skill to console the young lady for her mother's death. But the younger Glendinning stood up in defence of her property, and with a positiveness which had hitherto made no part of his character, declared, that now the kind lady was dead, the book was Mary's, and no one but Mary should have it.

"But if it is not a fit book for Mary to read, my dear boy," said the Father gently; "you would not wish it to remain with her."

"The lady read it," answered the young champion of property; "and so it could not be wrong—it shall not be taken away.—I wonder where Halbert is?—listening to the bravading tales of gay Christie, I reckon—he is always wishing for fighting, and now he is out of the way."

"Why, Edward, you would not fight with me, who am both a priest and an old man?"

"If you were as good a priest as the Pope, and as old as the hills to boot, you shall not carry away Mary's book without her leave. I will do battle for it."

"But see you, my love," said the Monk, amused with the resolute friendship manifested by the boy, "I do not take it; I only borrow it; and I leave in its place my own gay missal, as a pledge I will bring it again."

Edward opened the missal with eager curiosity, and glanced at the pictures with which it was illustrated. "Saint George and the dragon —Halbert will like that—and Saint Michael brandishing his sword over the head of the Wicked One—and that will do for Halbert too— And see the Saint John leading his lamb in the wilderness, with his little cross made of reeds, and his scrip and staff—that shall be my favourite—and where shall we find one for poor Mary?—here is a beautiful woman weeping and lamenting herself."

"That is Saint Mary Magdalen repenting of her sins, my dear boy," said the Father.

"That will not suit *our* Mary; for she commits no faults, and is never angry with us, but when we do something wrong."

"Then," said the Father, "I will shew you a Mary, who will protect her and you, and all good children. See how fairly she is represented with her gown covered with golden stars."

The boy was lost in wonder at the portrait of the Virgin, which the Sub-Prior turned up to him.

"This," he said, "is really like our sweet Mary; and I think I will let you take away the black book, that has no such goodly shews in it, and leave this for Mary instead. But you must promise to bring back the book, good Father—for now I think upon it, Mary may like that best which was her mother's."

"I will certainly return," said the Monk, evading his answer, "and perhaps I may teach you to write and read such beautiful letters as you see there written, and to paint them blue, green, and yellow, and to blazon them with gold."

"Ay, and to make such figures as these blessed Saints, and especially these two Marys?" said the boy.

"With their blessing," said the Sub-Prior, "I can teach you that art too, so far as I am myself capable of shewing, and you of learning it."

"Then," said Edward, "will I paint Mary's picture—And remember you are to bring back the black book; that you must promise me."

The Sub-Prior, anxious to get rid of the boy's pertinacity, and to set forward on his return to the convent, without having any farther interview with Christie the galloper, answered by giving the promise Edward required, mounted his mule, and set forth on his return homeward.

The November day was well spent ere the Sub-Prior resumed his journey; for the difficulty of the road, and the various delays which he had met with at the tower, had detained him longer than he purposed.

A chill easterly wind was sighing among the withered leaves, and stripping some of them from the hold they had yet retained on the parent trees.

"Even so," said the Monk, "our prospects in this vale of time grow more disconsolate as the stream of years passes on. Little have I gained by my journey, save the certainty that heresy is busy amongst us with more than her usual activity, and that the spirit of insulting religious orders, and plundering the Church's property, so general in the eastern districts of Scotland, has now come nearer home."

The tread of a horse which came up behind him, interrupted his reverie, and he soon saw he was mounted by the same wild rider whom he had left at the tower.

"Good even, my son, and benedicite," said the Sub-Prior as he passed; but the rude soldier scarce acknowledged the greeting, by bending his head; and dashing the spurs into his horse, went on at a pace which soon left the Monk and his mule far behind. "And there," thought the Sub-Prior, "goes another plague of the times—a fellow whose birth designed him to cultivate the earth, but who is perverted by the unhallowed and unchristian divisions of the country, into a daring dissolute robber. The barons of Scotland are now turned masterful thieves and ruffians, oppressing the poor by violence, and wasting the Church, by extorting free-quarters from abbeys and priories, without either shame or reason.—I fear me I shall be too late to counsel the Abbot to make a stand against these daring *sorners*.*—I must make haste." He struck his mule with the riding-wand accordingly; but, instead of mending her pace, the animal suddenly started from the path, and the rider's utmost efforts could not force her forward.

"Art thou, too, infected with the spirit of the times?" said the Sub-Prior; "thou wert wont to be ready and serviceable, and art now as restive as any wild jack-man or stubborn heretic of them all."

While he was contending with the startled animal, a voice, like that of a female, chaunted in his ear, or at least very close to it,

> "Good evening, Sir Priest, and so late as you ride,
> With your mule so fair, and your mantle so wide;
> But ride you through valley, or ride you o'er hill,
> There is one that has warrant to wait on you still.
>> Back, back,
>> The volume black!
> I have a warrant to carry it back."

* To *sorne*, in Scotland, is to exact free quarters against the will of the landlord. It is declared equivalent to theft by a statute passed in the year 1455. The great chieftains oppressed the Monasteries very much by exactions of this nature. The community of Aberbrothwick complained of an Earl of Angus, I think, who was in the regular habit of visiting them once a year, with a train of a thousand horse, and abiding till the whole winter provisions of the convent were exhausted.

The Sub-Prior looked around, but neither bush nor brake was near which could conceal an ambushed songstress. "May Our Lady have mercy on me!" he said; "I trust my senses have not forsaken me—yet how my thoughts should arrange themselves into rhimes which I despise, and music which I care nought for, or why there should be the sound of a female voice in ears, to which its melody has been so long indifferent, baffles my comprehension, and almost realizes the vision of Philip the Sacristan.—Come, good mule, betake thee to the path, and let us hence while our judgment serves us."

But the mule stood as if it had been rooted to the spot, backed from the point to which it was pressed by its rider, and by her ears laid close into her neck, and her eyes almost starting from their sockets, testified that she was under great terror.

While the Sub-Prior, by alternate threats and soothing, endeavoured to reclaim the wayward animal to her duty, the wild musical voice was again heard close beside him.

> "What ho! Sir Prior, and came you but here
> To conjure a book from a dead woman's bier?
> Sain you, and save you, be wary and wise,
> Ride back with the book or you'll pay for your prize.
> Back, back,
> There's death on the track!
> In the name of my master, I bid thee bear back."

"In the name of MY Master," said the astonished Monk, "that name before which all created things tremble, I conjure thee to say what thou art that hauntest me thus?"

The same voice replied,

> "That which is neither ill nor well,
> That which belongs not to Heaven nor to hell,
> A wreath of the mist, a bubble of the stream,
> 'Twixt a waking thought and a sleeping dream;
> A form that men spy
> With the half shut eye,
> In the beams of the setting sun am I."

"This is more than simple fantasy," said the Sub-Prior rousing himself; though, notwithstanding the natural hardihood of his temper, the sensible presence of a supernatural being so near him, failed not to make his blood run cold and his hair bristle. "I charge thee," he said aloud, "be thine errand what it will, to depart and trouble me no more!—False spirit, thou canst not appal any save those who do the work negligently."

The voice immediately answered:

> "Vainly, Sir Prior, would'st thou bar me my right!
> Like the star when it shoots, I can dart through the night;
> I can dance on the torrent and ride on the air,

> And travel the world with the bonnie night-mare.
>   Again, again,
>   At the crook of the glen,
> Where bickers the burnie, I'll meet thee again."

The road was now apparently left open; for the mule collected herself, and changed from her posture of terror to one which promised advance, although a profuse perspiration, and general trembling of the joints, indicated the bodily terror she had undergone.

"I used to doubt the existence of Cabalists and Rosicrucians," thought the Sub-Prior, "but by my Holy Order, I know no longer what to say!—My pulse beats temperately—my hand is cool—I am fasting from every thing but sin, and possessed of my ordinary faculties. Either some fiend is permitted to bewilder me, or the tales of Cornelius Agrippa, Paracelsus, and others who treat of occult philosophy, are not without foundation. At the crook of the glen?—I could have well desired to avoid a second meeting, but I am on the service of the church, and the gates of hell shall not prevail against me."

He moved onward accordingly, but with precaution, and not without fear; for he neither knew the manner in which, or the place where, his journey might be next interrupted by his invisible attendant. He descended the glen without interruption for about a mile further, when, just at a spot where the brook approached the steep hill, with a winding so abrupt as to leave scarcely room for a horse to pass, the mule was again visited with the same symptoms of terror which had before interrupted her course. Better acquainted than before with the cause of her restiveness, the Priest employed no effort to make her proceed, but addressed himself to the object, which he doubted not was the same that had formerly interrupted him, in the words of solemn exorcism prescribed by the church of Rome on such occasions.

In reply to his demand, the voice again sung;—

> "Men of good are bold as sackless,*
> Men of rude are wild and reckless.
>   Lie thou still
>   In the nook of the hill,
> For those are before thee that wish thee ill."

While the Sub-Prior listened, with his head turned in the direction from which the sounds seemed to come, he felt as if something rushed against him; and ere he could discover the cause, he was pushed from his saddle with gentle but irresistible force. Before he reached the ground his senses were gone, and he lay long in a state of insensibility; for the sunset had not ceased to gild the top of the distant hill when he fell,—and when he again became conscious of existence, the pale

* *Sackless*—Innocent.

moon was gleaming on the landscape. He awakened in a state of terror, from which, for a few minutes, he found it difficult to shake himself free. At length he sate up on the grass, and became sensible, by repeated exertion, that the only personal injury which he had sustained was the numbness arising from extreme cold. The motion of something near him made the blood again run to his heart, and by a sudden effort he started up, and, looking around, saw to his relief that the noise was occasioned by the footsteps of his own mule. The peaceable animal had remained quietly beside her master during his trance, browsing on the grass which grew plentifully in that sequestered nook.

With some exertion he collected himself, remounted the animal, and meditating upon his wild adventure, descended the glen till its junction with the broader valley through which the Tweed winds. The draw-bridge was readily dropped at his first summons, and so much had he won upon the heart of the churlish warden, that Peter appeared himself with a lantern to shew the Sub-Prior his way over the perilous pass.

"By my sooth, sir," he said, holding the light up to Father Eustace's face; "you look sore travelled and deadly pale—but a little matter serves to weary you out, you men of the cell. I now who speak to you—I have ridden—before I was perched up here on this pillar betwixt wind and water—it may be thirty Scots miles before I broke my fast, and have had the red of a bramble rose in my cheek all the while—But will you taste some food, or a cup of distilled waters?"

"I may not," said Father Eustace, "being under a vow—but I thank you for your kindness, and pray you to give what I may not accept to the next poor pilgrim who comes hither pale and fainting, for so it shall be the better both with him here, and with you hereafter."

"By my faith, and I will do so," said Peter Bridge-Ward, "even for thy sake—It is strange now, how this Sub-Prior gets round one's heart more than the rest of these cowled gentry, that think of nothing but quaffing and stuffing—Wife, I say—wife—we will give a cup of distilled waters and a crust of bread unto the next pilgrim that comes over; and ye may keep for the purpose the grunds of the last greybeard,* and the ill-baked bannock which the bairns couldna eat."

While Peter issued these charitable, and, at the same time, prudent injunctions, the Sub-Prior, whose mild interference had awakened the Bridge-Ward to such an act of unwonted generosity, was pacing onward to the Monastery. In the way, he had to commune with and subdue his own rebellious heart, an enemy, he was sensible, more

* An old-fashioned name for an earthen jar for holding spirits.

formidable than any which the external powers of Satan could place in his way.

Father Eustace had indeed strong temptation to suppress the extraordinary incident which had befallen him, which he was the more reluctant to confess, because he had passed so severe a judgment upon Father Philip, who, as he was now not unwilling to allow, had, on his return from Glendearg, encountered obstacles somewhat similar to his own. Of this the Sub-Prior was the more convinced, when, feeling in his bosom for the Book which he had brought off from the Tower of Glendearg, he found it was amissing, which he could only account for by supposing it had been stolen from him during his trance.

"If I confess this strange visitation," thought the Sub-Prior, "I become the ridicule of all my brethren—I whom the Primate sent hither to be a watch, as it were, and a check upon their follies. I give the Abbot an advantage over me which I shall never again recover, and Heaven only knows how he may abuse it, in his foolish simplicity, to the dishonour and loss of Holy Kirk.—But then, if I make not true confession of my shame, with what face can I again presume to admonish or restrain others?—Avow, proud heart," continued he, addressing himself, "that the weal of Holy Church interests thee less in this matter than thine own humiliation—Yes, Heaven has punished thee even in that point in which thou didst deem thyself most strong, in thy spiritual pride and thy carnal wisdom. Thou has laughed at, and derided the inexperience of thy brethren—stoop thyself in turn to their derision—tell what they may not believe—affirm that which they will ascribe to idle fear, or perhaps to wilful falsehood—sustain the disgrace of a silly visionary, or a wilful deceiver.—Be it so; I will do my duty, and make ample confession to my Superior—if the discharge of this duty destroys my usefulness in this house, God and Our Lady will send me where I can better serve them."

There was no little merit in the resolution thus piously and generously formed by Father Eustace. To men of any rank the esteem of their order is naturally most dear; but in the monastic establishment, cut off, as the brethren are, from other objects of ambition, as well as from all exterior friendship and relationship, the place which they hold in the opinion of each other is all in all.

But the consciousness how much he should rejoice the Abbot and most of the other Monks of Saint Mary's, who were impatient of the unauthorized yet irresistible controul, which he was wont to exercise in the affairs of the convent by a confession which would put him in a ludicrous, or perhaps even in a criminal point of view, could not weigh with Father Eustace in comparison with the duty which his belief enjoined.

As, strong in his feelings of duty, he approached the exterior gate of the Monastery, he was surprised to see torches gleaming, and men assembled around it, some on horseback, some on foot, while several of the Monks, distinguished through the night by their white scapularies, were making themselves busy amongst the crowd. The Sub-Prior was received with a unanimous shout of joy, which at once made him sensible that he had himself been the object of their anxiety.

"There he is! there he is! God be thanked—there he is, hale and fear!" exclaimed the vassals; while the Monks exclaimed "*Te Deum laudamus*—the blood of thy servants is precious in thy sight!"

"What is the matter, children? what is the matter, my brethren?" said Father Eustace, dismounting at the gate.

"Nay, brother, if thou know'st not, we will not tell thee till thou art in the refectory," answered the Monks; "Suffice it that the Lord Abbot had ordered these, our zealous and faithful vassals, instantly to set forth to guard thee from imminent peril—Ye may ungirth your horses, children, and dismiss—and, to-morrow, each who was at this rendezvous may send to the convent kitchen for a quarter of a yard of roast-beef, and a black-jack full of double ale."

The vassals dispersed with joyful acclamation, and the Monks with equal jubilee, conducted the Sub-Prior into the refectory.

Chapter Ten

Here we stand—
Woundless and well, may Heaven's high name be bless'd for't!
As erst, ere treason couch'd a lance against us.
                    DECKER

No SOONER was the Sub-Prior carried into the refectory by his rejoicing companions, than the first person on whom he fixed his eye proved to be Christie of the Clinthill. He was seated in the chimney-corner, fettered and guarded, his features drawn into that air of sulky and turbid resolution with which those hardened in guilt are accustomed to view the approach of punishment. But as the Sub-Prior drew near to him, his face assumed a more wild and startled expression, while he exclaimed—"The devil! the devil himself, brings the dead back upon the living!"

"Nay," said a Monk to him, "say rather, that Our Lady foils the attempts of the wicked on her faithful servants—our dear brother lives and moves."

"Lives and moves!" said the ruffian, rising and shuffling towards the Sub-Prior as well as his chains would permit; "nay, then I will never trust ashen shaft and steel point more—It is even so," he added, as he gazed on the Sub-Prior with astonishment; "neither wem nor wound—not so much as a rent in his frock!"

"And whence should my wound have come?" said Father Eustace.

"From the good lance that never failed me so foully before," replied Christie of the Clinthill.

"Heaven absolve thee for thy purpose!" said the Sub-Prior; "wouldst thou have slain a servant of the altar?"

"To choose!" answered Christie, "the Fifemen say, an' the whole pack of ye were slain, there were more lost at Flodden."

"Villain! art thou heretic as well as murderer?"

"Not I, by Saint Giles," replied the rider; "I listened blithely enough to the Laird of Monance, when he told me ye were all cheats and knaves; but when he would have had me go hear one Wiseheart, a gospeller, as they call him, he might as well have persuaded the wild colt that had flung one rider to kneel down and help another into the saddle."

"There is some goodness about him yet," said the Sacristan to the Abbot, who at that moment entered—"He refused to hear a heretic preacher."

"The better for him in the next world," answered the Abbot. "Prepare for death, my son—we deliver thee over to the secular arm of our Baillie, for execution on the Gallow-hill by peep of light."

"Amen!" said the ruffian; "'tis the end I must have come by sooner or later—and what care I whether I feed the crows at Saint Mary's or at Carlisle?"

"Let me implore your reverent patience for an instant," said the Sub-Prior; "until I shall enquire"——

"What!" exclaimed the Abbot, observing him for the first time—"Our dear brother restored to us when his life was unhoped for!— nay, kneel not to a sinner like me—stand up—thou hast my blessing. When this villain came to the gate, accused by his own evil conscience, and crying out he had murdered thee, I thought that the pillar of our main aisle had fallen—no more shall a life so precious be exposed to such risks, as occur in this Border country; no longer shall one beloved and rescued of Heaven hold so low a station in the church, as that of a poor Sub-Prior—I will write by express to the Primate for thy speedy removal and advancement."

"Nay, but let me understand," said the Sub-Prior; "did this soldier say that he had slain me?"

"That he had transfixed you," answered the Abbot, "in full career with his lance—but it seems he had taken an indifferent aim. But no sooner didst thou fall to the ground mortally gored, as he deemed, with his weapon, than our blessed Patroness appeared to him, as he averred"——

"I averred no such thing," said the prisoner; "I said a woman in white interrupted me, as I was about to examine the priest's cassock, for they are usually well lined—she had a bull-rush in her hand, with one touch of which she struck me from my horse, as I might strike down a child of four years old with an iron mace—and then, like a singing fiend as she was, she sung to me,

> 'Thank the holly-bush
> That nods on thy brow;
> Or with this slender rush
> I had strangled thee now.'

I gathered myself up with fear and difficulty, threw myself on my horse, and came hither like a fool to get myself hanged for a rogue."

"Thou seest, honoured brother," said the Abbot to the Sub-Prior, "in what favour thou art with our blessed Patroness, that she herself becomes the guardian of thy paths—Not since the days of our blessed founder hath she shewn such grace to any one. All unworthy were we to hold spiritual superiority over thee, and we pray thee to prepare for thy speedy removal to Aberbrothock."

"Alas! my lord and father," said the Sub-Prior, "your words pierce my very soul—under the seal of confession will I presently tell thee why I conceive myself rather the baffled sport of a spirit of another sort, than the protected favourite of the heavenly powers. But first let me ask this unhappy man a question or two."

"Do as ye list," replied the Abbot—"but you shall not convince me that it is fitting you remain in this inferior office in the convent of Saint Mary."

"I would ask of this poor man," said Father Eustace, "for what purpose he nourished the thought of putting to death one who never did him evil."

"Ay! but thou didst menace me with evil," said the ruffian, "and no one but a fool is menaced twice. Doest thou not remember what you said touching the Primate and Lord James, and the black pool of Jedwood? Didst thou think me fool enough to wait till thou hadst betrayed me to the sack and the fork? There were small wisdom in that methinks—as little as in coming hither to tell my own misdeeds— I think the devil was in me when I took this road—I might have remembered the proverb, 'Never Friar forgot feud.'"

"And was it solely for that—for that only hasty word of mine, uttered in a moment of impatience, and forgotten ere it was well spoken?" said Father Eustace.

"Ay! for that, and for the love of thy gold crucifix," said Christie of the Clinthill.

"Gracious heaven! and could the yellow metal—the glittering earth —so far overcome every sense of what is thereby represented?— Father Abbot, I pray, as a dear boon, you will deliver this guilty person to my mercy."

"Nay, brother," interposed the Sacristan, "to your doom if you will, not to your mercy—remember, we are not all equally favoured by our blessed Lady, nor is it likely that every frock in the Convent will serve as a coat of proof when a lance is couched against it."

"For that very reason," said the Sub-Prior, "I would not that for my worthless self the community were to fall at feud with Julian of Avenel, this man's master."

"Our Lady forbid!" said the Sacristan, "he is a second Julian the Apostate."

"With our reverend father the Abbot's permission then," said Father Eustace, "I desire this man be freed from his chains, and suffered to depart uninjured;—And here, friend," he added, giving him the golden crucifix, "is the image for which thou wert willing to stain thy hands with murther—view it well, and may it inspire thee with other and better thoughts than those which referred to it as a piece of bullion. Part with it, nevertheless, if thy necessities require, and get thee one of such coarse substance that mammon shall have no share in any of the reflections to which it gives rise. It was the bequest of a dear friend to me; but dearer service can it never do than that of winning a soul to heaven."

The Borderer, now freed from his chains, stood gazing alternately on the Sub-Prior and on the golden crucifix. "By Saint Giles," said he, "I understand ye not!—an ye give me gold for couching my lance at thee, what would you give me to level it at a heretic?"

"The Church," said the Sub-Prior, "will try the effect of her spiritual censures to bring these stray sheep again into the fold, ere she employ the edge of the sword of Saint Peter."

"Ay, but," said the ruffian, "they say the Primate recommends a little strangling and burning in aid both of censure and of sword. But fare ye weel, I owe you a life, and it may be I will not forget my debt."

The Baillie now came bustling in, dressed in his blue coat and bandaliers, and attended by two or three halberdiers. "I have been a thought too late in waiting upon your reverend lordship. I am grown somewhat fatter since the field of Pinkie, and my leathern coat slips not on so soon as it was wont—but the dungeon is ready, and though, as I said, I have been some what late"——

Here his intended prisoner walked gravely up to the officer's nose, to his great amazement.

"You have been indeed somewhat late, Baillie," said he, "and I am greatly obligated to your buff-coat, and to the time you took to put it on. If the secular arm had arrived some quarter of an hour sooner, I had been out of the reach of spiritual grace—but as it is, I wish you good even, and a safe riddance out of your garment of durance, in which you have much the air of a hog in armour."

Wroth was the Baillie with this comparison, and exclaimed in ire ——"An' it were not for the presence of the venerable Lord Abbot, thou knave"——

"Nay, an' thou would'st try conclusions," said Christie of the Clint-hill, "I will meet thee at day-break by Saint Mary's well."

"Hardened wretch," said Father Eustace, "art thou but this instant delivered from death, and doest thou so soon nurse thoughts of slaughter?"

"I shall meet with thee ere it be long, thou knave," said the Baillie, "and teach thee thine Oremus."

"I shall meet thy cattle in a moonlight night, before that day," said he of the Clinthill.

"I shall have thee by the neck one misty morning, thou strong thief," answered the secular officer of the church.

"Thou art thyself as strong a thief as ever rode," retorted Christie; "and if the worms were once feasting on that fat carcase of thine, I might well hope to have thine office, by favour of these reverend men."

"A cast of their office, and a cast of mine," answered the Baillie; "a cord and a confessor, that is all thou wilt have from us."

"Sirs," said the Sub-Prior, observing that his brethren began to take more interest than was exactly decorous in this wrangling betwixt justice and iniquity, "I pray you both to depart—Master Baillie, retire with your halberdiers, and trouble not the man whom we have dismissed.—And thou, Christie, or whatever be thy name, take thy departure, and remember thou owest thy life to the Lord Abbot's clemency."

"Nay, as to that," answered Christie, "I judge that I owe it to your own—but impute it to whom ye list, I owe a life among ye, and there is an end." And whistling as he went, he left the apartment, seeming as if he held the life which he had forfeited not worthy farther thanks.

"Obstinate even to brutality!" said Father Eustace; "and yet who knows but some better ore may lie under so rude an exterior."

"Save a thief from the gallows," said the Sacristan—"you know the rest of the proverb; and admitting, as may Heaven grant, that our life and limb are safe from this outrageous knave, who shall insure our meal and our malt, our herds and our flocks?"

"Marry, that will I, my brethren," said an aged Monk. "Ah, brethren, you little know what may be made of a repentant robber. In Abbot Ingelram's days—ay, and I remember them as it were yesterday—the freebooters were the best welcome men that came to Saint Mary's. Ay, they paid tithe of every drove that they brought over from the South, and because they were something lightly come by, I have known them make the tithe a seventh—that is, if their confessor knew his business —ay, when we saw from the tower a score of fat bullocks, or a drove of sheep coming down the valley, with two or three stout men-at-arms behind them, with their glittering steel caps, and their black-jacks, and their long lances, the good Lord Abbot Ingelram was wont to say —he was a merry man—there come the tithes of the spoilers of the Egyptians! Ay, and I have seen the famous John the Armstrang,—a fair man he was and a goodly, the more pity that hemp was ever heckled for him—I have seen him come into the Abbey-Church with nine tassells of gold in his bonnet, and every tassell made of nine English nobles, and he would go from chapel to chapel, and from image to image, and from altar to altar, on his knees—and leave here a tassell, and there a noble, till there was as little gold on his bonnet as on my hood—you will find no such Border thieves now!"

"No truly, Brother Nicolas," answered the Abbot; "they are more apt to take any gold the Church has left, than to bequeath or bestow any—and for cattle, beshrew me if I think they care whether beeves have fed on the meadows of Lanercost Abbey or of Saint Mary's."

"There is no good thing left in them," said Father Nicolas; "they are clean naught—Ah, the thieves that I have seen!—such proper men! and as pitiful as proper, and as pious as pitiful!"

"It skills not talking of it, Brother Nicolas," said the Abbot; "and I will now dismiss you, my brethren, holding your meeting upon this our inquisition concerning the danger of our reverend Sub-Prior, instead of the attendance on the lauds this evening—Yet let the bells be duly rung for the edification of the laymen without, and also that the novices may give due reverence.—And now, benedicite, brethren! the cellarer will bestow on each a grace-cup and a morsel as ye pass the buttery, for ye have been turmoiled and anxious, and dangerous it is to fall asleep in such case on an empty stomach."

"*Gratias agimus quam maximas, Domine reverendissime,*" replied the brethren, departing in their due order.

But the Sub-Prior remained behind, and falling on his knees before the Abbot, as he was about to withdraw, craved him to hear under the seal of confession the adventures of the day. The reverend Lord

Abbot yawned, and would have alleged fatigue; but to Father Eustace, of all men, he was ashamed to shew indifference in his religious duties. The confession, therefore, proceeded, in which Father Eustace told all the extraordinary circumstances which had befallen him during the journey. And being questioned by the Abbot, whether he was not conscious of any secret sin, through which he might have been subjected for a time to the delusions of evil spirits, the Sub-Prior admitted with frank avowal, that he thought he might have deserved such a penance for having judged with unfraternal rigour of the report of Father Philip the Sacristan.

"Heaven," said the penitent, "may have been willing to convince me, not only that he can at pleasure open a communication betwixt us and beings of a different, and, as we word it, supernatural class, but also to punish our pride of superior wisdom, or superior courage, or superior learning."

It is well said that virtue is its own reward; and I question if duty was ever more completely recompensed, than by the audience which the reverend Abbot so unwillingly yielded to the confession of his Sub-Prior. To find the object of his fear shall we say, or of his envy, or of both, accusing himself of the very error with which he had so often tacitly charged him, was at once a corroboration of his judgment, a soothing of his pride, and an allaying of his fears. The sense of triumph, however, rather increased than diminished his natural good-humour; and so far was Abbot Boniface from being disposed to tyrannize over his Sub-Prior, in consequence of this discovery, that in his exhortation he hovered somewhat ludicrously betwixt the natural expression of his own gratified vanity, and his timid reluctance to hurt the feelings of Father Eustace.

"My brother," said he, *ex cathedra*, "it cannot have escaped your judicious observation, that we have often declined our own judgment in favour of your opinion, even about those matters which most nearly concerned the community. Nevertheless, grieved were we, could you think that we did this either because we deemed our own opinion less pregnant, or our wit more shallow, than that of our other brethren. For it is done exclusively to give our younger brethren, such as your much esteemed self, my dearest brother, that courage which is necessary to a free deliverance of your opinion,—we oftimes setting apart our proper judgment, that our inferiors, and especially our dear brother the Sub-Prior, may be comforted and encouraged in proposing valiantly his own thoughts. Which our deference and humility may, in some sort, have produced in your mind, most reverend brother, that self-opinion of parts and knowledge, which hath led unfortunately to your over-estimating your own faculties, and thereby subjecting yourself, as is but too visible, to the japes and mockeries of evil spirits. For it is assured that Heaven always holdeth us in the least esteem when we deem of ourselves most highly; and also, on the other hand, it may be that we have somewhat departed from what became our high seat in this Abbey, in suffering ourself to be too much guided, and even as it were controuled, by the voice of our inferior. Wherefore," continued the Lord Abbot, "in both of us such faults shall and must be amended—you hereafter presuming less upon your gifts and carnal wisdom, and I taking heed not so easily to relinquish mine own opinion for that of one lower in place and in office. Nevertheless, we would not that we should thereby lose the high advantage which we have derived, and may yet derive, from your wise counsel, which hath been so often recommended to us by our most reverend Primate. Wherefore, on affairs of high moment, we will call you to our presence in private and listen to your opinion, which, if it shall agree with our own, we will deliver to the chapter, as emanating directly from ourselves; thus sparing you, dearest brother, that seeming victory which is so apt to engender spiritual pride, and avoiding ourselves the temptation of falling into that modest facility of opinion, whereby our office is lessened and our person (were that of consequence) rendered less important in the eyes of the community over which we preside."

Notwithstanding the high notions which, as a rigid Catholic, Father Eustace entertained of the sacrament, as his church call it, of confession, there was some danger that a sense of the ridiculous might have stolen on him, when he heard his Superior, with such simple cunning, lay out a little plan for availing himself of the Sub-Prior's wisdom and experience, while he took the whole credit to himself. Yet his conscience immediately told him that he was right.

"I should have thought more," he reflected, "of the spiritual Superior, and less of the individual. I should have spread my mantle over the frailties of my spiritual father, and done what I might to support his character, and, of course, to extend his utility among the brethren, as well as with others. The Abbot cannot be humbled, but what the community must be humbled in his person. Her boast is, that over all her children, especially over those called to places of distinction, she can diffuse those gifts which are necessary to render them illustrious."

Actuated by these sentiments, Father Eustace frankly assented to the charge which his Superior, even in that moment of authority, had rather intimated than made, and signified his humble acquiescence in any mode of communicating his counsel which might be most agreeable to the Lord Abbot, and might best remove from himself all temptation to glory in his own wisdom. He then prayed the reverend father to assign him such penance as might best suit his offence, intimating at the same time, that he had already fasted the whole day.

"And it is that I complain of," answered the Abbot, instead of giving him credit for his abstinence; "it is of these very penances, fasts, and vigils, which we complain; as tending only to generate air and fumes of vanity, which, ascending from the stomach into the head, do but puff us up with vain glory and self opinion. It is meet and beseeming that novices should undergo fasts and vigils; for some part of every community must fast, and young stomachs may best endure it. Besides, in them it abates wicked thoughts, and the desire of worldly delights. But, reverend brother, for those to fast who are dead and mortified to the world, as I and thou, is work of supererogation, and is but the mother of spiritual pride. Wherefore, I enjoin thee, most reverend brother, go to the buttery, and drink two cups at least of good wine, eating withal a comfortable morsel, such as may best suit thy taste and stomach. And in respect that thine own opinion of thy own wisdom hath at times made thee less conformable to, and companionable with, thy weaker and less learned brethren, I enjoin thee, during the said repast, to chuse for thy companion, our reverend brother Nicolas, and, without interruption or impatience, to listen for a stricken hour to his narratives, concerning those things which befell in the times of our venerable predecessor, Abbot Ingelram, on whose soul may Heaven have mercy! And for such holy exercises as may further advantage your soul, and expiate the fault whereof you have contritely and humbly avowed yourself guilty, we will ponder upon that matter, and announce our will to you the next morning."

It was remarkable, that after this memorable evening, the feelings of the worthy Abbot towards his adviser were much more kindly and friendly than when he deemed the Sub-Prior the impeccable and infallible person, in whose garment of virtue and wisdom no flaw was to be discerned. It seemed as if this avowal of his own imperfections had recommended Father Eustace to the friendship of his Superior, although at the same time this increase of benevolence was attended with some circumstances, which, to a man of the Sub-Prior's natural elevation of mind and temper, were more grievous than even undergoing the legends of the dull and verbose Father Nicolas. For instance, the Abbot seldom mentioned him to the other monks, without designing him our beloved Brother Eustace, poor man!—And now and then he used to warn the younger brethren against the snares of vain-glory and spiritual pride, which Satan sets for the more rigidly righteous, with such looks and demonstrations as did all but expressly designate the Sub-Prior as one who had fallen at one time under such delusions. Upon such occasions, it required all the votive obedience of a monk, all the philosophical discipline of the schools, and all the patience of a Christian, to enable Father Eustace to endure the pompous and patronizing parade of his honest, but somewhat thickheaded Superior. He began himself to be desirous of leaving the Monastery, or at least he manifestly declined to interfere with its affairs, in that marked and authoritative manner, which he had at first practised.

Chapter Eleven

You call this education, do you not?
Why 'tis the forced march of a herd of bullocks
Before a shouting drover. The glad van
Move on at ease, and pause a while to snatch
A passing morsel from the dewy green-sward,
While all the blows, the oaths, the indignation,
Fall on the croupe of the ill-fated laggard
That cripples in the rear.

Old Play

TWO OR THREE YEARS glided on, during which the storm of the approaching alteration in church government became each day louder and more perilous. Owing to the circumstances which we have intimated in the end of the last chapter, the Sub-Prior Eustace appeared to have altered considerably his habits of life. He afforded, on all extraordinary occasions, to the Abbot, whether privately, or in the assembled chapter, the support of his wisdom and experience. But in his ordinary habits he seemed now to live more for himself, and less for the community, than had been his former practice.

He often absented himself for whole days from the convent; and as the adventure of Glendearg dwelt deeply on his memory, he was repeatedly induced to visit that lonely tower, and to take an interest in the orphans who had their shelter under its roof. Besides, he felt a deep anxiety to know whether the volume which he had lost, when so strangely preserved from the lance of the murderer, had again found its way back to the tower of Glendearg. "It was strange," he thought, "that a spirit," for such he could not help judging the being whose voice he had heard, "should, on the one side, seek the advancement of heresy, and, on the other, interpose to save the life of a zealous Catholic priest."

But from no enquiry which he made at the various inhabitants of the Tower of Glendearg could he learn that the copy of the translated Scriptures, after which he made such diligent enquiry, had again been seen by any of them.

In the meanwhile the good father's occasional visits were of no small consequence to Edward Glendinning and to Mary Avenel. The former displayed a power for apprehending and retaining whatever was taught him, which filled Father Eustace with admiration. He was at once acute and industrious, alert and accurate; one of those rare combinations of talent and industry, which are seldom combined save in the most fortunate subjects.

It was the earnest desire of Father Eustace that the excellent qualities thus early displayed by Edward should be educated to the service of the church, to which he thought the youth's own consent might be easily attained, as he was of a calm, contemplative, retired habit, and seemed to consider knowledge as the principal object, and its enlargement as the greatest pleasure, in life. As to the mother, the Sub-Prior had little doubt that, trained as she was to view the Monks of Saint Mary's with such profound reverence, she would be but too happy in an opportunity of enrolling one of her sons in its honoured community. But the good Father proved to be mistaken in both these particulars.

When he spoke to Elspet Glendinning of that which a mother best loves to hear—the proficiency and abilities of her son—she listened with a delighted ear. But when Father Eustace hinted at the duty of dedicating to the service of the church, talents which seemed fitted to defend and to adorn it, the dame endeavoured always to shift the subject; and if pressed farther, enlarged on her own incapacity, as a lone woman, to manage the feu—on the advantage which her neighbours of the township were often taking of her unprotected state, and on the wish she had that Edward might fill his father's place, remain in the little tower, and close her eyes.

On such occasions the Sub-Prior would answer, that even in a worldly point of view the welfare of the family would be best consulted by one of the sons entering into the community of St Mary's, as it was not to be supposed that he would fail to afford his family the important protection which he could then easily extend towards them. What could be a more pleasing prospect than to see him high in honour? or what more sweet than to have the last duties rendered to her by a son, revered for his holiness of life and exemplary manners? Besides, he endeavoured to impress upon the dame that her eldest son, Halbert, whose bold temper and headstrong indulgence of a wandering humour rendered him incapable of learning, was for that reason, as well as that he was her eldest born, fittest to bustle through the affairs of the world, and manage the little fief.

Elspet durst not directly dissent from what was proposed, for fear of giving displeasure, and yet she always had something to say against it. Halbert, she said, was not like any of the neighbour boys; he was taller by the head, and stronger by the half, than any boy of his years within the Halidome. But he was fit for no peaceful work that could be devised. If he liked a book ill, he liked a plough or a pattle worse. He had scoured his father's old broad-sword, suspended it by a belt round his waist, and seldom stirred without it. He was a sweet boy and a gentle if speak him fair, but cross him and he was a born devil. "In a word," she said, bursting into tears, "deprive me of Edward, good father, and ye bereave my house of prop and pillar; for my heart tells me that Halbert will take to his father's gait, and die his father's death."

When the conversation came to this crisis, the good-humoured Monk was always content to drop the discussion for the time, trusting some opportunity would occur of removing her prejudices, for such he thought them, against Edward's proposed destination.

When, leaving the mother, the Sub-Prior addressed himself to the son, animating his zeal for knowledge, and pointing out how amply it might be gratified should he agree to take holy orders, he found the same repugnance which Dame Elspet had exhibited. Edward pleaded a want of sufficient vocation to so serious a profession, his reluctance to leave his mother and other objections, which the Sub-Prior treated as evasive.

"I plainly perceive," said he one day, in answer to them, "that the devil has his factors as well as Heaven, and that they are equally, or alas! perhaps more active, in bespeaking for their master the first of the market. I trust, young man, that neither idleness, nor licentious pleasure, nor the love of worldly gain and worldly grandeur, the chief baits with which the great Fisher of souls conceals his hook, are the causes of your declining the career to which I would incite you. But above all I trust—but above all I hope—that the vanity of superior knowledge, a sin with which those who have made proficiency in learning are most frequently beset, has not led you into the awful hazard of listening to the dangerous doctrines which are now afloat concerning religion. Better for you that you were as grossly ignorant as the beasts which perish, than that the pride of knowledge should induce you to lend ear to the voice of the heretics." Edward Glendinning listened to the rebuke with a downcast look, and failed not, when it was concluded, earnestly to vindicate himself from the charge of having pushed his studies into any subjects which the Church inhibited; and so the Monk was left to form vain conjectures respecting the cause of his reluctance to embrace the monastic state.

It is an old proverb, used by Chaucer, and quoted by Elizabeth, that "the greatest clerks are not the wisest men;" and it is as true as if the poet had not rhimed, or the queen reasoned on it. If Father Eustace had not had his thoughts turned so much to the progress of heresy, and so little to what was passing in the little tower, he might have read, in the speaking eye of Mary Avenel, now a girl of fourteen or fifteen, reasons which might disincline her youthful companion towards the monastic vows. I have said, that she also was a promising pupil of the good father, upon whom her innocent and infantine beauty had an effect of which he was himself, perhaps, unconscious. Her rank and expectations entitled her to be taught the arts of reading and writing, and each lesson which the Monk assigned her was conned over in company with Edward, and by him explained and re-explained, and again illustrated, until she became perfectly mistress of it.

In the beginning of their studies, Halbert had been their school companion. But the boldness and impatience of his disposition soon quarrelled with an occupation, in which, without assiduity and unremitted attention, no progress was to be expected. The Sub-Prior's visits were at irregular intervals, and often weeks would intervene between them, in which case Halbert was sure to forget all that had been prescribed for him to learn, and much which he had partly acquired before. His deficiences on these occasions gave him pain, but it was not of that sort which produces amendment.

For a time, like all who are fond of idleness, he endeavoured to detach the attention of his brother and Mary Avenel from their task, rather than to learn his own, and such dialogues as the following would ensue.

"Take your bonnet, Edward, and make haste—the Laird of Hunter's-hope is at the head of the glen with his hounds."

"I care not, Halbert," answered the younger brother; "two brace of dogs may kill a deer without my being there to see them, and I must help Mary Avenel with her lesson."

"Ay! you will labour at the Monk's lessons till you turn monk yourself," answered Halbert.—"Mary, will you with me, and I will shew you the cushat's nest I told you of?"

"I cannot go with you, Halbert," answered Mary, "because I must study this lesson—it will take me long to learn it—I am sorry I am so dull, for if I could get my task as fast as Edward, I should like to go with you."

"Should you, indeed?" said Halbert; "then I will wait for you—and, what is more, I will try to get my lesson also."

With a smile and a sigh he took up the primer, and began heavily to con over the task which had been assigned him. As if banished from the society of the two others, he sate sad and solitary in one of the deep window-recesses, and after in vain struggling with the difficulties of his task, and his disinclination to learn it, he found himself involuntarily engaged in watching the movements of the other two students, instead of toiling any longer.

The picture which Halbert looked upon was delightful in itself, but somehow or other it afforded very little pleasure to him. The beautiful girl, with looks of simple, yet earnest anxiety, was bent on disentangling those intricacies which obstructed her progress to knowledge, and looking ever and anon to Edward for assistance, while, seated close by her side, and watchful to remove every obstacle from her way, he seemed at once to be proud of the progress which his pupil made, and of the assistance which he was able to render her. There was a bond betwixt them, a strong and interesting tie, the desire of obtaining knowledge, the pride of surmounting difficulties.

Feeling most acutely, yet ignorant of the nature and source of his own emotion, Halbert could no longer endure to look upon this quiet scene, but, starting up, dashed his book from him, and exclaimed aloud,—"To the fiend I bequeath all books, and the dreamers that make them!—I would a score of Southron would come up the glen, and we should learn how little all this muttering and scribbling is worth."

Mary Avenel and his brother both started, and looked at Halbert with surprise, while he went on with great animation, his features swelling, and the tears starting into his eyes as he spoke.—"Yes, Mary —I wish a score of Southron came up the glen this very day; and you should see one good hand, and one good sword, do more to protect you than all the books that were ever opened, and all the pens that ever grew on a goose's wing."

Mary looked a little surprised and a little frightened at his vehemence, but instantly replied affectionately, "You are vexed, Halbert, because you do not get your lesson so fast as Edward can—and so am I, for I am as stupid as you—But come, and Edward shall sit betwixt us and teach us."

"He shall not teach *me*," said Halbert, in the same angry mood; "I never can teach *him* to do any thing that is honourable and manly, and he shall not teach *me* any of his monkish tricks.—I hate the Monks, with their drawling nasal tone like so many frogs, and their long black petticoats like so many women, and their reverences, and their lordships, and their lazy vassals, that do nothing but paddle in the mire with plough and harrow, from Yule to Michaelmass. I will call none lord, but him who wears a sword to make his title good; and I will call none man, but he that can bear himself manlike and masterful."

"For Heaven's sake, peace, brother," said Edward; "if such words were taken and reported out of the house, they would be our mother's ruin."

"Report them yourself then, and they will be *your* making, and nobody's marring save mine own. Say, that Halbert Glendinning will never be vassal to an old man with a cowl and a shaven crown, while there are twenty barons who wear casque and plume that lack bold followers. Let them grant you these wretched acres, and much meal may they bear you to make your peasantly *brochan*." He left the room hastily, but instantly returned, and continued to speak with the same tone of quick and irritated feeling. "And you need not think so much, neither of you, and especially you, Edward, need not think so much of your parchment book there, and your cunning in reading it. By my faith I will soon learn to read as well as you—for I know a better teacher than your grim old Monk, and a better book than his painted breviary—and since you like scholar-craft so well, Mary Avenel, you will see whether Edward or I have most of it." He left the apartment and came not again.

"What can be the matter with him?" said Mary, following Halbert with her eyes from the window, as with hasty and unequal steps he ran up the wild glen.—"Where can your brother be going, Edward?—what book?—what teacher does he talk of?"

"It avails not guessing," said Edward. "Halbert is angry he knows not why, and speaks of he knows not what—let us go again to our lessons, and he will come home when he has tired himself with scrambling among the crags as usual."

But Mary's anxiety on account of Halbert seemed more deeply rooted. She declined prosecuting the task in which they had been so pleasingly engaged, under the excuse of a head-ache; nor could Edward prevail upon her to resume it again that morning.

Meanwhile Halbert, his head unbonnetted, his features swelled with jealous anger, and the tear still in his eye, sped up the wild and upper extremity of the little valley of Glendearg with the speed of a roe-buck, chusing, as if in desperate defiance of the difficulties of the way, the wildest and most dangerous paths, and voluntarily exposing himself an hundred times to dangers which he might have escaped by turning a little aside from them. It seemed as if he wished his course to be as straight as that of the arrow to its mark.

He arrived at length in a narrow and secluded *cleugh*, or deep ravine, which ran down into the valley, and contributed a scanty rivulet to the supply of the brook by which Glendearg is watered. Up this he sped with the same precipitate haste which had marked his departure from the tower, nor did he pause and look around, until he had reached the fountain from which the rivulet had its rise.

Here Halbert stopped short, and cast a gloomy, and almost a frightened glance around him. A huge rock rose in front, from a cleft of which grew a wild holly-tree, whose dark green branches rustled over the spring which arose beneath. The banks on either hand rose so high, and approached each other so closely, that it was only when the sun was in its meridian height, and during the summer solstice, that its rays could reach the bottom of the chasm in which he now stood. But it was now summer, and the hour was noon, so that the unwonted reflection of the sun was dancing in the pellucid fountain.

"It is the season and the hour," said Halbert to himself; "and now if I dared I might soon become wiser than Edward with all his pains! Mary should see whether he alone is fit to be consulted, and to sit by her side, and hang over her as she reads, and point out every word and every letter. And she loves me better than him—I am sure she does—for she comes of noble blood, and scorns sloth and cowardice.—And do I myself not stand here slothful and cowardly as any priest of them all?—Why should I fear to call upon this form—this shape?—Already have I endured the vision, and why not again?—What can it do to me, who am a man of lith and limb, and have by my side my father's sword? Does my heart beat—do my hairs bristle, at the thought of calling up a painted shadow, and how should I face a band of Southron in flesh and blood? By the soul of the first Glendonwyne I will make proof of the charm!"

He cast the leathern brogue or buskin from his right foot, planted himself in a firm posture, unsheathed his sword, and first looking around to collect his resolution, he bowed three times deliberately towards the holly-tree, and as often to the little fountain, repeating at the same time, with a determined voice, the following rhymes:

> "Thrice to the holly brake—
>   Thrice to the well:—
> I bid thee awake,
>   White Maid of Avenel!
> Noon gleams on the Lake—
>   Noon glows on the Fell—
> Wake thee, O wake,
>   White Maid of Avenel."

These lines were hardly uttered, when there stood the figure of a female clothed in white, within three steps of Halbert Glendinning.

> I guess 'twas frightful there to see
> A lady richly clad as she—
> Beautiful exceedingly.*

END OF VOLUME FIRST

---

* Coleridge's Christabelle.

THE MONASTERY

VOLUME II

Chapter One

There's something in that ancient superstition,
Which, erring as it is, our fancy loves.
The spring that, with its thousand crystal bubbles,
Bursts from the bosom of some desert rock
In secret solitude, may well be deem'd
The haunt of something purer, more refin'd,
And mightier than ourselves.

Old Play

YOUNG HALBERT GLENDINNING had scarcely pronounced the mystical rhymes, than, as we have mentioned in the conclusion of the last chapter, an appearance, as of a beautiful female, dressed in white, stood within two yards of him. His terror for the moment overcame his natural courage, as well as the strong resolution which he had formed, that the figure which he had now twice seen should not a third time daunt him. But it would seem there is something thrilling and abhorrent to flesh and blood, in the consciousness that we stand in presence of a being in form like to ourselves, but so different in faculties and nature, that we can neither understand its purposes, nor calculate its means of pursuing them.

Halbert stood silent and gasped for breath, his hairs erecting themselves on his head—his mouth open—his eyes fixed—and, as the sole remaining sign of his late determined purpose, his sword pointed towards the apparition. At length, with a voice of ineffable sweetness, the White Lady, for by that name we shall distinguish this being, sung, or rather chaunted, the following lines:—

"Youth of the dark eye, wherefore did'st thou call me?
Wherefore art thou here, if terrors can appal thee?
He that seeks to deal with us must know nor fear, nor failing;
To coward and churl our speech is dark, our gifts are unavailing.

The breeze that brought me hither now, must sweep Egyptian ground,
The fleecy cloud on which I ride for Araby is bound;
The fleecy cloud is drifting by, the breeze sighs for my stay,
For I must sail a thousand miles before the close of day."

The astonishment of Halbert began once more to give way to his resolution, and he gained voice enough to say, though with a faultering accent, "In the name of God, what art thou?" The answer was in melody of a different tone and measure.

"What I am I must not show—
What I am thou could'st not know—
Something betwixt heaven and hell—
Something that neither stood nor fell—
Something that through thy wit or will
May work thee good—may work thee ill.
Neither substance quite, nor shadow,
Haunting lonely moor and meadow,
Dancing by the haunted spring,
Riding on the whirlwind's wing;
Aping in fantastic fashion
Every change of human passion,
While o'er our frozen minds they pass,
Like shadows from the mirror'd glass.
Wayward, fickle is our mood,
Hovering betwixt bad and good,
Happier than brief-dated man,
Living ten times o'er his span;
Far less happy, for we have
Help nor hope beyond the grave!
Man awakes to joy or sorrow;
Our's the sleep that knows no morrow.
This is all that I can show—
This is all that thou may'st know."

The White Lady paused, and seemed to await an answer; but, as Halbert hesitated how to frame his speech, the vision seemed gradually to fade, and become more and more incorporeal. Justly guessing this to be a symptom of her disappearance, Halbert compelled himself to say,—"Lady, when I saw you in the glen, and when you brought back the black book of Mary of Avenel, thou didst say I should one day learn to read it."

The White Lady replied,

"Ay! and I taught thee the word and the spell,
To waken me here by the Fairies' Well.
But thou hast loved the heron and hawk,
More than to seek my haunted walk;
And thou hast loved the lance and the sword,
More than good text and holy word;
And thou hast loved the deer to track,
More than the lines and the letters black;
And thou art a ranger of moss and wood,
And scornest the nurture of gentle blood."

"I will do so no longer, fair maiden," said Halbert; "I desire to learn
—and thou didst promise me, that when I did so desire, thou wouldest
be my helper. And I am no longer afraid of thy presence, and I am no
longer regardless of instruction." As he uttered these words the figure
of the White Maiden grew gradually as distinct as it had been
at first; and what had well nigh faded into an ill-defined and colourless shadow, again assumed an appearance at least of corporeal consistency, although the hues were less vivid, and the outline of the
figure less distinct and defined,—so at least it seemed to Halbert,—
than those of an ordinary inhabitant of the earth. "Wilt thou grant my
request," he said, "fair Lady, and give to my keeping the holy book
which Mary of Avenel has so often wept for?"

The White Lady replied,

> "Thy craven fear my truth accused,
> Thine idlehood my trust abused;
> He that draws to harbour late,
> Must sleep without, or burst the gate.
> There is a star for thee which burn'd,
> Its influence wanes, its course is turn'd;
> Valour and constancy alone
> Can bring thee back the chance that's flown."

"If I have been a loiterer, Lady," answered young Glendinning,
"thou shalt now find me willing to press forward with double speed.
Other thoughts have filled my mind, other thoughts have engaged my
heart within a brief period—and by heaven, other occupations shall
henceforward fill up my time. I have lived in this day the space of years
—I came hither a boy—I will return a man—a man, such as may
converse not only with his own kind, but with whatever God permits to
be visible to him. I will learn the contents of that mysterious volume—
I will learn why the Lady of Avenel loved it—why the priests feared,
and would have stolen it—why thou didst twice recover it from their
hands.—What mystery is wrapt in it?—Speak, I conjure thee." The
Lady assumed an air peculiarly sad and solemn, as, drooping her
head, and folding her arms on her bosom, she replied:

> "Within that awful volume lies
> The mystery of mysteries!
> Happiest they of human race,
> To whom God has granted grace
> To read, to fear, to hope, to pray,
> To lift the latch, and find the way;
> And better had they ne'er been born,
> Who read to doubt, or read to scorn."

"Give me the volume, Lady," said young Glendinning. "They call
me idle—they call me dull—in this pursuit my industry shall not fail;
nor, with God's blessing, shall my understanding. Give me the
volume." The apparition again replied:

> "Many a fathom dark and deep
> I have laid the book to sleep;
> Ethereal fires around it glowing—
> Ethereal music ever flowing—
>   The sacred pledge of Heav'n
> All things revere,
> Each in their sphere,
>   Save man for whom 'twas giv'n:
> Lend thy hand, and thou shalt spy
> Things ne'er seen by mortal eye."

Halbert Glendinning boldly reached his hand to the White Lady.
"Fearst thou to go with me?" she said, as his hand trembled at the soft and cold touch of her own—

> "Fearst thou to go with me?
> Still it is free to thee
>   A peasant to dwell;
> Thou may'st drive the dull steer,
> And chace the king's deer,
> But never more come near
>   This haunted well."

"If what thou sayest be true," said the undaunted boy, "my destinies are higher than thine own. There shall be neither well nor wood which I dare not visit. No fear of aught, natural or supernatural, shall bar my path through my native valley."

He had scarce uttered these words when they both descended through the earth, with a rapidity which took away Halbert's breath and every other sensation, saving that of being hurried on with the utmost velocity. At length they stopped with a shock so sudden, that the mortal journeyer through this unknown space must have been thrown down with violence, had he not been upheld by his supernatural companion.

It was more than a minute, ere, looking around him, he beheld a grotto, or natural cavern, composed of the most splendid spars and crystals, which returned in a thousand prismatic hues the light of a brilliant flame that glowed on an altar of alabaster. This altar, with its fire, formed the central point of the grotto, which was of a round form, and very high in the roof, resembling in some respect the dome of a cathedral. Corresponding to the four points of the compass, there went off four long galleries or arcades, constructed of the same brilliant materials with the dome itself, and the termination of which was lost in darkness.

No human imagination can conceive, or words suffice to describe, the glorious radiance, which, shot fiercely forth by the flame, was returned from so many hundred thousand points of reflection, afforded by the sparry pillars and their numerous angular crystals.

The fire itself did not remain steady and unmoved, but rose and fell, sometimes ascending in a brilliant pyramid of condensed flame half way up the lofty expanse, and again fading into a softer and more rosy hue, and hovering as it were on the surface of the altar to collect its strength for another brilliant exertion. There was no visible fuel by which it was fed, nor did it emit either smoke or vapour of any kind.

What was of all the most remarkable, the black volume so often mentioned lay not only unconsumed, but untouched in the slightest degree amid this intensity of fire, which, while it seemed to be of force sufficient to melt adamant, had no effect whatever on the sacred book thus subjected to its utmost influence.

The White Lady, having paused long enough to let young Glendinning take a complete survey of what was around him, now said, in her usual chaunt,

> "There lies the volume thou boldly has sought;
> Touch it, and take it, 'twill dearly be bought."

Familiarized in some degree with marvels, and desperately desirous of shewing the courage he had boasted, Halbert plunged his hand, without hesitation, into the flame, trusting by the rapidity of the motion to snatch out the volume before the fire could greatly affect him. But he was greatly disappointed. The flame instantly caught upon his sleeve, and though he withdrew his hand immediately, yet his arm was so dreadfully scorched, that he had well nigh screamed with pain. He suppressed the natural expression of anguish, however, and only intimated the agony which he felt by a contortion and a muttered groan. The White Lady passed her cold hand over his arm, and, ere she finished the following metrical chaunt, his pain was entirely gone, and no mark of the scorching was visible:

> "Rash thy deed,
> Mortal weed
> To immortal flames applying;
> Rasher trust
> Has thing of dust,
> On his own weak worth relying:
> Strip thee of such fences vain,
> Strip, and prove thy luck again."

Obedient to what he understood to be the meaning of his conductress, Halbert bared his arm to the shoulder, throwing down the remains of his sleeve, which no sooner touched the floor on which he stood than it collected itself together, shrivelled itself up, and was without any visible fire reduced to light tinder, which a sudden breath of wind dispersed into empty space. The White Lady, observing the surprise of the youth, immediately repeated—

> "Mortal warp and mortal woof,
> Cannot brook this charmed roof;
> All that mortal art hath wrought,
> In our cell returns to nought.
> The minted gold returns to clay,
> The polish'd diamond melts away;
> All is alter'd, all is flown,
> Nought stands fast but truth alone.
> Not for that thy quest give o'er:
> Courage! prove thy chance once more."

Emboldened by her words, Halbert Glendinning made a second effort, and, plunging his bare arm into the flame, took out the sacred volume without feeling either heat or inconvenience of any kind. Astonished, and almost terrified at his own success, he beheld the flame collect itself, and shoot up into one long and final stream, which seemed as if it would ascend to the very roof of the cavern, and then, sinking as suddenly, became totally extinguished. The deepest darkness ensued; but Halbert had no time to consider his situation, for the White Lady had already caught his hand, and they ascended to upper air with the same velocity with which they had sunk into the earth.

They stood by the fountain in the Corri-nan-shian when they emerged from the bowels of the earth; but on casting a bewildered glance around him, the youth was surprised to observe, that the shadows had fallen far to the east, and that the day was well nigh spent. He gazed on his conductress for explanation, but her figure began to fade before his eyes—her cheeks grew paler, her features less distinct, her form became shadowy, and blended itself with the mist which was ascending the hollow ravine. What had late the symmetry of form, and the delicate, yet clear hues of feminine beauty, now resembled the flitting and pale ghost of some maiden who has died for love, as it is seen, indistinctly and by moon-light, by her perjured lover.

"Stay, spirit," said the youth, emboldened by his success in the subterranean dome, "thy kindness must not leave me, as one encumbered with a weapon he knows not how to wield. Thou must teach me the art to read and understand this volume; else what avails it me that I possess it?"

But the figure of the White Lady still waned before his eye, until it became an outline as pale and indistinct as that of the moon, when the winter morning is far advanced; and ere she had ended the following chaunt, she was entirely invisible:—

> "Alas! alas!
> Not ours the grace
> These holy characters to trace:
> Idle forms of painted air,
> Not to us is given to share
> The boon bestow'd on Adam's race.

> With patience bide,
> Heaven will provide
> The fitting time, the fitting guide."

The form was already gone, and now the voice itself had melted away in melancholy cadence, softening, as if the Being who spoke had been slowly wafted from the spot where she had commenced her melody. It was at this moment that Halbert felt the extremity of the terror which he had hitherto so manfully suppressed. The very necessity of exertion had given him spirit to make it, and the presence of the mysterious Being, while it was a subject of fear in itself, had nevertheless given him the sense of a protector's being near to him. It was when he could reflect with composure on what had passed, that a cold tremor shot across his limbs, his hair bristled, and he was afraid to look around lest he should find at his elbow something more frightful than the first vision. A breeze arising suddenly realized the beautiful and wild idea of the most imaginative of our modern bards*—

> It fann'd his cheek, it raised his hair,
> Like a meadow gale in spring;
> It mingled strangely with his fears,
> Yet it felt like a welcoming.

The youth stood silent and astonished for a few minutes. It seemed to him that the extraordinary Being he had seen, half his terror, half his protectress, was still hovering on the gale which swept past him, and that she might again make herself sensible to his organ of sight. "Speak!" he said, wildly tossing his arms, "speak yet again—be once more present, lovely vision!—thrice have I now seen thee, yet the idea of thy invisible presence around or beside me, makes my heart beat faster than if the earth yawned and gave up a demon." But neither sound nor appearance indicated the presence of the White Lady, and nothing preternatural beyond what he had already witnessed, was again audible or visible. Halbert, in the mean while, by the very exertion of again inviting the presence of this mysterious Being, had recovered his natural audacity. He looked around once more, and resumed his solitary path down the valley into whose recesses he had penetrated.

Nothing could be more strongly contrasted than the storm of passion with which he had bounded over stock and crag, in order to plunge himself into the Corri-nan-shian, and the sobered mood in which he now returned homeward, industriously seeking out the most practicable path, not from a wish to avoid danger, but that he might not by bodily exertion distract his attention, deeply fixed on the extraordinary scene which he had witnessed. In the former case, he had

* Coleridge.

sought by hazard and bodily exertion to indulge at once the fiery excitation of passion, and to banish the cause of the excitement from his recollection; while now he studiously avoided all interruption to his contemplative walk, lest the difficulties of the way should interfere with, or disturb, his own deep reflections. Thus slowly pacing forth his course, with the air of a pilgrim rather than a deer-hunter, Halbert about the close of evening regained his paternal tower.

Chapter Two

The Miller was of manly make,
To meet him was na mows;
There durst na ten come him to take,
Sae noited he their pows.
Christ's Kirk on the Green

IT WAS AFTER SUNSET, as we have already stated, when Halbert Glendinning returned to the abode of his father. The hour of dinner was at noon, and that of supper about an hour after sunset at this period of the year. The former had passed without Halbert's appearing; but this was no uncommon circumstance, for the chase or any other pastime which occurred, made Halbert a frequent neglecter of hours; and his mother, though angry and disappointed when she saw him not at table, was so much accustomed to his occasional absence, and knew so little how to teach him more regularity, that a testy observation was almost all the censure with which such omissions were visited.

On the present occasion, however, the wrath of good Dame Elspet soared a little higher than usual. It was not merely on account of the special tup's-head and trotters, the haggis and the side of mutton, with which her table was set forth, but also because of the arrival of no less a person than Hob Miller, as he was universally termed, though the man's name was Happer.

The object of the Miller's visit to the tower of Glendearg was, like those embassies which potentates send to each other's courts, partly ostensible, partly politic. In outward shew, Hob came to visit his friends of the Halidome, and share the festivity common among country folks, after the barn-yard has been filled, and to renew old intimacies by new conviviality. But in very truth he also came to have an eye upon the contents of each stack, and to obtain such information respecting the extent of the crop reaped and gathered in by each feuar, as might prevent the possibility of *abstracted multures*.

All the world knows that the cultivators of each barony or regality, temporal or spiritual, in Scotland, are obliged to bring their corn to be grinded at the mill of the territory, for which they pay a heavy charge, called *intown multures*. I could speak to the thirlage of *invecta et illata* too, but let that pass. I have said enough to intimate that I talk not without book. Those of *Sucken*, or enthralled ground, were liable in penalties, if, deviating from this thirlage, (or thraldom) they carried their grain to another mill. Now such another, erected on the lands of a lay-baron, lay within a tempting and convenient distance of Glendearg; and the Miller was so obliging, and his charges so moderate, that it required Hob Miller's utmost vigilance to prevent evasions of his right of monopoly.

The most effectual means he could devise was this shew of good fellowship and neighbourly friendship,—under colour of which he made his annual cruise through the barony—numbered every corn-stack, and computed its contents by the boll, so that he could give a shrewd hint afterwards whether or not the grist came to the right mill.

Dame Elspet, like her compeers, was obliged to take these domiciliary visits in the sense of politeness; but in her case they had not occurred since her husband's death, probably because the tower of Glendearg was distant, and there was but a trifling quantity of arable or *infield* land attached to it. This year there had been, upon some speculation of old Martin's, several bolls sown in the outfield, which, the season being fine, had ripened remarkably well. Perhaps this circumstance occasioned the honest Miller's including Glendearg, on this occasion, in his annual round.

Dame Glendinning received with pleasure a visit which she used formerly only to endure with patience; and she had changed her view of the matter chiefly, if not entirely, because Hob had brought with him his daughter Mysie, of whose features she could give so slight an account, but whose dress she had described so accurately to the Sub-Prior.

Hitherto this girl had been an object of very trifling consideration in the eyes of the good widow; but the Sub-Prior's particular and somewhat mysterious enquiries had set her brains to work on the subject of Mysie of the Mill. And she had here asked a broad question, and there she had thrown out an inuendo, and there again she had gradually led on to a conversation on the subject of poor Mysie. And from all enquiries and investigations she had collected, that Mysie was a dark-eyed laughter-loving wench, with cherry-cheeks, and a skin as white as her father's finest bolted flour, out of which was made the Abbot's own wastel-bread. For her temper, she sung and laughed from morning to night; and for her fortune—a material article—besides that which the Miller might have amassed by means of his proverbial golden thumb, Mysie was to inherit a good handsome lump of land, with a prospect of the mill and mill-acres descending to her husband on an easy lease, if a fair word were spoken in season to the Abbot, and to the Prior, and to the Sub-Prior, and to the Sacristan, and so forth.

By turning and again turning these advantages over in her own mind, Elspet at length came to be of opinion, that the only way to save her son Halbert from a life of "spur, spear, and snafle," as they called that of the border-riders, from the dint of a cloth-yard shaft, or the loop of an inch-cord, was, that he should marry and settle, and that Mysie Happer should be his destined bride.

As if to her wish, Hob Miller arrived on his strong-built mare, bearing on a pillion behind him the lovely Mysie, with cheeks like a peony-rose, (if Dame Glendinning had ever seen one,) spirits all afloat with rustic coquetry, and a profusion of hair as black as ebony. The *beau-ideal* which Dame Glendinning had been bodying forth in her imagination, became unexpectedly realized in the buxom form of Mysie Happer, whom, in the course of half an hour, she settled upon as the maiden who was to fix the restless and untutored Halbert. True, Mysie, as the dame soon saw, was like to love dancing round a may-pole as well as managing a domestic establishment, and Halbert was like to break more heads than grind sacks of corn. But then a miller should always be of manly make, and has been described so since the days of Chaucer and James I.* Indeed to be able to outdo and bully the whole *Sucken*, (once more we use this barbarous phrase,) in all athletic exercises, was one way to render easy the collection of dues which men would have disputed with a less formidable champion. Then, as to the deficiences of the miller's wife, the dame was of opinion they might be supplied by the activity of the miller's mother. "I will keep house for the young folks myself, for the tower is grown very lonely," thought Dame Glendinning, "and to live near the kirk will be mair comfortable in my auld age—And then Edward may agree with his brother about the feu, more especial as he is a favourite with the Sub-Prior—and then he may live in the auld tower like his worthy father before him—And who kens but Mary Avenel, high-blood as she is, may e'en draw in her stool to the chimney-nook, and sit down here for good and a'?—It's true she has no tocher, but the like of her

---

* The verse we have chosen for a motto, is from a poem imputed to James I. of Scotland. As for the Miller who figures amongst the Canterbury pilgrims, besides his sword and buckler, he boasted other attributes, all of which, but especially the last, shew that he relied more on the strength of the outside than the inside of his scull.

> The miller was a stout carl for the nones,
> Full big he was of brawn, and eke of bones;
> That proved well, for wheresoe'er he cam,
> At wrastling he wold bear away the ram;
> He was short-shoulder'd, broad, a thick gnar.
> There n'as no door that he n'old heave of bar,
> Or break it at a running with his head, &c.

for beauty and sense ne'er crossed my een, and I have kenn'd every
wench in the Halidome of Saint Mary's—ay, and their mothers that
bore them—Ay, she is a sweet and a lovely creature as ever tied snood
over brown hair—Ay, and then, though her uncle keeps her out of her
ain for the present time, yet it is to be thought the grey-goose-shaft
will find a hole in his coat of proof, as, God help us! it has done in
many a better man's—and, moreover, if they should stand on their
pedigree and gentle race, Edward might say to them—that is to her
gentle kith and kin, 'whilk o' ye was her best friend when she came
down the glen to Glendearg in a misty evening, on a beast mair like a
cuddie than aught else?'—And if they tax him with churl's blood,
Edward might say, that, forbye the old proverb, how

> Gentle deed
> Makes gentle bleid;

yet, moreover, there comes no churl's blood from Glendinning or
Brydone, for, says Edward"——

The hoarse voice of the Miller at this moment recalled the dame
from her reverie, and compelled her to remember that if she meant to
realize her airy castle, she must begin by laying the foundation in
civility to her guest and his daughter, whom she was at that moment
most strangely neglecting, though her whole plan turned on conciliating their favour and good opinion, and that, in fact, while arranging
matters for so intimate a union with her company, she was suffering
them to sit unnoticed, and in their riding gear, as if about to resume
their journey. "And so I say, dame," concluded the Miller, (for she
had not marked the beginning of his speech,) "an ye be so busied with
your housewife-skep, or aught else, why, Mysie and I will trot our
ways down the glen again to Johnie Broxmouth's, who pressed us right
kindly to bide with him."

Starting at once from her dream of marriages and inter-marriages,
mills, mill-lands and baronies, Dame Elspet felt for a moment like the
milk-maid in the fable, when she overset the pitcher, on the contents
of which so many golden dreams were founded. But the foundation of
Dame Glendinning's hopes was only tottering, not over-thrown,
and she hastened to restore its equilibrium. Instead of attempting to
account for her absence of mind and want of attention to her guests,
which she might have found something difficult, she assumed the
offensive, like an able general when he finds it necessary, by a bold
attack, to disguise his weakness.

A loud exclamation she made, and a passionate complaint she set
up against the unkindness of her old friend, who could, for an instant
doubt the heartiness of her welcome to him and to his hopeful daughter; and then to think of his going back to John Broxmouth's, when the

auld tower stood where it did, and had room in it for a friend or two in the worst of times—and he too a neighbour that her umquhile Simon, blessed be his cast, used to think the best friend he had in the Halidome! And on she went, urging her complaint with so much seriousness that she had well nigh imposed on herself as well as upon Hob Miller, who had no mind to take anything in dudgeon; and as it suited his plans to pass the night at Glendearg, would have been equally contented to do so even had his reception been less vehemently hospitable.

To all Elspet's expostulations on the unkindness of his proposal to leave her dwelling, he answered composedly, "Nay, dame, what could I tell? Ye might have had other grist to grind, for ye looked as if ye scarce saw us—Or what know I? ye might bear in mind the words Martin and I had about the last barley ye sawed—for I ken dry multures* will sometimes stick in the throat. A man seeks but his awn, and yet folks shall hold him for both miller and miller's man, that is miller and knave,† all the country over."

"Alas! that you will say so, neighbour Hob," said Dame Elspet, "or that Martin should have had any words with you about the mill-dues. I will chide him roundly for it, I promise you, on the faith of a true widow. You know full well that a lone woman is sore put upon by her servants."

"Nay, dame," said the Miller, unbuckling the broad belt which made fast his cloak, and served, at the same time, to suspend by his side a swingeing Andra Ferrara, "bear no grudge at Martin, for I bear none—I take it on me as a thing of mine office to maintain my right of multure, lock, and goupen.‡ And reason good, for, as the old song says,

I live by my mill, God bless her,
She's parent, child, and wife.

The poor old slut, I am beholden to her for my living, and bound to stand by her, as I say to my mill-knaves, in right and in wrong. And so should every honest fellow stand by his bread-winner.—And so, Mysie, ye may doff your cloak since our neighbour is so kindly glad to see us—why, I think, we are as blythe to see her—not one in the

* Dry multures were a fine, or compensation in money, for not grinding at the mill of the thirl. It was, and is, accounted a vexatious exaction.

† The under miller, is in the language of thirlage, called the knave, which indeed signified originally his lad, (*Knabé*—German,) but by degrees came to be taken in a worse sense. In the old translation of the Bible, Paul is made to term himself the knave of our Saviour. The allowance of meal taken by the miller's servant was termed knave-ship.

‡ The multure was the regular exaction for grinding the meal. The *lock*, (signifying a small quantity,) and the *goupen* or handful, were additional perquisites demanded by the miller, and submitted to or resisted by the *Suckener* as circumstances permitted. These and other petty dues were called in general the *Sequels*.

Halidome pays their multure more duly, sequels, arriage, and carriage, and mill-services, used and wont."

With that the Miller hung his ample cloak without further ceremony upon a huge pair of stag's antlers, which adorned at once the
naked walls of the tower, and served for what are vulgarly called cloak-
pins.

In the meanwhile, Dame Elspet assisted to disembarrass the damsel whom she destined for her future daughter-in-law, of her hood,
mantle, and the rest of her riding gear, giving her to appear as
beseemed the buxom daughter of the wealthy Miller, gay and goodly,
in a white kirtle, the seams of which were embroidered with green
silken lace or fringe, entwined with some silver thread. An anxious
glance did Elspet cast upon the good-humoured face, which was now
more fully shown to her, and was only obscured by a quantity of raven
black hair, which the maid of the mill had restrained by a snood of
green silk, embroidered with silver, corresponding to the trimmings of
her kirtle. The countenance itself was exceedingly comely—the eyes
black, large, and roguishly good-humoured—the mouth was small—
the lips well formed, though somewhat full—the teeth were pearly
white—and the chin had a very seducing dimple in it. The form
belonging to this pleasant and joyous face was full and round, and firm
and fair. It might become coarse and masculine some years hence,
which is the common fault of Scottish beauty; but in Mysie's sixteenth
year she had the shape of an Hebe. The anxious Elspet, with all her
maternal partiality, could not help admitting within herself, that a
better man than Halbert might go further and fare worse. She looked
a little giddy, and Halbert was not nineteen; still it was time he should
be settled, for to that point the dame always returned; and here was an
excellent opportunity.

The simple cunning of Dame Elspet now exhausted itself in commendations of her fair guest, from the snood, as they say, to the single-
soled shoes. Mysie listened and blushed with pleasure for the first five
minutes; but ere ten had elapsed, she began to view the old lady's
compliments rather as subjects of mirth than of vanity, and was much
more disposed to laugh at than to be flattered by them, for Nature had
mingled the good-humour with which she had endowed the damsel
with no small portion of shrewdness. Even Hob himself began to tire
of hearing his daughter's praises, and broke in with, "Ay, ay, she is a
clever quean enough; and, were she five years older, she shall lay a
loaded sack on an *aver** with e'er a lass in the Halidome. But I hae
been looking for your two sons, dame. Men say down-bye, that Halbert's turned a wild springald, and that we may have word of him from

* *Aver*—properly a horse of labour.

Westmoreland one moonlight night or another"——

"God forbid, my good neighbour; God, in his mercy, forbid!" said Dame Glendinning earnestly; for it was touching the very key-note of her apprehensions, to hint any probability that Halbert might become one of the marauders so common in the age and country. But, fearful of having betrayed too much alarm on this subject, she immediately added, "That though, since the sad rout at Pinkie-cleuch, she had been all of a tremble when a gun or a spear was named, or when men spoke of fighting; yet, thank to God and Our Lady, her sons were like to live and die honest and peaceful tenants to the Abbey, as their father might have done, but for that awful hosting which he went forth to, with mony a brave man who never returned."

"Ye need not tell me of it, dame," said the Miller, "since I was there myself, and made two pair of legs (and these were not mine, but my mare's,) worth one pair of hands. I judged how it would be, when I saw our host break ranks, with rushing on through that broken ploughed field, and so as they had made a pricker of me, I e'en pricked off with myself while the play was good."

"Ay, ay, neighbour," said the dame, "ye were aye a wise and a wary man; if my Simon had had your wit, he might have been here to speak about it this day: But he was aye cracking of his good blood and his high kindred, and less would not serve him than to bide the bang to the last, with the earls, and knights, and squires, that had no wives to greet for them, or else had wives that cared not how soon they were widows; but that is not for the like of us. But touching my son Halbert, there is no fear of him; for if it should be his misfortune to be in the like case, he has the best pair of heels in the Halidome, and could run almost as fast as your mare herself."

"Is this he, neighbour?" quoth the Miller.

"No," replied the mother; "that is my youngest son, Edward, who can read and write like the Lord Abbot himself, if it were not a sin to say so."

"Ay," said the Miller; "and is that the young clerk the Sub-Prior thinks so much upon?—they say he will come far ben that lad—wha kens but he may come to be Sub-Prior himself?—as broken a ship has come to land."

"To be a Prior, neighbour Miller," said Edward, "a man must first be a priest, and for that I judge I have little vocation."

"He will take to the pleugh-pettle, neighbour," said the good dame; "and so will Halbert too, I trust. I wish you saw Halbert.—Edward, where is your brother?"

"Hunting, I think," replied Edward; "at least he left us this morning to join the Laird of Hunter's-hope and his hounds. I have heard them baying in the glen all day."

"And if I had heard that music," said the Miller, "it would have done my heart good—ay, and may be taken me two or three miles out of my road. When I was the Miller of Morebattle's knave, I have followed the hounds from Eckford to the foot of Hounam-law— followed them on foot, Dame Glendinning, ay, and led the chace when the Laird of Cessford and his gay riders were all thrown out by the mosses and gills. I brought the stag on my back to Hounam Cross, when the dogs had pulled him down. I think I see the old grey knight, as he sate so upright on his strong war-horse, all white with foam; and 'Miller,' said he to me, 'an' thou turn thy back on the mill, and wend with me, I will make a man of thee.' But I chose rather to abide by clap and happer, and the better luck was mine; for the proud Percy caused hang five of the Laird's henchmen at Alnwick for burning a rickle of houses some gate beyond Fowberry."

"Ah, neighbour, neighbour," said Dame Glendinning, "you were aye wise and ware—but if you like hunting, I must say Halbert's the lad to please you. He hath all those fair holiday-terms of hawk and hound as ready in his mouth as Tom with the tod's-tail, that is the Lord Abbot's ranger."

"Ranges he not homeward at dinner-time, dame," demanded the Miller; "for we call noon the dinner-hour at Kennaquhair?"

The widow was forced to admit, that, even at this important period of the day, Halbert was frequently absent; at which the Miller shook his head, intimating, at the same time, some allusion to the proverb of MacFarlane's geese, which "liked their play better than their meat."*

That the delay of dinner might not increase the Miller's disposition to prejudge Halbert, Dame Glendinning called lustily on Mary Avenel to take her task of entertaining Mysie Happer, while she herself rushed to the kitchen, and, entering at once upon the province of Tibb Tacket, rummaged among trenchers and dishes, snatched pots from the fire, and placed pans and gridirons on it, accompanying her own feats of personal activity with such a continued list of injunctions to Tibb, that Tibb at length lost patience, and said, "Here was as muckle wark about meating an auld miller, as if they had been to banquet the blood of Bruce." But this, as it was supposed to be spoken aside, Dame Glendinning did not think it convenient to hear.

* A breed of wild-geese, which long frequented the uppermost island in Loch-Lomond, called Inch-Tavoe, were supposed to have some mysterious connection with the ancient family of MacFarlane of that ilk, and it is said were never seen after the ruin and extinction of that house. Why they were said to like their play better than their meat, I could never learn, but the proverb is in general use. The MacFarlanes had a house and garden upon that same island of Inch-Tavoe.

Chapter Three

Nay, let me have the friends who eat my victuals,
As various as my dishes. The feast's naught,
Where one huge plate predominates.—John Plaintext,
He shall be mighty beef, our English staple;
The worthy Alderman, a butter'd dumpling;
Yon pair of whisker'd Cornets, ruff and rees;
Their friend the Dandy, a green goose in sippets.
And so the board is spread at once and fill'd
On the same principle—Variety.

New Play

"AND WHAT brave lass is this?" said Hob Miller, as Mary Avenel entered the apartment to supply the absence of Dame Elspet Glendinning.

"The young Lady of Avenel, father," said the Maid of the Mill, dropping as low a curtsey as her rustic manners enabled her to make. The Miller, her father, doffed his bonnet, and made his reverence, not altogether so low perhaps as if the young lady had appeared in the pride of rank and riches, yet so as to give high birth the due homage which the Scots for a length of time scrupulously rendered to it.

Indeed, from having had her mother's example before her for so many years, and from a native sense of propriety and even of dignity, Mary Avenel had acquired a demeanour, which marked her title to consideration, and effectually checked any attempt at great familiarity on the part of those who might be her associates in her present situation, but could not well be termed her equals. She was by nature mild, pensive, and contemplative, gentle in disposition, and most placable when accidentally offended; but still she was of a retired and reserved habit, and shunned to mix in ordinary sports, even when the rare occurrence of a fair or wake gave her an opportunity to mingle with companions of her own age. If at such scenes she was seen for an instant, she appeared to behold them with the composed indifference of one to whom their gaiety was matter of no interest; and who seemed only desirous to glide away from the scene as soon as she possibly could.

Something also had transpired concerning her being born on Allhallow Eve, and the powers with which that circumstance was supposed to invest her over the invisible world. And from all these particulars combined, the young men and women of the Halidome used to distinguish Mary among themselves by the name of the Spirit of Avenel, as if the fair but fragile form, the beautiful but rather colourless cheek, the dark blue eye, and the shady hair, had belonged rather to the immaterial than the substantial world. The general tradition of the White Lady, who was supposed to wait on the fortunes of the family of Avenel, gave a sort of zest to this piece of rural wit. It gave great offence, however, to the two sons of Simon Glendinning, and when the expression was in their presence applied to the young lady, Edward was wont to check the petulance of those who used it by strength of argument, and Halbert by strength of arm. In such cases Halbert had this advantage, that although he could render no aid to his brother's argument, yet when circumstances required it in his own personal manner of taking up the affair, he was sure to have that of Edward, who never indeed himself commenced a fray, but on the other hand, did not testify any reluctance to enter into combat on Halbert's behalf or in his rescue.

But the zealous attachment of the two youths, being themselves, from the retired situation in which they dwelt, comparative strangers in the Halidome, did not serve in any degree to alter the feelings of the inhabitants towards the young lady, who seemed to have dropped amongst them from out of another sphere of life. Still, however, she was regarded with respect, if not with fondness; and the attention of the Sub-Prior to the family, not to mention the formidable name of Julian Avenel, which every new incident of these tumultuous times tended to render more famous, attached to his niece a certain importance. So that some aspired to her acquaintance out of pride, while the more timid of the feuars were anxious to inculcate upon their children the necessity of being respectful to the noble orphan. So that Mary Avenel, little loved because little known, was regarded with a mysterious awe, partly derived from fear of her uncle's moss-troopers, and partly from her own retired and distant habits, enhanced by the superstitious opinions of the time and country.

It was not without some portion of this awe, that Mysie felt herself left alone in company with a young person so distant in rank, and so different in bearing from herself; for her worthy father had taken the first opportunity to step out unobserved, in order to mark how the barn-yard was filled, and what prospect it afforded of grist to the mill. In youth, however, there is a sort of free-masonry, which, without much conversation, teaches young persons to estimate each other's character, and places them at ease on the briefest acquaintance. It is only when taught deceit by the commerce of the world, that we learn to shroud our character from observation; and to disguise our real sentiments from those with whom we are placed in communion.

Accordingly, the two young women were soon engaged in such objects of interest as best became their age. They visited Mary

Avenel's pigeons, which she nursed with the tenderness of a mother; they turned over her slender stores of finery, which yet contained some articles which excited the respect of her companion, though Mysie was too good-humoured to nourish envy. A golden rosary, and some female ornaments marking superior rank, had been rescued in the moment of their utmost adversity, more by Tibb Tacket's presence of mind, than by the care of their owner, who was at that sad moment too much sunk in deep grief to pay any attention to such circumstances. They struck Mysie with a deep impression of veneration; for, excepting what the Lord Abbot and the convent might possess, she did not believe there was so much real gold in the world as was exhibited in these few trinkets; and Mary, however sage and serious, was not above being pleased with the admiration of her rustic companion.

Nothing, indeed, could exhibit a stranger contrast than the appearance of the two girls;—the good-humoured laughter-loving countenance of the Maid of the Mill, who stood gazing with unrepressed astonishment on whatever was in her inexperienced eye rare and costly, and with a humble, and at the same time cheerful acquiescence in her inferiority, asking all the little queries about the use and value of the ornaments, while Mary Avenel, with her quiet composed dignity and placidity of manner, produced them one after another for the amusement of her companion.

As they became gradually more familiar, Mysie of the Mill was just venturing to ask, why Mary Avenel never appeared at the May-pole, and to express her wonder when the young lady said she disliked dancing, when a trampling of horses at the gate of the tower interrupted their conversation.

Mysie flew to the shot-window, in the full ardour of unrestrained female curiosity. "Saint Mary! sweet lady! here come two well-mounted gallants—will you step this way to look at them?"

"No," said Mary Avenel, "you shall tell me who they are."

"Well—if you like it better," said Mysie—"but how shall I know them?—stay, I do know one of them, and so do you, lady—he is a blythe man—somewhat light of hand they say, but the gallants of these days think no great harm of that. He is your uncle's henchman, that they call Christie of the Clinthill; and he has not his old green jerkin, and the rusty black jack over it, but a scarlet cloak, laid down with silver lace three inches broad, and a breast-plate you might see to dress your hair in, as well as in that keeking-glass in the ivory frame that you shewed me even now—come, dear lady, come to the shot-window and see him."

"If it be the man you mean, Mysie," replied the orphan of Avenel, "I will see him soon enough, for either the pleasure or comfort the sight will give me."

"Nay, but if you will not come to see gay Christie," replied the Maid of the Mill, her face flushed with eager curiosity, "come and tell me who the gallant is that is with him—the handsomest—the very love-somest young man I ever saw with sight."

"It is my foster-brother, Halbert Glendinning," said Mary, with apparent indifference; for she had been accustomed to call the sons of Elspet her foster-brethren, and to live with them as if they had been her brothers in earnest.

"Nay, by Our Lady, that it is not," said Mysie; "I know the favour of both the Glendinnings well, and I think this rider be not of our country. He has a crimson velvet bonnet, and long brown hair falling down under it, and a beard on his upper lip, and his chin clean and close shaved, and a sky-blue jerkin, slashed and lined with white sattin, and trunk-hose to suit, and no weapon but a rapier and dagger —Well, if I was a man, I would never wear weapon but the rapier! it is so slender and becoming, instead of having a cart-load of iron at my back, like my father's broad-sword, with its great rusty basket-hilt. Do you not delight in the rapier and poniard, lady?"

"The best sword," answered Mary, "if I must needs answer a question of the sort, is that which is drawn in the best cause, and which is best used when it is out of the scabbard."

"But can you not guess who this stranger should be?" said Mysie.

"Indeed, I cannot even attempt it; but to judge by his companion, it is no matter how little he is known," replied Mary.

"My benison on his bonny face," said Mysie, "if he is not going to alight here!—now, I am as much pleased as if my father had given me the silver ear-rings he has promised me so often; nay, you had as well come to the window, for you must see him by and bye whether you will or not."

I do not know how much sooner Mary Avenel might have sought the point of observation, if she had not been scared from it by the unrestrained curiosity expressed by her buxom friend; but at length the same feeling prevailed over her sense of dignity, and satisfied with having displayed all the indifference that was necessary in point of decorum, she no longer thought it necessary to restrain her curiosity.

From the out-shot or projecting window she could indeed perceive, that Christie of the Clinthill was attended on the present occasion by a very gay and gallant cavalier, who, from the nobleness of his countenance and manner, his rich and handsome dress, and the shewy appearance of his horse and furniture, must, she agreed with her new friend, be a person of some consequence.

Christie also seemed conscious of something, which made him call out with more than his usual insolence of manner, "What, ho! so ho! the house! Churl peasants, will no one answer when I call?—Ho! Martin,—Tibb,—Dame Glendinning!—a murrain on you, must we stand keeping our horses in the cold here, and they steaming with heat, when we have ridden so sharply?"

At length he was obeyed, and old Martin made his appearance. "Ha!" said Christie, "art thou there, old True-penny?—here, stable me these steeds, and see them well bedded, and stretch thine old limbs by rubbing them down; and see thou quit not the stable till there is not a turned hair on either of them."

Martin took the horses to the stable as commanded, but suppressed not his indignation a moment after he could vent it with safety. "Would not any one think," said he to Jasper, an old ploughman, who, in coming to his assistance, had heard Christie's imperious injunctions, "that this loon, this Christie of the Clinthill, was laird or lord at the least of him? No such thing, man! I remember him a little dirty turnspit boy in the house of Avenel, that every body on a frosty morning like this warmed his fingers by kicking or cuffing!—And now he is a gentleman, and swears, d—n him and renounce him, as if the gentlemen could not so much as keep their own wickedness to themselves, without the like of him going to hell in their very company, and by the same road. I have as much a mind as ever I had to my dinner, to go back and tell him to sort his horse himself, since he is as able as I am."

"Hout tout, man!" answered Jasper, "keep a calm sough—better to fleech a fool than fight with him."

Martin acknowledged the truth of the proverb, and, much comforted therewith, betook himself to cleaning the stranger's horse with great assiduity, remarking, it was a pleasure to handle a handsome nag, and turning over the other to the charge of Jasper. Nor was it until Christie's commands were literally complied with, that he deemed it proper, after washing himself, to join the party in the spence; not for the purpose of waiting upon them, as a mere modern reader might possibly expect, but that he might have share of dinner in their company.

In the mean while Christie had presented his companion to Dame Glendinning as Sir Piercie Shafton, a friend of his and of his master, come to spend three or four days with little din in the tower. The good dame could not conceive how she was entitled to such an honour, and would fain have pleaded her want of every sort of convenience to entertain a guest of that quality. And, indeed, the visitor, when he cast his eyes round the bare walls, eyed the huge black chimney, scrutinized the meagre and broken furniture of the apartment, and beheld the embarrassment of the mistress of the family, intimated great reluctance to intrude upon Dame Glendinning a visit, which could scarce, from all appearances, prove otherwise than an inconvenience to her, and a penance to himself.

But the reluctant hostess and her guest had to do with an inexorable man, who silenced all expostulation with, "such was his master's pleasure. And, moreover," he continued, "though the Baron of Avenel's will must, and ought to prove law to all within ten miles around him, yet here, dame," he said, "is a letter from your petticoated baron, the lord-priest yonder, who enjoins you, as you regard his pleasure, that you afford to this good knight such decent accommodation as is in your power, suffering him to live as privately as he shall desire. And for you, Sir Piercie Shafton," continued Christie, "you will judge for yourself, whether secrecy and safety is not more your object even now, than soft beds and high cheer. And do not judge of the dame's goods by the semblance of her cottage; for you will see by the dinner she is about to spread for us, that the vassal of the kirk is seldom found with her basket bare."

While he thus laboured to reconcile Sir Piercie Shafton to his fate, the widow having consulted her son Edward on the real import of the Lord Abbot's injunction, and having found that Christie had given a true exposition, saw nothing else left for her save to make that fate as easy as she could to the stranger. He himself also seemed reconciled to his lot by some feeling probably of strong necessity, and accepted with a good grace the hospitality which the dame offered with a very indifferent one.

In fact, the dinner which soon smoked before the assembled guests, was of that substantial kind which warrants plenty and comfort. Dame Glendinning had cooked it after her best manner; and, delighted with the handsome appearance which her good cheer made when placed on the table, forgot both her plans and the vexations which interrupted them, in the hospitable duty of pressing her assembled visitors to eat and drink, watching every trencher as it waxed empty, and loading it with fresh supplies ere the guest could utter a negative.

In the meanwhile the company attentively regarded each other's motions, and seemed endeavouring to form a judgment of each other's character. Sir Piercie Shafton condescended to speak to no one but to Mary Avenel, and on her he conferred exactly the same familiar and compassionate, though somewhat scornful sort of attention, which a pretty fellow of these days will sometimes condescend to bestow on a country miss, when there is no prettier or more fashionable woman present. The manner indeed was different, for the etiquette of those times did not permit Sir Piercie Shafton to pick his teeth or to yawn, or to gabble like the beggar whose tongue (as he says) was cut out by the Turks, or to affect deafness or blindness, or any other infirmity of the organs. But though the embroidery of his conversation was different, the groundwork was the same, and the high-flown and ornate compliments with which the gallant knight of the sixteenth century interlarded his conversation, were as much the offspring of egotism and self-conceit, as the jargon of the coxcombs of our own days.

The English knight was, however, something daunted at finding that Mary Avenel listened with an air of indifference, and answered with wonderful brevity, to all the fine things which ought, as he conceived, to have dazzled her with their brilliancy, and puzzled her by their obscurity. But if he was disappointed in making the desired, or rather the expected impression, upon her whom he addressed, Sir Piercie Shafton's discourse was marvellous in the ears of Mysie the Miller's daughter, and not the less so that she did not comprehend the meaning of a single word which he uttered. Indeed, the gallant knight's language was far too courtly to be understood by persons of intelligence more acute than Mysie's.

It was about this time, that the "only rare poet of his time, the witty, comical, facetiously-quick, and quickly-facetious John Lylly—he that sate at Apollo's table, and to whom Phœbus gave a wreath of his own bays without snatching"*—he, in short, who wrote that singularly coxcomical work, called *Euphues and his England*, was in the very zenith of his absurdity and reputation. The quaint, forced, and unnatural style which he introduced by his "Anatomy of Wit," had a fashion as rapid as it was momentary—all the court ladies were his scholars, and to *parler Euphuisme*, was as necessary a qualification of a courtly gallant, as those of understanding how to use his rapier or to dance a measure.

It was no wonder that the Maid of the Mill was soon as effectually blinded by the intricacies of this erudite and courtly style of conversation, as she had ever been by the dust of her father's own meal-sacks. But there she sate with her mouth and eyes as open as the mill-door and the two windows, shewing teeth as white as her father's bolted flour, and endeavouring to secure a word or two for her own future use out of the pearls of rhetoric which Sir Piercie Shafton scattered around him with such bounteous profusion.

---

* Such and yet more extravagant are the compliments paid to this author by his editor Blount. Notwithstanding all exaggeration, Lylly was really a man of wit and imagination, though both were deformed by the most unnatural affectation that ever disgraced a printed page.

For the male part of the company, Edward felt ashamed of his own manner and slowness of speech, when he observed the handsome young courtier, with an ease and volubility of which he had no conception, run over all the common-place topics of high-flown gallantry. It is true, the good sense and natural taste of young Glendinning soon informed him that the gallant cavalier was speaking nonsense. But, alas! where is the man of modest merit, and real talent, who has not suffered from being out-shone in conversation, and outstripped in the race of life, by men of less reserve, and of qualities more showy, though less substantial? and well constituted must the mind be, that can yield up the prize without envy to competitors more unworthy than himself.

Edward Glendinning had no such philosophy. While he despised the jargon of the gay cavalier, he envied the facility with which he could run on, as well as the courtly grace of his tone and expression, and the perfect ease and elegance with which he offered all the little acts of politeness to which the duties of the table gave opportunity. And if I am to speak truth, I must own that he envied these qualities the more, as they were all exercised in Mary Avenel's service, and, although only so far accepted as they could not be refused, intimated a wish on the stranger's part to place himself in her good graces, as the only person in the room to whom he thought it worth while to recommend himself. His title, rank, and very handsome figure, together with some sparks of wit and spirit which flashed across the cloud of nonsense which he uttered, rendered him, as the words of the old song say, "a lad for a lady's viewing." So that poor Edward, with all his real worth and acquired knowledge, in his home-spun doublet, blue cap, and deer-skin trowsers, looked like a clown beside the courtier, and, feeling the full inferiority, nourished no good will to him by whom he was eclipsed.

Christie, on the other hand, so soon as he had satisfied to the full a commodious appetite, by means of which persons of his profession could, like the wolf and eagle, gorge themselves with as much food at one meal as might serve them for several days, began also to feel himself more in the back ground than he liked to be. This worthy had, amongst his other good qualities, an excellent opinion of himself; and, being of a bold and forward disposition, had no mind to be thrown into the shade by any one. With that impudent familiarity which such persons mistake for graceful ease, he broke in upon the knight's finest speeches with as little remorse as he would have driven the point of his lance through a laced doublet.

Sir Piercie Shafton, a man of rank and high birth, by no means encouraged or endured this familiarity, and requited the intruder either with total neglect, or such laconic replies, as intimated sovereign contempt for the rude spearman, who affected to converse with him upon terms of equality.

The Miller held his peace; for, as his usual conversation turned chiefly on his clapper and toll dish, he had no mind to brag of his wealth in presence of Christie of the Clinthill, or to intrude his discourse on the English cavalier.

A little specimen of the conversation may not be out of place here, were it but to shew young ladies what fine things they have lost by living when Euphuism is out of fashion.

"Credit me, fairest lady," said the knight, "that such is the cunning of our English courtiers of the hodiernal strain, that, as they have infinitely refined upon the plain and rustical discourse of our fathers, which, as I may say, more beseemed the mouths of country roisterers in a May-game than that of courtly gallants in a galliard, so I hold it ineffably and unutterably improbable, that those who may succeed us in that garden of wit and courtesy shall alter or amend it. Venus delighteth but in the language of Mercury, Bucephalus will stoop to none but Alexander, no one can sound Apollo's pipe but Orpheus."

"Valiant sir," said Mary, who could scarce help laughing, "we have but to rejoice in the chance which hath honoured this solitude with a glimpse of the sun of courtesy, though it rather blinds than enlightens us."

"Pretty and quaint, fairest lady," answered the Euphuist. "Ah that I had with me my Anatomy of Wit—that all-to-be-unparalleled volume—that quintessence of human wit—that treasury of quaint invention—that exquisitely-pleasant-to-read, and inevitably-necessary-to-be-remembered manual of all that is worthy to be known—which indoctrines the rude in civility, the dull in intellectuality, the heavy in jocosity, the blunt in gentility, the vulgar in nobility, and all of them in that unutterable perfection of human utterance, that eloquence which no other eloquence is sufficient to praise, that art which, when we call it by its own name of Euphuism, we bestow on it its richest panegyric."

"By Saint Mary," said Christie of the Clinthill, "if your worship had told me you had left such wealth as you talk of at Prudhoe Castle, Long Aikie and I would have had them off with us if man and horse could have carried them; but you told us of no treasure that I wot of, save the silver tongs for turning up your moustachios."

The Knight treated this intruder's mistake—for certainly Christie had no idea that all these epithets which sounded so rich and splendid, were lavished upon a small quarto volume—with a stare, and then turning again to Mary Avenel, the only person whom he thought worthy to address, he proceeded in his strain of high-flown oratory.

"Even thus," said he, "do hogs contemn the splendour of oriental pearls; even thus are the delicacies of a choice repast in vain offered to the long-eared grazer of the common, who turneth from them to devour a thistle. Surely as idle is it to pour forth the treasures of oratory before the eyes of the ignorant, and to spread the dainties of the intellectual banquet before those who are, morally and metaphysically speaking, no better than asses."

"Sir Knight, since that is your quality," said Edward, "we cannot strive with you in loftiness of language; but I pray you in fair courtesy, while you honour my father's house with your presence, to spare us such vile comparisons."

"Peace, good villagio," said the knight, gracefully waving his hand, "I prithee peace, kind rustic; and you, my guide, whom I may scarce call honest, let me prevail upon thee to imitate the laudable taciturnity of that honest yeoman, who sits as mute as a mill-post, and of that comely damsel, who seems as with her ears she drunk in what she did not altogether comprehend, even as a palfrey listeneth to a lute, whereof howsoever he knoweth not the gamut."

"Marvellous fine words," at length said Dame Glendinning, who began to be tired of sitting so long silent, "marvellous fine words, neighbour Happer, are they not?"

"Brave words—very brave words—very exceeding pyet words," answered the Miller; "nevertheless, to speak my mind, a lippy of bran were worth a bushel o' them."

"I think so too, under his worship's favour," answered Christie of the Clinthill. "I well remember that at the race of Morham, as we called it, near Berwick, I took a young Southron fellow out of saddle with my lance, and cast him, it might be, a gad's length from his nag; and so, as he had some gold on his laced doublet, I deemed he might ha' the like on it in his pocket too, though that is a rule that does not aye hold good—So I was speaking to him of ransom, and out he comes with a handful of such terms as his honour there hath gleaned up, and craved me of mercy, as I was a true son of Mars, and such like."

"And obtained no mercy at thy hand, I dare be sworn," said the knight, who deigned not to speak Euphuism excepting to the ladies.

"In truth," replied Christie, "I would have thrust my lance down his throat, but just then they flung open that accursed postern gate, and forth pricked old Hunsdon, and Henry Carey, and as many fellows at their heels as turned the chace northward again. So I e'en pricked Bayard with the spur and went off with the rest; for a man should ride when he may not wrestle, as they say in Tynedale."

"Trust me," said the knight, again turning to Mary Avenel, "if I do not pity you, lady, who, being of noble blood, are thus in a manner compelled to abide in the cottage of the ignorant, like the precious stone in the head of a toad, or like a precious garland on the head of an ass—But soft, what gallant have we here, whose garb savoureth more of the rustic than doth his demeanour, and whose looks seem more lofty than his habit? even as"——

"I pray you, Sir Knight," said Mary, "to spare your courtly similitudes for refined ears, and give me leave to name unto you my foster-brother, Halbert Glendinning."

"The son of the good dame of the cottage, as I opine," answered the English knight; "for by some such name did my guide discriminate the mistress of this mansion, which you, madam, enrich with your presence.—And yet, touching this juvenal, he hath that about him which belongeth to higher birth, for all are not black who dig coals"——

"Nor all white who are millers," said honest Hob, glad to get in a word, as they say, edge-ways.

Halbert, who had sustained the glance of the Englishman with some impatience, and knew not what to make of his manner and language, replied with some asperity, "Sir Knight—we have in this land of Scotland an ancient saying, 'Scorn not the bush that bields you.' You are a guest in my father's house to shelter you from danger, if I am rightly informed by the domestics. Scoff not its homeliness or that of its inmates—ye might long have abidden at the court of England, ere we had sought your favour or cumbered you with our society. Since your fate has sent you hither amongst us, be contented with such fare and such converse as we can afford you, and scorn us not for our kindness; for the Scots wear short patience and long swords."

All eyes were turned on Halbert while he was thus speaking, and there was a general feeling that his countenance had an expression of intelligence, and his person an air of dignity, which they had never before observed. Whether it was that the wonderful Being with whom he had so lately held communication, had bestowed on him a grace and dignity of look and bearing which he had not before, or whether the being conversant in high matters, and called to a destiny beyond that of other men, had a natural effect in giving becoming confidence to his language and manner, we pretend not to determine. But it was evident to all, that, from this day, young Halbert was an altered man; that he acted with the steadiness, promptitude, and determination which belonged to riper years, and bore himself with the manners which appertained to higher rank.

The knight took the rebuke with good humour. "By mine honour," he said, "thou hast reason on thy side, good juvenal—nevertheless, I spoke not as in ridicule of the roof which relieves me, but rather in

your own praise, to whom, if this roof be native, thou may'st nevertheless rise from its lowliness; even as the lark, which maketh his humble
nest in the furrow, ascendeth towards the sun, as well as the eagle
which buildeth her eyry in the cliff."

This high-flown discourse was interrupted by Dame Glendinning,
who, with all the busy anxiety of a mother, was loading her son's
trencher with food, and dinning in his ear her reproaches on account
of his prolonged absence. "And see," she said, "that you do not one
day get such a sight while you are walking about among the haunts of
them—that are not of our flesh and bone, as befell Mungo Murray
when he slept on the greensward-ring of the Auld Kirkhill at sun-set,
and wakened at day-break in the wild hills of Breadalbane. And see
that when ye are looking for deer, the red stag does not gaul you as it
did Diccon Thorburn, who never cast the wound that he took from a
buck's-horn. And see, when you go swaggering about with a long
broad-sword by your side, whilk it becomes no peaceful man to do,
that you dinna meet with them that have broad-sword and lance both
—there are enow of rank riders in this land that neither fear God nor
regard man."

Here her eye "in a fine frenzy rolling," fell full upon that of Christie
of the Clinthill, and at once her fears for having given offence interrupted the current of maternal rebuke, which, like rebuke matrimo-
nial, may be often better meant than timed. There was something of
sly and watchful significance in Christie's eye, an eye grey, keen,
fierce, yet wily, formed to express at once cunning and malice, which
made the dame instantly conjecture she had said too much, while she
saw in imagination her twelve goodly cows go lowing down the glen in
a moonlight night, with half a score of Border spearmen at their heels.

Her voice, therefore, sunk from the elevated tone of maternal
authority into a whimpering apologetic sort of strain, and she proceeded to say, "It is no that I have any ill thoughts of the Border riders,
for Tibb Tacket there has often heard me say that I thought spear and
bridle as natural to a Border-man as a pen to a priest, or a feather-fan
to a lady—Have not you heard me say it, Tibb?"

Tibb shewed something less than the expected alacrity in attesting
her mistress's deep respect for the freebooters of the southland hills;
but, thus conjured, did at length reply, "Hout ay, mistress, I'se warrant I have heard you say something like that."

"Mother!" said Halbert, in a firm and commanding tone of voice,
"what or whom is it that you fear under my father's roof?—I well hope
that it harbours not a guest in whose presence you are afraid to say
your pleasure to me or my brother? I am sorry I have been detained so
late, being ignorant of the fair company which I should encounter on

my return.—I pray you let this excuse suffice; and what satisfies you, will, I trust, be nothing less than acceptable to your guests."

An answer calculated so justly betwixt the submission due to his parent, and the natural feeling of dignity in one who was by birth master of the mansion, excited universal satisfaction. And as Elspet herself confessed to Tibb on the same evening, "She did not think it had been in the callant—till that night, he took pets and passions if he was spoke to, and lap through the house like a four-year-auld at the least word of advice that was minted at him—And now he spoke as grave and as douce as the Lord Abbot himself. She kenn'd na," she said, "what might be the upshot of it, but it was like he was a wonderfu' callant even now."

The party then fell asunder, the young men retiring to their apartments, the elder to their household cares. While Christie went to see his horse properly accommodated, Edward betook himself to his book, and Halbert, who was as ingenious in employing his hands as he had hitherto appeared imperfect in mental exertion, applied himself to constructing a place of concealment in the floor of his apartment by raising a plank, beneath which he resolved to deposit that copy of the Holy Scriptures which had been so strangely regained from the possession of men and spirits.

In the meanwhile, Sir Piercie Shafton sate still as a stone in the chair in which he had deposited himself, his hands folded on the stomach, his legs stretched straight out before him and resting upon the heels, his eyes cast up to the ceiling as if he had meant to count every mesh of every cobweb with which the arched roof was canopied, wearing at the same time a face of as solemn and imperturbable gravity, as if his existence had depended on the accuracy of his calculation.

He could scarce be roused from his listless state of contemplative absorption so as to take some supper, a meal at which the younger females appeared not. Sir Piercie stared around twice or thrice as if he missed something; but he asked not for them, and only evinced his sense of a proper audience being a wanting, by his abstraction and absence of mind, seldom speaking until he was twice addressed, and then replying, without trope or figure, in that plain English, which nobody could speak better when he had a mind.

Christie, finding himself in undisturbed possession of the conversation, indulged all who chose to listen with details of his own wild and inglorious warfare, while Dame Elspet's curch bristled with horror, and Tibb Tacket, rejoiced to find herself once more in the company of a jack-man, listened to his tales, like Desdemona to Othello's, with undisguised delight. Meantime the two brother Glendinnings were each wrapped up in his own reflections, and only interrupted in them by the signal to move bed-ward.

Chapter Four

He strikes no coin 'tis true, but coins new phrases,
And vends them forth as knaves vend gilded counters,
Which wise men scorn, and fools accept in payment.
Old Play

IN THE MORNING, Christie of the Clinthill was nowhere to be seen. As this worthy personage did seldom pique himself on sounding a trumpet before his movements, no one was surprised at his moonlight departure, though some alarm was excited lest he had not made it empty-handed. So, in the language of the national ballad,

Some ran to cupboard, and some to kist,
But nought was gone that could be mist.

All was in order, the key of the stable left above the door, and that of the iron-grate in the inside of the lock. In short, the retreat had been made with scrupulous attention to the security of the garrison, and so far Christie left them nothing to complain of.

The safety of the premises was ascertained by Halbert, who, instead of catching up a gun or a cross-bow, and sallying out for the day as had been his frequent custom, now, with a gravity beyond his years, took a survey of all around the tower, and then returned to the spence, or public apartment, in which, at the early hour of seven, the morning-meal was prepared.

There he found the Euphuist in the same elegant posture of abstruse calculation which he had exhibited on the preceding evening, his arms folded in the same angle, his eyes turned up to the same cobwebs, and his heels resting on the ground as before. Tired of this affectation of indolent importance, and not much flattered with his guest's persevering in it to the last, Halbert resolved at once to break the ice, being determined to know what circumstances had brought to the Tower of Glendearg a guest at once so supercilious and so silent.

"Sir Knight," said he with some firmness, "I have twice given you good morning, to which the absence of your mind hath, I presume, prevented you from yielding attention or from making return. This exchange of courtesy is at your pleasure—But, as what I have farther to say concerns your comfort and your motions in an especial manner, I will entreat you to give me some signs of attention, that I may be sure I am not wasting my words on a monumental image."

At this unexpected address, Sir Piercie Shafton opened his eyes, and treated the speaker to a broad stare; but, as Halbert returned the glance without either confusion or dismay, the knight thought proper to change his posture, raise up his body, draw in his legs, fix his eyes on young Glendinning, and assume the appearance of one who listens to what is said to him. Nay, to make his purpose more evident, he gave voice to his resolution in these words, "Speak, we do hear."

"Sir Knight," said the youth, "it is the custom of this Halidome, or patrimony of Saint Mary's, to trouble with enquiries no guests who receive our hospitality, providing they tarry in our house only for a single revolution of the sun. We know that both criminals and debtors come hither for sanctuary, and we scorn to extort from the pilgrim, whom chance may make a guest, an avowal of the cause of his pilgrimage and penance. But when one so high above our rank as yourself, Sir Knight, and especially one to whom the possession of such preeminence is not indifferent, shews his determination to be our guest for a longer time, it is our usage to require to know from him whence he comes, and what is the cause of his journey?"

The English knight gaped twice or thrice before he answered, and then replied in a bantering tone. "Truly, good villagio, your question hath in it somewhat of embarrassment; for you ask me of things concerning which I am not as yet altogether determined what answer I may find it convenient to make. Let it suffice thee, kind juvenal, that thou has the Lord Abbot's authority for treating me to the best of that power of thine, which, indeed, may not always so well suffice for my accommodation as either of us would desire."

"I must have a more precise answer than this, Sir Knight," said the young Glendinning.

"Friend," said the knight, "be not outrageous—it may suit your northern manners thus to press harshly upon the secrets of thy betters; but believe me, that even as the lute, struck by an unskilful hand, doeth produce only discords, so"——At this moment the door of the apartment opened, and Mary Avenel presented herself—"But who can talk of discords," said the knight, assuming his complimentary vein and humour, "when the soul of harmony descends upon us in the presence of surpassing beauty! For even as foxes, wolves, and other animals void of sense and reason, do fly from the presence of the resplendent sun of heaven when he arises in his glory, so do strife, wrath, and all ireful passions retreat, and as it were scud away, from the face which now beams upon us, with power to compose our angry passions, illuminate our errors and difficulties, sooth our wounded minds, and lull to rest our disorderly apprehensions; for as the heat and warmth of the eye of day is to the material and physical world, so is the eye which I now bow down before to that of the intellectual microcosm."

He concluded with a profound bow; and Mary Avenel, gazing from one to the other, and plainly seeing that something was amiss, could only say, "For heaven's sake, what is the meaning of this?"

The newly acquired tact and intelligence of her foster-brother was as yet insufficient to enable him to give an answer. He was quite uncertain how he ought to deal with a guest, who, preserving a singularly high tone of assumed superiority and importance, seemed nevertheless so little serious in what he said, that it was quite impossible to discern with accuracy whether he was in jest or earnest.

Forming, however, the internal resolution to bring Sir Piercie Shafton to a reckoning at a more fit place and season, he resolved to prosecute the matter no farther at present; and the entrance of his mother with the damsel of the Mill, and the return of the honest Miller from the stack-yard, where he had been numbering and calculating the probable amount of the season's grist, rendered further discussion impossible for the moment.

In the course of the calculation, it could not but strike the man of meal and grind-stones, that, after the church's dues were paid, and after all which he himself could by any means whatsoever deduct from the crop, still the residue which must revert to Dame Glendinning could not be less than considerable. I wot not if this led the honest Miller to nourish any plans similar to those adopted by Elspet; but it is certain that he accepted with grateful alacrity an invitation which the dame gave to his daughter, to remain a week or two as her guest at Glendearg.

The principal persons being thus in high good humour with each other, all business gave place to the hilarity of the morning repast; and so much did Sir Piercie appear gratified by the attention which was paid to every word that he uttered by the nut-brown Mysie, that, notwithstanding his high birth and distinguished quality, he bestowed on her some of the more ordinary and second-rate tropes of his elocution.

Mary Avenel, when relieved from the awkwardness of feeling the full weight of his conversation addressed to herself, enjoyed it much more; and the good knight, encouraged by these conciliating marks of approbation from the sex, for whose sake he cultivated his oratorical talents, made speedy intimation of his purpose to be more communicative than he had shewn himself in his conversation with Halbert Glendinning, and gave them to understand, that it was in consequence of some pressing danger that he was at present their involuntary guest.

The conclusion of the breakfast was signal for the separation of the company. The Miller went to prepare for his departure; his daughter to arrange matters for her unexpected stay; Edward was summoned to consultation by Martin concerning some agricultural matter, in which Halbert could not be brought to interest himself; the dame left the room upon her household concerns, and Mary was in the act of following her, when she suddenly recollected, that if she did so, the strange knight and Halbert must be left alone together, at the risk of another quarrel.

The maiden no sooner observed this circumstance, than she instantly returned from the door of the apartment, and, seating herself in a small stone window-seat, resolved to maintain that curb which she was sensible her presence imposed on Halbert Glendinning, of whose quick temper she had some apprehensions.

The stranger marked her motions, and, either interpreting them as inviting his society, or obedient to those laws of gallantry which permitted him not to leave a lady in silence and solitude, he instantly placed himself near to her side, and opened the conversation as follows:

"Credit me, fair lady," he said, addressing Mary Avenel, "it much rejoiceth me, being as I am a banished man from the delights of mine own country, that I shall find here, in this obscure and sylvan cottage of the north, a fair form and a candid soul, with whom I may explain my mutual sentiments. And let me pray you in particular, lovely lady, that, according to the universal custom now predominant in our court, the garden of superior wits, you will exchange with me some epithet whereby you may mark my devotion to your service. Be henceforward named, for example, my Protection, and let me be your Affability."

"Our northern and country manners, Sir Knight, do not permit us to exchange epithets with those to whom we are strangers," replied Mary Avenel.

"Nay, but see now," said the knight, "how you are startled! even as the unbroken steed which swerves aside from the shaking of a handkerchief, though he must in time encounter the waving of a pennon. This courtly exchange of epithets of honour, is no more than the compliments which pass between Valour and Beauty, wherever they meet, and under whatever circumstances. Elizabeth of England herself calls Philip Sidney her Courage, and he in return calls that princess his Inspiration. Wherefore, my fair Protection, for by such epithet it shall be mine to denominate you"——

"Not without the young lady's consent, sir," answered Halbert; "most truly do I hope your courtly and quaint breeding will not so far prevail over the more ordinary rules of behaviour."

"Fair tenant of an indifferent copy-hold," replied the knight, with the same coolness and civility of mien, but in a tone somewhat more lofty than he used to the young lady, "we do not, in the southern parts, much intermingle discourse, save with those with whom we may stand on some footing of equality; and I must, in all discretion, remind you, that the necessity which makes us inhabitants of the same cabin, doth not place us otherwise on a level with each other."

"By Saint Mary," replied young Glendinning, "it is my thought that it does; for plain men hold, that he who asks the shelter is indebted to him who gives it; and so far, therefore, is our rank equalized while this roof covers us both."

"Thou art altogether deceived," answered Sir Piercie; "and that thou mayst fully adapt thyself to our relative condition, know that I account not myself thy guest, but that of thy master, the Lord Abbot of Saint Mary's, who, for reasons best known to himself and me, chuseth to administer his hospitality to me through the means of thee, his servant and vassal, who art therefore, in good truth, as passive an instrument of my accommodation as this ill-made and rugged joint-stool on which I sit, or as the wooden trencher from which I eat my coarse commons. Wherefore," he added, turning to Mary, "fairest mistress, or rather as I said before, most lovely Protection"*——

Mary Avenel was about to reply to him, when the stern, fierce, and resentful expression of voice and countenance with which Halbert exclaimed, "Not the King of Scotland, did he live, should use me thus!" induced her to throw herself between him and the stranger, exclaiming, "For God's sake, Halbert, beware what you do!"

"Fear not, fairest Protection," replied Sir Piercie, with the utmost serenity, "that I can be provoked by this rustical and mistaught juvenal to do aught misbecoming your presence or mine own dignity; for as soon shall the gunner's linstock give fire unto the icicle, as the spark of passion inflame my blood, tempered as it is to serenity by the respect due to the presence of my gracious Protection."

"You may well call her your protection, Sir Knight," said Halbert; "by Saint Andrew, it is the only sensible word I have heard you speak

---

* There are many instances to be met with in the ancient drama of this whimsical and conceited custom of persons who formed an intimacy, distinguishing each other by some quaint epithet. In *Every Man out of his Humour*, there is a humorous debate upon the names most fit to bind the relation betwixt Sogliardo and Cavaliero Shift, which ends by adopting those of Countenance and Resolution. What is more to the point is the speech of Hedon, a voluptuary and a courtier in *Cynthia's Revels*. "You know that I call Madam Philantia my HONOUR, and she calls me her AMBITION. Now, when I meet her in the presence, anon, I will come to her and say, 'Sweet Honour, I have hitherto contented my sense with the lilies of your hand, but now I will taste the roses of your lip.' To which she cannot but blushing answer, 'Nay, now you are too ambitious;' and then do I reply, 'I cannot be too ambitious of Honour, sweet lady.' Wilt not be good?"—I think there is some remnant of this foppery preserved in masonic lodges.

—but we may meet where her protection shall no longer afford you shelter."

"Fairest Protection," continued the courtier, not even honouring with a look, far less with a direct reply, the threat of the incensed Halbert, "doubt not that thy faithful Affability will be more commoved by the speech of this rudesby, than the bright and serene moon is perturbed by the baying of the cottage-cur, proud of the height of his own dung-hill, which, in his conceit, lifteth him nearer unto the majestic luminary."

To what lengths so unsavoury a simile might have driven Halbert's indignation, is left uncertain; for at that moment Edward rushed into the apartment with the intelligence that two most important officers of the Convent, the Kitchener and Refectioner, were just arrived with a sumpter-mule, loaded with provisions, announcing that the Lord Abbot, the Sub-Prior, and the Sacristan, were on their way hither. A circumstance so very extraordinary had never been recorded in the annals of Saint Mary's, or in the traditions of Glendearg, though there was a faint legendary report that a Lord Abbot had dined there in old days, after having been bewildered in a hunting expedition amongst the wilds which lie to the northward. But that the present Lord Abbot should have taken a voluntary journey to so wild and dreary a spot, the very Kamschatka of the Halidome, was a thing never dreamed of, and the news excited the greatest surprise in all the members of the family, saving Halbert alone.

This fiery youth was too full of the insult he had received to think of any thing as unconnected with it. "I am glad of it," he said; "I am glad the Abbot comes hither. I will know of him by what right this stranger is sent hither to domineer over us under our father's roof, as we were slaves and not freemen. I will tell the proud priest to his beard"——

"Alas! alas! my brother," said Edward, "think what these words may cost thee."

"And what will, or what can they cost me," said Halbert, "that I should sacrifice my human feelings and my justifiable resentment to the fear of what the Abbot can do?"

"Our mother—our mother!" exclaimed Edward; "think, if she is deprived of her home, expelled from her property, how can you amend what your rashness may ruin?"

"It is too true, by Heaven," said Halbert, striking his forehead. Then, stamping his foot against the floor to express the full energy of the passion to which he dared no longer give vent, he turned round and left the apartment.

Mary Avenel looked at the stranger knight, while she was endeavouring to frame a request that he would not report the intemperate violence of her foster-brother to the prejudice of his family, in the mind of the Abbot. But Sir Piercie, the very pink of courtesy, conjectured her meaning from her embarrassment, and waited not to be entreated.

"Credit me, fairest Protection," said he, "your Affability is less than capable of seeing or hearing, far less of reciting or reiterating, aught of an unseemly nature which may have chanced while I enjoyed the Elysium of your presence. The winds of idle passion may indeed rudely agitate the bosom of the rude; but the heart of the courtier is polished to resist them, as the frozen lake receives not the influence of the breeze. Even so"——

The voice of Dame Glendinning, in shrill summons, here demanded Mary Avenel's attendance, who instantly obeyed, not a little glad to escape from the compliments and similies of this court-like gallant. Nor was it apparently less a relief on his part; for no sooner was she past the threshold of the room, than he exchanged the look of formal and elaborate politeness which had accompanied each word he had uttered hitherto, for an expression of the utmost lassitude and ennui; and after indulging in one or two portentous yawns, broke forth into a soliloquy.

"What the foul fiend sent this wench hither? As if it were not sufficient plague to be harboured in a hovel that would hardly serve for a dog's-kennel in England, baited by a rude peasant-boy, and dependant on the faith of a mercenary ruffian, but I cannot even have time to muse over my own mishap, but must come aloft, frisk, fidget, and make speeches to please this pale hectic phantom, because she has gentle blood in her veins! By mine honour, setting prejudice aside, the mill-wench is the more attractive metal of the two—But patienza, Piercie Shafton, thou must not lose thy well-earned claim to be accounted a devout servant of the fair sex, a witty-brained, prompt, and accomplished courtier. Rather thank Heaven, Piercie Shafton, which hath sent thee a subject, wherein, without derogating from thy rank, (since the honours of the Avenel family are beyond dispute,) thou may'st find a whet-stone for thy witty compliments, a strop whereon to sharpen thine acute ingine, a butt whereat to shoot the arrows of thy gallantry. For even as a Bilboa blade, the more it is rubbed the brighter and the sharper will it prove, so——But what need I waste my stock of similitudes in holding converse with myself?—Yonder comes the monkish retinue, like some half score of crows winging their way slowly up the valley—I hope, a'gad, they have not forgotten my trunk-mails of apparel amid the ample provision they have made for their own belly-timber—Mercy, a'gad, I were finely holped up if the vesture has miscarried among the thievish Borderers!"

Stung by this reflection, he ran hastily down stairs, and caused his horse to be saddled, that he might, as soon as possible, ascertain this important point, by meeting the Lord Abbot and his retinue as they came up the glen. He had not ridden a mile before he met them advancing with the slowness and decorum which became persons of their dignity and profession. The knight failed not to greet the Lord Abbot with all the formal compliments with which men of rank at that period exchanged courtesies. He had the good fortune to find that his maills were numbered among the train of baggage which attended upon the party; and, satisfied in that particular, he turned his horse's head, and accompanied the Abbot to the tower of Glendearg.

Great, in the meanwhile, had been the turmoil of the good Dame Elspet and her coadjutors, to prepare for the fitting reception of the Father Lord Abbot and his retinue. The Monks had indeed taken care not to trust too much to the state of her pantry; but she was not the less anxious to make such additions as might enable her to claim the thanks of her feudal lord and spiritual father. Meeting Halbert, as, with his blood on fire, he returned from his altercation with her guest, she commanded him instantly to go forth to the hill, and not to return without venison; reminding him that he was apt enough to go thither for his own pleasure, and must now do so for the credit of the house.

The Miller, who was now hastening his journey homewards, promised to send up some salmon by his own servant. Dame Elspet, who by this time thought she had guests enough, had begun to repent of her invitation to poor Mysie, and was just considering by what means, short of giving offence, she could send off the Maid of the Mill behind her father, and adjourn all her own aerial architecture till some future opportunity, when this unexpected generosity on the part of the sire rendered any present attempt to return his daughter on his hands too highly ungracious to be thought further on. So the Miller departed alone on his homeward journey.

Dame Elspet's sense of hospitality proved in this instance its own reward; for Mysie had dwelt too near the convent to be altogether ignorant of the noble art of cookery, which her father patronized to the extent of consuming on festival days such dainties as his daughter could prepare in emulation of the luxuries of the Abbot's kitchen. Stripping, therefore, her holiday kirtle, and adopting a dress more suitable to the occasion, the good-humoured maiden stripped her snowy arms above the elbows; and, as Elspet acknowledged, in the language of the time and country, took "entire and aefauld part with her" in the labours of the day; shewing unparalleled talent, and indefatigable industry, in the preparation of *mortreux*, *blanc-manger*, and heaven knows what delicacies besides, which Dame Glendinning, unassisted by her skill, dared not even have dreamed of presenting.

Leaving this able substitute in the kitchen, and regretting that Mary Avenel was so brought up, that she could entrust nothing to her care, unless it might be seeing the great chamber strewed with fresh rushes, and ornamented with such flowers and branches as the season afforded, Dame Elspet hastily donned her best attire, and with a beating heart presented herself at the door of her little tower, to make her obeisance to the Lord Abbot as he crossed her humble threshold. Edward stood by his mother, and felt the same palpitation, which his philosophy was at a loss to account for. He was yet to learn how long it is ere our reason learns to triumph over the force of external circumstances, and how much our feelings are affected by novelty, and blunted by use and habit.

On the present occasion, he witnessed with wonder and awe the approach of some half a score of riders, sober men upon sober palfreys, muffled in their long black garments, and only relieved by their white scapularies, shewing more like a funeral procession than aught else, and not quickening their pace beyond that which permitted easy conversation and easy digestion. The sobriety of the show was indeed somewhat enlivened by the presence of Sir Piercie Shafton, who, to shew his skill in the manege was not inferior to his other accomplishments, kept alternately pressing and checking his gay courser, forcing him to piaffe, to caracole, to passage, and to do all the other feats of the school, to the great annoyance of the Lord Abbot, the wonted sobriety of whose palfrey became at length discomposed by the vivacity of its companion, while the dignitary kept crying out in bodily alarm, "I do pray you, sir—Sir Knight—good now, Sir Piercie —Be quiet, Benedict, there is a good steed—soh, poor fellow!" and uttering all the other precatory and soothing exclamations by which a timid horseman usually bespeaks the favour of a frisky companion, or of his own unquiet nag, and concluding the bead-roll with a sincere *Deo gratias* so soon as he alighted in the court-yard of the little tower of Glendearg.

The inhabitants unanimously knelt down to kiss the hand of the Lord Abbot, a ceremony which even the Monks were often condemned to. Good Abbot Boniface was too much fluttered by the incidents of the later part of his journey, to go through this ceremony with much solemnity, or indeed with much patience. He kept wiping his brow with a snow-white handkerchief with one hand, while another was abandoned to the homage of his vassals; and then signing the cross with his outstretched arm, and exclaiming, "Bless ye—bless ye, my children!" he hastened into the house and murmured not a little at the darkness and steepness of the rugged winding-stair, whereby he at length scaled the spence destined for his entertainment, and, overcome with fatigue, threw himself, I do not say into an easy chair, but into the easiest the apartment afforded.

Chapter Five

A courtier extraordinary, who by diet
Of meats and drinks, his temperate exercise,
Choice music, frequent baths, his horary shifts
Of shirts and waistcoats, means to immortalize
Mortality itself, and makes the essence
Of his whole happiness the trim of court.
Magnetic Lady

WHEN THE LORD ABBOT had suddenly and superciliously vanished from the eyes of his expectant vassals, the Sub-Prior made amends for the negligence of his principal, by the kind and affectionate greeting which he gave to all the members of the family, but especially to Dame Elspet, her foster-daughter, and her son Edward. "Where," he even condescended to enquire, "is that naughty Nimrod, Halbert?—He hath not yet, I trust, turned, like his great prototype, his hunting-spear against man?"

"O no, an it please your reverence," said Dame Glendinning, "Halbert is up the glen to get some venison, or surely he would not have been absent when such a day of honour dawned upon me and mine."

"O, to get savoury meat such as our soul loveth," murmured the Sub-Prior, "it has been at all times an acceptable gift.—I bid you good morrow, my good dame, as I must attend upon his lordship the Father Abbot."

"And O, reverend sir," said the good widow, detaining him, "if it might but be your pleasure to take part with us if there is any thing wrong; and if there is any thing wanted, to say that it is just coming, or to make some excuse as your learning best knows how. Every bit of vassail and silver work have we been spoiled of since Pinkie Cleugh, when I lost poor Simon Glendinning, that was warst of a'!"

"Never mind—never fear," said the Sub-Prior, gently extricating his garment from the anxious grasp of Dame Elspet, "the Refectioner has with him the Abbot's plate and drinking cups; and I pray you to believe that whatever is short in your entertainment will be deemed amply made up in your good-will."

So saying, he escaped from her and went into the spence, where such preparations as haste permitted were making for the noon collation of the Abbot and the English knight. Here he found the Lord

Abbot, for whom a cushion, composed of all the plaids in the house, had been unable to render Simon's huge elbow-chair a soft or comfortable place of rest.

"Benedicite!" said Abbot Boniface, "now marry fie upon these hard benches with all my heart—they are as uneasy as the *scabella* of our novices. Saint Jude be with us, Sir Knight, how have you contrived to pass over the night in this dungeon? An your bed was no softer than your seat, you might as well have slept on the stone couch of Saint Pacomius. After trotting a full ten miles, a man needs a softer seat than has fallen to my hard lot."

With sympathizing faces, the Sacristan and the Refectioner ran to raise up the Lord Abbot, and to adjust his seat to his mind, which was at length accomplished in some sort, although he continued alternately to bewail his fatigue, and to exult in the conscious sense of having discharged an arduous duty. "You errant cavaliers," said he, addressing the knight, "may now perceive that others have their travail and their toils to undergo as well as your honoured faculty. And this I will say for myself and the soldiers of Saint Mary, among whom I may be termed captain, that it is not our wont to flinch from the heat of the service, or to withdraw from the good fight. No, by Saint Mary!—no sooner did I learn that you were here, and dared not for certain reasons come to the Monastery, where with as good will, and with more convenience, we might have given you a better reception, than, striking the table with my hammer, I called a brother—Timothy, said I, let them saddle Benedict—let them saddle my black palfrey, and bid the Sub-Prior and some half score of attendance be in readiness to-morrow after matins—we would ride to Glendearg.—Brother Timothy stared, thinking, I imagine, that his ears had scarce done him justice—but I repeated my commands, and, said I, let the Kitchener and Refectioner go before to aid the poor vassals to whom the place belongs in making a suitable collation. So that you will consider, good Sir Piercie, our mutual incommodities, and forgive whatever you may find amiss."

"By my faith," said Sir Piercie Shafton, "there is nothing to forgive —If you spiritual warriors have to submit to the grievous incommodities which your lordship narrates, it would ill become me, a sinful and secular man, to complain of a bed as hard as a board, of broth which relished as if made of burnt wool, of flesh which, in its sable and singed shape, seemed to put me on a level with Richard Cœur-de-Lion, when he eat up the head of a Moor carbonadoed, and of other viands savouring rather of the rusticity of this northern region."

"By the good saints, sir," said the Abbot, somewhat touched in point of his character for hospitality, of which he was in truth a most faithful and zealous professor, "it grieves me to the heart that you have found our vassals no better provided for your reception—Yet I crave leave to observe, that if Sir Piercie Shafton's affairs had permitted him to honour with his company our poor house of Saint Mary's, he might have had less to complain of in respect of easements."

"To give your lordship the reasons," said Sir Piercie Shafton, "why I could not at this present time approach your dwelling, or avail myself of its well-known and undoubted hospitality, craves either some delay, or," looking around him, "a limited audience."

The Lord Abbot immediately issued his mandate to the Refectioner: "Hie thee to the kitchen, brother Hilarius, and there make enquiry at our brother the Kitchener, within what time he opines that our collation may be prepared, since sin and sorrow it were, considering the hardships of this noble and gallant knight, no whit mentioning or weighing those we ourselves have endured, if we were now either to advance or retard the hour of refection before or beyond the time when the viands are fit to be set before us."

Brother Hilarius parted with an eager alertness to execute the will of his superior, and returned with the assurance, that punctually at one after noon would the collation be ready.

"Before that time," said the accurate Refectioner, "the wafers, flamms, and pastry-meat, will scarce have had the just degree of fire, which learned pottingers prescribe as fittest for the body; and if it should be past one o'clock, were it but ten minutes, our brother the Kitchener opines, that the haunch of venison would suffer in spite of the skill of the little turn-broche whom he has recommended to your holiness by his praises."

"How!" said the Abbot, "a haunch of venison!—from whence comes that dainty? I remember not thou didst intimate its presence in thy hampers of vivers."

"So please your holiness and lordship," said the Refectioner; "he is a son of the woman of the house who hath shot it and sent it in—killed but now; yet, as the animal-heat hath not left the body, the Kitchener undertakes it shall eat as tender as a young chicken—and this youth hath a special gift in shooting deer, and never misses the heart or the brain; so that the blood is not driven through the flesh, as happens too often with us. It is a hart of grease—your holiness has seldom seen such a haunch."

"Silence, Brother Hilarius," said the Abbot, wiping his mouth; "it is not beseeming our order to talk of food so earnestly, especially as we must oft have our animal powers exhausted by fasting, and be accessible (as being ever mere mortals) to those signs of longing (he again wiped his mouth) which arise on the mention of victuals to an hungry man.—Minute down, however, the name of that youth—it is fitting merit should be rewarded, and he shall hereafter be a *frater ad succurendum* in the kitchen and buttery."

"Alas! reverend Father, and my good lord," replied the Refectioner, "I did enquire after the youth, and I learn he is one who prefers the casque to the cowl, and the sword of the flesh to the weapons of the spirit."

"And if it be so," said the Abbot, "see that thou retain him as a deputy-keeper and man-at-arms, and not as a lay brother of the Monastery—for old Tallboy, our forester, waxes dim-eyed, and hath twice spoiled a noble buck, by hitting him unwarily on the haunch. Ah! 'tis a foul fault, the abusing by evil-killing, evil-dressing, evil-appetite, or otherwise, the good creatures indulged to us for our use. Wherefore, secure us the services of this youth, Brother Hilarius, in the way that may best suit him.—And now, Sir Piercie Shafton, since the fates have assigned us a space of well nigh an hour, ere we dare hope to enjoy more than the vapour or savour of our repast, may I pray you, of your courtesy, to tell me the cause of this visit; and, above all, to inform us, why you will not approach our more pleasant and better furnished *hospitium?*"

"Reverend Father, and my very good lord," said Sir Piercie Shafton, "your wisdom well knows that there are stone-walls which have ears, and that is to be looked to in matters which concern a man's head."

The Abbot signed to his attendants, excepting the Sub-Prior, to leave the room, and then said, "Your valour, Sir Piercie, may freely unburthen yourself before our faithful friend and counsellor Father Eustace, the benefits of whose advice we may too soon lose, inasmuch as his merits will speedily recommend him to an higher station, in which, we trust, he may find the blessing of a friend and adviser as valuable as himself, since I may say of him, as our claustral rhime goeth,[*]

> Dixit Abbas ad prioris,
> Tu es homo boni moris,
> Quia semper sanioris
>   Mihi das concilia.

Indeed," he added, "the office of Sub-Prior is altogether beneath our dear brother; nor can we elevate him unto that of Prior, which, for certain reasons, is at present kept vacant amongst us. Howbeit, Father Eustace is fully possessed of my confidence, and worthy of yours, and well may it be said of him, *Intravit in secretis nostris.*"

---

[*] The rest of this doggrel rhime may be found in Fosbrooke's learned work on British Monachism.

Sir Piercie Shafton bowed to the reverend brethren, and, heaving a sigh, as if he would have burst his steel-cuirass, he thus commenced his speech.

"Certes, reverend sirs, I may well heave such a suspiration, who have, as it were, exchanged heaven for purgatory, leaving the lightsome sphere of the royal court of England, for a remote nook in this inaccessible desert—quitting the tilt-yard, where I was ever ready among my compeers to splinter a lance, either for the love of honour, or for the honour of love, in order to couch my knightly spear against base and pilfering besognios and marauders—exchanging the lighted halls, wherein I used nimbly to pace the swift coranto, or to move with a loftier grace in the stately galliard, for this rugged and decayed dungeon of rusty-coloured stone—quitting the gay theatre, for the solitary chimney-nook of a Scottish dog-house—bartering the sounds of the soul-ravishing lute, and the love-awakening viol-de-gamba, for the discordant squeak of a northern bag-pipe—above all, exchanging the smiles of these beauties, who form a galaxy around the throne of England, for the cold courtesy of an untaught damsel, and the bewildered stare of a miller's maiden. More might I say, of the exchange of the conversation of gallant knights and gay courtiers of mine own order and capacity, whose conceits are bright and vivid as the lightning, for that of monks and churchmen—but it were discourteous to urge that topic."

The Abbot listened to this list of complaints with great round eyes, which evinced no exact intelligence of the orator's meaning; and when the knight paused to take breath, he looked with a doubtful and enquiring eye at the Sub-Prior, not well knowing in what tone he should reply to an exordium so extraordinary. The Sub-Prior accordingly stepped in to the relief of his principal.

"We deeply sympathize with you, Sir Knight, in the several mortifications and hardships to which fate has subjected you, particularly in that which has thrown you into the society of those, who, as they were conscious they deserved not such an honour, so neither did they at all desire it. But all this goes little way to expound the cause of this train of disasters, or, in plainer words, the reason which has compelled you into a situation having so few charms for you."

"Gentle and reverend sir," replied the knight, "forgive an unhappy person, who, in giving a history of his miseries, dilateth upon their extremity, even as he who, having fallen from a precipice, looketh upward to measure the height from which he hath been precipitated."

"Yea, but," said Father Eustace, "methinks it were wiser in him to tell those who come to lift him up, which of his bones have been broken."

"You, reverend sir," said the knight, "have, in the encounter of our wits, made a fair attaint;* whereas I might be in some sort said to have broken my staff across. Pardon me, grave sir, that I speak the language of the tilt-yard, which is doubtless strange to your reverend ears.— Ah! brave resort of the noble, the fair, and the gay!—Ah! throne of love, and citadel of honour!—Ah! celestial beauties, by whose bright eyes it is graced! Never more shall Piercie Shafton advance, the centre of your radiant glances, couch his lance, and spur his horse at the sound of the spirit-stirring trumpets, nobly called the voice of war —never more shall he baffle his adversary's encounter boldly, break his spear dexterously, and ambling around the lovely circle, receive the rewards with which beauty honours chivalry!"

Here he paused, wrung his hands, looked upward, and seemed lost in contemplation of his own fallen fortunes.

"Mad, very mad," whispered the Abbot to the Sub-Prior; "I would we were fairly shot of him, for of a truth, I expect he will proceed from raving to mischief—Were we not better call up the rest of the brethren?"

But the Sub-Prior knew better than his Superior how to distinguish the jargon of affectation from the ravings of insanity, and although the extremity of the knight's passion seemed altogether fantastic, yet he was not ignorant to what extravagancies the fashion of the day can conduct its votaries.

Allowing, therefore, two minutes space to permit the knight's enthusiastic feelings to exhaust themselves, he again gravely reminded him that the Lord Abbot had undertaken a journey, unwonted to his age and habits, solely to learn in what he could serve Sir Piercie Shafton—that it was altogether impossible he could do so without his receiving distinct information of the situation in which he had now sought refuge in Scotland—"The day wore on," he observed, looking at the window; "and if the Abbot should be obliged to return to the Monastery without obtaining the necessary intelligence, the regret might be mutual, but the inconvenience was like to be all on Sir Piercie's own side."

The hint was not thrown away.

"O, goddess of courtesy!" said the knight, "can I have so far forgotten thy behests, as to make this good prelate's ease and time a sacrifice to my vain complaints! Know, then, most worthy, and not less worshipful, that I, your poor visitor and guest, am by birth nearly

---

* *Attaint* was a term of tilting used to express the champion's having *attained* his mark, or, in other words, struck his lance straight and fair against the helmet, or breast of his adversary. Whereas to break the lance across, intimated a total failure in directing the point of the weapon on the object of his aim.

bound to the Piercie of Northumberland, whose fame is so widely blown through all parts of the world where English worth hath been known. Now this present Earl of Northumberland, of whom I propose to give you the brief history"——

"It is altogether unnecessary," said the Abbot; "we know him well to be a good and true nobleman, and a sworn upholder of our Catholic faith, in the spite of the heretical woman who now sits upon the throne of England. And it is specially as his kinsman, and as knowing that ye partake with him in such devout and faithful belief and adherence to our holy mother church, that we say to you, Sir Piercie Shafton, that ye be heartily welcome to us, and that an we wist how, we would labour to do you good service in your extremity."

"For such kind offer, I rest your most humble debtor," said Sir Piercie; "nor need I at this moment say more than that my Right Honourable Cousin of Northumberland, having devised with me and some others the choice and picked spirits of the age, how and by what means the worship of God, according to the Catholic church, might be again introduced into this distracted kingdom of England, (even as one deviseth, by the assistance of his friend, to catch and to bridle a run-away steed,) it pleased him so deeply to entrust me in those communications, that my personal safety becomes as it were entwined or complicated therewith. Natheless, as we have had sudden reason to believe, this Princess Elizabeth, who maintaineth around her a sort of counsellors skilful in tracking whatever schemes may be pursued for bringing her title into challenge, or for erecting again the discipline of the Catholic church, has obtained certain knowledge of the trains which we had laid before we could give fire unto them. Wherefore, my Right Honourable Cousin of Northumberland, thinking it best belike that one man should take both blame and shame for the whole, did lay the burthen of all this trafficking upon my back; with which I am the rather content to bear, in that he hath always shewn himself my kind and honourable kinsman, as well as that my estate, I wot not how, hath of late been somewhat insufficient to maintain the expence of those braveries, wherewith it is incumbent on us, who are chosen and selected spirits, to distinguish ourselves from the vulgar."

"So that possibly," said the Sub-Prior, "your private affairs rendered a foreign journey less incommodious to you than it might have been to the noble earl, your right worthy cousin."

"You are right, reverend sir," answered the courtier; "*rem acu*—you have touched the point with a needle—My cost and expences had been indeed somewhat lavish at the late triumphs and tourneys, and the flat-capp'd citizens had shewn themselves unwilling to furnish my pocket for new gallantries for the honour of the nation, as well as for mine own peculiar glory—and, to speak truth, it was in some part the hope of seeing these matters amended that led me to desire a new world in England."

"So that the miscarriage of your public enterprize, with the derangement of your own private affairs," said the Sub-Prior, "have induced you to seek Scotland as a place of refuge."

"*Rem acu*, once again," said Sir Piercie; "and not without good cause, since my neck, had I remained, might have been brought within the circumstances of an halter—And so speedy was my journey northward, that I had but time to exchange my murrey-coloured doublet of Genoa velvet, thickly laid over with goldsmith's work, for this cuirass, which was made by Bonamico of Milan, and travelled northward with all speed, judging that I might do well to visit my Right Honourable Cousin of Northumberland at one of his numerous castles. But as I posted towards Alnwick, even with the speed of a star, which, darting from its native sphere, shoots wildly downwards, I was met at Northallerton by one Henry Vaughan, a servant of my right honourable kinsman, who shewed me, that as then I might not with my safety come to his presence, seeing that in obedience to orders from his court, he was obliged to issue out letters for my incarceration."

"This," said the Abbot, "seems but hard measure on the part of your honourable kinsman."

"It might be so judged, my lord," replied Sir Piercie; "nevertheless I will stand to the death for the honour of my Right Honourable Cousin of Northumberland. Also, Henry Vaughan gave me, from my said cousin, a good horse, and a purse of gold, with two Border-prickers as they are called, for my guides, who conducted me, by such roads and bye-paths as have never been seen since the days of Sir Lancelot and Sir Tristrem, into this kingdom of Scotland, and to the house of a certain baron, or one who holds the style of such, called Julian Avenel, with whom I found such reception as the place and party could afford."

"And that," said the Abbot, "must have been right wretched; for, to judge from the appetite which Julian sheweth when abroad, he hath not, I judge, over-abundant provision at home."

"You are right, sir—your reverence is in the right—we had but lenten fare, and, what was worse, a score to clear at the departure; for though this Julian Avenel called us to no reckoning, yet he did so extravagantly admire the fashion of my poniard—the *poignet* being of silver exquisitely hatched, and indeed the weapon being altogether a piece of exceeding rare device and beauty—that in faith I could not for very shame's sake but pray his acceptance of it, words which he gave me not the trouble of repeating twice, before he had stuck it into his greasy buff-belt, where, credit me, reverend sir, it shewed more like a butcher's knife than a gentleman's dagger."

"So goodly a gift might at least have purchased you a few days hospitality," said Father Eustace.

"Reverend sir," said Sir Piercie, "had I abidden with him, I should have been complimented out of every remnant of my wardrobe—actually flayed, by the hospitable gods I swear it! Sir, he secured my spare doublet, and had a pluck at my gally-gaskins—I was enforced to beat a retreat before I was altogether unrigged. In good time I received a letter from my right honourable cousin, shewing me that he had written to you in my behalf, and sent to your charge two mails filled with wearing apparel—namely, my rich crimson silk doublet, slashed out and lined with cloth of gold, which I wore at the last revels, with baldric and trimmings to correspond—also two pair black silk slops, with hanging garters of carnation silk—also the flesh-coloured silken doublet, with the trimmings of fur, in which I danced the salvage man at the Gray's-Inn mumming—also"——

"Sir Knight," said the Sub-Prior, "I pray you to spare the further inventory of your wardrope—the Monks of Saint Mary's are no free-booting barons, and whatever part of your vestments have arrived at our house, have been this day faithfully brought hither, with the mails which contained them. I may presume from what has been said, as we have indeed been in sort given to understand by the Earl of Northumberland, that your desire is to remain for the present as unknown and as unnoticed, as may be consistent with your high worth and distinction?"

"Alas, reverend father!" replied the courtier, "a blade when it is in the scabbard cannot give lustre, a diamond when it is in the casket cannot give light, and worth, when it is compelled by circumstances to obscure itself, cannot draw observation—my retreat can only attract the admiration of those few to whom circumstances permit its displaying itself."

"I conceive now, my venerable father and lord," said the Sub-Prior, "that your wisdom will assign such a course of conduct to this noble knight, as may be alike consistent with his safety, and with the weal of the community. For you wot well what perilous strides have been made in these audacious days, to the destruction of all ecclesiastical foundations, and that our holy community has been repeatedly menaced. Hitherto they have found no flaw in our raiment; but a party friendly as well to the Queen of England, as to the heretical doctrines of her schismatical church, or even to worse and wilder forms of heresy, prevails now at the court of our sovereign, who dare not yield to her suffering clergy the protection she would gladly extend to them."

"My lord, and reverend sir," said the knight, "I will gladly relieve ye of my presence while ye canvass this matter at your freedom; and to speak truly, I am desirous to see in what case the chamberlain of my noble kinsman hath found my wardrope, and how he hath packed the same, and whether it has suffered from the journey—there are four suits of as pure and elegant device as ever the fancy of a fair lady doated upon, every one having a treble and appropriate change of ribbons, trimmings, and fringes, which, in case of need, may as it were renew each of them, and multiply the four into twelve.—There is also my sad-coloured riding-suit, and three cut-work shirts with falling bands—I pray you, pardon me—I must needs see how matters stand with them without farther dallying."

Thus speaking, he left the room; and the Sub-Prior, looking after him significantly, added, "Where the treasure is will the heart be also."

"Saint Mary preserve our wits!" said the Abbot, stunned with the knight's abundance of words; "were man's brains ever so stuffed with silk and broad-cloth, cut-work, and I wot not what besides!—and what could move the Earl of Northumberland to assume for his bosom counsellor, in matters of depth and danger, such a feather-brained coxcomb as this!"

"Had he been other than what he is, venerable father," said the Sub-Prior, "he had been less fitted for the part of scape-goat, to which his right honourable cousin had probably destined him from the commencement, in case of their plot failing. I know something of this Piercie Shafton. The legitimacy of his mother's descent from the Piercie family, the point on which he is most jealous, hath been called in question. If hair-brained courage, and an outrageous spirit of gallantry, can make good his pretensions to the high lineage he claims, these qualities have never been denied him. For the rest, he is one of the ruffling gallants of the time, like Rowland Yorke, Stukely, and others, who wear out their fortunes, and endanger their lives, in idle braveries, in order that they may be the only choice gallants of the time; and afterwards endeavour to repair their estate, by engaging in the desperate plots and conspiracies which wiser heads have devised. To use one of his own conceited similitudes, such courageous fools resemble hawks, which the wiser conspirator keeps hooded and blindfolded on his wrist until the quarry is on the wing, and who are then flown at them."

"Saint Mary," said the Abbot, "he were an evil guest to introduce into our quiet household. Our young monks make bustle enough, and more than is beseeming God's servants, about their outward attire already—this knight were enough to turn their brains, from the

Vestiarius down to the very scullion boy."

"A worse evil might follow," said the Sub-Prior: "In these bad days, the patrimony of the church is bought and sold, forfeited and distrained, as if it were the unhallowed soil appertaining to a secular baron. Think what penalty awaits us, were we convicted of harbouring a rebel to Her whom they call the Queen of England! There would neither be wanting Scottish parasites to beg the lands of the foundation, nor an army from England to burn and harry the Halidome. The men of Scotland were once Scotsmen, firm and united in their love to their country, and throwing every other consideration aside when the frontier was menaced—now they are—what shall I call them—the one part French, the other part English, considering their dear native country merely as a prize-fighting stage, upon which foreigners are welcome to decide their quarrels."

"Benedicite," replied the Abbot, "they are indeed slippery and evil times."

"And therefore," said Father Eustace, "we must walk warily—we must not, for example, bring this man—this Sir Piercie Shafton, to our house of Saint Mary's."

"But how then shall we dispose of him?" replied the Abbot; "bethink thee that he is a sufferer for Holy Church's sake—that his patron, the Earl of Northumberland, hath been our friend, and that, lying so near us, he may work us weal or woe according as we deal with his kinsman."

"And, accordingly," said the Sub-Prior, "for these reasons, as well as for discharge of the great duty of Christian charity, I would protect and relieve this man. Let him not go back to Julian Avenel—this unconscientious baron would not stick to plunder the exiled stranger —Let him remain here—the spot is secluded, and if the accommodation be beneath his quality, discovery will become the less likely. We will make such means for his convenience as we can devise."

"Will he be persuaded, thinkest thou?" said the Abbot; "I will leave my own travelling bed for his repose, and send up a suitable easy-chair."

"With such easements," said the Sub-Prior, "he must not complain; and then if threatened by any sudden danger, he can soon come down to the sanctuary, where we will harbour him in secret until means can be devised of dismissing him in safety."

"Were we not better," said the Abbot, "send him on to the court, and get rid of him at once?"

"Ay, but at the expence of our friends—this butterfly may fold his wings, and lie under cover in the cold air of Glendearg; but were he at Holyrood, he would, did his life depend on it, expand his spangled drapery in the eyes of the queen and court—Rather than fail of distinction, he would sue for love to our gracious sovereign—the eyes of all men would be upon him in the course of three short days, and the international peace of the two ends of the island endangered for a creature, who, like a silly moth, cannot abstain from fluttering round a light."

"Thou hast prevailed with me, Father Eustace," said the Abbot, "and it will go hard but I improve on thy plan—I will send up in secret, not only household stuff, but wine and wassell-bread. There is a young swankie here who shoots venison well. I will give him directions to see that the knight lacks none."

"Whatever accommodation he can have, which infers not a risk of discovery," said the Sub-Prior, "it is our duty to afford him."

"Nay," said the Abbot, "we will do more, and will instantly dispatch an express servant to the keeper of our revestry to send us such things as he may want, even this night. See it done, good father."

"I will," answered Father Eustace; "but I hear the gull clamorous for some one to truss his points.* He will be fortunate if he lights on any one here, who can do him the office of groom of the chamber."

"I would he would appear," said the Abbot, "for here comes the Refectioner with the collation—By my faith, the ride hath given me a sharp appetite."

Chapter Six

> I'll seek for other aid— Spirits, they say,
> Flit round invisible, as thick as motes
> Dance in the sunbeam. If that spell
> Or necromancer's sigil can compel them,
> They shall hold council with me.
>   JAMES DUFF

THE READER'S attention must be recalled to Halbert Glendinning, who had left the tower of Glendearg immediately after his quarrel with its new guest Sir Piercie Shafton. As he walked with a rapid pace up the glen, old Martin followed him, beseeching him to be less hasty.

"Halbert," said the old man, "you will never live to have white hair, if you take fire thus at every spark of provocation."

"And why should I wish it, old man," said Halbert, "if I am to be the butt that every fool may aim a shaft of scorn against?—What avails it, old man, that you yourself move, sleep and wake, eat thy niggard meal, and repose on thy hard pallet?—Why art thou so well pleased that the

---

* The points were the strings of cord or ribbon, (so called, because *pointed* with metal like the laces of women's stays), which attached the doublet to the hose. They were very numerous, and required assistance to tie them properly, which was called *trussing*.

morning should call you up to daily toil, and the evening again lay you down a wearied-out wretch? Were it not better sleep and wake no more, than to undergo this dull exchange of labour for insensibility, and of insensibility for labour?"

"God help me," answered Martin, "there may be truth in what thou sayest—but walk slower, for my old limbs cannot keep pace with your young legs—walk slower, I say, and I will tell thee why age, though unlovely, is yet endurable."

"Speak on then," said Halbert, slackening his pace; "but remember we must seek venison to refresh the fatigues of these holy men, who will this morning have achieved a journey of six miles—and if we reach not the Brocksburn head, we are scarce like to see an antler."

"Then know, my good Halbert," said Martin, "whom I love as my own son, that I am satisfied to live till death calls me, because my Maker wills it. Aye, and although I spend what men call a hard life, pinched with cold in winter, and burned with heat in summer, though I feed hard and sleep hard, and am held mean and despised, yet I bethink me, that were I of no use on the face of this fair creation, God would withdraw me from it."

"Thou poor old man," said Halbert, "and can such a vain conceit as this of thy fancied use, reconcile thee to a world where thou playst so poor a part?"

"My part was nearly as poor," said Martin, "my person nearly as much despised, the day that I saved my mistress and her child from perishing in the wilderness."

"Right, Martin," answered Halbert, grasping his hand; "there, indeed, thou didst what might be a sufficient apology for a whole life of insignificance."

"And do you account it for nothing, Halbert, that I should have the power of giving you a lesson of patience and submission to the destinies of Providence? Methinks there is use for the grey hairs in the land, were it but to instruct the green head by precept and by example."

Halbert held down his face, and remained silent for a minute or two, and then resumed his discourse: "Martin, seest thou ought changed in me of late?"

"Surely," said Martin. "I have always known you hasty, wild, and inconsiderate, rude, and prompt to speak at the volley and without reflection; but now, methinks, your bearing, without losing its natural fire, has something in it of force and dignity which it had not before. It seems as if you had fallen asleep a carle, and awakened a gentleman."

"Thou canst judge, then, of noble bearing?" said Halbert.

"Surely," answered Martin, "in some sort I can; for I have travelled through court, and camp, and city, with my master Walter Avenel, although he could do nothing for me but give me room for two score of sheep on the hill—And surely even now, while I speak with you, I feel sensible that my language is more refined than it is my wont to use, and that—though I know not the reason—the rude northern dialect, so familiar to my tongue, has given place to a more town-bred speech."

"And this change in thyself and me, thou can'st by no means account for?"

"Change!" replied Martin, "by Our Lady, it is not so much a change which I feel, as a recalling and renewal of sentiments and expressions which I had some thirty years since, ere Tibb and I set up our humble household. It is singular, that your society should have this sort of influence over me, Halbert, and that I should never have experienced it ere now."

"Think'st thou," said Halbert, "thou seest in me aught that can raise me from this base, low and despised state, into one where I may rank with those proud men, who now despise my clownish poverty?"

Martin paused an instant, and then answered, "Doubtless you may, Halbert; as broken a ship has come to land. Heard ye never of Hughie Dun, who left this Halidome some thirty-five years gone by? —a deliverly fellow was Hughie—could read and write like a priest, and could wield brand and buckler with the best of the riders. I mind him well—the like of him was never seen in the Halidome of Saint Mary's, and so was seen of the preferment that God sent him."

"And what was that?" said Halbert, his eyes sparkling with eagerness.

"Nothing less," answered Martin, "than body-servant to the Archbishop of Saint Andrews!"

Halbert's countenance fell.—"A servant—and to a priest? Was this all that knowledge and activity could raise him to?"

Martin, in his turn, looked with wistful surprise in the face of his young friend. "And to what could fortune lead him farther?" answered he. "The son of a kirk-feuar is not the stuff that lords and knights are made of—courage and scholar-craft cannot change churl's blood into gentle blood, I trow. I have heard, forbye, that Hughie Dun left a good five hundred punds of Scots money to his only daughter, and that she married the Bailie of Pittenweem."

At this moment, and while Halbert was embarrassed with devising a suitable answer, a deer bounded across their path. In an instant the cross-bow was at the youth's shoulder, the bolt whistled, and the deer, after giving one bound upright, dropt dead on the green sward.

"There lies the venison our dame wanted," said Martin; "who would have thought of an out-lying stag being so low down the glen at this season?—And it is a hart of grease too—in full season, and three inches of fat on the brisket. Now this is all your luck, Halbert, that follows you, go where you like. Were you to put in for it, I would warrant you were made one of the Abbot's yeomen-prickers, and ride about in a purple doublet as bold as the best."

"Tush, man," answered Halbert, "I will serve the Queen, or no one. Take thou care to have down the venison to the tower, since they expect it. I will on to the moss. I have two or three bird-bolts at my girdle, and it may be I shall find wild-fowl."

He hastened his pace, and was soon out of sight. Martin paused for a moment, and looked after him. "There goes the making of a right gallant stripling, an' ambition have not the spoiling of him—Serve the Queen, said he? By my faith, and she hath worse servants, from all that I e'er heard of them. And wherefore should he not keep a high heart? They that ettle to the top of the ladder will at least get up some rounds. They that mint* at a gown of gold, will always get a sleeve of it. But come, sir, (addressing the stag) you shall go to Glendearg on my two legs somewhat more slowly than you were frisking it even now on your own four nimble shanks. Nay by my faith, if you be so heavy, I will content me with the best of you, and that's the haunch and the nombles, and e'en heave up the rest on the old oak-tree yonder, and come for it with one of the yauds."†

While Martin returned to Glendearg with the venison, Halbert prosecuted his walk, breathing more easily since he was free of his companion. "The domestic of a proud and lazy priest—body-squire to the Arch-bishop of Saint Andrews," he repeated to himself; "and this, with the privilege of allying his blood with the Bailie of Pittenweem, is thought a preferment worth a brave man struggling for;— nay more, a preferment which, if attained, should crown the hopes, past, present, and to come, of the son of a kirk-vassal! By Heaven, but that I find in me a reluctance to practise their acts of nocturnal rapine, I would rather take the jack and lance, and join with the Border-riders.—Something I will do. Here, degraded and dishonoured, I will not live the scorn of each whiffling stranger from the South, because, forsooth, he wears tinkling spurs on a tawny boot. This thing—this phantom, be it what it will, I will see it once more. Since I spoke with her, and touched her hand, thoughts and feelings have dawned on me, of which my former life had not even dreamed; and shall I, who feel my father's glen too narrow for my expanding spirit, brook to be

---

* *Mint*—aim at.

† *Yauds*—horses; more particularly horses of labour.

bearded in it by this vain gew-gaw of a courtier, and in the sight too of Mary Avenel? I will not stoop to it—by Heaven!"

As he spoke thus, he arrived in the sequestered glen of Corri-nan-shian, as it verged upon the hour of noon. A few moments he remained looking upon the fountain, and doubting in his own mind with what countenance the White Lady might receive him. She had not indeed expressly forbidden his again evoking her; but yet there was something like such a prohibition implied in the farewell, which recommended him to wait for another guide.

Halbert Glendinning did not long, however, allow himself to pause. Hardihood was the natural characteristic of his mind; and under the expansion and modification which his feelings had lately undergone, it had been augmented rather than diminished. He drew his sword, undid the buskin from his foot, bowed three times with deliberation towards the fountain, and as often towards the tree, and repeated the same rhyme as formerly.—

> "Thrice to the holly-brake—
>   Thrice to the well:—
> I bid thee awake,
>   White Maid of Avenel.
> Noon gleams on the lake—
>   Noon glows on the fell—
> Wake thee, O wake,
>   White Maid of Avenel."

His eye was on the holly-bush as he spoke the last line; and it was not without an involuntary shuddering that he saw the air betwixt his eye and that object become more dim, and condense as it were into the faint appearance of a form, through which, however, so thin and transparent was the first appearance of the phantom, he could still discover the outline of the bush, as through a veil of fine crape. Gradually, however, it darkened into a more substantial appearance, and the White Lady stood before him with displeasure on her brow. She spoke, and her speech was still song, or rather measured chaunt; but, as if now more familiar, it flowed occasionally in modulated blank-verse, and at other times in the lyrical measure which she had used at their former meeting.

> "This is the day when the fairy kind
> Sit weeping alone for their hopeless lot,
> And the wood-maiden sighs to the sighing wind,
> And the mer-maiden weeps in her crystal grot;
> For this is the day that a deed was wrought,
> In which we have neither part nor share,
> For the children of clay was salvation bought,
> But not for the forms of sea or air!
> And ever the mortal is most forlorn,
> Who meeteth our race on the Friday morn."

"Spirit," said Halbert Glendinning, boldly, "it is bootless to threaten one who holds his life at no rate. Thine anger can but slay me; nor do I think thy power extendeth, or thy will stretcheth, so far. The terrors which your race practice upon others, are vain against me. My heart is hardened against fear, as by a sense of despair. If I am, as thy words infer, of a race more peculiarly the care of Heaven than thine, it is mine to call, and must be thine to answer. I am the nobler."

As he spoke, the figure looked upon him with a fierce and ireful countenance, which, without losing the resemblance of that which it usually exhibited, had a wilder and more exaggerated cast of features. The eyes seemed to contract and become more fiery, and slight convulsions passed over the face, as if it was about to be transformed into something hideous. The whole appearance resembled those faces which the imagination summons up when it is disturbed by laudanum, but which do not remain under its command, and, beautiful in their first appearance, become wild and grotesque ere we can arrest them.

But when Halbert had concluded his bold speech, the White Lady stood before him with the same pale, fixed, and melancholy aspect, which she usually bore. He had expected the agitation which she exhibited would conclude in some frightful metamorphosis. Folding her arms on her bosom, the phantom replied,

> "Daring youth! for thee it is well,
> Here calling me in haunted dell,
> That thy heart has not quail'd,
> Nor thy courage fail'd,
> And that thou could'st brook
> The angry look
> Of Her of Avenel.
> Did one limb shiver,
> Or an eye-lid quiver,
> Thou were lost for ever.
> Though I am form'd from the ether blue,
> And my blood is of the unfallen dew,
> And thou art framed of mud and dust,
> 'Tis thine to speak, reply I must."

"I demand of thee, then," said the youth, "by what charm it is that I am thus altered in mind and in wishes—that I think no longer of deer or dog, of bow or bolt—that my soul spurns the bounds of this obscure glen—that my blood boils at an insult from one by whose stirrup I would some days since have run for a whole summer's morn, contented and honoured by the notice of a single word? Why do I now seek to mate me with princes, knights and nobles?—Am I the same, who but yesterday, as it were, slumbered in contented obscurity, but who am to-day awakened to glory and ambition?—Speak—tell me, if thou canst, the meaning of this change?—Am I spell-bound—or have

I till now been under the influence of a spell, that I feel as another, yet am conscious of being the same? Speak, and tell me, is it to thy influence that the change is owing?"

The White Lady replied,

> "A mightier wizard far than I
> Wields o'er the universe his power;
> Him owns the eagle in the sky,
> The turtle in the bower.
> Changeful in shape, yet mightiest still,
> He wields the heart of man at will,
> From ill to good, from good to ill,
> In cot and castle-tower."

"Speak not thus darkly," said the youth, colouring so deeply, that face, neck, and hands were in a sanguine glow; "make me sensible of thy purpose."

The spirit answered,

> "Ask thy heart, whose secret cell
> Is fill'd with Mary Avenel!
> Ask thy pride, why scornful look
> In Mary's view it will not brook?
> Ask it, why thou seek'st to rise
> Among the mighty and the wise,—
> Why thou spurn'st thy lowly lot,—
> Why thy pastimes are forgot,—
> Why thou would'st in bloody strife
> Mend thy luck or lose thy life?
> Ask thy heart, and it shall tell,
> Sighing from its secret cell,
> 'Tis for Mary Avenel."

"Tell me, then," said Halbert, his cheek still deeply crimsoned, "thou who has said to me that which I dare not say to myself, by what means shall I urge my passion—by what means make it known?"

The White Lady replied,—

> "Do not ask me;
> On doubts like these thou can'st not task me.
> We only see the passing show
> Of human passions' ebb and flow;
> And view the pageant's idle glance
> As mortals eye the northern dance,
> When thousand streamers, flashing bright,
> Career it o'er the brow of night,
> And gazers mark their changeful gleams,
> But feel no influence from their beams."

"Yet thine own fate," replied Halbert, "unless men greatly err, is linked with that of mortals?"

The phantom answered,—

> "By ties mysterious linked, our fated race
> Holds strange connection with the sons of men.
> The star that rose upon the House of Avenel,

> When Norman Ulric first assumed the name,
> That star, when culminating in its orbit,
> Shot from its sphere a drop of diamond dew,
> And this bright font received it—and a Spirit
> Rose from the fountain, and her date of life
> Hath co-existence with the House of Avenel,
> And with the star that rules it."

"Speak yet more plain," answered young Glendinning; "of this I can nothing. Say, what hath forged thy wierded* link of destiny with the House of Avenel? say, especially, what fate now overhangs that house?"

The White Lady replied,—

> "Look on my girdle—on this thread of gold—
> 'Tis fine as web of lightest gossamer,
> And, but there is a spell on't, would not bind,
> Light as they are, the folds of my thin robe.
> But when 'twas donn'd, it was a massive chain,
> Such as might bind the champion of the Jews,
> Even when his locks were longest—it hath dwindled,
> Hath minished in its substance and its strength,
> As sunk the greatness of the House of Avenel.
> When this frail thread gives way, I to the elements
> Resign the principles of life they lent me.
> Ask me no more of this!—the stars forbid it."

"Then can'st thou read the stars," answered the youth, "and may'st tell me the fate of my passion, if thou can'st not aid it?"

The White Lady again replied,—

> "Dim burns the once bright star of Avenel,
> Dim as the beacon when the morn is nigh,
> And the o'er-wearied warder leaves the light-house;
> There is an influence sorrowful and fearful,
> That dogs its downward course. Disastrous passion,
> Fierce hate and rivalry, are in the aspect
> That lowers upon its fortunes."

"And rivalry?" repeated Glendinning; "it is then as I feared!—But shall that English silk-worm presume to beard me in my father's house, and in the presence of Mary Avenel?—Give me to meet him, spirit—give me to do away the vain distinction of rank on which he refuses me the combat. Place us on equal terms, and gleam the stars with what aspect they will, the sword of my father shall controul their influences."

She answered as promptly as before,

> "Complain not on me, child of clay,
> If to thy harm I yield the way.
> We, who soar thy sphere above,
> Know not aught of hate or love;
> As will or wisdom rules thy mood,
> My gifts to evil turn or good."

* _Wierded_—fated.

"Give me to redeem my honour," said Halbert Glendinning
——give me to retort on my proud rival the insults he has thrown on
me, and let the rest fare as it will. If I cannot revenge my wrong, I
shall sleep quiet, and know nought of my disgrace."

The phantom failed not to reply,

> "When Piercie Shafton boasteth high,
> Let this token meet his eye.
> The sun is westering from the dell,
> Thy wish is granted—fare thee well!"

As the White Lady spoke or sung these last words, she undid from
her locks a silver bodkin around which they were twisted, and gave it
to Halbert Glendinning; then shaking her dishevelled hair till it fell
like a veil around her, the outlines of her form gradually became as
diffuse as her flowing tresses, her countenance grew pale as the moon
in her first quarter, her features became indistinguishable, and she
melted into the air.

Habit inures us to wonders; but the youth did not find himself
alone by the fountain without experiencing, though in a much less
degree, the revulsion of spirits which he had felt upon the phantom's
former disappearance. A doubt strongly pressed upon his mind,
whether it were safe to avail himself of the gifts of a spirit which did not
even pretend to belong to the class of angels, and might, for aught he
knew, have a much worse lineage than that which she was pleased to
avow. "I will speak of it," he said, "to Edward, who is clerkly learned,
and will tell me what I should do. And yet, no—Edward is scrupulous
and wary.—I will prove the effect of her gift on Sir Piercie Shafton if
he again braves me, and by the issue, I will be myself a sufficient judge
whether there is danger in resorting to her counsels. Home, then,
home—and we shall soon learn whether that home shall longer hold
me; for not again will I brook insult, with my father's sword by my
side, and Mary for the spectator of my disgrace."

Chapter Seben

> I give thee eighteenpence a-day,
>   And my bow shalt thou bear,
> And over all the north country,
>   I make thee chief rydere.
> And I thirteenpence a-day, quoth the quene,
>   By god and by my faye,
> Come fetch thy payment when thou wilt,
>   No man shall say thee nay.
>   *William of Cloudesley*

THE MANNERS of the age did not permit the inhabitants of Glendearg to partake of the collation which was placed in the spence of that

ancient tower, before the Lord Abbot and his attendants, and Sir Piercie Shafton. Dame Glendinning was excluded, both by inferiority of rank and by sex; for, (though it was a rule often neglected,) the superior of Saint Mary's was debarred from taking his meals in female society. To Mary Avenel the latter, and to Edward Glendinning the former, incapacity attached; but it pleased his lordship to require their presence in the apartment, and to say sundry kind words to them upon the ready and hospitable reception which they had afforded him.

The smoking haunch now stood upon the table; a napkin, white as snow, was, with due reverence, tucked under the chin of the Abbot by the Refectioner; and nought was wanting to commence the repast, save the presence of Sir Piercie Shafton, who at length appeared, glittering like the sun, in a carnation-velvet doublet, slashed and puffed out with cloth of silver, his hat of the newest block, surrounded by a hat-band of goldsmith's work, while around his neck he wore a collar of gold, set with rubies and topazes so rich, that it vindicated his anxiety for the safety of his baggage from being entirely founded upon his love of mere finery. This gorgeous collar or chain, resembling those worn by the knights of the highest orders of chivalry, fell down on his breast, and terminated in a medallion.

"We waited for Sir Piercie Shafton," said the Abbot, hastily assuming his place in the great chair which the Kitchener advanced to the table with ready hand.

"I pray your pardon, reverend father and my good lord," replied that pink of courtesy; "I did but wait to cast my riding slough, and to transmew myself into some civil form meeter for this worshipful company."

"I cannot but praise your gallantry, Sir Knight," said the Abbot, "and your prudence also, for chusing the fitting time to appear thus adorned. Certes, had that goodly chain been visible in some part of your late progress, there was risk that the lawful owner might have parted company therewith."

"This chain, said your reverence?" answered Sir Piercie; "surely it is but a toy, a trifle, a slight thing which shews but poorly with this doublet—marry, when I wear that of the murrey-coloured, double-piled Genoa velvet, puffed out with ciprus, the gems, being relieved and set off by the darker and more grave ground of the stuff, show like stars giving a lustre through dark clouds."

"I nothing doubt it," said the Abbot, "but I pray you to sit down at the board."

But Sir Piercie had now got into his element, and was not easily interrupted—"I own," he continued, "that slight as the toy is, it might perchance have had some captivation for Julian—Santa Maria!" said

he, interrupting himself; "what was I about to say, and my fair and
beauteous Protection, or shall I rather term her my Discretion, here in
presence—Indiscreet had it been in your Affability, O most lovely
Discretion, to have suffered a stray word to have broke out of the pen-
fold of his mouth, that might overleap the fence of civility, and trespass
on the manor of decorum."

"Marry!" said the Abbot, somewhat impatiently, "the greatest discretion that I can see in the matter is, to eat our victuals being hot—
Father Eustace, say the Benedicite, and cut up the haunch."

The Sub-Prior readily obeyed the first part of the Abbot's injunction, but paused upon the second—"It is Friday, most reverend," he
said in Latin, desirous that the hint should escape, if possible, the ears
of the stranger.

"We are travellers," said the Abbot in reply, "and *viatoribus licitum
est*—you know the canon—a traveller must eat what food his hard fate
sets before him.—I grant you all a dispensation to eat flesh this day,
conditionally that you, brethren, say the Confiteor at curfew time, that
the knight give alms to his ability, and that all and each of you fast from
flesh on such day within the next month that shall seem most convenient; wherefore fall to and eat your food with cheerful countenances,
and you, Father Refectioner, *da mixtus*."

While the Abbot was thus stating the conditions on which his indulgence was granted, he had already half finished a slice of the noble
haunch, and now washed it down with a flagon of rhenish, modestly
tempered with water.

"Well is it said," he observed, as he requested from the Refectioner
another slice, "that virtue is its own reward; for though this is but
humble fare, and hastily prepared, and eaten in a poor chamber, I do
not remember me of having had such an appetite since I was a simple
brother in the Abbey of Dundrennan, and was wont to labour in the
garden from morning until nones, when our Abbot struck the *cymbalum*. Then would I enter keen with hunger, parched with thirst, (*da
mihi vinum quæso, et merum sit*,) and partake with appetite of whatever
was set before us, according to our rule; feast or fast-day, *caritas* or
penitentia, was the same to me. I had no stomach complaints then,
which now crave both the aid of wine and choice cookery, to render
my food acceptable to my palate, and easy of digestion."

"It may be, holy father," said the Sub-Prior, "an occasional ride to
the extremity of Saint Mary's patrimony, may have the same happy
effect on your health as the air of the garden at Dundrennan."

"Perchance, with our patroness's blessing, such progresses may
advantage us," said the Abbot; "having an especial eye that our venison is carefully killed by some woodsman that is master of his craft."

"If the Lord Abbot will permit me," said the Kitchener, "I think the best way to assure his lordship on that important point, would be to retain as a yeoman-pricker, or deputy-ranger, the eldest son of this good woman, Dame Glendinning, who is here to wait upon us. I should know by mine office what belongs to killing of game, and I can safely pronounce that never saw I, or any other *coquinarius*, a bolt so justly shot. It has cloven the very heart of the buck."

"What speak you to us of one good shot, father," said Sir Piercie; "I would avise you that such no more maketh a shooter, than doth one swallow make a summer—I have seen this springald of whom you speak, and if his hand can send forth his shafts as boldly as his tongue doth utter presumptuous speeches, I will own him as good an archer as Robin Hood."

"Marry," said the Abbot, "and it is fitting we know the truth of this matter from the dame herself, for ill-advised were we to give way to any rashness in this matter, whereby the bounties which heaven and our patroness provide might be unskilfully mangled, and rendered unfit for worthy men's use.—Stand forth, therefore, Dame Glendinning, and tell to us, as thy liege lord and spiritual Superior, using plainness and truth, without either fear or favour, as being a matter wherein we are deeply interested, Doth this son of thine use his bow as well as the Father Kitchener avers to us?"

"So please your noble fatherhood," answered Dame Glendinning, with a deep courtesy; "I should know somewhat of archery to my cost, seeing my husband—God assoilzie him!—was slain in the field of Pinkie with an arrow-shot, while he was fighting under the Kirk's banner, as became a liege vassal of the Halidome. He was a valiant man, please your reverence, and an honest; and saving that he loved a bit of venison, and shifted for his living at a time as Border-men will sometimes do, I wot nought of sin that he did. And yet, though I have paid for mass after mass to the matter of a forty shilling, besides a quarter of wheat and four firlots of rye, I can have no assurance yet that he has been delivered from purgatory."

"Dame," said the Lord Abbot, "this shall be looked into heedfully; and since thy husband fell, as thou sayest, in the Kirk's quarrel, and under her banner, rely upon it that we will have him out of purgatory forthwith—that is, always providing he be there.—But it is not of thy husband whom we now devise to speak, but of thy son; not of a shot Scotsman, but of a shot deer—Wherefore I say, answer me to the point, is thy son a practised archer, ay or no?"

"Alack! my reverend lord," answered the widow; "and my croft would be better tilled, if I could answer your reverence that he is not.—Practised archer!—marry, holy sir, I would he would practise something else—cross-bow and long-bow, hand-gun and hack-but, falconet and saker, he can shoot with them all. And if it would please this right honourable gentleman, our guest, to hold out his hat at the distance of an hundred yards, our Halbert shall send shaft, bolt, or bullet through it, (so the right honourable gentleman swerve not, but hold out steady,) and I will forfeit a quarter of barley if he touch but a knot of his ribbands. I have seen our old Martin do as much, and so has our right reverend the Sub-Prior, if he be pleased to remember it."

"I am not like to forget it, dame," said Father Eustace; "for I knew not which most to admire, the composure of the young marksman, or the steadiness of the old mark. Yet I presume not to advise Sir Piercie Shafton to subject his valuable beaver, and yet more valuable person, to such a risk, unless it should be his own especial pleasure."

"Be assured it is not," said Sir Piercie Shafton, something hastily, "be well assured, holy father, that it is not. I dispute not the lad's qualities, for which your reverence vouches. But bows are but wood, strings are but flax, or the silk worm excrement at best—archers are but men, fingers may slip, eyes may dazzle, the blindest may hit the butt, the best marker may shoot a bow's length beside. Therefore will we no perilous experiments."

"Be that as you will, Sir Piercie," said the Abbot; "meantime we will name this youth bow-bearer in the forest granted to us by good King David, that the chase might recreate our wearied spirits, the flesh of the deer improve our poor commons, and the hides cover the books of our library; thus tending at once to the sustenance of body and soul."

"Kneel down, woman, kneel down," said the Refectioner and the Kitchener, with one voice, to Dame Glendinning, "and kiss his lord-ship's hand, for the grace which he has granted to thy son."

They then, as if they had been chaunting the service and the responses, set off in a sort of duetto, enumerating the advantages of the situation.

"A green gown and a pair of leathern gally-gaskins every Pente-cost," said the Kitchener.

"Four merks by the year at Candlemas," answered the Refectioner.

"An hogshead of ale at Martlemas, of the double strike, and single ale at pleasure, as he shall agree with the Cellarer"——

"Who is a reasonable man," said the Abbot, "and will encourage an active servant of the convent."

"A mess of broth and a dole of mutton or beef, at the Kitchener's, on each high holiday," resumed the Kitchener.

"The gang of two cows and a palfrey on Our Lady's meadow," answered his brother officer.

"An ox-hide to make buskins of yearly, because of the brambles," echoed the Kitchener.

"And various other perquisites, *quæ nunc præscribere longum,*" said the Abbot, summing, with his own lordly voice, the advantages attached to the office of conventual bow-bearer.

Dame Glendinning was all this while on her knees, her head mechanically turning from the one church-officer to the other, which, as they stood one on each side of her, had much the appearance of a figure moved by clock-work, and so soon as they were silent, most devoutly did she kiss the munificent hand of the Abbot. Conscious, however, of Halbert's intractability in some points, she could not help qualifying her grateful and reiterated thanks for the Abbot's bountiful proffer, with a hope that Halbert would see his wisdom, and accept of it.

"How," said the Abbot, bending his brows, "accept of it? woman, is thy son in his right wits?"

Elspet, stunned by the tone in which this question was asked, was altogether unable to reply to it. Indeed, any answer she might have made could hardly have been heard, as it pleased the two office-bearers of the Abbot's table again to re-commence their alternate dialogue.

"Refuse?" said the Kitchener.

"Refuse?" answered the Refectioner, echoing the other's word in a tone of still louder astonishment.

"Refuse four merks by the year!" said the one.

"Ale and beer—broth and mutton—cow's-grass and palfrey's!" shouted the Kitchener.

"Gown and galligaskins!" responded the Refectioner.

"A moment's patience, my brethren," answered the Sub-Prior, "and let us not be thus astonished before cause is afforded of our amazement. This good dame best knoweth the temper and spirit of her son—thus much I can say, that it lieth not towards letters or learning, of which I have in vain endeavoured to instil in him some tincture. Nevertheless, he is a youth of no common spirit, but much like those (in my weak judgment) whom God raises up among a people when he meaneth that their deliverance shall be wrought out with strength of hand and valour of heart.—Such men we have seen marked by a waywardness, and even an obstinacy of character, which hath appeared intractability and stupidity to those among whom they walked and were conversant, until the very opportunity hath arrived in which it was the will of Providence that they should be the fitting instrument of great things."

"Now, in good time hast thou spoken, Father Eustace," said the

Abbot; "and we will see this swankie before we decide upon the means of employing him.—How say you, Sir Piercie Shafton, is it not the court fashion to suit the man to the office, and not the office to the man?"

"So please your reverence and lordship," answered the Northumbrian knight, "I do partly, that is, in some sort, subscribe to what your wisdom hath delivered. Nevertheless, under reverence of the Sub-Prior, we do not look for gallant leaders and national deliverers in the hovels of the mean common people. Credit me, that if there be some flashes of natural spirit about this young person, which I am not called upon to dispute, (though I have seldom seen that presumption and arrogance was made good upon the upshot by deed and action,) yet still these will prove unable to distinguish him, save in his own limited and lowly sphere—even as the glow-worm, which makes a goodly shew among the grass of the field, would be of little avail if deposited in a beacon-grate."

"Now, in good time," said the Sub-Prior, "and here comes the young huntsman to speak for himself;" for, being placed opposite to the window, he could observe Halbert as he ascended the little mound on which the tower was situated.

"Summon him to our presence," said the Lord Abbot; and with an obedient start the two attendant monks went off with emulous alertness. Dame Glendinning sprung away at the same moment, partly to gain an instant to recommend obedience to her son, partly to prevail with him to change his apparel, before coming in presence of the Abbot. But the Kitchener and Refectioner, both speaking at once, had already seized each an arm, and were leading Halbert in triumph into the apartment, so that she could only ejaculate, "His will be done—but an he had but had on him his Sunday's hose!"

Limited and humble as this desire was, the fates did not grant it, for Halbert Glendinning was hurried into the presence of the Lord Abbot and his party without a word of explanation, and without a moment's time being allowed to assume his holiday hose, which, in the language of the time, implied both breeches and stockings.

Yet though thus suddenly presented, and the centre of all eyes, there was something in Halbert's appearance which commanded a certain degree of respect from the company into which he was so unceremoniously intruded, and the greater part of whom were disposed to consider him with hauteur, if not with absolute contempt. But his appearance and reception we must devote to another chapter.

Chapter Eight

Now chuse thee, gallant, betwixt wealth and honour;
There lies the pelf, in sum to bear thee through
The dance of youth, and the turmoil of manhood,
Yet leave enough for age's chimney-corner;
But an thou grasp to it, farewell Ambition,
Farewell each hope of bettering thy condition,
And raising thy low rank above the churl's
That tills the earth for bread.

Old Play

IT IS NECESSARY to dwell for some brief space on the appearance and demeanour of young Glendinning, ere we proceed to describe his interview, at this momentous crisis of his life, with the Abbot of Saint Mary's.

Halbert was now about nineteen years old, tall and active rather than strong, yet of that hardy confirmation of limb and sinew, which promises great strength when the growth shall be complete and the system confirmed. He was perfectly well made, and like most men who have that advantage, possessed a grace and natural ease of manner and carriage, which prevented his height from being the distinguishing part of his external appearance. It was not until you had compared his stature with that of those amongst, or near to whom he stood, that you became sensible that the young Glendinning was upwards of six feet high. In the combination of unusual height, with perfect symmetry, ease, and grace of carriage, the young heir of Glendearg, notwithstanding his rustic birth and education, had greatly the advantage even of Sir Piercie Shafton himself, whose stature was lower, and his limbs, though there was no particular point to object to, were on the whole less exactly proportioned. On the other hand, Sir Piercie's very handsome countenance afforded him as decided an advantage over the Scotsman, as regularity of features and brilliance of complexion could give over traits which were rather strongly marked than beautiful, and upon whose complexion the "skyey influences," to which he was constantly exposed, had blended the red and white into the purely nut-brown hue, which coloured alike cheeks, neck, and forehead, and blushed only in a darker glow upon the former.—Halbert's eyes supplied a marked and distinguished part of his physiognomy. They were large and of a hazel colour, and sparkled in moments of animation, with such uncommon brilliancy, that it seemed as if they actually emitted light. Nature had closely curled the locks of dark-brown hair, which relieved and set off the features, such as we have described them, displaying a bold and animated disposition much more than might have been expected from his situation, or from his previous manners, which hitherto had seemed bashful, homely, and awkward.

Halbert's dress was certainly not of that description which sets off to the best advantage a presence of itself prepossessing. His jerkin and hose were of coarse russet cloth, and his cap of the same. A belt round his waist served at once to sustain the broad-sword which we have already mentioned, and to hold five or six arrows and bird-bolts, which were stuck into it on the right side, along with a large knife hilted with buck-horn, or, as it was then called, a dudgeon dagger. To complete his dress, we must notice his loose buskins of deer's-hide, formed so as to draw up on the leg as high as the knee, or at pleasure to be thrust down lower than the calves. These were generally used at the period by such as either had their principal occupation, or their chief pleasure, in sylvan sports, as they served to protect the legs against the rough and tangled thickets into which the pursuit of game frequently led them.—And these trifling particulars complete his external appearance.

It is not so easy to do justice to the manner in which young Glendinning's soul spoke through his eyes, when ushered so suddenly into the company of those whom his earliest education had taught him to treat with awe and reverence. The degree of embarrassment which his demeanour evinced, had nothing in it either meanly servile, or utterly disconcerted. It was no more than became a generous and ingenuous youth of a bold spirit, but totally inexperienced, who should for the first time be called upon to think and act for himself in such society, and under such disadvantageous circumstances. There was not in his carriage a grain either of forwardness or of timidity, which a friend could have wished away.

He kneeled and kissed the Abbot's hand, then rose, and retiring two paces, bowed respectfully to the circle around, smiling gently as he received an encouraging nod from the Sub-Prior, to whom alone he was personally known, and blushing as he encountered the anxious look of Mary Avenel, who beheld with painful interest the sort of ordeal to which her foster-brother was about to be subjected. Recovering from the transient flurry of spirits into which the encounter of her glance had thrown him, he stood composedly awaiting till the Abbot should express his pleasure.

The ingenuous expression of countenance, noble form, and graceful attitude of the young man, failed not to prepossess in his favour the churchmen in whose presence he stood. The Abbot looked round and exchanged a gracious and approving glance with his counsellor Father Eustace, although probably the appointment of a ranger, or bow-bearer, was one in which he might have been disposed to proceed without the Sub-Prior's advice, were it but to shew his own free agency. But the good mien of the young man now in nomination was such, that he rather hastened to exchange congratulation on meeting with so proper a subject of promotion, than to indulge any other feeling. Father Eustace enjoyed the pleasure which a well-constituted mind derives from seeing a benefit light on a deserving object; for as he had not seen Halbert since circumstances had made a material change in his manner and feelings, he scarce doubted that the proffered appointment would, notwithstanding his mother's uncertainty, suit the disposition of a youth who had appeared devoted to woodland sports, and a foe alike to sedentary or settled occupation. The Refectioner and Kitchener were so well pleased with Halbert's prepossessing appearance, that they seemed to think that the salary, emoluments, and perquisites, the dole, the grazing, the gown, and the galligaskins, could scarce be better bestowed than on the active and graceful figure before them.

Sir Piercie Shafton, whether from being more deeply engaged in his own cogitations, or that the subject was unworthy his notice, did not seem to partake of the general feeling of approbation excited by the young man's presence. He sate with his eyes half shut, and his arms folded, appearing to be wrapped in contemplations of a nature deeper than those arising out of the scene before him. But, notwithstanding his seeming abstraction and absence of mind, there was a flutter of vanity in Sir Piercie's very handsome countenance, an occasional change of posture from one striking attitude (or what he conceived to be such,) to another, and an occasional stolen glance at the female part of the company, to spy how far he succeeded in rivetting their attention, which gave a marked advantage, in comparison, to the less regular and more harsh features of Halbert Glendinning, with their composed, manly, and deliberate expression of mental fortitude.

Of the females belonging to the family of Glendearg, the Miller's daughter alone had her mind sufficiently at leisure to admire, from time to time, the graceful attitudes of Sir Piercie Shafton; for both Mary Avenel and Dame Glendinning were waiting in anxiety and apprehension the answer which Halbert was to return to the Abbot's proposal, and fearfully anticipating the consequences of his probable refusal. The conduct of his brother Edward was, for a lad constitutionally shy, respectful, and even timid, at once affectionate and noble. This younger son of Dame Elspet had stood unnoticed in a corner, after the Abbot, at the request of the Sub-Prior, had honoured him with some passing notice, and asked him a few common-place questions about his progress in Donatus, and in the *Promptuarium Parvu-*

lorum, without waiting for the answers. From his corner he now glided round to his brother's side, and keeping a little behind him, slid his right hand into the huntsman's left, and by a gentle pressure, which Halbert instantly and ardently returned, expressed at once his interest in his situation, and his resolution to share his fate.

The groupe was thus arranged, when, after the pause of two or three minutes, which he employed in slowly sipping his cup of wine, in order that he might enter on his proposal with due and deliberate dignity, the Abbot at length expressed himself thus:

"My son—we your lawful superior, and the Abbot, under God's favour, of the community of Saint Mary's, have heard of your manifold good gifts—a-hem—especially touching wood-craft—and the huntsman-like fashion in which you strike your game, truly and as a yeoman should, not abusing Heaven's good benefits by spoiling the flesh, as is too often seen in careless rangers. A-hem." He made here a pause, but observing that Glendinning only replied to his compliment by a bow, he proceeded,—"My son, we commend your modesty; nevertheless, we will that thou should'st speak freely to us touching that which we have premeditated for thine advancement, meaning to confer on thee the office of bow-bearer and ranger, as well over the chases and forests wherein our house hath privilege by the gifts of pious kings and nobles, whose souls now enjoy the fruits of their bounties to the church, as to those which belong to us in exclusive right of property and perpetuity. Thy knee, my son—that we may, with our own hand, and without loss of time, induct thee into office."

"Kneel down," said the Kitchener on the one side; and "Kneel down," said the Refectioner on the other.

But Halbert Glendinning remained standing.

"Were it to shew gratitude and good-will for your reverend lordship's noble offer, I could not," he said, "kneel low enow, or remain long enough kneeling. But I may not kneel to take investiture of your noble gift, my Lord Abbot, being a man determined to seek my fortune otherwise."

"How is that, sir?" said the Abbot, knitting his brows; "do I hear you speak aright? and do you, a born vassal of the Halidome, at the moment when I am destining to you such a noble expression of my good will, propose exchanging my service for that of any other?"

"My lord," said Halbert Glendinning, "it grieves me to think you hold me capable of undervaluing your gracious offer, or of exchanging your service for another. But your noble proffer doth but hasten the execution of a resolution which I have long since formed."

"Ay, my son," said the Abbot, "is it indeed so?—right early have you learned to form resolutions without consulting those on whom you naturally depend. And what may it be, this sagacious resolution, if I may so far pray you?"

"To yield up to my brother and mother," answered Halbert, "mine interest in the fief of Glendearg, lately possessed by my father, Simon Glendinning: and having prayed your lordship to be the same kind and generous master to them, that your predecessors, the venerable Abbots of Saint Mary's, have been to my fathers in time past, for myself, I am determined to seek my fortune where I may best find it."

Dame Glendinning here ventured, emboldened by maternal anxiety, to break silence with an exclamation of "O my son!" Edward, clinging to his brother's side, half spoke, half whispered a similar ejaculation, of "Brother! brother!"

The Sub-Prior took up the matter in a tone of graver reprehension, which, as he conceived, the interest he had always taken in the family of Glendearg required at his hand.

"Wilful young man," he said, "what folly can urge thee to push back the hand that is stretched out to aid thee? What visionary aim hast thou before thee, that can compensate for the decent and sufficient independence which thou art now rejecting with scorn?"

"Four marks by the year, duly and truly," said the Kitchener.

"Cow's-grass, doublet, and galligaskins," answered the Refectioner.

"Peace, my brethren," said the Sub-Prior; "and may it please your lordship, venerable father, upon my petition, to allow this headstrong youth a day for consideration, and it shall be my part so to endoctrinate him, as to convince him what is due on this occasion to your lordship, to his family, and to himself."

"Your kindness, reverend father," said the youth, "craves my dearest thanks—it is the continuance of a long train of benevolence towards me, for which I give you my gratitude, for I have nothing else to offer. It is my mishap, not your fault, that your intentions have been frustrated. But my present resolution is fixed and unalterable. I cannot accept the generous offer of the Lord Abbot; my fate calls me elsewhere, to scenes where I shall end it or mend it."

"By Our Lady," said the Abbot, "I think the youth be mad indeed—Or that you, Sir Piercie, judged of him most truly, when you prophesied that he would prove unfit for the promotion we designed him—it may be you knew something of this wayward humour before?"

"By the mass, not I," answered Sir Piercie Shafton, with his usual indifference. "I but judged of him from his birth and breeding; for seldom doth a good hawk come out of a kite's egg."

"Thou art thyself a kite, and a kestrel to boot," replied Halbert Glendinning, without a moment's hesitation.

"This in our presence, and to a man of worship!" said the Abbot, the blood rushing to his face.

"Yes, my lord," answered the youth; "even in your presence I return to this gay man's face, the causeless dishonour which he has flung on my name. My brave father, who fell in the cause of his country, demands that justice at the hands of his son!"

"Unmannered boy!" said the Abbot.

"Nay, my good lord," said the knight, "praying pardon for the coarse interruption, let me pray you not to be wroth with this rustical —Credit me, the north wind shall as soon puff one of your rocks from its basis, as ought which I hold so slight and inconsiderate as the churlish speech of an untaught churl, shall move the spleen of Piercie Shafton."

"Proud as you are, Sir Knight," said Halbert, "in your imagined superiority, be not too confident that thou can'st not be moved."

"Faith, by nothing that thou can'st urge," said Sir Piercie.

"Knowest thou then this token?" said young Glendinning, offering to him the silver bodkin which he had received from the White Lady.

Never was such an instant change, from the most contemptuous serenity, to the most furious state of passion, as that which Sir Piercie Shafton exhibited. It was the difference between a cannon standing loaded in its embrazure, and the same gun when touched by the linstock. He started up, every limb quivering with rage, and his features so inflamed and agitated by passion, that he more resembled a demoniac, than a man under the regulation of reason. He clenched both his fists, and thrusting them forward, offered them furiously at the face of Glendinning, who was even himself startled at the frantic state of excitation which his action had occasioned. The next moment he withdrew them, struck his open palm against his own forehead, and rushed out of the room in a state of indescribable agitation. The whole matter had been so sudden, that no person present had time to interfere.

When Sir Piercie Shafton had left the apartment, there was a moment's pause of astonishment; and then a general demand that Halbert Glendinning should instantly explain by what means he had produced such a violent change in the deportment of the English cavalier.

"I did nought to him," answered Halbert Glendinning, "but what you all saw—am I to answer for the fantastic freaks of humour?"

"Boy," said the Abbot, in his most authoritative manner, "these subterfuges shall not avail thee. This is not a man to be driven from his temperament without some sufficient cause. That cause was given by thee, and must have been known to thee. I command thee, as thou wilt save thyself from worse measure, to explain to me by what means thou hast moved our friend thus—We chuse not that our vassals shall drive our guests mad in our very presence, and we remain ignorant of the means whereby their purpose is effected."

"So may it please your reverence, I did but show him this token," said Halbert Glendinning, delivering it at the same time to the Abbot, who looked at it with much attention, and then, shaking his head, gravely delivered it to the Sub-Prior, without speaking a word.

Father Eustace looked at the mysterious token with some attention; and then addressing Halbert in a severe voice, said, "Young man, if thou wouldest not have us suspect thee of some strange double-dealing in this matter, let us instantly know whence thou had'st this token, and how it possesses an influence on Sir Piercie Shafton?"—It would have been extremely difficult for Halbert, thus hard pressed, to have either evaded or answered so puzzling a question. To have avowed the truth might, in these times, have occasioned his being burned at a stake, although, in ours, his confession would only have gained for him the credit of a liar beyond all rational credibility. He was fortunately relieved by the return of Sir Piercie Shafton himself, whose ear caught, as he entered, the sound of the Sub-Prior's question.

Without waiting until Halbert Glendinning replied, he came forward whispering to him as he passed, "Be secret—thou shalt have the satisfaction thou hast dared to seek for."

When he returned to his place, there were still marks of discomposure on his brow; but, becoming apparently collected and calm, he looked round him, and apologized for the indecorum of which he had been guilty, which he ascribed to sudden and severe indisposition. All were silent, and looked on each other with some surprise.

The Lord Abbot gave orders for all to retire from the apartment, save himself, Sir Piercie Shafton, and the Sub-Prior. "And have an eye," he added, "on that bold youth, that he escape not; for if he hath practised by charm, or otherwise, on the health of our worshipful guest, I swear by the alb and mitre which I wear, that his punishment shall be most exemplary."

"My lord and venerable father," said Halbert, bowing respectfully, "fear not that I will abide my doom. I think you will best learn from the worshipful knight himself, what is the cause of his distemperature, and how slight my share has been in it."

"Be assured," said the knight, without looking up, however, while he spoke, "I will satisfy the Lord Abbot."

With these words the company retired, and with them young Glendinning.

When the Abbot, the Sub-Prior, and the English knight were left alone, Father Eustace, contrary to his custom, could not help speaking the first. "Expound unto us, noble sir," he said, "by what mysterious means the production of this simple toy could so far move your spirit, and overcome your patience, after you had shewn yourself proof to all the provocation offered by this self-sufficient and singular youth?"

The knight took the silver bodkin from the good father's hand, looked at it with great composure, and having examined it all over, returned it to the Sub-Prior, saying at the same time, "In truth, venerable father, I cannot but marvel, that the wisdom implied alike in your silver hairs, and in your eminent rank, should, like to a babbling hound (excuse the similitude) open thus loudly on a false scent. I were, indeed, more slight to be moved than the leaves of the aspin tree, which wag at the least breath of heaven, could I be moved by such a trifle as this, which in no way concerns me more than if the same quantity of silver were stricken into so many groats. Truth is, that from my youth upward, I have been subjected to such a malady as you saw me visited with even now—a cruel and searching pain, which goeth through nerve and bone, even as a good brand in the hands of a brave soldier sheers through limb and sinew—but it passes away speedily, as you yourselves may judge."

"Still," said the Sub-Prior, "this will not account for the youth offering to you this piece of silver, as a token by which you were to understand something, and, as we must needs conjecture, something disagreeable."

"Your reverence is to conjecture what you will," said Sir Piercie; "but I cannot pretend to lay your judgment on the right scent when I see it at fault. I hope I am not liable to be called upon to account for the foolish actions of a malapert boy?"

"Assuredly," said the Sub-Prior, "we shall prosecute no enquiry which is disagreeable to our guest. Nevertheless," said he, looking to his Superior, "this chance may, in some sort, alter the plan your lordship had formed for your worshipful guest's residence for a brief term in this tower, as a place alike of secrecy and of security; both of which, in the terms which we now stand on with England, are circumstances to be desired."

"In truth," said the Abbot, "and the doubt is well thought on, were it as well removed. For I scarce know in the Halidome so fitting a place of refuge, yet see I not how to recommend it to our worshipful guest, considering the unrestrained petulance of this headstrong youth."

"Tush! reverend sirs,—what would you make of me?" said Sir Piercie Shafton. "I protest, by mine honour, I would abide in this house, to chuse. What! I take no exceptions at the youth for shewing a flash of spirit, though the spark may light on mine own hand. I honour the lad for it. I protest I will abide here, and he shall aid me in striking down a deer. I must needs be friends with him, an he be such a shot; and we will speedily send down to my Lord Abbot a buck of the first head, killed so artificially as shall satisfy even the reverend Kitchener."

This was said with such apparent ease and good-humour, that the Abbot made no farther observation on what had passed, but proceeded to acquaint his guest with the details of furniture, hangings, provisions, and so forth, which he purposed to send up to the Tower of Glendearg for his accommodation. This discourse, seasoned with a cup or two of wine, served to prolong the time until the reverend Abbot ordered his cavalcade to prepare for their return to the Monastery.

"As we have," he said, "in the course of this our toilsome journey, lost our meridian,* indulgence shall be given to those of our attendance who shall, from very weariness, be unable to attend the duty at prime,† and this by way of misericord or *indulgentia*."‡

Having benevolently intimated a boon to his faithful followers, which he probably judged would be far from unacceptable, the good Abbot, seeing all ready for his journey, bestowed his blessing on the assembled household—gave his hand to be kissed by Dame Glendinning—himself kissed the cheek of Mary Avenel, and even of the Miller's maiden, when they approached to render him the same homage—commanded Halbert to rule his temper, and to be aiding and obedient in all things to the English knight—admonished Edward to be *discipulus impiger atque strenuus*—then took a courteous farewell of Sir Piercie Shafton, advising him to lie close, for fear of the English Borderers, who might be employed to kidnap him; and, having discharged these various offices of courtesy, moved forth to the courtyard, followed by the whole establishment. Here, with a heavy sigh approached to a groan, the venerable father heaved himself upon his palfrey, whose dark purple housings swept the ground; and, greatly comforted that the discretion of the animal's pace would be no longer disturbed by the gambadoes of Sir Piercie and his prancing warhorse, he set forth at a sober and steady trot upon his return to the Monastery.

* The hour of repose at noon, which, in the middle ages, was employed in slumber, and which the monastic rules of nocturnal vigils rendered necessary.

† *Prime* was the midnight service of the Monks.

‡ *Misericord*, according to the learned work of Fosbrooke on British Monachism, meant not only an indulgence, or exoneration from particular duties, but also a particular apartment in a Convent, where the Monks assembled to enjoy such indulgences or allowances as were granted beyond the rule.

When the Sub-Prior had mounted to accompany his principal, his eye sought out Halbert, who, partly hidden by a projection of the outward wall of the court, stood apart from, and gazing upon the departing cavalcade, and the groupe which assembled around them. Unsatisfied with the explanation he had received concerning the mysterious transaction of the silver bodkin, yet interesting himself in the youth, of whose character he had formed a favourable idea, the worthy Monk resolved to take an early opportunity of investigating that matter. In the meanwhile, he looked upon Halbert with a serious and warning aspect, and held up his finger to him as he signed farewell. He then joined the rest of the churchmen, and followed his Superior down the valley.

Chapter Nine

> I hope you'll give me cause to think you noble,
> And do me right with your sword, sir, as becomes
> One gentleman of honour to another;
> All this is fair, sir—let us make no days on't,
> I'll lead your way.
>
> *Love's Pilgrimage*

THE LOOK and sign of warning which the Sub-Prior gave to Halbert Glendinning as they parted, went to his heart; for although he had profited much less than Edward by the good man's instructions, he had a sincere reverence for his person; and even the short time he had had for deliberation, tended to shew him he was embarked in a perilous adventure. The nature of the provocation which he had given to Sir Piercie Shafton he could not even conjecture; but he saw that it was of a mortal quality, and he was now to abide the consequences.

That he might not force these consequences forward by any premature renewal of their quarrel, he resolved to walk apart for an hour, and consider on what terms he was to meet this haughty foreigner. The time seemed propitious for his doing so without having the appearance of wilfully shunning the stranger, as all the members of the little household were dispersing either to perform such tasks as had been interrupted by the arrival of the dignitaries, or to put in order what had been deranged by their visit.

Leaving the tower, therefore, and descending, unobserved as he thought, the knoll on which it stood, Halbert gained the little piece of level ground which extended betwixt the descent of the hill, and the first sweep made by the brook after washing the foot of the eminence on which the tower was situated, where a few straggling birch and oak trees served to screen him from observation. But scarce had he reached the spot, when he was surprised to feel a smart tap upon his shoulder, and, turning around, he perceived he had been closely followed by Sir Piercie Shafton.

When, whether from our state of animal spirits, want of confidence in the justice of our cause, or any other motive, our own courage happens to be in a wavering condition, nothing tends so much alto-gether to disconcert us as a great appearance of promptitude on the part of our antagonist. Halbert Glendinning, both morally and consti-tutionally intrepid, was nevertheless somewhat troubled at seeing the stranger, whose resentment he had provoked, appear at once before him, and with an aspect which boded hostility. But though his heart might beat somewhat thicker, he was too high-spirited to exhibit any external signs of emotion.—"What is your pleasure, Sir Piercie?" he said to the English knight, enduring without apparent discomposure all the terrors which his antagonist had summoned into his aspect.

"What is my pleasure?" answered Sir Piercie; "a goodly question after the part you have acted towards me. Young man, I know not what infatuation has led thee to place thyself in direct and insolent opposi-tion to one who is a guest of thy liege-lord the Abbot, and who, even from the courtesy due to thy mother's roof, had a right to remain there uninsulted. Neither do I ask, or care, by what means thou hast become possessed of the fatal secret by which thou hast dared to offer me open shame. But I must now tell thee, that the possession of it hath cost thee thy life."

"Not, I trust, if my hand and sword can defend it," replied Halbert, boldly.

"True," said the Englishman, "I mean not to deprive thee of thy fair chance of self-defence. I am only sorry to think, that, young and country-bred as thou art, it can but little avail thee. But thou must be well aware, that in this quarrel I shall use no terms of quarter."

"Rely on it, proud man," answered the youth, "that I shall ask none; and although thou speakest as if I lay already at thy feet, trust me, that as I am determined never to ask thy mercy, so I am not fearful of needing it."

"Thou wilt then," said the knight, "do nothing to avert the certain fate which thou hast provoked with such wantonness?"

"And how were that to be purchased?" replied Halbert Glendin-ning, more with the wish of obtaining some farther insight into the terms on which he stood with this stranger, than to make him the submission which he might require.

"Explain to me instantly," said Sir Piercie, "without equivocation or delay, by what means thou wert enabled to wound my honour so deeply—and shouldst thou point out to me by so doing an enemy more worthy of my resentment, I will permit thine own obscure insignificance to draw a veil over thine insolence."

"This is too high a flight," said Glendinning, fiercely, "for thine own presumption to soar without being checked at. Thou hast come to my father's house, as well as I can guess, a fugitive and an exile, and thy first greeting to its inhabitants has been that of contempt and injury. By what means I have been able to retort that contempt, let thine own conscience tell thee. Enough for me that I stand on the privilege of a free Scottish-man, and will brook no insult unreturned, and no injury unrequited."

"It is well then," said Sir Piercie Shafton; "we will dispute this matter to-morrow morning with our swords. Let the time be daybreak, and do thou assign the place. We will go forth as if to strike a deer."

"Content," replied Halbert Glendinning; "I will guide thee to a spot where an hundred men might fight and fall without any chance of interruption."

"It is well," answered Sir Piercie Shafton. "Here then we part.— Many will say, that in thus indulging the right of a gentleman to the son of a clod-breaking peasant, I derogate from my sphere, even as the blessed sun would derogate should he condescend to compare and match his golden beams with the twinkle of a pale, blinking, expiring, gross-fed taper. But no consideration of rank shall prevent my avenging the insult thou hast offered me. We bear a smooth face, observe me, Sir Villagio, before the worshipful inmates of yonder cabin, and to-morrow we try conclusions with our swords." So saying, he turned away towards the tower.

It may not be unworthy of notice, that in the last speech only, had Sir Piercie used some of those flowers of rhetoric which characterised the usual style of his conversation. Apparently, a sense of wounded honour, and the deep desire of vindicating his injured feelings, had proved too strong for the fantastic affectation of his acquired habits. Indeed, such is usually the influence of energy of mind, when called forth and exerted, that Sir Piercie Shafton had never appeared in the eyes of his youthful antagonist half so much deserving of esteem and respect as in this brief dialogue, by which they exchanged mutual defiance. As he followed him slowly to the tower, he could not help thinking to himself, that, had the English knight always displayed this superior tone of bearing and feeling, he would not probably have felt so earnestly disposed to take offence at his hand. Mortal offence, however, had been exchanged, and the matter was to be put to mortal arbitrement.

The family met at the evening meal, when Sir Piercie Shafton

extended the benignity of his countenance and the graces of his conversation far more generally over the party than he had hitherto condescended to do. The greater part of his attention was, of course, still
engrossed by his divine and inimitable Discretion, as he chose to term
Mary Avenel; but, nevertheless, there were interjectional flourishes
to the maid of the mill, under the title of Comely Damsel, and to the
dame, under that of Worthy Matron. Nay, lest he should fail to excite
their admiration by the graces of his rhetoric, he generously, and
without solicitation, added those of his voice; and after regretting
bitterly the absence of his viol-de-gambo, he regaled them with a
song, "which," said he, "the inimitable Astrophel, whom mortals call
Philip Sidney, composed in the non-age of his muse, to shew the
world what they are to expect from his riper years, and which will one
day see the light in that un-to-be-paralleled perfection of human wit,
which he hath addressed to his sister, the matchless Parthenope,
whom men call Countess of Pembroke; a work," he continued,
"whereof his friendship hath permitted me, though unworthy, to be an
occasional partaker, and whereof I may well say, that the deep afflictive tale which awakeneth our sorrows, is so relieved with brilliant
similitudes, dulcet descriptions, pleasant poems, and engaging inter-
ludes, that they seem as the stars of the firmament, beautifying the
dusky robe of night. And though I wot well how much the lovely and
quaint language will suffer by my widowed voice, widowed in that it is
no longer matched by my beloved viol-de-gambo, I shall assay to give
you a taste of the ravishing sweetness of the poesy of the un-to-be-
imitated Astrophel."

So saying, he sung without mercy or remorse about five hundred
verses, of which the two first and the four last may suffice for a
specimen—

> What tongue can her perfections tell,
> On whose each part all pens may dwell.
> *   *   *   *   *
> Of whose high praise and praiseful bliss,
> Goodness the pen, Heaven paper is;
> The ink immortal fame doth send,
> As I began so must I end.

As Sir Piercie Shafton always sung with his eyes half shut, it was not
until, agreeable to the promise of his poetry, he had fairly made an
end, that, looking round, he discovered that the greater part of his
audience had, in the meanwhile, yielded to the charms of repose.
Mary Avenel, indeed, from a natural sense of politeness, had contrived to keep awake through all the prolixities of the divine Astrophel;
but Mysie was in dreams transported back to the dusty atmosphere of
her father's mill. Edward himself, who had given his attention for

some time, had at length fallen fast asleep; and the good dame's nose, could its tones have been put under regulation, might have supplied the bass of the lamented viol-de-gambo. Halbert alone, who had no temptation to give way to the charms of slumber, remained awake with his eyes fixed on the songster; not that he was better entertained with the words, or more ravished with the execution, than the rest of the company, but rather because he admired, or perhaps envied, the composure, which could thus spend the evening in interminable madrigals, when the next morning was to be devoted to deadly combat. Yet it struck his natural acuteness of observation, that the eye of the gallant cavalier did now and then, furtively as it were, seek a glance of his countenance, as if to discover how he was taking this exhibition of his antagonist's composure and serenity of mind.

"He shall read nothing in my countenance," thought Halbert, proudly, "that can make him think my indifference less than his own."

And taking from a shelf a bag full of miscellaneous matters collected for the purpose, he began with great industry to dress hooks, and had finished half-a-dozen of flies (we are enabled, for the benefit of those who admire the antiquities of the gentle art of angling, to state that they were brown hackles,) by the time that Sir Piercie had arrived at the conclusion of his long-winded strophes of the divine Astrophel. So that he also testified a magnanimous contempt of that which to-morrow should bring forth.

As it now waxed late, the family at Glendearg separated for the evening; Sir Piercie first saying to the dame that "her son Albert"——

"Halbert," said Elspet, with emphasis, "Halbert; after his goodsire, Halbert Brydone."

"Well, then, I have prayed your son Halbert, that we may strive to-morrow with the sun's earliness to wake a stag from his lair, that I may see whether he be as prompt at that sport as fame bespeaks him."

"Alas! sir," answered Dame Elspet, "he is but too prompt, an you talk of promptitude, at any thing that has steel at one end of it and mischief at the other. But he is at your honourable disposal, and I trust you will teach him how obedience is due to our venerable father and lord, the Abbot, and prevail with him to take the bow-bearer's place in fee; for, as the two worthy monks said, it will be a great help to a widow-woman."

"Trust me, good dame," replied Sir Piercie, "it is my purpose so to endoctrinate him, touching his conduct and bearing towards his betters, that he shall not lightly depart from the reverence due to them.—We meet, then, beneath the birch-trees in the plain," he said, looking to Halbert, "so soon as the eye of day hath opened its lids."—Halbert answered with a sign of acquiescence, and the knight proceeded, "And now, having wished to my fairest Discretion those pleasant dreams which wave their pinions around the couch of sleeping beauty, and to this comely damsel the bounties of Morpheus, and to all others the common good-night, I will crave you leave to depart to my place of rest, though I may say with the poet,

> Ah rest!—no rest but change of place and posture;
> Ah sleep!—no sleep but worn-out Nature's swooning;
> Ah bed!—no bed but cushion filled with stones:
> Rest, sleep, or bed, await not on an exile."

With a delicate obeisance he left the room, evading Dame Glendinning, who hastened to assure him he would find his accommodations for repose much more agreeable than they had been the night before, there having been store of warm coverlids, and a soft feather-bed, sent up from the Abbey. But the good Knight probably thought that the grace and effect of his exit would be diminished, if he were recalled from his heroics to discuss such sublunary and domestic topics, and therefore hastened away without waiting to hear her out.

"A pleasant gentleman," said Dame Glendinning, looking after him; "but I will warrant him an humourous*—And sings a sweet song, though it is somewhat of the longest—well, I make mine avow he is goodly company—I wonder when he will go away."

Having thus expressed her respect for her guest, not without intimation that she was heartily tired of his company, the good dame gave the signal for the family to disperse, and laid her injunctions on Halbert to attend Sir Piercie Shafton at- day-break, as he had required.

When stretched on his pallet by his brother's side, Halbert had no small cause to envy the sound sleep which instantly settled on the eyes of Edward, but refused him any share of its influence. He saw now too well what the spirit had darkly indicated, that, in granting the boon which he had asked so unadvisedly, she had contributed more to his harm than to his good. He was now sensible, too late, of the various dangers and inconveniences with which his dearest friends were threatened, alike by his discomfiture or his success in the approaching duel. If he fell, he might say personally, "good night all." But it was not the less certain that he should leave a dreadful legacy of distress and embarrassment to his mother and family,—an anticipation which by no means tended to render the front of death, in itself a griesly object, more agreeable to the imagination. The vengeance of the Abbot, his conscience told him, was sure to descend on his mother and brother, or could only be averted by the generosity of the victor—And Mary

---

* *Humourous*—full of whims—thus Shakspeare, "humourous as winter."—The vulgar word humour-some comes nearest to the meaning.

Avenel—he should have shewn himself, if he succumbed in the present combat, as inefficient in protecting her, as he had been unnecessarily active in bringing disaster on her, and on the house in which she had been protected from infancy. And to this view of the case were to be added all those embittered and anxious feelings with which the bravest men, even in a better or less doubtful quarrel, regard the issue of a deadly conflict, the first time when it has been their fate to engage in an affair of that nature.

But however disconsolate the prospect seemed in the event of his being conquered, Halbert could expect from victory little more than the safety of his own life, and the gratification of his wounded pride. To his friends—to his mother and brother—especially to Mary Avenel—the consequences of his triumph would be more certain destruction than the contingency of his defeat and death. If the English knight survived, he might in courtesy extend his protection to them; but if he fell, nothing was likely to screen them from the vindictive measures which the Abbot and convent would surely adopt against the violation of the peace of the Halidome, and the slaughter of a protected guest by one of their own vassals, within whose house they had lodged him for shelter. These thoughts, in which neither view of the case augured aught short of ruin to his family, and that ruin entirely brought on by his own rashness, were thorns in Halbert Glendinning's pillow, and deprived his soul of peace, and his eyes of slumber.

There appeared no middle course, saving one which was marked by degradation, and which, even if he stooped to it, was by no means free of danger. He might indeed confess to the English knight the strange circumstances which led to his presenting him with the token which the White Lady, (in her displeasure as it now seemed,) had given him, that he might offer it to Sir Piercie Shafton. But to this avowal his pride could not stoop, and reason, who is wonderfully ready to be of counsel with pride on such occasions, offered many arguments to shew it would be useless as well as mean so far to degrade himself. "If I tell a tale so wonderful," thought he, "shall I not either be stigmatized as a liar, or punished as a wizard?—Were Sir Piercie Shafton generous, noble, and benevolent, as the champions of whom we hear in romance, I might indeed gain his ear, and, without demeaning myself, escape from the situation in which I am placed. But he is—or at least seems to be—self-conceited, arrogant, vain, and presumptuous—I should but humble myself in vain—And I will not humble myself!" said he, starting out of bed, grasping to his broad-sword, and brandishing it in the light of the moon, which streamed through the deep niche that served them as a window;

when, to his extreme surprise and terror, an airy form stood in the moonlight, but intercepted not the reflection on the floor. Dimly as it was expressed, the sound of the voice soon made him sensible he saw the White Lady.

At no time had her presence seemed so terrific to him; for when he had invoked her, it was with the expectation of the apparition, and the determination to abide the issue. But now she had come uncalled, and her presence impressed him with a sense of approaching misfortune, and with the hideous apprehension that he had associated himself with a demon, over whose motions he had no controul, and of whose powers and quality he had no certain knowledge. He remained, therefore, in mute terror, gazing on the apparition, which chaunted or recited in cadence the following lines—

> "He whose heart for vengeance sued,
> Must not shrink from shedding blood;
> The knot that thou hast tied with word,
> Thou must loose by edge of sword."

"Avaunt thee, false Spirit!" said Halbert Glendinning; "I have bought thy advice too dearly already—Begone, in the name of God!"

The Spirit laughed; and the cold unnatural sound of her laughter had something in it more fearful than the usual melancholy tones of her voice. She then replied.

> "You have summon'd me once—you have summon'd me twice,
> And without e'er a summons I come to you thrice.
> Unask'd for, unsued for, you came to my glen,
> Unsued and unask'd, I am with you again."

Halbert Glendinning gave way for a moment to terror, and called on his brother, "Edward! waken, waken, for Our Lady's sake!"

Edward awaked accordingly, and asked what he wanted.

"Look out," said Halbert, "look up! seest thou no one in the room?"

"No, upon my good word," said Edward, looking out.

"What, seest thou nothing in the moon-shine upon the floor there?"

"No, nothing," answered Edward, "save thyself, resting on thy naked sword. I tell thee, Halbert, thou shouldst trust more to thy spiritual arms, and less to those of steel and iron. For this many a night hast thou started and moaned, and cried out of fighting, and of spectres, and of goblins—thy sleep hath not refreshed thee—thy waking hath been a dream.—Credit me, dear Halbert, say the *Pater* and *Credo*, resign thyself to the protection of God, and thou will sleep sound and wake in comfort."

"It may be," said Halbert slowly, and having his eye still bent on the female form which to him seemed distinctly visible,—"it may be—But tell me, dear Edward, seest thou no one on the chamber floor but me?"

"No one," answered Edward, raising himself on his elbow; "dear brother, lay aside thy weapon, say thy prayers, and lay thee down to rest."

While he thus spoke, the Spirit smiled at Halbert as if in scorn; her wan cheek faded in the wan moonlight even before the smile had passed away, and Halbert himself no longer beheld the vision to which he had so anxiously solicited his brother's attention. "May God preserve my wits!" he said, as, laying aside his weapon, he again threw himself on his bed.

"Amen! my dearest brother," answered Edward; "but we must not provoke that heaven in our wantonness which we invoke in our misery. —Be not angry with me, my dear brother—I know not why you have totally of late estranged yourself from me—It is true, I am neither so athletic in body, nor so alert in courage, as you have been from infancy; yet, till lately, you have not absolutely cast off my society— Believe me, I have wept in secret, though I forbore to intrude myself on your privacy. The time has been when you held me not so cheap; and when, if I could not follow the game so closely, or mark it so truly as you, I could fill up our intervals of pastime with pleasant tales of the olden times, which I had read or heard, and which could win your attention as we sate and eat our provision by some pleasant spring— but now I have, though I know not why, lost thy regard and affection. Nay, toss not thy arms about thee thus wildly," said the younger brother; "from thy strange dreams, I fear some touch of fever hath affected thy blood—let me draw closer around thee thy mantle."

"Forbear," said Halbert—"your care is needless—your complaints are without reason—your fears on my account are in vain."

"Nay, but hear me, brother," said Edward. "Your speech in sleep, and now even your waking dreams, are of beings which belong not to this world or to our race—Our good Father Eustace says, that howbeit we may not do well to receive all idle tales of goblins and spectres, yet there is warrant from holy Scripture to believe, that the fiends haunt waste and solitary places; and that those who frequent such wildernesses alone, are the prey, or the sport of these wandering demons. And therefore, I pray thee, brother, let me go with you when you go next up the glen, where, as you well know, there be places of evil reputation—Thou carest not for my escort; but, Halbert, such dangers are more safely encountered by the wise in judgment, than by the bold in bosom; and though I have small cause to boast of my own wisdom, yet I have that which ariseth from the written knowledge of elder times."

There was a moment during this discourse, when Halbert had well nigh come to the resolution of disburthening his own breast, by entrusting Edward with all that weighed upon it. But when his brother reminded him that this was the morning of a high holiday, and that, setting aside all other business or pleasure, he ought to go to the Monastery and shrive himself before Father Eustace, who would that day occupy the confessional, pride stepped in and confirmed his wavering resolution. "I will not avow," he thought, "a tale so extraordinary, that I may be considered as an impostor or something worse—I will not fly from this Englishman, whose arm and sword may be no better than my own—my fathers have faced his betters, were he as much distinguished in battle as he is by his quaint discourse."

Pride, which has been said to save man, and woman too, from falling, has yet a stronger influence on the mind when it embraces the cause of passion, and seldom fails to render it victorious over conscience and reason. His mind once determined, though to the worser course, Halbert at length slept sound, and was only awakened by the dawn of day.

Chapter Ten

Indifferent, but indifferent-pshaw, he doth it not
Like one who is his craft's master—ne'er the less
I have seen a clown confer a bloody coxcomb
On one who was a master of defence.

Old Play

WITH THE FIRST grey peep of dawn, Halbert Glendinning arose and hastened to dress himself, girt on his weapon, and took a cross-bow in his hand, as if his usual sport had been his sole object. He groped his way down the dark and winding stair-case, and undid, with as little noise as possible, the fastenings of the inner door, and of the exterior iron grate. At length he stood free in the court-yard, and looking up to the tower, saw a signal made with a kerchief from the window. Nothing doubting that it was his antagonist, he paused expecting him. But it was Mary Avenel, who glided like a spirit from under the low and rugged portal.

Halbert was much surprised, and felt, he knew not why, like one caught in the act of a meditated trespass. The presence of Mary Avenel had till that moment never given him pain. She spoke too in a tone where sorrow seemed to mingle with reproach, while she asked him with emphasis, "What he was about to do?"

He shewed his cross-bow, and was about to express the pretext he had meditated, when Mary interrupted him.

"Not so, Halbert—that evasion were unworthy of one whose word has hitherto been truth. You meditate not the destruction of the deer —your hand and your heart are aimed at other game—you seek to do battle with this stranger."

"And wherefore should I quarrel with our guest?" answered Halbert, blushing deeply.

"There are, indeed, many reasons why you should not," replied the maiden, "nor is there one of avail wherefore you should—yet, nevertheless, such a quarrel you are now searching after."

"Why should you suppose so, Mary?" said Halbert, endeavouring to hide his conscious purpose,—"he is my mother's guest—he is protected by the Abbot and the community, who are our masters—he is of high degree also, and wherefore should you think that I can, or dare, resent a hasty word, which he has perchance thrown out against me more from the wantonness of his wit, than the purpose of his heart?"

"Alas!" answered the maiden, "the very asking that question puts your resolution beyond a doubt. Since your childhood you were ever daring, seeking danger rather than avoiding it—delighting in whatever had the air of adventure and of courage; and it is not from fear that you will now blench from your purpose—O let it then be from pity!—from pity, Halbert, to your aged mother, whom your death or victory will alike deprive of the comfort and stay of her age."

"She has my brother Edward," said Halbert, turning sullenly from her.

"She has indeed," said Mary Avenel, "the calm, the noble-minded, the considerate Edward, who has thy courage, Halbert, without thy fiery rashness,—thy generous spirit, with more of reason to guide it. He would not have heard his mother, would not have heard his adopted sister, beseech him in vain not to ruin himself, and tear up their future hopes of happiness and protection."

Halbert's heart swelled as he replied to this reproach, "Well—what avails it speaking?—you have him that is better than me—wiser, more considerate,—braver for aught that I know—You are provided with a protector, and need care no more for me."

Again he turned to depart, but Mary Avenel laid her hand on his arm so gently that he scarce felt her hold, yet felt that it was impossible for him to shake it off. There he stood, one foot advanced to leave the court-yard, but so little determined on departure, that he resembled a traveller arrested by the spell of a magician, and unable either to quit the attitude of motion, or to proceed on his course.

Mary Avenel availed herself of his state of suspense. "Hear me," she said, "hear me, Halbert—I am an orphan, and even Heaven hears the orphan—I have been the companion of your infancy, and if *you* will not hear me for an instant, from whom may Mary Avenel claim so poor a boon?"

"I hear you," said Halbert Glendinning, "but be brief, dear Mary—You mistake the nature of my business—it is but a morning of summer sport which we propose."

"Say not thus," said the maiden, interrupting him, "say not thus to me—Others thou may'st deceive, me thou canst not—There has been that in me from the earliest youth, which fraud flies from, and which imposture cannot deceive. For what fate has given me such a power I know not; but, bred an ignorant maiden in this sequestered valley, mine eyes can too often see what man would most willingly hide. I can judge of the dark purpose, though it is hid under the smiling brow, and a glance of the eye says more to me than oaths and protestations do to others."

"Then," said Halbert, "if thou canst so read the human heart,—say, dear Mary—what doest thou see in mine?—tell me that—say that what thou seest—what thou readest in this bosom, does not offend thee—say but *that*, and thou shall be the guide of my actions, and mould me now and henceforward to honour or to dishonour at thy own free will."

Mary Avenel became first red, and then deadly pale, as Halbert Glendinning spoke. But when, turning round at the close of his address, he took her hand, she gently withdrew it, and replied, "I cannot read the heart, Halbert, and I would not by my will know aught of yours, save what beseems us both—I only can judge of signs, words, and actions of little outward import, more truly than those around me, as my eyes, thou knowst, have seen objects not presented to those of others."

"Let them gaze then on one whom they shall never see more," said Halbert, once more turning from her, and rushing out of the court-yard without again looking back.

Mary Avenel gave a faint scream, and clasped both her hands firmly on her forehead and eyes. She had been a minute in this attitude, when she was thus greeted by a voice from behind: "Generously done, my most clement Discretion, to hide those brilliant eyes from the far inferior beams which even now begin to gild the eastern horizon—certes, peril there were that Phœbus, outshone in splendour, might in very shamefacedness turn back his car, and rather leave the world in darkness, than incur the disgrace of such an encounter—Credit me, lovely Discretion"——

But as Sir Piercie Shafton (the reader will readily set down these flowers of eloquence to the proper owner,) attempted to take Mary

Avenel's hand, in order to proceed in his speech, she shook him abruptly off, and regarding him with an eye which evinced terror and agitation, rushed past him into the tower.

The knight stood looking after her with a countenance in which contempt was strongly mingled with mortification. "By my knighthood!" he ejaculated, "I have thrown away upon this rude rustic Phidelé a speech which the proudest beauty at the court of Felicia (so let me call the Elysium from which I am banished!) might have termed the very mattins of Cupid. Hard and inexorable was the fate that sent thee hither, Piercie Shafton, to waste thy wit upon country wenches, and thy valour upon hob-nailed clowns! But that insult—that affront—had it been offered to me by the lowest plebeian, he must have died for it by my hand, in respect the enormity of the offence doth countervail the inequality of him by whom it was given. I trust I shall find this clownish roisterer not less willing to deal in blows than in taunts."

While he held this conversation with himself, Sir Piercie Shafton was hastening to the little tuft of birch trees which had been assigned as the place of meeting. He greeted his antagonist with a courtly salutation, followed by this commentary: "I pray of you to observe, that I doff my hat to you, though so much my inferior in rank, without derogation on my part, inasmuch as my having so far honoured you in receiving and admitting your defiance, doth, in the judgment of the best martialists, in some sort and for the time, raise you to a level with me—an honour which you may and ought to account cheaply purchased, even with the loss of your life, if such should chance to be the issue of this duello."

"For which condescension," said Halbert, "I have to thank the token which I presented to you."

The knight changed colour, and grinded his teeth with rage ——"Draw your weapon!" said he to Glendinning.

"Not in this spot," answered the youth; "we will be liable to interruption—Follow me, and I will bring you to a place where we will encounter no such risk."

He proceeded to walk up the glen, resolving that their place of combat should be in the entrance of the Corri-nan-shian, both because the spot, lying under the reputation of being haunted, was very little frequented, and also because he regarded it as a place which to him might be termed fated, and which he therefore resolved should witness his death or victory.

They walked up the glen for some time in silence, like honourable enemies who did not wish to contend with words, and who had nothing friendly to exchange with each other. Silence, however, was always an irksome state with Sir Piercie, and, moreover, his anger was usually a hasty and short-lived passion. As, therefore, he went forth, in his own idea, in all love and honour towards his antagonist, he saw not any cause for submitting longer to the very painful restraint of positive silence. He began by complimenting Halbert on the alert activity with which he surmounted the obstacles and impediments of the way.

"Trust me," said he, "worthy rustic, we have not a lighter or a firmer step in our courtlike revels, and if duly set forth by a silk hose, and trained unto that stately exercise, your leg would make an indifferent good shew in a pavin or a galliard. And I doubt nothing," he added, "that you have availed yourself of some opportunity to improve yourself in the art of fence, which is more akin than dancing to our present purpose?"

"I know nothing more of fencing," said Halbert, "than hath been taught me by an old shepherd of ours, called Martin, and at whiles a lesson from Christie of the Clinthill—for the rest, I must trust to good sword, strong arm, and sound heart."

"Marry and I am glad of it, young Audacity, (I will call you my Audacity, and you may call me your Condescension, while we are on these terms of unnatural equality,) I am glad of your ignorance with all my heart. For we martialists proportion the punishments which we inflict upon our opposites, to the length and hazard of the efforts wherewith they oppose themselves to us. And I see not why you, being but a tyro, may not be held sufficiently punished for your outrecuidance and orgulous presumption, by the loss of an ear, an eye, or even of a finger, accompanied by some flesh-wound of depth and severity, suited to your error—whereas, had you been able to stand more effectually on your defence, I see not how less than your life could have atoned sufficiently for your presumption."

"Now, by God and Our Lady," said Halbert, unable any longer to restrain himself, "thou art thyself over-presumptuous, who speakst thus daringly of the issue of a combat which is not yet even begun— Are you a god, that you already dispose of my life and limbs? or are you a judge on the justice-air, telling at your ease and without risk, how the head and quarters of a condemned criminal are to be disposed of?"

"Not so—O thou, whom I have well permitted to call thyself my Audacity! I, thy Condescension, am neither a god to judge the issue of the combat before it is fought, nor a judge to dispose at my ease and in safety of the limbs and head of a condemned criminal. But I am an indifferent good master of fence, being the first pupil of the first master of the first school of fence that our royal England affords, the said master being no other than the truly noble, and all-unutterably-skilful Vincentio Saviolo, from whom I learned the firm step, quick

eye, and nimble hand—of which qualities thou, O my most rustical
Audacity, art full like to reap the fruits so soon as we shall reach a place
of ground fitting for such experiments."

They had now reached the gorge of the ravine where Halbert had at
first intended to stop; but when he observed the narrowness of the
level ground, he began to consider that it was only by superior agility
that he could expect to make up his deficiency in the science, as it was
called, of defence. He found no spot which afforded sufficient room
to traverse for this purpose, until he reached the well-known fountain,
by whose margin, and in front of the huge rock from which it sprung,
was an amphitheatre of level turf, of small space indeed, compared
with the great height of the cliffs with which it was surrounded on
every point save that from which the rivulet issued forth, yet large
enough for their present purpose.

When they had reached this spot of ground, fitted well by its gloom
and sequestered situation to be a scene of mortal strife, both were
surprised to observe that a grave was dug close by the foot of the rock
with great neatness and regularity, the green turf being laid down
upon the one side, and the earth thrown out in a heap upon the other.
A mattock and shovel lay by the verge of the grave.

Sir Piercie Shafton bent his eye with unusual seriousness upon
Halbert Glendinning, as he asked him sternly, "Does this bode
treason, young man? And have you purpose to set upon me here as in
an emboscata or place of vantage?"

"Not on my part, by heaven!" answered the youth; "I told no one of
our purpose, nor would I for the throne of Scotland take odds against
a single arm."

"I believe thou wouldest not, mine Audacity," said the knight,
resuming the affected manner which was become a second nature to
him; "nevertheless this fosse is curiously well shaped, and might be
the master-piece of Nature's last bed-maker, I would say the sexton.
Wherefore, let us be thankful to chance, or some unknown friend,
who hath thus provided for one of us the decencies of sepulture, and
let us proceed to determine which shall have the advantage of enjoying
this place of undisturbed slumber."

So saying, he stripped off his doublet and cloak, which he folded up
with great care, and deposited upon a large stone, while Halbert
Glendinning, not without some emotion, followed his example. Their
vicinity to the favourite haunt of the White Lady led him to form some
conjectures concerning the incident of the grave. "It must have been
her work!" he thought: "the Spirit foresaw and has provided for the
fatal event of the combat—I must return from this place a homicide,
or I must remain here for ever!"

The bridge seemed now broken down behind him, and the chance of coming off honourably without killing or being killed, (the hope of which issue has cheered the sinking heart of many a duellist,) seemed now to be altogether removed. Yet the very desperation of his situation gave him, on an instant's reflection, both firmness and courage, as it presented to him one sole alternative, conquest, namely, or death.

"As we are here," said Sir Piercie Shafton, "unaccompanied by any patrons or seconds, it were well you should pass your hand over my sides, as I shall over yours; not that I suspect you to use any quaint device of privy armour, but in order to comply with the ancient and laudable custom practised on all such occasions."

While, complying with his antagonist's humour, Halbert Glendinning went through this ceremony, Sir Piercie Shafton did not fail to solicit his attention to the quality and fineness of his wrought and embroidered shirt—"In this very shirt," said he, "O mine Audacity! —I say in this very garment, in which I am now to combat a Scottish rustic like thyself, it was my envied lot to lead the winning party at that wondrous match at ballon, made betwixt the divine Astrophel, (our matchless Sidney,) and the right honourable my very good lord of Oxford. All the beauties of Felicia, (by which name I distinguish our beloved England,) stood in the gallery, waving their kerchiefs at each turn of the game, and cheering the winners by their plaudits. After which noble sport we were refreshed by a suitable banquet, whereat it pleased the noble Urania, (being the unmatched Countess of Pembroke,) to accommodate me with her own fan for the cooling my somewhat too much inflamed visage, to requite which courtesy, I said, casting my features into a smiling yet melancholy fashion, O divinest Urania! receive again that too fatal gift, which not like the Zephyr cooleth, but like the hot breath of the Sirocco heateth yet more that which is already inflamed. Whereupon looking upon me somewhat scornfully, yet not so but what the experienced courtier might perceive a certain cast of approbative affection"——

Here the knight was interrupted by Halbert, who had waited with courteous patience for some little time, till he found, that far from drawing to a close, Sir Piercie seemed rather inclined to wax prolix in his reminiscences.

"Sir Knight," said the youth, "if this matter be not very much to the purpose, we will, if you object not, proceed to that which we have in hand. You should have abidden in England had you desired to waste time in words, for here we spend it in blows."

"I crave your pardon, most rustical Audacity," answered Sir Piercie; "truly I become oblivious of every thing beside, when the recollections of the divine court of Felicia press upon my weakened memory, even as a saint is dazzled when he bethinks him of the beatific vision. Ah felicitous Feliciana! delicate nurse of the fair, chosen abode of the wise, the birth-place and cradle of nobility, the temple of courtesy, the fane of sprightly chivalry—Ah heavenly court, or rather courtly heaven! cheered with dances, lulled asleep with harmony, wakened with sprightly sports and tourneys, decored with silks and tissues, glittering with diamonds and jewels, standing on end with double-piled velvets, satins, and satinettas!"

"The token, Sir Knight, the token!" exclaimed Halbert Glendinning, who, impatient of Sir Piercie's interminable oratory, reminded him of the ground of their quarrel, as the best way to compel him to attend to the purpose of their meeting.

And he judged right; for Sir Piercie Shafton no sooner heard him speak, than he exclaimed, "Thy death-hour has struck—betake thee to thy sword—Via!"

Both swords were unsheathed, and the combatants commenced their engagement. Halbert felt immediately that, as he had expected, he was far inferior to his adversary in the management of his weapon. Sir Piercie Shafton had taken no more than his own share of real merit, when he termed himself an absolutely good fencer; and Glendinning soon felt that he would have great difficulty in escaping with life and honour from such a master of the sword. The English knight was master of all the mystery of the *stoccata*, *imbrocata*, *punto-reverso*, *incartata*, and so forth, which the Italian masters of defence had lately introduced into general practice. But Glendinning, on his part, was no novice in the principles of the art, according to the old Scottish fashion, and possessed the first of all qualities, a steady and collected disposition. At first, being desirous to try the skill, and become acquainted with the play of his enemy, he stood on his defence, keeping his foot, hand, eye, and body in perfect unison, and holding his sword short, and with the point towards his antagonist's face, so that Sir Piercie, in order to assail him, was obliged to make actual passes, and could not avail himself of his skill in making feints; while, on the other hand, Halbert was prompt to parry these attacks, either by shifting his ground, or with the sword. The consequence was, that after two or three sharp attempts on the part of Sir Piercie, which were evaded or disconcerted by the address of his antagonist, he began to assume the defensive in his turn, fearful of giving some advantage by being repeatedly the assailant. But Halbert Glendinning was too cautious to press on an antagonist whose dexterity had already more than once placed him within a hair's-breadth of death, which he had only escaped by uncommon watchfulness and agility.

When each had made a feint or two, there was therefore a pause in the conflict, both as if by one assent dropping their swords' point, and looking on each other for a moment without speaking. At length Halbert Glendinning, who felt perhaps more uneasy on account of his family, than he had done before he had displayed his own courage, and proved the strength of his antagonist, could not help saying, "Is our subject of quarrel, Sir Knight, so mortal, that one of our two bodies must needs fill up that grave?—or may we with honour, having proved ourselves against each other, sheathe our swords and depart friends?"

"Valiant and most rustical Audacity," said the Southron Knight, "to no man on earth could you have put a question on the code of honour, who was more capable of rendering you a reason. Let us pause for the space of one venue, until I give you my opinion on this dependence;* for certain it is, that brave men should not run upon their fate like brute and furious wild beasts, but should slay each other deliberately, decently, and with reason. Therefore, if we coolly examine the state of our dependence, we may the better apprehend whether the sisters three have doomed one of us to expiate the same with his blood—does thou understand me?"

"I have heard Father Eustace," said Halbert, after a moment's recollection, "speak of the three furies, with their thread and their shears."

"Enough—enough,"—interrupted Sir Piercie Shafton, crimson with a new fit of rage, "the thread of thy life is spun!"

And with these words he attacked with the utmost ferocity the Scottish youth, who had but just time to throw himself into a posture of defence. But the rash fury of the assailant, as frequently happens, disappointed its own purpose; for, as he made a desperate thrust, Halbert Glendinning avoided it, and, ere the knight could recover his weapon, requited him (to use his own language) with a resolute stoccata, which passed through his body, and Sir Piercie Shafton fell to the ground.

---

* *Dependence*—A phrase among the brethren of the sword for an existing quarrel.

Chapter Eleven

Yes, life hath left him—every busy thought,
Each fiery passion, every strong affection,
The sense of outward ill and inward sorrow,
Are fled at once from the pale trunk before me;
And I have given that which spoke and moved,
Thought, acted, suffered as a living man,
To be a ghastly form of bloody clay,
Soon the foul food for reptiles.

Old Play

I BELIEVE few successful duellists (if the word successful can be applied to a superiority so fatal,) have beheld their dead antagonist stretched on earth at their feet, without wishing they could redeem with their own blood that which it has been their fate to spill. Least of all could such indifference be the lot of so young a man as Halbert Glendinning, who, unused to the sight of human blood, was not only struck with sorrow, but with terror, when he beheld Sir Piercie Shafton lie stretched on the green-sward before him, vomiting gore as if impelled by the strokes of a pump. He threw his bloody sword on the ground, and hastened to kneel down and support him, vainly striving, at the same time, to staunch his wound, which seemed rather to bleed inwardly than externally.

The unfortunate knight spoke at intervals, when the syncope would permit him, and his words, so far as intelligible, partook of his affected and conceited, yet not ungenerous character.

"Most rustical youth," he said, "thy fortune hath prevailed over knightly skill—and Audacity hath overcome Condescension—Even as the kite hath sometimes hawked at and struck down the falcon-gentle.—Fly and save thyself!—take my purse—it is in the nether pocket of my carnation-coloured hose—and is worth a clown's acceptance.—See that my mails, with my vestments, be sent to the Monastery of Saint Mary's—(here his voice grew weak, and his mind and recollection seemed to waver)—I bestow the cut velvet jerkin, with close breeches conforming—for—Oh!—the good of my soul."

"Be of good comfort, sir," said Halbert, half distracted with his agony of pity and remorse. "I trust you shall yet do well—O for a leach!"

"Were there twenty physicians, O most generous Audacity, and that were a grave spectacle—I might not survive—my life is ebbing fast.—Commend me to the rustical nymph whom I called my Discretion—O Claridiana!—true empress of this bleeding heart—which now bleedeth in sad earnest!—Place me on the ground at my length, most rustical victor, born to quench the pride of the burning light of the most felicitous court of Feliciana—O saints and angels—knights and ladies—masques and theatres—quaint devices—chain-work and broidery—love, honour, and beauty!"——

While muttering these last words, which slid from him, as it were unawares, while doubtless he was recalling to mind the glories of the English court, the gallant Sir Piercie Shafton stretched out his limbs—groaned deeply, shut his eyes, and became motionless.

The victor tore his hair for very sorrow, as he looked on the pale countenance of his victim. Life, he thought, had not utterly fled, but without better aid than his own, he saw not how it could be preserved.

"Why," he exclaimed, in vain penitence, "why did I provoke him to an issue so fatal! Would to God I had submitted to the worst insult man could receive from man, rather than be the bloody instrument of this bloody deed—and doubly cursed be this evil-boding spot, which, haunted as I knew it to be by a witch or a devil, I yet chose for the place of combat! In any other place, save this, there had been help to be gotten by speed of foot, or by uplifting of voice—but here there is no one to be found by search, no one to hear my shouts, save the evil spirit which has counselled this mischief. It is not her hour—I will essay the spell howsoever; and if she can give me aid, she *shall* do it, or know of what a madman is capable even against those of another world!"

He spurned his bloody shoe from his foot, and repeated the spell with which the reader is well acquainted; but there was neither voice, apparition, nor signal of answer. The youth, in the impatience of his despair, and with the rash hardihood which formed the basis of his character, shouted aloud, "Witch—Sorceress—Fiend!—art thou deaf to my cries of help, and so ready to appear and answer those of vengeance? Arise and speak to me, or I will choke up thy fountain, tear down thy holly-bush, and leave thy haunt as waste and bare, as thy fatal assistance has made me waste of comfort and bare of counsel!"—This furious and raving invocation was suddenly interrupted by a distant sound, resembling a hollo, from the gorge of the ravine. "Now may Saint Mary be praised," said the youth, hastily fastening his sandal, "I hear the voice of some living man, who may give me counsel and help in this fearful extremity."

Having donned his sandal, Halbert Glendinning, hollowing at intervals, in answer to the sound which he had heard, ran with the speed of a hunted buck down the rugged defile, as if paradise had been before him, hell and all her furies behind, and his eternal happiness or misery had depended upon the speed which he exerted. In a space incredibly short for any one but a Scottish mountaineer having his nerves strung by the deepest and most passionate interest, the youth reached the entrance of the ravine, through which the rill that flows down Corri-nan-shian discharges itself, and unites with the brook that waters the little valley of Glendearg.

Here he paused, and looked around him upwards and downwards through the glen, without perceiving a human form. His heart sank within him. But the windings of the glen intercepted his prospect, and the person, whose voice he had heard, might, therefore, be at no great distance, though not obvious to his sight. The branches of an oak tree, which shot straight out from the face of a tall cliff, proffered to his bold spirit, steady head, and active limbs, the means of ascending it as a place of out-look, although the enterprize was what most men would have shrunk from. But by one bound from the earth, the active youth caught hold of the lower branch, and swung himself up into the tree, and in a minute more gained the top of the cliff, from which he could easily descry a human figure descending the valley. It was not that of a shepherd, or of a hunter, and scarce any others used to traverse this deserted solitude, especially coming from the north, since the reader may remember that the brook took its rise from an extensive and dangerous morass which lay in that direction.

But Halbert Glendinning did not pause to consider who the traveller might be, or what might be the purpose of his journey. To know that he saw a human being, and might receive, in the extremity of his distress, the countenance and advice of a fellow-creature, was enough for him at the moment. He threw himself from the pinnacle of the cliff once more into the arms of the projecting oak-tree, whose boughs waved in middle air, anchored by the roots in a huge rift, or chasm of the rock. Catching at the branch which was nearest to him, he dropped himself from that height upon the ground; and such was the athletic springiness of his youthful sinews, that he pitched there as lightly, and with as little injury, as the falcon stooping from her wheel.

To resume his race at full speed up the glen, was the work of an instant; and, as he turned angle after angle of the indented banks of the valley, without meeting that which he sought, he became half afraid that the form which he had seen at such a distance had already melted into thin air, and was either a deception of his own imagination, or of the elementary spirits by which the valley was supposed to be haunted.

But, to his inexpressible joy, as he turned around the base of a huge and distinguished crag, he saw, straight before and very near to him, a person, whose dress, as he viewed it hastily, resembled that of a pilgrim.

He was a man in advanced life, and wearing a long beard, having on his head a large slouched hat, without either band or broach. His dress was a tunic of black serge, which, like those commonly called hussar-cloaks, had an upper part, which covered the arms and fell down over the lower; a small scrip and bottle, which hung at his back, with a stout staff in his hand, completed his equipage. His step was feeble, like that of one exhausted by a toilsome journey.

"Save ye, good father!" said the youth. "God and Our Lady have sent you to my assistance."

"And in what, my son, can so frail a creature as I am be of service to you?" said the old man, not a little surprised at being thus accosted by so handsome a youth, his features discomposed by anxiety, his face flushed with exertion, his hands and much of his dress stained with blood.

"A man bleeds to death in the valley here, hard by. Come with me—come with me! You are aged—you have experience—you have at least your senses—and mine have well nigh left me."

"A man—and bleeding to death—and here in this desolate spot?" said the stranger.

"Stay not to question it, father," said the youth, "but come instantly to his rescue—follow me—follow me, without an instant's delay."

"Nay, but my son," said the old man, "we do not thus lightly follow the guides who present themselves thus suddenly in the bosom of a howling wilderness. Ere I follow thee, thou must expound to me thy name, thy purpose, and the cause."

"There is no time to expound anything," said Halbert; "I tell thee a man's life is at stake, and thou must come to aid, or I will carry thee thither by force!"

"Nay, thou shalt not need," said the traveller; "if it indeed be as thou sayest, I will follow thee of free-will—the rather that I am not wholly unskilled in leach-craft, and have in my scrip that which may do thy friend a service—Yet walk more slowly, I pray thee, for I am already well nigh fore-spent with travel."

With the indignant impatience of the fiery steed when compelled by his rider to keep pace with some slow drudge upon the highway, Halbert accompanied the way-farer, burning with anxiety which he endeavoured to subdue, that he might not alarm his companion, who was obviously afraid to trust him. When they reached the place where they were to turn off the wider glen into the Corri, the traveller made a doubtful pause as if unwilling to leave the broader path. "Young man," he said, "if thou meanest aught but good to these grey hairs, thou will gain little by thy cruelty. I have no earthly treasure to tempt either robber or murderer."

"And I," said the youth, "am neither—and yet—God of Heaven! I *may* be a murderer, unless your aid comes in time to this wounded wretch!"

"Is it even so?" said the traveller; "and do human passions disturb the breast of nature even in her deepest solitude?—yet why should I marvel that where darkness abides the works of darkness should abound?—By its fruits is the tree known.—Lead on, unhappy youth —I follow thee!"

And with better will to the journey than he had evinced hitherto, the stranger exerted himself to the uttermost, and seemed to forget his own fatigue in his efforts to keep pace with his impatient guide.

What was the surprise of Halbert Glendinning, when, upon arriving at the fatal spot, he saw no appearance of the body of Sir Piercie Shafton! The traces of the fray were otherwise sufficiently visible. The knight's cloak had indeed vanished as well as the body, but his doublet remained where he had laid it down, and the turf on which he had been stretched was stained with blood in many a dark crimson spot.

As he gazed round him in terror and astonishment, Halbert's eyes fell upon the place of sepulture which had so lately appeared to gape for a victim. It was no longer open, and it seemed that earth had received the expected tenant; for the usual narrow hillock was piled over what had lately been an open grave, and the green sod was adjusted over all with the accuracy of an experienced sexton. Halbert stood aghast. The idea rushed on his mind irresistibly, that the earth-heap before him enclosed what had lately been a living, moving, and sentient fellow-creature, whom, on little provocation, his fell act had reduced to a clod of the valley, as senseless and as cold as the turf under which he rested. The hand that scooped the grave had completed its work; and whose hand could it be save that of the mysterious being of doubtful quality, whom his rashness had invoked, and whom he had suffered to intermingle in his destinies?

As he stood with clasped hands and uplifted eyes, bitterly rueing his rashness, he was roused by the voice of the stranger, whose suspicions of his guide had again been awakened, by finding the scene so different from what Halbert had led him to expect—"Young man," he said, "hast thou baited thy tongue with falsehood, to cut perhaps only a few days from the life of one whom Nature will soon call home, without guilt on thy part to hasten his journey?"

"By the blessed Heaven!—by our dear Lady!" ejaculated Halbert——

"Swear not at all!" said the stranger, interrupting him, "neither by Heaven, for it is God's throne—nor by earth, for it is his footstool— nor by the creatures whom he hath made, for they are but earth and clay as we are. Let thy yea be yea, and thy nay nay. Tell me in a word, why and for what purpose thou hast feigned a tale, to lead a bewildered traveller yet farther astray?"

"As I am Christian man," said Glendinning, "I left him here bleeding to death—and now I nowhere spy him, and much I doubt that the tomb thou seest has closed on his mortal remains!"

"And who is he for whose fate thou art so anxious?" said the stranger; "or how is it possible that this wounded man could have been either removed from, or interred in, a place so solitary?"

"His name," said Halbert, after a moment's pause, "is Piercie Shafton—there, on that very spot, I left him bleeding; and what power has conveyed him hence, I know no more than thou doest."

"Piercie Shafton?" said the stranger, "Sir Piercie Shafton of Wilverton, a kinsman, as it is said, of the great Piercie of Northumberland? If thou hast slain him, to return to the territories of the proud Abbot is to give thy neck to the gallows. He is well known that Piercie Shafton; the meddling tool of wiser plotters—a hair-brained trafficker in treason—a champion of the Pope, employed as a forlorn hope by those more politic heads, who have more will to work mischief than valour to encounter danger.—Come with me, youth, and save thyself from the evil consequences of this deed—guide me to the castle of Avenel, and thy reward shall be protection and safety."

Again Halbert paused, and summoned his mind to a hasty council. The vengeance with which the Abbot was likely to visit the slaughter of Shafton, his friend and in some measure his guest, was likely to be severe; yet, in the various contingencies which he had considered previous to their duel, he had unaccountably omitted to reflect what was to be his line of conduct in case of Sir Piercie falling by his hand. If he returned to Glendearg, he was sure to draw on his whole family, including Mary Avenel, the resentment of the Abbot and community; whereas it was possible that flight might make him regarded as the sole author of the deed, and might avert the indignation of the Monks from the rest of the inhabitants of his paternal tower. Halbert recollected also the favour expressed for the household, and especially for Edward, by the Sub-Prior; and he conceived that he could, by communicating his own guilt to that worthy ecclesiastic, when at a distance from Glendearg, secure his powerful interposition in favour of his family. These thoughts rapidly passed through his mind, and he determined on flight. The stranger's company and his promised protection came in aid of that resolution; but he was unable to reconcile the invitation which the old man gave him to accompany him for safety to the castle of Avenel, with the connections of Julian, the present usurper of that inheritance. "Good father," he said, "I fear that you

mistake the man with whom you wish me to harbour. Avenel guided
Piercie Shafton into Scotland, and his hench-man, Christie of the
Clinthill, brought the southron hither."

"Of that," said the old man, "I am well aware—yet if thou wilt trust
to me, as I have shewn no reluctance to confide in thee, thou shalt find
with Julian Avenel welcome, or at least safety."

"Father," replied Halbert, "though I can ill reconcile what thou
sayest to what Julian Avenel hath done, yet caring little about the
safety of a creature so lost as myself, and as thy words seem those of
truth and honesty, and finally as thou didst render thyself frankly up to
my conduct, I will return the confidence thou hast shewn, and accompany thee to the castle of Avenel by a road which thou thyself couldst
never have discovered." He led the way, and the old man followed for
some time in silence.

Chapter Twelve

'Tis when the wound is stiffening with the cold,
The warrior first feels pain—'tis when the heat
And fiery fever of his soul is passed,
The sinner feels remorse.
                                        Old Play

THE FEELINGS of compunction with which Halbert Glendinning
was visited upon this painful occasion, were deeper than belonged to
an age and country in which human life was held so cheap. They fell
far short certainly of those which might have afflicted a mind regu-
lated by better religious precepts, and more strictly trained under
social laws; but still they were deep and severely felt, and divided in
Halbert's bosom even the regret with which he parted from Mary
Avenel and the tower of his fathers.

The old traveller walked silently by his side for some time, and then
addressed him.—"My son, it has been said that sorrow must speak or
die—Why art thou so much cast down?—tell me thy unhappy tale,
and it may be that my grey head may devise counsel and aid for your
young life."

"Alas!" said Halbert Glendinning, "can you wonder why I am cast
down?—I am at this instant a fugitive from my father's house, from
my mother, and from my friends, and I bear on my hand the blood of a
man who injured me but in idle words, which I have thus bloodily
requited. My heart now tells me I have done evil—it were harder than
these rocks if it could bear unmoved the thought, that I have sent this
man to a long account, un-houseled and unshrieved!"

"Pause there, my son," said the traveller. "That thou hast defaced

God's image in thy neighbour's person—that thou hast sent dust to dust in idle wrath or idler pride, is indeed a sin of the deepest dye—that thou hast cut short the space which Heaven might have allowed him for repentance, makes it yet more deadly—but for all this there is balm in Gilead."

"I understand you not, father," said Halbert, struck by the solemn tone which was assumed by his companion.

The old man proceeded. "Thou hast slain thine enemy—it was a cruel deed: thou hast cut him off perchance in his sins—it is a fearful aggravation. Do yet by my counsel, and in lieu of him whom thou hast perchance consigned to the kingdom of Satan, let thine efforts wrest another subject from the reign of the Evil One."

"I understand you, father," said Halbert; "thou would'st have me atone for my rashness by doing service to the soul of my adversary—But how may this be? I have no money to purchase masses, and gladly would I go barefooted to the Holy Land to free his spirit from Purgatory, only that"——

"My son," said the old man, interrupting him, "the sinner for whose redemption I entreat you to labour, is not the dead but the living. It is not for the soul of thine enemy I would exhort thee to pray—that has already had its final doom from a Judge as merciful as he is just; nor, wert thou to coin that rock into ducats, and obtain a mass for each one, would it avail the departed spirit. Where the tree hath fallen, it must lie—but the sapling which hath in it yet the vigour and juice of life, may be bended to the point to which it ought to incline."

"Art thou a priest, father," said the young man, "or by what commission doest thou talk of such high matters?"

"By that of my Almighty Master," said the traveller, "under whose banner I am an enlisted soldier."

Halbert's acquaintance with religious matters was no deeper than could be derived from the Archbishop of Saint Andrews' Catechism, and the pamphlet called the Twa-pennie Faith, both which were industriously circulated and recommended by the Monks of Saint Mary's. Yet, however indifferent and superficial a theologian, he began to suspect that he was now in company with one of the gospellers, or heretics, before whose influence the ancient system of religion now tottered to the very foundation. Bred up, as may well be presumed, in a holy horror against these formidable sectaries, the youth's first feelings were those of a loyal and devoted church vassal. "Old man," said he, "wert thou able to make good with thy hand the words that thy tongue hath spoken against our Holy Mother Church, we should have tried upon this moor which of our creeds hath the better champion."

"Nay," said the stranger, "if thou art a true champion of Rome, thou wilt not pause from thy purpose because thou hast the odds of years and of strength on thy side. Hearken to me, my son. I have shewed thee how to make thy peace with heaven, and thou hast rejected my proffer. I will now shew thee how thou shalt make thy reconciliation with the powers of this world. Take this grey head from the frail body which supports it—carry it to the chair of the proud Abbot Boniface; and when thou tellest him thou hast slain Piercie Shafton, and his ire rises at the deed, lay the head of Henry Warden at his foot, and thou shalt have praise instead of censure."

Halbert Glendinning stepped back in surprise. "What! are you that Henry Warden so famous among the heretics, that even Knox's name is scarce more frequently in their mouths? Art thou he, and darest thou to approach the Halidome of Saint Mary's?"

"I am Henry Warden of a surety," said the old man, "far unworthy to be named in the same breath with Knox, but yet willing to venture on whatever dangers my Master's service may call me to."

"Hearken to me then," said Halbert; "to slay thee, I have no heart —to make thee prisoner, were equally to bring thy blood on my head —to leave thee in this wild without a guide, were little better. I will conduct thee, as I promised, in safety to the castle of Avenel; but breathe not, while we are on the journey, a word against the doctrines of the holy church of which I am an unworthy—but though an ignorant, a zealous member.—When thou art there arrived, beware of thyself—there is a high price upon thy head, and Julian Avenel loves the glance of gold bonnet-pieces."*

"Yet thou sayst not, that for lucre he would sell the blood of his guest?"

"Not if thou comest an invited stranger, relying on his faith," said the youth; "evil as Julian may be, he dare not break the rites of hospitality; for, loose as we are in all other ties, these are respected amongst us even to idolatry, and his nearest relations would think it incumbent on them to spill his blood themselves, to efface the disgrace such treason would bring upon their name and lineage. But if thou goest self-invited, and without assurance of safety, I promise thee the risk is great."

"I am in God's hand," answered the preacher, for such was Henry Warden; "it is on his errand that I traverse these wilds amidst dangers of every kind; while I am useful for my Master's service they shall not prevail against me, and when, like the barren fig-tree, I can no

---

* A gold coin of James V., the most beautiful in the Scottish series; so called because the effigies of the sovereign is represented wearing a bonnet.

longer produce fruit, what imports it when or by whom the axe is laid to the root?"

"Your courage and devotion," said Glendinning, "are worthy of a better cause."

"That," said Warden, "cannot be—mine is the very best."

They continued their journey in silence, Halbert Glendinning tracing with the utmost accuracy the mazes of the dangerous and intricate morasses and hills which divided the Halidome from the barony of Avenel. From time to time he was obliged to stop, in order to assist his companion to cross the black intervals of quaking bog, called in the Scottish dialect *hags*, by which the firmer parts of the morass were intersected.

"Courage, old man," said Halbert, as he saw his companion almost exhausted with fatigue, "we shall soon be upon hard ground. And yet soft as this moss is, I have seen the merry falconers go through it as light as deer when the quarry was upon the flight."

"True, my son," answered Warden, "for so I will still call you though you term me no longer father; and even so doth headlong youth pursue its pleasures, without regard to the mire and the peril of the paths through which they are hurried."

"I have already told thee," answered Halbert Glendinning, sternly, "that I will hear nothing from thee that savours of doctrine."

"Nay, but, my son," answered Warden, "thy spiritual father himself would surely not dispute the truth of what I have now spoken for your edification."

"Glendinning stoutly replied, "I know not how that may be—but I wot well it is the fashion of your brotherhood to bait your hook with fair discourse, and to hold yourselves up as angels of light, that you may the better extend the kingdom of darkness."

"May God," replied the preacher, "pardon those who have thus reported of his servants! I will not offend thee, my son, by being instant out of season—thou speakest but as thou art taught—yet sure I trust that so goodly a youth will be still rescued, like a brand from the burning."

While he thus spoke, the verge of the morass was attained, and their path lay on the declivity. Green-sward it was, and, viewed from a distance, chequered with its narrow and verdant line the dark-brown heath which it traversed, though the distinction was not so easily traced when they were walking on it. The old man pursued his journey with comparative ease, and unwilling again to awaken the jealous zeal of his young companion for the Roman faith, he discoursed on other matters. The tone of his conversation was still grave, moral, and instructive. He had travelled much, and knew both the language and manners of other countries, concerning which Halbert Glendinning, already anticipating the possibility of being obliged to quit Scotland for the deed he had done, was naturally and anxiously desirous of information. By degrees he was more attracted by the charms of the stranger's conversation than he was repelled by the dread of his dangerous character as a heretic, and Halbert had called him father more than once, ere the turrets of Avenel Castle came in view.

The situation of this ancient fortress was remarkable. It occupied a small rocky islet in a mountain lake, or *tarn*, as such a piece of water is called in Westmoreland. The lake might be about a mile in circumference, surrounded by hills of considerable height, which, except where old trees and brushwood occupied the ravines that divided them from each other, were bare and heathy. The surprise of the spectator was chiefly excited by finding so large a piece of water situated in that high and mountainous region, and the landscape around had features which might rather be termed wild, than either romantic or sublime. Yet the scene was not without its charms. Under the burning sun of summer, the clear azure of the deep unruffled lake refreshed the eye, and impressed the mind with a pleasing feeling of deep solitude. In winter, when the snow lay on the mountains around, these dazzling masses appeared to ascend far beyond their wonted and natural height, while the lake, which stretched beneath, and filled their bosom with all its frozen waves, lay like the surface of a darkened and broken mirror around the black and rocky islet, and the walls of the grey castle with which it was crowned.

As the castle occupied, either with its principal buildings, or with its flanking and outward walls, every projecting point of the rock which served as its site, it seemed as completely surrounded by water as the nest of a wild swan, save where a narrow causeway extended betwixt the islet and the shore. But it was larger in appearance than in reality; and of the buildings which it actually contained, many had become ruinous and uninhabitable. In the times of the grandeur of the Avenel family, these had been occupied by a considerable garrison of followers and retainers, but they were now in a great measure deserted; and Julian Avenel would probably have fixed his habitation in a residence better suited to his diminished fortunes, had it not been for the great security which the situation of the old castle afforded to a man of his precarious and perilous mode of life. Indeed, in this respect, the spot could scarce have been more happily chosen, for it could be rendered almost completely inaccessible at the pleasure of the inhabitant. The distance betwixt the nearest shore and the islet was not indeed above an hundred yards; but then the causeway which connected them was extremely narrow, and completely divided by two cuts, one in the mid-way between the islet and shore, and another close under the outward gate of the castle. These formed a formidable, and almost insurmountable interruption to any hostile approach. Each was defended by a draw-bridge, one of which, being that nearest to the castle, was regularly raised at all times during the day, and both were lifted at night.

The situation of Julian Avenel, engaged in a variety of feuds, and a party to almost every dark and mysterious transaction which was on foot in that wild and military frontier, required all these precautions for his security. His own ambiguous and doubtful course of policy had increased these dangers; for as he made professions to both parties in the state, and occasionally united more actively with either the one or other, as chanced best to serve his immediate purpose, he could not be said to have either firm allies and protectors, or determined enemies. His life was a life of expedients and of peril; and while, in pursuit of his interest he made all the doubles which he thought necessary to attain his object, he often over-ran his prey, and missed that which he might have gained by observing a straighter course.

Chapter Thirteen

I'll walk on tiptoe; arm my eye with caution,
My heart with courage, and my hand with weapon,
Like him who ventures on a lion's den.
                                        Old Play

WHEN, ISSUING from the gorge of a pass which terminated upon the lake, the travellers came in sight of the ancient castle of Avenel, the old man paused, and resting upon his pilgrim's staff, looked with earnest attention upon the scene before him. The castle was, as we have said, in many places ruinous, as was evident, even at this distance, by the broken, rugged, and irregular outline of the walls and of the towers. In others it seemed more entire, and a pillar of dark smoke, which ascended from the chimnies of the donjon, and spread its long dusky pennon through the clear ether, indicated that it was inhabited. But no corn-fields or enclosed pasture-grounds on the side of the lake shewed that provident attention to comfort and subsistence which usually appeared near the houses of the greater, and even of the lesser barons. There were no cottages with their patches of infield, and their little crofts and gardens, surrounded by rows of massive sycamores; no church with its simple tower in the valley; no herds of sheep among the hills; no cattle on the lower ground; nothing which intimated the occasional prosecution of the arts of peace and of industry. It was plain that the inhabitants, whether few or numerous, must be considered as the garrison of the castle, living within its defended precincts, and subsisting themselves by means which were other than peaceful.

Probably it was with this conviction that the old man, gazing on the castle, muttered to himself, "*Lapis offensionis et petra scandali,*" and then, turning to Halbert Glendinning, he added, "We may say of yonder fort as King James did of another fastness in this province, that he who built it was a thief in his heart."

"But it was not so," answered Glendinning; "yonder castle was builded by the old lords of Avenel, men as much beloved in peace as they were respected in war—they were the bulwark of the frontiers against foreigners, and the protectors of the natives from domestic oppression—the present usurper of their inheritance no more resembles them, than the night-prowling owl resembles a falcon, because she may build on the same rock."

"This Julian Avenel holds no high place, then, in the love and regard of his neighbours?" said Warden.

"So little," answered Halbert, "that besides the jack-men and riders with whom he has associated himself, and of whom he has many at his disposal, I know of few who voluntarily associate with him. He has been more than once outlawed both by England and Scotland, his lands declared forfeited, and his head set at a price. But in these unquiet times, a man so daring as Julian Avenel has ever found some friends willing to protect him against the penalties of the law, on condition of his secret services."

"You describe a dangerous man," replied Warden.

"You may have experience of that," replied the youth, "if you deal not the more warily;—though it may well be that he also has forsaken the communion of the church, and gone astray in the paths of heresy."

"What thy blindness terms the path of heresy," answered the reformer, "is indeed the straight and narrow way, wherein he who walks turns not aside, whether for worldly wealth or for worldly passion.—Would to God this man were moved by no other and no worse spirit than that which prompts my poor endeavours to extend the kingdom of Heaven! This Baron of Avenel is personally unknown to me, is not of our congregation or of our counsel; yet I bear to him charges touching my safety, from those whom he must fear if he does not respect them, and upon that assurance I will venture upon his hold—I am now sufficiently refreshed by these few minutes of repose."

"Take then this advice for your safety," said Halbert, "and believe that it is founded upon the usage of this country and its inhabitants. If you can better shift for yourself, go not to the castle of Avenel—if you do risk going thither, obtain from him, if possible, his safe conduct, and beware that he swears it by the Black Rood—And lastly, observe whether he eats with you at the board, or pledges you in the cup; for if he gives you not these signs of welcome, his thoughts are evil towards you."

"Alas!" said the preacher, "I have no better earthly refuge for the present than these frowning towers, but I go thither trusting to aid which is not of this earth—But thou, good youth, needest thou trust thyself in this dangerous den?"

"I," answered Halbert, "am in no danger. I am well known to Christie of Clinthill, the henchman of this Julian Avenel; and, what is a yet better protection, I have nothing either to provoke malice or to tempt plunder."

The tramp of a steed, which clattered along the shingly banks of the loch, was now heard behind them; and, when they looked back, a rider was visible, his steel cap, and the point of his long lance glancing in the setting sun, as he rode rapidly towards them.

Halbert Glendinning soon recognized Christie of the Clinthill, and made his companion aware that the henchman of Julian Avenel was approaching.

"Ha, youngling!" said Christie to Halbert, as he came up to them, "thou hast made good my word at last, and come to take service with my noble master, hast thou not? Thou shalt find me a good friend and a true; and ere Saint Barnaby come round again, thou shalt know every pass betwixt Millburn Plain and Netherby, as if thou hadst been born with a jack on thy back, and a lance in thy hand.—What old carle hast thou with thee?—He is not of the brotherhood of Saint Mary's—at least he has not the buist of these black cattle."

"He is a way-faring man," said Halbert, "who has concerns with Julian of Avenel. For myself, I intend to go to Edinburgh to see the court and the Queen, and when I return hither we will talk of your proffer. Meantime, as thou hast often invited me to the castle, I crave hospitality there to-night for myself and my companion."

"For thyself and welcome, young comrade; but we harbour no pilgrims, nor aught that looks like a pilgrim."

"So please you," said Warden, "I have letters of commendation to thy master from a sure friend, whom he will right willingly oblige in higher matters than in affording me a brief protection—And I am no pilgrim, but renounce the same, with all its superstitious observances."

He offered his letters to the horseman, who shook his head.

"These," he said, "are matters for my master, and it will be well if he can read them himself; for me, sword and lance are my book and psalter, and have been since I was twelve years old. But I will guide you to the castle, and the Baron of Avenel will himself judge of your errand."

By this time the party had reached the causeway, along which Christie advanced at a trot, intimating his presence to the warders within the castle by a shrill and peculiar whistle. At this signal the farther draw-bridge was lowered. The horseman passed it, and disappeared under the gloomy portal which was beyond it.

Glendinning and his companion advancing more leisurely along the rugged causeway, stood at length under the same gateway, over which frowned, in dark red free-stone, the ancient armorial bearings of the house of Avenel, which represented a female figure shrouded and muffled, which occupied the whole field. The cause of their assuming so singular a device was uncertain, but the figure was generally supposed to represent the mysterious being called the White Lady of Avenel.* The sight of this mouldering shield awakened in the mind of Halbert the strange circumstances which had connected his fate with that of Mary Avenel, and with the doings of the spiritual being who was attached to her house, and whom he saw here represented in stone, as he had before seen her effigy upon the seal ring of Walter Avenel, which, with other trinkets formerly mentioned, had been saved from pillage, and brought to Glendearg, when Mary's mother was driven from her habitation.

"You sigh, my son," said the old man, observing the impression made on his youthful companion's countenance, but mistaking the cause; "if you fear to enter, we may yet return."

"That can ye not," said Christie of the Clinthill, who emerged at that instant from a side door under the arch-way. "Look yonder, and chuse whether you will return skimming the water like a wild-duck, or winging the air like a plover."

They looked, and saw that the draw-bridge which they had just crossed was again raised, and now interposed its planks betwixt the setting sun and the portal of the castle, deepening the gloom of the arch under which they stood. Christie laughed and bid them follow him, saying, by way of encouragement, into Halbert's ear, "Answer boldly and readily to whatever the Baron asks you—never stop to pick your words, and above all shew no fear of him—the devil is not so black as he is painted."

As he spoke thus, he introduced them into the large stone-hall, at the upper end of which blazed a huge fire of wood. The long oaken table, which as usual occupied the midst of the apartment, was covered with rude preparations for the evening meal of the Baron and his

---

* There is an ancient English family which bears, or did bear, a phantom passant sable in a field argent.

chief domestics, five or six of whom, strong athletic savage-looking men, paced up and down the lower end of the hall, which rang to the jarring clang of their long swords that clashed as they moved, and to the heavy tramp of their high-heeled jack-boots. Iron jacks, or coats of buff, formed the principal part of their dress, and steel-bonnets, or large slouched hats with Spanish plumes drooping backwards, were their head attire.

The Baron of Avenel was one of those tall muscular martial figures which are the favourite subjects of Salvator Rosa. He wore a cloak which had been once gaily trimmed, but which, by long wear and frequent exposure to the weather, was now faded in its colours. Thrown negligently about his tall person, it partly hid and partly shewed a short doublet of buff, under which was in some places visible that light shirt of mail which was called a *secret*, because worn instead of more ostensible armour to protect against private assassination. A leathern belt sustained a large and heavy sword on the one side, and on the other that gay poniard which had once called Sir Piercie Shafton master, of which the hatchments and gildings were already much defaced, either by rough usage or neglect.

Notwithstanding the rudeness of his apparel, Julian Avenel's manner and countenance had far more elevation than those of the attendance which surrounded him. He might be fifty or upwards, for his dark hair was mingled with grey, but age had neither tamed the fire of his eye or the enterprize of his disposition. His countenance had been handsome, for beauty was an attribute of the family; but the lines were roughened by fatigue and exposure to the weather, and rendered coarse by the habitual indulgence of violent passions.

He seemed in deep and moody reflection, and was pacing at a distance from his dependants along the upper end of the hall, sometimes stopping from time to time to caress and feed a goss-hawk, which sate upon his wrist, with its jesses (i. e. the leathern straps fixed to its legs,) wrapt around his finger. The bird, which seemed not insensible to its master's attention, answered his caresses by ruffling forwards its feathers, and pecking playfully at his hand. At such intervals the Baron smiled, but instantly resumed the darksome air of sullen meditation. He did not even deign to look upon an object, which few could have passed and repassed so often without bestowing on it a transient glance.

This was a woman of exceeding beauty, rather gaily than richly attired, who sate on a low seat close by the huge hall chimney. The gold chains round her neck and arms,—the gay gown of green which swept the floor,—the silver-embroidered girdle, with its bunch of keys depending in housewifely pride by a silver chain,—the yellow

silken *couvrechef* (Scotticé *curch*) which was disposed around her
head, and partly concealed her dark profusion of hair,—above all, the
circumstance so delicately touched in the old ballad, that "the girdle
was too short," the "gown of green all too wide," for the wearer's
present shape, would have intimated the Baron's Lady. But then the
lowly seat,—the expression of deep melancholy, which was changed
into a timid smile whenever she saw the least chance of catching the
eye of Julian Avenel,—the subdued look of grief, and the starting tear
for which that constrained smile was again exchanged when she saw
herself entirely disregarded,—these were not attributes of a wife, or
they were those of a dejected and afflicted one.

Julian Avenel, as we have said, continued to pace the hall without
paying any of that mute attention which is rendered to almost
every female either by affection or courtesy. He seemed totally
unconscious of her presence, or of that of his attendants, and
was only roused from his own dark reflections by the attention
he paid to the falcon, to which, however, the lady seemed to attend,
as if studying either to find an opportunity of speaking to the
Baron, or of finding something enigmatical in the expressions which
he used to the bird. All this the strangers had time enough to
remark; for no sooner had they entered the apartment, than their
usher, Christie of the Clinthill, after exchanging a significant glance
with the menials or troopers at the lower end of the apartment,
signed to Halbert Glendinning and to his companion to stand still
near the door, while he himself, advancing nearer the table, placed
himself in such a situation as to catch the Baron's observation
when he should be disposed to look around, but without presuming
to intrude himself on his master's attention. Indeed the look of
this man, naturally bold, hardy, and audacious, seemed totally
changed when he was in presence of his master, and resembled
the dejected and cowering manner of a quarrelsome dog when
rebuked by his owner, or when he finds himself obliged to deprecate
the violence of a superior adversary of his own species.

In spite of the novelty of his own situation, and every painful feeling
connected with it, Halbert felt his curiosity interested in the female,
who sate by the chimney unnoticed and unregarded. He marked with
what keen and trembling solicitude she watched the broken words of
Julian, and how her glance stole towards him, ready to be averted upon
the slightest chance of his perceiving himself to be watched.

Meantime he went on with his dalliance with his feathered favourite, now giving, now withholding the morsel with which he was about
to feed the bird, and so exciting its appetite and gratifying it by turns.
"What, more yet?—thou foul kite, thou wouldst never have done—

give thee part thou wilt have all—Ay, prune thy feathers, and prink thyself gay—much thou wilt make of it now—doest think I know thee not?—doest think I see not that all that ruffling and pluming of wing and feathers is not for thy master, but to try what thou canst make of him, thou greedy gled?—well—there—take it then, and rejoice thyself—little boon goes far with thee, and with all thy sex—and so it should."

He ceased to look on the bird, and again traversed the apartment. Then taking another small piece of meat from the trencher, on which it was placed ready cut for his use, he began once again to tempt and teaze the bird, by offering and withdrawing it, until he awakened its wild and bold disposition. "What! struggling, fluttering, aiming at me with beak and single?* So la! So la! wouldst mount? wouldst fly? the jesses are round thy clutches, fool—thou canst neither stir nor soar, but by my will—Beware thou come to reclaim, wench—else I will wring thy head off one of these days—Well, have it then, and well fare thou with it.—So ho, Jenkin!" One of the attendants stepped forward —"Take the foul gled hence to the mew—I am weary of her—Look well to her casting and to her bathing—we will see her fly to-morrow. —How now, Christie, so soon returned!"

Christie advanced to his master, and gave an account of himself and his journey, in the way in which a police-officer holds communication with his magistrate, that is, as much by signs as by words.

"Noble sir," said that worthy satellite, "the Laird of ——," he named no place, but pointed with his finger in a south-western direction,—"may not ride with you the day he purposed, because the Lord Warden has threatened that he will——"

Here another blank, intelligibly enough made up by the speaker touching his own neck with his left fore-finger, and leaning his head a little to one side.

"Cowardly caitiff!" said Julian; "by Heaven! the whole world turns sheer naught—it is not worth a brave man living in—Ye may ride a day and night, and never see a feather wave or hear a horse prance—the spirit of our fathers is dead amongst us—the very brutes are degenerated—the cattle we bring home at our life's risk are mere carrion— Our hawks are riflers†—our hounds are turn-spits and trindle-tails— our men are women, and our women are——"

He looked at the female for the first time, and stopped short in the midst of what he was about to say, though there was something so contemptuous in the glance, that the blank might have been thus filled

---

* In the *kindly* language of hawking, as Lady Juliana Berners terms it, hawks' talons are called their *singles*.

† So termed when they only caught their prey by the feathers.

up—"Our women are such as she is." He said it not however, and, as if desirous of attracting his attention at all risks, and in whatever manner, she rose and came forwards to him, but with a timorousness ill-disguised by affected gaiety.—"Our women, Julian—what would you say of the women?"

"Nothing," answered Julian Avenel, "at least nothing but that they are kind-hearted wenches like thyself, Kate." The female coloured deeply, and returned to her seat.—"And what strangers hast thou brought with thee, Christie, that stand yonder like two stone statues?" said the Baron.

"The taller," said Christie, "is, so please you, a young fellow called Halbert Glendinning, the eldest son of the old widow at Glendearg."

"What brings him here?" said the Baron; "hath he any message from Mary Avenel?"

"Not as I think," said Christie; "the youth is roving the country—he was always a wild slip, for I have known him since he was the height of my sword."

"What qualities hath he?" said the Baron.

"All manner of qualities," answered his follower—"he can strike a buck, track a deer, fly a hawk, hallow to a hound—he shoots in the long and cross-bow to a hair's-breadth—wields a lance or sword like myself nearly—backs a horse manfully and fairly—I wot not what more a man need to do to make him a gallant companion."

"And who," said the Baron, "is the old miser who stands beside him?"

"Some cast of a priest as I fancy—he says he is charged with letters to you."

"Bid them come forward," said the Baron; and no sooner had they approached him more nearly, than, struck by the fine form and strength displayed by Halbert Glendinning, he addressed him thus: —"I am told, young swankie, that you are roaming the world to seek your fortune—if you will serve Julian Avenel, you may find it without going farther."

"So please you," answered Glendinning, "something has chanced to me that makes it better I should leave this land, and I am bound for Edinburgh."

"What!—thou hast stricken some of the king's deer, I warrant,—or lightened the meadows of Saint Mary's of some of their beeves—or thou hast taken a moonlight leap over the Border?"

"No, sir," said Halbert, "my case is entirely different."

"Then I warrant thee thou hast stabbed some brother churl in a fray about a wench—thou art a likely lad to wrangle in such a cause."

Ineffably disgusted at his tone and manner, Halbert Glendinning remained silent while the thought darted across his mind, what would Julian Avenel have said, had he known the quarrel, of which he spoke so lightly, had arisen on account of his own brother's daughter.—"But be thy cause of flight what it will," said Julian in continuation, "doest thou think the law or its emissaries can follow thee into this island, or arrest thee under the standard of Avenel?—look at the depth of the lake, the strength of the walls, the length of the causeway—look at my men, and think if they are like to see a comrade injured, or if I, their master, am a man to desert a faithful follower, in good or evil. I tell thee, it shall be an eternal day of truce betwixt thee and justice as they call it, from the instant thou hast put my colours into thy cap—thou shalt ride by the Warden's nose as thou wouldest pass an old market-woman, and ne'er a cur which follows him shall dare to bay at thee!"

"I thank you for your offers, noble sir," replied Halbert, "but I must answer in brief, that I cannot profit by them—my fortunes lead me elsewhere."

"Thou art a self-willed fool for thy pains," said Julian, turning from him; and signing to Christie to approach, he whispered in his ear, "There is promise in that young fellow's looks, Christie, and we want men of limbs and sinews so compacted—those thou hast brought to me of late are the mere refuse of mankind, wretches scarce worth the arrow that ends them: this youngster is limbed like Saint George. Ply him with wine and wassail—let the wenches weave their meshes about him like spiders—thou understandest?" Christie gave a sagacious nod of intelligence, and fell back to a respectful distance from his master. —"And thou, old man," said the Baron, turning to the elder traveller, "hast thou been roaming the world after fortune too?—it seems not she has fallen into thy way."

"So please you," replied Warden, "I were perhaps more to be pitied than I am now, had I indeed met with that fortune, which, like others, I have sought in my greener days."

"Nay, understand me, friend," said the Baron; "if thou art satisfied with thy buckram gown and long staff, I also am well content thou shouldst be as poor and contemptible as is good for the health of thy body and soul—All I care to know of thee is, the cause which hath brought thee to my castle, where few crows of thy kind care to settle. Thou art, I warrant thee, some ejected monk of a suppressed convent, paying in his old days the price of the luxurious idleness in which he spent his youth—ay, or it may be some pilgrim with a budget of lies from Saint James of Compostella, or Our Lady's of Loretto; or thou mayst be some pardoner with his budget of reliques from Rome, forgiving sins at a penny a dozen, and one to the tale—Ay, I guess why I find thee in this boy's company, and doubtless thou wouldest have such a strapping lad as he to carry thy wallet, and relieve thy lazy shoulders; but by the mass, I will cross thy cunning. I make my vow to sun and moon, I will not see a proper lad so misleard as to run the country with an old knave, like Simmie and his brother.* Away with thee!" he added, rising in wrath, and speaking so fast as to give no opportunity of answer, being probably determined to terrify the elder guest into an abrupt flight—"Away with thee, with thy clouted coat, scrip, and scallop-shells, or, by the name of Avenel, I will have them loose the hounds on thee."

Warden waited with the greatest patience until Julian Avenel, astonished that the threats and violence of his language made no impression on him, paused in a sort of wonder, and said in a less imperious tone, "Why the fiend doest thou not answer me?"

"When you have done speaking," said Warden, in the same composed manner, "it will be full time to reply."

"Say on, man, in the devil's name—but take heed—beg not here—were it but for the rinds of cheese, the refuse of the rats, or a morsel that my dogs would turn from—neither a grain of meal, nor the nineteenth part of a gray groat, will I give to any feigned limmar of thy coat."

"It may be," answered Warden, "that you would have less quarrel with my coat if you knew what it covers. I am neither friar nor mendicant, and would be right glad to hear thy testimony against these foul deceivers of God's church, and usurpers of his rights over the Christian flock, were it given in Christian charity."

"And who or what art thou, man," said Avenel, "that thou comest to this Border land, and art neither monk, nor soldier, nor broken man?"

"I am an humble teacher of the holy word," answered Warden. "This letter from a most noble person will speak why I am here at this present time."

He delivered the letter to the Baron, who regarded the seal with some surprise, and then looked on the letter itself, which seemed to excite still more. He then looked fixedly at the stranger, and said, in a menacing tone, "I think thou darest not betray me, or deceive me?"

"I am not the man to attempt either," was the concise reply.

Julian Avenel carried the letter to the window, where he perused, or at least attempted to peruse it more than once, often looking from the paper and gazing on the stranger who had delivered it, as if he meant to read the purport of the missive in the face of the messenger. Julian at length called to the female,—"Catherine, bestir thee, and fetch me presently that letter which I bade thee keep ready at hand in thy casket,

---

* Two *quæstionarii*, or begging friars, whose accoutrements and roguery make the subject of an old Scottish satirical poem.

having no sure lockfast place of my own."

Catherine went with the readiness of one willing to be employed; and as she walked, the situation which requires a wider gown and a longer girdle, and in which woman claims from man a double propor- tion of the most anxious care, was still more visible than before. She soon returned with the paper, and was rewarded with a cold—"I thank thee, wench—thou art a careful secretary."

This second paper he also perused and reperused more than once, and still, as he read it, bent from time to time a wary and observant eye upon Henry Warden. This examination and re-examination, though both the man and the place were dangerous, the preacher endured with the most composed and steady countenance, seeming, under the eagle, or rather the vulture eye of the Baron, as unmoved as under the gaze of an ordinary and peaceful peasant. At length Julian Avenel folded both papers, and having put them into the pocket of his cloak, cleared his brow, and coming forward, addressed his female compan- ion. "Catherine," said he, "I have done this good man injustice, when I mistook him for one of the drones of Rome. He is a preacher, Catherine—a preacher of the—the new doctrine of the Lords of the Congregation."

"The doctrine of the blessed Scriptures," said the preacher, "puri- fied from the devices of men."

"Sayest thou?" said Julian Avenel—"Well, thou mayst call it what thou lists; but to me it is recommended, because it flings off all those sottish dreams about saints and angels and devils, and unhorses the lazy monks that have ridden us so long, and spur-galled us so hard. No more masses and corpse-gifts, no more tithes and offerings to make men poor—no more prayers or psalms to make men cowards—no more christenings and penances, and confessions and marriages."

"So please you," said Henry Warden, "it is against the corruptions, not against the fundamental doctrines of the church, which we desire to renovate, and not to abolish."

"Pr'ythee, peace, man," said the Baron; "we of the laity care not what you set up, so you pull merrily down what stands in our way. Specially it suits well with us of the Southland fells; for it is our profession to turn the world upside down, and we live ever the blithest life when the downer side is uppermost."

Warden would have replied; but the Baron allowed him not time, striking the table with the hilt of his dagger, and crying out,—"Ho! you loitering knaves, bring our supper-meal quickly—see you not this holy man is exhausted for lack of food?—heard ye ever of priest or preacher that devoured not his five meals a-day?"

The attendants bustled to and fro, and speedily brought in several large smoking platters, filled with huge pieces of beef, boiled and roasted, but without any variety whatsoever; without vegetables, and almost without bread, though there was at the upper end a few oat-cakes in a basket. Julian Avenel made a sort of apology to Warden.

"You have been commended to our care, Sir Preacher, since that is your style, by a person whom we highly honour."

"I am assured," said Warden, "that the most noble Lord"——

"Pr'ythee, peace, man," said Avenel; "what need of naming names, so we understand each other? I meant but to speak in reference to your safety and comfort, of which he desires us to be chary. Now, for your safety, look at my walls and water. But touching your comfort, we have no corn of our own, and the meal-girnels of the south are less easily transported than their beeves, seeing they have no legs to walk upon. But what though? a stoup of wine thou shalt have, and of the best—thou shalt sit betwixt Catherine and me at the board-end.— And, Christie, do thou look to the young springald, and call to the cellarer for a flagon of the best."

The Baron took his wonted seat at the upper end of the board; his Catherine sate down, and courteously pointed a seat betwixt them for their reverent guest. But notwithstanding the influence both of hunger and fatigue, Henry Warden retained his standing posture.

Chapter Fourteen

When lovely woman stoops to folly,
And finds too late that men betray——
*   *   *   *   *

JULIAN AVENEL saw with surprise the demeanour of the reverend stranger. "Beshrew me," he said, "these new-fashioned religioners have fast-days, I warrant me—the old ones used to confer these blessings chiefly on the laity."

"We acknowledge no such rule," said the preacher—"We hold that our faith consists not in using or abstaining from special meats on special days; and in fasting we rend our hearts, and not our gar-ments."

"The better—the better for yourselves, and the worse for Tom Tailor," said the Baron; "but come, sit down, or if thou needs must, e'en give us a cast of thy office—mutter thy charm."

"Sir Baron," said the preacher, "I am in a strange land, where neither mine office nor my doctrine are known, and where, it would seem, both are greatly misunderstood. It is my duty so to bear me, that in my person, however unworthy, my Master's dignity may be respected, and that sin may take no confidence from relaxation of the bonds of discipline."

"Ho la! halt there," said the Baron; "thou wert sent hither for thy safety, but not, I think, to preach to, or controul me. What is it thou wouldst have, Sir Preacher? remember thou speakest to one somewhat short of patience, who loves a short health and a long draught."

"In a word, then," said Henry Warden, "that lady"——

"How?" said the Baron, starting—"what of her?—what hast thou to say of that dame?"

"Is she thy house-dame?" said the preacher, after a moment's pause, in which he seemed to seek for the best mode of expressing what he had to say—"Is she in brief thy wife?"

The unfortunate young woman pressed both her hands on her face, as if to hide it, but the deep blush which crimsoned her brow and neck, shewed that her cheeks were also glowing; and the bursting tears which found their way betwixt her slender fingers, bore witness to her sorrow, as well as to her shame.

"Now, by my father's ashes!" said the Baron, rising and spurning from him his footstool with such violence, that it hit the wall on the opposite side of the apartment—then instantly constraining himself, he muttered, "What need to run myself into trouble for a fool's word?"—then resuming his seat, he answered coldly and scornfully—"No, Sir Priest or Sir Preacher, Catherine is not my wife—Cease thy whimpering, thou foolish wench—she is not my wife, but she is handfasted with me, and that makes her as honest a woman."

"Handfasted?"—repeated Warden.

"Knowst thou not that rite, holy man?" said Avenel, in the same tone of derision; "then I will tell thee—we Border-men are more wary than your inland clowns of Fife and Lothian—no jump in the dark for us—no clenching the fetters for ever around our wrists till we know how they will wear with us—we take our wives, like our horses, upon trial. When we are handfasted, as we term it, we are man and wife for a year and day—that space gone by, each may chuse another mate, or, at their pleasure, may call the priest to marry them for life—And this we call handfasting."

"Then," said the preacher, "I tell thee, noble Baron, in brotherly love to thy soul, it is a custom licentious, gross, and corrupted, and, if persisted in, dangerous, yea, damnable. It binds thee to the frailer being while she is the object of desire—it relieves thee when she is most the subject of pity—it gives all to brutal sense, and nothing to generous and gentle affection. I say to thee, that he who can meditate the breach of such an engagement, abandoning the deluded woman and the helpless off-spring, is worse than the birds of prey; for of them the males remain with their mates until the nestlings can take wing. Above all, I say it is contrary to the pure Christian doctrine, which assigns woman to man as the partner of his labour, the soother of his evil, his helpmate in peril, his friend in affliction; not as the toy of his looser hours, or as a flower, which, once cropped, he may throw aside at pleasure."

"Now, by the Saints, a most virtuous homily!" said the Baron; "quaintly conceived and curiously pronounced, and to a well chosen congregation. Hark ye, Sir Gospeller! trow ye to have a fool in hand? Know I not that your sect rose by bluff Harry Tudor, merely because ye aided him to change *his* Kate; and wherefore should I not use the same Christian liberty with *mine?* Tush, man! bless the good food, and meddle not with what concerns thee not—thou hast no gull in Julian Avenel."

"He gulls and cheats himself," said the preacher; "should he even incline to do that poor sharer of his domestic cares the imperfect justice that remains to him, can he now raise her to the rank of a pure and uncontaminated matron?—can he deprive his child of the misery of owing his birth to a mother who has erred? He can indeed give them both the rank, the status of a married wife and of a lawful son; but, in opinion, their names will be smirched and sullied with a stain which his tardy efforts cannot entirely efface. Yet render it to them, Baron of Avenel, render to them this late and imperfect justice. Bid me bind you together for ever, and celebrate the day of your bridal, not with feasting or was-sell, but with sorrow for past sin, and the resolution to commence a better life. Happy then will have the chance been that has drawn me to this castle, though I come driven by calamity, and unknowing where my course is bound, like a leaf travelling on the north wind."

The plain, and even coarse features of the zealous speaker, were warmed at once and ennobled by the dignity of his enthusiasm; and the wild Baron, lawless as he was, and accustomed to spurn at controul, whether of religious or moral law, felt, for the first time perhaps in his life, that he was under subjection to a mind superior to his own. He sate mute and suspended in his deliberations, hesitating betwixt anger and shame, yet borne down by the weight of the just rebuke thus boldly fulminated against him.

The unfortunate young woman, conceiving hopes from her tyrant's silence and apparent indecision, forgot both her fear and shame in her timid expectation that Avenel would relent; and fixing upon him her anxious and beseeching eyes, gradually drew near and nearer to his seat, till at length, laying a trembling hand on his cloak, she ventured to utter, "O noble Julian, listen to the good man!"

The speech and the motion were ill-timed, and wrought in that proud and wayward spirit the reverse of her wishes.

Julian Avenel started up in fury, exclaiming, "What! thou foolish callet, art thou confederate with this strolling vagabond, whom thou has heard beard me in my own hall! Hence with thee, and think that I am proof both to male and female hypocrisy!"

The poor girl started back, astounded at his voice of thunder and looks of fury, and, turning pale as death, endeavoured to obey his orders, and tottered towards the door. Her limbs failed her in the attempt, and she fell on the stone floor in a manner which her situation might have rendered fatal—The blood gushed from her face.—Halbert Glendinning brooked not a sight so brutal, but, uttering a deep imprecation, started from his seat, and laid his hand on his sword, under the strong impulse of passing it through the body of the cruel and hard-hearted ruffian. But Christie of the Clinthill, guessing his intention, threw his arms around him, and prevented him from stirring to execute his purpose.

The impulse to such a dangerous act of violence was indeed but momentary, as it instantly appeared that Avenel himself, shocked at the effects of his violence, was lifting up and endeavouring to sooth in his own way the terrified Catherine.

"Peace," he said, "prithee peace, thou silly minion—why, Kate, though I listen not to this tramping preacher, I said not what might happen, an thou doest bear me a stout boy. There—there—dry thy tears—call thy women.—So ho!—where be these queans?—Christie—Rowley—Hutcheon—drag them hither by the hair of the head."

A half dozen of startled wild-looking females rushed into the room, and bore out her who might be either termed their mistress or their companion. She shewed little sign of life, except by groaning faintly and keeping her hand on her side.

No sooner had this luckless female been conveyed from the apartment, than the Baron, advancing to the table, filled and drunk a deep goblet of wine; then, putting an obvious restraint on his passions, turned to the preacher, who stood horror-struck at the scene he had witnessed, and said, "You have borne too hard on us, Sir Preacher—but coming with the commendations which you have brought me, I doubt not but your meaning was good. But we are a wilder folk than you inland men of Fife and Lothian. Be advised, therefore, by me—Spur not an unbroken horse—put not your plough-share too deep into new land—Preach to us spiritual liberty, and we will hearken to you.—But we will give no way to spiritual bondage.—Sit, therefore, down, and pledge me in old sack, and we will talk over other matters."

"It is *from* spiritual bondage," said the preacher, in the same tone of admonitory reproof, "that I came to deliver you—it is from a bondage more fearful than that of the heaviest earthly gyves—it is from your own evil passions."

"Sit down," said Avenel, fiercely; "sit down while the play is good —else by my father's crest and by my mother's honour"——

"Now," whispered Christie of the Clinthill to Halbert, "if he refuse to sit down, I would not give a grey groat for his head."

"Lord Baron," said Warden, "thou hast placed me in extremity. But if the question be, whether I am to hide the light which I am commanded to shew forth, or to lose the light of this world, my choice is made. I say to thee, like the Holy Baptist to Herod, it is not lawful for thee to have this woman; and I say it, though bonds and death be the consequence, counting my life as nothing in comparison of the ministry to which I am called."

Julian Avenel, enraged at the firmness of this reply, flung from his right hand the cup in which he was about to drink to his guest, and from the other cast off the hawk, which flew wildly through the apartment. His first motion was to lay hand upon his dagger. But changing his resolution, he exclaimed, "To the dungeon with this insolent stroller!—I will hear no man speak a word for him.—Look to the falcon, Christie, thou fool—an she escape, I will dispatch you after her every man—Away with that hypocritical dreamer!—drag him hence if he resists."

He was obeyed in both points.—Christie of the Clinthill arrested the hawk's flight, by putting his foot on her jesses, and so holding her fast, while Henry Warden was led off, without having shewn the slightest symptom of terror, by two of the Baron's satellites. Julian Avenel walked the apartment for a short space in sullen silence, and dispatching one of his attendants with a whispered message, which probably related to the health of the unfortunate Catherine, he said aloud, "These rash and meddling priests—by Heaven! they make us worse than we would be without them."

The answer which he presently received seemed somewhat to pacify his angry mood, and he took his place at the board, commanding his retinue to do the like. All sate down in silence, and began their repast.

During the meal, Christie in vain attempted to engage his youthful companion in carousal, or, at least, in conversation. Halbert Glendinning pleaded fatigue, and expressed himself unwilling to taste any liquor stronger than the heather-ale, which was at that time frequently used at meals. Thus every effort at joviality died away, until the Baron, striking his hand against the table, as if impatient of the long unbroken silence, called out aloud, "What, ho! my masters

—are ye Border-riders, and sit as mute over your meal as a mess of monks and friars?—Some one sing, if no one list to speak: Meat eaten without either mirth or music, is ill of digestion.—Louis," he added, speaking to one of the youngest of his followers, "thou art ready enough to sing when no one bids thee."

The young man looked first at his master, then up to the arched roof of the hall, then drank off the horn of ale, or wine, which stood before him, and with a rough, yet not unmelodious voice, sung the following ditty to the ancient air of "Blue Bonnets over the Border."

1.

March, march, Ettrick and Teviotdale,
  Why the deil dinna ye march forward in order;
March, march, Eskdale and Liddesdale,
  All the blue bonnets are bound for the Border.
    Many a banner spread,
    Flutters above your head,
  Many a crest that is famous in story,
    Mount, and make ready then,
    Sons of the mountain glen,
  Fight for the Queen and our old Scottish glory.

2.

Come from the hills where your hirsels are grazing,
  Come from the glens of the buck and the roe;
Come to the crag where the beacon is blazing,
  Come with the buckler, the lance, and the bow.
    Trumpets are sounding,
    War-steeds are bounding,
  Stand to your arms then, and march in good order,
    England shall many a day
    Tell of the bloody fray,
  When the Blue Bonnets came over the Border.

The song, rude as it was, had in it that warlike character which at any other time would have roused Halbert's spirit; but at present the charm of minstrelsy had no effect upon him. He made it his request to Christie to suffer him to retire to rest, a request with which that worthy person, seeing no chance of making a favourable impression on his intended proselyte in his present humour, was at length pleased to comply. But no Serjeant Kite, who ever practised the profession of recruiting, was more attentive that his object should not escape him, than was Christie of the Clinthill. He indeed conducted Halbert Glendinning to a small apartment overlooking the lake, which was accommodated with a truckle bed. But before quitting him, Christie took special care to give a look to the bars which crossed the outside of the window, and when he left the apartment, he failed not to give the key a double turn; circumstances which convinced young Glendinning that there was no intention of suffering him to depart from the

Castle of Avenel at his own time and pleasure. He judged it, however, most prudent to let these alarming symptoms pass without observation.

No sooner did he find himself in undisturbed solitude, than he ran rapidly over the events of the day in his recollection, and to his surprise found that his own precarious fate, and even the death of Piercie Shafton, made less impression on him than the singularly bold and determined conduct of his companion, Henry Warden. Providence, which suits its implements to the end they are to achieve, had awakened in the cause of Reformation in Scotland, a body of preachers of more energy than refinement, bold in spirit, and strong in faith, contemners of whatever stood betwixt them and their principal object, and seeking the advancement of the Great Cause in which they laboured by the roughest road, provided it were the shortest. The soft breeze may wave the willow, but it requires the voice of the tempest to agitate the boughs of the oak; and, accordingly, to milder hearers, and in less rude ages, their manners would have been ill-adapted, but they were singularly successful in their mission to the people to whom it was addressed.

Owing to these reasons, Halbert Glendinning, who had resisted and repelled the arguments of the preacher, was forcibly struck by the firmness of his demeanour in the dispute with Julian Avenel. It might be discourteous, and most certainly it was incautious, to choose such a place and such an audience, for upbraiding with his transgressions a baron, whom both manners and situation placed in full possession of independent power. But the conduct of the preacher was uncompromising, firm, manly, and obviously grounded upon the deepest conviction which duty and principle could afford; and Glendinning, who had viewed the conduct of Avenel with the deepest abhorrence, was proportionally interested in the brave old man, who had ventured life rather than withhold the censure due to guilt. This pitch of virtue seemed to him to be in religion what was demanded by chivalry of her votaries in war; an absolute surrender of all selfish feelings, and a combination of every energy proper to the human mind, to discharge the task which duty demanded.

Halbert was at the period when youth is most open to generous emotions, and knows best how to appreciate them in others, and he felt, though he hardly knew why, that, whether catholic or heretic, the safety of this man deeply interested him. Curiosity mingled with the feeling, and led him to wonder what the nature of those doctrines could be, which stole their votary so completely from himself, and devoted him to chains or to death as their sworn champion. He had indeed been told of saints and martyrs of former days, who had braved

for their religious faith the extremity of death and torture. But their
spirit of enthusiastic devotion had long slept in the ease and indolent
habits of their successors, and their adventures, like those of knights-
errant, were rather read for amusement than for edification. A new
impulse had been necessary to re-kindle the energies of religious zeal,
and that impulse was now operating in favour of a purer religion, with
one of whose truest votaries the youth had now met for the first time.

The sense that he himself was a prisoner, under the power of this
savage chieftain, by no means diminished Halbert's interest in the fate
of his fellow-sufferer, while he determined at the same time so far to
emulate his fortitude, that neither threats nor suffering should compel
him to enter into the service of such a master. The possibility of escape
next occurred to him, and though with little hope of effecting it in that
way, Glendinning proceeded to examine more particularly the window of the apartment.

The apartment was situated in the first storey of the castle, and was
not so far from the rock on which it was founded, but what an active
and bold man might with little assistance descend to a shelve of the
rock which was immediately below the window, and from thence
either leap or drop himself down into the lake which lay below his eye,
clear and blue in the placid light of a full summer's moon.—"Were I
once placed on that ledge," thought Glendinning, "Julian Avenel and
Christie had seen the last of me." The size of the window favoured
such an attempt, but the stancheons or iron bars seemed to form an
insurmountable obstacle.

While Halbert Glendinning gazed from the window with that
eagerness of hope which was prompted by the energy of his character
and his determination not to yield to circumstances, his ear caught
some sounds from below, and listening with more attention, he could
distinguish the voice of the preacher engaged in his solitary devotions.
To open a correspondence with him became immediately his object,
and failing to do so by less marked sounds, he at length ventured to
speak, and was answered from beneath—"Is it thou, my son?" The
voice of the prisoner now sounded more plain than when it was first
heard, for Warden had approached the small aperture, which, serving
his prison for a window, opened just betwixt the wall and the rock, and
admitted a scanty portion of light through a wall of immense thickness. This *soupirail* being placed exactly under Halbert's window,
permitted the prisoners to converse in a low tone, when Halbert
declared his intention to escape, and the possibility he saw of achiev-
ing his purpose, but for the iron stancheons of the window—"Prove
their strength, my son, in the name of God!" said the preacher.
Halbert obeyed him more in despair than hope, but to his great

astonishment, and somewhat to his terror, the bar parted asunder near the bottom, and the longer part being easily bent outwards and not secured with lead in the upper socket, dropt out into Halbert's hand. He immediately whispered, but as energetically as a whisper could be expressed—"By Heaven, the bar has given way in my hand!"

"Thank Heaven, my son, instead of swearing by it," answered Warden from his dungeon.

With little effort Halbert Glendinning forced himself through the opening thus wonderfully effected, and using his leathern sword-belt as a rope to assist him, let himself safely drop upon the shelf of rock upon which the preacher's window opened. But through this no passage could be effected, being scarce larger than a loop-hole for musketry, and apparently constructed for that purpose.

"Is there no means by which I can assist your escape, my father?" said Halbert.

"There is none, my son," answered the preacher; "but if thou wilt ensure my safety, that may be in thy power."

"I will labour earnestly for it," said the youth.

"Take then a letter which I will presently write, for I have the means of light and writing materials in my scrip—Hasten towards Edinburgh, and on the way thou wilt meet a body of horse marching southwards—Give this to their leader, and acquaint him of the state in which thou hast left me. It may hap that thy doing so will advantage thyself."

In a minute or two the light of a taper gleamed through the shot-hole, and very shortly after, the preacher, with the assistance of his staff, pushed a billet to Glendinning through the window.

"God bless thee, my son," said the old man, "and complete the marvellous work which he has begun!"

"Amen!" answered Halbert, with solemnity, and proceeded on his enterprize.

He hesitated a moment whether he should attempt to descend to the edge of the water; but the steepness of the rock, and darkness of the night, rendered the enterprize too dangerous. He clasped his hands above his head, boldly sprung from the precipice, shooting himself forward into the air as far as he could for fear of sunken rocks, and alighted on the lake, head foremost, with such force as sunk him for a minute below the surface. But strong, long-breathed, and well accustomed to such exercise, Halbert, even though encumbered with his sword, dived and rose like a sea-fowl, and swam across the lake in the northern direction. When he landed and looked back on the castle, he could observe that the alarm had been given, for lights glanced from window to window, and he heard the draw-bridge lowered, and the tread of horses' feet upon the causeway. But, little alarmed for the consequence of a pursuit during the darkness, he wrung the water from his dress, and, plunging into the moors, directed his course to the north-east by the assistance of the polar star.

END OF VOLUME SECOND

THE MONASTERY

VOLUME III

Chapter One

Why, what an intricate impeach is this!
I think you all have drank of Circe's cup.
If here you hous'd him, here he would have been;
If he were mad, he would not plead so coldly.
Comedy of Errors

LEAVING FOR THE PRESENT Halbert Glendinning to the guidance of his courage and his fortune, our story returns to the tower of
Glendearg, where matters in the meanwhile took place, with which it
is most fitting that the reader should be acquainted.

The meal was prepared at noontide with all the care which Elspet
and Tibb, assisted by the various accommodations which had been
supplied from the Monastery, could bestow on it. Their dialogue ran
on as usual in the intervals of their labour, partly as between mistress
and servant, partly as maintained by gossips of nearly equal quality.

"Look to the minced meat, Tibb," said Elspet; "and turn the
broach even, thou good-for-nothing Simmie,—thy wits are harrying
bird's nests, child.—Weel, Tibb—this is a fasheous job, this Sir
Piercie lying leaguer with us up here, and wha kens for how lang?"

"A fasheous job indeed," answered her faithful attendant, "and
little good did the name ever bring to fair Scotland. Ye may have your
hands fuller of them than they are yet—Mony a sair heart have the
Percies given to Scots wife and bairns with their pricking on the
Borders. There was Hotspur, and mony mair of that bloody kindred,
have sate in our skirts since Malcolm's time, as Martin says!"

"Martin should keep a weel-scrapeit tongue in his head," said
Elspet, "and not slander the kin of any body that guestens at Glendearg; forbye, that Sir Piercie Shafton is much respected with the
holy fathers of the community, and they will make up to us ony

fasherie that we have with him, either by good word or good deed, I'se warrant them. He is a considerate lord the Lord Abbot."

"And weel he likes a saft seat to his hinder end," said Tibb; "I have seen a belted baron sit on a bare bench and find nae fault. But an ye are pleased, mistress, I am pleased."

"Now, in good time, here comes Mysie of the Mill.—And whare hae ye been, lass, for a's gaen wrang without you?" said Elspet.

"I just gaed a blink up the burn," said Mysie, "for the young lady has lain down on her bed, and is no just that weel—So I gaed a gliff up the burn."

"To see the young lads come hame frae the sport, I will warrant you," said Elspet. "Ay, ay, Tibb, that's the way the young folk guide us, Tibbie—leave us to do the wark, and out to the play themsells."

"Ne'er a bit of that, mistress," said the Maid of the Mill, stripping her pretty round arms, and looking actively and good-humouredly round for some duty which she could discharge, "but just—I thought ye might like to ken if they were coming back, just to get the dinner forward."

"And saw you ought of them then?" demanded Elspet.

"Not the least tokening," said Mysie, "though I got to the head of a knowe, and though the English knight's beautiful white feather could have been seen over all the bushes in the Shaw."

"The knight's white feather!" said Dame Glendinning; "ye are a sillie hempie—my Halbert's high head will be seen farther than his feather, let it be as white as it like, I trow."

Mysie made no answer, but began to knead dough for wastel cake with all dispatch, observing Sir Piercie had partaken of that dainty and commended it upon the preceding day. And presently, in order to place on the fire the *girdle* or iron plate on which these cates were to be baked, she displaced a stew-pan in which some of Tibb's delicacies were submitted to the action of the kitchen fire. Tibb muttered betwixt her teeth—"And it is the broth for my sick bairn, that maun make room for the dainty Southron's wastel bread! It was a blithe time in Wight Wallace's days, or Good King Robert's, when the pock-puddings gat naething here but hard straiks and bloody crowns. But we will see how it will a' end."

Elspet did not think it proper to notice these discontented expressions of Tibbie, but they sunk into her mind; for she was apt to consider her as a sort of authority in matters of war and policy, with which her former experience as bower-woman at Avenel Castle made her better acquainted than were the peaceful inhabitants of the Hali-dome. She only spoke, however, to express her surprise that the hunters did not return.

"An they come not back the sooner," said Tibb, "they will fare the waur, for the meat will be roasted to a cinder—and there is poor Simmie that can turn the spit nae langer: the bairn is melting like an icicle in warm water—Gang awa, bairn, and take a mouthful of the caller air, and I will turn the broach till ye come back."

"Rin up to the bartizan at the tower head, callant," said Dame Glendinning, "the air will be callerer there than ony gate else, and bring us word if our Halbert and the gentleman are coming down the glen."

The boy lingered long enough to allow his substitute, Tibb Tacket, heartily to tire of her own generosity, and of his cricket-stool by the side of a huge fire. He at length returned with the news that he had seen nobody.

The matter was not remarkable so far as Halbert Glendinning was concerned, for, patient alike of want and of fatigue, it was no uncommon circumstance for him to remain in the wilds till curfew time. But nobody had given Sir Piercie Shafton credit for being so keen a sportsman, and the idea of an Englishman preferring the chase to his dinner was altogether inconsistent with their preconceptions of the national character. Amidst wondering and conjecturing, the usual dinner-hour passed long away; and the inmates of the tower, taking a hasty meal themselves, adjourned their more solemn preparation until the hunters' return at night, since it seemed now certain that their sport had either carried them to a greater distance, or engaged them for a longer time than had been expected.

About four hours after noon, arrived (not the expected sportsmen,) but an unlooked for visitant, the Sub-Prior from the Monastery. The scene of the preceding day had dwelt on the mind of Father Eustace, who was of that keen and penetrating cast of mind which loves not to leave unascertained whatever of mysterious is subjected to its enquiry. His kindness was interested in the family of Glendearg, which he had now known for a long time; and besides, the community was interested in the preservation of the peace betwixt Sir Piercie Shafton and his youthful host, since whatever might draw public attention on the former, could not fail to be prejudicial to the Monastery, which was already threatened by the hand of power. He found the family assembled all but Mary Avenel, and was informed that Halbert Glendinning had accompanied the stranger on a day's sport. So far was well. They had not returned; but when did youth and sport conceive themselves bound by set hours? and the circumstance excited no alarm in his mind.

While he was conversing with Edward Glendinning touching his progress in the studies he had pointed out to him, they were startled by a shriek from Mary Avenel's apartment, which drew the whole family in headlong haste to her apartment. They found her in a swoon in the arms of old Martin, who was bitterly accusing himself of having killed her. So indeed it seemed, for her pale features and closed eyes argued rather a dead corpse than a living person. The whole family were instantly in tumult. Snatching her from Martin's arms with the eagerness of affectionate terror, Edward bore her to the casement, that she might receive the influence of the open air. The Sub-Prior, who, like many of his profession, had some knowledge of medicine, hastened to prescribe the readiest remedies which occurred to him, and the terrified females contended with, and impeded each other, in their rival efforts to be useful.

"It has been ane of her weary ghaists," said Dame Glendinning.

"It is just a trembling on her spirits, as her blessed mother used to have," said Tibb.

"It is some ill news has come ower her," said the miller's maiden, while burnt feathers, cold water, and all the usual means of restoring suspended animation, were employed alternately, and with little effect.

At length a new assistant, who had joined the groupe unobserved, tendered his aid in the following terms:—"How is this, my most fair Discretion? What cause hath moved her ruby current of life to rush back to the citadel of the heart, leaving pale those features in which it should have delighted to meander for ever?—Let me approach her," he said, "with this sovereign essence, distilled by the fair hands of the divine Urania, and powerful to recall fugitive life, even if it were trembling on the verge of departure."

Thus speaking, Sir Piercie Shafton kneeled down, and most gracefully presented to the nostrils of Mary Avenel a silver pouncet-box, exquisitely chased, containing a sponge dipped in the essence which he recommended so highly. Yes, gentle reader, it was Sir Piercie Shafton himself who thus unexpectedly proffered his good offices! his cheek, indeed, very pale, and some part of his dress stained with blood, but not otherwise appearing different from what he was on the preceding evening. But no sooner had Mary Avenel opened her eyes, and fixed them on the figure of the officious courtier, than she screamed faintly, and exclaimed,—"Secure the murtherer!"

Those present stood aghast with astonishment, and none more so than the Euphuist, who found himself accused so suddenly and so strangely by the patient whom he was endeavouring to succour, but who repelled his attempts to yield her assistance with all the energy of abhorrence.

"Take him away," she exclaimed—"take away the murtherer!"

"Now, by my knighthood," answered Sir Piercie, "your lovely faculties either of mind or body are, O my most fair Discretion, obnubilated by some strange hallucination. For either your eyes do not discern that it is Piercie Shafton, your most devoted Affability, who now stands before you, or else, your eyes discerning truly, your mind hath most erroneously concluded that he hath been guilty of some delict or violence to which his hand is a stranger. No murther, O most scornful Discretion, hath been this day done, saving but that which your angry glances are now performing on your most devoted captive."

He was here interrupted by the Sub-Prior, who had, in the mean time, been speaking with Martin apart, and had received from him an account of the circumstances, which, suddenly communicated to Mary Avenel, had thrown her into this state. "Sir Knight," said the Sub-Prior, in a very solemn tone, yet with some hesitation, "appearances have been communicated to us of a nature so extraordinary, that —reluctant as I am to exercise such authority over a guest of our venerable community, I am constrained to request from you an explanation of them. You left this tower early in the morning, accompanied with a youth, Halbert Glendinning, the eldest son of this good dame, and you return hither without him. Where, and at what hour, did you part company from him?"

The English knight paused for a moment, and then replied,—"I marvel that your reverence employs so grave a tone to enforce so slight a question. I parted with Halbert Glendinning some hour or twain after sunrise."

"And at what place, I pray you?" said the Monk.

"In a deep ravine, where a fountain rises at the base of a huge rock; an earth-born Titan, which heaveth up its grey head"——

"Spare us further description," said the Sub-Prior; "we know the spot. But that youth hath not since been heard of, and it will fall on you to account for him."

"My bairn! my bairn!" exclaimed Dame Glendinning. "Yes, holy father, make the villain account for my bairn!"

"I swear, good woman, by bread and by water, which are the props of our life"——

"Swear by wine and wastel bread, for these are the props of *thy* life, thou greedy Southron!" said Dame Glendinning;—"a base belly-god, to come here to eat the best, and practise on our lives that give it to him!"

"I tell thee, woman," said Sir Piercie Shafton, "I did but go with thy son to the hunting."

"A black hunting it has been to him, poor bairn," replied Tibb;

"and sae I said it wad prove, since I first saw the false Southron snout of thee—little good comes of a Piercie's hunting, from Chevy-Chace till now."

"Be silent, woman," said the Sub-Prior, "and touch not the English knight. We do not yet know any thing beyond suspicion."

"We will have his heart's blood," said Dame Glendinning; and, seconded by the faithful Tibbie, she made such a sudden onslaught on the unlucky Euphuist, as must have terminated in something serious, had not the Monk, aided by Mysie Happer, interposed to protect him from their fury. Edward had left the apartment the instant the disturbance broke out, and he now entered, sword in hand, followed by Martin and Jasper, the one having a hunting-spear in his hand, the other a cross-bow.

"Keep the door," he said to his two attendants; "shoot him or stab him without mercy, should he attempt to break forth; if he offers an escape, by Heaven he shall die!"

"How now, Edward," said the Sub-Prior; "how is this that you so far forget yourself? meditating violence to a guest, and in my presence, who represent your liege lord?"

Edward stepped forward with his drawn sword in his hand. "Pardon me, reverend father," he said, "but in this matter the voice of nature speaks louder and stronger than yours. I turn my sword's point against this proud man, and I demand of him the blood of my brother —the blood of my father's son—of the heir of our name! If he denies to give me a true account of him, he shall not deny me vengeance."

Embarrassed as he was, Sir Piercie Shafton shewed no personal fear. "Put up thy sword," he said, "young man—not in the same day does Piercie Shafton contend with two peasants."

"Hear him! he confesses the deed, holy father," said Edward.

"Be patient, my son," said the Sub-Prior, endeavouring to sooth the feelings which he could not otherwise controul, "be patient—thou wilt attain the ends of justice better through my means than thine own violence—And you, women, be silent—Tibb, remove your mistress and Mary Avenel."

When Tibb had, with the assistance of the other females of the household, borne the poor mother and Mary Avenel into separate apartments, and while Edward, still keeping his sword in his hand, hastily traversed the room, as if to prevent the possibility of Sir Piercie Shafton's escape, the Sub-Prior insisted upon knowing from the perplexed knight the particulars which he knew respecting Halbert Glendinning. His situation became extremely embarrassing, for what he might with safety have told of the issue of their combat was so revolting to his pride, that he could not bring himself to enter into the detail;

and of Halbert's actual fate he knew, as the reader is well aware, absolutely nothing.

The Father in the meanwhile pressed him with remonstrances, and prayed him to observe, he would greatly prejudice himself by declining to give a full account of the transactions of the day. "You cannot deny," he said, "that yesterday you seemed to take the most violent offence at this unfortunate youth; and that you suppressed your resentment so suddenly, as to impress us all with surprise. Last night you proposed to him this day's hunting party, and you set out together by break of day. You parted, you said, at the fountain near the rock, about an hour or twain after sunrise, and it appears that before you parted you had been at strife together."

"I said not so," replied the knight. "Here is a coil, indeed, about the absence of a rustical bondsman, who, I dare say, hath gone off (if he be gone) to join the next rascally band of freebooters! Ye ask me, a knight, and of the Piercie's lineage, to account for such an insignificant fugitive; and I answer,—let me know the price of his head, and I will pay it to your convent-treasurer."

"You admit, then, that you have slain my brother," said Edward, interfering once more. "I will presently shew you at what price we Scots rate the lives of our friends."

"Peace, Edward, peace—I entreat—I command thee," said the Sub-Prior. "And you, Sir Knight, think better of us than to suppose you may spend Scottish blood, and reckon for it as for wine spilt in a drunken revel. This youth was no bondsman—thou well knowst, that in thine own land thou hadst not dared to lift thy sword against the meanest subject of England, but what her laws would have called thee to answer for the deed. Do not hope it will be otherwise here, for you will but deceive yourself."

"You drive me beyond my patience," said the Euphuist, "even as the over-driven ox is urged into madness—What can I tell you of a young fellow whom I have not seen since the second hour after sunrise?"

"But you can explain in what circumstances you parted with him," said the Monk.

"What *are* the circumstances, in the devil's name, which you desire should be explained?—for although I protest against this constraint as alike unworthy and inhospitable, yet would I willingly end this fray, providing that by words it may be ended," said the knight.

"If these end it not," said Edward, "blows shall, and that full speedily."

"Peace, impatient boy," said the Sub-Prior; "and do you, Sir Piercie Shafton, acquaint me why the ground is bloody by the verge of the fountain in Corri-nan-shian, where, as you say yourself, you parted from Halbert Glendinning?"

Resolute not to avow his defeat if possibly he could avoid it, the knight answered in a haughty tone, that he supposed it was no unusual thing to find the turf bloody where hunters had slain a deer.

"And did you bury your game as well as kill it?" said the Monk. "We must know from you who is the tenant of that grave—that newly-made grave, beside the very fountain whose margin is so deeply crimsoned with blood?—Thou seest thou canst not evade me; therefore be ingenuous, and tell us the fate of this unhappy youth, whose body is doubtless lying under that bloody turf."

"If it be," said Sir Piercie, "they must have buried him alive; for I swear to thee, reverend father, that this rustic juvenal parted from me in perfect health. Let the grave be searched, and if his body be found, then deal with me as ye list."

"It is not my sphere to determine thy fate, Sir Knight, but that of the Lord Abbot, and the right reverend Chapter—it is but my duty to collect such information as may best possess their wisdom with the matters which have chanced."

"Might I presume so far, reverend father," said the knight, "I should wish to know the author and evidence of all these suspicions, so unfoundedly urged against me."

"It is soon told," said the Sub-Prior; "nor do I wish to disguise it, if it can avail you in your defence. This maiden, Mary Avenel, apprehending that you nourished malice against her foster-brother under a friendly brow, did advisedly send up the old man, Martin Tacket, to follow your footsteps and to prevent mischief. But it seems that your evil passions had outrun precaution; for, when he came up to the spot, guided by your footsteps upon the dew, he found but the bloody turf and the new-covered grave; and after long and vain search through the wilds after Halbert and yourself, he brought back the sorrowful news to her who had sent him."

"Saw he not my doublet, I pray you?" said Sir Piercie Shafton; "for when I came to myself I found myself wrapped in my cloak, but without my under garment, as your reverence may observe."

So saying, he opened his cloak, forgetting, with his characteristical inconsistence, that he shewed his shirt stained with blood.

"How! cruel man," said the Monk, when he observed this confirmation of his suspicions; "wilt thou deny thy guilt, even while thou bearest on thy person the blood thou hast shed?—Wilt thou longer deny that thy rash hand has robbed a mother of a son, our community of a vassal, the Queen of Scotland of a liege subject? and what canst thou expect, but that, at the least, we deliver thee up to England, as undeserving our further protection?"

"By the Saints!" said the knight, now driven to extremity, "if this blood be the witness against me, it is but rebel blood, since this morning at sun-rise it flowed within my own veins."

"How were that possible, Sir Piercie Shafton," said the Monk, "since I see no wound from whence it can have flowed?"

"That," said the knight, "is the most mysterious part of the transaction—See here!"

So saying, he undid his shirt-collar, and opening his bosom, shewed the spot through which Halbert's sword had passed, but already cicatrized, and bearing the appearance of a wound lately healed.

"This exhausts my patience, Sir Knight," said the Sub-Prior, "and is adding insult to violence and injury. Do you hold me for a child or an ideot, that you pretend to make me believe that the fresh blood with which your shirt is stained, flowed from a wound which has been healed for weeks or months? Unhappy mocker, think'st thou thus to blind us?—too well do we know that it is the blood of your victim, wrestling with you in the desperate and mortal struggle, which has thus dyed your apparel."

The knight, after a moment's recollection, said, in reply, "I will be open with you, my father—bid these men stand out of ear-shot, and I will tell you all I know of this mysterious business; and muse not, good father, though it may pass thy wit to expound it, for I avouch to you it is too dark for mine."

The Monk commanded Edward and the two men to withdraw, assuring the former that his conference with the prisoner would be brief, and giving him permission to keep watch at the door of the apartment; without which allowance he might, perhaps, have had some difficulty in procuring his absence. Edward had no sooner left the chamber, than he dispatched messengers to one or two families of the Halidome, with whose sons his brother and he sometimes associated, to tell them Halbert Glendinning had been murdered by an Englishman, and to require them to repair to the tower of Glendearg without delay. The duty of revenge in such cases was held so sacred, that he had no reason to doubt they would instantly come with such assistance as would ensure the detention of the prisoner. He then locked the doors of the tower, both inner and outer, and also the gate of the court-yard. Having taken these precautions, he made a hasty visit to the females of the family, exhausting himself in efforts to console them, and in protestations that he would have vengeance for his murdered brother.

Chapter Two

Now, by Our Lady, Sheriff, 'tis hard reckoning,
That I, with every odds of birth and barony,
Should be detain'd here for the casual loss
Of a wild forester, whose utmost having
Is but the brazen buckle of the belt
In which he sticks his hedge knife.
Old Play

WHILE EDWARD was making preparations for securing and punishing the supposed murderer of his brother, with an intense thirst for vengeance which had not hitherto shewn itself as part of his character, Sir Piercie Shafton made such communication as it pleased him to the Sub-Prior, who listened with great attention, though the knight's narrative was none of the clearest, especially as his self-conceit led him to conceal or abridge the details which were necessary for comprehending it.

"You are to know," he said, "reverend father, that this rustical juvenal having chosen to offer me, in the presence of your venerable Superior, yourself, and other excellent and worthy persons, besides the damsel Mary Avenel, whom I term my Discretion in all honour and kindness, a gross insult, rendered yet more intolerable by the time and place, my just resentment did so gain the mastery over my discretion, that I resolved to allow him the privileges of an equal, and to indulge him with the combat."

"But, Sir Knight," said the Sub-Prior, "you still leave two matters very obscure. First, why the token he presented to you gave you so much offence, as I with others witnessed; and then again, how this youth, whom you then met for the first, or, at least, the second time, knew so much of your history as enabled him so deeply to move you?"

The knight coloured very deeply.

"For your first query," he said, "most reverend father, we will, if you please, prætermit it as nothing essential to the matter in hand; and for the second—I protest to you that I know as little of his means of knowledge as you do, and that I am well nigh persuaded he deals with Sathanas, of which more anon.—Well, sir—In the evening I failed not to veil my purpose with a pleasant brow, as is the custom amongst us martialists, who never display the bloody colours of defiance in our countenance, until our hand is armed to fight under them. I amused the fair Discretion with some canzonettes, and other toys, which could not but be ravishing to her inexperienced ears. I arose in the morning, met my antagonist, who, to say truth, for an inexperi-

enced villagio, comported himself as stoutly as I could have desired.—
So coming to the encounter, reverend sir, I did try his metal with some
half-a-dozen of downright passes, with any one of which I could have
been through his body, only that I was loth to take so fatal an advantage, but rather mixing mercy with my just indignation, studied to
inflict upon him some flesh-wound of no very fatal quality. But, sir, in
the midst of my clemency, he being instigated, I think, by the devil, did
follow up his first offence with some insult of the same nature. Whereupon being eager to punish him, I made an estramazone, and my foot
slipping at the same time,—not from any fault of fence on my part, or
any advantage of skill on his, but the devil having, as I said, taken up
the matter in hand, and the grass being slippery,—ere I recovered my
position I encountered his sword, which he had advanced, with my
undefended person, so that, as I think, I was in some sort run through
the body. My juvenal, being beyond measure appalled at his own
unexpected and unmerited success in this strange encounter, takes
the flight and leaves me there, and I fall you into a dead swoon for the
lack of the blood I had lost so foolishly—And when I awake, as from a
sound sleep, I find myself lying, an it like you, wrapt up in my cloak at
the foot of one of the birch-trees which stand together in a clump near
to this place. I feel my limbs, and experience little pain, but much
weakness—I put my hand to the wound—it was whole and skinned
over as you now see it—I rise and come hither; and in these words you
have my whole day's story."

"I can only reply to so strange a tale," answered the Monk, "that it is
scarce possible that Sir Piercie Shafton can expect me to credit it.
Here is a quarrel whose cause you conceal,—a wound received in the
morning, of which there is no recent appearance at sun-set,—a grave
filled up, in which no body is deposited,—the vanquished found alive
and well,—the victor departed no man knows whither. These things,
Sir Knight, hang not so well together, that I should receive them as
gospel."

"Reverend father," answered Sir Piercie Shafton, "I pray you, in
the first place, to observe, that if I offer peaceful and civil justification
of that which I have already averred to be true, I do so only in devout
deference to your dress and to your order, protesting, that to any other
opposite, saving a man of religion, a lady, or my liege prince, I would
not deign to support that which I had once averred, otherwise than
with the point of my good sword. And so much being premised, I have
to add, that I can but gage my honour as a gentleman, and my faith as a
catholic Christian, that the things which I have described to you have
happened to me as I have described them, and not otherwise."

"It is a deep assertion, Sir Knight," answered the Sub-Prior; "yet, bethink you, it is only an assertion, and that no earthly reason can be alleged why things should be believed which are so contrary to reason. Let me pray you to say whether the grave, which has been seen at your place of combat, was open or closed when your encounter took place?"

"Reverend father," said the knight, "I will veil from you nothing, but shew you each secret of my bosom, even as the pure fountain revealeth the smallest pebble which graces the sand at the bottom of its crystal mirror"——

"Speak to me in plain terms, for the love of heaven," said the Monk; "these holiday phrases belong not to solemn affairs—Was the grave open when your conflict began?"

"It was," answered the knight, "I acknowledge it; even as he that acknowledgeth"——

"Nay, I pray thee, fair son, forbear these similitudes, and observe me. On yesterday even no grave was found in that place, for old Martin chanced, contrary to his wont, to go thither in quest of a strayed sheep. At break of day, by your own confession, a grave was opened in that spot, and there a combat was fought—only one of the combatants appears, and he is covered with blood, and to all appearance woundless."—Here the knight made a gesture of impatience. ——"Nay, fair son, hear me but one moment—the grave is closed and covered by the sod—what can we believe, but that it conceals the bloody corpse of the fallen duellist?"

"By Heaven, it cannot!" said the knight, "unless the juvenal hath slain himself, and buried himself, in order to place me in the predicament of his murderer."

"The grave shall doubtless be explored, and that by to-morrow's dawn," said the Monk; "I will see it done with mine own eyes."

"But," said the prisoner, "I protest against all evidence which may arise from its contents, and do insist beforehand, that whatever may be found in that grave shall not prejudicate me in my defence. I have been so haunted by diabolical deceptions in this matter, that what do I know but that the devil may assume the form of this rustical juvenal, in order to procure my further vexation?—I protest unto you, holy father, it is my very thought that there is witchcraft in all that hath befallen me since I entered into this northern land, in which men say that sorceries do abound. I, who am held in awe and regard even by the prime gallants in the court of Feliciana, have been here bearded and taunted by a clod-treading clown. I, whom Vincentio Saviolo termed his nimblest and most agile disciple, was, to speak briefly, foiled by a cow-boy, who knew no more of fence than is used at every country wake. I am run, as it seemed to me, thorough the body, with a very sufficient stoccata, and faint on the spot; and yet, when I recover, I find myself without either wem or wound, and lacking nothing of my apparel, saving my murrey-coloured doublet, slashed with satin, which I will pray may be enquired after, lest the devil, who transported me, should have dropped it in his passage among some of the trees or bushes—it being a choice and most fanciful piece of raiment, which I wore for the first time at the Queen's pageant in Southwark."

"Sir Knight," said the Monk, "you do again go astray from this matter. I enquire of you concerning that which concerns the life of another man, and, it may be, touches your own also, and you answer me with a tale of an old doublet!"

"Old?" exclaimed the knight; "now, by the gods and saints, if there be a gallant at the British Court more fancifully considerate, and more considerately fanciful, more quaintly curious, and more curiously quaint, in frequent changes of all rich articles of vesture, becoming one who may be accounted point-de-vice a courtier, I will give you leave to term me a slave and a liar."

The Monk thought, but did not say, that he had already acquired right to doubt the veracity of the Euphuist, considering the marvellous tale which he had told. Yet his own strange adventure, and that of Father Philip, rushed on his mind, and forbade his coming to any conclusion. He contented himself, therefore, with observing, that these were certainly strange incidents, and requested to know if Sir Piercie Shafton had any other reason for suspecting himself to be in a manner so particularly selected for the sport of sorcery and witchcraft.

"Sir Sub-Prior," said the Euphuist, "the most extraordinary circumstance remains behind, which alone, had I neither been bearded in dispute, nor foiled in combat, nor wounded and cured in the space of a few hours, would nevertheless of itself, and without any other corroborative, compel me to believe myself the subject of some malevolent fascination. Reverend sir, it is not to your ears that men should tell tales of love and gallantry, nor is Sir Piercie Shafton one who, to any ears whatsoever, is wont to boast of his fair acceptance with the choice and prime beauties of the court; insomuch that a lady, none of the least resplendent constellations which revolve in that hemisphere of honour, pleasure, and beauty, but whose name I here prætermit, was wont to call me her Taciturnity. Nevertheless truth must be spoken; and I cannot but allow, as the general report of the court, allowed in camps and echoed back by city and country, that in the alacrity of the accost, the tender delicacy of the regard, the facetiousness of the address, the adopting and pursuing of the fancy, the solemn close, and the graceful fall-off, Piercie Shafton was accounted the only gallant of the time, and so well accepted amongst the choicer beauties of the age, that no silk-hosed reveller of the presence-chamber or plumed jouster of the tilt-yard approached him by a bow's length in the ladies' regard, being the mark at which every well-born and generous juvenal aimeth his shaft. Nevertheless, reverend sir, having found in this rude place something which by blood and birth might be termed a lady, and being desirous to keep my gallant humour in exercise as well as to shew my sworn devotion to the sex in general, I did shoot off some arrows of compliment at this Mary Avenel, terming her my Discretion, with other quaint and well-imagined courtesies, rather bestowed out of my bounty than her merit, or perchance like unto the boyish fowler who rather than not exercise his bird-piece, will shoot at crows or magpies for lack of better game"——

"Mary Avenel is much obliged by your notice," answered the Monk; "but to what does all this detail of past and present gallantry conduct us?"

"Marry, to this conclusion," answered the knight; "that either this my Discretion, or I myself, am little less than bewitched; for, instead of receiving my accost with a grateful bow, answering my regard with a suppressed smile, accompanying my falling-off or departure with a slight sigh, honours with which I protest to you the noblest dancers and proudest beauties in Feliciana have graced my poor services, she hath paid me as little and as cold regard as if I had been some hob-nailed clown of these bleak mountains! Nay, this very day, while I was in the act of kneeling at her feet to render her the succours of this pungent quintessence of purest spirit distilled by the fairest hands of the court of Feliciana, she pushed me from her with looks which savoured of repugnance, and, as I think, thrust at me with her foot as if to spurn me from her presence. These things, reverend father, are strange, portentous, unnatural, and befall not in the current of mortal affairs, but are symptomatic of sorcery and fascination. So that having given to your reverence a perfect, simple, and plain account of all that I know concerning this matter, I leave it to your wisdom to solve what may be found soluble in the same, it being my purpose to-morrow, with the peep of dawn, to set forward towards Edinburgh."

"I grieve to be an interruption to your designs, Sir Knight," said the Monk, "but that may hardly be."

"How, reverend father!" said the knight, with an air of the utmost surprise; "if what you say respects my departure, understand that it *must* be, for I have so resolved it."

"Sir Knight," reiterated the Sub-Prior, "I must once more repeat, this *cannot* be, until the Abbot's pleasure be known in the matter."

"Reverend sir," said the knight, drawing himself up with great dignity, "I desire my hearty and thankful commendations to the

Abbot; but in this matter I have nothing to do with his reverend pleasure, designing only to consult my own."

"Pardon me," said the Sub-Prior; "the Lord Abbot hath in this matter a voice potential."

Sir Piercie Shafton's colour began to rise—"I marvel," he said, "to hear your reverence talk thus—What! will you, for the imaginary death of a rude low-born frampler and wrangler, venture to impinge upon the liberty of a kinsman of the house of Piercie?"

"Sir Knight," returned the Sub-Prior civilly, "your high lineage and your kindling anger, will avail you nothing in this matter—You shall not come here to seek a shelter, and then spill our blood as if it were water."

"I tell you," said the knight, "once more, as I have told you already, that there was no blood spilled but mine own!"

"That remains to be proved," replied the Sub-Prior; "we of the community of Saint Mary's of Kennaquhair, use not to take fairy tales in exchange for the lives of our liege vassals."

"We of the house of Piercie," answered Shafton, "brook neither threats nor restraint—I say I will travel to-morrow, happen what may!"

"And I," answered the Sub-Prior, in the same tone of determination, "say that I will break your journey, come what will!"

"Who shall gainsay me," said the knight, "if I make my way by force?"

"You will judge wisely to think ere you make such an attempt," answered the Monk, with composure; "there are men enough in the Halidome to vindicate its rights over those who dare to infringe them."

"My cousin of Northumberland will know how to revenge this usage to a beloved kinsman so near to his blood," said the Englishman.

"The Lord Abbot will know how to protect the rights of his territory, both with the temporal and spiritual sword," said the Monk. "Besides, consider, were we to send you to your kinsman at Alnwick or Warkworth to-morrow, he dared do nothing but transmit you in fetters to the Queen of England. Bethink, Sir Knight, that you stand on slippery ground, and reconcile yourself to be a prisoner in this place until the Abbot shall decide the matter. There are armed men enow to countervail all your efforts at escape. Let patience and resignation therefore arm you to a necessary submission."

So saying, he clapped his hands, and called aloud. Edward entered, accompanied by two young men who had already joined him, and were well armed.

"Edward," said the Sub-Prior, "you will supply the English knight here in this spense with suitable food and accommodation for the night, treating him with as much kindness as if nothing had happened between you. But you will place a sufficient guard, and look carefully that he make not his escape. Should he attempt to break forth, resist him to the death; but in no other case harm a hair of his head, as you will be answerable."

Edward Glendinning replied,—"That I may obey your commands, reverend sir, I will not again offer myself to this person's presence; for shame it were to me to break the peace of the Halidome, but not less shame to leave my brother's death unavenged."

As he spoke, his lips grew livid, the blood forsook his cheek, and he was about to leave the apartment, when the Sub-Prior recalled him, and said in a solemn tone,—"Edward, I have known you from infancy —I have done what lay within my reach to be of use to you—I say nothing of what you owe to me as the representative of your spiritual superior—I say nothing of the duty from the vassal to the Sub-Prior —But Father Eustace expects from the pupil whom he has nurtured —he expects from Edward Glendinning, that he will not, by any deed of sudden violence, however justified in his own mind by the provocation, break through the respect due to public justice, or that which I have an especial right to claim from him."

"Fear nothing, my reverend father, for so in an hundred senses I may well term you," said the young man; "fear not, I would say, that I will in any thing diminish the respect I owe to the venerable community by whom we have so long been protected, far less that I will do aught which can be personally less than respectful to you. But the blood of my brother must not cry for vengeance in vain—your Reverence knows our Border creed."

"'Vengeance is mine, saith the Lord, and I will requite it,'" answered the Monk. "The heathenish custom of deadly feud which prevails in this land, through which each man seeks vengeance at his own hand when the death of a friend or kinsman has chanced, hath already deluged our dales with the blood of Scottish men, spilled by the hands of countrymen and kindred—it were endless to count up the fatal results. On the Eastern Border, the Homes are at feud with the Swintons and Cockburns; in our Middle Marches, the Scotts and Kerrs have spilled as much brave blood in domestic feud as might have fought a pitched field in England, could they but have forgiven and forgotten a casual rencounter that placed their names in opposition. On the West, the Johnstones are at war with the Maxwells, the Jardines with the Bells, drawing with them the flower of the country which should place their breasts as a bulwark against England, into private and bloody warfare, of which it is the only end to waste and impair the forces of the country, already divided in itself. Do not, my dear son Edward, permit this bloody prejudice to master your mind. I cannot ask you to think of the crime supposed as if the blood spilled had been less dear to you—Alas! I know that is impossible. But I do require you, in proportion to your interest in the supposed sufferer, (for as yet the whole is matter of supposition) to bear on your mind the evidence on which the guilt of the accused person must be tried. He hath spoken with me, and I confess his tale is so extraordinary, that I should have, without a moment's hesitation, rejected it as incredible, but that an affair which chanced to myself in this very glen—More of that another time—suffice it for the present to say, that from what I have myself experienced, I deem it possible, that, extraordinary as Sir Piercie Shafton's story may seem, I hold it not utterly impossible."

"Father," said Edward Glendinning, when he saw that his preceptor paused, unwilling farther to explain on what grounds he was inclined to give a certain credit to Sir Piercie Shafton's story, while he admitted it as improbable—"Father to me you have been in every sense. You know that my hand grasps more readily to the book than to the sword; and that I lack utterly the ready and bold spirit which distinguished"——here his voice faultered, and he paused for a moment, and then went on with resolution and rapidity—"I would say, that I am unequal to Halbert in promptitude of heart and of hand —But Halbert is gone, and I stand his representative and that of my father—his successor in all his rights (while he said this, his eyes shot fire,) and bound to assert and maintain them as he would have done— therefore I am a changed man, increased in courage as in my rights and pretensions. And, reverend father, respectfully, but plainly and firmly do I say, his blood, if it has been shed by this man, shall be atoned—Halbert shall not sleep neglected in his lonely grave, as if with him the spirit of my father had ceased for ever. His blood flows in my veins, and while his has been poured forth unrequited, mine will permit me no rest. My poverty and meanness of rank shall not be his protection. My calm nature and peaceful studies shall not be his protection. Even the obligations, holy father, which I acknowledge to you, shall not be his protection. I await with patience the judgment of the Abbot and chapter, for the slaughter of one of their most anciently descended vassals. If they do right to my brother's memory, it is well. But mark me, father, if they shall fail in rendering me that justice, I bear a heart and a hand which, although I love not such extremities, are capable of remedying such an error. He who takes up my brother's succession, must avenge his death."

The Monk perceived with surprise, that Edward, with his extreme diffidence, humility, and obedient assiduity, for such were his general characteristics, had still boiling in his veins the wild principles of those from whom he was descended, and by whom he was surrounded. His eyes sparkled, his frame was agitated, and the extremity of his desire of vengeance seemed to give a vehemence to his manner resembling the restlessness of joy.

"May God help us," said Father Eustace, "for frail wretches as we are, we cannot help ourselves under sudden and strong temptation.— Edward, I will rely on your word that you do nothing rashly."

"That will I not," said Edward,—"that, my better than father, I surely will not. But the blood of my brother—the tears of my mother— and—and—and of Mary Avenel, shall not be shed in vain—I will not deceive you, father—if this Piercie Shafton have slain my brother, he dies, if the whole blood of the whole house of Piercie were in his veins."

There was a deep and solemn determination in the utterance of Edward Glendinning, expressive of a rooted resolution. The Sub-Prior sighed deeply, and for the moment yielded to circumstances, and urged the acquiescence of his pupil no further. He commanded lights to be placed in the lower chamber, which for a time he paced in silence.

A thousand ideas, and even differing principles, debated with each other in his bosom. He greatly doubted the English knight's account of the duel, and of what had followed it. Yet the extraordinary and supernatural circumstances which had befallen the Sacristan and himself in that very glen, prevented him from being absolutely incredulous on the score of the wonderful wound and recovery of Sir Piercie Shafton, and prevented him from at once condemning as impossible that which was altogether improbable. Then he was at a loss how to controul the fraternal affections of Edward, with respect to whom he felt something like the keeper of a wild animal, a lion's whelp or tiger's cub, which he has held under his command from infancy, but which, when grown to maturity, on some sudden provocation displays his fangs and talons, erects his crest, resumes his savage nature, and bids defiance at once to his keeper and to all mankind.

How to restrain and mitigate an ire which the universal example of the times rendered deadly and inveterate, was sufficient cause of anxiety to Father Eustace. But he had also to consider the situation of his community, dishonoured and degraded by submitting to suffer the slaughter of a vassal to pass unavenged; a circumstance which of itself might in these difficult times have afforded pretext for a revolt among their wavering adherents, or, on the other hand, exposed the community to imminent danger, should they proceed against a subject of

England of high degree, connected with the house of Northumberland and other northern families of high rank, who, as they possessed the means, could not be supposed to lack inclination to wreak upon the patrimony of Saint Mary of Kennaquhair, any violence which might be offered to their kinsman.

In either case, the Sub-Prior well knew that the ostensible cause of feud, insurrection, or incursion, being once afforded, the case would not be ruled either by reason or by evidence, and he groaned in spirit when, upon counting up the chances which arose in this ambiguous dilemma, he found he had only a choice of difficulties. He was a monk, but he felt also as a man, indignant at the supposed slaughter of young Glendinning by a man skilful in all the practice of arms, in which the vassal of the Monastery was most likely to be deficient; and to aid the resentment which he felt for the loss of a youth whom he had known from infancy, came in full force the sense of dishonour arising to his community from passing over so gross an insult unavenged. Then the light in which it might be viewed by those who at present presided in the stormy Court of Scotland, attached as they were to the reformation, and allied by common faith and common interest with Queen Elizabeth, was a formidable subject of apprehension. The Sub-Prior well knew how they lusted after the revenues of the church (to express it in the ordinary phrase of the religious of the time) and how readily they would grasp at such a pretext for encroaching on those of Saint Mary's, as would be afforded by the suffering to pass unpunished the death of a native Scotsman by a Catholic Englishman, rebel to Queen Elizabeth.

On the other hand, to deliver up to England, or, which was nearly the same thing, to the Scottish administration, an English knight leagued with the Piercie by kindred and political intrigue, a faithful follower of the Catholic Church, who had fled to the Halidome for protection, was, in the estimation of the Sub-Prior, an act most unworthy in itself and meriting the malediction of heaven, besides being, moreover, fraught with great temporal risk. If the government of Scotland was now almost entirely in the hands of the Protestant party, the Queen was still a Catholic, and there was no knowing when, amid the sudden changes which agitated that tumultuous country, she might find herself at the head of her own affairs, and able to protect those of her own faith. Then if the Court of England and its Queen were zealously Protestant, the northern counties, whose friendship or enmity were of most consequence in the first instance to the community of Saint Mary's, contained many Catholics, the heads of whom were able, and must be supposed willing, to avenge any injury suffered by Sir Piercie Shafton.

On either side, the Sub-Prior, thinking, according to his sense of duty, most anxiously for the safety and welfare of his Monastery, saw the greatest risk of damage, blame, inroad, and confiscation. The only course on which he could determine, was to stand by the helm like a resolute pilot, watch every contingency, do his best to weather each reef and shoal, and commit the rest to heaven and his patroness.

As he left the apartment, the knight called after him, beseeching he would order his trunk-mails to be sent into this apartment, understanding he was to be guarded here for the night, as he wished to make some alteration in his apparel.

"Ay, ay," said the Monk, muttering as he went up the winding stair, "carry him his trumpery with all dispatch. Alas! that man, with so many noble objects of pursuit, will amuse himself like a jack-an-ape, with a laced jerkin and a cap and bells!—I must now to the melancholy work of consoling that which is well nigh inconsolable, a mother weeping for her first-born."

Advancing, after a gentle knock, into the apartment of the women, he found that Mary Avenel was retired to bed, extremely indisposed, and that Dame Glendinning and Tibb were indulging their sorrows by the side of a decaying fire, and by the light of a small iron lamp, or cruize, as it was termed. Poor Elspet's apron was thrown over her head, and bitterly did she sob and weep for "her beautiful, her brave, —the very image of her dear Simon Glendinning, the stay of her widowhood and the support of her old age."

The faithful Tibb echoed her complaints, and, more violently clamorous, made deep promises of revenge on Sir Piercie Shafton, if there was "a man left in the south that could draw a whinger, or a woman that could thraw a rape." The presence of the Sub-Prior imposed silence on these clamours. He sate down by the unfortunate mother, and essayed, by such topics as his religion and reason suggested, to interrupt the current of Dame Glendinning's feelings. But the attempt was in vain. She listened, indeed, with some little interest, while he pledged his word and his interest with the Abbot, that the family which had lost their eldest-born by means of a guest received at his command, should experience particular protection at the hand of the community; and that the fief which had belonged to Simon Glendinning should, with extended bounds and added privileges, be conferred on Edward.

But it was only for a very brief space that the mother's sobs were apparently softer, and her grief more mild. She soon blamed herself for casting a moment's thought "upon warld's gear, while poor Halbert was lying stretched in his bloody shirt." The Sub-Prior was not more fortunate when he promised that Halbert's body "should be removed to hallowed ground, and his soul secured by the prayers of the church in his behalf." Grief would have its natural course, and the voice of the comforter was wasted in vain.

Chapter Three

He is at liberty, I have ventured for him!
—————if the law
Find and condemn me for't, some living wenches,
Some honest-hearted maids will sing my dirge,
And tell to memory my death was noble,
Dying almost a martyr.
Two Noble Kinsmen

THE SUB-PRIOR of Saint Mary's, in taking his departure from the spence in which Sir Piercie Shafton was confined, and in which some preparations were made for his passing the night as the room which might be most conveniently guarded, left more than one perplexed person behind him. There was connected with this apartment, and opening into it, a small *outshot*, or projecting part of the building, occupied by a little sleeping apartment, which, upon ordinary occasions, was that of Mary Avenel, and which, in the unusual number of guests who had come to the tower on the former evening, had also accommodated Mysie Happer, the Miller's daughter; for anciently, as well as in the present day, a Scottish house was usually rather too narrow and limited for the extent of the owner's hospitality, and some shift and contrivance was necessary, upon any unusual occasion, to ensure the accommodation of all the guests.

The fatal news of Halbert Glendinning's death had thrown all former arrangements into confusion. Mary Avenel, whose case required immediate attention, had been transported into the apartment hitherto occupied by Halbert and his brother, as the latter proposed to watch all night, in order to prevent the escape of the prisoner. Poor Mysie had been altogether overlooked, and had naturally enough betaken herself to the little apartment which she had hitherto occupied, ignorant that the spence, through which lay the only access to it, was to be the sleeping apartment of Sir Piercie Shafton. The measures taken for securing him there had been so sudden, that she was not aware of it, until she found that the other females had been removed from the spence by the Sub-Prior's direction, and having once missed the opportunity of retreating along with them, bashfulness, and the high respect which she was taught to bear to the monks, prevented her venturing forth alone, and intruding herself on the presence of Father Eustace, while in secret conference with the Southern Englishman. There appeared no remedy but to wait till their interview was over; and, as the door was thin, and did not shut very closely, she could hear every word which passed betwixt them.

It thus happened, that without any intended intrusion on her part, she became privy to the whole conversation of the Sub-Prior and the English knight, and could also observe from the window of her little retreat, that more than one of the young men summoned by Edward arrived successively at the tower. These circumstances led her to entertain most serious apprehension that the life of Sir Piercie Shafton was in great and instant peril.

Woman is naturally compassionate, not less willingly so when youth and fair features are on the side of him who claims her sympathy. The handsome presence, elaborate dress and address of Sir Piercie Shafton, which had failed to make any favourable impression on the grave and lofty character of Mary Avenel, had completely dazzled and bewildered the poor Maid of the Mill. The knight had perceived this result, and flattered by seeing that his merit was not universally under-rated, he had bestowed on Mysie a good deal more of his courtesy than in his opinion her rank warranted. It was not cast away, but received with a devout sense of his condescension, and with gratitude for his personal notice, which, joined to her fears for his safety, and the natural tenderness of her disposition, began to make wild work in her heart.

"To be sure it was very wrong in him to slay Halbert Glendinning," (it was thus she argued the case with herself,) "but then he was a gentleman born, and a soldier, and so gentle and courteous withal, that she was sure the quarrel had been all of young Glendinning's own seeking; for it was well known that both these lads were so taken up with that Mary Avenel, that they never looked at another lass in the Halidome, more than if they were of a different degree. And then Halbert's dress was as clownish as his manners were haughty; and this poor young gentleman, (who was habited like any prince,) banished from his own land, was first drawn into a quarrel by a rude brangler, and then persecuted and like to be put to death by his kin and allies."

Mysie wept bitterly at the thought, and then her heart rising against such cruelty and oppression to a defenceless stranger, who dressed with so much skill, and spoke with so much grace, she began to consider whether she could not render him some assistance in this extremity.

Her mind was now entirely altered from its original purpose. At first her only anxiety had been to find the means of escaping from the interior apartment, without being noticed by any one; but now she began to think that heaven had placed her there for the safety and protection of the persecuted stranger. She was of a simple and affectionate, but at the same time an alert and enterprizing character, possessing more than female strength of body, and more than female courage, though with feelings as capable of being bewildered with gallantry of dress and language, as a fine gentleman of any generation would have desired to exercise his talents upon. "I will save him," she thought, "that is the first thing to be resolved—and then I wonder what he will say to the poor Miller's maiden, that has done for him what all the dainty dames in London or Holyrood would have feared to venture upon."

Prudence began to pull her sleeve as she indulged speculations so hazardous, and hinted to her that the warmer Sir Piercie Shafton's gratitude might prove, it was the more likely to be fraught with danger to his benefactress. Alas! poor Prudence, thou mayst say with our moral teacher,

> I preach for ever, but I preach in vain.

The Miller's maiden, while you pour your warning into her unwilling bosom, has glanced her eye on the small mirror by which she has placed her little lamp, and it returns to her a countenance and eyes, pretty and sparkling at all times, but ennobled at present with the energy of expression proper to those who have dared to form, and stand prepared to execute, deeds of generous audacity.

"Will these features—will these eyes, joined to the benefit I am about to confer upon Sir Piercie Shafton, do nothing to removing the distance of rank between us?"

Such was the question which female vanity asked at fancy; and though even fancy dared not answer in a ready affirmative, a middle conclusion was adopted—"Let us first succour the gallant youth, and trust to fortune for the rest."

Banishing, therefore, from her mind every thing that was personal to herself, the rash but generous girl turned her whole thoughts to the means of executing this enterprize.

The difficulties which interposed were of no ordinary nature. The vengeance of the men of that country, in case of deadly feud, that is, in cases of a quarrel excited by the slaughter of any of their relations, was one of their most marked characteristics; and Edward, however gentle in other respects, was so fond of his brother, that there could be no doubt that he would be as signal in his revenge as the customs of the country authorized. There were to be passed the inner door of the apartment, the two gates of the tower itself, and the gate of the court-yard, ere the prisoner was at liberty; and then a guide and means of flight were to be provided, otherwise ultimate escape was impossible. But where the will of woman is strongly bent on the accomplishment of such a purpose, her wit is seldom baffled by difficulties, however embarrassing.

The Sub-Prior had not long left the apartment, ere Mysie had devised a scheme, daring indeed, but likely to be successful if dexterously conducted. It was necessary, however, that she should remain where she was till so late an hour, that all in the tower should have betaken themselves to repose, excepting those whose duty made them watchers. The interval she employed in watching the movements of the person in whose service she was thus boldly a volunteer.

She could hear Sir Piercie Shafton pace the floor to and fro, in reflection doubtless on his own untoward fate and precarious situation. By and bye she heard him making a rustling among his trunks, which, agreeable to the order of the Sub-Prior, had been placed in the apartment to which he was confined, and which he was probably amusing more melancholy reflections by examining and arranging. Then she could hear him resume his walk through the room, and as if his spirits had been somewhat relieved and elevated by the survey of his wardrope, she could distinguish that at one turn he half recited a sonnet, at another half whistled a galliard, and at the third hummed a saraband. At length she could hear that he extended himself on the temporary couch which had been allotted to him, after muttering his prayers hastily, and in a short time she concluded he must be fast asleep.

She employed the moments which intervened in considering her enterprize under every different aspect; and dangerous as it was, the steady review which she took of the various perils accompanying her purpose, furnished her with plausible devices for obviating them. Love and generous compassion, which give singly such powerful impulse to the female heart, were in this case united, and championed her to the last extremity of hazard.

It was an hour past midnight. All in the tower slept soundly but those who had undertaken to guard the English prisoner; or if sorrow and suffering drove sleep from the bed of Dame Glendinning and her foster-daughter, they were too much wrapt in their own griefs to attend to external sounds. The means of striking light were at hand in the small apartment, and thus the Miller's maiden was enabled to light and trim a small lamp. With a trembling step and throbbing heart, she undid the door which separated her from the apartment in which the Southron knight was confined, and almost flinched from her fixed purpose, when she found herself in the same room with the sleeping prisoner. She scarce trusted herself to look upon him, as he lay wrapped in his cloak, and fast asleep upon the pallet bed, but turned her eyes away while she gently pulled his mantle, with no more force than was just equal to awaken him. He moved not until she had twitched his cloak a second and a third time, and then at length looking up, was about to make an exclamation in the suddenness of his surprise.

Mysie's bashfulness was conquered by her fear. She placed her finger on her lips, in token that he must observe the most strict silence, then pointed to the door to intimate that it was watched.

Sir Piercie Shafton now collected himself, and sat upright on his couch. He gazed with surprise on the graceful figure of the young woman who stood before him; her well-formed person, her flowing hair, and the outline of her features, shown dimly, and yet to advantage, by the partial and feeble light which she held in her hand. The romantic imagination of the gallant would soon have coined some compliment proper for the occasion, but Mysie left him not time.

"I come," she said, "to save your life, which is else in great peril—if you answer me, speak as low as you can, for they have centinelled your door with armed men."

"Comeliest of miller's daughters," answered Sir Piercie, who by this time was sitting upright on his couch, "dread nothing for my safety. Credit me, that, as in very truth, I have not spilled the red puddle (which these villagios call the blood) of their most uncivil relation, so I am under no apprehension whatever for the issue of this restraint, seeing that it cannot but be harmless to me. Natheless, to thee, O most Molendinar beauty, I return the thanks which thy courtesy may justly claim."

"Nay, but Sir Knight," answered the maiden, in a whisper as low as it was tremulous; "I deserve no thanks, unless you will act by my counsel. Edward Glendinning hath sent for Dan of the Howlet-hirst, and young Adie of Aikenshaw, and they are come with three men more, and with bow, and jack, and spear, and I heard them say to each other, and to Edward as they alighted in the court, that they would have amends for the death of their kinsman, if the monk's cowl should smoke for it—And the vassals are so wilful now, that the Abbot himself dare not controul them, for fear they turn heretics, and refuse to pay their feu-duties."

"In faith," said Sir Piercie Shafton, "it may be a shrewd temptation, and perchance the Monks may rid themselves of trouble and cumber, by handing me over the march to Sir John Foster or Lord Hunsdon, the English wardens, and so make peace with their vassals and with England at once. Fairest Molinara, I will for once walk by thy rede, and if thou doest contrive to extricate me from this vile kennel, I will so celebrate thy wit and beauty, that the Baker's nymph of Raphael d'Urbino shall seem but a gypsey in comparison of my Molinara."

"I pray you, then, be silent," said the Miller's daughter; "for if your speech betrays that you are awake, my scheme fails utterly, and it is Heaven's mercy and Our Lady's that we are not already overheard and discovered."

"I am silent," replied the Southron, "even as the starless night—but yet—if this contrivance of thine should endanger thy safety, fair and no less kind than fair damsel, it were utterly unworthy of me to accept it at thy hand."

"Do not think of me," said Mysie, hastily; "I am safe—I shall take thought for myself, if I once saw you out of this dangerous dwelling—if you would provide yourself with any part of your apparel or goods, lose no time."

The knight *did*, however, lose some time, ere he could settle in his own mind what to take and what to abandon of his wardrope, each article of which seemed endeared to him by recollection of the feasts and revels at which it had been exhibited. For some little while Mysie left him to make his selections at leisure, for she herself had also some preparations to make for flight. But when, returning from the apartment into which she had retired, with a small bundle in her hand, she found him still indecisive, she insisted in plain terms, that he should either make up his baggage for the enterprize, or give it up entirely. Thus urged, the disconsolate knight hastily made up a few clothes into a bundle, regarded his mails with a mute expression of sorrow, and intimated his readiness to wait upon his kind guide.

She led the way to the door of the apartment, and motioning to the knight to stand close behind her, tapped once or twice at the door. She was at length answered by Edward Glendinning, who demanded to know who knocked within, and what they desired?

"Speak low," said Mysie Happer, "or you will awaken the English knight—it is I, Mysie Happer, who knock—I wish to get out—you have locked me up and I was obliged to wait till the Southron slept."

"Locked you up!" replied Edward, in surprise.

"Yes," answered the Miller's daughter, "you have locked me in this room—I was in Mary Avenel's sleeping apartment."

"And can you not remain there till morning," replied Edward, "since it has so chanced?"

"What!" said the Miller's daughter, in a tone of offended delicacy, "I remain here a moment longer than I can get out without discovery? —I would not for all the Halidome of Saint Mary's, remain a minute longer in the neighbourhood of a man's apartment than I can help it— for whom, or for what do you hold me? I promise you, my father's daughter has been better brought up than to put in peril her good name."

"Come forth then, and get to thy chamber in silence," said Edward.

So saying, he undid the bolt. The stair-case without was in utter darkness, as Mysie had before ascertained. So soon as she stept out, she took hold of Edward as if to support herself, thus interposing her person betwixt him and Sir Piercie Shafton, by whom she was closely followed. Thus screened from observation, the Englishman slipped past on tiptoe, unshod and in silence, while the damsel complained to Edward that she wanted a light.

"I cannot get you a light," said he, "for I cannot leave this post; but there is fire below."

"I will sit below till morning," said the Maid of the Mill; and, tripping down stairs, heard Edward bolt and bar the door of the now tenantless apartment with vain caution.

At the foot of the stair which she descended, she found the object of her care waiting her farther directions. She recommended to him the most absolute silence, which, for once in his life, he seemed not unwilling to observe, conducted him with as much caution as if he were walking on cracked ice, to a dark recess, used for depositing wood, and instructed him to ensconce himself behind the faggots. She herself lighted her lamp once more at the kitchen-fire, and took her distaff and spindle, that she might not seem to be unemployed, in case any one came into the apartment. From time to time, however, she stole towards the window on tiptoe, to catch the first glance of the dawn, for the farther prosecution of her adventurous project. At length she saw, to her great joy, the first peep of the morning brighten upon the grey clouds of the east, and clasping her hands together, thanked Our Lady for the sight, and implored protection during the remainder of her enterprize. Ere she had finished her prayer, she started at feeling a man's arm across her shoulder, while a rough voice spoke in her ear—"What! menseful Mysie of the Mill so soon at her prayers?—now, benison on the bonny eyes that open so early!—I'll have a kiss for good morrow's sake."

Dan of the Howlet-hirst, for he was the gallant who paid Mysie this compliment, suited the word with the action, and the action, as is usual in such cases of rustic gallantry, was rewarded with a cuff, which Dan received as a fine gentleman receives a rap with a fan, but which, delivered by the energetic arm of the Miller's maiden, would have certainly astonished a less robust gallant.

"How now, Sir Coxcomb!" said she, "and must you be away from your guard over the English knight, to plague quiet folks with your horse-tricks!"

"Truly you are mistaken, pretty Mysie," said the clown, "for I have not yet relieved Edward at his post; and were it not a shame to let him stay any longer, by my faith, I could find it in my heart not to quit you these two hours."

"O, you have hours and hours enough to see any one," said Mysie; "but you must think of the distress of the household even now, and get Edward to sleep for a while, for he has awaked watch this whole night."

"I will have another kiss first," answered Dan of the Howlet-hirst.

But Mysie was now on her guard, and, conscious perhaps of the vicinity of the wood-hole, offered such strenuous resistance, that the swain cursed the nymph's bad humour with very unpastoral phrase and emphasis, and ran up stairs to relieve the guard of his comrade. Stealing to the door, she heard the new centinel hold a brief conversation with Edward, after which the latter withdrew, and the former entered upon the duties of his watch.

Mysie suffered him to walk there a little while undisturbed, until the dawning became more general, by which time she supposed he might have digested her coyness, and then presenting herself before the watchful centinel, demanded of him "the keys of the outer tower, and of the court-yard gate."

"And for what purpose?" answered the warder.

"To milk the cows, and drive them out to their pasture," said Mysie; "you would not have the poor beasts kept in the byre a' morning, and the family in such distress, that there is fiend ane fit to do a turn but the byre-woman and myself?"

"And where is the byre-woman?" said Dan.

"Sitting with me in the kitchen, in case these distressed folks want any thing."

"There are the keys then, Mysie Dorts," said the centinel.

"Many thanks, Dan Ne'er-do-weel," answered the Maid of the Mill, and escaped down stairs in a moment.

To hasten to the wood-hole, and there to robe the English knight in a short-gown and petticoat, which she had provided for the purpose, was the work of another moment. She then undid the gates of the tower, and made towards the byre, or cow-house, which stood in one corner of the court-yard. Sir Piercie Shafton remonstrated against the delay which this would occasion.

"Fair and generous Molinara," he said, "were we not better undo the outward gate, and make the best of our way hence, even like a pair of sea-mews who make towards shelter of the rocks as the storm waxes high?"

"We must drive out the cows first," said Mysie, "for a sin it were to spoil the poor widow's cattle, both for her sake and the poor beasts' own; and I have no mind any one shall leave the tower in a hurry to follow us. Besides, you must have your horse, for you will need a fleet one ere all be done."

So saying, she locked and double-locked both the inward and outward door of the tower, proceeded to the cow-house, turned out the cattle, and giving the knight his own horse to lead, drove them before her out at the court-yard gate, intending to return for her own palfrey. But the noise attending this operation caught the wakeful attention of Edward, who, starting to the bartizan, called to know what the matter was?

Mysie answered with great readiness, that "she was driving out the cows, for that they would be spoiled by want of looking to."

"I thank thee, kind maiden," said Edward—"and yet," he added, after a moment's pause, "what damsel is that thou hast with thee?"

Mysie was about to answer, when Sir Piercie Shafton, who did not apparently desire that the great work of his liberation should be executed without the interposition of his own ingenuity, exclaimed from beneath, "I am she, O most bucolical juvenal, under whose charge is placed the milky mothers of the herd."

"Hell and darkness!" exclaimed Edward, in a transport of fury and astonishment, "it is Piercie Shafton—What! treason! treason!—ho! —Dan—Jasper—Martin—the villain escapes!"

"To horse, to horse!" cried Mysie, and in an instant mounted behind the knight, who was already in the saddle.

Edward caught up a cross-bow, and let fly a bolt, which whistled so near Mysie's ear, that she called to her companion,—"Spur—spur, Sir Knight!—the next will not miss us.—Had it been Halbert instead of Edward who bent that bow, we had been dead men."

The knight pressed his horse, which dashed through the cows, and down the knoll on which the tower was situated. Then taking the road down the valley, the gallant animal, reckless of its double burthen, soon conveyed them out of hearing of the tumult and alarm with which their departure filled the tower of Glendearg.

Thus it strangely happened, that two men were flying in different directions at the same time, each accused of being the other's murderer.

Chapter Four

——Sure he cannot
Be so unmanly as to leave me here;
If he do, maids will not so easily
Trust men again.
The Two Noble Kinsmen

THE KNIGHT continued to keep the good horse at a pace as quick as the road permitted, until they had cleared the valley of Glendearg, and entered upon the broad dale of the Tweed, which now rolled before them in crystal beauty, displaying on its opposite bank the huge grey Monastery of Saint Mary's, its towers and pinnacles scarce yet touched by the newly-risen sun, so deeply the edifice lies shrouded under the mountains which rise to the southward.

Turning to the left, the knight continued his road down the northern bank of the river, until they arrived nearly opposite to the weir, or dam-dike, where Father Philip had concluded his extraordinary aquatic excursion.

Sir Piercie Shafton, whose brain seldom admitted more than one idea at a time, had hitherto pushed forward without very distinctly considering where he was going. But the sight of the Monastery so near to him, reminded him that he was still on dangerous ground, and that he must necessarily provide for his safety by chusing some settled plan of escape. The situation of his guide and deliverer also occurred to him, for he was far from being either selfish or ungrateful. He listened, and discovered that the Miller's daughter was sobbing and weeping bitterly as she rested her head on his shoulder.

"What ails thee," he said, "my generous Molinara?—is there aught that Piercie Shafton can do which may shew his gratitude to his deliverer?" Mysie pointed with her finger across the river, but ventured not to turn her eyes in that direction. "Nay, but speak plain, most generous damsel, for I swear to you that I comprehend nought by this extension of thy fair digit."

"Yonder is my father's house," said Mysie, in a voice interrupted by the increasing burst of her sorrow.

"And I was carrying thee discourteously to a distance from thy habitation?" said Shafton, imagining he had found out the source of her grief. "Woe worth the hour that Piercie Shafton, in attention to his own safety, neglected the accommodation of any female, far less of his most beneficent liberatrice. Dismount then, O lovely Molinara, unless thou wouldst rather that I should transport thee on horseback to the house of thy molendinary father, which, if thou sayst the word, I am prompt to do so, defying all dangers which may arise to me personally, whether by monk or miller."

Mysie suppressed her sobs, and with considerable difficulty muttered her desire to alight, and take her fortune by herself. Sir Piercie Shafton, too devoted a squire of dames to consider the most lowly as exempted from respectful attention, independent of the claims which the Miller's maiden possessed over him, dismounted instantly from his horse, and received in his arms the poor girl, who still wept bitterly, and when placed on the ground, seemed scarce able to support herself, or at least still clung, though, as it seemed, unconsciously, to the support he had afforded. He carried her to a weeping birchtree, which grew on the green-sward bank around which the road winded, and, placing her on the ground beneath it, exhorted her to compose herself. A strong touch of natural feeling struggled with, and half overcame his acquired affectation, while he said, "Credit me, most generous damsel, the service you have done to Piercie Shafton he would have deemed too dearly bought, had he foreseen it was to cost you these tears and singults. Shew me the cause of your grief, and if I can do aught to remove it, believe that the rights you have acquired over me will make your commands sacred as those of an empress. Speak then, fair Molinara, and command him whom fortune hath rendered at once your debtor and your champion. What are your orders?"

"Only that you will fly and save yourself," said Mysie, mustering up her utmost efforts to utter these few words.

"Yet," said the knight, "let me not leave you without some token of remembrance." Mysie would have said there needed none, and most truly would she have spoken, could she have spoken for weeping. "Piercie Shafton is poor," he continued, "but let this chain testify he is not ungrateful to his deliverer."

He took from his neck the rich chain and medallion we have formerly mentioned, and put it into the powerless hand of the poor maiden, who neither received nor rejected it, but, occupied with more intense feelings, seemed scarce aware of what he was doing.

"We shall meet again," said Sir Piercie Shafton, "at least I trust so —meanwhile, weep no more, fair Molinara, an thou lovest me."

The phrase of conjuration was but used as an ordinary commonplace expression of the time, but bore a deeper sense to poor Mysie's ear. She dried her tears, and when the knight, in all kind and chivalrous courtesy, stooped to embrace her at their parting, she rose humbly up to receive the proffered honour in a posture of more deference, and meekly and gratefully accepted the offered salute. Sir Piercie Shafton mounted his horse, and began to ride off. But curiosity, or perhaps a stronger feeling, soon induced him to look back, when he beheld the Miller's daughter standing still motionless on the spot where they had parted, her eyes turned after him, and the unheeded chain hanging from her hand.

It was at this moment that a glimpse of the real state of Mysie's affections, and of the motive from which she had acted in the whole matter, glanced on Sir Piercie Shafton's mind. The gallants of that age, disinterested, aspiring, and lofty-minded even in their cox-combry, were strangers to those degrading and mischievous pursuits which are usually termed low amours. They did not "chase the humble maidens of the plain," or degrade their own rank, to deprive rural innocence of peace and virtue. It followed, of course, that as conquests in this class were no part of their ambition, they were in most cases totally overlooked and unsuspected, when they were casually made. The companion of Astrophel, and flower of the tilt-yard of Feliciana, had no more idea that his graces and good parts could attach the love of Mysie Happer, than a first-rate beauty in the boxes dreams of the fatal wound which her charms may inflict on some romantic attorney's apprentice in the pit. I suppose, in any ordinary case, the pride of rank and distinction would have pronounced on the humble admirer the doom which Beau Fielding denounced against the whole female world, "Let them look and die." But the obligations under which he lay to the enamoured maiden, Miller's daughter as she was, precluded the possibility of Sir Piercie's treating the matter *en cavalier*, and much embarrassed, yet a little flattered at the same time, he rode back to try what could be done for the damsel's relief.

The innate modesty of poor Mysie could not prevent her shewing too obvious signs of joy at Sir Piercie Shafton's return. She was betrayed by the sparkle of the rekindling eye, and a caress which, however timidly bestowed, she could not help giving to the neck of the horse which brought back the beloved rider.

"What farther can I do for you, kind Molinara?" said Sir Piercie Shafton, himself hesitating and blushing; for, to the grace of Queen Bess's age be it spoken, her courtiers wore more iron on their breasts than brass on their foreheads, and even amid their vanities preserved still the decaying spirit of chivalry, which inspired of yore the very gentle perfect Knight of Chaucer,

> Who in his port was modest as a maid.

Mysie blushed deeply, with her eyes fixed on the ground, and Sir Piercie proceeded in the same tone of embarrassed kindness. "Are you afraid to return home alone, my kind Molinara?—would you that I should accompany you?"

"Alas!" said Mysie, looking up, and her cheek changing from scarlet to pale, "I have no home left."

"How! no home?" said Shafton; "says my generous Molinara she hath no home, when yonder stands the house of her father, and but a crystal stream between?"

"Alas!" answered the Miller's maiden, "I have no longer either home or father. He is a devoted servant to the Abbey—I have offended the Abbot, and if I return home my father will kill me."

"He dare not injure thee, by heaven!" said Sir Piercie; "I swear to thee by my honour and knighthood, that the forces of my cousin of Northumberland shall lay the Monastery so flat, that a horse shall not stumble as he rides over it, if they should dare to injure a hair of your head. Therefore be hopeful and content, kind Mysinda, and know you have obliged one who can and will avenge the slightest wrong offered to you."

He sprung from his horse as he spoke, and, in the animation of his argument, grasped the willing hand of Mysie, (or Mysinda as he had now christened her.) He gazed too upon full black eyes, fixed upon his own with an expression which, however subdued by maidenly shame, it was impossible to mistake, on cheeks where something like hope began to restore the natural colour, and on two lips which, like double rose-buds, were kept a little apart by expectation, and shewed within a line of teeth as white as pearl. All this was dangerous to look upon, and Sir Piercie Shafton, after repeating with less and less force his request that the fair Mysinda would allow him to carry her to her father's, ended by asking the fair Mysinda to go along with him—"At least," he added, "until I shall be able to conduct you to a place of safety."

Mysie Happer made no answer; but, blushing scarlet betwixt joy and shame, mutely expressed her willingness to accompany the Southron Knight, by knitting her bundle closer, and preparing to resume her seat en croupe. "And what is your pleasure that I should do with this?" she said, holding up the chain as if she had been for the first time aware that it was in her hand.

"Keep it, fairest Mysinda, for my sake," said the knight.

"Not so, sir," answered Mysie, gravely; "the maidens of my country take no such gifts from their superiors, and I need no token to remind me of this morning."

Most earnestly and courteously did the knight urge her acceptance of the proposed guerdon, but on this point Mysie was resolute; feeling perhaps, that to accept of any thing bearing the appearance of reward, would be to place the service she had rendered him on a mercenary footing. In short, she would only agree to conceal the chain, lest it might prove the means of detecting the owner, until Sir Piercie should be placed in perfect safety.

They mounted and resumed their journey, of which Mysie, as bold and sharp-witted in some points as she was simple and susceptible in others, now took in some degree the direction, having only enquired its general destination, and learned that Sir Piercie Shafton desired to go to Edinburgh, where he hoped to find friends and protection. Possessed of this information, Mysie availed herself of her local knowledge to get as soon as possible out of the bounds of the Hali-dome, and into those of a temporal baron, supposed to be addicted to the reformed doctrines, and upon whose limits, at least, she thought their pursuers would not attempt to hazard any violence. She was not indeed very apprehensive of a pursuit, reckoning with some confid-ence that the inhabitants of the Tower of Glendearg would find it a matter of difficulty to surmount the obstacles arising from their own bolts and bars, with which she had carefully secured them before setting forth on the retreat.

They journeyed on, therefore, in tolerable security, and Sir Piercie Shafton found leisure to amuse the time in high-flown speeches and long anecdotes of the court of Feliciana, to which Mysie bent an ear not a whit less attentive, that she did not understand one word out of three which was uttered by her fellow traveller. She listened, however, and admired upon trust, as many a wise man has been contented to treat the conversation of a handsome but silly mistress. As for Sir Piercie, he was in his element; and, well assured of the interest and full approbation of his auditor, he went on spouting Euphuism of more than usual obscurity, and at more than usual length. Thus passed the morning, and noon brought them within sight of a winding stream, on the side of which arose an ancient baronial castle, sur-rounded by some large trees. At a small distance from the gate of the mansion, extended, as in those days was usual, a straggling hamlet, having a church in the centre.

"There are two hostelries in this Kirktown," said Mysie, "but the worst is best for our purpose; for it stands apart from the other houses, and I ken the man weel, for he has dealt with my father for malt."

This *causa scientiæ*, to use a lawyer's phrase, was ill chosen for Mysie's purpose; for Sir Piercie Shafton had, by dint of his own loquacity, been talking himself all this while into a high esteem for his fellow-traveller, and, pleased with the gracious reception which she afforded to his powers of conversation, had well nigh forgotten that she was not herself one of those high-born beauties of whom he was recounting so many stories, when this unlucky speech at once placed the most disadvantageous circumstances attending her lineage under his immediate recollection. He said nothing however. What indeed could he say? Nothing was so natural as that a miller's daughter should be acquainted with the publicans who dealt with her father for malt, and all that was to be wondered at was the concurrence of events which had rendered such a female the companion and guide of Sir Piercie Shafton of Wilverton, kinsman of the great Earl of Northumberland, whom princes and sovereigns themselves termed cousin, because of the Piercie blood.* He felt the disgrace of strolling the country with a miller's maiden on the crupper behind him, and was even ungrateful enough to feel some emotions of shame, when he halted his horse at the door of the little inn.

But the alert intelligence of Mysie Happer spared him farther sense of derogation, by instantly springing from the horse, and cramming the ears of mine host, who came out with his mouth agape to receive a guest of the knight's appearance, with an imagined tale, in which circumstance on circumstance were huddled so fast, as to astonish Sir Piercie Shafton, whose own invention was none of the most brilliant. She explained to the publican that this was a great English knight travelling from the Monastery to the Court of Scotland, after having paid his vows to Saint Mary, and that she had been directed to conduct him so far on the road; and that Ball, her palfrey, had fallen by the way, because he had been over-wrought with carrying home the last melder of corn to the portioner of Langhope; and that she had turned in Ball to graze in the Tasker's park near Cripplecross, for he had stood as still as Lot's wife with very weariness; and that the knight had courteously insisted she should ride behind him, and that she had brought him to her kenn'd friend's hostlery rather than to proud Peter Peddie's, who got his malt at the Mellerstane mills; and that he must get the best that the house afforded, and that he must get it ready in a moment of time, and that she was ready to help in the kitchen.

All this ran glibly off the tongue without pause on the part of Mysie Happer, or doubt on that of the landlord. The guest's horse was conducted to the stable, and he himself installed in the cleanest corner and best seat which the place afforded. Mysie, ever active and officious, was at once engaged in preparing food, in spreading the table, and in making all the better arrangements which her experience could suggest, for the honour and comfort of her companion. He would fain have resisted this; for while it was impossible not to be gratified with the eager and alert kindness which was so active in his service, he felt an undefinable pain in seeing Mysinda

---

* Froissart tells us somewhere (the readers of romances are indifferent to accurate reference) that the King of France called one of the Piercies cousin, because of the blood of Northumberland.

engaged in these menial services, and discharging them, moreover, as one to whom they were but too familiar. And yet this jarring feeling was mixed with, and perhaps balanced by, the extreme grace with which the neat-handed maiden executed the tasks, however mean in themselves, and gave to the wretched corner of a miserable inn of the period, the air of a bower in which an enamoured fairy, or at least a shepherdess of Arcadia, was displaying, with unavailing solicitude, her designs on the heart of some knight, destined by fortune to higher thoughts, and a more splendid union.

The lightness and grace with which Mysie covered the little round table with a snow-white cloth, and arranged upon it the hastily-roasted capon, with its accompanying stoup of Bourdeaux, were but plebeian graces in themselves; but yet there were very flattering ideas excited by each glance. She was so very well made, agile and graceful at once, with her hand and arm as white as snow, and her face in which a smile contended with a blush, and her eyes which looked ever at Shafton when he looked elsewhere, and were dropped at once when they encountered his, that she was irresistible. In fine, the affectionate delicacy of her whole demeanour, joined to the promptitude and boldness she had so lately evinced, tended to ennoble the services she had rendered, as if Love had taught her to adopt them, or as if some

> ————sweet engaging Grace
> Put on some clothes to come abroad,
> And took a waiter's place.

But, on the other hand, came the damning reflection, that these duties were not taught her by Love, to serve the beloved only, but arose from the positive habits of a miller's daughter, accustomed, doubtless, to render the same service to every wealthier churl who frequented her father's mill. This stopped the mouth of Vanity, and of the love which Vanity had been hatching, as effectually as a peck of literal flour would have done.

Amidst this variety of emotions, Sir Piercie Shafton forgot not to ask the object of them to sit down and partake the good cheer which she had been so anxious to provide and to place in order. He expected that this invitation would have been bashfully perhaps, but certainly most thankfully, accepted. But he was partly flattered, and partly piqued, by the mixture of deference and resolution with which Mysie declined his invitation. And immediately after, she vanished from the apartment, leaving the Euphuist to consider whether he was most gratified or displeased by her disappearance.

In fact, this was a point on which he would have found it difficult to make up his mind, had there been any necessity for it. As there was none, he drank a cup or two of claret, and sang (to himself) a strophe

or two of the canzonettes of the divine Astrophel. But in spite both of
wine and of Sir Philip Sidney, the connection in which he now stood,
and that which he was in future to hold, with the lovely Molinara,
or Mysinda, as he had been pleased to denominate Mysie Happer,
recurred to his mind. The fashion of the times (as we have already
noticed) fortunately coincided with his own natural generosity of
disposition, which indeed amounted almost to extravagance, in pro-
hibiting, as a deadly sin, alike against gallantry, chivalry, and morality,
his rewarding the good offices he had received from this poor maiden,
by abusing any of the advantages which her confidence in his honour
had afforded. To do Sir Piercie justice, it was an idea which never
entered into his head; and he would probably have dealt the most
scientific *imbrocata*, *stoccata*, or *punto reverso*, which the school of Vincent Saviolo had taught him, to any man who had dared to suggest to
him such selfish and ungrateful meanness. On the other hand, he was
a man, and foresaw various circumstances which might render their
journey together in this intimate fashion a scandal and a snare. Moreover, he was a coxcomb and a courtier, and felt there was something
ridiculous in travelling the land with a miller's daughter behind his
saddle, giving rise to suspicions not very creditable to either, and to
ludicrous constructions, so far as he himself was concerned.

"I would," he said half aloud, "that, if such might be done without
harm or discredit to the too-ambitious, yet too-well distinguishing
Molinara, she and I were fairly severed, and bound on our different
courses; even as we see the goodly vessel bound for the distant seas
hoist sails and bear away into the deep, while the humble fly-boat
carries to shore those friends, who, with wounded hearts and watery
eyes, have committed to their higher destinies the more daring adventurers by whom the fair frigate is manned."

He had scarce uttered the wish when it was gratified; for the host
entered to say that his worshipful knighthood's horse was ready to be
brought forth as he had desired; and on his enquiry for "the—the—
damsel—that is—the young woman"——

"Mysie Happer," said the landlord, "has returned to her father's;
but she bade me say, you could not miss the road for Edinburgh, in
respect it was neither far way nor foul gate."

It is seldom we are exactly blessed with the precise fulfilment of our
wishes at the moment when we utter them; perhaps because Heaven
wisely withholds what, if granted, would be often received with ingratitude. So at least it chanced in the present instance; for when mine
host said that Mysie was returned homeward, the knight was tempted
to reply, with an ejaculation of surprise and vexation, and a hasty
demand, whither and when she had departed? The first emotion his

prudence suppressed, the second found utterance.

"Where is she gane?" said the host, gazing on him, and repeating his question—"She is gane hame to her father's, it is like—And she gaed just when she gave orders about your worship's horse, and saw it weel fed, (she might have trusted me, but millers and millers' kin think a' body as thief-like as themselves) an' she's three miles on the gate by this time."

"Is she gone, then?" muttered Sir Piercie, making two or three hasty strides through the narrow apartment—"Is she gone?—well, then, let her go. She could have had but disgrace by abiding by me, and I little credit by her society. That I should have thought there was such difficulty in shaking her off! I warrant she is by this time laughing with some clown she has encountered; and my rich chain will prove a good dowry.—And ought it not to prove so? and has she not deserved it, were it ten times more valuable?—Piercie Shafton! Piercie Shafton! doest thou grudge thy deliverer the guerdon she hath so dearly won? The selfish air of this northern land hath infected thee, Piercie Shafton, and blighted the blossoms of thy generosity, even as it is said to shrivel the flowers of the mulberry.—Yet I thought," he added, after a moment's pause, "that she would not so easily and voluntarily have parted from me. But it skills not thinking of it.—Cast my reckoning, mine host, and let your groom lead forth my nag."

The good host seemed also to have some mental point to discuss, for he answered not instantly, debating perhaps whether his conscience would bear a double charge for the same guests. Apparently his conscience replied in the negative, though not without hesitation, for he at length replied—"It's daffing to lee; it winna deny that the lawing is clean paid. Ne'ertheless, if your worshipful knighthood pleases to give aught for increase of trouble"——

"How!" said the knight; "the reckoning paid?—and by whom, I pray you?"

"E'en by Mysie Happer, if truth maun be spoken, as I said before," answered the honest landlord, with as many compunctious visitings for telling the verity as another might have felt for making a lie in the circumstances—"And out of the monies supplied for your honour's journey by the Abbot, as she tauld to me. And laith were I to surcharge any gentleman that darkens my doors." He added, in the confidence of honesty which his frank avowal entitled him to entertain, "Nevertheless, as I said before, if it pleases your knighthood of free good will to consider extraordinary trouble"——

The knight cut short his argument, by throwing the landlord a rose-noble, which probably doubled the value of a Scottish reckoning, though it would have defrayed but a half one at the Three Cranes of the Vintry. The bounty so much delighted mine host, that he ran to fill the stirrup-cup (for which no charge was ever made) from a butt yet charier than that which he had pierced for the former stoup. The knight paced slowly to horse, partook of his courtesy, and thanked him with the stiff condescension of the court of Elizabeth; then mounted and followed the northern path, which was pointed out as the nearest to Edinburgh, and which, though very unlike a modern highway, bore yet so distinct a resemblance to a public and frequented road as not to be easily mistaken.

"I shall not need her guidance it seems," said he to himself, as he rode slowly onward; "and I suppose that was one reason of her abrupt departure, so different from what one might have expected.—Well, I am well rid of her—do we not pray to be liberated from temptation? Yet that she should have erred so much in estimation of her own situation and mine, as to think of defraying the reckoning! I would I saw her once more, but to explain to her the solecism of which her inexperience hath rendered her guilty. And I fear," he added, as he emerged from some straggling trees, and looked out upon a wild moorish country, composed of a succession of swelling lumpish hills, "I shall soon want the aid of this Ariadne, who might afford me a clue through the recesses of yonder mountainous labyrinth."

As the knight thus communed with himself, his attention was caught by the sound of a horse's footsteps; and a lad, mounted on a little grey Scottish nag, about fourteen hands high, coming along a path which led from behind the trees, joined him on the high-road, if it could be termed such.

The dress of the lad was completely village-fashion, yet neat and handsome in appearance. He had a jerkin of grey cloth slashed and trimmed, with black hose of the same, with deer-skin rullions or sandals, and handsome silver spurs. A cloak of a dark mulberry colour was closely drawn round the upper part of his person, and the cape in part muffled his face, which was also obscured by his bonnet of black velvet cloth and its little plume of feathers.

Sir Piercie Shafton, fond of society, desirous also to have a guide, and, moreover, prepossessed in favour of so handsome a youth, failed not to ask him whence he came, and whither he was going. The youth looked another way, as he answered, that he was going to Edinburgh, "to seek service in some nobleman's family."

"I fear me you have run away from your last master," said Sir Piercie, "since you dare not look me in the face while you answer my question."

"Indeed, sir, I have not," answered the lad bashfully, while, as if with reluctance, he turned round his face, and instantly withdrew it. It was but a glance, but the discovery was complete. There was no mistaking the dark full eye, the cheek in which much embarrassment could not altogether disguise an expression of comic humour, and the whole figure at once betrayed, under her metamorphosis, the Maid of the Mill. The recognition was joyful, and Sir Piercie Shafton was too much pleased to have regained his companion to remember the various good reasons which had consoled him for losing her.

To his questions respecting her dress, she answered that she had obtained it in the town from a friend: it was the holiday suit of a son of her's, who had taken the field with his liege-lord, the baron of the land. She had borrowed the suit under pretence she meant to play in some mumming or rural masquerade. She had left, she said, her own apparel in exchange, which was better worth ten crowns than this was worth four.

"And the nag, my ingenious Molinara," said Sir Piercie, "whence comes the nag?"

"I borrowed him from our host at the Gled's-Nest," she replied; and added, half stifling a laugh, "he has sent to get, instead of it, our Ball, which I left in the Tasker's park at Cripplecross. He will be lucky if he find it there."

"But, then, the poor man will lose his horse, most argute Mysinda?" said Sir Piercie Shafton, whose English notions of property were a little startled at a mode of acquisition more congenial to the ideas of a miller's daughter (and he a Border miller to boot) than with those of an English person of quality.

"And if he does lose his horse," said Mysie, laughing, "surely he is not the first man on the marches who has had such a mischance. But he will be no loser, for I warrant him stop the value out of monies that he has owed my father this many a day."

"But then your father will be the loser," objected yet again the pertinacious uprightness of Sir Piercie Shafton.

"What signifies it now to talk of my father?" said the damsel pettishly; then instantly changing to a tone of deep feeling, she added, "My father has this day lost that, which will make him hold light the loss of all the gear he has left."

Struck with the accents of remorseful sorrow in which his companion uttered these few words, the English knight felt himself bound 1 oth in honour and conscience to expostulate with her as strongly as he could, on the risks of the step which she had now taken, and on the propriety of her returning to her father's house. The matter of his discourse, though adorned with many unnecessary flourishes, was honourable both to his head and heart.

The Maid of the Mill listened to his flowing periods with her head sunk on her bosom as she rode, like one in deep thought or deeper sorrow. When he had finished, she raised up her countenance, looked full on the knight, and replied with great firmness—"If you are weary of my company, Sir Piercie Shafton, you have but to say so, and the miller's daughter will be no farther cumber to you. And do not think I will be a burthen to you, if we travel together to Edinburgh—I have wit enough and pride enough to be a willing burthen to no man. But if you reject not my company at present, and fear not it will be burthensome to you hereafter, speak no more to me of returning back. All that you can say to me, I have said to myself; and that I am now here, is a sign that I have said it to no purpose. Let this subject, therefore, be for ever ended betwixt us. I have already, in some small fashion, been useful to you, and the time may come I may be more so; for this is not your land of England, where men say justice is done with little fear or favour to great and to small. But it is a land where men do by the strong hand, and defend by the ready wit, and I know better than you the perils you are exposed to."

Sir Piercie Shafton was somewhat mortified to find that the damsel conceived her presence useful to him as a protectress as well as guide, and said something of seeking protection from nought save his own arm and his good sword. Mysie answered very quietly, that she nothing doubted his bravery; but it was that very quality of bravery which was most likely to involve him in danger. Sir Piercie Shafton, whose head never kept very long in any continued train of thinking, acquiesced without much reply; resolving in his own mind that the maiden only used this apology to disguise her real motive of affection to his person. The romance of the situation flattered his vanity and elevated his imagination, as placing him in the situation of one of those romantic heroes of whom he had read the histories, where similar transformations made a distinguished figure.

He took many a side-long glance at his page, whose habits of country sport and country exercise had rendered her quite adequate to sustain the character she had assumed. She managed the little nag with dexterity, and even with grace; nor did any thing appear which could have betrayed her disguise, excepting when a bashful consciousness of her companion's eyes being fixed on her, gave her an appearance of temporary embarrassment, which greatly added to her beauty.

The couple rode forward as in the morning, pleased with themselves and with each other, until they arrived at the village where they were to repose for the night, and where all the inhabitants of the little inn, both male and female, joined in extolling the good grace and handsome countenance of the English knight, and the uncommon beauty of his youthful attendant.

It was here that Mysie Happer first made Sir Piercie Shafton sensible of the reserved manner in which she proposed to live with him. She announced him as her master, and, waiting upon him with the reverent demeanour of an actual domestic, permitted not the least approach to familiarity, not even such as the knight might with the utmost innocence have ventured upon. For example, Sir Piercie, who, as we know, was a great connoisseur in dress, was detailing to her the advantageous change which he proposed to make in her attire so soon as they should reach Edinburgh, by arraying her in his own colours of pink and carnation. Mysie Happer listened with great complacency to the unction with which he dilated upon welts, laces, slashes, and trimmings, until, carried away by the enthusiasm with which he was asserting the superiority of the falling band over the Spanish ruff, he approached his hand, in the way of illustration, towards the collar of his page's doublet. She instantly stepped back, and gravely reminded him that she was alone, and under his protection.

"You cannot but remember the cause which has brought me here," she continued; "make the least approach to any familiarity, which you would not offer to a princess surrounded by her court, and you have seen the last of the Miller's daughter—She will vanish as the chaff disappears from the shieling-hill,* when the west wind blows."

"I do protest, fair Molinara," said Sir Piercie Shafton—But the fair Molinara had disappeared before his protest could be uttered. "A most singular wench," said he to himself; "and by this hand as discreet as she is fair-featured—Certes, shame it were to offer her scathe or dishonour! She makes similes, too, though somewhat savouring of her condition. Had she but read Euphues, and forgotten that accursed mill and shieling-hill, it is my thought that her converse would be broidered with as many and as choice pearls of compliment, as that of the most rhetorical lady in the Court of Feliciana. I trust she means to return to bear me company."

But that was no part of Mysie's prudential scheme. It was then drawing to dusk, and he saw her not again until the next morning, when the horses were brought to the door that they might prosecute their journey.

But our story here necessarily leaves the English knight and his page, to return to the tower of Glendearg.

* The place where corn was winnowed, while that operation was performed by the hand, was called in Scotland the Sheiling-hill.

Chapter Five

You call it an ill angel—it may be so;
But sure I am, among the ranks which fell,
'Tis the first fiend ere counsell'd man to rise,
And win the bliss himself had forfeited.
Old Play

WE MUST RESUME our narrative at the period when Mary Avenel
was conveyed to the apartment which had been formerly occupied by
the two Glendinnings, and when her faithful attendant Tibbie had
exhausted herself in useless attempts to compose and to comfort her.
Father Eustace had also dealt forth with well-meant kindness those
apothegms and dogmata of consolation, which friendship almost
always offers to grief, though they are uniformly offered in vain. She
was at length left to indulge in the desolation of her own sorrowful
feelings. She felt as those, who, loving for the first time, have lost what
they loved, before time and repeated calamity have taught them that
every loss is to a certain extent reparable or endurable.

Such grief may be conceived better than it can be described, as is
well known to those who have experienced it. But Mary Avenel had
been taught by the peculiarity of her situation, to regard herself as the
Child of Destiny; and the melancholy and reflecting turn of her
disposition gave to her sorrows a depth and breadth peculiar to her
character. The grave—and it was a bloody grave—had closed, as she
supposed, over the youth to whom she was secretly, but most warmly
attached; the force and ardour of Halbert's character bearing a singular correspondence to the energy of which her own was capable. Her
sorrow did not exhaust itself in sighs or in tears, but when the first
shock had passed away, collected itself with deep and steady meditation, to collect and calculate, like a bankrupt debtor, the full amount of
her loss. It seemed as if all that connected her with earth, had vanished
with this broken tie. She had never dared to anticipate the probability
of an ultimate union with Halbert, yet now his supposed fall seemed
that of the only tree which was to shelter her from the storm. She
respected the more gentle character, and more peaceful attainments
of the younger Glendinning; but it had not escaped her (what never
indeed escaped woman in such circumstances,) that he was not indisposed to place them in competition with what she, the daughter of a
proud and warlike race, deemed the more manly qualities of his elder
brother; and there is no time when a woman does so little justice to the
character of a surviving lover, as when comparing him with the preferred rival of whom she has been recently deprived.

The motherly, but coarse kindness of Dame Glendinning, and the doating fondness of her old domestic, seemed now the only kind feelings of which she formed the object; and she could not but reflect how little these were to be compared with the devoted attachment of a high-souled youth, whom the least glance of her eye could command, as the high-mettled steed is governed by the bridle of the rider. It was when plunged amongst these desolating reflections, that Mary Avenel felt the void of mind, arising from the narrow and bigotted ignorance in which Rome then educated the children of her church. Their whole religion was a ritual, and their prayers were the formal iteration of unknown words, which, in the hour of affliction, could yield but little consolation to those who from habit resorted to them. Unused to the practice of mental devotion, and of personal approach to the Divine Presence by prayer, she could not help exclaiming in her distress, "There is no aid for me on earth, and I know not how to ask it from heaven!"

As she spoke thus in her agony of sorrow, she cast her eyes into the apartment, and saw the mysterious Spirit, which waited upon the fortunes of her house, standing in the moonlight in the midst of the room. The same form, as the reader knows, had more than once offered itself to her sight; and either her native boldness of mind or some peculiar quality attached to her from her birth, had made her look upon it without shrinking. But the White Lady of Avenel was now more distinctly visible, and more closely present than she had ever before seemed to be, and Mary was appalled by her presence. She would, however, have spoken; but there ran a tradition, that though others who had seen the White Lady had asked questions and received answers, yet those of the house of Avenel who had ventured to speak to her, had never long survived the colloquy. The figure besides, as, sitting up in her bed, Mary Avenel gazed on it intently, seemed by her gestures to caution her to keep silence, and at the same time to bespeak attention.

The White Lady then seemed to press one of the planks of the floor with her foot, while, in her usual low, melancholy, and musical chaunt, she repeated the following verses:

> "Maiden, whose sorrows wail the Living Dead,
>   Whose eyes shall commune with the Dead Alive,
> Maiden, attend! Beneath my foot lies hid
>   The Word, the Law, the Path, which thou doest strive
> To find, and canst not find.—Could Spirits shed
>   Tears for their lot, it were my lot to weep,
> Shewing the road which I shall never tread,
>   Though my foot points it—Sleep, eternal sleep,
> Dark, long, and cold forgetfulness my lot!—
>   But do not thou at human ills repine,

> Secure there lies full guerdon in this spot
>   For all the woes that wait frail Adam's line—
> Stoop then and make it your's,—I may not make it mine!"

The phantom stooped towards the floor as she concluded, as if with the purpose of laying her hand on the board on which she stood. But ere she had completed that gesture, her form became indistinct, was presently only like the shade of a fleecy cloud, which passed betwixt earth and the moon, and was presently altogether invisible.

A strong impression of fear, the first which she had experienced in her life to any agitating extent, seized upon the mind of Mary Avenel, and for a minute she felt a disposition to faint. She repelled it, however, mustered her courage, and addressed herself to saints and angels, as her church recommended. Broken slumbers at length stole on her exhausted mind and frame, and she slept until the dawn was about to arise, when she was awakened by the cry of "Treason! treason! follow, follow!" which arose in the tower, when it was found that Piercie Shafton had made his escape.

Apprehensive of some new misfortune, Mary Avenel hastily arranged the dress which she had not laid aside, and venturing to quit her chamber, learned from Tibb, who, with her grey hairs dishevelled like those of a sybil, was flying from room to room, that the bloody Southron villain had made his escape, and that Halbert Glendinning, poor bairn, would sleep unrevenged and unquiet in his bloody grave. In the under apartments, the young men were roaring like thunder, and venting in oaths and exclamations against the fugitives the rage which they experienced in finding themselves locked up within the tower, and debarred from their vindictive pursuit by the wily precaution of Mysie Happer. The authoritative voice of the Sub-Prior commanding silence was next heard; upon which Mary Avenel, whose turn of feeling did not lead her to enter into counsel or society with the rest of the party, again retired to her solitary chamber.

The rest of the family held counsel in the spence, Edward almost beside himself with anger, and the Sub-Prior himself not a little offended at the effrontery of Mysie Happer in attempting such a scheme, as well as at the mingled boldness and dexterity with which it had been executed. But neither surprise nor anger availed aught. The windows, well secured with iron bars for keeping assailants out, proved now as effectual for detaining the inhabitants within. The battlements were open indeed, but without ladder or ropes to act as a substitute for wings, there was no possibility of descending from them. They easily succeeded in alarming the inhabitants of the cottages beyond the precincts of the court; but the men had been called in to strengthen the guard for the night, and only women and children remained, who could contribute nothing in the emergency, except their useless exclamations of surprise, and there were no neighbours for miles around. Dame Elspet, however, though drowned in tears, was not so unmindful of external affairs but what she could find voice enough to tell the women and children without, to "leave their skirl-ing, and look after the seven cows that she couldna get minded, what wi' the awfu' distraction of her mind, what wi' that fause slut having locked them up in their ain tower as fast as if they had been in the Jeddart tolbooth."

Meanwhile, the men finding other modes of exit impossible, unanimously concluded to force the doors with such tools as the house afforded for the purpose. These were not very proper for the occasion, and the strength of the doors was very great. The interior one, formed of oak, occupied them for three mortal hours, and there was little prospect of the iron door being forced in double the time.

While they were engaged in this ungrateful toil, Mary Avenel had with much less labour acquired exact knowledge of what the Spirit had intimated in her mystic rhyme. On examining the spot which the phantom had indicated by her gestures, it was not difficult to discover that a board had been loosened, which might be raised at pleasure. On removing this piece of plank, Mary Avenel was astonished to find the Black Book, well remembered by her as her mother's favourite study, of which she immediately took possession, with as much joy as her present situation rendered her capable of feeling.

Ignorant in a great measure of its contents, Mary Avenel had been taught from her infancy to hold this volume in sacred veneration. It is probable that the deceased Lady of Walter Avenel only postponed initiating her daughter into the mysteries of the Divine Word, until she should be better able to comprehend both the lessons which it taught, and the risk at which, in these times, they were studied. Death interposed, and removed her before the times became favourable to the reformers, and before her daughter was so far advanced in age as to be fit to receive religious instruction of this deep import. But the affectionate mother had made preparations for the earthly work which she had most at heart. There were slips of paper inserted in the work, in which, by an appeal to, and a comparison of various passages in holy writ, the errors and human inventions with which the Church of Rome had defaced the simple edifice of Christianity, as erected by its divine architect, were pointed out. These controversial topics were treated with a spirit of calmness and christian charity, which might have been an example to the theologians of the period; but they were clearly, fairly, and plainly argued, and supported by the necessary proofs and references. Other papers there were which had no reference whatsoever to polemics, but were the simple effusions of a devout mind communing with itself. Among these was one frequently used, as it seemed from the state of the manuscript, on which the mother of Mary had transcribed and placed together those affecting texts to which the heart has recourse in affliction, and which assure us at once of the sympathy and protection afforded to the children of the promise. In Mary Avenel's state of mind, these attracted her above all the other lessons, which, coming from a hand so dear, had reached her at a time so critical, and in a manner so touching. She read the affecting promise, "I will never leave thee nor forsake thee," and the consoling exhortation, "Call upon me in the day of trouble, and I will deliver thee." She read them, and her heart acquiesced in the conclusion, Surely this is the word of God.

There are those to whom a sense of religion has come in storm and tempest; there are those whom it has summoned amid scenes of revelry and idle vanity; there are those, too, who have heard its "still small voice" amid rural leisure and placid contentment. But perhaps the knowledge which causeth not to err, is most frequently impressed upon the mind during seasons of affliction; and tears are the softened showers which cause the seed of heaven to spring and take root in the human breast. At least it was thus with Mary Avenel. She was insensible to the discordant noise which rang below, the clang of bars and the jarring symphony of the levers which they used to force them, the measured shout of the labouring inmates as they combined their strength for each heave, and gave time with their voices to the exertion of their arms, and their deeply muttered vows of revenge on the fugitives who had bequeathed them at their departure a task so toilsome and difficult. Not all this din, combined in hideous concert, and expressive of aught but peace, love, and forgiveness, could divert Mary Avenel from the new course of study on which she had so singularly entered. "The serenity of heaven," she said, "is above me; the sounds which are beneath are but those of earth and earthly passion."

Meanwhile the noon was passed, and little impression was made on the iron grate, when they who laboured at it received a sudden reinforcement by the unexpected arrival of Christie of the Clinthill. He came at the head of a small party, consisting of four horsemen, who bore in their caps the sprig of holly, which was the badge of Avenel.

"What ho! my masters," he said, "I bring you a prisoner."

"You had better have brought us liberty," said Dan of the Howlethirst.

Christie looked at the state of affairs with great surprise. "An I were to be hanged for it," he said, "as I may for as little a matter, I could not forbear laughing at seeing men peeping through their own bars like so many rats in a rat-trap, and he with the beard behind, like the oldest rat of the cellar."

"Hush, thou unmannered knave," said Edward, "it is the Sub-Prior, and this is neither time, place, nor company, for your ruffian jests."

"What ho! is my young master malapert?" said Christie; "why, man, were he my own carnal father, instead of being father to half the world, I would have my laugh out—and now it is over, I must assist you I reckon, for you are setting very greenly about this gear—put the pinch nearer the staple, man, and hand me an iron crow through the grate, for that's the fowl to fly away with a wicket on its shoulders. I have broke into as many such grates as you have teeth in your young head—ay and broke out of them too, as the captain of the Castle of Lochmaben knows full well."

Christie did not boast more skill than he really possessed; for, applying their combined strength, under the direction of that experienced engineer, bolt and staple gave way before them, and in less than half an hour, the grate, which had so long repelled their force, stood open before them.

"And now," said Edward, "to horse, my mates, and pursue the villain Shafton!"

"Halt there," said Christie of the Clinthill; "pursue your guest, my master's friend and my own?—there go two words to that bargain. What the foul fiend would you pursue him for?"

"Let me pass," said Edward, vehemently, "I will be staid by no man —the villain has murdered my brother."

"What says he?" said Christie, turning to the others; "murdered? who is murdered, and by whom?"

"The Englishman, Sir Piercie Shafton," said Dan of the Howlet-hirst, "has murdered young Halbert Glendinning yesterday morning, and we are all risen to the fray."

"It is a bedlam business, I think," said Christie. "Here I find you all locked up in your own tower, and I find it is to prevent you revenging a murder that was never committed!"

"I tell you," said Edward, "that my brother was slain and buried yesterday morning by this false Englishman."

"And I tell you," answered Christie, "that I saw him alive and well last night. I would I knew his trick of getting out of the grave; most men find it more hard to break through a green sod than a grated door."

Every body now paused, and looked on Christie in astonishment, until the Sub-Prior, who had hitherto avoided communication with him, came up and required earnestly to know, whether he meant really to maintain that Halbert Glendinning lived.

"Father," said he, with more respect than he usually shewed to any one save his master, "I confess I may sometimes jest with those of your coat, but not with you; because, as you may partly recollect, I owe you a life. It is certain as the sun is in heaven, that Halbert Glendinning supped at the house of my master the Baron of Avenel last night, and that he came thither in company with an old man, of whom more anon."

"And where is he now?"

"The devil only can answer that question," replied Christie, "for the devil has possessed the whole family I think. He took fright, the foolish lad, at something or other that our Baron did in his moody humour, and so he jumped into the lake and swam ashore like a wild-duck. Robin of Redcastle spoiled a good gelding in chasing him this morning."

"And why did he chase the youth?" said the Sub-Prior; "what harm had he done?"

"None that I know of," said Christie; "but such was the Baron's order, being in his mood, and all the world having gone mad, as I said before."

"Whither away so fast, Edward?" said the Monk.

"To Corri-nan-shian, Father," answered the youth. "Martin and Dan, take pick-axe and mattock, and follow me if you be men."

"Right," said the Monk, "and fail not to give us instant notice what you find."

"If you find aught there like Halbert Glendinning," said Christie, hollowing after Edward, "I will be bound to eat him unsalted.—'Tis a sight to see now how that fellow takes the bent!—it is in the time of action men see what lads are made of. Halbert was aye skipping up and down like a roe, and his brother used to sit in the chimney-nook with his book and sic like trash—But the lad was like a loaded hack-but, whilk will stand in the corner as quiet as any old carle's crutch until ye draw the trigger, and then there is nought but flash and smoke.—But here comes my prisoner; and, setting other matters aside, I must pray a word with you, Sir Sub-Prior, respecting him. I came on before to treat about him, but I was interrupted with this fasherie."

As he spoke, two more of Avenel's troopers rode into the court-yard, leading betwixt them a horse, on which, with his hands bound to his side, sate the reformed preacher, Henry Warden.

Chapter Six

At school I knew him—a sharp-witted youth,
Grave, thoughtful, and reserved amongst his mates,
Turning the hours of sport and food to labour,
Starving his body to inform his mind.

Old Play

THE SUB-PRIOR, upon the Borderer's request, had not failed to return into the tower, into which he was followed by Christie of the Clinthill, who, shutting the door of the apartment, drew near and began his discourse with an air of great confidence and familiarity.

"My master," he said, "sends me with his commendations to you, Sir Sub-Prior, above all the community of Saint Mary's, and more specially than even to the Abbot himself; for though he be termed my lord, and so forth, all the world kens that you are the tongue of the trump."

"If you have aught to say to me concerning the community," said the Sub-Prior, "it were well you proceeded in it without further delay. Time presses, and the fate of young Glendinning dwells on my mind."

"I will be caution for him, body for body," said Christie. "I do protest to you, as sure as I am a living man, so surely is he one."

"Should I not tell his unhappy mother the joyful tidings?" said Father Eustace,—"and yet better wait till they return from searching the grave. Well, Sir Jack-man, your message to me from your master?"

"My lord and master," said Christie, "hath good reason to believe that, from the information of certain back-friends, whom he will reward at more leisure, your reverend community hath been led to deem him ill attached to Holy Church, allied with heretics and those who favour heresy, and a hungerer after the spoils of your Abbey."

"Be brief, good hench-man," said the Sub-Prior, "for the devil is ever most to be feared when he preacheth."

"Briefly, then—my master desires your friendship; and to excuse himself from the maligners' calumnies, he sends to your Abbot that Henry Warden, whose sermons have turned the world upside down, to be dealt with as Holy Church directs, and as the Abbot's pleasure may determine."

The Sub-Prior's eyes sparkled at the intelligence, for it had been accounted a matter of great importance that this man should be arrested, possessed, as he was known to be, of so much zeal and popularity, that scarce the preaching of Knox himself had been more awakening to the people, and more formidable to the Church of Rome.

In fact, that ancient system, which so well accommodated its doctrines to the wants and wishes of a barbarous age, had, since the art of
printing, and the gradual diffusion of knowledge, lain floating many a
rood like some huge Leviathan, into which ten thousand reforming
fishers were darting their harpoons. The Roman Church of Scotland,
in particular, was at her last gasp, actually blowing blood and water, yet
still with unremitted, though animal exertions, maintaining the conflict with the assailants, who on every side were plunging their
weapons into her bulky body. In many large towns, the monasteries
had been suppressed by the fury of the populace; in other places, their
possessions had been usurped by the power of the reformed nobles;
but still the hierarchy made a part of the common law of the realm, and
might claim both its property and privileges wherever it had the means
of asserting them. The Community of Saint Mary's of Kennaquhair
was considered as being particularly in this situation. They had
retained, undiminished, their territorial power and influence; and the
great barons in the neighbourhood, partly from their attachment to
the party in the state who yet upheld the old system of religion, partly
because each grudged the share of the prey which the others must
necessarily claim, had as yet abstained from despoiling the Halidome.
The Community were also understood to be protected by the powerful Earls of Northumberland and Westmoreland, whose zealous
attachment to the Catholic faith caused at a later period the great
rebellion of the tenth of Elizabeth.

Thus happily placed, it was supposed by the friends of the decaying
cause of the Roman Catholic faith, that some determined example of
courage and resolution, exercised where the franchises of the church
were yet entire, and her jurisdiction undisputed, might awe the progress of the new opinions into inactivity; and, protected by the laws
which still existed, and by the favour of the sovereign, might be the
means of securing the territory which Rome yet preserved in Scotland, and perhaps of recovering that which she had lost.

The matter had been considered more than once by the northern
Catholics of Scotland, and they had held communication with those of
the south. Father Eustace, devoted by his public and private vows, had
caught the flame, and had eagerly advised that they should execute the
doom of heresy on the first reformed preacher, or, according to his
sense, on the first heretic of eminence, who should venture within the
precincts of the Halidome. A heart naturally kind and noble, was, in
this instance, as it has been in many more, deceived by its own generosity. Father Eustace would have been a bad administrator of the
inquisitorial power in Spain, where that power was omnipotent, and
where judgment was exercised without danger to those who inflicted

it. In such a situation his rigour might have relented in favour of the criminal, whom it was at his pleasure to crush or to place at freedom. But in Scotland, during this crisis, the case was entirely different. The question was, whether one of the spirituality dared, at the hazard of his own life, step forward to assert and exercise the rights of the church. Was there any one who would venture to wield the thunder in her cause, or must it remain like that in the hand of a painted Jupiter, the object of derision instead of terror? The crisis was calculated to awake the soul of Eustace, for it comprized the question, whether he dared, at all hazards to himself, to execute with stoical severity a measure which, according to the general opinion, was to be advantageous to the church, and, according to ancient law, and to his firm belief, was not only justifiable but meritorious.

While such resolutions were agitated amongst the catholics, chance placed a victim within their grasp. Henry Warden had, with the animation proper to the enthusiastic reformers of the age, transgressed, in the vehemence of his zeal, the bounds of the discretional liberty allowed to his sect so far, that it was thought the Queen's personal dignity was concerned in bringing him to justice. He fled from Edinburgh, with recommendations, however, from Lord James Stewart, afterwards the celebrated Earl of Moray, to some of the Border chieftains of inferior rank, who were privately conjured to procure him safe passage into England. One of the principal to whom such recommendation was addressed, was Julian Avenel, for as yet, and for a considerable time afterwards, the correspondence and interest of Lord James lay rather with the subordinate leaders than with the chiefs of great power, and men of distinguished influence upon the Border. Julian Avenel had intrigued without scruple with both parties —yet bad as he was, he certainly would not have practised aught against the guest whom Lord James had recommended to his hospitality, had it not been for what he termed the preacher's officious intermeddling in his family affairs. But when he had determined to make Warden rue the lecture he had read him, and the scene of public scandal which he had caused in his hall, Julian resolved, with the constitutional shrewdness of his disposition, to combine his vengeance with his interest. And therefore, instead of doing violence on the person of Henry Warden within his own castle, he determined to deliver him up to the Community of Saint Mary's, and at once make them the instruments of his own revenge, and found a claim of personal recompence either in money, or in a grant of Abbey-lands at a low quit-rent, which last began now to be the established form in which the temporal nobles plundered the spirituality.

The Sub-Prior, therefore, of Saint Mary's unexpectedly saw the stedfast, active, and inflexible enemy of the church delivered into his hand, and felt himself called upon to make good his promises to the friends of the catholic faith, by quenching heresy in the blood of one of its most zealous professors.

To the honour of Father Eustace's heart more than his consistency, the communication that Henry Warden was placed within his power, struck him with more sorrow than triumph; but his next feelings were those of exultation. "It is sad," he said to himself, "to cause human suffering, it is awful to cause human blood be spilled; but the judge to whom the sword of Saint Paul, as well as the keys of Saint Peter, are confided, must not flinch from his task. Our weapon returns into our own bosom, if not wielded with a steady and unrelenting hand against the irreconcileable enemies of the Holy Church. *Pereat iste!* It is the doom he has incurred, and were all the heretics in Scotland armed and at his back, they should not prevent its being pronounced, and, if possible, enforced.—Bring the heretic before me," he said, issuing his commands aloud, and in a tone of authority.

Henry Warden was led in, his hands still bound, but his feet at liberty.

"Clear the apartment," said the Sub-Prior, "of all but the necessary guard on the prisoner."

All retired excepting Christie of the Clinthill, who, having dismissed the inferior troopers whom he commanded, unsheathed his sword, and placed himself beside the door, as if taking upon him the character of centinel.

The judge and the accused met face to face, but in that of both was enthroned the noble confidence of rectitude. The Monk was about, at the utmost risk to himself and his community, to exercise what in his ignorance he conceived to be his duty. The preacher, actuated by a better informed, yet not a more ardent zeal, was prompt to submit to execution for God's sake, and to seal, were it necessary, his mission with his blood. Placed at such a distance of time as better enables us to appreciate the tendency of the principles on which they severally acted, we cannot doubt to which the palm ought to be awarded. But the zeal of Father Eustace was as free from passion and personal views as if it had been exerted in a better cause.

They approached each other, armed each and prepared for intellectual conflict, and perusing each other with their eyes, as if either hoped to spy out some defect, some chasm in the armour of his antagonist. As they gazed on each other, old recollections began to awake in either bosom, at the sight of features long unseen and much altered, but not forgotten. The brow of the Sub-Prior dismissed by degrees its frown of command, the look of calm yet stern defiance gradually vanished from that of Warden, and both lost for an instant that of gloomy solemnity. They had been ancient and intimate friends in youth at a foreign university, but had been long separated from each other; and the change of name, which the preacher had adopted from motives of safety, and the Monk from the common custom of the convent, had prevented the possibility of their hitherto recognizing each other in the opposed parts which they had been playing in the great polemical and political drama. But now the Sub-Prior exclaimed, "Henry Wellwood!"—the preacher replied, "William Allan!"—and, stirred by the old familiar names, and never-to-be-forgotten recollections of college studies and college intimacy, their hands were for a moment locked in each other.

"Remove his bonds," said the Sub-Prior, and assisted Christie in performing that office with his own hands, although the prisoner scarcely would consent to be unbound, repeating with emphasis, that he rejoiced in the cause for which he suffered shame. When his hands were at liberty, however, he shewed his sense of the kindness by again exchanging a grasp and a look of kindness with the Sub-Prior.

The salute was frank and generous on either side, yet it was but the friendly recognition and greeting which is wont to take place betwixt adverse champions, who do nothing in hate but all in honour. As each felt the pressure of the situation in which they stood, he quitted the grasp of the other's hands, and fell back, confronting each other with looks more calm and sorrowful than expressive of any other passion. The Sub-Prior was the first to speak. "And is this then the end of that restless activity of mind, that bold and indefatigable love of truth that urged investigation to its utmost limits, and seemed to take heaven itself by storm—is this the termination of Wellwood's career?—and having known and loved him during the best years of our youth, do we meet in our old age as judge and criminal?"

"Not as judge and criminal," said Henry Warden, for to avoid confusion we describe him by his later name—"Not as judge and criminal do we meet, but as a misguided oppressor and his ready and devoted victim. I, too, may ask, are these the harvest of the rich hopes excited by the classical learning, acute logical powers, and varied knowledge of William Allan, that he should sink to be the solitary drone of a cell, graced only above the swarm with the high commission of executing Roman malice on all who oppose her?"

"Not to thee," answered the Sub-Prior, "be assured—not unto thee, nor unto mortal man, will I render an account of the power with which the church may have invested me. It was granted but as a deposit for her welfare—for her welfare it shall at every risk be exercised, without fear and without favour."

"I expected no less from your misguided zeal," answered the preacher; "and in me have you met one on whom you may fearlessly exercise your authority, secure that his mind at least will defy your influence, as the snows of that Mount Blanc which we saw together, shrink not under the heat of the summer sun."

"I do believe thee," said the Sub-Prior, "I do believe that thine is indeed metal unmalleable by force. Let it yield then to persuasion. Let us debate these matters of faith, as we once were wont to conduct our scholastic disputes, when hours, nay days, glided past in the mutual exercise of our intellectual powers. It may be thou may'st yet hear the voice of the shepherd, and return to the universal fold."

"No, Allan," replied the prisoner, "this is no vain question, devised by dreaming scholiasts, on which they may whet their intellectual faculties until the very metal be wasted away. The errors which I combat are like those fiends which are only cast out by fasting and prayer. Alas! not many wise, not many learned are chosen—the cottage and the hamlet shall in our days bear witness against the schools and their disciples. Thy very wisdom, which is foolishness, hath made thee, as the Greeks of old, hold as foolishness that which is the only true wisdom."

"This," said the Sub-Prior, sternly, "is the mere cant of ignorant enthusiasm, which appealeth from learning and from authority, from the sure guidance of that lamp which God hath afforded us in the Councils and in the Fathers of the Church, to a rash, self-willed, and arbitrary interpretation of the Scriptures, wrested according to the private opinion of each speculating heretic."

"I disdain to reply to the charge," replied Warden. "The question at issue between your church and mine, is, whether we will be judged by the Holy Scriptures, or by the devices and decisions of men not less subject to err than ourselves, and who have defaced our holy religion with vain devices, reared up idols of stone and wood, in form of those, who, when they lived, were but sinful creatures, to share the worship due only to the Creator—established a toll-house betwixt heaven and hell, that profitable purgatory of which the Pope keeps the keys, and like an iniquitous judge commutes punishment for bribes"——

"Silence, blasphemer," said the Sub-Prior, sternly, "or I will have thy blatant obloquy stopped with a gag."

"Ay," replied Warden, "such is the freedom of the Christian conference to which Rome's priests so kindly invite us—the gag—the rack—the axe is the *ultima ratio Romæ*. But know thou, mine ancient friend, that the character of thine ancient companion is not so changed by age, but what he still dares to endure for the cause of truth all that thy proud hierarchy shall dare to inflict."

"Of that," said the Monk, "I nothing doubt—thou wert ever a lion to turn against the spear of the hunter, not a stag to be dismayed by the sound of his bugle."—He walked through the room in silence. "Well-wood," he said at length, "we can no longer be friends—our faith, our hope, our anchor on futurity, is no longer the same."

"Deep is my sorrow that thou speakest truth. May God so judge me," said the Reformer, "as I would buy the conversion of a soul like thine with my dearest heart's blood."

"To thee, and with better reason, do I return the wish," replied the Sub-Prior; "it is such an arm as thine that should defend the bul-warks of the church, and it is now directing the battering-ram against them, and rendering practicable the breach through which all that is greedy, and all that is base, and all that is mutable and hot-headed in this innovating age, already hope to advance to destruction and to spoil. But since such is our fate, that we can no longer fight side by side as friends, let us at least act as generous enemies. You cannot have forgotten,

> O gran bontà dei cavalieri antiqui
> Erano nemici eran' de fede diversa—

Although, perhaps," he added, stopping short in his quotation, "your new faith forbids you to reserve a place in your memory, even for what high poets have recorded of loyal faith and generous sentiment."

"The faith of Buchanan," replied the preacher, "the faith of Buch-anan and of Beza cannot be unfriendly to literature. But the poet you have quoted affords strains fitter for a dissolute court than for a convent."

"I might retort on your Theodore Beza," said the Sub-Prior, smil-ing; "but I hate the judgment that, like the flesh-fly, skims over whatever is sound, to detect and settle upon some spot which is tainted. But to the purpose. If I conduct thee or send thee a prisoner to Saint Mary's, thou art to-night a tenant of the dungeon, to-morrow a burthen to the gibbet-tree. If I were to let thee go hence at large, I were thereby wronging the Holy Church, and breaking mine own solemn vow. Other resolutions may be adopted in the capital, or better times may speedily ensue. Wilt thou remain a true prisoner upon thy parole, rescue or no rescue, as is the phrase amongst the warriors of this country? Wilt thou solemnly promise that thou wilt do so, and that at my summons thou wilt present thyself before the Abbot and Chap-ter at Saint Mary's, and that thou wilt not stir from this house above a quarter of a mile in any direction? Wilt thou, I say, engage me thy word for this, and such is the sure trust which I repose in thy good faith, that thou shalt remain here unharmed and unsecured, a prisoner at large, subject only to appear before our court when called upon."

The preacher paused—"I am unwilling," he said, "to fetter my native liberty by any self-adopted engagement. But I am already in your power, and you may bind me to my answer. By such promise, to abide within a certain limit, and to appear when called upon, I renounce not any liberty which I at present possess, and am free to exercise; but, on the contrary, being in bonds, and at your mercy, I acquire thereby a liberty which I at present possess not. I will therefore accept of thy proffer, as what is courteously offered on thy part, and may be honourably accepted on mine."

"Stay yet," said the Sub-Prior, "one important part of thy engagement is forgotten—thou art further to promise, that while thus left at liberty, thou wilt not preach or teach, directly or indirectly, any of those pestilent heresies by which so many souls have been in this our day won over from the kingdom of light to the kingdom of darkness."

"There we break off our treaty," said Warden, firmly—"Woe unto me if I preach not the Gospel!"

The Sub-Prior's countenance became clouded, and he again paced the apartment, and muttered, "A plague upon the self-willed fool!" then stopped short in his walk, and proceeded in his argument.— Why, by thine own reasoning, Henry, thy refusal here is but peevish obstinacy. It is in my power to place you where your preaching can reach no human ear; in promising therefore to abstain from it, you grant nothing which you have it in your power to refuse."

"I know not that," replied Henry Warden; "thou mayst indeed cast me into a dungeon, but can I foretel that my Master hath not taskwork for me to perform even in that dreary mansion? The chains of saints have, ere now, been the means of breaking the bonds of Satan— in a prison holy Paul found the jailor whom he brought to believe the word of salvation, he and all his house."

"Nay," said the Sub-Prior, in a tone betwixt anger and scorn, "if you match yourself with the blessed Apostle, it were time we had done —prepare to endure what thy folly, as well as thy heresy, deserves.— Bind him, soldier."

With proud submission to his fate, and regarding the Sub-Prior with something which almost amounted to a smile of superiority, the preacher placed his arms so that the bonds could be again fastened round him.

"Spare me not," he said to Christie; for even that ruffian hesitated to draw the cord straitly.

The Sub-Prior, meanwhile, looked at him from under his cowl, which he had drawn over his head, and partly over his face, as if he wished to shade his own emotions. They were those of a huntsman within point-blank shot of a noble stag, yet is too much struck with his majesty of front and of antler to take aim at him. They were those of a fowler, who, levelling his gun at a magnificent eagle, is yet reluctant to use his advantage when he sees the noble sovereign of the birds pruning himself in proud defiance of whatever may be attempted against him. The heart of the Sub-Prior (bigotted as he was) relented, and he doubted if he ought to purchase by a rigorous discharge of what he deemed his duty, the remorse he might afterwards feel for the death of one so nobly independent in thought and character, the friend, besides, of his own happiest years, during which they had, side by side, striven in the noble race of knowledge, and indulged their intervals of repose in the lighter studies of classical and general letters.

The Sub-Prior's hand pressed his half-o'ershadowed cheek, and his eye, more completely obscured, was bent on the ground, as if to hide the workings of his relenting nature.

"Were but Edward safe from the infection," he thought to himself —"Edward, whose eager and enthusiastic mind presses forward in the chase of all that hath even the shadow of knowledge, I might trust this enthusiast with the women, after due caution to them that they cannot, without guilt, attend to his reveries."

As the Sub-Prior revolved these thoughts, and delayed the definitive order which was to determine the fate of the prisoner a sudden noise at the entrance of the tower diverted his attention for an instant, and, his cheek and brow inflamed with all the glow of heat and determination, Edward Glendinning rushed into the room.

Chapter Seven

Then in my gown of sober gray
    Along the mountain path I'll wander,
And wind my solitary way
    To the sad shrine that courts me yonder.

There, in the calm monastic shade,
    All injuries may be forgiven;
And there for thee, obdurate maid,
    My orisons shall rise to heaven.
    The Cruel Lady of the Mountains

THE FIRST WORDS which Edward uttered were,—"My brother is safe, reverend father—he is safe, thank God, and lives!—there is not in Corri-nan-shian a grave, nor a vestige of a grave—the turf around the fountain has neither been disturbed by pick-axe, spade, or mattock, since the deer's-hair first sprang there—he lives as surely as I live!"

The earnestness of the youth—the vivacity with which he looked
and moved—the springy step, outstretched hand, and ardent eye,
reminded Henry Warden of Halbert, so lately his guide. The brothers
had indeed a strong family resemblance, though Halbert was far more
athletic and active in his person, taller and better knit in the limbs, and
though Edward had, on ordinary occasions, a look of more habitual
acuteness and more profound reflection. The preacher was interested
as well as the Sub-Prior.

"Of whom do you speak, my son?" he said, in a tone as unconcerned as if his own fate had not been at the same instant trembling in
the balance, and as if dungeon and death did not appear to be his
instant doom—"Of whom, I say, speak you? If of a youth somewhat
older than you seem to be—brown-haired, open-featured, taller and
stronger than you appear, yet having much of the same air and of the
same tone of voice—if such a one is the brother whom you seek, it may
be I can tell you news of him."

"Speak then, for Heaven's sake," said Edward—"life or death lies
on thy tongue."

The Sub-Prior joined eagerly in the same request, and without
waiting to be urged, the preacher gave a minute account of the circumstances under which he met the elder Glendinning, with so exact
a description of his person, that there remained no doubt as to his
identity. When he mentioned that Halbert Glendinning had conducted him to the dell in which they found the grass bloody, and a
grave newly closed, and told how the youth accused himself of the
slaughter of Sir Piercie Shafton, the Sub-Prior looked on Edward
with astonishment.

"Didst thou not say, even now," he said, "that there was no vestige
of a grave in that spot?"

"No more vestige of the earth having been removed than if the turf
had grown there since the days of Adam," replied Edward Glendinning. "It is true," he added, "that the adjacent grass was trampled and
bloody."

"These are delusions of the Enemy," said the Sub-Prior, crossing
himself.—"Christian men may no longer doubt of it."

"But an' it were so," said Warden, "Christian men might better
guard themselves by the sword of prayer than by the idle form of a
cabalistical spell."

"The badge of our salvation," said the Sub-Prior, "cannot be so
termed: the sign of the cross disarmeth all evil spirits."

"Ay," answered Henry Warden, apt and armed for controversy;
"but it should be borne in the heart, not scored with the fingers in the
air. That very impassive air, through which your hand passes, shall as

soon bear the imprint of your action, as the external action shall avail the fond bigot who substitutes vain motions of the body, idle genuflections, and signs of the cross, for the living and heart-born duties of faith and good-works."

"I pity thee," said the Sub-Prior, as actively ready for polemics as himself,—"I pity thee, Henry, and reply not to thee. Thou mayst as well winnow forth and measure the ocean with a sieve, as mete out the power of holy words, deeds, and signs, by the erring gauge of thine own reason."

"Not by mine own reason would I mete them," said Warden; "but by His holy Word, that unfading and unerring lamp of our paths, compared to which human reason is but as a glimmering and fading taper, and your boasted tradition only a misleading wild-fire. Shew me your Scripture warrant for ascribing virtue to such vain signs and motions."

"I offered thee a fair field of debate," said the Sub-Prior, "which thou didst refuse. I will not at present resume the controversy."

"Were these my last accents," said the reformer, "and were they uttered at the stake, half-choked with smoke, and as the faggots kindled into a blaze around me, with that last utterance I would testify against the superstitious devices of Rome."

The Sub-Prior suppressed with pain the controversial answer which arose to his lips, and, turning to Edward Glendinning, he said, "there could be now no doubt that his mother ought presently to be informed that her son lived."

"I told you that two hours since," said Christie of the Clinthill, "an' you would have believed me. But it seems you are more willing to take the word of an old grey sorner, whose life has been spent in pattering heresy, than mine, though I never rode a foray in my life without duly saying my pater-noster."

"Go then," said Father Eustace to Edward; "let thy sorrowing mother know that her son is restored to her from the grave, like the child of the widow of Zarephthah; at the intercession," he added, looking at Henry Warden, "of the blessed Saint whom I invoked in his behalf."

"Deceived thyself," said Warden, instantly, "thou art a deceiver of others. It was no dead man, no creature of clay, whom the blessed Tishbite invoked, when, stung by the reproach of the Shunamite woman, he prayed that her son's soul might come into him again."

"It was by his intercession, however," repeated the Sub-Prior; "for what says the Vulgate? Thus is it written: '*Et exaudivit Dominus vocem Helie; et reversa est anima pueri intra eum, et revixit;*'—and thinkst thou the intercession of a glorified saint is more feeble than when he walks on earth, shrouded in a tabernacle of clay, and seeing but with the eye of flesh?"

During this controversy Edward Glendinning appeared restless and impatient, agitated by some strong internal feeling, but whether of joy, grief, or expectation, his countenance did not expressly declare. He took now the unusual freedom to break in upon the discourse of the Sub-Prior, who, notwithstanding his resolution to the contrary, was obviously kindling in the spirit of controversy, which Edward diverted by conjuring his reverence to allow him to speak a few words in private.

"Remove the prisoner," said the Sub-Prior to Christie; "look to him carefully that he escape not; but for thy life do him no injury."

His commands being obeyed, Edward and the Monk were left alone, when the Sub-Prior thus addressed him.

"What hath come over thee, Edward, that thy eye kindles so wildly, and thy cheek is thus changing from scarlet to pale? Why didst thou break in so hastily and unadvisedly upon the argument with which I was prostrating yonder heretic? And wherefore does thou not tell thy mother that her son is restored to her by the intercession, as Holy Church well warrants us to believe, of blessed Saint Benedict, the patron of our Order? For if ever my prayers were put forth to him with zeal, it hath been in behalf of this house, and thine eyes have seen the result—go and tell it to thy mother."

"I must tell her then," said Edward, "that if she has regained one son, another is lost to her."

"What meanest thou, Edward? what language is this?" said the Sub-Prior.

"Father," said the youth, kneeling down to him, "my sin and my shame shall be told thee, and thou shalt witness my penance with thine own eyes."

"I comprehend thee not," said the Sub-Prior. "What canst thou have done to deserve such self-accusation?—Hast thou too listened," he added, knitting his brows, "to the demon of heresy, ever most effectual tempter of those, who, like yonder unhappy man, are distinguished by their love of knowledge?"

"I am guiltless in that matter," answered Glendinning, "nor have presumed to think otherwise than thou, my kind father, has taught, and than the church allows."

"And what is it then, my son," said the Sub-Prior, kindly, "which thus afflicts thy conscience? speak it me, that I may answer thee in the words of comfort; for the Church's mercy is great to those obedient children who doubt not her power."

"My confession will require her mercy," replied Edward. "My

brother Halbert—so kind, so brave, so gentle, who spoke not, thought not, acted not, but in love to me, whose hand had aided me in every difficulty, whose eye watched over me like the eagle's over her nestlings, when they prove their first flight from the eyrie—this brother, so kind, so gentle, so affectionate—I heard of his sudden, his bloody, his violent death, and I rejoiced—I heard of his unexpected restoration, and I sorrowed."

"Edward," said the father, "thou art beside thyself—what could urge thee to such odious ingratitude—in your hurry of spirits you have mistaken the confused tenor of your feelings—Go, my son, pray, compose thy mind—we will speak of this another time."

"No, father, no," said Edward vehemently, "now, or never!—I will find the means to tame this rebellious heart of mine, or I will tear it out of my bosom—Mistake its passions?—no, father, grief can ill be mistaken for joy—all wept, all shrieked around me—my mother—the menials—She, too, the cause of my crime—all wept—And I?—I could hardly disguise my brutal and insane joy, under the appearance of revenge—Brother, I said, I cannot give thee tears, but I will give thee blood—Yes, father, as I counted hour after hour, while I kept watch upon the English prisoner, and said, I am an hour nearer to hope and to happiness"——

"I understand thee not, Edward," said the Monk, "nor can I conceive in what way thy brother's supposed murder should have affected thee with such unnatural joy—Surely the sordid desire to succeed him in his small possessions"——

"Perish the paltry trash!" said Edward with the same emotion. "No, father, it was rivalry—it was jealous rage—it was the love of Mary Avenel that rendered me the unnatural wretch I confess myself!"

"Of Mary Avenel!" said the priest—"of a lady so high above either of you in name and rank? How dared Halbert—how dared you, presume to lift your eye to her but in honour and respect, as to a superior of another degree from your's?"

"When did Love wait for the sanction of Heraldry?" replied Edward; "and in what but a line of dead ancestors was Mary, our mother's guest and foster-child, different from us, with whom she was brought up?—Enough, we loved—we both loved her!—but the passion of Halbert was requited. He knew it not, he saw it not—but I was sharper-eyed. I saw that even when I was more approved, Halbert was more beloved. With me she would sit for hours at our common task with the cold simplicity and indifference of a sister, but with Halbert she trusted not herself. She changed colour, she was fluttered when he approached her; and when he left her, she was sad, pensive, and solitary. I bore all this—I saw my rival's advancing progress in her affections—I bore it, father, and yet I hated him not—I could not hate him!"

"And well for thee that thou didst not," said the father; "wild and headlong as thou art, wouldst thou hate thy brother for partaking in thine own folly?"

"Father," replied Edward, "the world esteems thee wise, and holds thy knowledge of mankind high; but thy question shews that thou has never loved. It was by an effort that I saved myself from hating my kind and affectionate brother, who, all unsuspicious of my rivalry, was perpetually loading me with kindness. Nay, there were moods of my mind, in which I could return that kindness for a time with energetic enthusiasm. Never did I feel this so strongly as on the night which parted us. But I could not help rejoicing when he was swept from my path—could not help sorrowing when he was again restored to be a stumbling-block in my paths."

"May God be gracious to thee, my son!" said the Monk; "this is an awful state of mind. Even in such evil mood did the first murtherer rise up against his brother, because Abel's was the more acceptable sacrifice."

"I will wrestle with the demon which has haunted me, father," replied the youth firmly—"I will wrestle with him, and I will subdue him. But first I must remove from the scenes which are to follow here. I cannot endure that I should see Mary Avenel's eyes again flash with joy at the restoration of her lover. It were a sight to make a second Cain of me. My fierce, turbid, and transitory joy discharged itself in a thirst to commit homicide, and how can I estimate the frenzy of my despair?"

"Madman!" said the Sub-Prior, "at what dreadful crime does thy fury drive?"

"My lot is determined, father," said Edward, in a resolved tone; "I will embrace the spiritual state which you have so oft recommended. It is my purpose to return with you to Saint Mary's, and with the permission of the Holy Virgin and of Saint Benedict, to offer my profession to the Abbot."

"Not now, my son," said the Sub-Prior, "not in this distemperature of mind. The wise and good accept not gifts which are made in heat of blood, and which may be after repented of; and shall we make our offerings to Wisdom and to Goodness itself with less of solemn resolution and deep devotion of mind, than is necessary to make them acceptable to our own frail companions in this valley of darkness? This I say to thee, my son, not as meaning to deter thee from the good path thou art now inclined to prefer, but that thou may'st make thy vocation and thine election sure."

"There are actions, father," returned Edward, "which brook no delay, and this is one. It must be done this very *now*, or it may never be done. Let me go with you—let me not behold the return of Halbert into this house. Shame, and the sense of injustice I have already done him, will join with these dreadful passions which urge me to do him yet farther wrong. Let me then go with you."

"With me, my son," said the Sub-Prior, "thou shalt surely go; but our rule, as well as reason and good order, require that you should dwell a space with us as a probationer or novice, before taking upon thee those final vows, which, sequestering for ever from the world, dedicate thee to the service of Heaven."

"And when shall we set forth, father?" said the youth, as eagerly as if the journey which he was now undertaking led to the pleasures of a summer holiday.

"Go, then," said the Sub-Prior, yielding to his impetuosity—"go, then, and command them to prepare for our departure.—Yet stay," he said, as Edward, with all the awakened enthusiasm of his character, darted from his presence; "come hither, my son, and kneel down."

Edward obeyed, and kneeled down before him. Notwithstanding his slight figure and thin features, the Sub-Prior could, from the energy of his tone, and the earnestness of his devotional manner, impress his pupils and his penitents with no ordinary feelings of personal reverence. His heart always was, as well as seemed to be, in the duty which he was immediately performing; and the spiritual guide who thus shews a deep conviction of the importance of his office, seldom fails to impress a similar feeling upon his hearers. Upon such occasions as the present, his puny body seemed to assume more majestic stature—his spare and emaciated countenance bore a bolder, loftier, and more commanding port—his voice, always beautiful, trembled as labouring under the immediate impulse of the Divinity—and his whole demeanour seemed to bespeak, not the mere ordinary man, but the organ of the Church in which she had vested her high power for delivering sinners from their load of iniquity.

"Hast thou, my fair son," said he, "faithfully recounted the circumstances which have thus suddenly determined thee to a religious life?"

"The sins I have confessed, my father," answered Edward, "but I have not yet told a strange appearance, which, acting on my mind, hath, I think, aided to determine my resolution."

"Say it, then, now," returned the Sub-Prior; "it is thy duty to leave me uninstructed in nought, so that thereby I may understand the temptation that besets thee."

"I tell it with unwillingness," said Edward; "for although, God wot,

I speak but the mere truth, yet even while my tongue speaks it as truth, my own ears receive it as fable."

"Yet say the whole," said Father Eustace; "neither fear rebuke from me, seeing I may know reasons for receiving as true that which others might regard as fabulous."

"Know, then, father," replied Edward, "that betwixt hope and despair—and, heavens! what an hope!—the hope to find the corpse mangled and crushed hastily in amongst the bloody clay which the foot of the scornful victor had trod down upon my good, my gentle, my courageous brother,—I sped to the glen called Corri-nan-shian; but, as your reverence has been already informed, neither the grave which my unhallowed wishes had in spite of my better self longed to see, nor any appearance of the earth having been opened, was visible in the solitary spot where Martin had, at morning yesterday, seen the fatal hillock. You know our dalesmen, father? The place hath an evil name, and this deception of the sight inclined them to leave it. My companions became affrighted, and hastened down the glen as men caught in trespass. My hopes were too much blighted, my mind too much agitated, to fear either the living or the dead. I descended the glen more slowly than they, often looking back, and not ill-pleased with the poltroonery of my companions, which left me to my own perplexed and moody humour, and induced them to hasten into the broader dale. They were already out of sight, and lost amongst the windings of the glen, when, looking back, I saw a female form standing beside the fountain"——

"How, my fair son?" said the Sub-Prior, "beware you jest not with your present situation."

"I jest not, father," answered the youth; "it may be I shall never jest again—surely not for many a day. I saw, I say, the form of a female clad in white, such—such as the Spirit which haunts the house of Avenel is supposed to be. Believe me, my father, for, by heaven and earth, I say nought but what I saw with these eyes!"

"I believe thee, my son," said the Monk; "proceed in thy strange story."

"The apparition," said Edward Glendinning, "sung, and thus run her lay; for, strange as it may seem to you, her words abide by my remembrance though only once heard, as if they had been sung to me from infancy upward:

'Thou who seek'st my fountain lone,
With thoughts and hopes thou darest not own;
Whose heart within leap'd wildly glad
When most his brow seem'd dark and sad;
Hie thee back, thou find'st not here
Corpse or coffin, grave or bier;

The Dead Alive is gone and fled—
Go thou, and join the Living Dead!

'The Living Dead, whose sober brow
Oft shrouds such thoughts as thou hast now;
Whose hearts within are seldom cured
Of passions by their vows abjured;
Where, under sad and solemn show,
Vain hopes are nursed, wild wishes glow.
Seek the convent's vaulted room,
Prayer and vigil be thy doom;
Doff the green, and don the gray,
To the cloister hence away!'"

"'Tis a wild lay," answered the Sub-Prior, "and chaunted, I fear me, with no good end. But we have power to turn the machinations of Satan to his shame. Edward, thou shalt go with me as thou desirest—thou shalt prove the life for which I have long thought thee best fitted—thou shalt aid, my son, this trembling hand of mine to sustain the Holy Ark, which rude unhallowed men press rashly forward to touch and to profane.—Wilt thou not first see thy mother?"

"I will see no one," said Edward hastily; "I will risk nothing that may shake the purpose of my heart. From Saint Mary's they shall learn my destination—all of them shall learn it. My mother—Mary Avenel—my restored and happy brother—they shall all know that Edward lives no longer to the world to be a clog on their happiness. Mary shall no longer need to constrain her looks and expressions to coldness, because I am nigh. She shall no longer"——

"My son," said the Sub-Prior, interrupting him, "it is not by looking back on the vanities and vexations of this world that we fit ourselves for the discharge of duties which are not of it. Go, get our horses ready, and as we descend the glen together I will teach thee the truths through which the fathers and wise men of old had that precious alchemy which can convert suffering into happiness."

Chapter Eight

Now on my faith this gear is all entangled,
Like to the yarn-clew of the drowsy knitter,
Dragg'd by the frolic kitten thro' the cabin,
While the good dame sits nodding o'er the fire—
Masters, attend; 'twill crave some skill to clear it.
                                        Old Play

EDWARD, with the speed of one who doubts the steadiness of his own resolution, hastened to prepare the horses for their departure, and at the same time thanked and dismissed the neighbours who had come to his assistance, and who were not a little surprised both at the suddenness of his proposed departure, and at the turn affairs had taken.

"Here's cold hospitality," quoth Dan of the Howlet-hirst to his comrades; "I trow the Glendinnings may die and come alive right oft ere I put foot in stirrup again for the matter."

Martin soothed them by placing food and liquor before them. They ate sullenly, however, and departed in bad humour.

The joyful news that Halbert Glendinning lived, was quickly communicated through the sorrowing family. The mother wept and thanked Heaven alternately; until her habits of domestic economy awakening as her feelings became calmer, she observed, "It would be an unco task to mend the yetts, and what were they to do while they were broken in that fashion? At open doors dogs come in."

Tibb remarked, "She aye thought Halbert was ower glegg at his weapon to be killed sae easily by ony Piercie o' them a'—they might say of these Southrons as they liked, but they had not the pith and wind of a canny Scot, when it came to close grips."

On Mary Avenel the impression was inconceivably deeper. She had but newly learned to pray, and it seemed to her that her prayers had been instantly answered—that the compassion of Heaven, which she had learned to implore in the words of Scripture, had descended upon her after a manner almost miraculous, and recalled the dead from the grave at the sound of her lamentation. There was a dangerous degree of enthusiasm in this train of feeling, but it originated in the purest devotion.

A silken and embroidered muffler, one of the few articles of more costly attire which she possessed, was devoted to the purpose of wrapping up and concealing the sacred volume, which henceforth she was to regard as her chiefest treasure, lamenting only that, for want of a fitting interpreter, much must remain to her a book closed and a fountain sealed. She was unaware of the yet greater danger she incurred, of putting an imperfect or even false sense upon some of the doctrines which appeared most comprehensible. But Heaven had provided against both these hazards.

While Edward was preparing the horses, Christie of the Clinthill again solicited his orders respecting the reformed preacher Henry Warden, and again the worthy Monk laboured to reconcile in his own mind his compassion, and the esteem which, almost in spite of himself, he could not help feeling for his ancient companion, with the duty which he owed to the church. The unexpected resolution of Edward had removed, he thought, the chief objection to his being left at Glendearg.

"If I carry this Wellwood, or Warden, to the Monastery," he

thought, "he must die—die in his heresy—perish body and soul—and though such a measure was once thought advisable, to strike terror into the heretics, such is now their daily-increasing strength, that it may rather rouse them to fury and to revenge. True, he refuses to pledge himself to abstain from sowing his tares among the wheat. But the ground here is too barren to receive them. I fear not his making impression on these poor women, the vassals of the church, and bred up in due obedience to her behests. The keen, searching, enquiring, and bold disposition of Edward, might have afforded fuel to the fire; but that is removed, and there is nothing left which the flame may catch to.—Thus shall he have no power to spread his evil doctrines abroad, and yet his life shall be preserved, and it may be his soul rescued as a prey from the fowler's net. I will myself contend with him in argument; for when we studied in common, I yielded not to him, and surely the cause for which I struggle will support me, were I yet more weak than I deem myself. Were this man reclaimed from his errors, an hundred-fold more advantage would arise to the church from his spiritual regeneration, than from his temporal death."

Having finished these meditations, in which there was at once goodness of disposition and narrowness of principle, a considerable portion of self-opinion, and no small degree of self-delusion, the Sub-Prior commanded the prisoner to be brought into his presence.

"Henry," he said, "whatever a rigid sense of duty may demand of me, ancient friendship and Christian compassion forbid me to lead thee to assured death. Thou wert wont to be generous, though stern and stubborn in thy resolves; let not thy sense of what thine erring thoughts term duty, draw thee farther than mine have done. Remember, that every sheep whom thou shalt here lead astray from the fold, will be demanded in time and through eternity of him who hath left thee the liberty of doing such evil. I ask no engagement of thee, save that thou remain a prisoner on thy word at this tower, and will appear when summoned."

"Thou hast found an invention to bind my hands," replied the preacher, "more sure than would have been the heaviest shackles in the prison of thy convent. I will not rashly do what may endanger thee with thy unhappy superiors, and I will be the more cautious, because, if we had farther opportunity of conference, I trust thine own soul may yet be rescued as a brand from the burning, and that casting from thee the livery of Anti-Christ, that trader in human sins and human souls, I may yet assist thee to lay hold on the Rock of Ages."

The Sub-Prior heard this sentiment, so similar to that which had occurred to himself, with the same kindling feelings with which the game-cock hears and replies to the challenge of his rival.

"I bless God and Our Lady," said he, drawing himself up, "that my faith is already anchored on that Rock on which Saint Peter founded his church."

"It is a perversion of the text," said the eager Henry Warden, "grounded upon a vain play upon words—a most idle paronamasia."

The controversy would have been rekindled, and in all probability, —for what can ensure the good temper and moderation of polemics? —it might have ended in the preacher's being transported a captive to the Monastery, had not Christie of the Clinthill observed it was growing late, and that he having to descend the glen, which had no good reputation, cared not greatly for travelling there after sunset. The Sub-Prior, therefore, stifled his desire of argument, and again telling the preacher that he trusted to his gratitude and generosity, he bade him farewell.

"Be assured, mine old friend," replied Warden, "that no willing act of mine shall be to thy prejudice. But if my Master shall place work before me, I must obey God rather than man."

These two men, both excellent from natural disposition and acquired knowledge, had more points of similarity than they themselves would have admitted. In truth, the chief distinction betwixt them was, that the Catholic, defending a religion which afforded little interest to the feelings, had, in his devotion to the cause he espoused, more of the head than of the heart, and was politic, cautious, and artful; while the Protestant, acting under the strong impulse of more lately adopted conviction, and feeling, as he justly might, a more animated confidence in his cause, was more enthusiastic, eager, and precipitate in his desire to advance it. The priest would have been contented to defend, the preacher aspired to conquer; and, of course, the impulse by which the latter was governed, was more active and more decisive. They could not part from each other without a second pressure of hands, while each looked in the face of his old companion, as he bade him adieu, with a countenance strongly expressive of sorrow, affection, and pity.

Father Eustace then explained briefly to Dame Glendinning, that this person was to be her guest for some days, discharging her and her whole household, under high spiritual censures, to hold any conversation with him on subjects of religion, but commanding her to attend to his wants in all other particulars.

"May Our Lady forgive me, reverend father," said Dame Glendinning, somewhat dismayed at this intelligence, "but I must needs say, that ower mony guests have been the ruin of mony a house, and I trow they will bring down Glendearg. First came the Lady of Avenel, (her soul be at rest—she meant nae ill,) but she brought with her as mony bogles and fairies, as hae kept the house in care ever since, sae that we have been living as it were in a dream. And then came that English knight, if it please you, and if he hasna killed my son outright, he has chased him aff the gate, and it may be lang eneugh ere I see him again —forbye the damage done to door and outer-door. And now your reverence has given me the charge of a heretic, who, it is like, may bring the great horned devil himself down upon us all; and they say that it is neither door nor window will serve him, but he will take away the side of the auld tower alang with him. Nevertheless, reverend father, your pleasure is doubtless to be done to our power."

"Go to, woman," said the Sub-Prior; "send for workmen from the clachan, and let them charge the expence of these repairs to the Community, and I will give the treasurer warrant to allow them. Moreover, in settling the rental-mails, and feu-duties, thou shalt have allowance for the trouble and charges to which thou art now put, and I will cause strict search to be made after thy son."

The dame curtsied deep and low at each favourable expression; and when the Sub-Prior had done speaking, she added her farther hope that his reverence would hold some communing with her gossip the Miller, concerning the fate of his daughter, and expound to him that the chance had by no means happened through any negligence on her part.

"I sair doubt me, father," she said, "if Mysie finds her way back to the mill in a hurry; but it was all her father's own fault that let her run lamping about the country, riding on bare-backed nags, and never settling to do a turn of wark within doors, unless it were to dress dainties at dinner-time for his ain kyte."

"You remind me, dame, of another matter of urgency," said Father Eustace; "and, God knows, too many of them press on me at this moment. This English knight must be sought out, and explanation given to him of these most strange chances. The giddy girl must also be recovered. If she hath suffered in reputation by this unhappy mistake, I will not hold myself innocent of the disgrace. Yet how to find them out I know not."

"So please you," said Christie of the Clinthill, "I am willing to take the chace, and bring them back by fair means or foul; for though you have always looked as black as night at me, whenever we have forgathered, yet I have not forgotten that had it not been for you, my neck would have kenned the weight of my four quarters. If any man can track the tread of them, I will say in the face of both Merse and Teviotdale, and take the Forest to-boot, that I am that man. But first I have matters to treat of on my master's score, if you will permit me to ride down the glen with you."

"Nay, but my friend," said the Sub-Prior, "thou should'st remember I have but slender cause to trust thee for a companion through a place so solitary."

"Tush! tush!" said the Jack-man, "fear me not; I had the worst too surely to begin that sport again. Besides, have I not said a dozen of times, I owe you a life? and when I owe a man either a good turn or a bad, I never fail to pay it sooner or later. Moreover, beshrew me if I care to go alone down the glen, or even with my troopers, who are, every loon of them, as much devil's bairns as I am myself; whereas, if your reverence, since that is the word, take beads and psalter, and I come alone with jack and spear, you will make the devils take the air, and I will make all human enemies take the earth."

Edward here entered, and told his reverence that his horse was prepared. At this instant his eye caught his mother's, and the resolution which he had so strongly formed was staggered when he recollected the necessity of bidding her farewell. The Sub-Prior saw his embarrassment, and came to his relief.

"Dame," he said, "I forgot to mention that your son Edward goes with me to Saint Mary's, and will not return for two or three days."

"You will be wishing to help him to recover his brother—may the saints reward your kindness!"

The Sub-Prior returned the benediction which in this instance he had not very well deserved, and he and Edward set forth on their route. They were presently followed by Christie, who came up with his followers at such a speedy pace, as intimated sufficiently that his wish to obtain spiritual convoy through the glen, was extremely sincere. He had, however, other matters to stimulate his speed, for he was desirous to communicate to the Sub-Prior a message from his master Julian, connected with the delivery of the prisoner Warden; and having requested the Sub-Prior to ride with him a few yards before Edward and the troopers of his own party, he thus addressed him—sometimes interrupting his discourse in a manner testifying that his fear of supernatural beings was not altogether lulled to rest by his confidence in the sanctity of his fellow-traveller.

"My master," said the rider, "deemed he had sent you an acceptable gift in that old heretic preacher; but it seems, from the slight care you have taken of him, that you make small account of the boon."

"Nay," said the Sub-Prior, "do not thus judge of it. The Community must account highly of the service, and will reward it to thy master in goodly fashion. But this man and I are old friends, and I trust to bring him back from the paths of perdition."

"Nay," said the rider, "when I saw you shake hands at the beginning, I counted that you would fight it all out in love and honour, and that there would be no extreme dealings betwixt ye—however, it is all one to my master—Saint Mary! what call you yon, Sir Monk?"

"The branch of a willow streaming across the path betwixt us and the sky."

"Beshrew me," said Christie, "if it looked not like a man's hand holding a sword.—But touching my master, he, like a prudent man, hath kept himself aloof in these broken times, until he could see with precision what footing he was to stand upon. Right tempting offers he hath had from the Lords of Congregation, whom you call heretics; and at one time he was minded, to be plain with you, to have taken their way—for he was assured that the Lord James was coming this road at the head of a round body of cavalry. And accordingly Lord James did so far reckon upon him, that he sent this man Warden, or whatsoever be his name, to my master's protection, as an assured friend; and, moreover, with tidings that he himself was marching hitherward at the head of a strong body of horse."

"Now, Our Lady forefend!" said the Sub-Prior.

"Amen!" answered Christie, "did your reverence see aught?"

"Nothing whatever," replied the Monk; "it was thy tale which wrested from me that exclamation."

"And it was with some cause, for if Lord James should come hither, your Halidome would smoke for it. But be of good cheer—that expedition is ended before it was begun. The Baron of Avenel had sure news that Lord James has been fain to march westward with his merry-men, to protect Lord Semple against Cassilis and the Kennedies. By my faith, it will cost him a brush; for wot ye what they say of that name,—

> From Wigton to the foot of Ayr,
>   And all bedown the Crooks of Cree;
> No man may think to tenant there,
>   Unless he serve Saint Kennedie."

"Then," said the Sub-Prior, "the Lord James's purpose of coming southwards being broken, cost this person, Henry Warden, a cold reception at Avenel Castle."

"It would not have been altogether so rough a one," said the moss-trooper; "for my master was in heavy thought what to do in these unsettled times, and would scarce have hazarded misusing a man sent to him by so terrible a leader as the Lord James. But, to speak the plain truth, some busy devil tempted the old man to meddle with my master's Christian liberty of hand-fasting with Catherine of Newport. So that broke the wand of peace between them, and now ye may have my master, and all the force he can make, at your devotion, for Lord James never forgave wrong done to him; and if he come by the upper-

hand, he will have Julian's head if there were never another of the
name, as it is like there is not, excepting the bit slip of a lassie yonder.
And now I have told you more of my master's affairs than he would
thank me for; but you have done me a frank turn once, and I may need
one at your hands again."

"Thy frankness," said the Sub-Prior, "shall assuredly advantage
thee; for much it concerns the church in these broken times to know
the purposes and motives of those around us. But what is it that thy
master expects from us in reward of good service; for I esteem him
one of those who are not willing to work without their hire?"

"Nay, that I can tell you flatly; for Lord James had promised him, in
case he would be of his faction in these parts, an easy tack of the teind-
sheaves of his own Barony of Avenel, together with the lands of
Cranberry-moor, which lie interjected with his own. And he will look
for no less at your hand."

"But there is old Gilbert of Cranberry-moor," said the Sub-Prior,
"what are we to make of him? The heretic Lord James may take on
him to dispone upon the goods and lands of the Halidome at his
pleasure, because, doubtless, but for the protection of God, and the
baronage which yet remain faithful to their creed, he may despoil us of
them by force. But while they are the property of the Community, we
may not take steadings from ancient and faithful vassals, to gratify the
covetousness of those who serve God only from the lucre of gain."

"By the mass," said Christie, "it is well talking, Sir Priest; but when
ye consider that Gilbert has but two half-starved cowardly peasants to
follow him, and but an auld jaded aver to ride upon, fitter for the
plough than for manly service; and that the Baron of Avenel never
rides with fewer than ten jack-men at his back, and oftener with fifty,
bodin in all that effeirs to war as if they were to do battle for a kingdom,
and mounted on nags that nicker at the clash of a sword, as if it were
the clank of the lid of a corn-chest—I say, when ye have computed all
this, you may guess which course will best serve your Monastery."

"Friend," said the Monk, "I would willingly purchase thy master's
assistance on his own terms, since times leave us no better means of
defence against the sacrilegious spoliation of heresy; but to take from
a poor man his patrimony"——

"For that matter," said the rider, "his seat would scarce be a soft
one, if my master thought that Gilbert's interest stood betwixt him and
what he wishes. The Halidome has land enough, and Gilbert may be
quartered elsewhere."

"We will consider the possibility of so disposing the matter," said
the Monk, "and will expect in consequence your master's most active
assistance, with all the followers he can make to join in the defence of

the Halidome, against any force by which it may be threatened."

"A man's hand and a mailed glove on that," said the jack-man. "They call us marauders, thieves, and what not; but the side we take we hold by—And I will be blithe when my Baron comes to a point which side he will take, for the castle is a kind of hell, (Our Lady forgive me for naming such a word in this place!) while he is in his mood, studying how he may best advantage himself. And now, Heaven be praised, we are in the open valley, and I may swear a round oath, should aught happen to provoke it."

"My friend," said the Sub-Prior, "thou has little merit in abstaining from oaths or blasphemy, if it be only out of fear of evil spirits."

"Nay, I am not quite a church vassal yet," said the jack-man, "and if you link the curb too tight on a young horse, I promise you he will rear —why, it is much for me to forbear old customs on any account whatsoever."

The night being fine, they forded the river at the spot where the Sacristan met with his unhappy encounter with the Spirit. So soon as they arrived at the gate of the Monastery, the porter in waiting eagerly exclaimed, "Reverend father, the Lord Abbot is most anxious for your presence."

"Let these strangers be carried to the guest hall and treated with the best by the Cellarer; reminding them, however, of that modesty and decency of conduct which becometh guests in a house like this."

"But the Lord Abbot demands you instantly, my venerable brother," said Father Philip, arriving in great haste. "I have not seen him more discouraged or desolate of counsel since the field of Pinkie-cleugh was stricken."

"I come, my good brother, I come," said Father Eustace. "I pray thee, good brother, let this youth Edward Glendinning be conveyed to the Chamber of the Novices, and placed under their instructor. God has touched his heart, and he proposeth laying aside the vanities of the world, to become a brother of our holy order; which, if his good parts be matched with fitting docility and humility, he may one day live to adorn."

"My very venerable brother," exclaimed old Father Nicolas, who came hobbling with a third summons to the Sub-Prior, "I pray thee to hasten to our worshipful Lord Abbot.—The holy patroness be with us! never saw I Abbot of the House of Saint Mary's in such consternation; and yet I remember me well when Father Ingelram had the news of Flodden-field."

"I come, I come, venerable brother," said Father Eustace—And having repeatedly ejaculated, "I come!" he at last went to the Abbot in good earnest.

Chapter Nine

It is not texts will do it—Church artillery
Are silenced soon by real ordnance,
And canons are but vain opposed to cannons.
Go, coin your crosier, melt your church plate down,
Bid the starved soldier banquet in your halls,
And quaff your long-saved hogsheads—Turn them out
Thus primed with your good cheer, to guard your walls,
And they will venture for't.——

Old Play

THE ABBOT received his counsellor with a tremulous eagerness of welcome, which announced to the Sub-Prior an extreme agitation of spirits, and the utmost want of good counsel. There was neither mazer-dish nor standing-cup upon the little table, at the elbow of his huge chair of state; his beads alone lay there, and it seemed as if he had been telling them in his extremity of distress. Beside the beads was placed the mitre of the Abbot, of an antique form, and blazing with precious stones, and the rich and highly-embossed crosier rested against the same table.

The Sacristan and old Father Nicolas had followed the Sub-Prior into the Abbot's apartment, perhaps with the hope of learning something of the important matter which seemed to be in hand. They were not mistaken; for, after having ushered in the Sub-Prior, and being themselves in the act of retiring, the Abbot made them a signal to remain.

"My brethren," he said, "it is well known to you with what painful zeal we have overseen the weighty affairs of this house committed to our unworthy hand—your bread hath been given to you, and your water hath been sure—I have not wasted the revenues of the Convent on vain pleasures, as hunting or hawking, or in change of rich cope and alb, or in feasting idle bards and jesters, saving those, who, according to old wont, were received in time of Christmas and Easter. Neither have I enriched either mine own relations nor strange women, at the expence of the Patrimony."

"There has not been such a Lord Abbot," said Father Nicolas, "to my knowledge, since the days of Abbot Ingelram, who"——

At that portentous word, which always preluded a long story, the Abbot broke in.

"May God have mercy on his soul!—we talk not of him now.— What I would know of you, my brethren, is, whether I have, in your mind, faithfully discharged the duties of mine office?"

"There has never been subject of complaint," answered the Sub-Prior.

The Sacristan, more diffuse, enumerated the various acts of indulgence and kindness which the mild government of Abbot Boniface had conferred on the brotherhood of Saint Mary's—the *indulgentiæ* —the *gratias*—the *biberes*—the weekly mess of boiled almonds—the enlarged accommodation of the refectory—the better arrangement of the cellarage—the improvement of the revenue of the Monastery— the diminution of the privations of the brethren.

"You might have added, my brother," said the Abbot, listening with melancholy acquiescence to the detail of his own merits, "that I caused to be built that curious screen, which secureth the cloisters from the north-eastern wind.—But all these things avail nothing—As we read in holy Machabee, *Capta est civitas per voluntatem Dei*. It hath cost me no little thought, no common toil, to keep these weighty matters in such order as you have seen them—there was both barn and binn to be kept full—Infirmary, dormitory, guest-hall, and refectory, to be looked to—processions to be made, confessions to be heard, strangers to be entertained, *veniæ* to be granted or refused; and I warrant me, when every one of you was asleep in your cell, the Abbot hath lain awake for a full hour by the bell, thinking how these matters might be ordered seemly and suitably."

"May we ask, reverend my lord," said the Sub-Prior, "what additional care has now been thrown on you, since your discourse seems to point that way?"

"Marry, this it is," said the Abbot. "The talk is not now of *biberes*, or of *caritas*, or of boiled almonds, but of an English band coming against us from Hexham, commanded by Sir John Foster; nor is it of the screening us from the east wind, but how to escape Lord James Stuart, who cometh to lay waste and destroy with his heretic soldiers."

"I thought that purpose had been broken by the feud between Semple and the Kennedies," said the Sub-Prior, hastily.

"They have accorded that matter at expence of the church as usual," said the Abbot; "the Earl of Cassilis is to have the tiend sheaves of his lands, which were given to the house of Corseregal, and he has stricken hands with Stuart, who is now called Moray.— *Principes convenerunt in unum adversus Dominum*.—There are the letters."

The Sub-Prior took the letters, which had come by express messenger from the Primate of Scotland, who still laboured to uphold the tottering fabric of the system under which he was at length buried, and stepping towards the lamp, read them with an air of deep and settled attention—the Sacristan and Father Nicolas looked as helplessly at each other, as the denizens of the poultry-yard when the hawk soars over it. The Abbot seemed bowed down with the extremity of sorrowful apprehension, but kept his eye timorously fixed on the Sub-Prior, as if striving to catch some comfort from the expression of his countenance. When at length he beheld that, after a second intent perusal of the letters, he remained still silent and full of thought, he asked him in an anxious tone, "What is to be done?"

"Our duty must be done," answered the Sub-Prior, "and the rest is in the hands of God."

"Our duty—our duty," answered the Abbot impatiently; "doubtless we are to do our duty, but what is that duty? or how will it serve us? —Will bell, book, and candle drive back the English heretics? or will Moray care for psalms and antiphonars? or can I fight for the Halidome, like Judas Maccabeus, against those profane Nicanors? or send the Sacristan against this new Holofernes, to bring back his head in a basket?"

"True, my Lord Abbot," said the Sub-Prior, "we cannot fight with carnal weapons, it is alike contrary to our habit and vow; but we can die for our Convent and for our Order. Besides, we can arm those who will and can fight. The English are but few in number, trusting, it would seem, that they will be joined by Moray, whose march has been interrupted. If Foster, with his Cumberland and Hexhamshire bandits, ventures to march into Scotland, to pillage and despoil our House, we will levy our vassals, and, I trust, will be found strong enough to give him battle."

"In the blessed name of Our Lady," said the Abbot, "think you that I am Petrus Eremita, to go forth the leader of an host?"

"Nay," said the Sub-Prior, "let some man skilled in war lead our people—there is Julian Avenel, an approved soldier."

"But a scoffer, a debauched person, and, in brief, a man of Belial," quoth the Abbot.

"Still," said the Monk, "we must use his ministry in that to which he has been brought up—we can guerdon him richly, and indeed I already know the price of his service. The English, it is expected, will presently set forth, hoping here to seize upon Piercie Shafton, whose refuge being taken with us, they make the pretext of this unheard-of inroad."

"It is even so," said the Abbot; "I never judged that his body of satin and his brain of feathers boded us much good."

"Yet we must have his assistance, if possible," said the Sub-Prior; "he may interest in our behalf the great Piercie, of whose friendship he boasts, and that good and faithful Lord may break Foster's purpose. I will dispatch that jack-man after him with all speed.—Chiefly, however, I trust to the military spirit of the land, which will not suffer peace to be broken on the frontier with patience. Credit me, my lord, it will bring to our side the hands of many, whose hearts may have gone astray after strange doctrines. The great chiefs and barons will be ashamed to let the vassals of peaceful monks fight unaided against the old enemies of England."

"It may be," said the Abbot, "that Foster will wait for Moray, whose purpose hitherward is but delayed for a short space."

"By the rood, he will not," said the Sub-Prior; "we know this Sir John Foster—a pestilent heretic, he will long to destroy the church—a born Borderer, he will thirst to plunder her of her wealth—a Border-warden, he will be eager to ride in Scotland—there are too many causes to urge him on—if he joins with Moray, he will have at best but an auxiliary's share of the spoil—if he comes hither before him, he will reckon on the whole harvest of depredation as his own. Julian Avenel also has, as I have heard, some spite against Sir John Foster; they will fight when they meet with double determination. Sacristan, send for our bailiff—where is the roll of fencible men liable to do suit and service to the Halidome?—Send off to the Baron of Meigallot—he can raise threescore horse and better—Say to him the Monastery will compound with him for the customs of his bridge, which have been in controversy, if he will shew himself a friend at such a pinch.—And now, my lord, let us compute our possible numbers, and those of the enemy, that human blood be not spilled in vain. Let us therefore calculate"——

"My brain is dizzied with the emergency," said the poor Abbot—"I am not, I think, more a coward than others, so far as my own person is concerned; but speak to me of marching and collecting soldiers, and calculating forces, and you may as well tell of it to the youngest novice of a nunnery. But my resolution is taken. Brethren," he said, rising up and coming forward with that dignity which his comely person enabled him to assume, "hear for the last time the voice of your Abbot Boniface. I have done for you the best that I could—in quieter times I had perhaps done better, for it was for quiet that I sought the cloister, which has been to me a place of turmoil, as much as if I had sate in the receipt of custom, or ridden forth as leader of an armed host. But now matters turn worse and worse, and I, as I grow old, am less able to struggle with them. Also, it becomes me not to hold a place, whereof the duties, through my default or misfortune, may be but imperfectly filled by me. Wherefore I have resolved to demit this mine high office, so that the order of these matters may presently devolve upon Father Eustatius here present, our well-beloved Sub-Prior; and I now rejoice that he hath not been provided according to his merits elsewhere, seeing that I well hope he will succeed to the mitre and staff which it is my present purpose to lay down."

"In the name of Our Lady, do nothing hastily, my lord," said Father Nicolas—"I do remember that when the worthy Abbot Ingelram, being in his ninetieth year, for I warrant you he could remember when Benedict the Thirteenth was deposed, and being ill at ease and bed-fast, the brethren rounded in his ear that he were better resign his office—and what said he, being a pleasant man? marry, that while he could crook his little finger, he would keep hold of the crosier with it."

The Sacristan also strongly remonstrated against the resolution of his Superior, and set down the insufficiency he pleaded to the native modesty of his disposition. The Abbot listened in downcast silence; even flattery could not win his ear.

Father Eustace took a nobler tone with his disconcerted and dejected Superior. "My Lord Abbot," he said, "if I have been silent concerning the virtues with which you have governed this house, do not think I am unaware of them. I know that no man ever brought to your high office a more sincere wish to do well to all mankind; and if your rule has not been marked with the bold lines which sometimes distinguished your spiritual predecessors, their faults have equally been strangers to your character."

"I did not believe," said the Abbot, turning his looks to Father Eustace with some surprise, "that you, father, of all men, would have done me this justice."

"In your absence," said the Sub-Prior, "I have ever done it more fully. Do not lose the good opinion which all men entertain of you, by renouncing your office when your care is most needed."

"But, my brother," said the Abbot, "I leave a more able in my place."

"That you do not," said Eustace; "because it is not necessary you should resign, in order to possess the use of whatever experience or talent I may be accounted master of. I have been long enough in this profession to know that the individual qualities which any of us may possess, are not his own, but the property of the Community, and only so far useful when they promote the general advantage. If you care not in person, my lord, to deal with this troublesome matter, let me implore you to go instantly to Edinburgh, and make what friends you can in our behalf, while I in your absence will, as Sub-Prior, do my duty in defence of the Halidome. If I succeed, may the honour and praise be yours, and if I fail, let the disgrace and shame be mine own."

The Abbot mused for a space, and then replied,—"No, Father Eustatius, you shall not conquer me by your generosity. In times like these, this house must have stronger pilotage than my weak hands afford; and he who steers the vessel must be chief of the crew. Shame were it to accept the praise of other men's labours; and, in my poor mind, all the praise which can be bestowed on him who undertakes a task so perilous and perplexing, is a meed beneath his merits. Misfortune to him would deprive him of an iota of it! Assume, therefore, your authority to-night, and proceed in the preparations you judge necessary. Let the Chapter be summoned to-morrow after we have heard mass, and all shall be ordered as I have told you. Benedicite, my brethren!—peace be with you! may the new Abbot-expectant sleep as sound as he who is about to resign his mitre."

They retired, affected even to tears. The good Abbot had shewn a point of his character to which they were strangers. Even Father Eustace had held his spiritual superior hitherto as a good-humoured, indolent, self-indulgent man, whose chief merit was an absence of gross faults; so that this sacrifice of power to a sense of duty, even if a little alloyed by the meaner motives of fear and apprehended difficulties, raised him considerably in the Sub-Prior's estimation. He even felt an aversion to profit by the resignation of the Abbot Boniface, and in a manner to arise on his ruins; but this sentiment did not long contend with those arising out of the good of the church. It could not be denied that Boniface was entirely unfitted for his situation in the present crisis, and that the Sub-Prior felt that he himself, acting merely as a delegate, could scarce take the decisive measures which the time required; the weal of the Community therefore demanded his elevation. If, besides, there crept in a feeling of an high dignity attained, and the native exultation of a haughty spirit called to contend with the imminent dangers attached to a post of such distinction, these sentiments were so cunningly blended and amalgamated with others of a more disinterested nature, that as the Sub-Prior himself was unconscious of their agency, we, who have a regard for him, are not solicitous to detect it.

The Abbot-elect bore a more ample port than formerly, when giving such directions as the pressing circumstances of the times required; and those who approached him could perceive an unusual kindling of his falcon eye, and an unusual flush upon his pale and faded cheek. With briefness and precision he wrote and dictated various letters to different barons, acquainting them with the meditated invasion of the Halidome by the English, and conjuring them to lend aid and assistance as in a common cause. The temptation of advantage was held out to those whom he judged less sensible of the cause of honour, and all were urged by the motives of patriotism and ancient animosity to the English. The time had been when no such exhortations would have been necessary. But so essential was Elizabeth's aid to the reformed party in Scotland, and so strong was that party almost everywhere, that there was reason to believe a great many would observe neutrality on the present occasion, even if they did not go the length of uniting with the English against the Catholics.

When Father Eustace considered the number of the immediate vassals of the church whose aid he might legally command, his heart sunk at the thoughts of ranking them under the banner of the fierce and profligate Julian Avenel.

"Were the young enthusiast Halbert Glendinning to be found," thought Father Eustace in his anxiety, "I would have risked the battle under his leading, young as he is, and with better hope of God's blessing. But the bailiff is now too infirm, nor know I a Chief of name whom I might trust in this important matter better than this Avenel." —He touched a bell which stood on the table, and commanded Christie of the Clinthill to be brought before him.—"Thou owest me a life," said he to that person on his entrance, "and I may do thee another good turn if thou be'st sincere with me."

Christie had already drained two standing-cups of wine, which would, on another occasion, have added to the insolence of his familiarity. But at present there was something in the augmented dignity of manner of Father Eustace, which imposed a restraint on him. Yet his answers partook of his usual character of undaunted assurance. He professed himself willing to return a true answer to all enquiries.

"Has the Baron (so styled) of Avenel any friendship with Sir John Foster, warden of the west marches of England?"

"Such friendship as is between the wild cat and the terrier," replied the rider.

"Will he do battle with him should they meet?"

"As surely," replied Christie, "as ever cock fought on Shrove-tide-even."

"And would he fight with Foster in the Church's quarrel?"

"On any quarrel, or upon no quarrel whatsoever," answered the jack-man.

"We will then write to him, letting him know, that if upon occasion of an apprehended incursion by Sir John Foster he will agree to join his force with ours, he shall lead our men, and be gratified for doing so to the extent of his wish. Yet one word more—Thou didst say thou couldst find out where the English knight Piercie Shafton has this day fled to?"

"That I can, and bring him back too, by fair means or force, as best likes your reverence."

"No force must be used upon him. Within what time wilt thou find him out?"

"Within thirty hours, so he have not crossed the Lothian firth—if it is to do you a pleasure, I will set off directly, and wind him as a sleuth-dog tracks the moss-trooper," answered Christie.

"Bring him hither then, and thou wilt deserve good at our hands, which I may soon have free means of bestowing on thee."

"Thanks to your reverence, I put myself in your reverence's hands. We of the spear and snafle walk something recklessly through life; but if a man were worse than he is, your reverence knows he must live, and that's not to be done without shifting, I trow."

"Peace, sir, and begone on thine errand—thou shalt have a letter from us to Sir Piercie."

Christie made two steps towards the door, then turning back and hesitating, like one who would make an impertinent pleasantry if he dared, he asked what he was to do with the wench Mysie Happer, whom the Southron knight had carried off with him.

"Am I to bring her hither, please your reverence?"

"Hither, you malapert knave?" said the churchman; "remember you to whom you speak?"

"No offence meant," replied Christie; "but if such is not your will, I could carry her to Avenel Castle, where well-favoured wench was never unwelcome."

"Bring the unfortunate girl to her father's, and break no scurril jests here," said the Sub-Prior—"See that thou guide her in all safety and honour."

"In safety, surely," said the rider, "and in such honour as her out-break has left her.—I bid your reverence farewell, I must be on horse before cock-crow."

"What, in the dark?—how knowst thou which way to go?"

"I tracked the knight's horse-tread as far as near to the ford, as we rode along together," said Christie, "and I observed it turn to the northward. He is for Edinburgh I will warrant you—so soon as day-light comes I will be on the road again. It is a kenspeckle hoof-mark, for the shoe was made by old Eckie of Cannobie—I would swear to the curve of the cawker." So saying, he departed.

"Hateful necessity," said Father Eustace, looking after him, "that makes necessary such implements as these. But, assailed as we are on all sides, and by all conditions of men, what alternative is left us?—But now let me to my most needful task."

The Abbot elect accordingly sate down to write letters, arrange orders, and take upon him the whole charge of an institution which tottered to its fall, with the same spirit of proud and devoted fortitude wherewith the commander of a fortress, reduced nearly to the last extremity, calculates what means remain to him to protract the fatal hour of successful storm. In the meanwhile Abbot Boniface, having given a few natural sighs to the downfall of the pre-eminence he had so long enjoyed amongst his brethren, fell fast asleep, leaving the whole cares and toils of office to his assistant and successor.

Chapter Ten

And when he came to broken briggs,
He slack'd his bow and swam;
And when he came to grass growing,
Set down his feet and ran.
                              Gil Morrice

WE RETURN to Halbert Glendinning, who, as our readers may remember, took the high road to Edinburgh. His intercourse with the preacher Henry Warden, from whom he received a letter at the moment of his deliverance, had been so brief that he had not even learned the name of the nobleman to whose care he was recommended. Something like a name had been spoken indeed, but he had only comprehended that he was to meet the chief advancing towards the south, at the head of a party of horse. When day dawned on his journey, he was in the same uncertainty. A better scholar would have been informed by the address of the letter, but Halbert had not so far profited by Father Eustace's lessons as to be able to decypher it. His mother-wit taught him that he must not, in these uncertain times, be too hasty in asking information of any one, and when, after a long day's journey, night surprised him near a little village, he began to be uncertain, and anxious concerning the issue of his journey.

In a poor country, hospitality is generally exercised freely, and Halbert, when he requested a night's quarters, did nothing either degrading or extraordinary. The old woman, to whom he made this request, granted it the more readily that she thought she saw some resemblance between Halbert and her son Saunders, who had been killed in one of the frays so common in the time. It is true, Saunders was a short, square-made fellow, with red hair and a freckled face, and somewhat bandy-legged, whereas the stranger was of a brown complexion, tall, and remarkably well made. Nevertheless, the widow was clear that there existed a general resemblance betwixt her guest and Saunders, and kindly pressed him to take share of her evening cheer. A pedlar, a man of about forty years old, was also her guest, who talked with great feeling of the misery of pursuing such a profession as his in the time of war and tumult.

"We think much of knights and soldiers," said he; "but the pedder-coffe who travels this land has need of more courage than them all. I am sure he maun face mair risk, God help him. Here have I come this length, trusting the godly Earl of Moray would be on his march to the Borders, for he was to have guestened with the Baron of Avenel; and instead of that comes news that he has gone westlandways about some tuilzie in Ayrshire. And what to do I wot not; for if I go to the south without a safeguard, the next bonny rider I meet might ease me of sack and pack, and maybe of my life to boot; and then, if I try to strike across the moors, I may be as ill off before I can join myself to that good Lord's company."

No one was quicker at catching a hint than Halbert Glendinning. He said he himself had a desire to go westward. The pedlar looked at him with a very doubtful air, when the old dame, who perhaps thought her young guest resembled the umquhile Saunders, not only in his looks, but in a certain pretty turn to slight-of-hand, which the defunct was supposed to have possessed, tipped him a wink, and assured the pedlar he need have no doubt that her young cousin was a true man.

"Cousin!" said the pedlar, "I thought you said this youth had been a stranger."

"Ill hearing makes ill rehearsing," said the landlady; "he is a stranger to me by eye-sight, but that does not make him a stranger to me by blood, more especially seeing his likeness to my son Saunders, poor bairn."

The pedlar's scruples and jealousies being thus removed, or at least silenced, the travellers agreed that they would proceed in company together the next morning by day-break, the pedlar acting as a guide to Glendinning, and the youth as a guard to the pedlar, until they should fall in with Moray's detachment of horse. It would appear that their landlady never doubted what was to be the event of this compact, for, taking Glendinning aside, she charged him "to be moderate with the poor body, but at all events, not to forget to take a piece of black say, to make the auld wife a new rokelay." Halbert laughed and took his leave.

It did not a little appal the pedlar, when, in the midst of a bleak heath, the young man told him the nature of the commission with which their hostess had charged him. He took heart, however, upon seeing the open, frank, and friendly demeanour of the youth, and vented his exclamations on the ungrateful old traitress. "I gave her," he said, "yester-e'en, nae farther gane, a yard of that very black say, to make her a couvre-chef; but I see it is ill done to teach the cat the way to the kirn."

Thus at ease on the intentions of his companion, for in those happy days the worst was always to be expected from a stranger, the pedlar acted as Halbert's guide over moss and moor, over hill and many a dale, in such a direction as might best lead them towards the route of Moray's party. At length they arrived upon the side of an eminence, which commanded a distant prospect over a tract of savage and desolate moorland, marshy and waste—an alternate change of shingly hill and level morass, only varied by blue stagnant pools of water. A scarce marked road winded like a serpent through this wilderness, and the pedlar, pointing to it, said—"The road from Edinburgh to Glasgow— here we must wait, and if Moray and his train be not already passed by, we shall soon see trace of them—unless some new purpose shall have altered their resolution; for in these blessed days no man, were he the nearest the throne, as this Earl of Moray may be, knows when he lays his head on his pillow at night where it is to lie upon the following even."

They paused accordingly, and sate down, the merchant cautiously using for a seat the box which contained his treasures, and not concealing from his companion that he wore under his cloak a pistolet hanging at his belt in case of need. He was courteous however, and offered Halbert a share of the provisions which he carried about him for refreshment. They were of the coarsest kind—oat-bread baked into cakes, oat-meal slaked with cold water, an onion or two, and a morsel of smoked ham, completed the feast. But such as it was, no Scotsman of the time, had his rank been much higher than that of Glendinning, would have refused to share in it, especially as the pedlar produced, with a mysterious air, a tup's-horn, which he carried slung from his shoulders, and which, when its contents were examined, produced to each party a clam-shell-full of excellent usquebaugh—a liquor strange to Halbert, for the strong waters known in the south of Scotland came from France, and in fact were but rarely used. The pedlar recommended it as excellent, said he had procured it in his last visit to the braes of Doune, where he had safely traded under the safe-conduct of the Laird of Buchanan. He also set an example to Halbert, by devoutly emptying the cup "to the speedy downfall of Anti-christ."

Their conviviality was scarce ended, ere a rising dust was seen on the road of which they commanded the prospect, and half a score of horsemen were dimly descried advancing at considerable speed, their casques glancing, and the points of their spears twinkling, as they caught a glimpse of the sun.

"These," said the pedlar, "must be the out-scourers of Moray's party; let us lie down in the peat-hagg, and keep ourselves out of sight."

"And why so?" said Halbert; "let us rather go down and make a signal to them."

"God forbid!" replied the pedlar; "do you ken so ill the customs of our Scottish nation? That plump of spears that are spurring on so fast will be commanded by the bastard of Morton, or some such daring fear-nothing as neither regards God nor man. It is their business, if they meet with any enemies, to pick quarrel, and clear the way of them; and the chief knows nothing what happens, coming up with his more discreet and moderate friends, it may be a full mile in the rear. Were we to go near these lads of the laird's belt, your letter would do you little good, and my pack would do me mickle black ill; they would tirl every steek of claithes from our back, fling us into a moss-hagg with a stone at our heels, naked as the hour that brought us into this cumbered and sinful world, and neither Moray nor any other man ever the wiser. But if he did come to ken of it, what might he help it?— it were accounted a mere mistake, and there were all the moan made. O credit me, youth, that when men draw cold steel on each other in their native country, they neither can nor may dwell deep on the offences of those whose swords are useful to them."

They suffered therefore the vanguard, as it might be termed, of the Earl of Moray's host to pass forward; and it was not long until a denser cloud of dust began to arise to the northward.

"Now," said the pedlar, "now let us hurry down the hill; for to tell the truth," said he, dragging Halbert along earnestly, "a Scottish noble's march is like a serpent—the head is furnished with fangs, and the tail hath its sting—the only harmless point of access is the main-body."

"I will hasten as fast as you will," said the youth, "but tell me why the rearward of such an army should be as dangerous as the van?"

"Because, as the van-guard consists of their picked wild desperates, resolute for mischief, such as neither fear God nor regard their fel-low-creatures, but understand themselves bound to hurry from the road whatsoever is displeasing to themselves, so the rear-guard con-sists of mis-proud serving men, who, being in charge of the baggage, take care to amend by their exactions upon travelling merchants and others, their own thefts on their master's property. You will hear the advanced *enfans perdus*, as the French call them, and so they are indeed, namely, children of the fall, singing unclean and fulsome ballads of sin and harlotrie—and then will come on the middle-ward, when you will hear canticles and psalms sung by the reforming nobles, and the gentry, and honest and pious clergy, by whom they are accom-panied—and last of all, you will find in the rear a legion of godless lacqueys and palfreniers, and horse-boys, talking of nothing but dicing, drinking, and drabbing."

As the pedlar spoke, they had reached the side of the high-road,

and Moray's main body was in sight, consisting of about three hundred horse, marching with great regularity, and in a closely compacted
body. Some of the troopers wore the liveries of their masters, but this
was not common. Most of them were dressed in such colours as
chance dictated. But, the majority being clad in blue cloth, and the
whole armed with cuirass and back-plate, with sleeves of mail, gaunt-
lets, and poldroons, and either mailed hose or strong jack-boots, they
had something of an uniform appearance. Many of the leaders were
clad in complete armour, and all in a certain half-military dress, which
no man of quality in these disturbed times ever felt himself sufficiently
safe to abandon.

The foremost of this party immediately rode up to the pedlar and to
Halbert Glendinning, and demanded of them who they were. The
pedlar told his story, the young Glendinning exhibited his letter,
which a gentleman carried to Moray. In an instant after, the word
"Halt!" was given through the squadron, and at once the onward
heavy tramp, which seemed the most distinctive attribute of the body,
ceased, and was heard no more. The command was announced that
the troop would halt here for an hour to refresh themselves and their
horses. The pedlar was assured of safe protection, and accommodated with the use of a baggage horse. But at the same time he was
ordered into the rear; a command which he reluctantly obeyed, and
not without wringing pathetically the hand of Halbert as he separated
from him.

The young heir of Glendearg was in the meanwhile conducted to a
plot of ground more raised, and therefore drier than the rest of the
moor. Here a carpet was flung on the ground by way of table-cloth,
and around it sate the leaders of the party, partaking of an entertainment as coarse, with relation to their rank, as that which Glendinning
had so lately shared might at present seem to men of his degree.
Moray himself rose as he came forwards, and advanced a step to meet
him. This celebrated person had in his person, as well as in his mind,
much of the admirable qualities of James V., his father. Had not the
stain of illegitimacy rested upon his birth, he would have filled the
Scottish throne with as much honour as any of the Stuart race. But
History, while she acknowledges his high talents, and much that was
princely, nay, royal, in his conduct, cannot forget that ambition led
him further than honour or loyalty warranted. Brave amongst the
bravest, fair in presence and in favour, skilful to manage the most
intricate affairs, to attach to himself those who were doubtful, to stun
and overwhelm, by the suddenness and intrepidity of his enterprizes,
those who were resolute in resistance, he attained, and as to personal
merit certainly deserved, the highest place in the kingdom. But he

abused, under the influence of strong temptation, the opportunities which his sister Mary's misfortunes and imprudence threw in his way; he supplanted his sovereign and benefactress in her power, and his history affords us one of those mixed characters, in which principle was so often sacrificed to policy, that we must condemn the statesman while we pity and regret the individual. Many events in his life countenance the charge that he himself aimed at the crown; and it is too true, that he countenanced the fatal expedient of establishing an English, that is, a foreign and an hostile interest, in the councils of Scotland. But his death may be received as an atonement for his offences, and may serve to shew how much more safe is the person of a real patriot, than that of the mere head of a faction, who is accounted answerable for the offences of his meanest attendants.

When Moray approached, the young rustic was naturally abashed at the dignity of his presence. The commanding form, and the countenance to which high and important thoughts were familiar, the features which bore the resemblance of Scotland's long line of kings, were well calculated to impress awe and reverence. His dress had little to distinguish him from the high-born nobles and barons by whom he was attended. A buff-coat, fairly embroidered with silken lace, supplied the place of armour; and a massive gold chain, with its medal, hung round his neck. His black velvet bonnet was decorated with a string of large and fair pearls, and with a small tufted feather; a long heavy sword was girt to his side, as the familiar companion of his hand; he wore gilded spurs on his boots, and these completed his equipage.

"This letter," he said, "is from the godly preacher of the word Henry Warden, young man—is it not so?" Halbert answered in the affirmative. "And he writes to us, it would seem, in some strait, and refers us to you for the circumstance. Let us know, I pray you, how things stand with him."

In some perturbation Halbert Glendinning gave an account of the circumstances which had accompanied the preacher's imprisonment. When he came to the discussion of the *handfasting* engagement, he was struck with the ominous and displeased expression of Moray's brows, and, contrary to all prudential and politic rule, seeing something was wrong, yet not well aware what that something was, had almost stopped short in his narrative.

"What ails the fool?" said the Earl, drawing his dark-red eye-brows together, while the same dusky glow kindled on his brow—"Hast thou not learned to tell a true tale without stammering?"

"So please you," answered Halbert with considerable address, "I have never before spoken in such a presence."

"He seems a modest youth," said Moray, turning to his next attend-

ant, "and yet one who in a good cause will neither fear friend nor foe.
—Speak on, friend, and speak freely."

Halbert then gave an account of the quarrel betwixt Julian Avenel
and the preacher, which the Earl, biting his lip the while, compelled
himself to listen to as a thing of indifference. At first he appeared even
to take the part of the Baron.

"Henry Warden," he said, "is too hot in his zeal. The law both of
God and of man maketh allowance for certain alliances, though not
strictly formal, and the issue of such may succeed."

This general declaration he expressed, accompanying it with a
glance around upon the few followers who were present at this interview. The most of them answered—"there is no contravening that;"
but one or two looked on the ground and were silent. Moray then
looked again at Glendinning, commanding him to say on what next
chanced, and not to omit any particular. When he mentioned the
manner in which Julian had cast from him his hand-fasted concubine,
Moray drew a deep breath, set his teeth hard, and laid his hand on the
hilt of his dagger. Casting his eyes once more around the circle, which
was now augmented by one or two of the reformed preachers, he
seemed to devour his rage in silence, and again commanded Halbert
to proceed. When he came to describe how Warden had been dragged
to a dungeon, the Earl seemed to have found the point at which he
might give vent to his own resentment, secure of the sympathy and
approbation of all who were present. "Judge you," he said, looking to
those around him, "judge you, my peers and noble gentlemen of
Scotland, betwixt me and this Julian Avenel—he hath broken his own
word, and hath violated my safe-conduct—and judge you also, my
reverend brethren, he hath put his hand forth upon a preacher of the
gospel, and perchance may sell his blood to the worshippers of Anti-
Christ."

"Let him die the death of a traitor," said the secular chiefs, "and let
his tongue be struck through with the hangman's fiery iron to avenge
his perjury."

"Let him go down to his place with Baal's priests," said the
preachers, "and be his ashes cast into Tophet."

Moray heard them with the smile of expected revenge; yet it is
probable that the brutal treatment of the female, whose circumstances
somewhat resembled those of the Earl's own mother, had its own
share in the grim smile which curled his sun-burned cheek and his
haughty lip. To Halbert Glendinning, when his narrative was finished, he spoke with great kindness.

"He is a bold and gallant youth," said he to those around, "and
formed of the stuff which becomes a bustling time. There are periods

when men's spirits shine bravely through them. I will know something more of him."

He questioned him more particularly concerning the Baron of Avenel's probable forces—the strength of his castle—the dispositions of his next heir, and this brought necessarily forwards the sad history of his brother's daughter, Mary Avenel, which was told with an embarrassment that did not escape Moray.

"Ha! Julian Avenel," he said, "and do you provoke my resentment, when you have so much more reason to deprecate my justice! I knew Walter Avenel, a true Scotsman and a good soldier. Our sister, the Queen, must right his daughter; and were her land restored, she would be a fitting bride to some brave man who may better merit our favour than the traitor Julian."—Then looking at Halbert, he said, "Art thou of gentle blood, young man?"

Halbert, with a faultering and uncertain voice, began to speak of his distant pretensions to claim a descent from the ancient Glendonwynes of Galloway, when Moray interrupted him with a smile.

"Nay, nay—leave pedigrees to bards and heralds—in our days, each man is the son of his own deeds. The glorious light of reformation hath shone alike on prince and peasant; and peasant as well as prince may be illustrated by fighting in its defence. It is a stirring world, where all may advance themselves who have stout hearts and strong arms. Tell me frankly why thou hast left thy father's house."

Halbert Glendinning made a frank confession of his duel with Piercie Shafton, and mentioned his supposed death.

"By my hand," said Moray, "thou art a bold sparrow-hawk to match thee so early with such a kite as Piercie Shafton. Queen Elizabeth would give her glove filled with gold crowns to know that meddling coxcomb to be under the sod. Would she not, Morton?"

"Ay, by my word, and esteem her glove a better gift than the crowns," replied Morton.

"But what shall we do with this young homicide," said Moray; "what will our preachers say?"

"Tell them of Moses and of Benaiah," said Morton; "it is but the smiting of an Egyptian when all is said out."

"Let it be so," said Moray, laughing; "but we will bury the tale as the prophet did the body in the sand. I will take care of this swankie.— Be near to us, Glendinning, since that is thy name. We retain thee as a squire of our household. The master of our house will see thee fully equipped and armed."

During the expedition which he was now engaged in, Moray found several opportunities of putting Glendinning's courage and presence of mind to the test, and he began to rise so rapidly in his esteem, that those who knew the Earl considered the youth's fortune as certain. One step only was wanting to raise him to a still higher degree of confidence and favour—it was the abjuration of the Popish religion. The ministers who attended upon Moray, and formed his chief support amongst the people, found an easy convert in Halbert Glendinning, who, from the beginning of his life, had never felt much devotion towards the Catholic faith, and who listened eagerly to more reasonable views of religion. By thus adopting the faith of his master, he became still nearer to him, and was constantly about his person during his prolonged stay in the west of Scotland, which the intractability of those whom the Earl had to deal with, protracted from day to day, and week to week.

Chapter Eleven

Faint the din of battle bray'd
Distant down the hollow wind;
War and terror fled before,
Wounds and death were left behind.
PENROSE

THE AUTUMN of the year was well advanced, when the Earl of Morton, one morning, rather unexpectedly, entered the antichamber of Moray, in which Halbert Glendinning was in waiting.

"Call your master, Halbert," said the Earl; "I have news for him from Teviotdale—and for you too, Glendinning."

"News! news! my Lord of Moray!" he exclaimed at the door of the Earl's bed-room, "come forth instantly." The Earl appeared, and greeted his ally, demanding eagerly his tidings.

"I have had a sure friend with me from the south," said Morton; "he has been at Saint Mary's Monastery, and brings important tidings."

"Of what complection?" said Moray, "and can you trust the bearer?"

"He is faithful, on my life," said Morton; "I wish all around your Lordship may prove equally so."

"At what, and whom, do you point?" said Moray.

"Here is the Egyptian of trusty Halbert Glendinning, our Southland Moses, come alive again, and flourishing, gay and bright as ever, in that Teviotdale Goshen, the Halidome of Kennaquhair."

"What mean you, my lord?" said Moray.

"Only that your new henchman has put a false tale upon you. Piercie Shafton is alive and well; by the same token that the gull is thought to be detained there by love to a miller's daughter, who roamed the country with him in disguise."

"Glendinning," said Moray, bending his brows into his darkest frown, "thou hast not, I trust, dared to bring me a lie in thy mouth, in order to win my confidence."

"My lord," said Halbert, "I am incapable of a lie. I should choke on one were my life to require that I pronounced it. I say, that this sword of my father was through the body—the point came out behind his back—the hilt pressed upon his breast-bone. And I will plunge it as deep in the body of any one who shall dare to charge me with falsehood."

"How, fellow!" said Morton, "wouldst thou beard a nobleman?"

"Be silent, Halbert," said Moray, "and you, my Lord of Morton, forbear him. I see truth written on his brow."

"I wish the inside of the manuscript may correspond with the superscription. Look to it, my lord, you will one day lose your life by too much confidence."

"And you will lose your friends by being too readily suspicious," answered Moray. "Enough of this—let me hear thy tidings."

"Sir John Foster," said Morton, "is to send a party into Scotland to waste the Halidome."

"How! without waiting my presence and permission?" said Moray —"he is mad—Will he come as enemy into the Queen's country?"

"He has Elizabeth's express orders," answered Morton, "and they are not to be trifled with. Indeed, his march has been more than once projected and laid aside during the time we have been here, and has caused much alarm at Kennaquhair. Boniface, the old Abbot, has resigned, and whom think you they have chosen in his place?"

"No one surely," said Moray; "they would presume to hold no election until the Queen's pleasure and mine were known?"

Morton shrugged his shoulders—"They have chosen the pupil of old Cardinal Beatoun, that wily determined champion of Rome, the bosom-friend of our busy Primate of Saint Andrew's. Eustace, late the Sub-Prior of Kennaquhair, is now its Abbot, and, like a second Pope Julius, is levying men and making musters to fight with Foster if he comes forward."

"We must prevent that meeting," said Moray hastily; "which ever party wins the day, it were a fatal encounter for us—Who commands the troop of the Abbot?"

"Our faithful old friend, Julian Avenel, nothing less," answered Morton.

"Glendinning," said Moray, "sound trumpets to horse directly, and let all who love us get on horseback without delay—Yes, my lord, this were indeed a painful dilemma. If we take part with our English friends, the country will cry shame on us—the very old wives will attack us with their rocks and distaffs—the very stones of the streets will rise up against us—we cannot set our face to such a deed of infamy. And my sister, whose confidence I already have such difficulty in preserving, will altogether withdraw it from me. Then, were we to oppose the English Warden, Elizabeth would call it a protecting of her enemies and what not, and we should lose her."

"The she dragon," said Morton, "is the best card in our pack, and yet I would not willingly stand still and see English blades carve Scots flesh—What say you to loitering by the way, marching fair and easy for fear of spoiling our horses? They might then fight dog fight bull, fight Abbot fight archer, and no one could blame us for what chanced when we were not present."

"All would blame us, James Douglas," replied Moray; "we should lose both sides—We had better advance with utmost celerity, and do what we can to keep the peace betwixt them.—I would the nag that brought Piercie Shafton hither had broken his neck over the highest heuch in Northumberland!—he is a proper coxcomb to make all this bustle about, and to occasion perhaps a national war."

"Had we known in time," said Douglas, "we might have had him privily waited upon as he entered the Borders; there are strapping lads enough would have rid us of him for the lucre of his spur-whang. But to the saddle, James Stuart, since so the phrase goes. I hear your trumpets sound to horse and away—we shall soon see which nag is best breathed."

Followed by a train of about three hundred well mounted men-at-arms, these two powerful barons directed their course to Dumfries, and from thence eastward to Teviotdale, marching at a rate, which, as Morton had foretold, soon disabled a good many of their horses, so that when they approached the scene of expected action, there were not above two hundred of their train remaining in a body, and of these most were mounted on steeds which had been sorely jaded.

They had hitherto been amused and agitated by various reports concerning the advance of the English soldiers, and the degree of resistance which the Abbot was able to oppose to them. But when they were six or seven miles from Saint Mary's of Kennaquhair, a gentleman of the country, whom Moray had summoned to attend him, and on whose intelligence he knew he could rely, arrived at the head of two or three servants, "bloody with spurring, fiery red with haste." According to his report, Sir John Foster, after several times announcing, and as often delaying his intended incursion, had at last been so stung with the news that Piercie Shafton was openly residing within the Halidome, that he determined to execute the commands of his mistress, which directed him, at every risk, to make himself master of the Euphuist's person. The Abbot's unceasing exertions had collected a body of men almost equal in number to those of the English Warden, but less practised in arms. They were united under the command of Julian Avenel, and it was apprehended they would join battle upon the banks of a small stream which forms the verge of the Halidome.

"Who knows the place?" said Moray.

"I do, my lord," answered Glendinning.

"'Tis well," said the Earl; "take a score of the best-mounted horse —make what haste thou canst, and announce to them that I am coming up instantly with a strong power, and will cut to pieces, without mercy, whichever party strikes the first blow.—Davidson," said he, to the gentleman who brought the intelligence, "thou shalt be my guide. Hie thee on, Glendinning—Say to Foster, I conjure him, as he respects his Mistress's service, that he will leave the matter in my hands. Say to the Abbot, I will burn the Monastery over his head, if he strikes stroke till I come—Tell the dog, Julian Avenel, that he hath already one deep score to settle with me—I will set his head on the top of the highest pinnacle of Saint Mary's if he presume to open another. Make haste, and spare not the spur for fear of spoiling horse-flesh."

"Your bidding shall be obeyed, my lord," said Glendinning; and chusing those whose horses were in best plight to be his attendants, he went off as fast as the jaded state of their cavalry permitted. Hill and hollow vanished from under the feet of the chargers.

They had not ridden above half the way, when they met stragglers coming off from the field, whose appearance announced that the conflict was begun. Two supported in their arms a third, their elder brother, who was pierced with an arrow through the body. Halbert, who knew them to belong to the Halidome, called them by their names, and questioned them of the state of the affray; but just then, in spite of their efforts to retain him in the saddle, their brother dropped from the horse, and they dismounted in haste to receive his last breath. From men thus engaged, no information was to be obtained. Glendinning, therefore, pushed on with his little troop, the more anxiously as he perceived more stragglers, bearing Saint Andrew's cross upon their caps and corslets, flying apparently from the field of battle. Most of these, when they were aware of a body of horsemen approaching on the road, held to the one hand or the other, at such a distance as precluded coming to speech of them. Others, whose fear was more intense, kept the onward road, galloping wildly as fast as their horses could carry them, and when questioned, only glared without reply on those who spoke to them, and rode on without drawing bridle. Several of these were also known to Halbert, who had therefore no doubt, from the circumstances in which he met them, that the men of the Halidome were defeated. He became now unspeakably anxious concerning the fate of his brother, who, he could not doubt, must have been engaged in the affray. He therefore increased the speed of his horse, so that not above five or six of his followers could keep up with him. At length he reached a little hill, at the descent of which, surrounded by a semi-circular sweep of the little stream, lay the plain which had been the scene of the skirmish.

It was a melancholy spectacle. War and terror, to use the expression of the poet, had rushed on to the pursuit, and left only wounds and death behind them. The battle had been stoutly contested, as was almost always the case with these Border skirmishes, where ancient hatred, and mutual injuries, made men stubborn in maintaining the cause of their country. Towards the middle of the plain, there lay several bodies who had fallen in the very act of grappling with the enemy, and there were seen countenances which still bore the stern expression of unextinguishable hate and defiance, hands which clasped the hilt of the broken falchion, or strove in vain to pluck the deadly arrow from the wound. Some were wounded; and, cowed of the courage they had lately shewn, were begging aid, and craving water, in a tone of melancholy depression, while others tried to teach the faultering tongue to pronounce some half-forgotten prayer, which, even when first learned, they had but half-understood. Halbert, uncertain what course he was next to pursue, rode through the plain to see if, among the dead or wounded, he could discover any traces of his brother Edward. He experienced no interruption from the English. A distant cloud of dust announced that they were still pursuing the scattered fugitives, and he guessed, that to approach them with his followers, until they were again under some command, would be to throw away his own life, and that of his men, whom the victors would instantly confound with the Scots, against whom they had been successful. He resolved, therefore, to pause until Moray came up with his forces, to which he was the more readily moved, as he heard the trumpets of the English Warden sounding the retreat and recall from the pursuit. He drew his men together, and made a stand in an advantageous spot of ground, which had been occupied by the Scots in the beginning of the action, and most fiercely disputed while the skirmish lasted.

While he stood here, Halbert's ear was assailed by the feeble moan of a woman, which he had not expected to hear amid that scene, until the retreat of the foes had permitted the relatives of the slain to approach, for the purpose of paying them the last duties. He looked with anxiety, and at length observed, that by the body of a knight in bright armour, whose crest, though soiled and broken, still shewed the marks of rank and birth, there sat a female, wrapt in a horseman's cloak, and holding something pressed against her bosom, which he soon discovered to be a child. He glanced towards the English. They advanced not, and the continued and prolonged sound of their trumpets, with the shouts of the leaders, announced that their powers would not be instantly re-assembled. He had, therefore, a moment to look after this unfortunate woman. He gave his horse to a spearman as he dismounted, and, approaching the unhappy female, asked her in the most soothing tone he could assume, whether he could assist her in her distress. She made him no direct answer; but endeavouring, with a trembling and unskilful hand, to undo the springs of the visor and gorget, said, in a tone of impatient grief, "O, he would recover instantly could I but give him air—land and living, life and honour, would I give for the power of undoing these cruel iron platings that suffocate him." He that would sooth sorrow must not argue on the vanity of the most deceitful hopes. The body lay as that of one whose last draught of vital air had been drawn, and who must never more have concern with the nether sky. But Halbert Glendinning failed not to raise the visor and cast loose the gorget, when, to his own surprise, he recognized the pale face of Julian Avenel. His last fight was over: the fierce and turbid spirit had departed in the strife in which it had so long delighted.

"Alas! he is gone," said Halbert, speaking to the young woman, in whom he had now no difficulty of knowing the unhappy Catherine.

"O, no, no, no!" she reiterated, "do not say so—he is not dead—he is but in a swoon. I have lain as long in one myself—and then his voice would rouse me when he spoke kindly, and said, Catherine, look up for my sake—And look up, Julian, for mine," she said, addressing the senseless corpse; "I know you do but counterfeit to frighten me, but I am not frightened," she added, with a hysterical attempt to laugh; and then instantly changing her tone entreated him, "Speak, were it but to curse my folly. O, the rudest word you ever said to me would now sound like the dearest you wasted on me before I gave you all. Lift him up," she said, "lift him up, for God's sake!—have you no compassion? He promised to wed me if I bore him a boy, and this child is so like to it's father!—how shall he keep his word, if you do not help me to awaken him?—Christie of the Clinthill, Rowley, Hutcheon! ye were constant at his feast, but ye fled from him at the fray, false villains as ye are!"

"Not I, by heaven," answered a dying man, who made some shift to raise himself on his elbow, and discovered to Halbert the well-known features of Christie; "I fled not a foot, and a man can but fight while his breath lasts—mine is going fast.—So, youngster," said he, looking at Glendinning, and seeing his military dress, "thou hast ta'en the basnet at last. It is a better cap to live in than to die in. I would chance had sent thy brother here instead—there was good in him—but thou art as wild, and wilt soon be as wicked as myself."

"God forbid!" said Halbert hastily.

"Marry, and amen, with all my heart," said the wounded man, "there will be company enow without thee where I am going. But God be praised I had no hand in that wickedness," said he, looking to poor Catherine; and with some exclamation in his mouth that sounded betwixt a prayer and a curse, the soul of Christie of the Clinthill took wing to the last accompt.

Deeply wrapt in the painful interest which these shocking events had excited, Glendinning neglected for a moment the recollection of his own situation and duties, and was first recalled to them by a trampling of horse, and the cry of Saint George for England, which the English soldiers still continued to use. His handful of men, for most of the stragglers had waited for Moray's coming up, remained on horseback, holding their lances upright, having no command either to submit or resist.

"There stands our Captain," said one of them, as a very superior band of English came up, the vanguard of Foster's party.

"Your Captain, with his sword sheathed, and on foot in the presence of his enemy? a raw soldier I warrant him," said the English leader. "So! ho! young man, is your dream out, and will you now answer me if you will fight or fly?"

"Neither," answered Halbert Glendinning, with great tranquillity.

"Then throw down thy sword and yield thee," answered the Englishman.

"Not till I can help myself no otherwise," said Halbert, with the same moderation of tone and manner.

"Art thou for thine own hand, friend, or to whom doest thou owe service?" replied the English Captain."

"To the noble Earl of Moray."

"Then thou servest," said the Southron, "the most disloyal nobleman who breathes—false both to England and Scotland."

"Thou liest!" said Glendinning, regardless of all consequences.

"Ha! art thou so hot now, and wert so cold but a minute since? I lie, do I? Wilt thou do battle with me in that quarrel?"

"With one to one—one to two—or two to five, as you list," said Halbert Glendinning; "grant me but a fair field."

"That thou shalt have. Stand back, my mates," said the brave

Englishman. "If I fall, give him fair play, and let him go off free with his people."

"Long life to the noble Captain," cried the soldiers, as impatient to see the duel as if it had been a bull-baiting.

"He will have a short life of it though," said the Serjeant, "if he, an old man of sixty, is to fight for any reason, or for no reason, every man he meets, and especially the young fellows he might be father to.— And here comes the Warden besides, to see the sword-play."

In fact, Sir John Foster came up with a considerable body of his horsemen, just as his Captain, whose age rendered him unequal to the combat with so strong and active a youth as Glendinning, lost his sword.

"Take it up for shame, old Stawarth Bolton," said the English Warden; "and thou, young man, tell me who and what thou art?"

"A follower of the Earl of Moray, who bore his will to your honour," answered Glendinning, "but here he comes to say it himself, I see the van of his horsemen come over the hills."

"Get into order, my masters," said Sir John Foster to his followers; "you that have broken your spears, draw your swords. We are something unprovided for a second field, but if yonder dark cloud on the hill-edge bring us foul weather, we must bear as bravely as our broken cloaks will bide it. Meanwhile, Stawarth, we have got the deer we have hunted for—here is Piercie Shafton hard and fast betwixt two troopers."

"Who, that lad?" said Bolton; "he is no more Piercie Shafton than I am. He hath his gay cloak indeed—Piercie Shafton is a round dozen of years older than that slip of roguery. I have known him since he was thus high. Did you never see him in the tilt-yard or in the presence?"

"To the devil with such vanities!" said Sir John Foster; "when had I leisure for them or anything else? For my life-time has she kept me to this hangman's office, chasing thieves one day and traitors another, in daily fear of my life—the lance never hung up in the hall, the foot never out of the stirrup, the saddles never off my nags' backs; and now, because I have been mistaken in the person of a man I never saw, I warrant me, the next letters from the Privy Council will rate me as I were a dog—a man were better dead than thus slaved and harassed."

A trumpet interrupted Foster's complaints, and a Scottish pursuivant who attended, declared "that the noble Earl of Moray desired, in all honour and safety, a personal conference with Sir John Foster, midway between their parties, with six of company in each, and ten free minutes to come and go."

"And now," said the Englishman, "comes another plague. I must go speak with yonder false Scot, and he knows how to frame his devices, to cast dust in the eyes of a plain man, as well as ever a knave in the north. I am no match for him in words, and for hard blows we are but too ill provided. Pursuivant, we grant the conference—And you, Sir Swordsman (speaking to young Glendinning,) draw off with your troopers to your own party—march—attend your Earl's trumpet.— Stawarth Bolton, put our troop in order, and be ready to move forward at the wagging of a finger.—Get you gone to your own friends, I tell you, Sir Squire, and loiter not here."

Notwithstanding this peremptory order, Halbert Glendinning could not help stopping to cast a look upon the unfortunate Catherine, who lay insensible of the danger of the trampling of so many horses around her, insensible, as the second glance assured him, of all and for ever. Glendinning almost rejoiced when he saw that the last misery of life was over, and that the hoofs of the war-horses, amongst which he was compelled to leave her, could only injure and deface a senseless corpse. He caught the infant from her arms, half ashamed of the shout of laughter which rose on all sides, at seeing an armed man in such a situation assume such an unwonted and inconvenient burthen.

"Shoulder your infant!" cried a harquebusier.

"Port your infant!" said a pikeman.

"Peace, ye brutes," said Stawarth Bolton, "and respect humanity in others, if you have none yourselves. I pardon the lad having done some discredit to my grey hairs, when I see him take care of that helpless creature, which ye would have trampled upon as if you had been littered of bitch-wolves, not born of women."

While this passed, the leaders on either side met in the neutral space betwixt the forces of either, and the Earl thus accosted the English Warden: "Is this fair or honest usage, Sir John, or for whom do you hold the Earl of Morton and myself, that you ride in Scotland with arrayed banner, fight, slay, and make prisoners at your own pleasure? Is it well done, think you, to spoil our land and shed our blood, after the many proofs we have given to your mistress of our devotion to her will, saving always the allegiance due to our own sovereign?"

"My Lord of Moray," answered Foster, "all the world knows you to be a man of quick ingine and deep wisdom, and these several weeks have you held me in hand with promising to arrest my sovereign mistress's rebel, this Piercie Shafton of Wilverton, and you have never kept your word, alleging turmoils in the west, and I wot not what other causes of hindrance. Now, since he has had the insolence to return hither, and live openly within ten miles of England, I could no longer, in plain duty to my mistress and queen, tarry upon your successive delays, and therefore I have used her force to take her rebel, by the strong hand, wherever I can find him."

"And is Piercie Shafton in your hands then?" said the Earl of Moray. "Be aware that I may not, without my own great shame, suffer you to remove him hence without doing battle."

"Will you, Lord Earl, after all the advantages you have received at the hands of the Queen of England, do battle in the cause of her rebel?" said Sir John Foster.

"Not so, Sir John," answered the Earl, "but I will fight to the death in defence of the liberties of our free kingdom of Scotland."

"By my faith," said Sir John Foster, "I am well content—my sword is not blunted with all it has done yet this day."

"By my honour, Sir John," said Sir George Heron of Chipchase, "there is but little reason we should fight these Scottish Lords e'en now, for I hold with old Stawarth Bolton, and believe yonder prisoner to be no more Piercie Shafton than it is the Earl of Northumberland; and you were but ill advised to break the peace betwixt the countries for a prisoner of less consequence."

"Sir George," replied Foster, "I have often heard you herons are afraid of hawks—nay, lay not hand on sword, man, I did but jest; and for this prisoner, let him be brought up hither, that we may see who or what he is—always under assurance, my Lords," he continued, addressing the Scots.

"Upon our word and honour," said Morton, "we will offer no violence."

The laugh turned against Sir John Foster considerably, when the prisoner, being brought up, proved not only a different person from Sir Piercie Shafton, but a female in man's attire.

"Pluck the mantle from the quean's face and cast her to the horse-boys," said Foster; "she has kept such company ere now, I warrant."

Even Moray was moved to laughter, no common thing with him, at the disappointment of the English Warden; but he would not permit any violence to be offered to the fair Molinara, who had thus a second time, at her own personal risk, rescued Sir Piercie Shafton, by taking his person upon her during the flight.

"You have already done more mischief than you can well answer," said the Earl, "and it were dishonour to me should I permit you to harm a hair of this young woman's head."

"My lord," said Morton, "if Sir John will ride apart with me but for one moment, I will shew him such reasons as shall make him content to depart, and to refer this unhappy day's work to the judgment of the Commissioners nominated to try offences on the Border."

He then led Sir John Foster aside, and spoke to him in this manner: —"Sir John Foster, I much marvel that a man who knows your Queen

Elizabeth as you do, should not know that if you hope any thing from her, it must be for doing her useful service, not for involving her in quarrels with her neighbours without any advantage. Sir Knight, I will speak frankly what I know to be true. Had you seized the true Piercie Shafton by this ill-advised inroad; and had your deed threatened, as most like it might, a breach between the countries, your politic Princess and her politic council would rather have disgraced Sir John Foster than entered into war in his behalf. But now that you have stricken short of your aim, you may rely on it you will have little thanks for carrying the matter farther. I will work thus far on the Earl of Moray, that he will undertake to dismiss Sir Piercie Shafton from the realm of Scotland. Be well advised, and let the matter now pass off— You will gain nothing by further violence, for if we fight, you, as the fewer and the weaker through your former action, will needs have the worse."

Sir John Foster listened with his head declining on his breast-plate.

"It is a cursed chance," he said, "and I shall have little thanks for my day's work."

He then rode up to Moray, and said, that in deference to his Lordship's presence and that of my Lord of Morton, he had come to the resolution of withdrawing himself, with his power, without farther proceedings.

"Stop there, Sir John Foster," said Moray, "I cannot permit you to retire in safety, unless you leave some one who may be surety to Scotland, that the injuries you have at present done us may be fully accounted for—you will reflect, that by permitting your retreat, I become accountable to my Sovereign, who will demand a reckoning of me for the blood of her subjects, if I suffer those who shed it to depart so easily."

"It shall never be told in England," said the Warden, "that John Foster gave pledges like a subdued man, and that on the very field on which he stands victorious.—But," he added, after a moment's pause, "if Stawarth Bolton wills to abide with you on his own free choice, I will say nothing against it; and, as I bethink me, it were better he should stay to see the dismissal of this same Piercie Shafton."

"I receive him as your hostage, nevertheless, and shall treat him as such," said the Earl of Moray. But Foster, turning away as if to give directions to Bolton and his men, affected not to hear this observation.

"There rides a faithful servant of his most beautiful and Sovereign Lady," said Moray aside to Morton. "Happy man! he knows not whether the execution of her commands may not cost him his head; and yet he is most certain that to leave them unexecuted will bring disgrace and death without reprieve. Happy are they who are not only subjected to the caprices of Dame Fortune, but held bound to account and be responsible for them, and that to a Sovereign as moody and fickle as her humorous ladyship herself!"

"We also have a female Sovereign, my lord," said Morton.

"We have so, Douglas," said the Earl, with a suppressed sigh; "but it remains to be seen how long a female hand can hold the reins of power, in a realm so wild as ours. We will now go on to Saint Mary's, and see ourselves after the state of that House.—Glendinning, look to that woman and protect her.—What the fiend, man, hast thou got in thine arms?—an infant, as I live—where couldest thou find such a charge, at such a place and moment?"

Halbert Glendinning briefly told the story. The Earl rode forwards to the place where the body of Julian Avenel lay, with his unhappy companion's arms wrapt around him, like the trunk of an uprooted oak borne down by the tempest with all its ivy garlands. Both were cold-dead. Moray was touched in an unwonted degree, remembering, perhaps, his own birth. "What have they to answer for, Douglas," he said, "who thus abuse the sweetest gifts of affection?"

The Earl of Morton, unhappy in his marriage, was a libertine in his amours.

"You must ask that question of Henry Warden, my lord, or of John Knox—I am but a wild counsellor in woman's matters."

"Forward to Saint Mary's," said the Earl; "pass the word on—Glendinning, give the infant to this same female cavalier, and let it be taken charge of. Let no dishonour be done to the dead bodies, and call on the country to bury or remove them. Forward, I say, my masters."

Chapter Twelve

Gone to be married?—Gone to swear a peace!
King John

THE NEWS of the lost battle, so quickly carried by the fugitives to the village and convent, had spread the greatest alarm through the inhabitants. The Sacristan and other Monks counselled flight; the Treasurer recommended that the church-plate should be offered as a tribute to bribe the English officer. The Abbot alone was unmoved and undaunted.

"My brethren," he said, "since God has not given our people victory in the combat, it must be because he requires of us, his spiritual soldiers, to fight the good fight of martyrdom, a conflict in which nothing but our own faint-hearted cowardice can make us fail of victory. Let us assume, then, the armour of faith, and prepare, if it be necessary, to die under the ruins of these shrines, to the service of which we have devoted ourselves. Highly honoured are we all in this distinguished summons, from our dear brother Nicolas, whose grey hairs have been preserved until they should be surrounded by the crown of martyrdom, down to my beloved son Edward, who, arriving at the vineyard at the latest hour of the day, is yet admitted to share its toils with those who have laboured from the morning. Be of good courage, my children. I dare not, like my sainted predecessors, promise to you that you shall be preserved by miracle—I and you are always unworthy of that especial interposition, which, in earlier times, turned the sword of sacrilege against the bosom of tyrants by whom it was wielded, daunted the hardened hearts of heretics with prodigies, and called down hosts of angels to defend the shrine of God and of the Virgin. Yet, by Heavenly aid, you shall this day see that your Father and Abbot will not disgrace the mitre which sits upon his brow. Go to your cells, my children, and exercise your private devotions. Array yourselves also in alb and cope, as for our most solemn festivals, and be ready, when the tolling of the large bell announces the approach of the enemy, to march forth to meet them in solemn procession. Let the church be opened to afford such refuge as it may to those of our vassals, who, from their exertion in this day's unhappy battle, or other cause, are particularly apprehensive of the rage of the enemy. Tell Sir Piercie Shafton, if he has escaped the fight"——

"I am here, most venerable Abbot," replied Sir Piercie; "and if it so seemeth meet to you, I will presently assemble such of the men as have escaped this escaramouche, and will renew the resistance, even unto the death. Certes, you will learn from all that I did my part in this unhappy matter. Had it pleased Julian Avenel to have attended to my counsel, specially in somewhat withdrawing of his main battle, even as you may have marked the heron eschew the stoop of the falcon, receiving him rather upon his beak than upon his wing, affairs, as I do conceive, might have had a different face, and we might then, in more bellicous manner, have maintained that affray. Nevertheless, I would not be understood to speak any thing in disregard of Julian Avenel, whom I saw fall fighting manfully with his face to his enemy, which hath banished from my memory the unseemly term of "meddling coxcomb," with which it pleased him something rashly to qualify my advice, and for which, had it pleased Heaven and the saints to have prolonged the life of that excellent person, I had it bound upon my soul to have put him to death with my own hand."

"Sir Piercie," said the Abbot, at length interrupting, "our time allows brief leisure to speak what might have been."

"You are right, most venerable Lord and Father," replied the incorrigible Euphuist; "the præterite, as grammarians have it, concerns frail mortality less than the future mood, and indeed our cogitations respect chiefly the present. In a word, I am willing to head all who will follow me, and offer such opposition as manhood and mortality may permit, to the advance of these English, though they be my own countrymen—and be assured, Piercie Shafton will measure his length, being five feet ten inches, on the ground as he stands, rather than give two yards in retreat, according to the usual motion in which we retrograde."

"I thank you, Sir Knight, and I doubt not that you would make your words good. But it is not the will of Heaven that carnal weapons should rescue us. We are called to endure, not to resist; and to waste the blood of our innocent commons in vain opposition becomes not men of my profession; they have my commands to resign the sword and spear,—God and our Lady have not blessed our banner."

"Bethink you, reverend lord," said Piercie Shafton, very eagerly, "ere you resign the defence that is in your power—there are many posts near the entry of this village, where brave men might live or die to the advantage; and I have this additional motive to make defence,— the safety, namely, of a fair friend, who, I hope, hath escaped the hands of the heretics."

"I understand you, Sir Piercie—you mean the daughter of our Convent's miller?"

"Reverend my lord," said Sir Piercie, not without hesitation, "the fair Mysinda is, as may be in some sort alleged, the daughter of one who mechanically prepareth corn to be manipulated into bread, without which we could not exist, and which is therefore a trade in itself honourable, nay necessary. Nevertheless, if the purest sentiments of a generous mind, streaming forth like the rays of the sun reflected by a diamond, may ennoble one, who is in some sort the daughter of a molendinary mechanic"——

"I have no time for all this, Sir Knight," said the Abbot; "be it enough to answer, that with our will we war no longer with carnal weapons. We of the spirituality will teach you of the temporality how to die in cold blood, our hands not clenched for resistance, but folded for prayer—our minds not filled with jealous hatred, but with Christian meekness and forgiveness—our ears not deafened nor our senses confused by the sound of clamorous instruments of war; but, on the contrary, our voices composed to Haleluiah, Kyrie-Eleison, and Salve Regina, and our blood temperate and cold, as those who think upon reconciling themselves with God, not of avenging themselves on their fellow-mortals."

"Lord Abbot," said Sir Piercie, "this is all nothing to the fate of my

Molinara, whom, I beseech you to observe, I will not abandon, while golden hilt and steel blade bide together on my falchion. I commanded her not to follow us to the field, and yet methought I saw her in her page's attire amongst the rear of the combatants."

"You must seek elsewhere for the person in whose fate you are so deeply interested," said the Abbot; "and at present I will pray of your knighthood to enquire concerning her at the church, in which all our more defenceless vassals have taken refuge. It is my advice to you, that you also abide by the horns of the altar; and Sir Piercie Shafton," he added, "be of one thing secure, that if you come to harm, it will involve the whole of this brotherhood; for never, I trust, will the meanest of us buy safety at the expence of surrendering a friend or a guest. Leave us, my son, and may God be your aid."

When Sir Piercie Shafton had departed, and the Abbot was about to betake himself to his own cell, he was surprised by an unknown person anxiously requiring a conference, who, being admitted, proved to be no other than Henry Warden. The Abbot started as he entered, and exclaimed, angrily,—"Ha! are the few hours that fate allows him who may last wear the mitre of this house, not to be excused from the intrusion of heresy? Doest thou come," he said, "to enjoy the hopes which fate holds out to thy demented and accursed sect, to see the besom of destruction sweep away the pride of old religion—to deface our shrines—to mutilate and lay waste the bodies of our benefactors, as well as their sepulchres—to destroy the pinnacles and carved work of God's house, and Our Lady's?"

"Peace, William Allan!" said the Protestant preacher, with dignified composure; "for none of these purposes do I come. I would have these stately shrines deprived of the idols which, no longer simply regarded as the effigies of the good and the wise, have become the objects of foul idolatry. I would otherwise have its ornaments subsist, unless as they are, or may be, a snare to the souls of men; and especially do I condemn those ravages which have been made by the heady fury of the people, stung into zeal against will-worship by bloody persecution. Against such wanton devastation I lift my testimony."

"Idle that thou art!" said the Abbot Eustace, interrupting him; "what signifies the pretext under which thou doest despoil the house of God? and why at this present emergence wilt thou insult the master of it by thy ill-omened presence?"

"Thou art unjust, William Allan," said Warden; "but I am not the less settled in my resolution. Thou hast protected me sometime since at the hazard of thy rank, and what I know thou holdest yet dearer, at the risk of thy reputation with thine own sect. Our party is now uppermost, and, believe me, I have come down the valley, in which thou didst quarter me for sequestration's sake, simply with the wish to keep my engagement to thee."

"Ay," answered the Abbot, "and it may be, that my listening to that worldly and infirm compassion which pleaded with me for thy life, is now avenged by this impending judgment. Heaven hath smitten, it may be, the erring shepherd, and scattered the flock."

"Think better of the Divine judgments," said Warden. "Not for thy sins, which are those of thy blinded education and circumstances; not for thy sins, William Allan, art thou stricken, but for the accumulated guilt which thy mis-named church hath accumulated on her head, and those of her votaries, by the errors and corruptions of ages."

"Now, by my sure belief in the Rock of Peter," said the Abbot, "thou doest re-kindle the last spark of human indignation for which my bosom has fuel—I thought I might not again have felt the impulse of earthly passion, and it is thy voice which once more calls me to an expression of human anger!—thou that comest to insult me in my hour of sorrow, with these blasphemous accusations of that church which hath kept the light of Christianity alive from the times of the Apostles until now."

"From the times of the Apostles?" said the preacher eagerly. "*Negatur, Gulielme Allan*—the primitive church differed as much from that of Rome, as light from darkness, which, did time permit, I should speedily prove. And worse doest thou judge, in saying I come to insult thee in thy hour of affliction, being here, God wot, with the Christian wish of fulfilling an engagement I had made to my host, and of rendering myself to thy will while thou hadst yet power to exercise aught upon me, and if it might so be, to mitigate in thy behalf the rage of the victors whom God hath sent as a scourge to thy obstinacy."

"I will none of thy intercession," said the Abbot, proudly; "the dignity to which the church has exalted me, never should have swelled my bosom more proudly in the time of the highest prosperity, than it doth at this crisis—I ask nothing of thee, but the assurance that my lenity to thee hath been the means of perverting no soul to Satan, that I have not given to the wolf any of the stray lambs whom the Great Shepherd of souls had entrusted to my charge."

"William Allan," answered the protestant, "I will be sincere with thee. What I promised I have kept—I have withheld my voice from speaking even good things. But it has pleased Heaven to call the maiden Mary Avenel to a better sense of faith than thou and all the disciples of Rome can teach. Her I have aided with my humble power —I have extricated her from the machinations of evil spirits, to which she and her house were exposed during the blindness of their Romish superstition, and, praise be to my Master, I have not reason to fear she will again be caught in thy snares."

"Wretched man!" said the Abbot, unable to suppress his rising indignation, "is it to the Abbot of Saint Mary's that you boast having won the soul of a dweller in Our Lady's Halidome to the paths of foul error and damning heresy?—Thou doest urge me, Wellwood, beyond what it becomes me to bear, and movest me to employ the few moments of power I may yet possess, in removing from the face of the earth one, whose qualities, given by God, have been so utterly perverted as thine to the service of Satan."

"Do thy pleasure," said the preacher; "thy vain wrath shall not prevent my doing my duty to advantage thee, where it may be done without neglecting my higher call. I go to the Earl of Moray."

Their conference, which was advancing fast into bitter disputation, was here interrupted by the deep and sullen toll of the largest and heaviest bell of the Convent, a sound famous in the chronicles of the Community, for dispelling of tempests, and putting to flight demons, but which now only announced danger, without affording any means of warding against it. Hastily repeating his orders, that all the brethren should attend in the choir, arrayed for solemn procession, the Abbot ascended to the battlements of the lofty Monastery, by his own private stair-case, and there met the Sacristan, who had been in the act of directing the tolling of the huge bell, which fell under his duty.

"It is the last time I shall discharge mine office, most venerable Father and Lord," said he to the Abbot, "for yonder come the Philistines; but I would not that the large bell of Saint Mary's should sound for the last time, otherwise than in true and full tone—I have been a sinful man for one of our holy profession," added he, looking upward, "yet may I presume to say, not a bell hath sounded out of tune from the tower of this house while Father Philip had the superintendence of the chime and the belfry."

The Abbot, without reply, cast his eyes towards the path, or road, which, winding around the mountain, descends upon Kennaquhair from the southward. He beheld at a distance a cloud of dust, and heard the neighing of many horses, while the occasional sparkle of the long line of spears, as they came downwards into the valley, announced that the band came thither in arms.

"Shame on my weakness!" said Abbot Eustace, dashing the tears from his eyes; "my sight is too much dimmed to observe their motions —look, my son Edward," for his favourite novice had again joined him, "and tell me what ensigns they bear."

"They are Scottish men, when all is done," exclaimed Edward—"I see the white crosses—it may be the Western Borderers, or Fernie-herst and his clan."

"Look at the banner," said the Abbot, "tell me what are the blaz-onries?"

"The arms of Scotland," said Edward, "the lion and its tressure—quartered, as I think, with three cushions—can it be the royal stand-ard?"

"Alas! no," said the Abbot, "it is that of the Earl of Moray—he hath assumed with his new conquest the badge of the valiant Randolph, and hath dropped from his hereditary coat the bend which indicates his own base birth—would to God he may not have blotted it also from his memory!"

"At least, my father," said Edward, "he will secure us from the violence of the southron."

"Ay, my son—as the shepherd secures a silly lamb from the wolf, which he destines in due time to his own banquet. Oh, my son, evil days are on us—a breach has been made in the walls of our sanctuary —thy brother hath fallen from the faith—such news brought my last secret intelligence—Moray has already spoken of rewarding his ser-vices with the hand of Mary Avenel."

"Of Mary Avenel!" said the novice, tottering towards and grasping hold of one of the carved pinnacles which adorned the proud battle-ment.

"Ay, of Mary Avenel, my son, who has also abjured the faith of her fathers. Weep not, my Edward, weep not, my beloved son! or weep for their apostacy, and not for their union—Bless God, my child, who hath called thee to himself, out of the tents of wickedness; but for the grace of Our Lady and Saint Benedict, thou also had been a cast-away."

"I endeavour, my father," said Edward, "I endeavour to forget—but it has been the thought of all my former life—Moray dare not forward a match so unequal in birth."

"He dares do what suits his purpose—The castle of Avenel is strong, and needs a good castellan, devoted to his service—for the difference of their birth, he will mind it no more than he would mind defacing the natural regularity of the ground, were it necessary he should track upon it military lines and entrenchments. But do not droop for that—Awaken thy soul within thee, my son. Think you part with a vain vision, an idle dream, nursed in solitude and inaction.—I weep not—yet what am I now like to lose?—Look round this fair fabric, gorgeous beyond the skill and wealth of our degenerate days— Look at these towers, where saints have dwelt, and where heroes have been buried—think that I, so briefly called to preside over the pious flock, which has dwelt here since the first light of Christianity, may be this day written down the last father of this holy community—Come, let us descend, and meet our fate—I see them approach near to the village."

The Abbot descended, the novice cast a glance around him; yet the sense of the danger impending over the stately structure, with which he was now united, was unable to banish the recollection of Mary Avenel.—"His brother's bride!"—he pulled the cowl over his face, and followed his Superior.

The whole bells of the Abbey now added their peal to the death-toll of the largest which had so long sounded. The Monks wept and prayed as they got themselves into the order of their procession for the last time, as seemed but too probable.

"It is well our Father Boniface hath retired to the inland," said Father Philip, "he could never have put over this day, it would have broken his heart."

"God be with the soul of Abbot Ingelram!" said old Father Nicolas, "there were no such doings in his days—they say we are to be put forth of the cloisters, and how I am to live any where else than I have lived for these seventy years, I wot not—the best is, that I have not long to live any where."

A few moments after this the great gate of the Abbey was flung open, and the procession moved slowly forward from beneath its huge and richly adorned gate-way.—Cross and banner, pix and chalice, shrines containing reliques, and censers steaming with incense, preceded and were intermingled with the long and solemn array of the brotherhood, in their long black gowns and cowls, with their white scapularies hanging over them, the various officers of the convent each displaying his proper badge of office. In the centre of the procession came the Abbot, surrounded and supported by his chief assistants. He was dressed in his habit of high solemnity, and appeared as much unconcerned as if he had been taking his usual part in some ordinary ceremony. After him came the inferior persons of the convent; the novices in their albs or white dresses, and the lay-brethren distinguished by their beards, which were seldom worn by the Fathers. Women and children, mixed with a few men, came in the rear, bewailing the apprehended desolation of their ancient sanctuary. They moved, however, in order, and restrained the marks of their sorrow to a low wailing sound, which rather mingled with than interrupted the measured chaunt of the monks.

In this order the procession entered the market-place of the little village of Kennaquhair, which was then, as now, distinguished by an ancient cross of curious workmanship, the gift of some former monarch of Scotland. Close by the cross, of much greater antiquity, and scarcely less honoured, was an immensely large oak-tree, which perhaps had witnessed the worship of the Druids, ere the stately Monastery to which it adjoined had raised its spires in honour of the Christian faith. Like the Bentang-tree of the African villages, or the Plaistow-oak mentioned in White's Natural History of Selbourne, this tree was the rendezvous of the villagers, and regarded with peculiar veneration, a feeling common to most nations, and which perhaps may be traced up to the remote period when patriarchs feasted angels under the oak at Mamre.

The Monks formed themselves each in their due place around the cross, while under the ruins of the aged tree crowded the old and the feeble, with others who felt the common alarm. When they had thus arranged themselves, there was a deep and solemn pause. The Monks stilled their chaunt, the lay populace hushed their lamentation, and all awaited in terror and silence the arrival of those heretical forces, whom they had been so long taught to regard with terror.

A distant trampling was at length heard, and the glance of spears was seen to shine through the trees above the village. The sounds increased, and became more thick, one close continuous rushing sound, in which the tread of hoofs was mingled with the ringing of armour. The horsemen soon appeared at the principal entrance which leads into the irregular square or market-place which forms the centre of the village. They entered two by two, slowly, and in the greatest order. The van continued to move on, riding round the open space, until they had attained the utmost point, and then turning their horses' heads to the street, stood fast; their companions followed in the same order, until the whole market-place was closely surrounded with soldiers, and the files who followed, making the same manœuvre, formed an inner line within those who had first arrived, until the place was begirt with a quadruple file of horsemen closely drawn up. There was now a pause, of which the Abbot availed himself, by commanding the brotherhood to raise the solemn chaunt *De profundis clamavi*. He looked around the armed ranks, to see what impression the solemn sounds made on them. All were silent, but the brows of some had an expression of contempt, and almost all the rest bore a look of indifference; their line had been too long taken to permit past feelings of enthusiasm to be anew awakened by a procession or by a hymn.

"Their hearts are hardened," said the Abbot to himself in dejection, but not in despair; "it remains to see whether those of their leaders are equally obdured."

The leaders, in the mean while, were advancing slowly, and Moray, with Morton, rode in deep conversation before a chosen band of their most distinguished followers, amongst whom came Halbert Glendinning. But the preacher Henry Warden, who, upon leaving the Monastery, had instantly joined them, was the only person admitted to their conference.

"You are determined then," said Morton to Moray, "to give the heiress of Avenel, with all her pretensions, to this nameless and obscure young man."

"Hath not Warden told you," said Moray, "that they have been bred together, and are lovers from their youth upward?"

"And that they are both," said Warden, "by means which may be almost termed miraculous, rescued from the delusions of Rome, and brought within the pale of the true church. My residence at Glendearg hath made me well acquainted with these things. Ill would it beseem my habit and my calling, to thrust myself into match-making and giving in marriage, but worse were it in me to see your Lordships do needless wrong to the feelings which are proper to our nature, and, being indulged honestly and under the restraints of religion, become a pledge of domestic quiet here, and future happiness in a better world. I say, that you will do ill to rend those ties asunder, and to give this maiden to this kinsman of Lord Morton, though Lord Morton's kinsman he be."

"These are fair reasons, my Lord of Moray," said Morton, "why you should refuse me so simple a boon as to bestow this silly damsel upon young Bennygask. Speak out plainly, my lord; say you would rather see the castle of Avenel in the hands of one who owes his name and existence solely to your favour, than in the power of a Douglas, and of my kinsman."

"My Lord of Morton," said Moray, "I have done nothing in this matter which should aggrieve you. This young man Glendinning has done me good service, and may do me more. My promise was in some degree passed to him, and that while Julian Avenel was alive, when aught beside the maiden's lily hand would have been hard to come by; whereas you never thought of such an alliance for your kinsman, till you saw Julian lie dead yonder on the field, and knew his land to be a waif free to the first who could seize it. Come, come, my lord, you do less than justice to your gallant kinsman, in wishing him a bride bred up under the milk-pail; for this girl is a peasant wench in all but the accident of birth. I thought you had more deep respect for the honour of the Douglasses."

"The honour of the Douglasses is safe in my keeping," answered Morton haughtily; "that of other ancient families may suffer as well as the name of Avenel, if rustics are to be matched with the blood of our ancient barons."

"This is but idle talking," answered Lord Moray; "in times like these we must look to men, and not to pedigrees. Hay was but a rustic before the battle of Loncarty—the bloody yoke actually dragged the plough ere it was blazoned on a crest by the herald. Times of action make princes into peasants, and boors into barons. All families have sprung from some one mean man; and it is well if they have never degenerated from his virtue who raised them first from obscurity."

"My Lord of Moray will please to except the House of Douglas," said Morton haughtily; "men have seen it in the tree, but never in the sapling—have seen it in the stream, but never in the fountain. In the earliest of our Scottish annals, the Black Douglas was powerful and distinguished as now."

"I bend to the honours of the house of Douglas," said Moray, somewhat ironically; "I am conscious we of the Royal House have little right to compete with them in dignity—what though we have worn crowns and carried sceptres for a few generations, if our genealogy moves no further back than to the humble *Alanus Dapifer!*"

Morton's cheek reddened as he was about to reply; but Henry Warden availed himself of the liberty which the Protestant clergy long possessed, and exerted it to interrupt a discussion which was becoming too eager and personal to be friendly.

"My lords," he said, "I must be bold in discharging the duty of my Master—it is shame and scandal to hear two nobles, whose hands have been so forward in the work of reformation, fall into discord about such vain follies as now occupy your thoughts. Bethink how long you have thought with one mind, seen with one eye, heard with one ear, confirmed by your union the congregation of the Church, appalled by your joint authority the congregation of Anti-christ; and will you now fall into discord, about an old decayed castle and a few barren hills, about the loves and likings of a humble spearman and a damsel bred in the same obscurity, or about the still vainer questions of idle genealogy?"

"The good man hath right, noble Douglas," said Moray, reaching him his hand, "our union is too essential to the good cause to be broken off upon such idle terms of dissention. I am fixed to gratify Glendinning in this matter—my promise is passed. The wars, in which I have had my share, have made many a family miserable; I will at least try if I may not make one happy. There are maids and manors enow in Scotland—I promise you, my noble ally, that young Benny-gask shall be richly wived."

"My lord," said Warden, "you speak nobly, and like a Christian. Alas! this is a land of hatred and bloodshed—let us not chace from thence the few traces that remain of gentle and domestic love.—And be not too eager for wealth to thy noble kinsman, my Lord of Morton, seeing contentment in the marriage-state no way depends on it."

"If you allude to my family misfortune," said Morton, whose Countess, wedded by him for her estate and honours, was insane in her mind, "the habit you wear, and the liberty, or rather licence, of your profession, protects you from my resentment."

"Alas! my lord," replied Warden, "how quick and sensitive is our self-love! When, pressing forward in our high calling, we point out the errors of the Sovereign, who praises our boldness more than the noble Morton? But touch we upon his own sore, which most needs lancing, and he shrinks from the faithful chirurgeon in fear and impatient anger."

"Enough of this, good and reverend sir," said Moray; "you transgress the prudence yourself recommended even now.—We are now close upon the village, and the proud Abbot is come forth at the head of his hive. Thou hast pleaded well for him, Warden, otherwise I had taken this occasion to pull down the nest, and chase away the rooks."

"Nay, but do not so," said Warden; "this William Allan, whom they call the Abbot Eustatius, is a man whose misfortunes would more prejudice our cause than his prosperity. You cannot inflict more than he will endure; and the more that he is made to bear, the higher will be the influence of his talents and his courage. In his conventual throne, he will be but coldly looked on—disliked it may be and envied. But let him travel through the land, an oppressed and impoverished man, and his patience, his eloquence, and learning, will win more hearts from the good cause, than all the mitred abbots of Scotland have been able to make prey of during the last hundred years."

"Tush! tush! man," said Morton, "the revenues of the Halidome will bring more men, spears, and horses into the field in one day, than his preaching in a whole lifetime. These are not the days of Peter the Hermit, when Monks could march armies from England to Jerusalem; but gold and good deeds will still do as much or more than ever. Had Julian Avenel had but a score or two more men this morning, Sir John Foster had not missed a worse welcome. I say, confiscating the monk's revenues is drawing his fang-teeth."

"We will surely lay him under contribution," said Moray, "and, moreover, if he desires to remain in his Abbey, he will do well to produce Piercie Shafton."

As he thus spoke, they entered the market-place, distinguished by their complete armour and their lofty plumes, as well as by the number of followers bearing their colours and badges. Both these powerful nobles, but more especially Moray, so nearly allied to the crown, had at that time a retinue and household not much inferior to that of

Scottish royalty. As they advanced into the market-place, a pursuivant, pressing forward from their train, addressed the Monks in these words:—"The Abbot of Saint Mary's is commanded to appear before the Earl of Moray."

"The Abbot of Saint Mary's," said Eustace, "is in the patrimony of his Convent superior to every temporal lord. Let the Earl of Moray, if he seeks him, come himself to his presence."

On receiving this answer Moray smiled scornfully, and, dismounting from his lofty saddle, he advanced, accompanied by Morton, and followed by others, to the body of Monks assembled around the cross. There was an appearance of shrinking among them at the approach of the heretic lord, so dreaded and so powerful. But the Abbot casting on them a glance of rebuke and encouragement, stepped forth from their ranks like a valiant leader, when he sees that his personal valour must be displayed to revive the drooping courage of his followers. "Lord James Stuart," he said, "or Earl of Moray, if that be thy title, I, Eustatius, Abbot of Saint Mary's, demand by what right you have filled our peaceful village, and surrounded our brethren with these bands of armed men? If hospitality is sought, we have never refused it to courteous asking—if violence be meant against peaceful churchmen, let us know at once the pretext and the object."

"Sir Abbot," said Moray, "your language would better have become another age, and a presence inferior to ours. We come not here to reply to your interrogations, but to demand of you why you have broken the peace, collecting your vassals in arms, and convocating the Queen's lieges, whereby many men have been slain, and much trouble, perchance breach of amity with England, is likely to arise?"

"*Lupus in fabula*," answered the Abbot scornfully. "The wolf accused the sheep of muddying the stream when he drank in it above her—but it served as a pretext for devouring her. Convocate the Queen's lieges? I did so to defend the Queen's land against foreigners. I did but my duty; and I regret I had not the means to do it more effectually."

"And was it also a part of your duty to receive and harbour the Queen of England's rebel and traitor; and to inflame a war betwixt England and Scotland?" said Moray.

"In my younger days, my lord," answered the Abbot, with the same intrepidity, "a war with England was no such dreaded matter; and not merely a mitred abbot, bound by his rule to shew hospitality and afford sanctuary to all, but the poorest Scottish peasant, would have been ashamed to have pleaded fear of the Queen of England, as the reason for shutting his door against a persecuted exile. But in those olden days, the English seldom saw the face of a Scottish nobleman, save through the bars of his visor."

"Monk!" said the Earl of Morton, sternly, "this insolence will little avail thee; the days are gone by when Rome's priests were permitted to brave noblemen with impunity; give us up this Piercie Shafton, or by my father's crest I will set thy Abbey in a bright flame!"

"And if thou dost, Lord of Morton, its ruins will tumble above the tombs of thine own ancestors. Be the issue as God wills, the Abbot of Saint Mary's gives up no one whom he hath promised to protect."

"Abbot!" said Moray, "bethink thee ere we are driven to deal roughly—the hands of these men," he said, pointing to the soldiers, "will make wild work among shrines and cells, if we are compelled to undertake a search for this Englishman."

"Ye shall not need," said a voice from the crowd; and, advancing gracefully before the Earls, the Euphuist flung from him the mantle in which he was muffled. "Via the cloud that shadowed Shafton!" said he; "behold, my Lords, the Knight of Wilverton, who spares you the guilt of violence and sacrilege."

"I protest before God and man against any infraction of the privileges of this house," said the Abbot, "by seizing upon the person of this noble knight. If there be yet spirit in a Scottish Parliament, we will make you hear of this elsewhere, my lords!"

"Spare your threats," said Moray, "it may be, my purpose with Sir Piercie Shafton is not such as thou doest suppose—Attach him, pursuivant, as our prisoner, rescue or no rescue."

"I yield myself," said the Euphuist, "reserving my right to defy my Lord of Moray and my Lord of Morton to single duel, even as one gentleman may demand satisfaction of another."

"You shall not want those who will answer your challenge, Sir Knight," replied Morton, "without aspiring to men above thine own degree."

"And where am I to find these superlative champions," said the English knight, "whose blood runs more pure than that of Piercie Shafton?"

"Here is a flight for you, my lord!" said Moray.

"As ever was flown by wild-goose," said Stawarth Bolton, who had now approached to the front of the party.

"Who dared to say that word?" said the Euphuist, his face crimson with rage.

"Tut! man," said Bolton, "make the best of it, thy mother's father was but a tailor, old Cross-stitch of Holderness—Why, what! because thou art a misproud bird, and despisest thine own natural lineage, and rufflest in unpaid silks and velvets, and keepst company with gallants and cutters, must we lose our memory for that? Thy mother, Moll Cross-stitch, was the prettiest wench in these parts—she was wedded by Wild Shafton of Wilverton, who, men say, was a-kin to the Piercie on the wrong side of the blanket."

"Help the knight to some strong waters," said Morton; "he hath fallen from such a height that he is stunned with the tumble."

In fact, Sir Piercie Shafton looked like a man stricken by a thunderbolt, while, notwithstanding the seriousness of the scene hitherto, no one of the presence, not even the Abbot himself, could refrain from laughing at the rueful and mortified expression of his face.

"Laugh on," he said at length, "laugh on, my masters—it is not for me to be offended—yet would I know full fain from that squire who is laughing with the loudest, how he had discovered this unhappy blot, in an otherwise spotless lineage, and for what purpose he hath made it known?"

"*I* make it known?" said Halbert Glendinning in astonishment, for to him this pathetic appeal was made, "I never heard the thing till this moment."

"Why, did not that old rude soldier learn it from thee?" said the Knight, in increasing amazement.

"Not I, by Heaven," said Bolton; "I never saw the youth in my life before."

"But you *have* seen him ere now, my worthy master," said Dame Glendinning, bursting in her turn from the crowd. "My son, this is Stawarth Bolton, to whom we owe life, and the means of preserving it—if he be prisoner, as seems most likely, use thine interest with these noble lords to be kind to the widow's friend."

"What, my Dame of the Glen," said Bolton, "thy brow is more withered, as well as mine, since we met last, but thy tongue holds the touch better than my arm. This boy of thine gave me the foil sorely this morning. The brown varlet has turned as stout a trooper as I prophesied; and where is white-head?"

"Alas!" said the mother, looking down, "Edward has taken orders, and become a monk of this Abbey."

"A monk and a soldier!—evil trades both, my good dame—better have made one a good master fashioner, like old Cross-stitch of Holderness. I sighed when I envied you the two bonnie children, but I sigh not now to call either the monk or the soldier mine own. The soldier dies in the field, the monk scarce lives in the cloister."

"My dearest mother," said Halbert, "where is Edward, can I not speak with him?"

"He has just left us for the present," said Father Philip, "upon a message from the Lord Abbot."

"And Mary, my dearest mother," said Halbert.—Mary Avenel was not far distant, and the three were soon withdrawn from the crowd to hear and relate their various chances of fortune.

While the subordinate personages thus disposed of themselves, the Abbot held serious discussion with the two Earls, and, partly yielding to their demands, partly defending himself with skill and eloquence, was enabled to make a composition for his Convent which left it provisionally in no worse situation than before. The Earls were the more reluctant to drive matters to extremity, since he protested, that if urged beyond what his conscience would comply with, he would throw the whole lands of the Monastery into the Queen of Scotland's hands, to be disposed at her pleasure. This would not have answered the views of the Earls, who were contented, for the time, with a moderate sacrifice of money and lands. Matters being so far settled, the Abbot became anxious for the fate of Sir Piercie Shafton, and implored mercy in his behalf.

"He is a coxcomb," he said, "my lords, but he is a generous, though a vain fool; and it is my firm belief you have this day done him more pain than if you had run a poniard into him."

"Run a needle you mean, Abbot," said the Earl of Morton; "by mine honour, I thought this grandson of a fashioner of doublets was descended from a crowned head at least."

"I hold with the Abbot," said Moray; "there were little honour in surrendering him to Elizabeth, but he shall be sent where he can do her no injury. Our pursuivant and Bolton shall escort him to Dunbar, and ship him off for Flanders.—But soft, here he comes, and leading a female, as I think."

"Lords and others," said the English knight with great solemnity, "make way for the Lady of Piercie Shafton—a secret which I listed not to make known, till fate, which hath betrayed what I vainly strove to conceal, makes me less desirous to hide that which I now announce to you."

"It is Mysie Happer the miller's daughter, on my life," said Tibb Tacket. "I thought the pride of these Piercies would have a fa'."

"It is indeed the lovely Mysinda," said the Knight, "whose merits towards her devoted servant deserved higher rank than he had to bestow."

"I suspect though," said Moray, "that we should not have heard of the miller's daughter being made a lady, had not the knight proved to be the grandson of a tailor."

"My Lord," said Sir Piercie Shafton, "it is poor valour to strike him that cannot smite again; and I hope you will consider what is due to a prisoner by the law of arms, and say nothing more on this odious subject. When I am once more mine own man, I will find a new road to dignity."

"*Shape* one, I presume," said the Earl of Morton.

"Nay, Douglas, you will drive him mad," said Moray; "besides, we have other matter in hand—I must see Warden wed Glendinning with Mary Avenel, and put him in possession of his wife's castle without delay. It will be best done ere our forces leave these parts."

"And I," said the Miller, "have the like grist to grind; for I hope some one of the good fathers will wed my wench with her gay bridegroom."

"It needs not," said Shafton, "the ceremonial hath been solemnly performed."

"It will not be the worse of another bolting," said the Miller; "it is always best to be sure, as I say when I chance to take multure twice from the same meal-sack."

"Stave the miller off him," said Moray, "or he will worry him dead. The Abbot, my lord, offers us the hospitality of the Convent; I move we should repair hither, Sir Piercie, and all of us. I must learn to know this Maid of Avenel—to-morrow I must act as her father—All Scotland shall see how Moray can reward a faithful servant."

Mary Avenel and her lover avoided meeting the Abbot, and took up their temporary abode in a house of the village, where next day their hands were united by the Protestant preacher, in presence of the two Earls. On the same day Piercie Shafton and his bride departed, under an escort which was to conduct him to the sea-side, and see him embark for the Low Countries. Early on the next morning the bands of the Earls were under march to the castle of Avenel, to invest the young bridegroom with the property of his wife, which was surrendered to them without opposition.

But not without those omens which seemed to mark every remarkable event which befell the fated family, did Mary take possession of the ancient castle of her forefathers. The same warlike form which had appeared more than once at Glendearg, was seen by Tibb Tacket and Martin, who returned with their young mistress to partake her altered fortunes. It glided before the cavalcade as they advanced upon the long causeway, paused at each draw-bridge, and flourished its hand, as in triumph, as it disappeared under the gloomy arch-way, which was surmounted by the insignia of the house of Avenel. The two trusty servants made their vision only known to Dame Glendinning, who, with much pride of heart, had accompanied her son to see him take his rank among the barons of the land. "O, my dear bairn!" she exclaimed, when she heard the tale; "the castle is a grand place to be sure, but I wish ye dinna a' desire to be back in the quiet braes of

Glendearg before the play be played out."

This natural reflection, springing from maternal anxiety, was soon forgotten amid the busy and pleasing task of examining and admiring the new habitation of her son.

While these affairs were passing, Edward had hidden himself and his sorrows in the paternal tower of Glendearg, where every object was full of matter for bitter reflection. The Abbot's kindness had dispatched him thither upon pretension of placing some papers belonging to the Abbey in safety and secrecy; but in reality to prevent his witnessing the triumph of his brother. Through the deserted apartments, the scene of so many bitter reflections, the unhappy youth stalked like a discontented ghost, conjuring up around him at every step new subjects for sorrow and for self-torment. Impatient, at length, of the state of irritation and agonized recollection in which he found himself, he rushed out and walked hastily up the glen, as if to shake off the load which hung upon his mind. The sun was setting when he reached the entrance of Corri-nan-shian, and the recollection of what he had seen when he last visited that haunted ravine, burst on his mind. He was in a humour, however, rather to seek out danger than to avoid it.

"I will face this mystic being," he said. "She foretold the fate which has wrapped me in this dress,—I will know whether she has ought else to tell me of a life which cannot but be miserable."

He failed not to see the White Spirit seated by her accustomed haunt, and singing in her usual low and sweet tone. While she sung she seemed to look with sorrow on her golden zone, which was now diminished to the fineness of a silken thread.

> "Fare thee well, thou Holly green!
> Thou shalt seldom now be seen,
> With all thy glittering garlands bending,
> As to greet my slow descending,
> Startling the bewilder'd hind,
> Who sees thee wave without a wind.
>
> "Farewell, Fountain! now not long
> Shalt thou murmur to my song,
> While thy crystal bubbles glancing,
> Keep the time in mystic dancing,
> Rise and swell, are burst and lost,
> Like mortal schemes by fortune crost.
>
> "The knot of fate at length is tied,
> The Churl is Lord, the Maid is Bride!
> Vainly did my magic sleight
> Send the lover from her sight;
> Wither bush, and perish well,
> Fall'n is lofty Avenel!"

The Vision seemed to weep while she sung; and the words impressed on Edward a melancholy belief, that the alliance of Mary with his brother might be fatal to them both.

———

Here terminates the First Part of the Benedictine's Manuscript. I have in vain endeavoured to ascertain the precise period of the story, as the dates cannot be exactly reconciled with those of the most accredited histories. But it is astonishing how careless the writers of Utopia are upon these important subjects. I observe that the learned Mr Laurence Templeton, in his late publication, entitled IVANHOE, has not only blessed the bed of Edward the Confessor with an off-spring unknown to history, with sundry other solecisms of the same kind, but has inverted the order of nature, and feasted his swine with acorns in the midst of summer. All that can be alleged by the warmest admirer of this author amounts to this,—that the circumstances objected to are just as true as the rest of the story; which appears to me (more especially in the matter of the acorns) to be a very imperfect defence, and that the author will do well to profit by Captain Absolute's advice to his servant, and never tell more lies than are indispensably necessary.

END OF VOLUME THIRD

ESSAY ON THE TEXT

1. THE GENESIS OF *THE MONASTERY*   2. THE COMPOSITION
OF *THE MONASTERY*: the Manuscript; from Manuscript to
First Edition   3. THE LATER EDITIONS: *Historical Romances*; the
Interleaved Set and the Magnum   4. THE PRESENT TEXT: emendations from the Manuscript [structural changes, punctuation, spelling,
verbal emendations, material omitted or added in the First Edition,
names]; emendations from later editions.

The following conventions are used in transcriptions from Scott's
manuscript: deletions are enclosed ⟨thus⟩ and insertions ↑thus↓. Editorial comments within quotations are designated by square brackets
[thus]. The same conventions are used as appropriate for indicating
variants between the printed editions.

1. THE GENESIS OF *THE MONASTERY*

In his introduction to the Magnum edition of *The Monastery*, Scott wrote
that 'It would be difficult to assign any good reason why the author of
Ivanhoe . . . should choose for the scene of his next attempt the celebrated ruins of Melrose, in the immediate neighbourhood of his own
residence',[1] and indeed *The Monastery* is not a text which can be traced
back to any obvious original source or idea. As a novel drawing on
Scott's surroundings, and revisiting some of the geographical, historical, and literary material used in his *Minstrelsy of the Scottish Border*
(1802–03), his poem *The Lay of the Last Minstrel* (1805), and his 'Essay
on Border Antiquities' (1814), *The Monastery* has a pervasive intertextual relationship with much of Scott's earlier work. The novel can be
seen not only as a 'change of system' from *Ivanhoe*, as Scott calls it in the
Magnum introduction, but also as a development of his interest in
Border history. However, *The Monastery* does mark a shift in Scott's
writing career in another very important way: he made changes to the
partnership of publishers which had held for the publication of most of
the previous Waverley Novels. The novels, printed in Edinburgh by
James Ballantyne, always had two publishers, one in Edinburgh and the
other in London. The principal publisher would manage the whole
work, and a co-publisher would advertise the novel in its own area, sell
the books at wholesale rates to bookshops and distribute them accordingly. The most common arrangement for the Waverley Novels was for
the Edinburgh firm of Constables to manage and oversee the work.
Evidence of the disruption of this arrangement comes with Scott's announcement on 2 August 1819 of his next novel to his agent, James
Ballantyne's younger brother John: 'A New Novel of the right cast—3
volumes—the subject is quite ready & very interesting—to be divided

into 3 shares—Longman to be manager'. Scott was excited by his new idea which seemed to give him scope to develop ideas about the historical novel: 'the subject is quite new. I am not afraid of working myself out—not that I should not soon do so were I to depend on my own limited invention but the range of the past and the present is at my disposal & that is inexhaustible.'[2] This seemingly straightforward proposition gives little indication of the history of mistrust and recriminations between the various parties involved in the novel's publication, or, as Scott himself put it 'the general distrust which strikes everywhere'.[3] Yet Scott's decision that the London firm of Longman and Co. should manage the novel was to colour the history of its production.

The arrangement with Longmans was not unprecedented as they had previously managed Scott's second novel, *Guy Mannering* (1815). Furthermore, Scott had used other firms in bringing out the Waverley Novels: in 1816 the first series of *Tales of My Landlord* had been published by the Edinburgh firm of Blackwoods (who managed it) and the London firm Murrays. Nevertheless, in the case of the novels leading up to *The Monastery*, the management had been in the hands of Constables, whose senior partner, Archibald Constable, had a long-standing antipathy to Longmans. Why then did Scott decide to ask Longmans to act as the managing publishers for *The Monastery*? The primary reason for this choice was that it would be financially expedient for the novel to be published in London. Scott's financial scheme turned on the exchange of bills. These, the currency in which Scott's publishing transactions were largely conducted, were promissory notes which could be sold to banks at a discount ('discounted'). The party issuing the bills would then be obliged to pay the full sum on a specified date. In practice, this meant that when contracts were signed with bills as author's profits, James or John Ballantyne would go to one of the Edinburgh banks and receive cash, the amount being less than the face value of the bill. The discount would represent the interest on what was a loan from the bank, and the bank's estimate of the risk it was taking in making the money available. In 1819 there seems to have been some rationing of this credit from the banks, with Scott referring in letters to 'ticklish times' and 'circumstances of the times . . . unfavourable' to credit transactions.[4] In Edinburgh, Constable had an immense load of discounted bills with the banks, and in late July he asked for the renewal of bills on novels already sold.[5] Meanwhile, the Ballantynes were suffering difficulties of their own, and on 1 August Scott wrote to James:

> I observe your unpleasant dilemma out of which I trust to help you. It is indeed at the unpleasant alternative of anticipating funds designed for the end of the month & beginning of next but the thing cannot be helpd. What is perhaps worst of all is the delay of the paper for Ivanhoe—had I known of it?—but this avails little now.[6]

The 'unpleasant dilemma' was a problem with cash-flow. Ballantyne's

Printing Office was producing an octavo collected edition under the title
Novels and Romances of the Author of Waverley which was a very
substantial and costly undertaking. Not enough cash was coming in: the
Printing Office was owed money by the *Edinburgh Weekly Journal* (a
newspaper edited by James himself), and their next project, *Ivanhoe*, was
held up because of a paper-shortage. Scott had been counting on the
profits from the new novel, which had been due to appear in September,
and he stated bluntly to John Ballantyne on 26 July: 'I have no spare cash
till Ivanhoe comes forth.'[7] Although his own credit appears to have
remained good, he was already committed to a sizeable additional outlay
of money for his extension of the Abbotsford estate. There was also the
matter of his eldest son Walter who had received an army commission
with all the costly clothing and equipment that this entailed. All these
commitments made it necessary for Scott to act quickly. If he had had
plans for a more leisurely successor to *Ivanhoe* these were abandoned in
favour of bringing forward his next novel and, as he wrote to John
Ballantyne on 2 August, 'adopting the plan *just now* which we thought of
for *September*'.[8] A new novel could not have been sold to Constable with
the printing of *Ivanhoe* (which he was managing) not yet completed, and
in any case Scott saw it as much more profitable to have the novel
published in London with the credit-worthy Longmans. The arrangement was that Scott would grant licences to sell the novel in the form of
three shares. A third would be distributed to Longmans, a third to the
Ballantynes, and the remaining third would be offered to Constable. In
the case of *The Monastery*, Longmans would manage the publication and
pay the author's advance, receiving bills from the other two parties. To
Scott, this represented a means of solving the cash-flow problems:
Constable and the Ballantynes would be able to have their bills discounted in London, thus clearing themselves, in Scott's words, 'of the
plague of Scotch bills just now'.[9] The primary motive, then, for
switching the management to Longmans was to alleviate the temporary
cash-flow problem. At the outset, in that letter of 2 August, Scott had
told John Ballantyne: 'it is by no means my intention to change
Constable on future occasions. I only want to give his credit a little
repose. I can never forget that he sells better than anyone.'[10]

Scott was in combative mood during the transactions over the new
novel's financial arrangements. John Ballantyne had already left Edinburgh to go to Brighton for his health, and was in London and Brighton
from 10 July to 26 August, conveniently placed to represent Scott in his
negotiations with Longmans. Letters from Scott to John record these
negotiations. In the letter of 2 August Scott estimated a profit of £4500
with an advance for himself 'of £800 at the least but £1000 will do much
better'.[11] John took this to mean an advance of £800 to £1000 on the
whole edition,[12] but Scott had intended the sum to represent an advance
on each of the three shares and he wrote again on 12 August, reminding

John sharply of his responsibilities for gaining the most favourable terms possible for the author: 'As to what you say of making advances comfortable they might be so to Messrs. Longman but they will not at all answer my purpose if less than £2400 is made forthcoming. I am pledging my time and leisure for *my own* convenience not *for theirs* & if they do not like the terms I do not desire to deal with them as it would not answer my purpose.'[13] Scott was determined to do well out of the deal and the following day (having just received a letter from John dated 10 August: such a letter would have taken three days to reach Edinburgh from London) he instructed John to negotiate for the author's profits to be half the total, and to secure half of this sum in advance in the form of bills from Longmans. Because Longmans were managing the publication, they would initially be responsible for the entirety of Scott's advance. Longmans would be granted a one-third share in the novel, the Ballantynes would be offered one-sixth each, and Constable the remaining third ('if he takes his share', as Scott added nervously, aware that Constable would not be pleased with his demotion).[14] Longmans would then take Constable's and the Ballantynes' bills in exchange for their advance on each share. Scott is very clear that this is the only possible way of breaking the credit dead-lock with the Scottish banks: 'Any arrangement short of this will not answer my turn.'[15]

In this letter of 13 August Scott supplies John with more detailed figures. Although he writes that he expects a print-run of 12,000, his calculations are based on a minimum run of 6000. He now reckons that there will be a 'profit' of £4000: 6000 copies at a wholesale price of £1, less print and paper of £2200, leaving in fact a sum of £3800. He argues that of this sum £2250 to himself as author and £1500 to the publishers is a fair distribution, and then demands an advance of £2250, or £750 per share. Longmans, however, had stipulated that the print-run should be 10,000 rather than 12,000, producing a pro rata profit of £3750.[16] This figure represents the original £1000 plus an additional £2750 won for him by John to make up the full author's profits as advance—Scott had done well out of the negotiations.

So far, the story of *The Monastery* (Scott first mentions that this is to be the title of the new novel in his letter to John Ballantyne of 13 August) is relatively self-contained. However, having once decided to bring forward the new novel to take advantage of the enforced hiatus of the *Ivanhoe* paper shortage, Scott could not keep the two works entirely separate. At this point, another factor begins to influence the genesis of *The Monastery*. Writing on 23 August to Lady Louisa Stuart, to whom he would be unlikely to confide his financial difficulties, Scott suggests another reason for his promoting Longmans to the senior position in the novel's publication:

> . . . I am trying an antiquarian story I mean one relating to old
> English times which is a great amusement to me. I have laid aside a

half-finished story on the dissolution of the Monasteries. When I
print them I shall put them into different shapes and publish them
with different people and so run the one against the other. I am
rather curious to know if I can be detected in both instances.[17]

According to this version, the change of publishers was to be an experiment with the reading public. Scott's stated intention was to publish
Ivanhoe in Edinburgh and *The Monastery* in London as unconnected
works, and with no clue as to the authorship of either, in order to see
whether readers would guess that they were written by the same person.
In the event, however, both novels appeared under the name of 'The
Author of Waverley'.[18] Although Scott's primary motive for the London
publication of *The Monastery* was financial, the ideas about anonymity
and authorship which he was entertaining in late August clearly stayed
with him as he wrote the novel's Introductory Epistles and he includes
them in Captain Clutterbuck's wranglings with the Author of Waverley.
The material circumstances of the novel's inception thus become insep-
arable from its themes, not only in the Introductory Epistles' allusions to
rival claims for the ownership of the text, but also in the body of the novel
itself, dealing as it does with the struggle for possession of a book.

This brings us back to Archibald Constable, who felt himself betrayed by Scott's decision to allow Longmans to manage *The Monastery*.
Scott had been wary from the start about Constable's involvement,
assuming, accurately, that the primary publisher of his previous works
would not be pleased to be relegated to second place on the title-page.
When announcing the plan for *The Monastery*'s publication to John
Ballantyne on 2 August he instructed that Constable's share 'is not to be
offerd to him till I[vanho]e is out as it would you are aware only raise
such a clamour as we had in May—when the thing is arranged he must
consent or go without'.[19] By the end of November, however, Constable
was apprised of Scott's plans for *The Monastery*, and he was not happy,
believing that the author had been excessive in negotiating his advance
and less than honest in his dealings with his old associates.[20] Although
Constable accepted his third share in *The Monastery*, he did not feel that
ridding himself of 'a plague of Scotch bills' was sufficient compensation
for his demotion to second billing on the novel's title-page. His letter
books reveal a continuing hostility to Longmans, a dissatisfaction with
Scott's timing of *The Monastery*, and constant suspicions that the new
novel would harm *Ivanhoe*. Constable remained sensitive to references
to *The Monastery* and tended to regard any advance notice of it as
unwelcome competition for *Ivanhoe*. On 23 October he complained
that 'Blackwoods Magazine announces the Monastry as forthcoming
from Pater noster Row evidently to injure Ivanhoe & its publishers'.[21]
Constable regarded Scott as having already secured himself very
favourable terms in the deal with Longmans and resented his plans to
push forward with *The Monastery* which he again saw as unwelcome

competition for *Ivanhoe*: 'I much fear that the author will injure all if he brings out the Monastery early in the year.'[22]

Almost every aspect of *The Monastery*'s production was viewed by Constable with deep suspicion. On Longmans' decision to price the books at eight shillings a volume, in comparison with the nine shillings then mooted for *Ivanhoe*, he complained that 'the Monastery, should it come out soon, being *cheaper*, may be equally popular, and come in the way of *Ivanhoe*'.[23] Longmans had kept the price down, in comparison with that of *Ivanhoe*, by using cheaper paper and a smaller format— another source of irritation for Constable who saw this as a way for Scott to evade responsibility for any negative outcome of the switch of publishers: 'if the Book falls through in any way which I dont think will be the case—all will be attributed to change of size without the Authors after steps being taken into Account'.[24]

Even more irritating for Constable than the *Blackwood's* announcement was a number of advertisements in the London *Morning Chronicle* (a daily newspaper which regularly carried notices of the Waverley Novels and was currently advertising *Ivanhoe*) for a spurious Fourth Series of *Tales of My Landlord* (the series title of a number of Scott's earlier novels). The exchanges that followed the appearance of these advertisements strongly prefigure the terms that Scott was to use in his Introductory Epistle from the Author to Captain Clutterbuck: 'As I give you no title to employ or use the firm of the copartnery we are about to form, I will announce my property in my title-page, and put my own buist on my own cattle, which the attorney tells me will be a crime to counterfeit' (29.24–27). The first full advertisement appeared on 18 October announcing a four-volume book from the pen of a fictional narrator already employed by the Author of Waverley: 'TALES of MY LANDLORD, collected and arranged by JEDEDIAH CLEISH-BOTHAM, Schoolmaster and Parish Clerk of Gandercleugh, containing "PONTEFRACT CASTLE"'.[25] When Constable spotted this he immediately saw it as part of the supposed anti-*Ivanhoe* conspiracy, writing to his partner Cadell that the advertisement was 'intended to take the public attention from Ivanhoe & to attempt injury to those concerned in it'.[26] Constable suspected a conspiracy, speculating on the possibility of a secret enemy in the *Morning Chronicle* offices and later proposed that Longmans themselves were part of the intrigue: 'on the subject of the Tales *4 Series* I suspect Longman & Co are the proprietors & the *underhand* advertiser'.[27] This suspicion was also later voiced in a letter from Constables: 'in order to give no countenance to the Trade supposing that both Books come from the same quarter as that which meets so fully Longman & Cys patronage, we have struck out their firm, which otherwise would have stood in the title page of *Ivanhoe*'.[28]

On 21 October the same advertisement appeared, and on the 28th the newspaper published a rejoinder from John Ballantyne in the form of a letter to the editor, quoting the advertisement, and continuing:

> I who have transacted betwixt the Publishers and the Author of these Works, as his agent, do, on my certain knowledge, assure you and the public, that this Author has no concern whatever with the catchpenny publication announced as above; and, although I have not his express authority for saying so, I am morally assured he will at no period send any further work to the public under the title of Tales of My Landlord.
>
> The copyright of the Tales of My Landlord, in 12 volumes, has been purchased by, and is now the property of Messrs. Constable and Company, who are taking legal measures to interdict the publication of this spurious work under this title, and to punish those concerned in it when they shall be discovered.[29]

The hand behind the advertisements, and probable author of the advertised novel, *Pontefract Castle*, was the London bookseller William Fearman who showed no fear either of being 'discovered' or of John's threats of legal action. On 30 October, Fearman put another advertisement, this time signed, in the *Morning Chronicle* and followed it with a letter in reply to John's 'ridiculous threat' against him. This letter enters enthusiastically into the games of anonymity and authorship which Scott was himself to play in the Author of Waverley's reply to Captain Clutterbuck:

> If, by the Author, you mean Jedediah Cleishbotham, I think (to say the least of it) you presume too much, when, without having read a line of the Fourth Series, you pronounce it 'spurious.' The Fourth Series, collected and arranged by Jedediah Cleishbotham, is no more spurious than the First, the Second, or the Third. It is for the Public to judge of that when they see the work, and certainly not for you, who have never seen it. That Jedediah will prosecute Jedediah, because Jedediah's stores have happily furnished a Fourth Series, is as little to be believed as feared.[30]

Privately, this provoked Constable's ire further and he contemplated taking legal advice on the matter of the property-rights of the 'real' Jedidiah.[31] However, he appears to have followed Cadell's advice that 'silence is the safest course—and cheapest'.[32].

The in-fighting in the publishing world did not end there. The firm of Hurst, Robinson & Co., Constable's London associates and the London publishers of *Ivanhoe*, entered the fray in the hope of acquiring the Ballantyne share of the novel. Hurst, Robinson & Co. appealed to Constable to help them get 3333 books to sell, even though their name was not on the title page.[33] Advance orders for *Ivanhoe* had been accumulating well, and on 18 December John O. Robinson wrote to Constable including, perhaps by way of encouragement, a reference to Constable's *bête noir*, his suspicion of the involvement of Longmans in the bogus *Tales of My Landlord*:

> I am glad you have bought all Ballantynes Copies of the Monastery

and I own I can see no reason why you should not offer them to us at
once without hesitation L & Co having once declined or deferred
buying them ... You will no doubt have a long Conversation with
Mr Cadell about the Monastery and it affords me pleasure to say
that L & Co have not yet sold all the 50 Copies of the *spurious* Tales
and I trust most of [them] will be shelvers ... 34

Letters between Constable and Cadell indicate that the campaign of
Hurst, Robinson & Co. had been underway from at least 2 December.35
Constable is at first uncertain as to how to proceed, telling Cadell that
facilitating the involvement of Hurst, Robinson & Co. would give Longmans cause for a grievance against their own firm. Cadell writes cryptic-
ally: 'Do what you can to lug Robinson into this. I have many things to tell
you at meeting to render this an object of importance.'36 Although there
is no record of this conversation, the whole affair of the involvement of
Hurst, Robinson & Co. is overlaid with the misgivings and distrust that
surrounded the publication of *The Monastery*. When, on 15 December,
Constable wrote to the London firm offering them his share of the books
to sell, he again brought in the question of Longmans: 'With regard to
The Monastry I have purchased John & Jas Ballantynes third share of
10,000 Copies which will give us the command of the Book, these
Copies I need not add I should wish to see in your hands but before
actually transferring the Books or transaction to you, I hold it to be
proper to have some communication with Messr Longman & Co in
order to prevent all misunderstanding with that house on the subject'.37

   The course of production of *The Monastery* is not fully documented.
We know that the printing of the novel began on or shortly before 29
November when Constable visited the Ballantyne printing office and
reported to Cadell that he 'saw the two first sheets of *the Monastery* and
was told they have plenty of Copy'.38 When Scott started writing is less
easy to establish. The first mention of the subject matter of *The Monastery* comes in Scott's letter to John Ballantyne of 2 August 1819 noted
above, in which it is apparent that he has been thinking about his next
novel for some time and indeed has discussed it with John. It is difficult
to pin-point exactly when Scott commenced writing the text itself as he
appears to have made at least one start on it while *Ivanhoe* was held up by
the paper delay. Scott's recollection, according to Lockhart, of *The
Monastery*'s composition was one of its imbrication with *Ivanhoe*: 'It was
a relief ... to interlay the scenery most familiar to me with the strange
world for which I had to draw so much on imagination.'39 The first
mention of this 'interlaying' is Scott's letter of 19 August to James
Ballantyne, informing him 'I have finishd the 2d. volume I[vanho]e and
am determined to let it rest since the paper is not come & take to the
other to save time.'40 Assuming that 'the other' is *The Monastery*, it is
possible that this is when Scott began to turn the subject matter announced to John Ballantyne on 2 August into a novel proper. However,

in his letter to Lady Louisa Stuart on 23 August (quoted above) Scott writes: 'I have laid aside a half-finished story on the dissolution of the Monasteries', suggesting that the novel was already far advanced, or even, as one interpreter has supposed, that it was commenced before *Ivanhoe*.[41] But 'half-finished' is a sufficiently vague term, and a letter to a friend who had no commercial interest in the progress of Scott's work has no claims to precision. From the evidence available we can safely assume that Scott's first brief period of writing *The Monastery* took place in August 1819 before he returned once again to *Ivanhoe*.[42]

There is no record of precisely when Scott recommenced *The Monastery*. He must have written the latter part of the introductory exchange after the Fearman affair which took place in later October. John Ballantyne records having read the 'admirable introductions to the Monastery' on 15 December, but the novel proper must have been underway again by then.[43] It seems likely that Scott resumed *The Monastery* shortly after completing *Ivanhoe*: the last sheet of the earlier novel was at press by 7 November and the following day he was writing to John that it was 'almost all finishd . . . and the M[onaster]y is begun and will proceed rapidly'.[44] Scott seems to have made good progress. When on 29 November Constable wrote to Cadell to report that he had seen the first two sheets of *The Monastery* he had been told that 'they have plenty of copy'. (Needless to say, Constable follows this up with his usual complaint: 'the Monastry following so close at the heels of *Ivanhoe* is a sad affair'.)[45] By the beginning of November Scott was worried about James Ballantyne's inability to press forward towards the printing of *Ivanhoe*, which was then being transcribed by the copyists for the typesetters. Scott is concerned that James cannot get *Ivanhoe* out until late December and *The Monastery* will not appear until February (in fact, publication was to be in March). He proposes a new plan to John: 'Now the fact is that the M[onaster]y will run either to four volumes or which is much better will make two parts of three volumes each.'[46] At this stage Scott clearly felt he had plenty of material to continue his current project, and felt confident enough in Longmans' management to assume, as he does in this letter, that they would continue with a second part, should the novel become two novels. This is, of course, precisely what happened, with the extended material being published by Longmans in three volumes as *The Abbot*.[47] Even so, Constable and Cadell had evidently attempted to wrest the management of the continuing Waverley Novels back into their own grasp, by means of a secret plan to persuade Scott to proceed with *Kenilworth* instead of the second part of *The Monastery*.[48]

Thereafter *The Monastery* appears to have moved quietly towards publication, although Constable may have hoped to hold it up as long as possible. Even as he was writing to booksellers and shippers assuring them of the novel's imminent availability, Constable privately informed Hurst, Robinson & Co. on 7 February that 'the Monastry will be out next month, but the truth is, we do not hurry it that Ivanhoe may have more time'.[49] Nevertheless, by the end of February the final volume was at the press.[50] On 18 March Constables wrote to Longmans to inform them that they had just sent down their copies to arrive in time for the Edinburgh publication date of 23 March 1820.[51] The London date of publication was 30 March, and the price £1 4s.[52] Sales were only moderate, with the novel apparently doing better in Edinburgh than in London. Constables, needless to say, blamed everything on Longmans.[53]

2. THE COMPOSITION OF *THE MONASTERY*

The Manuscript. The manuscript of *The Monastery* is in the Pierpont Morgan Library, New York.[54] It represents almost the whole of the novel as printed, terminating at 3.349.3 in the first edition (353.27 in the present text) with the words 'fineness of a silken thread'. These words come at the bottom of a leaf but the sentence finishes in mid-line with no tag-word, suggesting that Scott sent no further material to the transcriber with this last batch of manuscript and that the subsequent material was added later. The manuscript has two sizes of paper. The introductory epistles are written on folio leaves resulting from folding (and probably cutting) a sheet of paper in two. They thus have vertical chain-lines, and are larger (32 cm by 19.5 cm) than the rest of the manuscript. The remaining leaves measure 26 cm by 19 cm with some slight variations. These are quarto leaves from sheets folded and cut, then folded (and probably cut) again, resulting in horizontal chain-lines. All the paper appears to have come from A. Cowan and Son, at the Valleyfield works in Penicuik, and bears the watermark of a crowned crest[55] with the countermark 'VALLEYFIELD'. The paper for the introduction is dated 1816 and for the rest of the manuscript 1817. The 218 leaves of the manuscript are numbered in different ways. Scott numbers each folio in sequence (but with some blanks) starting afresh with each volume. A later librarian has added page-type numbers (recording the odd numbers on the rectos) and the manuscript includes leaves added later for binding purposes.[56]

Scott writes the novel on one side of each leaf. Additions are written either in the margin, or on the verso of the preceding leaf. Footnotes to the main text also appear on the versos. The manuscript, then, reveals much about how Scott wrote and revised *The Monastery*. Although the manuscript shows many local alterations, it is generally written in a sequential flow which does not indicate any major changes of plan in the novel's composition. The one exception is suggested by the unusual layout of the first leaf. Although Scott usually writes in narrowly spaced lines extending close to the top and bottom edges, the first folio is much more widely spaced and leaves a gap at the bottom. The next folio begins with the Burns stanza ' 'Tis said he was a soldier bred' but above this Scott has crossed out 'The Monastery / vole 1st. / Introduction'. The decision to cast the introductory matter in the form of an epistle from Captain Clutterbuck to the Author of Waverley was evidently taken after Scott had started the novel, and a leaf of new material was attached to the beginning. The end of the introduction also shows us how Scott worked. Although he finished the Author of Waverley's epistle on the verso he did not send this section of the novel to the printers at once, retaining it as he started the next section and using the verso of the last leaf for a new motto for the first chapter.

Scott wrote quickly. His numbering of chapters is inconsistent and results in repeated chapter numbers in the first edition.[57] Occasionally he added chapter divisions as an afterthought as is the case with Volume 2, Chapter 8—here he returns to the preceding chapter to insert the phrase ' ↑ But his appearance and reception we must devote to another chapter ↓ ' on the verso.[58] Not all the mottoes are present in the manuscript and at one point Scott instructs the intermediaries (the EEWN's collective name for the copyist, compositors, proof-readers, and James Ballantyne) to move a motto from one chapter to another: 'Take in motto prefixd to Chapter II which must be deleted in that place' (see 255.5–11).[59]

As had been the case with all the preceding novels, a transcript of the manuscript was made to preserve Scott's anonymity before the text went to the printers. In the case of *The Monastery*, the transcriber has in certain places copied Scott's verso additions into the recto text, allowing us to identify his handwriting as that of John Ballantyne,[60] and Scott's use of him in this capacity for *The Monastery* is in keeping with John's close association with the novel. The transcriber has left marks in the margin to annotate his dealings with manuscript. Simple crosses usually indicate a problem in deciphering, and figures probably indicate the folio number of the copied sheet. For example, at f. 34 the transcriber is on his 91st sheet of the copied text, and at f. 36 his 99th.

One of the most interesting points in the manuscript is the second appearance of the White Lady's song, 'Thrice to the holly brake'. When Scott wished to re-introduce the lyric in Volume 2 he used the corresponding section of uncorrected proof bearing the song from its first appearance in the previous volume; this fragment is the only surviving section of proof. On f. 107 Scott signals 'printed paper apart'. This proof version, attached to the verso of the previous leaf, differs from the final printed text in a number of ways. The proof 'I bid thee wake' (as in the manuscript) appears in the final text as 'I bid thee wake'. The word 'Noon' in the 5th line appears in the proof version as 'None' and has been corrected in pencil on the paper apart. It is also possible to trace differences on the reverse of the fragment of proof. This encompasses text corresponding to the end of 1.311 and the start of 1.312 in the first edition and has lower case 'a's in 'letter—and' and 'cowardice—and' (112.11–12 in the present text).

Scott's working changes are of various kinds. Small alterations within a line include false starts at a word, decisions to move an adjective to a noun later in the sentence, the replacement of a word to avoid repetition, and (less frequently) the cancellation of words to remove tautologies. Longer or later additions are naturally more substantive. Scott tends to revise more heavily at the beginning of chapters, and there are significantly more alterations to the first volume than in the rest of the manuscript, Captain Clutterbuck's Introductory Epistle in particular containing several long verso additions. Some examples taken from a sample leaf (f. 11) of this section in the manuscript (15.41–17.28 in the present text) reveal the different ways in which Scott made changes as he wrote and revised. There are small revisions made when he immediately deletes the word he has written: 'Avel' is a first attempt at 'Avenel'; Scott commences 'treas' before correcting to 'hidden treasure'. Other minor alterations are inserted above the line: the appropriate chronology of the Abbey's building is restored when 'is' is altered to 'was' in the phrase 'there is no part of this ancient structure with which you are not as well acquainted as was the mason who built it'. Further small changes appear in the margin: 'possession' is altered to 'recollection'; Captain Clutterbuck's name is corrected from the original 'Captain MacGruthers' tilbury. Finally, there is a long and interesting addition (indicated by a caret in the text) written out on the verso of the previous page which raises questions about the mysterious transmission of the history of the Avenel family. This passage runs from 'But if your information be correct' to 'in a foreign land'.

A large number of the smaller alterations throughout the manuscript are corrections or clarifications, but many are changes in register or meaning. These often involve the delineation of characters or their rhetoric. In an early description of Mysie, Scott writes first that she 'giggled' from morning to night, and then changes it to the more decorous 'laughd', despite incurring a repetition with 'laughter-loving' in the same paragraph (121.40). Scott's first attempt at 'Audacity', Piercie Shafton's Euphuistic name for Halbert, is the somewhat less inflated 'Hardihood' (198.18–19). Stawarth Bolton's honesty is reinforced in a change from 'affected to' to 'appeard to' in Elspet Glendinning's fear that he will carry off 'one or other of the little darlings which he appeared to covet so much' (42.8). Many of Scott's manuscript revisions reveal his attempts to keep track of the practical aspects of his plot: the names and ages of the characters, and where they are at any given time. This process was to continue throughout the various stages of the novel's development but we can clearly see Scott working at it in the manuscript. He does not seem always to assign names in advance to places or people: 'Hobs-Cleugh' is an initial name for the more Romantic 'Glendearg' (36.6). The joke about the name of Clutterbuck's fictional village took some time to work out. Scott first leaves a dash in the manuscript,

having deleted '⟨M⟩——' (for Melrose: 6.9). At the next three occurrences the village is given the name 'Nayqhair' (23.25, 30.15, 31.16).
The first of these is changed to '⟨R⟩Kennaquhair' and at its final appearance in the first volume (71.40) it appears as 'Kennaquair', its name
throughout the rest of the manuscript and in the first edition. Even once
a name has been established, Scott can slip up. Edward's name is corrected from 'Charles' (the name of Scott's own younger son) at 91.34,
and Scott has particular difficulty in remembering the name he has
assigned to Christie of Clinthill: the name is inserted once in place of
'the horseman' (88.43), once in place of 'The Soldier' (89.16), and five
times in place of 'Gilbert' (89.30, 34, 41; 90.10, 35); Scott fails to catch
the last 'Gilbert' (91.38) which is corrected in the first edition. Scott's
difficulty with names extends even to the question of keeping his own
name secret: the Introductory Epistle was originally signed 'Walter
Scott' which he scores out heavily in order to substitute 'Cuthbert
Clutterbuck' (23.24). He is also uncertain about ages: the age of the
child Mary (a matter not finalised until the 18mo edition of 1824) is
altered from being between six and seven, to between five and six (compare 46.5).

Longer verso additions often clarify where characters are and where
they are going, or bring early events back into focus. During the scene in
which Halbert and Warden are imprisoned in the castle of Avenel, Scott
starts a sentence with Warden telling the escaping Halbert to take a
letter 'which I had prepared in case a means of ⟨escape⟩ dispatching it
should occur' but, presumably recognising the implausibility of this
ruse, changes it in a verso addition to a letter 'which I will presently
write' (233.19). Scott adds the passage 'The measures taken . . . which
passed betwixt them' (255.35–256.4) to explain how Mysie comes to be
listening at the door, overhearing the conversation from the previous
chapter which tells her where Sir Piercie is to be locked up. A similar
example at 324.23–38 includes an additional piece of dialogue—from
Moray's 'Tell me frankly why thou hast left thy father's house' to his 'Be
near to us, Glendinning, since that is thy name'—which presents
again to the reader's attention the circumstances of Halbert's duel with
Piercie Shafton.

Other alterations affect the ideas in the narrative as well as its shape.
In the early scene in which the child Mary sees her father's ghost, Scott
makes some changes to build up the eerie atmosphere. The passage
'But the two or three domestics . . . the domestic circle was thus
arranged' (50.20–26) is added to remove the presence of the servants,
and the detail of the children's nervousness ('This night . . . vicinity of
the light': 50.38–41) is further inserted. Between these additions, Scott
cancels a passage which he may have felt to detract from this atmo-
spheric intensification with historical information: he initially continued
the sentence which ends 'upon the three children' (50.33) with 'who

had been prohibited to stir abroad that night from the general apprehension entertaind of an evening sacred to the exercise of magical practices and solemnized as was supposed by the annual festival⟨s⟩ of mischievous spirits'.

Some revisions reinforce tensions between the various parties. Scott adds phrases of dialogue before the duel between Halbert and Shafton which draw attention to their nationalities. At 200.16–17 the phrase 'I say in this very garment, in which I am now to combat a Scottish rustic like thyself' is a verso addition, as is Halbert's later rejoinder 'You should have abidden in England had you desired to waste time in words, for here we spend it in blows' (200.39–40). Religious differences are strengthened at 222.40–43 with a verso addition to Julian's list of the errors of Catholicism: 'or thou mayest be some pardoner . . . boy's company'. In similar vein, Halbert's incipient Protestantism is emphasised in the verso addition (231.42–232.7): 'He had indeed been told of saints and martyrs . . . now met for the first time'. In Volume 3 Scott adds a paragraph reinforcing the status of Warden as a hero of the Reformation ('Remove his bonds . . . yet it was': 288.13–19) and starts but then deletes a passage in which Moray, another Protestant hero, criticises Queen Elizabeth's sending of troops to Scotland. After 'master of the Euphuist's person' (328.2) Scott originally wrote '"Elizabeth may rue this" said Moray fiercely "she calculates too surely on"' but then changed his mind.

Finally, one of the most interesting manuscript issues arises early on in Scott's indecision about how to date Captain Clutterbuck's Epistle to the Author of Waverley (23). Unsure, perhaps, about insulting the reader's intelligence, he vacillates between including and deleting the specific date of April 1st: All Fools' Day. His original attempt is '——On the — day of — ⟨181⟩' but then, using carets below the blanks, he inserts '1st.' and 'April'. However, there is a further emendation on the verso of the preceding pages which reads 'Village of ⟨Nayquhair 1st. day⟩ ⟨R⟩Kennaquhair of April 18—'. This, rearranged, became the first edition reading, yet it seems likely that Scott had intended the verso '1st. day' to remain, cancelling it by accident in the late decision to change the name of the village.

From Manuscript to First Edition. As described above, the manuscript was transcribed, probably by John Ballantyne, and set from the transcription by the compositors. The first proofs would have been checked in the publishing house by proof-readers before second proofs were sent to Scott with silent changes as well as suggestions by James Ballantyne for further alterations.

With the exception of the tiny fragment already noted, no proofs of the first edition of *The Monastery* survive. However, four early American editions derive in part from proofs sent across the Atlantic, officially to

M. Carey & Son in Philadelphia, to speed up printing in that hotly competitive market. The portion of the Carey edition corresponding to the final gathering (P) of the first volume in the British edition (from 117.32 in the present text) was set from uncorrected second stage proofs, and from this one can deduce which verbal changes to the manuscript were made before Scott saw the proofs, and which (a much larger number) were made by Scott and his intermediaries in or after the second proofs. In the portion of Carey corresponding to the final gathering (O) of the second volume of the British edition (from 226.39 in the present text) there are several first-edition as opposed to manuscript readings, a number of which are clearly Scott's work. This portion was thus apparently set from third stage proofs, with only a handful of verbal corrections and many more non-verbal refinements remaining to be made by intermediaries. Most interesting is the final gathering (Q) of the third British volume, containing the last three pages of the novel. The manuscript stops with the words 'silken thread.', three lines into the gathering. All four of the American editions include the subsequent song, evidently derived from second stage proofs. Two of them end there, but the other two have the final two paragraphs with only one small non-verbal variation from the first-edition text. This indicates that Scott originally intended to end with 'silken thread.', that he then added the song, and at a subsequent stage appended the final two paragraphs.[61]

Scott would have assumed that the intermediaries would make many changes during the transformation of his manuscript to printed text. The manuscript is very lightly punctuated. Scott usually has a full-stop or tiny dash at the end of a sentence and always starts a sentence with a capital. He uses dashes freely for punctuation within sentences and to indicate changes of speaker. Speech is usually, but not always, indicated by quotation marks. There are few commas and still fewer colons, semi-colons and exclamation marks. The first edition introduces nearly sixteen thousand commas into the text, and at least one of the intermediaries has a preference for introducing semi-colons both where Scott has left a dash and when he has clearly indicated a new sentence. A simple illustration of the way punctuation is introduced into the manuscript can be given by comparing a passage in the two states:

> Mysie flew to the shot-window in the full ardour of unrestraind female curiosity "Saint Mary! sweet Lady here come too ⟨g⟩ well-mounted gallants—will you step this way to look at them".——
> No" said Mary Avenel "you shall tell me who they are"—"Well —if you like it better—but how shall I know them—stay I do know one of them and so do you lady—he is a blythe man— somewhat light of hand they say but the gallants of these days think no great harm of that. He is your uncle's henchman that they call Christie of the Clinthill and he has not his old green

jerkin and the rusty black-jack over it but a scarlet cloak laid
down with silver lace three inches broad and a breastplate you
might see to dress your hair in as well as in that ivory keeking-
glass in the ivory frame that you showd me even now—come
dear lady come to the shot-window and see him"——(MS, ff.
79r–8or)

Mysie flew to the shot-window, in the full ardour of unrestrained
female curiosity. "Saint Mary! sweet lady! here come two well-
mounted gallants, will you step this way to look at them?"

"No," said Mary Avenel, "you shall tell me who they are."

"Well, if you like it better," said Mysie—"but how shall I know
them?—Stay, I do know one of them, and so do you, lady; he is a
blythe man, somewhat light of hand they say, but the gallants of
these days think no great harm of that. He is your uncle's hench-
man, that they call Christie of the Clinthill; and he has not his old
green jerkin, and the rusty black jack over it, but a scarlet cloak, laid
down with silver lace three inches broad, and a breast-plate you
might see to dress your hair in, as well as in that keeking-glass in the
ivory frame that you shewed me even now. Come, dear lady, come
to the shot-window and see him." (Ed1, 2.33.3–24: compare
130.29–42 of the present text)

The intermediaries have set the conversation out in paragraphs as
speech (in this instance Scott has included all necessary speech marks,
which is not always the case) and have replaced Scott's dashes with a
variety of punctuation: commas, semi-colons, full stops. A question
mark has been inserted, and hyphens have also been altered: 'black-
jack' loses a hyphen and 'breastplate' gains one. The passage also indicates other ways in which the manuscript was regularised and tidied up.
Scott's habitual past-participle formation 'unrestraind' is changed to
'unrestrained'. The homophonic slip of 'too' for 'two' is caught, and the
repetition of 'ivory' is removed. Scott expected intermediaries to be alert
to repetition, not only in this instance of a word being anticipated, but
also when repeated words were too near to each other, in which case
synonyms would be provided. For example, in Father Philip's words to
the White Lady, 'thou hast been refused passage at the bridge by the
churlish keeper, and thy crossing may concern thee either for performance of a vow, or for some other weighty charge' (64.32–34), the word
'crossing' replaces a second 'passage'. Scott is also rather fond of the
word 'stream' in this scene, prompting the alternatives 'current' and
'watery fluid', the latter perhaps an emendation of James Ballantyne who
was fond of such epithets. Scott also has a predilection for the adjective
'little' throughout the manuscript and a number of these are removed.

After it left Scott's hands for the first time, the text went through a
gradual process of orthographic standardisation, although the text of the
first edition retains a considerable number of variant spellings and has
few very clear policies. Scott's 'risque' is changed throughout to the

more modern 'risk', and 'wardrope' to 'wardrobe'. The first edition tends to favour the modern distinction between 'council' and 'counsel' which is not clearly demarcated in the manuscript, and it often reverses the word order of Scott's 'said he' to 'he said'. On the other hand there seems to be no attempt to standardise Scott's variant spellings: 'murder' and 'murther', 'chase' and 'chace', 'choose' and 'chuse', 'shew' and 'show' are interchangeable in both texts. Sometimes the first edition introduces variations: Scott's 'dreamd' is rendered variously as 'dreamed' and 'dreamt'.

Many of the small changes between the manuscript and the first edition are to increase the indications that a character is speaking Scots, and intermediaries would keep an eye on this. For example in Martin's speech 'Blythely welcome ... living woman' (45.6–10), 'lady' is changed to 'leddy', 'good' to 'gude', and 'any' to 'ony'. The intermediaries were not always consistent in this matter, and Martin also uses the term 'lady' in the first edition. At one point, however, a Scots word 'bairn' is emended to 'child' (70.3) as the Abbot does not talk in Scots.

Intermediaries were also expected to correct factual errors or errors in sense. Once in the first edition a physical impossibility (or impracticality) is sorted: in the manuscript Christie rides 'into the court yard wall', emended to 'into the little court-yard' (86.29–30). One of the more interesting changes of this kind, in terms of the novel's relation to history, reveals Scott's uncertainty about precisely who was the Archbishop of St Andrews. The occupant of this position never appears but is often referred to, and we are told that it was his idea to place Father Eustace at the Monastery. In the manuscript Scott seems to have in mind the famous Cardinal Beaton: the Primate of Scotland is throughout referred to as 'wily', politically scheming, and a violent defender of Catholicism. As Christie puts it, 'the Primate recommends a little strangling and burning' (100.34–35). Scott is also clearly thinking of Beaton when Christie refers to a feud between the Primate and Norman Leslie, the leader of Beaton's eventual killers (89.2–3). Beaton, however, was killed in 1546, before the events of the novel, and was succeeded as Archbishop of St Andrews by John Hamilton, who had a reputation for tolerance of the reformers and who was not a Cardinal. In Volume 1 Scott originally writes of the 'Cardinal Primate' but the 'Cardinal' is removed in the first edition (88.22 and 88.41). By Volume 3 Scott has accepted this, writing of Beaton and 'the Primate of Saint Andrew's' as if these were two separate people, but still managing to associate Beaton with the Sub-Prior. Morton comments on Eustace's election to Abbot: 'They have chosen the pupil of old Cardinal Beatoun, that wily determined champion of Rome, the bosom-friend of our busy Primate of Saint Andrew's' (326.30–32).

Given the paucity of evidence regarding proofs of *The Monastery* it would be unwise to speculate too far on the instigators of changes between manuscript and first edition. Nevertheless, some were clearly not made by Scott: numerous changes to individual words are the result of misreadings. Thus, among many others, we find 'cautious' for 'courteous' (65.4), 'breaking on' for 'breathing in' (76.42), 'produce' for 'practice' (166.4), 'intention' for 'attention' (218.33), 'quarters' for 'guestens' (235.30), 'erect' for 'track' (342.37), and 'mendicant' for 'merchant' (319.14). Misreadings of this kind can have quite a dramatic effect on the sense of the text: the phrase 'nurse thoughts of slaughter' becomes the meaningless 'morse thoughts of slaughter' (101.15–16). The Sub-Prior's desire that the feuding Border families should 'place their breasts as a bulwark against England' becomes 'place their breach . . .' (250.43)—altogether a much less effective military strategy.

At other points an unusual or unclear word is abandoned altogether and another which seems appropriate to the context is inserted. This process can easily obscure the meaning of what Scott initially wrote, as in Piercie Shafton's quandary as to whether Mysie's 'affectionate delicacy' is a sign of her love for him or of her obligation to 'render the same service to every wealthier churl who frequented her father's mill' (270.28–29). Scott describes the latter as 'the positive habits of a miller's daughter', but 'positive' is not very clear and we may guess that an intermediary unfamiliar with the word's older meaning of 'conventional' has substituted a phrase with a decidedly different meaning: 'ordinary and natural'. Coincidentally the manuscript word 'natural' is mistaken for 'martial' in Shafton's estimation of Halbert's spirit (175.10). The intermediary may have been understandably influenced by the previous line, 'we do not look for gallant leaders and national deliverers in the hovels of the mean common people', but the sense of the speech is blurred as Sir Piercie is drawing a distinction between 'natural spirit' and social situation.

Conscious stylistic changes may also be attributed to the intermediaries. There is a general movement in the first edition to correct, or perhaps explain, some of Scott's period idioms, usually by the addition of words. This results in a rather more periphrastic text than that of the manuscript, as the following examples show. Often articles are added: 'few years since' becomes 'a few years since' (46.2), 'in strange manner' becomes 'in a strange manner' (80.25), and 'beyond Forth' becomes 'beyond the Forth' (39.31). Sometimes phrases are rearranged: 'our subject of quarrel' becomes 'the subject of our quarrel' (202.6), and 'were we not better call up the rest of the brethren' becomes 'were it not better to call' them (155.17). Sometimes more information is given: in the manuscript Mysie wears a white kirtle 'for the dust of the mill', but in the first edition this becomes 'to hide the dust of the mill' (82.20); and Moray's observation that Warden 'hath right' becomes 'hath spoken right' (346.33). The first edition often chooses a rather more 'polite' vocabulary than does Scott's original text. Thus Halbert's feelings of regret at being parted from Mary are transferred from his 'bosom' to the more neutral 'heart' (209.27) and Sir Piercie's hands are moved from his 'stomach' to the more elegant position of being folded on his 'breast' (140.24). Captain Clutterbuck's rather over-familiar reference to Flemish canons with whom he was billeted as 'jolly dogs' is altered to 'jolly fellows' (14.33). There is also some excision of potentially improper allusion to sexuality. Thus a reference to 'the bastard of Morton' becomes the more decorous 'some wild kinsman of Morton' (320.3) and the suggestion that Mysie is exposing herself to sexual danger is toned down: Scott originally makes reference to the advantages which 'an experienced gallant of a later school might have made of her rash attachment', a phrase which is replaced in the first edition by 'her confidence in his honour had afforded' (271.10–11).

Much of Scott's usual trouble with remembering names and ages gets sorted out at this stage. At 57.41 and 58.25 both Walter and Julian Avenel have their correct names restored in place of the manuscript 'William'. At a number of points Edward's name is changed from 'Charles' and Halbert's from 'Albert', this latter making Elspet's insistence that her son, whom Sir Piercie has just called 'Albert', is named 'Halbert; after his goodsire, Halbert Brydone' (189.26–27) something of an in-joke.[62] Most interesting, perhaps, is Scott's use of the name 'Anselm' for Father Eustace, the Sub-Prior (84.38 and 255.41), as this is the monastic name he was to give to Edward in *The Abbot* and indeed a 'Father Anselm' is the original possessor of the mouldering heart in the Introductory Epistle, changed in the first edition to 'the good father' (17.27). It is difficult to decide, given Scott's vagueness about names, whether he was planning ahead for the novel's sequel even at this early stage or whether he was simply using 'Anselm' as a generally ecclesiastical name. The first edition also goes some way to standardising the spelling of character names. The most important of these is that of Elspet Glendinning. Both manuscript and first edition start with 'Elspeth'. The first edition persists with this variant throughout, but Scott had originally diverged after the first eight Elspeths to a clear preponderance of Elspets. The first edition also irons out most, though not all, of Scott's uses of 'Murray' for 'Moray'.[63] Scott further appears to have had difficulty remembering how characters must age according to the novel's fictional time-span. When they are in fact teenagers, Halbert and Edward are repeatedly referred to as 'children', changed in the first edition to 'lads' or 'young folk' (80.39 and 81.1). Among other similar changes around this point, 'little man' becomes 'dear boy' (90.31) and 'my little fellow' becomes simply 'Edward' (90.38). Elspet's remaining 'bairns's' is explained by the addition of the phrase 'so her fondness still called them' (81.37–38). The reader is reminded of the advance in the boys' ages by the first edition's inclusion of Elspet's comment that Halbert will be 'sixteen come Whitsuntide' (81.7).

The major structural difference between manuscript and first edition is in the division between Volumes 1 and 2. In the manuscript, Scott ended the first volume after Chapter 10, pausing the novel on the highly suspenseful moment of the White Lady's appearance to Halbert after he has summoned her. The reader must then turn to the new volume which follows immediately on with the words 'Halbert Glendinning had scarcely pronounced the mystical rhymes, than, as we have mentioned in the conclusion of the last chapter, an appearance, as of a beautiful female, dressed in white, stood within two yards of him' (113.13–16). The first edition has a rather less adventurous volume division, ending the first volume after the culmination of Halbert's visit to the White Lady's cavern and commencing the next with the residents of Glendearg awaiting his return.

Few alterations affect the plot although there is a sense of the fate of Piercie Shafton being clarified retrospectively in light of the decision to take him to Dunbar and ship him off to Flanders. Thus Morton's belief that Moray will 'secure Sir Piercie Shafton at some more fitting time' is changed to 'dismiss Sir Piercie Shafton from the realm of Scotland' (335.11–12 and again at 335.35). Shafton's 'arrest' becomes his 'dismissal'. Not many longer passages are added in the first edition, those that are occurring in the third volume and pertaining to the development of Edward's character in this novel, and to the future development of Halbert in its successor. In Edward's long speech promising to avenge Halbert's supposed death, the section 'his successor in all his rights . . . my rights and pretensions' (251.25–28) is added, as is the end of his speech from 'His eyes sparkled' (252.3–5). A sentence in this speech which had evidently got out of control in the manuscript is rewritten: 'thus I say plainly but do not fear that while I say this I may do more against this man than that which I have said' becomes in the first edition the rather more pithy 'He who takes up my brother's succession, must avenge his death' (251.41–42).

Towards the end of the novel there are clear indications that Scott was thinking of the direction its sequel might take and that decisions about such developments were taken between the completion of the manuscript and the final printing. More precisely, it might be true to say that it was between manuscript and first edition that Scott decided to focus intimations of foreboding on the very end of the novel. In Volume 2, warnings in the manuscript about the doubled-edged powers offered by the White Lady are reduced in the first edition: the section of the song beginning 'When Piercie Shafton boasteth high' was originally preceded by the lines 'Never gift by fairy given/ Prosperd on a friday even' (169.6). The excision of these lines concentrates the White Lady's gloomy prophecy in the song added at the end of Volume 3. As well as the White Lady's threatening final song and the ominous sentence which follows it, Scott adds the section 'But not without these omens . . . of her son' (352.30–353.4). This passage, describing the reappearance of the ghost of Simon Glendinning and including Elspet's fear that her son may not be happy at the castle of Avenel, is the earliest sign that Scott was considering the changes in Halbert which we witness in the opening of *The Abbot* where, despite his marriage to Mary, he appears restless and discontented. The final reappearance of the author as narrator is also absent from the manuscript.

Some of the most interesting changes occur in the introductory epistles and these can be dealt with separately. We learn that Captain Clutterbuck's age was changed from 'approaching to sixty' to 'about fifty' (10.22: perhaps to make him a more plausible veteran of the Napoleonic Wars), and that Scott's first name for the Glendinning family was 'Cairncross' (16.6). From the Author's Epistle, we discover that the 'land of Utopia' (27.15) where the characters in novels come from was originally the less idyllic 'land of Chimæra', and that Scott did not at first feel it necessary to explain the joke about Maria Edgeworth's being the 'mother of the finest family in England' (27.14). The manuscript paragraph ends simply with 'You are not born of woman unless indeed in a figurative sense.' There also seems to have been some uncertainty about the phrase describing fictional editors in novels as 'gentlemen who may be termd Knights of the straw' which is changed in the first edition to the much more straightforward 'pseudo editors' (29.6–7). Scott may have been thinking of Samuel Butler's *Hudibras* but the phrase was evidently deemed unclear.

Of particular significance are the changes which have to do with the circumstances of the novel's publication. As shown earlier in this essay, Scott's publishers were infuriated by the appearance of newspaper advertisements for a Fourth Series of *Tales of My Landlord*. Scott, who treats the whole episode as a joke in *The Monastery*, initially named the supposed author of the advertisements, writing in the footnote about Jedidiah Cleishbotham: 'the person assuming his name in Mr Fearmans advertizement is an impostor', but the first edition reads simply 'the person assuming his name is an impostor' (29.38). It was evidently thought impolitic for the Author of Waverley himself to enter into the row over the advertisements by naming the perpetrator, and this section of the novel is also made less 'factual' by the excision of another sentence commenting on relations within the publishing world. After the Author's reference to John Ballantyne's 'match at single-stick with a brother publisher' (30.18) Scott initially included the explanatory comment: 'Remark I mean a metaphorical match at single-stick for it has occurd to Scottish publishers to be calld in to ⟨defend⟩ ↑match↓ themselves literally at this wholesome exercize'. This too is removed in the first edition, perhaps because the explanation that the match is 'metaphorical' was deemed unnecessary, or perhaps because Scott or James Ballantyne wanted to distance the novel from the arguments erupting between the Edinburgh and London arms of the publishing venture, or from those between Constable and John Ballantyne.

These final pages of the Author's Epistle are some of the most substantially altered in the whole novel. Scott also adds the passage 'You will find . . . penance' (30.5–8) in which 'The Author' expresses his anti-Catholic sentiments, as well as adding to his stern words to Captain Clutterbuck the sentence 'I can at pleasure . . . to any one' (29.34–36). There is also a good example of how decisions about what was acceptable in the text could vary over time or between intermediaries. In the manuscript Epistle, the Author uses the metaphor of branding cattle to assert his ownership of the text: 'I will to speak rurally put my own Buist on my own cattle'. In the first edition it seems as if someone has taken the decision that speaking rurally will not be clear enough, and the phrase is made much more obvious: 'I will announce my property in my title-page, and put my own mark on my own chattels' (29.25–26). By the end of Volume 2, however, the term 'buist' is included in Christie's comment that Warden 'is not of the brotherhood of Saint Mary's—at least he has not the buist of these black cattle', complete with a footnote to explain the term (216.25–27).

3. LATER EDITIONS

Although some copies of *The Monastery* bear the imprint 'second edition', all those examined have turned out to be first editions bound with a new title page. The next stages of the text were the three consecutive editions of Scott's *Historical Romances*, a collection consisting of *Ivanhoe*, *The Monastery*, *The Abbot*, and *Kenilworth*. For the complete re-publication of the Waverley Novels (the 'Magnum Opus') Scott revised the text afresh and the textual relationship to each other of the various editions is indicated in the following stemma:

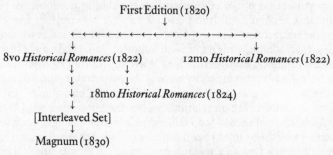

Historical Romances (1822) 12mo Historical Romances (1822)

First Edition (1820)

8vo Historical Romances (1822)   12mo Historical Romances (1822)

18mo Historical Romances (1824)

[Interleaved Set]

Magnum (1830)

Historical Romances. The method represented by the *Historical Romances* of republishing a set of the most recent Waverley Novels had already been established by the reissue of the novels before *Ivanhoe* under the title *Novels and Tales of the Author of Waverley*. The title of the new collection was suggested by Constable, whose idea it was, and Scott accepted £5000 for the copyright of all four novels.[64] With Constable in control, Longmans, the initial publishers of *The Monastery*, had no part in the new editions. The *Historical Romances* were published in three formats: octavo and duodecimo, both appearing in 1822, and an 18mo edition in 1824. The octavo and 18mo each had a print run of 5000 and the duodecimo one of 1500.[65]

None of these editions of the *Historical Romances* makes radical changes to the text though all have numerous small alterations. There is a certain amount of standardisation and modernisation of spelling in all of the formats: 'chuse' becomes 'choose', 'poney' becomes 'pony', 'countroul' becomes 'control', and 'faulter' becomes 'falter'. 'Enquiry' is usually changed to 'inquiry', and 'endoctrinate' to 'indoctrinate'. These changes are common to all the *Historical Romances* editions, but the 18mo has further modernisations of the spelling in a slight movement towards the standardisation of the plural of 'Abbey' and other 'ey' endings from 'Abbies' to 'Abbeys', 'vallies' to 'valleys', 'monies' to 'moneys'.

The octavo marks the first alterations of the text from the first edition on which it is based. Its most substantive change is in standardising the Earl of Moray's title to 'Murray'. (The first edition uses both versions but with a very clear preference for 'Moray'.) This change was also made in the subsequent editions. There is no obvious policy of repunctuation in the octavo, and changes are not very extensive. In general, there is a tendency to add commas, and to reverse the first edition's pattern of putting a long dash outside closing speech marks. However, commas are added and deleted in a way which sometimes changes the sense with varying results. For example, the first edition's 'disturbing, at such an hour and in such a place, the still, mute sanctity of the grave' (18.25–26), becomes 'disturbing, at such an hour, and in such a place, the still mute sanctity of the grave'. The octavo thus adds an unnecessary comma after 'hour', and removes one after 'still', changing the word from an adverb to an adjective and with it the meaning of the phrase. On the other hand, a more perceptive comma change is from the first edition's version of the sexton's 'when he died decently, I wad hae earded him' (20.5–6) to 'when he died, decently I wad hae earded him'. The octavo makes it clear that it is the burial rather than the death which is 'decent'.

Other octavo changes are more stylistic. Thus 'scholar-craft' is changed to 'school-craft' at 163.36 and the Sub-Prior's instructions to himself to 'affirm that which they will ascribe to idle fear, or perhaps to wilful falsehood—sustain the disgrace of a silly visionary, or a wilful deceiver' (96.27–29) is tidied up: the octavo rearranges the pattern of repeated words in the phrase to give 'affirm that which they will ascribe to idle fear, or perhaps to idle falsehood—sustain the disgrace of a silly visionary, or a wilful deceiver'. The octavo also makes a small number of verbal substitutions which alter the meaning. There is only a slight change of sense in its substitution of 'imposed' for 'incumbent' in the Sub-Prior's sense of the 'duty incumbent on him' (83.7), but a much greater disruption in the meaning is evident when 'dragons' is replaced by 'dragoons' in Elspet's description of the English raiders (53.33).

The duodecimo *Historical Romances* is an independent edition based on the first edition with no apparent reference to the octavo. It does correspond with the octavo in one substantive instance: the first edition's phrase 'perished from the way' (72.42) is altered to 'perished by the way' in all subsequent editions. However, as 'by the way' is the more common form, this is likely to be the result of independent changes in the octavo and duodecimo. Like the octavo, the duodecimo follows a policy of altering 'Moray' to 'Murray', though not till after the first two occurrences where it changes the first edition's 'Murray' to 'Moray'. The duodecimo is characterised by a tendency to introduce further commas and dashes. It also displays a preference for the forms 'seest', 'mayst', 'wouldst', 'canst' and so forth over the first edition's 'see'st', 'may'st', 'would'st', and 'can'st'. In general the duodecimo is a somewhat careless text introducing a number of omissions and mistakes. The repeated 'a gentleman' disappears from the young Mary's description of her father's ghost: 'it was a gentleman—a gentleman with a bright breast-plate' (52.27–28). Similarly, 'and wail' is omitted from Tibb's report that the White Lady 'is aye seen to yammer and wail' (56.9) and Tibb's name drops off Elspet's 'have you not heard me say it, Tibb?' (139.34). There is also some careless repetition: in Piercie Shafton's 'For your first query ... we will, if you please, prætermit it as nothing essential to the matter in hand' (244.31–32) the word 'matter' is changed to a second 'query'. A similar kind of eyeslip introduces the nonsensical answer 'you would have less quarrel with my groat if you knew what it covers' from Henry Warden to Julian Avenel's 'nor the nineteenth part of a gray groat, will I give to any feigned limmar of thy coat' (223.18–22). A change of plot is accidentally mooted when 'wench' is changed to 'wretch' in the Abbot's command: 'To-morrow cite the wench to appear before us' (75.16). Whoever was responsible for this change presumably believed the person in question was Father Philip and overlooked the discussion of Mysie Happer in the previous paragraph. As the duodecimo does not influence any other edition, these errors are unique to it and do not appear in either 18mo or the Magnum.

The 18mo is based not on the first edition but on the octavo; among the characteristic substantive changes in the octavo described above, 'dragoons', 'imposed', 'idle', and 'school-craft' feature in these two editions but not in the duodecimo.

Some care appears to have gone into the preparation of this edition. It is the only one to spot the discrepancy of the young Mary Avenel's age. In the first edition, Mary is told by her mother as they cross the moors to

Glendearg 'This is thy birthday, my sweet Mary' (45.43), yet in the very next paragraph the narrator is informing us that Mary is 'a lovely little girl between five and six years old'. Clearly, on her birthday she must be one or the other, and the 18mo settles for 'a lovely girl now just six years old'. (The Magnum, on which all texts after Scott's death are based, follows the octavo.) The 18mo makes a further innovation of its own which may perhaps be considered to go beyond the standing orders given to intermediaries for correcting the text. The Sub-Prior's new-found authority after his elevation to Abbot-elect is described thus: 'The Abbot-elect bore a more manly port than formerly' (314.32). Here 'manly' has been substituted for the 'ample' which appears in all previous editions. The idea behind this change is probably that Father Eustace is unlikely to have gained in physical size, but the novel has not previously suggested that there is anything unmanly about him. The 18mo alters the spelling of 'clue' to the older form 'clew' in Sir Piercie's phrase 'I shall soon want the aid of this Ariadne, who might afford me a clue through the recesses of yonder mountainous labyrinth' (273.20–21). As the later editions tend to modernise the spelling, this change to an earlier form can only be to emphasise the literal meaning of the word, a ball of thread which can be used to trace a path through a maze. This edition has a tendency to introduce further commas (either further to break up phrases or to replace dashes) and capitalisation ('Knight', 'Father', 'Catholic'). At least one of the compositors shows a fondness for the colon.

The Interleaved Set and the Magnum. After the 18mo *Historical Romances* of 1824 the text lay dormant for a time. In 1825 Scott had agreed to Constable's plan of a complete new edition of the Waverley Novels with the author's own emendations. Scott comments in his journal that this collection of the novels 'in a superior stile' would largely involve him in the addition of some historical and explanatory notes 'which are light work'.[66] The plan had to be deferred because of the financial crash of early 1826 which hit the publishing trade very badly (nearly ruining Scott in the process) but was revived in 1827 by Robert Cadell, Constable's erstwhile partner, who, following the wreckage of the crash, had now emerged as Scott's sole publisher.[67] Cadell planned a cheap, mass-market edition but maintained Constable's original scheme to produce a handsome, well-printed set with the author's revisions and the addition of notes. To facilitate Scott's work on the text, Constable had made up a set of the novels in the octavo format (in the case of *The Monastery* this was the first issue of the *Historical Romances*) with blank pages inserted between the printed ones. Both Scott's additions and the whole text then went through a further editing process at the hands of Cadell and the finished product was published in two volumes, representing Volumes 18 and 19 of the 'Magnum Opus' edition of the novels (so-called by Scott and all those involved in the publication although this was not an official name for the edition). Scott was working on the revision of *The Monastery* at the beginning of 1830. On 16 January he wrote to Cadell: 'I must have back the Abbot & Monastery bodyly my notes & all having a good deal to do to complete them.[68]

Although Scott now had a free rein to rework his text, his interest in *The Monastery* does not seem to have been very strongly revived by this opportunity, and this stage of *The Monastery* forms a contrast with his revisions of its highly successful predecessor, *Ivanhoe*. Compared with over 400 changes in *Ivanhoe*, the Interleaved Set of *The Monastery* records little more than 150.[69] For the new edition, Scott wrote an introduction in which he speculates on why *The Monastery* was comparatively poorly received and gives an account of some of his sources. He composed eleven lengthy notes, to be inserted at the end of chapters, supplying some historical background, ranging from the local history of the 'Drawbridge at Bridge-End' (Magnum, 18.72) to speculations about the 'Pedigree of the Douglas Family' (Magnum, 19.353). He also took the opportunity to extend the footnotes already in the text by introducing some new references to the parallels between Kennaquair and Melrose, and extending others including, for example, further details about the proverbial 'Macfarlane's Geese': in the interval between the first edition and the Interleaved Set, Scott has evidently found the answer to his quandary 'Why they were said to like their play better than their meat, I could never learn' (127.41–42). This phrase is now removed and James VI is credited with the saying. Information from these extended footnotes is introduced at the relevant points in the Explanatory Notes of the present edition.

Scott's changes to the text are not equally distributed across the novel and the end of the work seems to have particularly caught his attention: in a total of 37 chapters and the two introductions 34 changes occur in the last 5 chapters, which chiefly concern the battle and its aftermath. Scott's emendations vary in character from the addition of new ideas, to simple rearrangement of the text (sometimes for no very clear reason). For example, he includes a further joke about Maria Edgeworth as the mother of the novel: in recognition of her unmarried status, she is now credited with a miraculous birth with the addition of the phrase 'in her single blessedness' (in the Magnum 'in her state of single blessedness') to describe her. At the other end of the scale is the simple reshuffling of the phrase 'she well knew the man's character, which in fact she both disliked and feared' (90.5–6) to '. . . the character of the man whom in fact she both disliked and feared'.

Some of the changes are straightforward corrections. When sorting errors, Scott sometimes returns to the manuscript reading, and sometimes finds a third alternative. The manuscript 'tiend sheaves' is re-

stored from 'land-sheaves' (307.12–13) and a reference to the Lady of
Avenel's misfortunes which had 'drawn her to the Tower of Glendearg'
becomes once again 'driven her to the Tower of Glendearg' (83.36). In
the Introductory Epistle, Clutterbuck's landlady is again 'Mrs Grimslees' after having been 'Mrs Grinslees' in all printed texts (8.25, 29: Scott
overlooked the third occurrence at 8.35). Errors which had already
been picked up in later editions are again exposed in the octavo so that
obvious misreadings like 'dragoons' for 'dragons' (53.33), introduced
in the octavo and previously corrected in the duodecimo, need to be
amended again. A few times, Scott recognises a problem in the text but
does not return to the exact manuscript reading: 'the prisoners' was
originally a misreading of 'the presence' (350.9) but now Scott corrects
it to the more familiar 'those present'.

The most frequent revision is the further inclusion of dialogue appar-
atus ('said the Abbot', 'continued Sir Piercie') examples of which Scott
adds 6 times. In earlier stages of the text's history it was thought unnecessary to assign every single speech to a character if the speaker was
clear from the context. For the new edition, the attribution of speakers
has become more of a textual policy. Many of the other emendations
comprise the addition or substitution of a word or two for stylistic effect.
Scott balances out the phrase 'more danger in running away than in
standing' (4.13–14) by adding the word 'fast' to the end of it, and he
emphasises the contrast in 'the difference between a cannon standing
loaded in its embrazure, and the same gun when touched by the linstock'
(181.21–23) by replacing 'standing loaded' with 'lying quiet'. There is
also some retouching of grammar and syntax: 'is to send' becomes 'is
about to send' (326.19) and 'he took' (104.27) becomes 'he should
take'.

As there are not a great number of changes of more than a word or
two, we should be cautious about identifying patterns in Scott's revisions, but some trends do emerge. There is a certain amount of attention to Sir Piercie Shafton (who had been perceived by Scott as a cause
of the novel's lack of popularity). Sir Piercie gains a goatee beard: his
face, formerly 'close shaved' (131.15), now becomes 'close shaved, all
save a small patch on the point of the chin' to reflect Scott's sense of
Elizabethan fashions. There are also some small emendations to his
speeches: the more elevated 'brows' is substituted for 'head' (138.2) to
produce the phrase 'a precious garland on the brows of an ass', and an
unadorned mention of 'Halbert Glendinning' (239.25) becomes 'the
villagio whom you call Halbert Glendinning'. By contrast, Christie is
given a rougher cast of speech when his mild 'In truth' (137.36) is
replaced by the resounding 'By my Troggs', and a reminder of his less
than polite behaviour is inserted in a speech of Sir Piercie's: after the
sentence ending 'I was altogether unrigged' (158.9) Scott adds: 'That
Border knave his serving man has a pluck at me to and usurpd a scarlet

cassock and steel cuirass belonging to ⟨my⟩ the page of my body whom I was fain to leave behind me.—'. This last addition represents a faint tendency in the new additions to keep in focus characters not immediately engaged in a conversation. There is another example in Morton and Moray's discussion of Halbert's duel with Sir Piercie. Moray comments that Elizabeth would give a 'glove filled with gold crowns' to hear of Shafton's death and Morton replies that she would 'esteem her glove a better gift than her crown' (324.30–31), to which speech Scott adds 'which few border lads like this fellow will esteem just valuation' as the conversation is about to turn back to Halbert.

In general, Scott's additions are designed to elaborate rather than to alter the sense. Some of these elaborations, written several years after the initial inception of the text, may strike the reader as wordy or unnecessary. An example occurs in Scott's introduction of Catherine, where the text originally summed up her demeanour as 'not attributes of a wife, or they were those of a dejected and afflicted one' (219.10–11). Coming to revise the text, Scott seems not to trust the reader to notice that Catherine is pregnant and (rather coyly) replaces 'one' with 'female who had yielded her love on less than legitimate terms'. The urge to clarify leads to other substantive additions. After Piercie Shafton has told Mysie that he does not understand what she is pointing to ('I comprehend nought by this extension of thy fair digit': 264.31–32), Scott adds 'said the Knight who for once was puzzled as much as his own elegances of speech were wont to puzzle others', although this sentiment is perfectly clear from the context. A similar elaboration introduces an element of tautology into Edward's declaration that he will try to forget Mary Avenel. The octavo reads simply: 'I endeavour to forget; but it has been the thought of all my former life' (342.30–31), but Scott fills this out with: ' I endeavour to forget; but what I would now blot from memory has been the thought of all my former life'.

After the Interleaved copy left Scott's hands both James Ballantyne and Cadell are likely to have made changes both to the octavo text, and to Scott's new revisions. There is no record of whether or not Scott examined the proofs, but his own involvement in these final changes cannot be ruled out. Cadell transcribed Scott's changes before sending the text to the press and took the opportunity to edit Scott's additions and include some changes of his own. He commenced these activities, covered by the term 'revisal', on 27 January 1830, having concluded his work on *Ivanhoe* the previous day, and he completed them on 2 March.[70] On 5 March he revised the new Introduction,[71] and between 1 April and 11 May he was apparently dealing with proofs.[72] Volume 18 was published on 1 November 1830, and Volume 19 a month later.[73]

Some of Scott's phrasing is further revised in the Magnum. In the octavo (as in the first edition) we are told that Halbert displays 'one of those rare combinations of talent and industry, which are seldom combined save in the most fortunate subjects' (107.3–5). In the Interleaved Set Scott seems to have found 'subjects' unclear and elaborates with 'subjects of education', but this change was evidently deemed even more confusing, and the Magnum ends up with the more succinct and stylistically elegant 'combinations of talent and industry, which are seldom united'. The Sub-Prior complains (316.35–36) of the need to employ Christie: 'Hateful necessity . . . that makes necessary such implements as these.' Scott changes the phrase to 'renders indispensible such vile implements as these.' but the Magnum, spotting the repetition in 'necessity' and 'necessary', changes it again to 'obliges us to use such implements as these!'. The question of the Sub-Prior's apparent physical transformation on his accession to the office of Abbot is again raised. The octavo reads 'The Abbot-elect bore a more ample port than formerly' (314.32) and this, as discussed above, had been changed to 'manly port' in the 18mo. The Magnum finds another solution, changing 'bore a more ample port' to 'carried himself with more dignity'. A few errors that had come into the text with the first edition are corrected at this final stage. The original misreading of 'mendicant' for 'merchant' (319.14) is perceived as a mistake, but is changed to 'pedlar' (the usual designation of this character in the text). More usually, however, the verbal changes introduced into the Magnum seem the result of a turn to literalism: 'lost his sword' (332.11–12) is changed to 'was deprived of his sword' lest the reader should think Stawarth Bolton had merely mislaid his weapon in the heat of single combat.

The Magnum continues to emend the text according to the general instructions which had been followed by all intermediaries. There is some further avoidance of repetition: for example, 'Stripping, therefore, her holiday kirtle . . . the good-humoured maiden stripped her snowy arms' (148.38–40) becomes 'Laying aside, therefore . . . the good-humoured maiden bared her snowy arms'. The rather glaring repetition in 'This celebrated person had in his person' (321.32) is at last spotted and the second 'person' becomes 'appearance'. A small number of words are appropriately Scoticised in the dialogue of Scots-speaking characters. But the Magnum also changes what were probably perceived as stylistic infelicities: 'was a wild liver' (50.5) becomes 'led a wild and unsettled life', 'washing himself' (132.33) becomes 'fitting ablutions', and 'perusing each other with their eyes' (287.38) becomes 'intently regarding his opponent'. The Magnum also prefers certain word-forms over others: the spelling 'Stuart' is changed to 'Stewart', although Scott uses both in his Interleaved Set emendations, signalling a note on the 'Genealogy of the Stewarts' but composing the note under the title 'Pedigree of the Stuarts' (see Magnum, 19.394–95).[74] Throughout, the Magnum uses 'Scotch' rather than 'Scottish' and twice ignores Scott's corrections back to 'Scottish' in the Interleaved text.

The most common type of change practised in the Magnum is a

process of modernisation. The standardisation of spelling already noted throughout the editions of the *Historical Romances* is picked up again: frequent examples occur when 'shew' becomes 'show', 'chaunt' becomes 'chant', and 'relique' becomes 'relic'. The letter 'y' becomes 'i' in words such as 'siren', 'blithe', and 'silvan', and words ending in '-ize' tend to change to '-ise'. This is also true of verbal changes which often 'correct' the older or more unusual forms and constructions employed by Scott. Thus 'take little by' (29.19) becomes 'make little by', 'if speak him fair' (108.5) becomes 'if spoken fair', and 'awaked watch' (262.7) becomes 'kept watch'. The phrase 'chased our heaviest ... hours' (27.20) is possibly construed as a misreading and the first word is changed to 'cheered'. In general this has the effect of making the text rather more conventional.

Scott had done very little with the punctuation in the Interleaved Set, but now it undergoes some revision, largely the introduction of further punctuation marks. Perhaps the most striking change at this stage is the addition of exclamation marks. Some 50 are added, making a large total (particularly when it is considered that there were only 508 in the whole of the first edition). The Magnum also shows a preference for moving a long dash (indicating an interrupted speech) outside closing speech marks, and introduces a large number of hyphens into two-word phrases while making many hyphenated phrases into single words. Capital letters tend to be lowered (most conspicuously in the case of 'monk') with the exception of some religious terms ('Holy Kirk', 'Mother Church', and 'Heaven') which are capitalised.

4. THE PRESENT TEXT

The present text of *The Monastery* is based on the first edition but is emended by reference to the manuscript and occasionally to the later editions of the novel published in Scott's lifetime. The processes of editing Scott's novels for the Edinburgh Edition have so far shown the first edition in all cases to be the best basis for a modern edition and *The Monastery* is no exception. This was, after all, the edition which Scott saw fit to release to the public when he considered that the novel was finished, and it was also that in whose production he actively participated. The only other two states which clearly show Scott at work are the manuscript and the Magnum Opus. The latest changes clearly attributable to Scott occur in the Interleaved Set, the record of his changes intended for the Magnum Opus edition, and the Magnum would therefore have a claim for consideration as a base-text. In the case of *The Monastery*, however, this claim can be quickly discounted. It was ten years since Scott's initial conception of the text, and he cannot be said to have engaged in it as he had done with the first edition. His changes in the Interleaved text and the subsequent changes in the Magnum are largely mechanical. Where they do indicate new departures, these tend to simplify the novel, to modernise what was a deliberate sense of linguistic historicism, or to explain matters which were quite clear in the first place. To use the Magnum, then, would not add any significant creative contributions to the texts, but would include many of the errors introduced into the octavo *Historical Romances*, the edition on which the Magnum is based.

A better case for base-text might be made for the manuscript, which is almost complete and which, of course, is unequivocally the work of Scott. Although it might be said that the manuscript is the closest to Scott's initial conception of the novel, we must remember that this initial stage of writing included the understanding that intermediaries would make the routine changes which came under their general instructions: the introduction of complete punctuation, the avoidance of repetition of words in close proximity, and the correction of obvious errors of various sorts. The process of composition did not end with the completion of the manuscript. Taking this into consideration, the first edition can be seen as the first realisation of Scott's conception of *The Monastery* as a Waverley Novel, rather than as the first emendation of an 'original' text which preceded it. Nevertheless, the first edition is also the work of a number of different intermediaries, who may have lacked Scott's overview of the novel as a whole. As their function was primarily as transcriber, compositors, or proof-readers they were obliged to concentrate on the production of text and they sometimes correct mechanically rather than with a sense of the meaning. They were also working at speed and were always liable to introduce errors as well as correcting them. The first edition is the text which most accurately reflects the circumstances of the novel's production, but it might also be thought of as a victim of those circumstances, and it should be interpreted in the light of the manuscript as a clearer record of Scott's initial intentions. The intermediaries' instructions were general rather than particular and could not account for all eventualities. The first edition then cannot be regarded as entirely finalised or homogeneous, but rather as a basis from which to construct a text which is historically informed but which also answers the requirements of a modern reader.

The present edition takes the first edition as its base-text but introduces over 1300 emendations based on the manuscript. In the absence of surviving proofs, we cannot always be certain of the extent to which Scott was himself responsible for the changes between manuscript and first edition, but it is clear that the latter includes some serious misreadings, many of which have already been discussed in this essay. The first edition introduces a number of misreadings of the manuscript which, remaining uncorrected in the Magnum Opus upon which all following editions were based, have never before been restored to what Scott wrote. Striking among these, in that they constitute substantive changes in sense, are 'friend' for 'fiend' (76.24), 'breaking on' for 'breathing in'

(76.42), 'suddenly' for 'sullenly' (195.24), and 'printed' for 'painted' (111.11): these changes, and many similar ones, appear in print for the first time in the present text. Although straightforward misreading was the usual cause of error, the intermediaries were working at speed and were subject to its pressures: they sometimes copied not precisely what they saw, but what they expected to see, so that, for example, the White Lady's mocking 'Sir Prior' becomes the familiar 'Sub-Prior' at 93.17. They could also be subject to errors arising from homophones, 'rites' becoming 'rights' at 85.20. As more than one intermediary worked on the text, individual preferences (now unattributable) may have entered the text. Certain common words which do not have an appreciable effect on the sense appear in varying forms and spellings (for example 'on'/'upon', 'further'/'farther', 'round'/'around', 'betwixt'/'between', and 'shall'/'will'): in such cases Scott's manuscript reading is preferred.

In a very few cases, readings from the later editions published in Scott's lifetime are incorporated to correct errors in the first edition which are not distortions of the manuscript. The present text also includes a few editorial emendations, a number of which are accompanied by individual explanations in the Emendation List. The policy of emending with no obvious textual authority has been adopted only where there is a clear error in punctuation, grammar, or sense, as for example, when a speech ends with no full stop or closing speech marks at 254.42. In one final case, the phrase 'the Three Cranes or the Vintry' has been editorially emended to 'the Three Cranes of the Vintry' (272.43–273.1). This editorial correction of a factual error (the Three Cranes was an inn named after the cranes on the neighbouring Vintry wharf) is justified by reference to Scott's next-but-one novel, *Kenilworth*, which includes the phrase 'the Three Cranes, in the Vintry', indicating that Scott was aware that the Vintry was an area, not a hostelry.[75]

Emendations from the Manuscript. These take a number of different forms. The following examples are given to illustrate the pattern of changes made in the present text, and many others can be found in the full list of all emendations.

1] *Structural changes.* The present text restores Scott's original volume division between Volume 1 and Volume 2, coming at the end of Chapter 10. In the first edition, probably in order to even up the number of pages in each volume, the division was changed to the end of the following chapter. The present text, now physically in one volume, allows us to appreciate Scott's original end of the volume, dramatic and therefore likely to have been a deliberate choice rather than a miscalculation of the amount of text he had produced: the final chapter closes with the suspenseful and unexplained appearance of the White Lady to Halbert, with the reader having to turn to the next volume to discover the significance of her visitation. A second structural change is the moving of one of Scott's footnotes. As was observed earlier in this essay, one intermediary evidently decided that the phrase 'put my own buist on my own cattle' would either be incomprehensible to the average reader, or unsuitable diction for the style of the Author of Waverley, and substituted in the first edition the phrase 'put my own mark on my own chattels' (29.25–26). This occurs in Volume 1, but towards the end of Volume 2 (216.26–27) Scott uses the term again, this time in the speech of Christie of Clinthill, and includes a footnote explaining that the term means 'The brand or mark set upon sheep or cattle by their owners'. The present text restores the original 'buist' and transfers the footnote to the first occurrence.

2] *Punctuation.* Scott's system of punctuation is very different from that appearing in the first edition, but it is largely consistent and was easily 'translated' by intermediaries. But sometimes they overlooked instructions: Scott writes 'N.L.' ('new line') to indicate a new paragraph, and on the two occasions where this has been missed or ignored in the first edition his instruction is followed in this edition. Sometimes it is clear that the intermediaries, working at speed, simply have not understood Scott's intentions. We can see this in an exchange between Elspet and the Sub-Prior (80.22–27). Scott writes:

> "I desire first to know it from you Dame Glendinning" said the Monk and I again repeat it is your duty to explain it to me—This book you say which Father Philip removed from Glendearg"———
> "Was this morning returnd to us in strange manner" said the good widow. "Returnd?" said the Monk How mean you?"—

The intermediaries miss the division of speakers (Scott has not indicated a new line) and apportion the speech wrongly, resulting in the first-edition reading:

> "I desire first to know it from you, Dame Glendinning," said the Monk; "and I again repeat, it is your duty to tell it to me."
> "This book, if it please your reverence, which Father Philip removed from Glendearg, was this morning returned to us in a strange manner," said the good widow.

In general, however, the first edition's punctuation has been followed; it has been emended only where it is clearly misleading, or where Scott's manuscript sentence divisions have not been respected (for example at 238.8 where a full stop was replaced by a semi-colon). Although the punctuation can seem over-elaborate to a modern eye, it is in fact less formal than that of subsequent editions, especially those Victorian and twentieth-century texts which descend from the Magnum. Nevertheless, some further alterations, based on manuscript readings, have been made in the present text. One matter for consideration is the fact that intermediaries had to distinguish between dashes which indicated that other punctuation marks should be supplied, and dashes which Scott meant *as* dashes, the latter often occurring in direct speech to indicate excited or breathless communication.

An example of the present text's policy of restoring Scott's punctuation can be found at 130.29–42. The differences between manuscript and first edition in the passage 'Mysie flew to the shot-window . . . and see him' have already been discussed above (369–70), and all three versions can be compared to see how the present text adopts the manuscript's use of dashes to indicate excited speech and the flow of conversation. Here the present text is reproduced with the first edition variants in square parentheses:

> Mysie flew to the shot-window, in the full ardour of unrestrained female curiosity. "Saint Mary! sweet lady! here come two well-mounted gallants— [gallants,] will you step this way to look at them?"
>
> "No," said Mary Avenel, "you shall tell me who they are."
>
> "Well— [Well,] if you like it better," said Mysie—"but how shall I know them?—stay, [Stay,] I do know one of them, and so do you, lady—[lady;] he is a blythe man— [man,] somewhat light of hand they say, but the gallants of these days think no great harm of that. He is your uncle's henchman, that they call Christie of the Clinthill; and he has not his old green jerkin, and the rusty black jack over it, but a scarlet cloak, laid down with silver lace three inches broad, and a breast-plate you might see to dress your hair in, as well as in that keeking-glass in the ivory frame that you shewed me even now—come, [now. Come,] dear lady, come to the shot-window and see him."

The text itself indicates that Mysie's speech is to be taken as 'the full ardour of unrestrained female curiosity' and Scott further indicates Mysie's excited discourse by his inclusion in the manuscript of the first exclamation mark. The present edition follows up these indications by restoring manuscript dashes to represent the breaks in Mysie's speech. Scott's dashes are not random but are used to signal changes of direction, such as Mysie's turning to Mary to ask 'will you step this way to look at them?' or the parenthetical 'stay, I do know one of them, and so do you, lady' which in the manuscript is set off by dashes. The speech settles down in the middle for Mysie's detailed description of Christie (unpunctuated by Scott) and returns at the end of the paragraph to Mysie's more insistent instructions to Mary to come to the window, when Scott's dash is again restored in the present text.

Intermediaries are apt to introduce commas into the text; in the case of *The Monastery* over fifteen thousand commas are added to the first edition. Very often this procedure is entirely in keeping with their standing orders, but sometimes they change the rhythm of Scott's texts. This is particularly noticeable in instances of repeated words to portray excited or insistent speech: for example in Martin's distracted exclama-

tion 'Come awa—come awa—nae use in staying here langer' (45.17)
the manuscript dashes are replaced by commas in the first edition and
restored in the present text. At other times, commas can be semantically
disruptive. The first edition introduces the comma in this phrase of
Captain Clutterbuck's: 'At length he ended, with advising me . . . to
apply to some veteran of literature' (22.11–12). As the ending and the
advising are evidently coterminous, the comma is merely confusing.
Commas are retained unless they obscure the meaning (bearing in mind
the presentational conventions of Scott's day); the present edition aims
to restore the flow of Scott's original text, and in just over 80 cases
first-edition commas are either removed, or replaced with his original
dashes. Where Scott clearly indicates a comma, however, these are
retained even when they are not carried over into the first edition. This
is a very much rarer event than the addition of commas by intermediaries and occurs only seven times in the present text. Of these, two occur
in the same paragraph, a section which is quite instructive in the ways
Scott's punctuation, rudimentary though it is, can often be more precise
than the intermediaries gave him credit for. The manuscript reads
(f. 43r):

> There were opinions to be combated and refuted, practices to be
> enquired into hereticks to be detected and punishd, the fallen off to
> be reclaimd the wavering to be confirmd scandal to be removed
> from the clergy and the vigour of discipline to be reestablishd. Post
> upon Post arrived at the Monastery of Saint Mary's horses reeking
> and ⟨men⟩ riders exhausted this from the Privy Council, that from
> the Primate of Scotland and this other again from the Queen
> Mother exhorting approving condemning requesting advice ⟨and⟩
> upon this subject and requiring information upon that—

The first edition's interpretation of this passage (1.185) is as follows:

> There were opinions to be combatted and refuted—practices to be
> enquired into—heretics to be detected and punished—the fallen
> off to be reclaimed—the wavering to be confirmed—scandal to be
> removed from the clergy, and the vigour of discipline to be re-
> established. Post upon post arrived at the Monastery of St Mary's
> —horses reeking, and riders exhausted—this from the Privy
> Council, that from the Primate of Scotland, and this other again
> from the Queen Mother, exhorting, approving, condemning, re-
> questing advice upon this subject, and requiring information upon
> that.

Here the intermediaries have re-interpreted Scott's commas as a kind of
free indirect speech of the type for which he normally does use dashes,
and have duly inserted them throughout the passage. In this instance,
however, Scott has clearly, though not systematically, specified the use
of commas in the first sentence for what he intends to read as a list,
although he does not continue this explicit punctuation throughout the
passage. In the second sentence dashes (also inserted in the first

edition) are appropriate to set off the parenthetic phrase: 'horses reeking, and riders exhausted'. The present edition, emended both with manuscript punctuation and further editorial punctuation derived from the pattern of commas set by Scott, reads (67.37–68.5):

> There were opinions to be combatted and refuted, practices to be enquired into, heretics to be detected and punished, the fallen off to be reclaimed, the wavering to be confirmed, scandal to be removed from the clergy, and the vigour of discipline to be re-established. Post upon post arrived at the Monastery of Saint Mary's— horses reeking, and riders exhausted—this from the Privy Council, that from the Primate of Scotland, and this other again from the Queen Mother, exhorting, approving, condemning, requesting advice upon this subject, and requiring information upon that.

Apart from the ubiquitous dash and a number of commas, Scott's use of other punctuation is rare in the manuscript and where it does occur can be taken to indicate a conscious decision on his part. The present text thus preserves most of Scott's specific punctuation restoring nine exclamation marks, five colons, four semi-colons, and two question marks. Intermediaries also tend to remove capital letters in the manuscript—often, in the process, removing particular significances assigned by Scott. He clearly wishes the phrase 'to Wisdom and to Goodness' to denote personifications of these moral qualities, but the first edition's 'to wisdom and to goodness' (297.38) loses this effect. Sometimes the first edition, rather oddly, will capitalise one part of a phrase but not the other. The dancing master's 'Weekly Practising' (4.25), clearly a well-known village event, loses its first capital, and Clutterbuck's grand phrase 'the Sovereign of the Kingdom' (4.36) loses its second. Where there is no indication of a deliberate policy of capitalisation the lower case of the manuscript is followed. For example: in the Introductory Epistle the first edition twice capitalises the 'Ruins' of the monastery, perhaps to indicate that they were a specific tourist attraction. Scott does not do so, however, and as the first edition more frequently uses the lower-case 'ruins' his reading is preferred.

3] *Spelling.* The first edition does not standardise variant spellings, and neither does the present text. However, as he wrote Scott made occasional errors—for example 'substance' for 'subsistence' (43.40), or 'ought' for 'aught' (84.11)—which were corrected unless the intermediaries could not make out the word intended, in which case they substituted another term or omitted the puzzling word. Thus the unusual word 'spars', which Scott writes as 'sparrs', becomes 'shuts' (73.39). When Scott writes (very unclearly) the words 'peansantly *brochan*' (111.5) the intermediaries, unable to guess the unfamiliar word 'peasantly', simply leave it out. The present text distinguishes between obvious spelling errors on Scott's part, and such misreadings on the part of intermediaries.

As Christopher Johnson has discovered in his edition of *The Abbot*, Scott is consistent in his choice of spellings which specify a particular pronunciation: 'Scott tended to write words as he heard them, particularly in dialogue.'[76] Examples, which occur at various points in the text, are (manuscript reading first) the group: 'knowst'/'knowest', 'doest'/'dost', and 'mayst'/'mayest'; as well as 'burned'/'burnt', 'dreamed'/'dreamt', and 'kneeled'/'knelt'. The manuscript is preferred in all these cases (both forms appear in the first edition). Although the intermediaries were instructed to standardise patterns of diction, including the regularisation of Scots and English speech, some work remains to be done where they have inappropriately anglicised Scots, although in some cases this is likely to be a misreading of Scott's vowels which can look very similar; examples of this kind of confusion are (manuscript reading first): 'lee'/'lie' (9.40), 'safter'/'softer' (55.24), and 'ane'/'one' (3.33). Also restored are Scott's use of older forms of words where these have been modernised in the first edition. Examples of this practice include 'account' for 'accompt' (331.13), 'handkerchief' for 'kerchief' (194.31), and 'wardrobe' for 'wardrope' (158.19 etc.).

4] *Verbal Emendations.* Obvious misreadings, many of which are identified in the earlier sections of this essay, are corrected. Certain characteristics of Scott's handwriting led to probable errors in transcription. Scott rarely dots 'i's, his 'e's and 'i's are quite similar, and in general his vowels can quite easily be taken for each other. The first edition consistently confuses the words 'in' and 'on', taking 'on' for 'in' 7 times and once the other way round. Scott's handwriting is the likely cause for other misreadings: his 'g' and 'q' can look alike, which accounts for the unusual word 'guestens' turning into the more familiar 'quarters' (235.30). Other easily confused letters lead to 'foragers' becoming 'forayers' (40.28), 'cleansing' becoming 'clearing' (59.14), and 'mumming' becoming 'mummery' (158.17) in the first edition, all of which occasion straightforward reversions to the manuscript in the present text.

A great number of words and phrases are substituted between the manuscript and first edition, and from the novels for which proofs survive we can see that Scott himself generally participated in this process. This calls for some care when restoring manuscript readings. Words unnecessarily introduced into the first edition are removed: the second 'call' is omitted in the present text from the first edition's 'that liquor which hosts call Sherry, and guests call Lisbon' (11.1).

The intermediaries' instructions to remove repetition are generally respected in the present text. On the other hand, Scott can include deliberate repetition for emphasis or contrast which may be removed mechanically by intermediaries. The present edition assumes this to be the case at 44.15–17 where Tibb says 'our leddy is half gane already . . . a word mair and she is gane outright' and Martin replies 'I could almost wish . . . we were a' then gane'. The first edition replaced the second 'gane' with 'dead', but this is to interrupt the incremental effect of the exchange.

The restoration of material changed or omitted because it might have caused offence calls for some fine decisions. The policy of the present text is to restore readings which are likely to have been changed by an intermediary on the grounds of taste, but to retain first-edition changes which mute Scott's initial references to the factual events surrounding the publication of *The Monastery* described in the opening section of this essay. The latter are likely to be the result of second thoughts on Scott's part (even if this rethinking was suggested to him by one or other of his assistants) and the manuscript reference to William Fearman and the elaboration of the warring publishers are not included here. However, Scott's original 'jolly dogs', Captain Clutterbuck's familiar term for the Flemish canons, is restored from the first edition's 'jolly fellows' (14.33) and the first edition's euphemistic 'some wild kinsman of Morton' returns to its original 'the bastard of Morton' (320.3). At 323.16 the first edition removes 'hand-fasted' from the phrase 'his hand-fasted concubine'. This may be an oversight, but seems more likely an attempt to remove any ambiguity the practice of hand-fasting may cast over Catherine's moral status, and the present edition restores 'hand-fasted'.

Intermediaries worked quickly and could misinterpret not only Scott's writing but also his syntax. In the first edition the Sub-Prior opines: 'if the drenching of Father Philip cometh of the Evil One, yet it may not have been altogether without his own personal fault' (74.38–40). But Scott had written that the drenching 'may not have been by his own personal intervention'. The intermediary has taken the pronoun 'his' to refer to Father Philip and has altered the sentence to make better sense of this attribution. In the manuscript, however, 'his' refers to the Evil One, and this reading is restored in the present text.

Some changes in the first edition give the impression of intermediaries tinkering with the text for no very obvious reason. The first edition's 21 reversals of Scott's 'said he' to 'he said' have all been restored to 'said he' in the present text. Other reversals of words—for example 'would certainly' to 'certainly would' (4.29) and 'created things' to 'things created' (93.25)—are seen as unnecessary interventions on the part of intermediaries and the manuscript has been preferred. These instances usually involve the transposition of two adjacent words, but on occasion sentences are rearranged to follow manuscript readings which made good sense in the first place. Other changes are the result of a clearer policy. Intermediaries seem to have been in general less confident than Scott that his readers would understand unfamiliar terms even when these can be fairly easily deduced from the context. Scott describes the Abbot seated in 'his high-backed chair, the grotesque carving of which terminated in a mitre', but in the first edition, 'carving' has been unnecessarily elaborated as 'carved back' (69.18). Similarly, in the manuscript the Author warned Captain Clutterbuck against imitating 'the autograph of any other successful Empiric—amounting . . . to nothing short of felony'. In the first edition the words 'a crime' (29.28) are added after the dash but as this introduces a note of tautology into the sentence Scott's original phrase has been preferred.

Scott had a good ear for older linguistic forms, but intermediaries often modernised his dialogue. Thus 'recruits to my troop' becomes 'recruits for my troop' (41.34); 'Is our subject of quarrel' becomes 'Is the subject of our quarrel' (202.5–6); in the phrase 'for either the pleasure or comfort the sight will give me' (131.1–2) 'for' becomes 'considering'; and 'with my safety' becomes 'with safety' (157.18). Where historical examples of Scott's manuscript phrasing can be found, as in all these cases, the present text restores it. A common instance of this phenomenon is the introduction of indefinite articles into the first edition. Although these often sound more familiar to the modern ear, Scott's idioms turn out to be historically correct so the manuscript readings are restored here. Examples of this tendency are (manuscript given first, first edition second): 'keep e'e'/'keep an e'e' (19.33); 'in strange manner'/'in a strange manner' (80.25); 'of tendency'/'of a tendency' (60.4); 'was matter of no interest'/'was a matter of no interest' (128.33); and 'strikes stroke'/'strikes a stroke' (328.18). Piercie Shafton's extravagant language gives rise to one or two problems for intermediaries: the parodic (on Scott's part) 'un-to-be-paralleled' appears in the first edition as a more familiar 'not-to-be-paralleled' (188.14). On the other hand, an intermediary coins a Shaftonism of his own: Scott's 'rustical' turns into 'rusticial' (136.13), an error which passed into the *Oxford English Dictionary* where it is listed as pseudo-archaic.

A large group of changes involves the use of plurals. Scott's final 's' can be quite rudimentary and easily missed, but at other times intermediaries seem to have added or removed plurals randomly, and in either case the present text follows the manuscript. Generally this does not radically affect the sense as, for example, when 'forward' is restored to 'forwards' (46.41, 218.34), or 'communications' to 'communication' (244.12). On occasion, however, the switching round of plurals can effect a change in meaning. This is the case when Scott's reference to Mary's right to 'the possessions of her fathers' becomes 'the possessions of her father' (49.1) altering the sense of an ancestral right to the concept of legal inheritance.

5] *Material omitted or added in the First Edition.* Sometimes manuscript material is omitted from the first edition because the intermediary's eye has slipped down or across the page. There is a clear example of this at 55.9–12. The intermediary encounters the following manuscript reading of Tibb's question: 'what does your leddy aye do wi that book in her hand—It's nae wonder that her bairn sees bogles if she is aye reading on that thick black book wi' the silver clasps?' But his eye slips from 'aye do' to 'aye reading' to produce the first edition's 'what does your leddy aye do reading on that thick black book wi' the silver clasps?'. A shorter example is the omission of the words 'the recesses of' in the phrase 'of the recesses of the libraries' (28.5–6). The present text restores missing material in all such cases. At other times words are simply left out for no obvious reason, and such occurrences are likely to be the result of straightforward lapses of attention on the part of intermediaries. In this way 'curiously and' drops out of the phrase 'curiously and secretly' (24.18–19), and similarly 'pleasant and joyous' becomes simply 'joyous' (125.21).

The manuscript's idiom can be more elliptic than that of the first edition; in an attempt to clarify, intermediaries can introduce a more wordy style than Scott's original which sometimes implies actions rather than detailing them. Among many examples of this marked characteristic of the first edition, the manuscript's 'assayd Shagram' becomes 'essayed to lead forward Shagram' (47.11) and 'a certain credit' becomes 'a certain degree of credit' (251.17). Scott's more pithy phraseology can often fall prey to the intermediaries' tendency to over-correct grammatically: the parallelism of the manuscript's 'Halbert was likely to break more heads than grind sacks of corn' is diluted when an intermediary changes the second half of the phrase to 'than he would grind sacks of corn' (122.20). This is a common feature of the first edition: 'I would abide in this house to chuse' becomes 'I would abide in this house were I to chuse' (183.42–43), and many other examples can be found in the Emendation List. Even when the syntax is clear, intermediaries are given to filling in plot details. At 258.6 a simple reference to Mysie's 'scheme' is somewhat laboriously elaborated into 'scheme for Sir Piercie Shafton's freedom'. The first edition can be over eager to spell out characters' actions; it introduces the word 'sitting' into the phrase 'the bairns were frighted to see a strange woman sitting there' (81.6) although we have just been told already that the White Lady was sitting by the burn. Similarly, the manuscript's description of Martin 'a few paces before' the little party on the way to Glendearg becomes 'walking a little before' despite the verbal repetition that this introduces (46.7). In all such cases in the present text the manuscript is considered sufficiently clear and more elegant stylistically.

6] *Names.* Scott often found it difficult to keep track of characters' names in his novels and some of the inconsistencies thus engendered in *The Monastery* are described above in the section 'The Manuscript'. Most names are standardised in the first edition, but not always according to their prevalence in the manuscript and the present text attempts to identify Scott's preferred spelling. Despite the manuscript's clear tendency towards 'Elspet' Glendinning this character's name is standardised to 'Elspeth' in the first edition. The present text prefers the form of names indicated by the manuscript and has restored 'Elspet'. The manuscript also shows a preference for the monks' names 'Nicolas' and 'Ingelram' and these versions have been adopted. Slightly more problematic is the name of the Earl of Moray whose title appears as both 'Moray' and 'Murray' in both manuscript and first edition but is standardised to 'Murray' in all subsequent texts. Both textual and extratextual evidence suggests that 'Moray' was Scott's preferred version: it is the prevalent spelling in both manuscript and first edition of *The Monastery*,[77] and it was Scott's initial spelling in the manuscript of *The Abbot* until James Ballantyne objected on the proof that 'The Earl of *Murray* is so much more kenspeckle than the Earl of *Moray*'.[78] The Edinburgh Edition therefore restores 'Moray' in both novels.

Emendations from Later Editions. Later editions are used sparingly for textual emendation and are only referred to when they offer suggestions for the correction of obvious errors in the first edition. Most of the emendations introduced from later editions correct punctuation, but it has been necessary at times to adopt later readings which make better sense than the first edition. The 18mo, for example, supplies the correction of Mary Avenel's age to 'just six years old' (46.5) when the first edition has her poised between five and six on the very day of her birthday.

Scott's revisions in the Interleaved Set have been used as the bases for two substantive changes. First, there is the question of Piercie Shafton's mother's maiden name. In the first edition she is called 'Moll Crossstitch' the daughter of 'old Overstitch of Holderness'. In the Interleaved Set, Scott recognises that it is more likely for Moll to have the same surname as her father, and changes it to 'Over-stitch'. The present text, however, respects Scott's original choice of name (which appears twice in the first edition to the single appearance of 'Overstitch') as well as his desire for consistency, and has both Moll and her father named 'Crossstitch' (349.41). Another alteration in the Interleaved Set requires the editor to discriminate between what Scott actually wrote in the manuscript, and his change of mind long after the original writing of the novel. The first edition (following the manuscript) has the Earl of Moray telling Halbert to ride to the Monastery and 'spare the spur, for fear of spoiling horse-flesh'. In the Interleaved Set Scott changes this to 'spare not the spur', thereby reversing the sense. The immediate context is ambiguous: Halbert sets off 'as fast as the jaded state of their cavalry permitted'. The general impetus of this section of the novel, however, is one of speed and haste, so in this case Scott's later revision has been accepted (because it probably inserts a word missing in the manuscript), and the Magnum reading, which omits the comma after 'spur', has been adopted (328.21).

NOTES

All manuscripts cited are in the National Library of Scotland unless otherwise stated. For the shortened forms of reference employed see pp. 441–42.

1 Magnum, 18.iii.
2 *Letters*, 5.443, 445.
3 *Letters*, 5.454: 12 August [1819], to John Ballantyne.
4 *Letters*, 5.392 ([15 April 1819]: see *The Bride of Lammermoor*, EEWN 7a, 273), 399 (21 June [1819]), both to John Ballantyne.
5 *Letters*, 5.424–25 [postmarked 26 July 1819]. Scott is writing to James Ballantyne telling him not to renew Constable's bills.
6 *Letters*, 5.438.
7 *Letters*, 5.428.
8 *Letters*, 5.443.
9 *Letters*, 5.457: 13 August [1819], to John Ballantyne.
10 *Letters*, 5.445.
11 *Letters*, 5.444.
12 This misapprehension is confirmed by a Longman commission ledger entry for 11 August registering the receipt of a bill for £333 6s. 8d. (one third of the £1000) from the Ballantynes, who were responsible for advancing one third of the author's profits. The Longman Archives are held at Reading University Library and the ledger entry is in Longman I.19.52.
13 *Letters*, 5.454. The sum of £2400 represents Scott's calculation of what would be due to him as an advance on profits of £2500 on a three-volume edition with a print-run of 12,000. The sum is a rounding-up of half of £4500 £2250). For the general operation of 'half-profits' see *The Antiquary*, EEWN 3, 364. For further details of the system see *The Abbot*, EEWN 10, 379–80.
14 *Letters*, 5.443.
15 *Letters*, 5.457.
16 *The Abbot*, EEWN 10, 380.
17 *Letters*, 5.474.
18 Discussed extensively in *Ivanhoe*, EEWN 8, 409–10.
19 *Letters*, 5.443.
20 MS 319, ff. 252–55: Constable to Robert Cadell, 30 November 1819.
21 MS 319, f. 177v: Constable to Cadell, 23 October 1819.
22 MS 23234, f. 39v: Constable to Cadell, 4 November 1819.
23 MS 23234, f. 42v: Constable to Cadell, 6 December 1819. In fact the selling price agreed for *Ivanhoe* was 30s. for the three volumes.
24 MS 319, f. 253r: Constable to Cadell, 30 November 1819. *Ivanhoe* was designed from the start as a superior product which would look different from its predecessors, being printed on better paper and in the larger octavo format. *The Monastery* reverted to the more usual 12mo format resulting in a book of slightly smaller dimensions.
25 *Morning Chronicle*, 18 October 1819. A shorter advertisement, not mentioning Jedediah Cleishbotham, had appeared on 14 October.
26 MS 319, f. 168r: Constable to Cadell, 17 October 1819.
27 MS 319, f. 252v: Constable to Cadell, 30 November 1819.
28 MS 790, p. 691. Constable explains in a letter to Cadell of 30 November (MS 319, f. 253r): 'I have struck out L & C's name from the title page— when the Book is reddy we shall send Rees a copy into which a note shall be

put telling him that their firm does not appear in the title in order to counteract an impression in the Trade & with the Public—that the *4th Series* comes from the same quarter.'

29 *Morning Chronicle*, 28 October 1819. According to Constable, John cleared this letter with Scott before dispatching it to the newspaper (MS 319, ff. 175v–76r). John's letter only served to increase Constable's suspicions of an enemy at work within the newspaper office: 'John B's letter is in the paper this morning but without the introductory remarks & in the very worst place of the paper yesterday there was a 3d edit of the advert. in the M.C which shews there is some one at hand inserting it' (MS 319, f. 193v).

30 *Morning Chronicle*, 30 October 1819.

31 Robert Cadell, Constable's partner, was not optimistic about the outcome of legal action: 'I doubt if we can do any thing as to this—Mr McDougal thinks we cannot without the authors name—and that of course *is imposs-ible*' (MS 323, f. 92v: 28 November 1819).

32 MS 323, f. 52r: Cadell to Constable, 8 November 1819.

33 The title page specifies as primary publishers Longman, Hurst, Rees, Orme and Brown. The Hurst named here was a partner in Longmans, and not the same as the Hurst of Hurst, Robinson & Co. There was clearly some discussion between Constables and Hurst, Robinson & Co. about the possibility of the latter's name also appearing on the title page on the grounds that they had bought a share of books, but Constable advised that 'L&Co would say that our doing so was a Violation of all proper dealing on such Occasions & might ere long propose to us the insertion of the name of Some Edinr Bookseller on some of ours & their Property Books because that Edinr. Booksr purchased largely of them' (MS 23619, f. 1v: Constables to Hurst, Robinson & Co., 2 February 1820).

34 MS 326, ff. 23r–24r.

35 MS 323, f. 98r: Cadell to Constable, 2 December 1819; MS 319, ff. 269v–70r: Constable to Cadell, 8 December 1819.

36 MS 323, f. 116r: 10 December 1819.

37 MS 23618, f. 152r–v.

38 MS 319, f. 248v. The printing of *The Monastery* then began before the final sheet of *Ivanhoe* went to press on 6 and 7 December (MS 319, ff. 262r, 266r: Constable to Cadell).

39 Lockhart, 4.350.

40 *Letters*, 5.465.

41 This is the conclusion of Herbert Grierson in his biography of Scott, *Sir Walter Scott, Bart.* (London, 1938), 175.

42 My reading of this letter agrees with Graham Tulloch's account of the chronological relationship between *The Monastery* and *Ivanhoe*. For an alternative reading see *The Abbot*, EEWN 10, 381, where Christopher John-son argues that Scott here either invents the story of having already started *The Monastery* to account for his apparent desertion of Constable, or simply mixes up the titles of the two novels.

43 MS 1812, f. 31v: photographic copy of John Ballantyne's Journal.

44 *Letters*, 6.6.

45 MS 319, ff. 248r, 249v.

46 *Letters*, 6.6. Constable communicated this information to Hurst, Robinson

&Co., with the evident assumption that they had probably already heard it, on 3 January 1820 (MS 23618, ff. 175r–76r).

47   *The Abbot* is a sequel in that it continues Halbert's story and that of the rescued child of Julian Avenel. In other respects it is a different kind of novel, with a much greater stress on historical figures, most notably Mary Queen of Scots. The bargain for *The Abbot*, then known simply as *The Monastery* 'second Class', or 'second branch', was struck at the end of December 1819. For the further history of *The Abbot*'s separate existence see *The Abbot*, EEWN 10, 384–86.

48   On 7 March 1820 Constables wrote to Hurst, Robinson & Co.: 'We fear the hope we entertained of having Kennilworth before the 2nd Monastery is vanished—we understand the original plan proceeds—we have, as you may suppose, done everything in our power to avert this—without success —we again beg that Kennilworth may be *very private*—' (MS 23619, f. 15v).

49   MS 790, p. 777.

50   MS 791, p. 4: Constables to Longman, Hurst & Co., 25 February 1820.

51   MS 791, p. 18. The books were sent by sea on the steamship *Lord Wellington*.

52   *Morning Chronicle*, 30 March 1820.

53   Constables, writing to Longmans, blamed them for the way they had handled the sales by subscription (MS 23619, f. 23r: 25 March 1820; f. 30r: 5 April 1820). On 15 April they advised Hurst, Robinson & Co. to let their copies go at sale terms (MS 23619, f. 35r) and on 22 April Constables had clearly given up on the novel, telling the London firm to 'do all you can to dispose of it' (MS 23619, f. 39v).

54   Pierpont Morgan MA 444.

55   Compare E. Heawood, *Watermarks Mainly in the 17th and 18th Centuries* (Hilversum, 1950), no. 1774.

56   For continuity of reference the folios have been renumbered throughout the manuscript in consecutive order and references are to these numbers. The different methods of pagination can be compared in the following chart:

Consecutive	Library	Scott
Volume 1		
1	1	[–] (sheet added)
2	3	[1]
3	5	2
4–70	7–139	3–69
71	141	[–]
Volume 2		
[–]	143	[–]
[–]	145	[–]
72	147	[–]
73	149	[–]
74–77	151–57	2–5
78–92	159–87	1–15
93	189	[–]
94–150	191–303	16–72

[–]	305	[–]
[–]	307	[–]
Volume 3		
151	309	[–]
152	311	[–]
153–79	313–65	2–28
180	365 [bis]	29
181–219	367–443	30–68

57   Chapters are numbered as follows:
Vol. 1: MS: 1–9, [no number], 10, Vol. 2, Ch. 1; Ed1: 1–9, 9, 10–11
Vol. 2: MS: 1, 2, 2, [no further numbers]; Ed1: 1, 2, 2, 3, 3–11
Vol. 3: MS: 1–8, [no further numbers]; Ed1: 1–12.
In this essay the chapter numbers used are those of the present text.

58   Other instances of belated chapter divisions are Vol. 1, Chs 4, 7, 10, and
11; and Vol. 3, Ch. 2 where both the motto and opening sentence appear as
a verso addition.

59   f. 164r. Mottoes are missing from Vol. 1, Chs 3, 7, 8, 10, 11, and 12; Vol. 2,
Chs 1, 4, 13, and 14; and Vol. 3, Chs 6, 11, and 12.

60   John probably also transcribed *The Antiquary* and may have transcribed *The
Tale of Old Mortality*: see EEWN 3, 367 and 4b, 367.

61   The four American editions are those published in 1820 by M. Carey &
Son, Philadelphia; Samuel H. Parker, Boston; Clayton & Kingsland, New
York; and J. Seymour, New York. On 2 February 1820 Constables wrote to
Hurst, Robinson & Co.: 'We send you with this under a sealed Cover Vol
1st. of the M. which you may wish to send across the Atlantic but the parcel
must on no account be opened but dispatched as recd the Second Volume
will follow when complete very shortly and after it we hope very speedily
Vol IIId—we think it more than probable that another Vol 1st. is already on
its Voyage' (MS 23619, f. 1r). For further information on the American
publishers' use of proof sheets see *The Abbot*, EEWN 10, 393, and *Kenilworth*, EEWN 11, 403. Parker and Clayton & Kingsland have the final two
paragraphs. For examples of changes made between manuscript and second proofs see the entries for 118.5 and 119.12 in the Emendation List,
and for an example of a change made after second proofs see the entry for
231.13.

62   The section of manuscript with the 'Albert' to 'Halbert' emendations
occurs in a packet already dispatched by Scott by the time he was writing
Elspet's protest about Halbert's name in Volume 2.

63   The manuscript has in total 16 'Elspeth's, 15 'Elspat's and 61 'Elspet's.
The manuscript starts with 8 consecutive instances of 'Murray', then re-
verts to 'Moray' with only 3 further exceptions; the first edition has only 3
instances of 'Murray'.

64   For details see *Ivanhoe*, EEWN 8, 429–31.

65   For an account of the production of the *Historical Romances* see *Kenilworth*,
EEWN 11, 409–12.

66   *Journal*, 48: 24 December 1825.

67   The full story of the Magnum Opus can be found in Jane Millgate, *Scott's
Last Edition: A Study in Publishing History* (Edinburgh, 1987).

68   *Letters*, 11.286.

69   For Scott's return to *The Monastery* in the Magnum introduction see Jane
       Millgate, 'From Deferral to Avoidance: The Problem of *The Monastery*', in
       Scott in Carnival, ed. J. H. Alexander and David Hewitt (Aberdeen, 1993),
       264–79.

70   MS 21020, ff. 6v–11v.

71   MS 21020, f. 12r.

72   On 15 April Cadell noted: 'revised some notes of Monastery in proof'; on 1
       April he had 'revised with Anne [his wife] part of Abbot and some
       notes to Monastery', and on 11 May he 'revised some notes in Monastery'
       (MS 21020, ff. 18r, 16r, 21r). James Ballantyne's involvement in changes
       at the proof stage of the Magnum is indicated in a letter to Cadell answering
       the accusation that he was charging too much for corrections to the printed
       text. Ballantyne writes on 30 December 1828: 'To this charge nobody can
       speak so distinctly as myself; because it is my alterations on the proofs
       which in a considerable degree give rise to it. These are often so numerous
       (all done, as I of course think, for the advantage of the work) that I am
       much surprised to find the charge so low' (MS 21060, f. 178v).

73   William B. Todd and Ann Bowden, *Sir Walter Scott: A Bibliographical
       History 1796–1832* (New Castle, Delaware, 1998), 897.

74   Jane Millgate notes that Scott indicated 'his preference for the spelling
       "Stewart" over "Stuart", and although he himself marked only some of the
       occurrences of the name in the interleaved volumes others were altered in
       another hand, presumably on the author's instructions' (Millgate, *Scott's
       Last Edition*, 76).

75   See *Kenilworth*, EEWN 11, 3.30–31, 18.2. The reading 'in' also occurs in a
       note, probably by Scott, in *The Ancient British Drama*, [ed. Robert Dodsley,
       rev. Walter Scott,] 3 vols (London, 1810), 2.381. But another note in the
       same work (1.93) has 'of'.

76   *The Abbot*, EEWN 10, 409.

77   For the instances of 'Moray' and 'Elspet' see note 62 above.

78   *The Abbot*, proof, p. 4: see *The Abbot*, EEWN 10, 406.

EMENDATION LIST

The base-text for this edition of *The Monastery* is a specific copy of the first edition, owned by the Edinburgh Edition of the Waverley Novels. All emendations to this base-text, whether verbal, orthographic, or punctuational, are listed below, with the exception of certain general categories of emendation described in the next paragraph, and of those errors which result from accidents of printing such as a letter dropping out, provided always that evidence for the 'correct' reading has been found in at least one other copy of the first edition.

The following proper names have been standardised, as explained in the Essay on the Text, 394–95: Elspet, Ingelram, Moray (for the Earl), and Nicolas. Inverted commas are sometimes found in the first edition for displayed verse quotations, sometimes not; the present text has standardised the inconsistent practices of the base-text by eliminating such inverted commas, except where they occur at the beginnings or ends of speeches. The typographic presentation of mottoes, volume and chapter headings, displayed quotations, and the opening words of chapters and volumes, has been standardised. Although it is clear that James Ballantyne and Co. had only one italic ligature for both 'æ' and 'æ', it so happens that all the italic ligatures in *The Monastery* are 'æ', so that no emendation is called for. Ambiguous end-of-line hyphens in the base-text have been interpreted in accordance with the following authorities (in descending order of priority): predominant first edition usage; octavo, duodecimo, and 18mo *Historical Romances*; Magnum; MS.

Each entry in the list below is keyed to the text by page and line number; the reference is followed by the new, EEWN reading, then in brackets the reason for the emendation, and after the slash the base-text reading that has been replaced.

The great majority of emendations are derived from the manuscript. Most merely involve the replacement of one reading by another, and these are listed with the simple explanation '(MS)'. The spelling and punctuation of some emendations from the manuscript have been normalised in accordance with the prevailing conventions of the base-text. And, although as far as possible emendations have been fitted into the existing base-text punctuation, at times it has been necessary to provide emendations with a base-text style of punctuation. Where the manuscript reading adopted by the EEWN has required editorial intervention to normalise spelling or punctuation, the exact manuscript reading is given in the form: '(MS actual reading)'. Where the new reading has required significant editorial interpretation of the manuscript, not anticipated by the first edition, the explanation is given in the form '(MS derived: actual reading)'. Occasionally, some explanation of

401

the editorial thinking behind an emendation is required, and this is provided in a brief note.

The following conventions are used in transcriptions from Scott's manuscript: deletions are enclosed ⟨thus⟩ and insertions ↑thus↓; superscript letters are lowered without comment; the letters 'N. L.' (new line) are Scott's own, and indicate that he wished a new paragraph to be opened, in spite of running on the text, whereas the words '[new paragraph]' are editorial and indicate that Scott opened a new paragraph on a new line.

In spite of the care taken by the intermediaries, some local confusions in the manuscript persisted into the first edition. When straightening these, the editor has studied the manuscript context so as to determine Scott's original intention, and where the original intention is discernible it is of course restored. But from time to time such confusions cannot be rectified in this way. In these circumstances, Scott's own corrections and revisions in the Interleaved Set have more authority than the proposals of other editions, but if the autograph portions of the Interleaved Set have nothing to offer, the reading from the earliest edition to offer a satisfactory solution is adopted as the neatest means of rectifying a fault. Readings from the later editions are indicated by '(8vo)', etc., or '(Magnum)'. Emendations which have not been anticipated by a contemporaneous edition are indicated by '(Editorial)'.

3.10	continuance. Not (MS) / continuance;—not
3.19	upon her stale (MS) / upon stale
3.20	lights (MS) / light
3.33	ane (MS) / one
4.16	*Ours* (MS) / *ours*
4.22	"bodle" (MS) / 'bodle'
4.25	Weekly (MS) / weekly
4.29	would certainly (MS) / certainly would
4.30	own use. As for personal vanity (MS) / own personal use. As for vanity
4.36	Kingdom (MS) / kingdom
5.3	"bothered" (MS "botherd") / bothered
5.5	"preaching" (MS) / preaching
5.7	superintend, and, besides that he (MS superintend and, besides that he) / superintend; and, besides, he
5.9	what not, was (MS) / what not—was
5.19	essay (MS) / Essay
5.19	feats (MS) / facts
5.29	of future (MS) / of their future
5.41	hustled (MS) / bustled
6.20	hands. [new paragraph] I . . . do. I (MS hands. N.L. I tried field sports but they would not do I) / hand. [new paragraph] I
6.22	yards (MS) / yard
6.26	time that I (MS) / time I
6.41	or the (MS) / nor the
7.6	ruins (MS) /·Ruins
7.19	oft (MS) / often
7.21	has told (MS) / had told
7.22	ony (MS) / any
7.25	or Saxon (MS) / and Saxon
7.26	unfrequently (MS) / infrequently

7.30	became enlarged. (MS began to expand.) / became enlarged;
7.41	eat (MS) / ate
8.24	mine (MS) / my
8.25	Grimslees (MS) / Grinslees
8.29	Grimslees (MS) / Grinslees
8.35	Grimslees (MS) / Grinslees
9.5	fool (MS) / fowl
9.5	egg-sauce (MS) / egg sauce
9.6	ask ye (MS) / ask you
9.8	him—and (MS him— ↑ and ... ↓) / him, and
9.9	virtuoso—A (MS) / virtuoso—a
9.11	waeter (MS) / water
9.13	saumon—and (MS) / saumon—And
9.14	brig (MS brigg) / draw-brig
9.25	ane at (MS) / ane, at
9.33	chattering. You (MS) / chattering; you
9.37	maist (MS) / most
9.40	lee (MS) / lie
9.43	be this (MS) / by this
10.6	ruins (MS) / Ruins
10.7	late'—and (MS) / late.' And
10.14	fool (MS) / fowl
10.15	up—the (MS) / up, the
10.40	preparative (MS) / preparation
10.42	fool (MS) / fowl
11.1	guests Lisbon (MS) / guests call Lisbon
11.17	all such local (MS) / all local
11.24	And (MS) / and
11.39	shewed (MS shewd) / shared
12.1	hands (MS) / hand
12.8	where (MS) / when
12.15	you have mentioned (MS you have mentiond) / you mentioned
12.21	by the learned Pinkerton (MS by the learnd Pinkerton) / by Pinkerton
13.12	said he (MS) / he said
13.22	grand (MS) / great
13.30	abstinence: let (MS) / abstinence; but, let
13.39	hams (MS) / kain
14.4	fasted." (8vo) / fasted.
14.33	dogs (MS) / fellows
14.41	were (MS) / was
15.5	Old Lady (MS derived: Old lady) / old lady
15.18	family of (MS) / family in
15.23	these (MS) / those
15.24	Great (MS) / great
16.14	been long (MS) / long been
16.40	ears (MS) / ear
16.43	Majesty (MS) / majesty
17.6	value men (MS) / value which men
17.12	occurrences (MS) / circumstances
17.18	revisit (MS) / visit
17.29	must have been indeed (MS) / must, indeed, have been
17.35	I will (MS) / I shall
18.6	there's ... way; but (MS there's plenty o' them a' about an' he's curious that way but) / there's plenty a' about, an' he's curious of them; but
18.21	which (MS) / "which

18.21   "canopied (MS) / canopied
18.24   something in (MS) / that in
19.5   stane." (8vo) / stane" (MS stane"—)
19.26   whispered yet solemn accents glided (MS whisperd yet solemn accents
        glided) / whispered, yet solemn accent, glided
19.29   away—Come (MS) / away, come
19.33   keep e'e (MS) / keep an e'e
19.39   syne—they (MS) / syne. They
20.2   ken—and (MS) / ken, and
20.3   lang or (MS) / lang ere
20.4   in it (MS) / in't
20.5   and when he died, decent I (MS derived: and he ⟨wa⟩ ⟨dead⟩ died
        decent I) / and when he died decently, I
        8vo reads 'and when he died, decently I'.
20.21   to mine honest friend David's (MS to mine honest friend Davids) / to
        David's
20.25   shoulders, d——ning (8vo) / shoulders, d——ning (MS shoulders
        d——ning)
21.25   task (MS) / book
21.32   undertake to (MS) / undertake or
21.34   controversy, sir, in (MS controversy Sir in) / controversy in
22.7   incompetence (MS) / incompetency
22.8   on (MS) / upon
22.11   ended with (MS) / ended, with
22.22   me that I (MS) / me I
23.1   Jedidiah (Editorial) / Jedediah
        The spelling is adopted in line with the decision made for the first series
        of *Tales of my Landlord*: see *The Black Dwarf*, EEWN 4a, 174.
23.23   Servt, (MS Servt.) / Servant,
23.26   *On the 1st day of April* 18— (MS) / — *of April* 18—
        See Essay on the Text, 368 for the exact MS form.
24.11   is better (MS) / are better
24.18   are curiously and secretly (MS) / are secretly
24.20   to (MS) / so
24.31   quote only (MS) / only quote
25.5   Jedidiah (Editorial) / Jedediah
25.12   beyond perhaps even (MS) / perhaps even beyond
25.15   arise where he listed, as (MS arise where he listed as) / arise, as
25.16   water in (MS) / water, in
25.25   well-informed, but (MS derived: well informed but) / well-informed,
        —but
25.33   attention ready at (MS) / attention at
25.34   talent (MS) / talents
26.2   Jedidiah (Editorial) / Jedediah
26.4   and the persecuted (MS) / and persecuted
26.12   the (MS) / a
26.33   named (MS) / called
26.36   special (MS) / especial
27.32   how it is, they (MS how it is they) / how, they
27.40   any (MS) / my
28.2   mine (MS) / my
28.5   of the recesses of the libraries (MS) / of the libraries
28.7   spiders (MS) / spider
28.15   what?—why, to (MS what—why to) / what?—to
28.18   we (MS) / to

28.23   country)—the truth is, that I (MS country)—the truth is that I) /
         country) the truth is, I
28.25   although (MS) / though
28.28   or (MS) / and
28.43   that (MS) / who
29.6   gentlemen . . . resemble (MS gentlemen who may be termd Knights of
         the straw resemble) / pseudo-editors resemble
         See Essay on the Text, 375.
29.17   Jedidiah (Editorial) / Jedediah
29.20   ought (MS) / aught
29.26   buist† on my own cattle (MS Buist on my own cattle) / mark on my own
         chattels
29.28   empiric—amounting (MS Empiric—amounting) / empiric—a crime
         amounting
29.30   on (MS) / in
29.38   Jedidiah (Editorial) / Jedediah
29.41   remnants (MS) / remnant
29.41   Mountain-folks (MS mountain-folks) / Mountain folks
29.42   Hard! that (MS) / Hard that
29.44   [footnote] (Editorial) / [no footnote]
         See Essay on the Text, 387.
30.2   hand (MS) / hands
30.13   Remember (MS) / remember
30.20   it (MS) / It
31.4   Monks! they (MS Monks! twas they) / Monks they
31.7   he (MS) / HE
31.22   the first David (MS the 1st. David) / David the First
31.23   country (MS) / county
32.20   the love (MS) / a love
33.6   agreeable (MS) / agreeably
33.11   heaths (MS) / sheep-walks
33.41   assail (MS) / assault
34.9   good-wife (MS) / good wife
34.10   garden gave (MS) / garden afforded
34.11   Lent (MS) / lent
34.12   turf, and (MS derived: turf and) / turf; and
34.21   owerloup" into England; and (MS owerloup" into England and) /
         owerloup;" and
34.28   on (MS) / upon
34.30   As to (MS) / As for
34.33   secluded (MS) / excluded
35.11   incursions; for (MS derived: incursions for) / invasions. For
35.19   and some pieces (MS) / and a few pieces
36.5   vantage (MS) / strength
36.9   twining (MS) / winding
37.27   here (MS) / there
38.18   as from hospitality (MS ⟨and⟩ ↑as↓ from hospitality) / as hospitality
38.18   wish is (MS) / wish of the landlord is
38.22   with (MS) / to
38.36   on (MS) / in
38.41   out all their (MS) / out their
39.28   properties (MS) / property
39.31   beyond Forth (MS) / beyond the Forth
39.38   discerned (MS discernd) / descried
40.2   stated . . . words, and (MS stated her intention in a few brief words and)

/ stated, in a few brief words, her intention, and

40.3 submit only because (MS) / submit, because

40.5 for (MS) / from

40.10 afford—your (MS derived: afford [end of line] your) / afford. Your

40.13 said that we (MS) / said we

40.15 Comrades—faces (MS Comrades—faces) / Comrades, face

40.17 he said (MS) / said he

40.28 foragers (MS) / forayers

41.2 these boys—are (MS these little men—are) / these boys. Are

41.19 meant (MS) / mean

41.26 Southron; and the Southron (MS Southron and the Southron) / southern; and the southern

41.34 recruits to (MS) / recruits for

42.18 'drive a prey' (MS "drive a prey") / drive a foray

42.20 Southron (MS) / southern

42.25 Southron (MS) / southern

42.29 Southron (MS) / southern

42.32 us (MS) / me

43.2 corns (MS) / corn

43.34 unconscious of the extent of her (MS) / unconscious of her

44.8 Crombie (MS) / Crumbie

44.15 flighering (MS) / fleightering

44.16 she is gane (MS derived: she is gone) / she's dead

44.17 a' then gane (MS all then gone) / a' gane

44.19 work and want (MS) / work or want

44.22 looks (MS) / look

44.26 Southron (MS) / southern

44.28 wi' (MS) / with

44.41 worst (MS) / low

45.9 life—And (MS) / life, and

45.17 awa—come awa—nae (MS) / awa, come awa, nae

45.18 mile (MS) / miles

45.18 ling (MS) / muir

45.33 way—the (MS) / way; the

45.33 for—there (MS derived: for there) / for. There

45.34 they"—— (MS they"—) / they——"

Interrupted speech is normally indicated by a long dash after, rather than before, the closing quotation marks.

45.37 girth-gate (MS) / girth gate

46.2 which, few (MS which few) / which, a few

46.4 girl now just six (18mo) / girl between five and six (MS as Ed 1)

The previous paragraph indicates that today is Mary's birthday.

46.5 gipsey-fashion (MS gipsy-fashion) / gipsey fashion

46.6 bedding, the (MS derived: bedding the) / bedding; the

46.7 side, Tibb (MS) / side; Tibb

46.7 a few paces (MS) / walking a little

46.8 round (MS) / around

46.22 tap (MS) / top

46.23 difficulty—the (MS) / difficulty. The

46.36 was now broken (MS) / was broken

46.37 some (MS) / great

46.41 forwards (MS) / forward

47.9 figure, but (MS derived: figure but) / figure; but

47.11 assayed Shagram (MS assayd Shagram) / essayed to lead forward Shagram

47.12   inflexible in (MS) / inflexible to
47.33   the first sight (MS) / the sight
47.37   the more humble (MS) / the humble
48.4   lady, true," (MS lady true") / lady,"
48.5   step in and (MS) / step and
48.20   o'er awed (MS) / unawed
49.1   fathers (MS) / father
49.14   other's (8vo) / others (MS as Ed1)
49.15   or (MS) / and
49.27   lay rather too (MS) / lay too
49.36   of the (MS) / of this
49.40   she had loved (MS) / she loved
50.3   further (MS) / farther
50.14   around (MS) / round
50.15   master and (MS Master and) / master or
50.18   their (MS) / the
51.10   with great personal (MS) / with personal
51.15   such a din (MS) / such din
51.20   subject (MS) / subjected
51.29   heaven (MS Heaven) / heavens
51.29   starting (MS) / rising
51.41   come tumbling yon (MS) / come yon
52.4   youngest (MS) / younger
52.7   cry (MS) / say
52.14   was . . . in (MS was a man, an armd man, in) / was an armed man in
52.19   either (MS) / neither
52.24   of the Clinthill (MS) / of Clint-hill
52.33   down ower his breast-plate; and (MS derived: down over his breast
        and) / down his breast ower his breast-plate; and
52.35   head"——— (MS) / head"—
        Ed1 has room for only a one-em dash.
52.38   turning (MS) / turned
53.7   but as (MS) / and as
53.11   himsel—Be (MS himsell—Be) / himself—be
53.16   Christie—tods (MS) / Christie; tods
53.18   wad (MS) / would
53.29   hae (MS) / has
53.30   goodman (MS) / good man
53.31   been (MS) / be
53.33   not . . . failed to (MS not in other circumstances have faild to) / not have
        failed in other circumstances to
53.34   country-folks (MS country folks) / country-folk
53.42   answered (MS answerd) / said
54.3   breast-plate—And (MS) / breast-plate; and
54.21   at (MS) / to
54.22   "Fie, fie! (MS Fie fie!) / Fie, fie,
54.24   day. But (MS) / day; but
54.25   breast-lace.—My (MS) / breast-lace. My
54.33   me—And (MS) / me; and
54.34   wad (MS) / would
54.35   it—and (MS) / it. And
54.35   whae (MS) / wha
54.36   Sair (MS) / sair
54.36   min' (MS derived: min) / mind
54.37   baith. But (MS both. But) / baith; but

54.41   moment—he (MS) / moment; he
54.43   believe that it (MS) / believe it
55.6   I could wish (MS) / I wish
55.10   do wi' . . . reading (MS do wi that book in her hand—It's nae wonder that her bairn sees bogles if she is aye reading) / do reading
55.12   clasps—there (MS clasps—And there) / clasps?—there
55.14   ballats (MS) / ballants
55.16   carlines (MS) / carlins
55.23   himsel (MS himsell) / himself
55.24   safter (MS) / softer
55.25   sights come mair (MS) / sights mair
55.36   mire cleughs—Certain (MS) / moss-haggs—certain
55.37   resisted (MS) / reisted
56.13   trow—can (MS) / trow. Can
56.19   quoth (MS) / said
56.20   grand privileges (MS) / great privileges
56.24   for (MS) / at
56.25   arising again—whilk (MS derived: arising again Whilk) / rising again, whilk
56.27   or (MS) / as
56.29   and cast (MS) / to cast
56.33   hersel (MS hersell) / herself
57.16   lip (MS) / lips
57.17   dim. Yet (MS) / dim; yet
57.27   could (MS) / would
57.32   confessor, the (Magnum) / confessor; the (MS Confessor the)
57.35   valiant—he (MS) / valiant; he
57.41   Knowst (MS) / Knowest
58.4   knowst (MS) / knowest
58.6   Ho! Ho! Ho! (MS) / Ho! ho! ho!
58.9   widow—he! (MS) / widow—He!
58.15   *Buts*—neither (MS) / *Buts;* neither
58.15   abbot—Father Philip, the (MS derived: Abbot—Father Philip the) / abbot, Father Philip; the
58.19   friars—And (MS) / friars—and
58.20   us—what would all Christendom—what would our brother Eustace think of us!" (MS) / us."
58.22   Monastery (MS) / monastery
58.27   Moreover there (MS) / moreover it
58.28   who have in their day been (MS) / who, in their day, have been
58.31   deterring them—for (MS) / deterring them, for
58.32   withholding them—for (MS) / withholding them, for
59.6   in his (MS) / on his
59.11   the dear leddy (MS) / the leddy
59.13   knowst (MS) / knowest
59.14   what—what (MS) / what—What
59.14   cleansing (MS) / clearing
59.25   Heaven!" (MS) / Heaven,"
59.30   ever (MS) / even
60.4   of tendency (MS) / of a tendency
60.5   exclamation (MS) / exclamations
60.13   So (MS) / so
60.26   precepts (MS) / principles
60.30   I abide (MS) / I will abide
60.31   Well (MS) / well

61.3   had but dealt (MS) / had dealt
61.22   congregation—And (MS) / congregation; and
61.23   sister,"—(for (MS derived: sister,—(for) / sister, for
61.23   into (MS) / unto
61.25   clergy—so (MS) / clergy, so
61.26   age—unbound (MS) / age, unbound
61.27   friars—whether (MS friars—neither) / friars, whether
61.29   Monks—and (MS) / Monks, and
61.30   Cistercian—Of (MS Cistercians Of) / Cistercian, of
61.32   Monastery (MS) / ministers
61.39   it—moreover (MS derived: it [end of line] moreover) / it. Moreover
61.41   woxen (MS) / waxen
62.12   to quick (MS) / of quick
62.33   which she . . . inconvenience (MS which she had hitherto proceeded to
         his no small inconvenience) / which, to his no small inconvenience, she
         had hitherto proceeded
62.40   fair (MS) / fine
63.19   betwixt (MS) / between
63.21   side, or (MS derived: side or) / side; or
63.22   way, keep (MS way keep) / way, might keep
63.22   until (MS untill) / till
63.36   man (MS) / men
63.40   a *heavy* (MS) / *a heavy*
64.1   bridge (MS) / draw-bridge
64.2   does (MS) / dost
64.6   reconnoitring through (MS) / reconnoitring the Monk through
64.12   unattended by (MS) / unattended to by
64.14   end (MS) / head
64.23   it there (MS) / it, there
64.24   rather the (MS) / rather under the
64.26   here at this (MS) / there at that
64.34   or for some (MS) / or some
64.35   on (MS) / at
64.36   then looked up in (MS then lookd up in) / then in
64.41   courteous (MS) / cautious
65.4   courteous (MS) / cautious
65.28   sing—thereby (MS) / sing, thereby
65.39   swollen (MS) / swolen
66.15   fishing—whom (MS) / fishing, whom
66.15   tonight (MS) / to night
67.7   Here (MS) / Now
67.28   charitable, perfectly good natured, and (MS charitable perfectly good
         natured and) / charitable, and
67.38   refuted, practices (MS) / refuted—practices
67.38   into, heretics (MS derived: into hereticts) / into—heretics
67.39   punished, the (MS punishd, the) / punished—the
67.39   reclaimed, the (MS derived: reclaimed the) / reclaimed—the
67.40   confirmed, scandal (MS derived: confirmd scandal) / confirmed—
         scandal
68.16   it. In short, Father (MS It. In short father) / it. [new paragraph] Father
68.24   who at length hardly (MS) / who hardly
         The words 'at length', inserted on the facing verso, were missed.
68.41   that his own health held (MS) / that it held
69.5   detached (MS detachd) / dispatched
69.10   served. And (MS) / served; and

69.18   carving (MS) / carved back
69.28   trouble—a (MS) / trouble. A
69.29   when frailties (MS) / when the frailties
69.37   Eustace were the (MS) / Eustace the
69.38   was (MS) / were
69.40   mine—And then (MS) / mine. Then
70.2   thus am I dishonoured (MS derived: thus I am I dishonord) / thus I am
        dishonoured
70.9   those (MS) / these
70.10   a hungry (MS) / a little hungry
70.12   howsoever (MS) / however
70.25   bowed (MS) / turned
70.34   inviting him to (MS) / inviting to
71.2   him and immediately (MS him and ⟨he⟩ immediately) / him, and he
        immediately
71.11   reverent (MS) / reverend
71.16   says—send (MS) / says, send
71.23   of Holy (MS) / of the Holy
71.28   to whatever (MS) / to do whatever
72.2   precessors and all successors (MS) / predecessors and successors
72.11   we put (MS) / they put
72.12   And (MS) / and
72.27   It (MS) / it
72.31   Good Cause (MS) / good cause
72.41   Abbot, crossing himself, "our (MS Abbot crossing himself our) /
        Abbot, "our
72.43   be not (MS) / not be
73.4   and all (MS) / and saw all
73.7   necessity (MS) / necessisty
73.19   bright (MS) / birght
73.23   Speak (Editorial) / speak
        A change of addressee calls for an initial capital.
73.30   throat; if (MS) / throat. If
73.34   unbeseeming (MS) / unbecoming
73.36   but go (MS) / go but
73.36   my (MS) / the
73.39   sparreth (MS) / shuts
74.1   man—so (MS man so) / man. So
74.6   has (MS) / hast
74.9   miller, "not (8vo) / miller; "not (MS Millar not)
74.13   Art (MS) / art
74.33   in the (MS) / inthe
74.34   wondrous (MS) / wonderful
74.34   Satan is permitted (MS) / Satan hath been permitted
74.35   forward (MS) / forth
74.39   been by his own personal intervention (MS) / been altogether without
        his own personal fault
75.10   admit—and (MS) / admit; and
75.14   into—it (MS) / into; it
76.24   fiend (MS) / friend
76.26   is our (MS) / may be
76.32   men's (8vo) / mens' (MS mens)
76.42   breathing in (MS) / breaking on
77.13   rags—it (MS) / rags; it
77.15   jangle (MS) / jingle

77.37   all save (MS) / all food, save
78.28   Amongst (MS) / Among
78.31   branches, and lay (Editorial) / branches, lay (MS branches lay)
        Scott originally began this sentence 'The leaves of the willows were
        altogether witherd and': he deleted the last three words, but in the
        resumed sentence he forgot to include an 'and' before 'lay'.
78.37   said he (MS) / he said
78.40   winter—But (MS winter—And) / winter; but
79.9   faded—but (MS) / faded; but
79.19   onwards (MS) / onward
79.31   said he (MS) / he said
79.33   thoughts. I (MS) / thoughts—I
79.34   senses—I (MS senses⟨"⟩ I) / senses. I
80.1   Convent—though (MS) / Convent, though
80.6   you—for (MS) / you, for
80.7   would (MS) / Would
80.17   reverence—it (MS) / reverence, it
80.19   for it (MS) / for she
80.23   explain . . . "Was (MS explain it to me. This book which Father Philip
        removed from Glendearg"——"Was) / tell it to me." [new paragraph]
        "This book, if it please your reverence, which Father Philip removed
        from Glendearg, was
80.25   in strange (MS) / in a strange
80.27   Returned? (MS Returnd?) / Returned!
80.29   this tower (MS) / the town
80.35   top—if (MS) / top, which, if
80.36   untouched, it will at (MS ↑ untouchd ↓ it will at) / untouched, must at
81.4   Gude (MS) / Good
81.6   So (MS) / so
81.6   woman there—all (MS) / woman sitting there, all
81.7   Halbert—who (MS) / Halbert, who
81.11   sense and listen (MS) / sense listen
81.16   it back with (MS) / it with
81.22   Philip?" said (MS derived: Philip said) / Philip," said
        The MS has a question-mark after 'reverence' in line 24: Scott probably
        intended to put this at the end of the preceding speech.
82.3   "that I did, as (MS "that I did as) / "as
82.4   A (MS) / a
82.11   attention (MS) / attentoin
82.20   wears—for the (MS) / wears, to hide the
82.22   Then (MS) / Then,
82.30   acquaintance (MS) / acquaintances
82.31   multures (MS) / multure
82.35   will (MS) / must
83.6   reflection how (MS) / reflection, considering how
83.24   volumes (MS) / volume
83.36   driven (MS) / drawn
83.40   of life (MS) / of the life
84.1   art (MS) / Art
84.3   also—O! the (Editorial) / also—O the (MS also—the)
84.5   there—for (MS) / there; for
84.11   ought (MS) / aught
85.2   doest (MS) / dost
85.3   than deadly (MS than Deadly) / than of deadly
85.4   mayst (MS) / mayest

85.20   rites (MS) / rights
85.20   her holy visitor—confessor (MS) / the holy visitor—who was confessor
86.21   Avenel's—and (MS) / Avenel's; and
86.23   Philip—though (MS) / Philip, though
86.25   thick—Simon's (MS) / thick. Simon's
87.3   community, lived (MS derived: community ↑ lived ... ↓) / community
        —lived
87.19   Christie of Clinthill (MS ↑ Christie of Clint-hill ↓) / Christie of the
        Clinthill
87.37   trouble—you (MS) / trouble, you
88.1   betwixt (MS) / between
88.2   of Clinthill (MS) / of the Clinthill
88.2   jackman—ye (MS) / jackman; ye
88.5   rude (MS) / rudely
88.14   sends this due (MS) / sends due
88.17   errand—think'st (MS errand—thinkst) / errand.—Think'st
88.38   consider—he (MS) / consider he
89.4   Norman—a (MS) / Norman a
89.7   priests—and (MS) / priests; and
89.8   and blessing (MS) / and his blessing
89.35   What (MS) / what
90.1   thee (MS) / thou
90.14   betwixt (MS) /between
91.6   that—and (MS) / that; and
91.7   too—And (MS) / too. And
91.10   favourite—and (MS) / favourite; and
91.34   And (MS) / and
91.43   purposed (MS) / proposed
92.2   stripping some of them (MS) / stripping them
92.6   save (MS) / saving
92.7   her (MS) / his
92.25   with the (MS) / with his
92.30   wert (MS) were
92.42   1455 (MS) / 1445
93.5   nought (MS) / not
93.17   Sir Prior (MS) / Sub-Prior
93.22   on (MS) / in
93.25   created things (MS) / things created
94.9   doubt the (MS) / doubtthe
94.12   faculties. Either (MS ↑ ... faculties. ↓ Either) / faculties—Either
94.15   foundation. At the crook of the glen?—I (MS) / foundation.—At the
        crook of the glen? I
94.15   have well desired (MS) / have desired
94.18   onward (MS) / around
94.21   further (MS) / farther
94.22   a spot (MS) / the spot
94.22   where the brook (MS) / wher ethebrook
94.36   are (MS) / be
95.20   sore (MS) / sorely
95.21   weary you out, you (MS) / weary out you
95.27   vow—but (MS) / vow; but
95.34   wife—we (MS) / wife, we
96.25   Thou has (MS) / thou hast
96.30   Superior—if (MS) / Superior. If
97.7   amongst (MS) / among

97.19 dismiss—and (MS) / dismiss; and
97.29 carried (MS) / hurried
98.6 me so foully before (MS me so fouly before) / me before
98.28 reverent (MS) / reverend
98.38 Sub-Prior (8vo) / Sub-prior (MS Subprior)
99.16 seest (MS) / see'st
99.23 soul—under (MS derived: soul under) / soul. Under
99.41 was it (MS) / it was
99.43 spoken?" said (Editorial) / spoken!" said (MS spoken said)
100.1 and for (MS) / and—for
100.8 remember (MS) / Remember
100.15 Apostate (MS) / apostate
100.16 then," said (MS then" said) / then, "said
100.18 And (Editorial) / and (MS as Ed1)
100.20 murther—view (MS) / murther. View
100.27 from his chains (MS) / from chains
100.29 not!—an (MS not—an) / not!—An
100.32 sheep again into (MS) / sheep into
100.42 wont—but (MS) / wont; but
101.6 grace—but (MS) / grace; but
101.15 nurse (MS) / morse
101.17 shall meet with (MS) / will meet with
101.18 Oremus (MS) / Oramus
101.19 shall meet thy (MS) / will meet thy
101.21 shall have (MS) / will have
101.31 pray you (MS) / pray "you
101.37 own—but (MS) / own; but
101.41 exterior." (MS derived: exterior"—) / exterior?"
101.43 life and limb (MS) / lives and limbs
102.36 brethren! the (MS brethren the) / brethren! The
102.38 case on an empty (MS) / case with empty
103.9 such a penance (MS) / such penance
103.18 of his (MS) / of the
103.20 so often tacitly (MS) / so tacitly
103.21 of his judgment (MS of his judgement) / of the Abbot's judgment
103.32 were we (MS) / would we be
103.35 is done (MS) / was done
104.5 ourself (MS) / ourselves
104.23 sacrament . . . there (MS Sacrament as his Church call it of Confession
       there) / sacrament of confession, as his church calls it, there
105.12 mother (MS) / matter
105.15 thine own opinion (MS) / thine opinion
105.17 thy weaker (MS) / the weaker
105.20 narratives (MS) / narration
105.23 fault (MS) / faults
105.25 to (MS) / unto
105.31 his Superior (MS) / the Superior
105.37 And / and
106.23 experience. But (MS) / experience; but
106.39 after (MS) / for
107.7 educated (MS) / dedicated
107.9 attained (MS attaind) / obtained
107.22 if (MS) / when
107.23 feu—on (MS) / feu; on
107.26 the little tower (MS) / the tower

107.42 boys; he (MS) / boys—he
108.3 broad-sword, suspended (MS derived: broad sword suspended) / broad-sword—suspended
108.8 gait (MS) / gates
108.18 profession, his (MS derived: profession his) / profession—his
108.21 said he (MS) / he said
108.23 alas! perhaps (MS alas perhaps) / alas! the former are perhaps
108.28 trust—but above (MS) / trust—above
108.29 knowledge, a (MS derived: knowlege a) / knowledge—a
108.30 beset, has (MS derived: beset has) / beset—has
109.2 eye (MS) / eyes
109.7 writing, and (MS derived: writing and) / writing;—and
109.25 Hunter's-hope (MS derived: Huntershope) / Colmslie
       This character is referred to as 'the Laird of Hunter's-hope' at 126.43. 'Hunter's-hope' is restored in 18mo.
109.30 you with (MS) / you go with
110.13 emotion (MS) / emotions
110.16 Southron (MS) / Southrons
110.19 brother both started (MS) / brother started
110.22 Southron (MS) / Southrons
110.28 can—and (MS) / can; and
110.41 taken and (MS taken &) / taken up and
111.5 your peasantly *brochan* (MS derived: your peansantly *brochan*) / your *brochan*
111.10 you—for (Editorial) / you; and—for (MS you and—for)
111.11 painted (MS) / printed
111.12 breviary—and (Editorial) / breviary; and (MS breviary and)
111.18 of?" (MS derived: of?"—) / of?
111.19 angry he (MS) / angry—he
111.20 what—let (MS) / what; let
111.37 by (MS) / with
112.7 now if I dared I (MS derived: now I dared I) / now I———I
       The unusually long dash in Ed1 may indicate a blank left by transcriber or compositor.
112.19 Glendonwyne (MS) / Glendinning
112.25 rhymes (MS rhimes) / rhyme
112.39 END OF VOLUME FIRST (MS End of Volume I) / [No text]
115.1 learn—and (MS learn—&) / learn; and
115.2 wouldest (MS) / wouldst
115.3 helper. And I (MS) / helper; I
115.36 mystery (MS) / mytery
115.40 find (MS) / force
115.42 scorn." (8vo) / scorn. (MS as Ed1)
116.7 their (MS) / his
116.12 Fearst (MS) / Fearest
116.14 Fearst (MS) / Fearest
116.25 these (MS) / the
116.37 respect (MS) / respects
117.2 condensed flame (MS) / condensaed flme
117.15 There (MS) / Here
117.19 by the rapidity of the motion to (MS) / to the rapidity of the motion, to
117.27 she finished (MS she finishd) / she had finished
117.28 pain was (MS pain ⟨had⟩ ↑ was ↓) / pain had
118.5 minted (MS) / molten

The American editions show that 'minted' was misread as 'mortal', corrected in proof to 'molten'.

118.35 read and understand (MS) / read, and to understand
119.12 of a protector's (MS of a protectors) / of protection

The American editions show that this change was made before the proofs were corrected by Scott, as were those at 120.4 and 120.7.

119.25 organ (MS) / organs
120.4 difficulties (MS) / difficulty
120.6 than a (MS) / than of a
120.7 of evening (MS) / of the evening
120.7 [no text] / END OF VOLUME FIRST. (MS End of Vol I)
120.17 Halbert's (MS Halberts) / Halbert
120.26 soared a little higher (MS) / soared higher
120.31 was, like those (MS was like those) / was like the purpose of those
121.6 another, erected (MS another erected) / another mill, erected
121.34 Mill. And (MS) / Mill; and
121.41 fortune—a material article—besides (MS) / fortune, a material article. besides
122.20 than grind (MS) / than he would grind
122.26 opinion they (MS) / opinion that they
122.37 amongst (MS) / among
122.30 age—And (MS) / age—and
122.39 than the (MS) / than that of the
122.31 more especial (MS) / more especially
122.32 Sub-Prior—and (MS derived: Sub-prior And) / Sub-Prior, and
122.33 him—And (MS) / him—and
122.42 wheresoe'er (MS where soe'er) / whersoe'er
123.1 een, and (MS derived: een and) / een; and
123.3 them—Ay (MS) / them—ay
123.4 hair—Ay (MS) / hair—ay
123.7 man's—and (MS mans—and) / man's.—And
123.8 them—that (MS) / them, that
123.28 ways (MS) / way
124.2 her umqhuile Simon (MS) / his umquhile gossip Simon
124.12 Ye (MS) / ye
124.13 Or (MS) / or
124.25 swingeing (MS) / swinging
124.25 Andra (MS) / Andrew
124.37 exaction (MS) / exactions
124.40 translation (MS) / translations
124.43 or handful (MS) / a handful
125.1 multure (MS) / multures
125.5 are vulgarly called (MS are vulgarly calld) / we vulgarly call
125.7 meanwhile (MS mean while) / meantime
125.21 this pleasant and joyous (MS this pleasant & joyous) / this joyous
125.26 further (MS) / farther
125.32 shoes (MS) / shoe
125.35 by (MS) / with
125.40 hae (MS) / have
126.7 sad (MS) / last
126.9 thank to (MS) / thanks to
126.12 who (MS) / that
126.34 upon?—they (MS upon—they) / upon? they
126.34 lad—wha (MS) / lad; wha
127.3 good—ay (MS good—aye) / good, ay

127.11   thou turn (MS) / thou wilt turn
127.17   ware—but (MS) / wary; but
127.28   lustily (MS) / hastily
127.38   breed (MS) / brood
127.30   upon (MS) / into
128.20   Scots (MS) / Scotch
128.24   at great familiarity (MS) / at familiarity
128.26   well be (MS) / be well
128.30   to mingle (MS) / of mingling
128.33   was matter (MS) / was a matter
128.33   interest; (MS) / interest,
129.12   on (MS) / in
129.25   children (MS) / children,
130.31   gallants—will (MS) / gallants, will
130.33   Well—if (MS) / Well, if
130.34   stay (MS) / Stay
130.34   lady—he (MS) / lady; he
130.35   man—somewhat (MS) / man, somewhat
130.41   now—come (MS) / now. Come
131.1   for (MS) / considering
131.5   him—the handsomest—the (MS) / him, the handsomest, the
131.28   here!—now (MS here—now) / here! Now
131.38   could indeed perceive (MS) / could perceive
132.8   True-penny?—here (MS true-penny—here) / True-penny? here
132.14   said he (MS) / he said
132.18   on (MS) / in
132.19   cuffing!—And (MS cuffing—And) / cuffing! and
132.26   sough—better (MS) / sough; better
132.31   turning (MS) / turned
132.35   have share (MS) / have his share
132.39   good dame (MS) / goo ddame
132.42   And (MS ⟨But⟩ And) / But
133.36   other's (8vo) / others (MS as Ed1)
133.38   other's (8vo) / others (MS as Ed1)
134.29   qualification of (MS) / qualification to
135.18   these (MS) / those
135.26   viewing." So (MS) / viewing;" so
136.1   intimated sovereign (MS) / intimated a sovereign
136.8   place here, were (MS place here were) / place, were
136.13   rustical (MS) / rusticial
136.35   me you (MS) / me that you
136.36   Aikie (MS) / Dickie
136.37   treasure that I (MS) / treasure I
137.14   thee (MS) / you
137.16   drunk (MS) / drank
137.27   Southron (MS Suthron) / southern
137.33   of (MS) / for
138.19   Knight—we (MS) / Knight, we
138.21   you.' You (MS you. ⟨"⟩ You) / you'—you
138.31   it was (MS) / it were
138.39   the manners (MS) / a manner
139.2   his humble (MS) / its humble
139.10   them—that (MS) / them that
139.13   ye (MS) / you
139.34   lady—Have not you (MS) / lady—and have you not

139.35 than the (MS) / than her
140.7   callant—till (MS) / callant. Till
140.9   him—And (MS derived: him And) / him, but
140.22 in the (MS) / on the
140.23 the stomach (MS) / his breast
140.34 being a wanting (MS) / being wanting
141.32 Glendearg (MS) / Glendinning
141.33 said he (MS) / he said
141.41 treated the speaker to a (MS) / afforded the speaker a
142.2   raise up his body (MS raise up his ⟨b⟩ body) / raise his eyes
142.5   Speak, (MS) / Speak!
142.6   Knight," said (MS Knight" said) / Knight, "said
142.18 tone. (MS) / tone,
142.22 has (MS) / hast
142.27 outrageous—it (MS) / outrageous. It
142.30 doeth produce only discords (MS) / doth produce discords
143.19 means whatsoever deduct (MS) / means deduct
143.42 was signal (MS) / was a signal
144.36 Sidney (MS) / Sydney
144.38 you"——(Magnum) / you——" (MS as Ed 1)
145.11 mayst (MS) / mayest
145.33 speak—but (MS) / speak; but
145.36 upon the names (MS) / upon names
145.38 is the (MS) / is in the
146.22 dreamed (MS dreamd) / dreamt
147.10 them, as (MS derived: them as) / them. As
147.11 breeze. Even (MS) / breeze, even
147.28 attractive metal of (MS) / attractive of
149.2   dreamed (MS dreamd) / dreamt
149.5   with fresh rushes (MS) / with rushes
149.22 shew his (MS) / shew that his
149.33 the little tower (MS) / the tower
149.38 later (MS) / latter
150.8   baths (MS) / bathe
150.14 eyes of (MS) / eyesof
150.24 murmured (MS murmurd) / muttered
150.29 might but be (MS) / might be
150.31 excuse as your (MS) / excuses your
150.33 a'! (MS a!) / a'.
151.12 raise up the (MS) / raise the
151.25 and bid (MS) / andbid
151.26 attendance (MS) / attendants
151.29 and, said I, let (MS and said I let) / and said, Let
152.16 before or beyond the (MS derived: beyond or before the) / beyond the
152.30 hampers (MS) / hamper
153.14 services (MS) / service
153.22 "your wisdom well knows that (MS derived: "it is well known to you
        [end of line] wisdom well knows that) / "it is well known to your
        wisdom that
153.23 that is (MS) / that secrecy is
154.38 their extremity (MS) / them extremely
155.2   might (MS) / may
155.7   advance, the (MS advance the) / advance, as the
155.16 shot (MS) / rid
155.17 Were we not better call (MS) / Were it not better to call

156.5 unnecessary," said (8vo) / unnecessary, "said (MS unnecessary" said)
156.30 back; with which I (MS back with which I) / back; which load I
157.8 had (MS) / if
157.9 And (MS) / and
157.10 murrey (MS) / peach
157.18 with my safety (MS) / with safety
158.17 mumming (MS) / mummery
158.19 wardrope—the (MS) / wardrobe. The
158.23 been in sort given (MS) / been given
158.36 well what (MS) / well, that
158.41 of her (MS) / of the
159.4 wardrope (MS) / wardrobe
159.18 besides!—and (MS besides—and) / besides! And
160.6 Her (MS) / her
160.9 love to (MS) / love of
160.21 Holy (MS) / holy
161.15 an express servant to (MS) / a servant express to
161.15 revestry (MS Revestry) / revestiary
162.1 call you (MS) / call thee
162.1 lay you (MS) / lay thee
162.7 slower, I say, and (MS slower I say and) / slower, and
162.7 thee (MS) / you
162.11 miles—and (MS) / miles; and
162.16 burned (MS burnd) / burnt
162.21 playst (MS) / playest
162.26 Halbert, grasping his hand; "there (MS Halbert grasping his hand "there) / Halbert; "there
162.31 in the land (MS) / on the old scalp
162.35 seest (MS) / see'st
162.35 ought (MS) / aught
163.4 And surely (MS) / and surely
163.12 renewal of sentiments (MS derived: renewal sentiments) / renewing sentiments
163.13 since (MS) / sine
163.18 low and despised (MS) / low, despised
163.22 by?—a (MS bye—a) / by? A
163.25 him well—the (MS) / him—the
163.36 of—courage (MS) / of. Courage
164.3 too—in (MS) / too, in
164.9 tower (MS) / Tower
164.15 Queen, said he? (MS derived: Queen said he?) / Queen! said he.
164.16 them (MS) / him
164.16 heart (MS) / head
164.31 attained (MS attaind) / allowed
164.40 dreamed; and (MS dreamd—And) / dreamed; but
165.2 it—by (MS) / it, by
165.29 could still discover (MS) / could discern
165.31 Gradually, however, it (MS Gradually however it) / But gradually it
166.2 slay me; nor (MS slay me nor) / slay; nor
166.4 practice (MS) / produce
166.7 nobler." (MS nobler—") / nobler being."
166.31 were (MS) / wert
166.42 princes, knights (MS princes knights) / princes and knights
167.1 another . . . being the (MS another yet am conscious of being the) / another being, yet am conscious of remaining the

167.31 has (MS) / hast
167.31 dare (MS) / dared
168.8 plain (MS) / plainly
168.9 can nothing (MS) / can understand nothing
168.10 say, especially (MS say especially) / Say, especially
169.28 counsels (MS council ↑ s ↓) / counsel
169.36 thee chief (MS) / thee the chief
169.37 quene (MS) / queen
170.17 being entirely founded (MS) / being founded
171.3 had ... to have suffered (MS derived: had ... to sufferd) / hath ... to
       suffer
171.15 you know (MS) / You know
171.26 requested (MS requestd) / required
173.5 so the (MS) / so that
173.18 best—archers (MS) / best; archers
173.21 we no (MS) / we try no
173.35 merks (MS) / marks
173.36 Martlemas (MS) / Marttemas
174.15 it? woman (MS) / it?—Woman
174.33 in him (MS) / into him
175.7 delivered. Nevertheless (MS) / delivered—Nevertheless
175.10 natural (MS) / martial
175.36 presented, and (MS presented and) / presented amid
176.8 churl's [new line] That tills (MS) / churls [new line] That till
176.13 interview ... Mary's. (MS interview at this momentous crisis of his life
       with the Abbot of Saint Marys.) / interview with the Abbot of Saint
       Mary's, at this momentous crisis of his life.
176.20 distinguishing (MS) / distinguishes
177.6 russet (MS) / rustic
179.15 rangers. A-hem (MS rangers. Ahem) / rangers—a-hem
179.30 enow (MS) / enough
180.1 And (MS) / But
180.13 graver (MS) / grave
180.26 lordship, to (MS Lordship to) / lordship, and to
180.35 indeed—Or (MS) / indeed—or
180.40 from (MS) / by
180.42 and a kestrel (MS) / and kestrel
181.11 ought (MS) / aught
181.39 for the (MS) / for his
182.4 their (MS) / that
182.11 wouldest (MS) / would'st
182.17 burned (MS burnd) / burnt
182.17 only have (MS) / have only
182.27 round (MS) / around
182.37 not that (MS) / not but that
182.39 has been in it (MS) / in it has been
183.11 like to a (MS) / like a
183.38 removed. For (MS) / removed; for
183.38 Halidome (MS) / Halisome
183.43 house, to chuse (MS house to chuse) / house were I to chuse
184.1 hand (MS) / head
184.16 attendance (MS) / attendant
184.32 approached (MS approachd) / approaching
185.41 screen (MS) / secure
186.2 his (MS) / the

186.17 me. Young (MS) / me!—Young
186.21 uninsulted (MS) / without meeting insult
188.14 un-to-be-paralleled (MS un-to-be-paralleld) / not-to-be-paralleled
188.15 hath (MS) / has
188.24 shall assay (MS) / will essay
188.36 must I (MS) / I must
189.12 this (MS) / the
189.16 a shelf (MS) / the shelf
189.24 at (MS) / of
189.25 Albert"——— (Magnum) / Albert———" (MS as Ed1)
190.9   or (MS) / nor
190.18 Glendinning, looking after him; "but (MS Glendinning looking after him "but) / Glendinning; "but
190.19 humourous (MS) / humorous
190.20 longest—well (MS) / longest.—Well
190.25 he had required (MS) / he required
190.32 than to his (MS) / than his
190.42 humourous as winter (MS) / humorous as Winter
191.7   deadly (MS) / doubful
191.28 the token (MS) / that token
191.39 is—or (MS) / is, or
191.39 be—self-conceited (MS be—selfconceited) / be, self-conceited
191.41 said he (MS) / he said
192.12 mute (MS) / mere
192.24 thrice. (MS) / thrice;
192.30 seest (MS) / see'st
192.33 seest (MS) / see'st
192.41 will (MS) / wilt
193.1   seest (MS) / see'st
193.16 from infancy (MS) / from your infancy
193.22 could win (MS) / excited even
194.11 own—my (MS) / own. My
194.17 sound (MS) / soundly
194.26 girt (MS) / girded
194.31 kerchief (MS) / handkerchief
195.24 sullenly (MS su⟨dd⟩↑ll↓enly) / suddenly
195.34 You (MS) / you
195.38 shake (MS derived) / strike
196.5   You (MS) / you
196.8   Others (MS) / others
196.8   deceive, me (MS deceive me) / deceive, but me
196.13 hide. I (MS) / hide—I
196.19 shall (MS) / shalt
196.25 by (MS) / of
196.28 knowst (MS) / knowest
196.38 certes (MS) / Certes
196.41 Discretion"——— (MS) / Discretion———"
197.20 pray of you (MS) / pray you
197.32 we will (MS) we would
198.4   the very painful (MS) / the painful
198.7   we (MS) / "we
198.31 speakst (MS) / speakest
198.36 so—O (MS) / so, O
198.39 criminal. But (MS) / criminal; but
198.43 Saviolo (Editorial) / Saviola (MS as Ed1)

199.28   wouldest (MS) / wouldst
199.31   sexton. Wherefore (MS Sexton. Wherefore) / sexton—Wherefore
199.39   form some conjectures (MS) / form conjectures
199.40   grave. "It (MS) / grave—"It
200.5   courage, as it presented (MS courage as it presented) / courage, and
         presented
200.8   hand over my sides (MS) / hands over my side
200.27   fashion, O (8vo) / fashion; O (MS fashion O)
200.41   rustical (MS) / rusticated
201.11   to attend to the (MS) / to the
202.5   Is our subject of quarrel (MS) / Is the subject of our quarrel
202.18   does (MS) / Dost
203.13   on earth (MS) / on the earth
203.27   Condescension—Even (MS) / Condescension, even
203.29   take (MS) / Take
203.34   Oh! (MS) / oh!
204.20   which (MS) / who
204.37   hollowing (MS) / hallooing
206.2   over (MS) / on
206.19   rescue—follow (MS rescue follow) / rescue. Follow
206.26   aid, or (MS aid or) / aid him, or
206.39   path. "Young (MS) / path—"Young
206.41   will (MS) / wilt
206.41   cruelty. I (MS) / cruelty—I
207.4   yet (MS) / Yet
208.4   am Christian (MS) / am a Christian
208.6   tomb thou (MS) / tomb that thou
208.27   unaccountably (MS) / unacountably
209.4   aware—yet (MS) / aware. Yet
209.27   bosom (MS) / heart
209.31   tell (MS) / Tell
209.36   hand (MS) / head
210.16   barefooted (MS) / barefoot
210.23   lie—but (MS) / lie. But
210.27   doest (MS) / dost
210.40   said he (MS) / he said
211.1   champion (MS) / soldier
211.7   it—carry (MS) / it, and carry
211.7   of the proud (MS) / of proud
211.28   sayst (MS) / sayest
211.37   the risk (MS risque) / thy risk
211.39   his (MS) / His
211.42   in (MS) / of
212.25   edification. (MS) / edification?
213.14   finding so large a (MS) / finding a
213.17   sublime. Yet (MS) / sublime; yet
213.27   of the rock which (MS) / of rock, which
214.36   their little crofts (MS) / their crofts
215.9   builded (MS) / built
215.10   war—they (MS) / war. They
215.12   oppression—the (MS) / oppression. The
215.14   she may build (MS) / she builds
215.15   Avenel holds no high place, then, in (MS Avenel holds no high place
         then in) / Avenel, then, holds no high place in
215.27   may well be (MS) / may be

215.28 paths (MS) / path
215.29 thy (MS) / your
215.31 passion (MS) / passions
216.9 of Clinthill (MS) / of the Clinthill
216.26 [no footnote] (Editorial) / [footnote]
       See Essay on the Text, 387.
217.27 a side (MS) / the side
217.28 wild-duck (MS) / wild duck
217.34 into (MS) / in
217.35 you—never (MS derived: you never) / you. Never
217.38 stone-hall (MS) / stone hall
218.21 attendance which (MS derived: attendands which) / attendants who
218.33 attention (MS) / intention
218.34 forwards (MS) / forward
220.15 wench—else (MS) / wench, else
220.29 leaning his head a (MS) / leaning a
220.32 Ye (MS) / ye
220.36 Our (MS) / our
220.37 women, and (MS derived: women and) / women—and
221.1 is." He (MS is"—He) / is." [new paragraph] He
221.3 forwards (MS) / forward
221.20 hallow (MS) / halloo
222.4 thy (MS) / the
222.6 look (MS) / Look
222.12 wouldest (MS) / would'st
222.12 market-woman (MS) / market-women
222.14 sir," (MS Sir") / sir,
222.39 youth—ay (MS) / youth.—Ay
222.40 Lady's (MS) / Lady
222.41 mayst (MS) / mayest
222.43 wouldest (MS) / wouldst
223.8 scallop-shells (MS) / scallop-shell
224.23 mayst (MS) / mayest
224.39 Ho (MS) / Ha
224.40 quickly—see (MS quickly see) / quickly. See
224.41 food?—heard (MS food—heard) / food? Heard
225.19 pointed a (MS) / pointed to a
225.20 reverent (MS Reverrent) / reverend
225.35 must, e'en (MS) / must e'en
225.36 office—mutter (MS) / office, mutter
226.5 remember (MS) / Remember
226.8 "How?" (8vo derived: "How!") / "How? (MS as Ed 1)
226.27 Knowst (MS) / Knowest
226.30 fetters for ever around (MS) / fetters around
226.34 And (MS) / and
227.15 He gulls and cheats (MS) / He hath gulled and cheated
227.15 preacher; "should (Editorial) / preacher, "should (MS preacher "should)
227.17 him, can (MS derived: him can) / him. Can
227.18 matron?—can (MS matron—can) / matron?—Can
227.19 owing his birth (MS) / owing birth
227.20 status of a married (MS) / state of married
227.20 in opinion (MS) / in public opinion
227.32 at controul, whether (MS at controul whether) / at the controul whether
228.1 in that (MS) / on that

228.5   has heard (MS) / hast seen
228.24   doest (MS) / dost
228.32   drunk (MS) / drank
229.5   honour"——(MS) / honour!"——
229.23   resists (MS) / resist
229.35   began their (MS) / begun the
229.43   called (MS calld) / cried
230.2   speak: meat (MS) / speak. Meat
230.8   before (MS) / beside
230.23   glens (MS) / glen
231.13   Great Cause (MS) / great cause
         The American editions show that the capitals were abandoned after the
         proofs had been corrected by Scott.
231.17   in less rude ages (MS derived: in a less rude ages) / in a less rude age
231.18   the people (MS) / the rude people
231.38   though (MS) / although
232.15   apartment. [new paragraph] The (MS) / Apartment. The
232.38   window, permitted (MS window permitted) / window, the contiguity
         permitted
232.42   their (MS) / thy
233.14   Is (MS) / Are
233.35   head, boldly (MS derived: head boldly) / head and boldly
233.38   and well accustomed (MS and well accustomd) / and accustomed
235.9   Leaving (Editorial) / The course of the story, leaving (MS ⟨on⟩ The
         course of the story leaving)
235.10   fortune, our story returns (MS fortune our story returns) / fortune,
         returns
235.20   Tibb—this (MS) / Tibb, this
235.26   mony mair (MS) / many more
235.29   guestens (MS) / quarters
236.1   we have (MS) / we may have
236.9   lain (MS) / been
236.15   pretty round (MS) / round pretty
236.16   which (MS) / that
236.27   observing Sir (MS) / observing that Sir
236.27   dainty and (MS) / dainty, and
236.34   days (MS) / day
236.34   Good (MS) / good
237.22   preparation (MS) / preparations
238.4   her. So (MS) / her; so
238.6   tumult. Snatching (MS) / tumult, snatching
238.7   terror, Edward (MS derived: terror Edward) / terror. Edward
238.8   air. The (MS) / air; the
238.22   her ruby (MS) / the ruby
238.28   kneeled (MS kneeld) / knelt
238.33   cheek (MS) / cheeks
238.39   accused so suddenly and so strangely (MS) / so suddenly and so strang-
         ely accused
238.40   but (MS) / and
239.6   hath (MS) / has
239.16   that—reluctant (MS) / that, reluctant
239.20   with (MS) / by
239.24   slight (MS) / light
239.29   head"——(MS derived: head——") / head, even as——"
239.36   life"——(MS) / life"—

240.2 thee—little (MS) / thee. Little
240.5 knight. We (MS) / knight; we
240.11 and he now (MS) / and now
240.27 man—not (MS) / man; not
240.35 When Tibb had, with (MS When Tibb had with) / While Tibb, with
240.36 borne (MS born) / bore
241.16 knight, and of (MS knight and of) / knight of
241.24 reckon for it (MS) / reckon it
241.25 knowst (MS) / knowest
242.7 grave—that (MS) / grave, that
242.9 seest (MS) / see'st
242.17 Chapter—it (MS) / Chapter—It
242.22 me." (MS derived: me—") / me?"
242.28 came up to (MS) / came to
242.39 thy (MS) / the
243.15 ideot (MS) / idiot
243.18 us?—too (MS us—too) / us? Too
243.25 mine." (MS mine"—) / mine own."
243.33 them Halbert (MS) / them that Halbert
244.12 communication (MS) / communications
244.27 this (MS) / the
245.17 fall you into (MS) / fall into
245.35 averred (MS averd) / attested
246.1 no earthly reason (MS) / no reason
246.9 mirror"—— (MS) / mirror, and as"——
246.10 Speak to me in (MS) / Speak in
246.12 your (MS) / the
246.15 thee (MS) / you
246.16 yesterday even (MS) / yesterday at even
246.35 my further (MS) / me farther
246.36 me since (MS) / me. Since
246.38 abound. I (MS) / abound, I
246.39 Saviolo (Editorial) / Saviola
246.43 thorough (MS) / through
247.1 stoccata (MS) / stocata
247.12 Old? (MS) / Old!
247.30 corroborative, compel (MS corroborative compell) / corroborative, have compelled
248.18 grateful (MS) / gratified
249.6 imaginary (MS) / imagined
249.8 a kinsman (MS) / the kinsman
249.22 will (MS) / may
249.35 dared (MS) / dare
250.23 I may (MS) / may I
250.34 dales (MS) / vales
250.35 kindred—it (MS) / kindred. It
250.41 West, the (MS west the) / West frontier, the
250.43 breasts (MS) / breach
251.12 suffice (MS) / Suffice
251.16 on (MS) / upon
251.17 certain credit (MS) / certain degree of credit
251.19 grasps (MS) / grasped
251.20 lack (MS) / lacked
251.21 here (MS) / Here
251.23 am (MS) / was

251.23 hand—But (MS hand ⟨where⟩ ↑ — ↓ But) / hand; but
251.36 await (MS) / wait
251.40 although (MS) / though
252.19 further (MS) / farther
253.25 Scotsman (MS) / Scotchman
253.25 Englishman, rebel (MS Englishman rebel) / Englishman, a rebel
254.5   contingency (MS) / contingence
254.27 was "a (MS) / "were a
254.31 feelings. But (MS) / feelings; but
254.35 hand (MS) / hands
254.36 which had belonged (MS which had belongd) / which belonged
254.41 "upon warld's (MS "upon warlds) / upon world's
254.42 shirt." (Editorial) / shirt (MS as Ed1)
255.42 usually (MS) / always
256.12 compassionate, not (MS) / compassionate, and not
257.29 us (MS) / me
258.6   scheme, daring (MS scheme daring) / scheme for Sir Piercie Shafton's
        freedom, daring
258.20 wardrope (MS) / wardrobe
258.22 hear that (MS) / understand that
260.11 shall (MS) / will
260.16 wardrope (MS) / wardrobe
260.25 mails (MS) / trunk-mails
260.25 of sorrow (MS) / of parting sorrow
260.30 they (MS) / was
260.32 knight—it (MS) / knight. It
260.33 up and (MS) / up—and
260.35 in this (MS) / up into this
260.42 it—for (MS) / it—For
261.36 word with the action (MS) / action with the word
262.24 fiend (MS) / na
263.8   this (MS) / the first
263.12 by (MS) / for
263.23 horse, to (MS) / horse! To
263.28 dead men." (MS dead men") / dead."
263.29 through (MS) / past
264.11 its towers and pinnacles scarce (MS) / whose towers and pinnacles were
        scarce
264.16 Philip had concluded (MS) / Philip concluded
264.31 this (MS) / the
264.34 increasing (MS) / increased
264.41 sayst (MS) / sayest
265.6   from respectful (MS) / from a respectful
265.21 Speak then (MS) / Speak, then
265.35 so—meanwhile (MS) / so; meanwhile
265.43 off. But (MS) / off, but
266.19 romantic attorney's apprentice (MS romantic attorneys apprentice) /
        attorney's romantic apprentice
266.22 die." But (MS) / die;" but
266.37 gentle perfect Knight (MS gentle perfect knight) / gentle Knight
269.3   with the publicans (MS) / with publicans
269.8   strolling the (MS) / strolling through the
270.2   And yet (MS) / Yet
270.4   the tasks (MS) / these tasks
270.14 agile and graceful at once, (MS) / agile at once and graceful,

270.21 as if Love . . . some (MS as if Love had taught her to adopt them or as if some) / as if some
270.27 positive (MS) / ordinary and natural
270.29 of Vanity (MS) / of vanity
270.30 which Vanity (MS) / which vanity
270.36 accepted. But (MS) / accepted; but
270.38 And immediately (MS And immediatly) / Immediately
270.43 a cup or two of (MS) / a few cups of
271.14 Saviolo (Editorial) / Saviola (MS as Ed1)
272.3   And (MS) / and
272.9   well (MS) / Well
272.16 doest (MS) / dost
272.30 paid?—and (MS) / paid? and
272.43 of (Editorial) / or (MS as Ed1)
        See Essay on the Text, 386.
273.13 her—do (MS) / her. Do
273.27 completely village-fashion (MS) / completely in village fashion
274.1   was but a (MS) / was a
274.9   friend: (MS) / friend;
274.21 Mysinda? (MS) / Mysinda,
274.28 warrant him stop (MS) / warrant he will stop
274.28 that (MS) / which
274.39 risks (MS) / risk
274.43 periods (MS) / period
275.6   Edinburgh—I (MS) / Edinburgh; I
276.4   reverent (MS) / reverend
276.22 But (MS) / but
277.11 Eustace had also (MS) / Eustace also
277.36 not indisposed to place them (MS) / disposed to place himself
278.7   amongst (MS) / among
278.22 peculiar quality (MS) / peculiarity
278.22 had made her (MS) / made her now
278.39 doest (MS) / dost
279.27 precaution (MS) / precautions
279.30 turn (MS) / tone
280.13 was very great (MS) / was great
281.5   assure (MS) / assures
281.24 shout (MS) / shouts
281.32 beneath (MS) / around
281.39 What ho! my (MS) / What, ho!—my
282.3   of (MS) / in
282.9   out—and (MS) / out. And
282.13 many such grates (MS) / many grates
283.3   said he (MS) / he said
283.13 that (MS) / which
283.20 I said (MS) / I have said
283.23 Father," answered (MS father" answerd) / Father, "answered
283.28 hollowing (MS) / hallooing
283.29 it (MS) / It
283.33 whilk (MS) / which
283.33 any old carle's crutch (MS any old carles crutch) / an old crutch
283.34 nought (MS) / nothing
284.10 with an air of great (MS) / with great
284.14 kens (MS) / knows
284.17 further (MS) / farther

285.39 heart naturally (MS) / heart, naturally
287.5   honour of Father Eustace's heart more than his (MS derived: honour
        more of father Eustaces ⟨consisten⟩ ↑ heart more ↓ than ↑ ⟨of⟩ ↓ his)
        / honour more of Father Eustace's heart than of his
288.7   opposed (MS) / opposite
288.9   Wellwood!"—the (MS Wellwood" the) / Wellwood!" and the
288.23 hands (MS) / hand
288.28 career?—and (MS career and) / career?—And
289.16 chosen—the (MS) / chosen; the
289.30 err (MS) / error
289.35 keys, and like (MS keys and like) / keys, like
289.36 bribes"—— (MS) / bribes, and"——
289.42 thine ancient (MS) / thy former
290.2   doubt—thou (MS) / doubt—Thou
290.3   by (MS) / at
290.5   friends—our (MS friends our) / friends. Our
291.12 further (MS) / farther
291.25 mayst (MS) / mayest
291.28 Satan—in (MS) / Satan. In
292.37 lives!—there (MS lives—there) / lives!—There
292.38 grave—the (MS grave the) / grave. The
292.40 there—he (MS) / there. He
293.11 if dungeon (MS) / if a dungeon
293.36 were (MS) / be
293.40 termed: the (MS termd: the) / termed—the
294.15 motions." (MS derived: motions—") / motions?"
294.42 thinkst (MS) / thinkest
295.18 does (MS) / dost
295.37 has taught, and (MS has taught and) / hast taught me, and
295.40 it me (MS) / it to me
296.10 pray, compose (MS pray compose) / pray, and compose
296.14 passions?—no (MS) / passions?—No
296.15 joy—all (MS) / joy—All
296.16 menials—She (MS) / menials—she
296.17 And I?—I (MS And I? I) / and I—I
296.33 Love (MS) / love
296.33 Heraldry (MS) / heraldry
296.36 her!—but (MS her—but) / her! But
297.4   headlong (MS) / headstrong
297.7   has (MS) / hast
297.30 resolved (MS resolvd) / resolute
297.38 Wisdom and to Goodness (MS) / wisdom and to goodness
298.3   you—let (MS) / you; let
298.15 "Go, then," said (MS "Go then said) / "Even now; if thou wilt," said
298.18 darted (MS) / hastened
299.37 remembrance . . . as (MS remembrance though only once heard as) /
        remembrance, as
300.15 desirest—thou (MS) / desirest; thou
300.18 rude (MS) / bold
301.15 ony Piercie (MS) / ony Sir Piercie
301.15 a'—they (MS) / a'. They
301.16 liked, but (MS derived: liked but) / liked; but
301.23 lamentation (MS) / lamentations
301.38 himself (MS) / him
302.1   soul—and (MS) / soul: And

302.3 heretics, such (MS heretics such) / heretics, yet such
302.5 wheat. But (MS) / wheat; but
302.26 erring (MS) / own
302.27 done. Remember (MS) / done Remember
302.41 this (MS) / the
303.7 polemics?—it might (MS polemics—it might) / polemics?—might
303.26 was more enthusiastic (MS) / was enthusiastic
303.31 while (MS) / and
304.5 door and outer-door (MS) / outer door and inner door
304.9 alang (MS) / along
304.12 these (MS) / their
304.19 his reverence (MS his Reverence) / the Sub-Prior
304.23 if (MS) / whether
304.26 wark (MS) / work
305.9 as I am myself (MS) / as myself
305.11 alone (MS) / along
305.18 he said (MS) / said he
305.20 brother—may (MS brother Halbert—may) / brother? May
305.31 Edward and (MS Edward &) / Edward, and
305.32 him—sometimes (MS) / him, sometimes
306.38 the plain truth (MS) / the truth
307.6 assuredly (MS) / surely
307.12 teind-sheaves (MS) / land-sheaves
307.14 interjected (MS) / intersected
307.21 force. But (MS) / force; but
308.10 has (MS) / hast
308.13 rear—why (MS) / rear—Why
308.21 guest hall and treated (MS Guest hall and treated) / great hall, and be treated
308.41 Eustace—and (MS) / Eustace—And
309.4 cannons (MS cannon ↑s↓) / cannon
309.8 walls (MS) / wall
309.31 and alb (MS) / or alb
309.35 has (MS) / hath
309.39 soul!—we (MS soul—we) / soul!— [end of line] —we
309.40 you (MS) / ye
310.24 on (MS) / upon
310.37 *convenerunt in unum* (MS) / *convenerunt unum*
311.33 brought up—we (MS brought—we) / brought up. We
312.10 a born (MS) / born a
312.12 Scotland—there (MS) / Scotland. There
312.13 on—if (MS) / on. If
312.18 where (MS) / Where
312.19 Meigallot—he (MS) / Meigallot; he
312.22 pinch (MS) / point
312.24 vain. Let (MS) / vain—Let
312.33 could—in (MS) / could; in
313.8 office—and (MS) / office And
313.25 ever (MS) / even
313.43 have stronger (MS) / have a stronger
314.9 may (MS) / May
314.14 an (MS) / the
314.19 arise (MS) / rise
314.26 attained (MS attaind) / obtained
315.24 any (MS) / "any

316.1 firth—if (MS firth if) / firth—If
316.20 where well-favoured (MS where well favourd) / where a well-favoured
316.28 knowst (MS) / knowest
316.30 it (MS) / the track
317.9 Set (MS) / Let
317.41 this (MS) / the
318.15 a wink (MS) / the wink
318.27 their (MS) / the
319.7 Glasgow—here (MS) / Glasgow. Here
319.9 them—unless (MS) / them, unless
319.11 this (MS) / the
319.14 merchant (MS) / mendicant
320.3 the bastard (MS) / some wild kinsman
320.5 quarrel (MS) / quarrels
320.10 back (MS) / backs
320.16 deep (MS) / deeply
320.24 sting—the (MS) / sting, the
320.37 harlotrie—and (MS) / harlotrie. And
320.39 accompanied—and (MS) / accompanied. And
321.5 But, the majority being (MS derived: But the majority being) / But the majority, being
321.19 would (MS) / should
321.30 shared might (MS) / shared, might
321.31 forwards (MS) / forward
322.29 circumstance (MS) / circumstances
323.8 and of man (MS) / of man
323.16 his hand-fasted concubine (MS) / his concubine
323.39 sun-burned (MS sun-burnd) / sun-burnt
324.5 forwards (MS) / forward
324.18 Nay, nay—leave (MS derived: Nay nay leave) / Nay—nay—leave
324.18 heralds—in (MS) / heralds. In
324.39 house (MS House) / horse
325.20 antichamber (MS) / antichambed
325.23 Teviotdale—and (MS) / Teviotdale; and
326.3 brows (MS) / brow
326.43 painful (MS) / fatal
327.2 streets (MS) / street
327.15 We had (MS) / we had
327.15 with utmost (MS) / with the utmost
327.18 Northumberland!—he (MS Northumberland—he) / Northumberland!—He
328.18 strikes stroke (MS) / strikes a stroke
328.21 spare not the spur for (Magnum) / spare the spur, for (MS as Ed 1)
329.11 pursuit (MS) / field
329.35 retreat and (MS) / retreat, and
329.42 relatives (MS) / relations
330.12 She (MS) / The mourner
330.22 over: (MS) / over,
330.33 him, "Speak (MS derived: him "Speak) / him to "speak
330.38 how (MS) / How
330.42 answered (MS answered) / said
331.4 last. It (MS derived: last—It) / last? it
331.13 accompt (MS) / account
331.40 in (MS) / on
332.6 reason, every (MS reason every) / reason, with every

332.32 life—the (MS) / life; the
333.3 conference—And (MS derived: conference—and) / conference, and
333.11 danger of (MS) / danger and of
333.24 you (MS) / ye
333.27 Earl thus accosted (MS) / Earl accosted
334.14 hold with (MS) / hold opinion with
335.6 like (MS) / likely
335.6 between (MS) / betwixt
335.13 You (MS) / you
336.10 couldest (MS) / couldst
336.22 woman's (MS womans) / women's
336.31 through (MS) / among
336.34 officer. The (MS) / officer; the
337.1 ruins (MS) / ruin
337.20 as it may to (MS) / as may be to
337.41 interrupting, "our (MS derived: interrupting our) / interrupting him, "our
338.5 these (MS) / the
338.6 countrymen—and (MS countrymen⟨"⟩—and) / countrymen; and
338.11 good. But (MS) / good; but
338.12 resist; and to waste (MS resist and to waste) / resist, and may not waste
338.13 vain opposition (MS) / vain—Fruitless opposition
338.41 on (MS) / of
338.43 is all nothing (MS) / is nothing
339.42 yet (MS) / still
340.3 engagement (MS) / engagements
340.16 an (MS) / the
340.17 anger!—thou that (MS) / anger! yes, it is thy voice that
340.20 until (MS untill) / till
340.23 as light (MS) / as did light
340.27 thou hadst (MS thou ⟨and should⟩ hadst) / it had·
341.5 won (MS) / misled
341.5 to (MS) / into
341.31 this (MS) / the
342.5 tressure—quartered, as (MS tressure—and as) / tressure, quartered, as
342.6 can (MS) / Can
342.8 Moray—he (MS Moray he) / Moray. He
342.15 son—as (MS) / son, as
342.17 us—a (MS) / us. A
342.18 faith—such (MS) / faith. Such
342.26 God, my child, who (MS God my child who) / God, who
342.30 forget—but (MS) / forget; but
342.34 service—for (MS) / service; for
342.37 track (MS) / erect
342.38 Awaken (MS) / awaken
342.40 not—yet (MS) / not, yet
342.40 lose? . . . Look at (MS lose Look round this fair fabric ⟨the⟩ gorgeous beyond the skill and wealth of our degenerate days Look at) / lose?—Look at
342.42 saints have dwelt (MS) / saints dwelt
342.43 think (MS) / Think
343.3 fate—I (MS) / fate. I
343.18 days—they (MS) / days.—They
343.19 cloisters, and (MS derived: cloisters and) / cloisters; and
343.19 than I (MS) / than where I

344.15 lamentation (MS) / lamentations
344.24 entered two (MS enterd two) / entered, two
344.41 obdured (MS) / obdurate
345.16 and, being (MS and being) / and which, being
345.20 this kinsman (MS) / the kinsman
346.15 what (MS) / What
346.23 Master—it is shame (MS) / Master. It is a shame
346.25 Bethink how (MS) / Bethink you how
346.33 hath right (MS) / hath spoken right
347.6 protects (MS) / protect
348.42 of the Queen of England (MS) / of England
348.43 those (MS) / these
349.5 impunity; give (MS) / impunity. Give
349.41 Cross-stitch (Editorial) / Overstitch
        See Essay on the Text, 395.
349.43 keepst (MS) / keepest
350.9 presence (MS) / prisoners
350.25 Bolton, to (MS Bolton to) / Bolton, he to
350.31 brown varlet (MS) / Brown Varlet
350.32 white-head (MS) / White Head
350.35 evil (MS) / Evil
350.35 dame—better (MS) / dame. Better
351.12 disposed at (MS) / disposed of at
352.7 parts." (MS) / parts.
352.16 him," said (8vo) / him,' said (MS him said)
352.19 this (MS) / the
353.8 pretension (MS) / pretence
353.21 said. "She (MS said. She) / said; "she
353.22 ought (MS) / aught

All end-of-line hyphens in the present text are soft unless included in the list below. The hyphens listed are hard and should be retained when quoting.

HISTORICAL NOTE

Chronology. As Scott himself points out, *The Monastery* does not map its plot directly onto actual historical events: 'the dates cannot be exactly reconciled with those of the most accredited histories' (354.6–7). Going by the historical markers mentioned, but not dated, in the text, the story is spread from the Battle of Pinkie in 1547 to at least 1562—the date at which Lord James Stewart became Earl of Moray. This gives a time-span of about fifteen years, but if the narrative is traced according to its own internal chronology the duration is somewhat shorter: Halbert is about nine or ten years old at 40.18 and about 19 from 176.15 until the end of the novel, spanning a period of nine or ten years. The only date specified in the text is 'the peace of 1550' (35.14). Perhaps Scott intended the reader to associate this with the immediate aftermath of Pinkie, for which no date is given, reducing the time scale by three years. A further implicit reduction (in line with Halbert's age) brings the date of the novel's close to about 1559, at the start of the Scottish Reformation.

Alternatively, a strict calculation from 1547 would see the novel ending in 1557, with a number of historical references brought forward. Such a temporal compression has the effect of moving events closer together and defining factions and oppositions. Most strikingly, the reign of Elizabeth I, who came to the throne in 1558, is moved back to coincide with the events of the novel. Although Mary Queen of Scots remains a rather shadowy figure in *The Monastery* her presence is nevertheless brought into focus: Scott implies that she is resident in Edinburgh (where Halbert aspires to see her at 216.29–30) whereas historically she spent the years 1548–61 in France. In terms of the development of Protestantism in Scotland Scott is again unspecific. Julian Avenel refers to the Lords of the Congregation, a group of Protestant nobles who acquired this title when they signed the 'First Band' committing themselves to the establishing of Protestantism in 1557 (224.19–20). The novel refers rather vaguely to the outburst of iconoclasm that led to the sacking of monasteries beginning in the summer of 1559: 'In many large towns, the monasteries had been suppressed by the fury of the populace' (285.9–10). But here again the novel does not foreground the events of history.

Historical Context. Scott clearly does not expect the reader to pay too much attention to dates; nevertheless the novel situates itself in some specific historical conditions. Opening shortly after the defeat of the Scots at the Battle of Pinkie, *The Monastery* alludes to the circumstances leading up to that climactic event. The death of James V, shortly after the early heavy defeat of the Scots by the English at the Battle of Solway Moss in 1542, left Scotland in a weakened state.

James was succeeded by his week-old daughter Mary, causing a power vacuum which was to be filled by regents during her minority reign. The infant Mary's future was fought over by factions seeking appeasement of or alliances with England and France. In 1543 James Hamilton, 2nd Earl of Arran, who was governor of Scotland from 1543 to 1554, agreed to the Treaties of Greenwich which promised the infant Mary as bride for Edward, heir of Henry VIII, but Henry increased his demands, and the Scottish Parliament rejected the treaties, instead confirming those with France. The following year saw Henry taking military action to try to enforce the marriage. This so-called 'Rough Wooing' (38.38–40), led by the Earl of Hertford, had the specific aim of causing as much destruction as possible and devastated the lands of Lothian and the Borders, leaving them in the condition lamented by Elspet in the novel's early chapters. A Scottish victory at Ancrum in 1545 was followed by another wave of English incursions which destroyed much farm-land by crop-burning. In 1547 Henry sent a further invading force under the leadership of Hertford, now Duke of Somerset. It was met on 10 September by a larger but significantly less well equipped Scottish army at Pinkie, the battle in which *The Monastery*'s Simon Glendinning loses his life (39.8–12). Their retreat cut off by the sea on one side and the river Esk on the other, the Scots suffered massive losses, and the subsequent occupation of a number of Scottish towns during the next two years gave the English a base for further harassment of Lothian and the Borders.[1]

Arran's rival for power was the widow of James V, Mary of Guise, who took over the regency in 1554. The daughter of the French Count of Guise, she sought to strengthen Scotland's position through alliances with France, long a part of Scottish political strategy. Meanwhile, her opponents among the Scottish ruling class (including a number of Border lairds), established alignments with the English. The Sub-Prior comments on the divided loyalties of the Scots: 'the one part French, the other part English, considering their dear native country merely as a prize-fighting stage' (160.11–13). The novel's political background is thus marked by a tense factionalism between a Catholic group pursuing the 'auld alliance' with France, and a pro-English group who were embracing Protestantism and seeking to limit the powers which the Catholic Queen Mary could wield on taking up her personal rule.

Most of Scott's characters in *The Monastery* are fictional, and historical figures such as Queen Mary or John Knox remain firmly in the background. The principal historical character to make an appearance is James Stewart, illegitimate son of James V and Earl of Moray from 1562. Even in his case, however, Scott reserves most of Moray's historically documented activities to *The Monastery*'s sequel, *The Abbot*. Moray appears only in the third volume of *The Monastery* on his way to sort out a rather vaguely reported 'tuilzie in Ayrshire' between the powerful Kennedy family and the Sempills (318.5). Moray never reaches the south-west corner of Scotland, being waylaid by the hostilities sparked off by the Monastery's sheltering of the Catholic Piercie

Shafton, so Scott is not obliged to fill in the details of the Earl's activities in Ayrshire.

Although Scott had available to him sources from John Knox to William Robertson detailing the abuses practised by the monastic orders prior to the Reformation, he is comparatively mild in his description of the religious life at St Mary's.[2] *The Monastery*'s most prominent censure of Catholicism targets the Church's opposition to the translation of the Bible into English. Scott's 'Black Book' is not easy to identify: no vernacular Bible was printed in Scotland until 1579. William Tyndale's translation of the New Testament was available in Scotland from about 1527, but as the text in *The Monastery* appears to be the whole Bible we must assume that Scott did not intend the reader to identify any particular translation.[3] Scott makes dark allusions to the fate of those caught reading the English text, yet the practice was made lawful from 1543 in an Act of Parliament by which, as Knox put it, 'it was made free to all men and women to read the Scriptures in their own tongue'.[4] Scott may, however, be conflating other examples from Knox who cites an earlier case of a man named Forrest, burned at the stake 'for none other crime but because he had a New Testament in English'.[5] Knox goes on to quote an Act of Parliament which stated 'That under pain of heresy, no man should read any part of the Scriptures in the English tongue', but no such Act is recorded.[6] There was, however, an Act of 1541 which forbade meetings in private houses to discuss the scripture without the presence of a University-educated theologian, which may account for the Lady of Avenel's nervousness in reading the scriptures to her assembled household.

While events of international and national politics inform *The Monastery*, the novel foregrounds some of the more localised events and practices in the Eastern part of the Scottish Border over which the centralised government had great difficulty maintaining control. The sixteenth-century Borders were characterised by cross-frontier raids and cattle-thefts as well as violent and protracted feuds between (and sometimes within) families. Order was imposed on the region by Scottish law-enforcing expeditions (a number of them conducted by the Earl of Moray) which targeted particular areas where known felons would be apprehended and frequently executed. Both Hawick and Jedburgh were the sites of the rounding-up and mass execution of Borderers. In addition to these forays, the territory on each side of the Border was divided into the East, Middle, and West Marches. Each March was governed by a Warden, usually supplied by prominent Border families, a number of whom appear or are mentioned in *The Monastery*.[7] Opposing Wardens from Scotland and England would meet from time to time on Days of Truce on which grievances could be heard, debts settled, and prisoners exchanged. Nevertheless, despite these systems for keeping order, the Borders remained a wild and unregulated area throughout the 1550s and 1560s.

Sources. *The Monastery* does not follow any formal written histories very closely, but it refers throughout to the local history Scott had already documented in his collection of ballads *Minstrelsy of the Scottish Border* (1802–03), his notes to *The Lay of the Last Minstrel* (1805: a poem also set in the neighbourhood of Melrose), and his essay on 'Border Antiquities' which prefaced the two-volume *The Border Antiquities of England and Scotland* (1814). Characters with old Border names, some of them featuring in ballads, are scattered throughout the text, although Scott does not make much use of any single story. There are some echoes, however, in the stand-off between Moray and Sir John Foster (Ch. 36), of 'The Raid of the Reidswire', a ballad commemorating a Day of Truce which got out of hand in 1575. In his introduction to this ballad in the *Minstrelsy*, Scott describes how the two Wardens, Sir John Carmichael and the same John Foster who appears in *The Monastery*, levelled accusations at each other, resulting in a bloody skirmish between Foster's Tynedale men and a body of Jedburgh townsfolk who turned up to swell the ranks of the Scots.[8]

Scott's principal source for information about sixteenth-century monastic life was Fosbrooke's *British Monachism* of 1802 (enlarged in 1817), a staunchly Protestant, and not very accurate, account of the habits, customs, and regulations of monastic orders, and the duties of various offices within the monastery. Apart from Abbot Ambrosius's love of food and wine (Fosbrooke comments on the monks' gluttony),[9] Scott is less critical of monastic behaviour than is Fosbrooke. Of particular note here is Scott's omission of the details, recorded in *British Monachism*, that the monks of Melrose had private gardens, and that they extracted private pensions from the revenue from the Abbey's feuars, or tenant farmers.[10]

For his characterisation of Sir Piercie Shafton, Scott refers the reader to works that appeared about twenty years after the events of the novel, John Lyly's *Euphues: The Anatomy of Wit* (1578) and *Euphues and his England* (1580). These tell the story of a fictional rake, but the plot is really the vehicle for debates, letters, and speeches demonstrating formal rhetorical patterns. Scott does not follow Lyly very closely, however, preferring to satirise Sir Piercie with the assistance of Jonson and Shakespeare, both of whose plays (identified in the Explanatory Notes) include portraits of pretentious users of over-wrought language. Sir Piercie further complicates the novel's historical chronology by referring to Philip Sidney, born in 1554, as if he were a grown man, and as Graham Tulloch points out, he is best seen as a composite of Elizabethan linguistic exuberance.[11]

Like Sir Piercie, the White Lady did not fare well in the early reviews of the novel. In a section of the Magnum introduction in which Scott attempts to account for her lack of success with the public, he suggests that she was based on the German writer Friedrich de La Motte Fouqué's early nineteenth-century tale of the water-nymph Undine, overlaid with some Celtic mythology, while Coleman Parsons has traced yet more influences from folklore and literature. The White Lady is a very heterogeneous creation indeed.[12]

Much of Scott's description in Clutterbuck's Introductory Epistle of 'Kennaquair', based on his local town of Melrose, is likely to have come from personal observation, though he owned at least two guide-books.[13] Although there is no official record before 1836, John Mason, in his *Border Tour* of 1826, estimated the population of Melrose at 500 people.[14] By the 1820s it was a prosperous settlement. Landowners had already profited from the 'improving operations' mentioned at 5.7, by which formerly common ground was enclosed and cultivated.[15] The town's increasingly well-known charms drew several wealthy families who, like Scott, also had residences in Edinburgh. A number of retired soldiers, like Captain Clutterbuck, settled there, prompting Scott to remark that 'the inhabitants of Melrose . . . always have a gaudeamus [convivial gathering], like honest men, on the anniversary of Waterloo'.[16] But the principal feature of Melrose was its Abbey. Melrose Abbey was founded by David I in 1136 and continued to expand until devastated by an English army in 1385 when the Abbey church was almost completely destroyed. The church was rebuilt on a bigger scale over the next century. Scott represents the Abbey in a better state of repair than it really was in the sixteenth century, and he also allows the monks a greater degree of autonomy than obtained following the enforced deposition of the last Abbot in 1541 and the appointment of the infant James Stewart (a younger half-brother of the Earl of Moray) as its Commendator (a secular position which allowed him to profit from the Abbey's revenues). Renewed hostilities from England during the 'Rough Wooing' saw the further desecration of the Abbey church, and despite the monks' protests to their Commendator no repairs were forthcoming. Following the Reformation in 1560 the monks renounced monasticism, but a dwindling number of them continued to live in the Abbey buildings until 1590.

Although the Abbey lands were sold off by the Crown, the Abbey church continued to be used by the townspeople of Melrose and a makeshift roof and screen walls were constructed within the old nave. In 1803 Dorothy Wordsworth, visiting the Abbey in the company of Scott, commented: 'within these beautiful walls is the ugliest church that was ever beheld'.[17] Nevertheless, the Abbey was becoming a notable tourist attraction, encouraged by Scott's own well-known description of it in the very popular *Lay of the Last Minstrel*. With the completion of a new parish church in 1810 repairs to the Abbey could be contemplated. The old makeshift church was cleared and eventually Scott, with the assistance of the Abbey's owner, the Duke of Buccleuch, was to oversee restoration work starting in 1822. Architecturally, Melrose was of an exceptionally complex and lavish design. Captain Clutterbuck refers vaguely to a historically composite style of 'Gothic or Saxon architraves, mullions and flying buttresses' (7.25–26). In fact, little remained of the Romanesque twelfth-century church, and the Gothic design of the arches was mixed with the influences of the English Perpendicular style, evident in the tall windows with their flowing tracery. John Bower's 1813 guide to the Abbey (lavishly dedicated to Scott) describes it as 'one of the most magnificent pieces of Gothic architecture in the kingdom, and the admiration of every beholder, for the lightness of its pillars, the variety of its sculpture, the beauty of its stones, and the symmetry of its parts'.[18] Although most of the monastic buildings had vanished, the church itself presented a substantial ruin with only the west end and the western part of the North wall gone.[19]

NOTES

1 See David H. Caldwell, 'The Battle of Pinkie', in *Scotland and War AD 79–1918*, ed. Norman Macdougall (Edinburgh, 1991), 61–94.

2 The Abbotsford library has two editions of John Knox's *The Historie of the Reformation of the Church of Scotland* dated 1644 (the first edition) and 1732 (*CLA*, 2). It also contains the third edition of William Robertson's *The History of Scotland during the Reigns of Queen Mary and of King James VI*, published in 1760 (*CLA*, 4): Robertson's *History* was first published in 1759.

3 For translations of the Bible circulating in Scotland see Jenny Wormald, *Court, Kirk, and Community: Scotland 1470–1625* (London, 1981), 104–05.

4 John Knox, *History of the Reformation in Scotland*, ed. William Croft Dickinson, 2 vols (London, 1949), 1.45.

5 Knox implies that this took place in 1524 but this seems to be a mistake for 1533, the date given in Robert Keith, *The History of the Affairs of Church and State in Scotland* (Edinburgh, 1834), 9. See Knox, *History of the Reformation in Scotland*, 1.22 and note.

6 Knox, *History of the Reformation in Scotland*, 1.43 and note 6.

7 Scott gives a description of the divisions of the Border and their Wardens in his 'Essay on Border Antiquities': *The Prose Works of Sir Walter Scott, Bart.*, 28 vols (Edinburgh, 1834–36), 7.2–153 (98–108).

8 *Minstrelsy of the Scottish Border*, ed. T. F. Henderson, 4 vols (Edinburgh, 1902), 2.18–19.

9 Thomas Dudley Fosbrooke, *British Monachism*, new enlarged edn (London, 1817), 297–304.

10 *British Monachism*, 375.

11 For a detailed study of Shafton's speech see Graham Tulloch, 'Sir Walter Scott's Excursion into Euphuism', *Neuphilologische Mitteilungen*, 78 (1977), 65–76.

12 Coleman O. Parsons, *Witchcraft and Demonology in Scott's Fiction* (Edinburgh, 1964), 158–62.

13 [Adam Milne], *A Description of the Parish of Melrose* (Edinburgh, 1743) and John Bower, *Descriptions of the Abbeys of Melrose and Old Melrose with their Traditions* (Kelso, 1813): both *CLA*, 6.

14 [John Mason], *The Border Tour* (Edinburgh, 1826), 121.

15 John H. Romanes, 'An Enclosure Proceeding in Melrose in the Year 1742', *Scottish Historical Review*, 13 (1916), 101–08.

16 J. G. Lockhart, *Memoirs of the Life of Sir Walter Scott, Bart.*, 7 vols (Edinburgh, 1837), 5.188.

17 Dorothy Wordsworth, *Recollections of a Tour made in Scotland*, ed. Carol Kyros Walker (New Haven, 1997), 206–07.

18 *Descriptions of the Abbeys of Melrose and Old Melrose with their Traditions*, 28.

19 For Melrose and its Abbey see Marguerite Wood and J. S. Richardson, *Melrose Abbey* (HMSO 1932: rev. edn Historic Scotland, 1995); Richard Fawcett, *Scottish Abbeys and Priories* (London, 1994); Ian B. Cowan and David E. Easson, *Medieval Religious Houses, Scotland*, 2nd edn (London, 1976); *Melrose 1826*, ed. D. M. Hood (Melrose, [1978]); Mark Dilworth, *Scottish Monasteries in the Late Middle Ages* (Edinburgh, 1995).

EXPLANATORY NOTES

In these notes a comprehensive attempt is made to identify Scott's sources, and all quotations, references, historical events, and historical personages, to explain proverbs, and to translate difficult or obscure language. (Phrases are explained in the notes while single words are treated in the glossary.) The notes are brief; they offer information rather than critical comment or exposition. When a quotation has not been recognised this is stated: any new information from readers will be welcomed. References are to standard editions, or to the editions Scott himself used. Books in the Abbotsford Library are identified by reference to the appropriate page of the *Catalogue of the Library at Abbotsford*. When quotations reproduce their sources accurately, the reference is given without comment. Verbal differences in the source are indicated by a prefatory 'see', while a general rather than a verbal indebtedness is indicated by 'compare'. Biblical references are to the Authorised Version. Plays by Shakespeare are cited without authorial ascription, and references are to *William Shakespeare: The Complete Works*, edited by Peter Alexander (London and Glasgow, 1951, frequently reprinted).

The following publications are distinguished by abbreviations, or are given without the names of their authors:

Berners   [Juliana Berners], *The Book Containing the Treatises of Hawking; Hunting; Coat-armour; Fishing; and Blasing of Arms*, ed. Joseph Haslewood (1496; repr. London, 1810): *CLA*, 208.

'Border Antiquities'   'Essay on Border Antiquities' (1814), in *Prose Works*, 7.3–153.

Canterbury Tales   Geoffrey Chaucer, *The Canterbury Tales* (written *c.* 1387–1400), in *The Riverside Chaucer*, 3rd edn, ed. Larry D. Benson (Oxford, 1988): see *CLA*, 42, 154, 155, 172, 239.

Chambers   Robert Chambers, *The Popular Rhymes of Scotland* (Edinburgh, 1826).

Cheviot   Andrew Cheviot, *Proverbs, Proverbial Expressions and Popular Rhymes of Scotland* (London, 1896).

CLA   [J. G. Cochrane], *Catalogue of the Library at Abbotsford* (Edinburgh, 1938).

EEWN   The Edinburgh Edition of the Waverley Novels (Edinburgh, 1993–).

Fosbrooke   Thomas Dudley Fosbrooke, *British Monachism; or, Manners and Customs of the Monks and Nuns of England*, new enlarged edn (London, 1817): see *CLA*, 184.

Letters   *The Letters of Sir Walter Scott*, ed. H. J. C. Grierson and others, 12 vols (London, 1932–37).

LLM   Walter Scott, *The Lay of the Last Minstrel* (Edinburgh, 1805).

Lockhart   J. G. Lockhart, *Memoirs of the Life of Sir Walter Scott, Bart.*, 7 vols (Edinburgh, 1837).

Lyly   *Complete Works of John Lyly*, ed. R. Warwick Bond, 3 vols (Oxford, 1902).

Magnum   Walter Scott, *Waverley Novels*, 48 vols (Edinburgh, 1829–33).

Minstrelsy   *Minstrelsy of the Scottish Border*, ed. T. F. Henderson, 4 vols (Edinburgh, 1902).

441

ODEP   *The Oxford Dictionary of English Proverbs*, 3rd edn, rev. F. P. Wilson (Oxford, 1970).

Percy   *Reliques of Ancient English Poetry*, [ed. Thomas Percy], 3 vols (London, 1765); see *CLA*, 172.

Poetical Works   *The Poetical Works of Sir Walter Scott, Bart.*, [ed. J. G. Lockhart], 12 vols (Edinburgh, 1833–34).

Prose Works   *The Prose Works of Sir Walter Scott, Bart.*, 28 vols (Edinburgh, 1834–36).

Ray   John Ray, *A Compleat Collection of English Proverbs*, 3rd edn (London, 1737): *CLA*, 169.

Tales of the East   *Tales of the East*, ed. Henry William Weber, 3 vols (Edinburgh, 1812): *CLA*, 43.

title-page   *Waverley* (1814) was Scott's first novel. His eighth novel, *Ivanhoe* (1820), was the first to be called a 'romance': it inaugurated Scott's movement into pre-17th-century (and sometimes non-Scottish) subject areas.

3.3 Clutterbuck   the name carries connotations both of untidiness and of a beau or dandy.

3.8–11 pretend to . . . pretend to   claim . . . lay claim to.

3.14 last interview . . . sister   Fergus and Flora MacIvor are the Jacobite siblings in *Waverley* (1814). In fact Fergus carefully spares Flora the distress of a last interview before his execution (Ch. 69).

3.15–16 Dandie Dinmont   a character in *Guy Mannering* (1815).

3.24 three volumes   the usual method of novel publication in the early 19th century.

3.29–4.3 Captain Grose . . . call it   see Robert Burns, 'On the Late Captain Grose's Peregrinations thro' Scotland, collecting the Antiquities of that Kingdom' (1789; rev. 1793), lines 25–30. The reference is to the celebrated antiquary Francis Grose (1731?–91).

4.6 the Scots Fuzileers   the Regiment of Scots Fuzileers, raised in 1678, numbered the 21st Regiment of Foot in 1751.

4.7–8 old David Stiles, Clerk to his Majesty's Signet   no such person is listed as a Writer to the Signet.

4.20 a red coat   the standard uniform for the British soldier.

4.41 half-pay   pension paid to officers after their retirement from the services. Half-pay for a captain in an infantry regiment at this time was set at 5s. a day or £92 a year. Half-pay, like full-pay, was supposed to be paid monthly but frequently fell into arrears.

4.42 set up his staff of rest   settled down. See Henry Brooke, *The Fool of Quality*, 5 vols (Dublin, 1765–70), 3.242.

5.7 improving operations   schemes to enclose and cultivate common ground; see also Historical Note, 438.

5.8–9 trustee-meetings . . . justices   the reference is to public and legal responsibilities of a laird. The most important boards of trustees at the period were the turnpike trusts concerned with the construction of new roads. Meetings would be held between the Lord Lieutenant of the county (an office established in 1794) and his deputies, most often concerned with the maintenance of public order in a period of social unrest. Head-courts were normally held three times a year: all freeholders were expected to attend, and their most important function was to oversee the annual revision of the elect-oral register. The local Justices of the Peace would meet quarterly to supervise the revenue, settle wages, and ensure the maintenance of existing transport facilities.

5.17 the Sermons of Mr Peden   Alexander Peden (1626-86) was a Presby-terian minister with a reputation for prophecy, persecuted by the Crown. His sermons were published as *The Lord's Trumpet* [Glasgow, 1720]: *CLA*, 67, and (Glasgow, 1739): *CLA*, 75.

5.17–19 Life of Jack the Giant-Queller . . . worthy this legendary character was the subject of many 18th-century chap-books. He was usually known as 'Giant-Killer', but 'Queller' was also current as in the ballad opera *Jack the Giant-Queller* (1749: libretto by H. Brooke, composer anonymous). The 'Essay' is almost certainly fictitious.

5.21–22 doing something . . . undone compare the General Confession for morning and evening prayer in the *Book of Common Prayer*: 'We have left undone those things which we ought to have done; And we have done those things which we ought not to have done'.

5.24 a blue coat with a red neck from the evidence of his dress, Captain Doolittle may have been an officer in the Royal Artillery. See D. Alistair Campbell, *The Dress of the Royal Artillery* (London, 1971), 9–10.

5.27 the system of Helvetius Claude-Adrien Helvétius (1715–71), a French philosopher, taught, in his posthumously published treatise *De l'Homme, de ses facultés intellectuelles et de son éducation* (On Man, his Faculties and his Education), 2 vols (London, 1773), that education should follow natural inclinations.

5.43–6.2 the East and West Indies . . . The French Captain Clutterbuck is a veteran of the French Revolutionary and Napoleonic Wars between 1793–1802 and 1803–15, during which the French and British fought for control of the trade routes to India and the West Indies. The British army conducted campaigns in Egypt in 1801 and 1807.

6.3 hussars mounted regiments noted for their ferocity.

6.5 the three per cents. consolidated annuities: government securities consolidated in 1751 into a single stock yielding an interest of three per cent.

6.9 Kennaquhair the subject of this pun on ' kenna where' ('know not where') is finally identified as Melrose in a note in the Magnum (18.xlvii).

6.11 otium cum dignitate *Latin* honourable leisure. The phrase is used by Cicero in a letter to one of his friends describing his own withdrawal from active political life in 54 BC: *ad Fam.*, 1.9.21.

6.30 pleasant men of Teviotdale the song has not been traced. Teviotdale is the valley of the River Teviot, which flows through Hawick and joins the Tweed at Kelso.

6.39–41 circulating library . . . people circulating libraries rented out books to all-comers and attracted a more frivolous reputation than subscription libraries which had a closed membership.

7.1 a half-bound trashy novel novels were sold in boards and bound by the purchaser; *half-binding* means binding the spine and the corners in leather.

7.19 Cicerone a guide skilled at explaining antiquities, after the Roman politician and orator Cicero.

7.25 Gothic or Saxon architraves *architraves* are the mouldings round an arch (a 19th-century use of the term). 'Saxon' referred, confusingly, to the Romanesque architecture of the Norman period, characterised by weighty pillars and semi-circular arches. This gave way to a lighter, more elaborate design known as 'Gothic' which employed pointed arches and formed most of the design of Melrose Abbey. See Historical Note, 438.

8.12 Morpheus the Greek god of dreams.

8.13 Dugdale's Monasticon *Monasticon Anglicanum: An Inventory of Abbeys and Monasteries, chiefly in England and Wales*, by William Dugdale (1605–86). *The Monasticon* was first published in Latin in 3 volumes (London, 1655–73) followed by an abridgement in English (London, 1693). Two further volumes were added by John Stevens in 1722–23. Melrose Abbey is not listed.

8.13 the library at A—— a coded reference to Scott's own library at Abbotsford. Dugdale's *Monasticon* is not listed in *CLA*.

8.17   Vanderhagen's best ale   Francis Vanhagen was the proprietor of
Melrose's brewery in 1820.

8.24   mine honest … the George   in a Magnum note (18.xlvii–xlviii)
Scott identifies the inn as the George, still in Melrose, and the landlord with its
former proprietor and local character David Kyle.

8.25   Mrs Grimslees   the name has no clear significance: possible over-
tones include 'grey-sleeves', 'grim lies', and 'grey shelter' (as in such local
Melrose place-names as Abbotslee and Broomielees).

8.26–27   minced collops   a dish of chopped meat.

8.36   and odd   and a few more.

8.37–38   petticoat government   rule by a woman.

9.9   sad-coloured stand of claiths   set of dark- or sober-coloured clothes.

9.11   the auld draw-brig   see note to 62.42–43.

9.13   sticking saumon   engaging in the sport of salmon-spearing, popular
in the Borders.

9.17   the strings of my knees   the drawstrings to secure breeches at the
knee.

9.18–19   as thick as three in a bed   proverbial: John Poole, *The Hole in the
Wall* (London, 1813), 26.

9.20–21   Doctor Samuel Johnson … Scotland   Johnson's record of this
tour undertaken in 1773 was published in 1775 as *A Journey to the Western Islands
of Scotland*.

9.43   as fou as a piper   proverbial: Cheviot, 158.

10.16–17   my Lord's boats   in a Magnum note (18.lii) Scott identifies
parties for spearing salmon arranged by 'the late kind and amiable Lord Som-
merville, an intimate friend of the author'. John Southey Somerville
(1765–1819), 15th Baron Somerville, built a sporting lodge on the Tweed for
this purpose.

10.18   at e'en   in the evening.

10.28–29   gambadoes … steel clasps   *gambadoes* were heavy leather
protectors for a rider's leg, secured by clasps. Moulded to fit over riding boots,
and resembling the outer halves of boots, they were attached to the saddle and
harness. In fashion from the 17th century, they were still being improved at the
time of the novel: in the *Annual Register* for 1823 (316), one R. Green is recorded
as having obtained a patent 'for improvements in constructing gambadoes, or
mud boots, and attaching spurs thereto'. For an illustration, see Doreen
Yarwood, *The Encyclopaedia of World Costume* (London, 1978), 43.

11.1   Sherry … Lisbon   sherry was a particularly fashionable drink in the
early 19th century, but during the Peninsular War (1808–14) when the sherry-
producing region of Jerez in Spain was in French possession, and in the years
following, exports to Britain were very low. Lisbon, a white wine from the
Estremadura province of Portugal (in which Britain always had a presence
during the War), was an acceptable although less fashionable alternative.

11.6   with a witness   with a vengeance; and no mistake.

11.9   downa be confuted   see Robert Burns, 'A Dream' (1786), line 29;
'confuted' is corrected to 'disputed' in the Magnum (18.liv).

11.15–16   Mr Deputy Register of Scotland   the Clerk Register was responsible for the administration of the national archives. In a Magnum note
(18.lv) Scott identifies Thomas Thomson (1768–1852), then Deputy Clerk
Register, who was prominent in arranging, binding, and indexing the archives.

11.21–23   Pluck from … stuff   see *Macbeth*, 5.3.43–44, 46.

11.24–25   old dogs … new tricks   proverbial (Ray, 99, 142; *ODEP*, 805).

**11.27–28   to exchange their own old Mumpsimus for his new Sump-
simus**   this refers to the story of a boorish priest who misread the Latin
sumpsimus as *mumpsimus* in the prayer during ablution after communion ('quod

ore sumpsimus', meaning 'which we have consumed with our mouth'). He refused to accept correction on the grounds that he didn't wish to change his old *mumpsimus* for some new *sumpsimus*. The anecdote came to be applied to a notion obstinately adhered to however unreasonably. It is related in Richard Pace, *De fructu qui ex doctrina percipitur, liber* (Basel, 1517), 80–81: see the edition and translation by Frank Manley and Richard S. Sylvester, *The Benefit of a Liberal Education* (New York, 1967), 100–03 and note 171.

11.28 **Humana perpessi sumus** *Latin* we have steadfastly endured the human state.

11.41 **De Haga** in a Magnum note (18.lvi) Scott identifies the modern Haig family of Bemerside on the River Tweed, E of Melrose.

12.2 **march-treason** a blanket offence to cover various crimes on the English side of the border, punishable by death. In 'Border Antiquities' (106), Scott uses the term to describe large numbers of crimes 'to prevent all inter-course . . . between the natives of the two kingdoms'.

12.5–6 **from a cromlech to a cairn . . . Danes or Druids** a *cromlech* is a stone circle and a *cairn* a pile of stones used as a memorial or a burial site. Both pre-date the Celtic and Norse periods of British history, but following the discoveries of the antiquarian William Stukeley (1687–1765) such ancient monuments became popularly associated with the Druids, the magician-priests of the Celts. Scott himself supported the Norse origin of ancient monuments, commenting: 'The idea that such circles were exclusively Druidical is now justly exploded' (Lockhart, 3.199).

12.10–11 **Allan Ramsay's story . . . Wife** 'The Monk and the Miller's Wife' (1728), a comic poem by Allan Ramsay (1684–1758), which tells how a St Andrews scholar sees a priest misbehaving with the local miller's wife and arranges for him to be beaten by her husband.

12.18–19 **post-horses** horses kept for hire. They were hired by a traveller for a stage (either for riding or drawing a coach) and were changed at the inn (or 'post') at the end of the stage. They might also be used for conveying mail to and from the post-office in Melrose.

12.21–22 **Pinkerton . . . Berwick** Ramsay's poem may have been sug-gested by 'The Friars of Berwick', a satire dating from *c.* 1480 which appears in John Pinkerton, *Ancient Scotish Poems* (London and Edinburgh, 1786: *CLA*, 173), 1.65–85. This collection used as one of its sources the Maitland Folio Manuscript of 15th- and 16th-century verse collected by Richard Maitland of Lethington (1496–1586): in the edition by W. A. Craigie, 3 vols (Edinburgh and London, 1919–27), 'The Friars' appears at 1.133–48.

12.24 **James V.** King of Scots, reigned 1513–42.

12.24–26 **the Italian novelist . . . fabliau** among the analogues of 'The Friars of Berwick' is the French *fabliau* (comic tale) *Le Povre Clerk*. The Italian novelist whom Captain Clutterbuck's visitor believes to have been an intermedi-ary between such a *fabliau* and Ramsay's 'The Monk and the Miller's Wife' has not been identified.

13.1 **the order of Saint Benedict** a monastic order following the rule of St Benedict (*c.* 480–*c.* 550).

13.2–4 **a community . . . the Revolution** there was no Scottish Bene-dictine community as such in France, but there were two Scots Colleges, one founded at Paris in 1325 and the other at Tournai (in the Spanish Netherlands, now in Belgium) in 1576; the latter eventually settled at Douai and became the main centre in France for English-speaking Catholics. The French Revolution brought suppression of religious orders in France, and the taking of monastic vows was banned by the National Assembly in 1790.

13.24–25 **A European potentate . . . faith** some of the Scottish monas-teries in Germany, known as the 'Schottenklöster', continued to function until the 19th century, but there is no specific historical parallel.

13.30 our vows of poverty and abstinence members of monastic orders generally take three vows: poverty, chastity and obedience.

13.36–39 two thousand pounds ... ale see [Adam Milne], *A Description of the Parish of Melrose* (Edinburgh, 1743), 30: *CLA*, 6. A *chalder* is a dry measure of varying capacity.

14.3–4 made gude ... fasted taken from an anonymous anti-Catholic satire, 'The Paip that Pagaine full of pryde', first published in the collection *The Gude and Godlie Ballatis* (Edinburgh, 1565): in the edition by A. F. Mitchell for the Scottish Text Society (Edinburgh, 1897) the satire appears at 204–07. Scott incorporates readings from the versions printed in *Scotish Poems of the Sixteenth Century*, [ed. J. G. Dalyell], 2 vols (Edinburgh, 1801), 2.191–94 (*CLA*, 173) and Allan Ramsay, *The Ever Green*, 2 vols (Edinburgh, 1724), 2.236–39 (*CLA*, 170).

14.5–6 it is difficult ... spilling proverbial: see *ODEP*, 160–61 where this example is given.

14.12–14 The noble folio collection ... Saint Maur the Maurists were a French Benedictine congregation founded in 1618 and devoted to historical scholarship. Scott owned a 16-volume set of their collection of historical documents, *Recueil des historiens des Gaules et de la France*, 16 vols (Paris, 1738–1814: *CLA*, 35).

14.31–32 Flanders ... campaign of 1793 Flanders is the western part of Belgium. France declared war on Britain and Holland on 1 February 1793; Captain Clutterbuck must have fought in Britain's first campaign in Flanders in that year.

14.35 Sans-Culottes *French* without breeches. The term was used during the French Revolution to denote ill-equipped and poorly dressed volunteers in the Revolutionary army.

14.35 fortune de la guerre *French* [that is] the fortune of war.

15.5–6 the Old Lady of Babylon the whore of Babylon (see Revelation Ch. 17), a common way of denoting the Roman Catholic church among Scottish Protestants.

15.17–20 the reigning family ... his present Majesty the Protestant Hanoverian royal family was established by the Act of Settlement of 1701 to prevent the succession of the Catholic Stewarts. At the time Scott wrote this section George III was still on the throne, but he died on 29 January 1820, two months before the novel's publication, and was succeeded by his son, George IV.

15.26 its holy pale its religious jurisdiction.

15.32 about the size of a regimental orderly-book by the end of the 18th century such a book would typically measure about 20 cm by 12 cm.

15.36–42 There is among ... its ruins there are three aisle chapels, containing the tombs of local families, at the W end of Melrose Abbey (from a total of eight forming the S side of the building). Each is entered through a Gothic archway.

16.5–8 the arms ... Avenel the coat of arms represents the union of the two families brought about by the marriage of Halbert Glendinning and Mary Avenel which takes place between *The Monastery* and its sequel *The Abbot*. Two family coats are impaled (combined by being placed side by side on one shield, separated by a vertical line down the middle): the (historical) Glendinning arms occupy the right (dexter) side of the shield, and the (perhaps fictitious) Avenel arms the left (sinister). Scott's description of the Glendinning arms is incomplete. Properly it is 'quarterly argent and sable a cross parted per cross indented, and countercharged of the same' (i.e. a cross with the normal straight outline, enclosing a cross with serrated edges, the silver and black colours of the cross

and background reversed in neighbouring quarters). The Avenel arms consist
here of three rowels (the small spiked revolving wheel on the end of a spur), but
contrast 217.10–12. The 'ancient family' of Avenel was prominent in the 12th
and 13th centuries. The Englishman Robert Avenel, settled by David I in
Eskdale, became a benefactor of Melrose Abbey and eventually a novice monk,
dying in 1185. The male line became extinct with Roger Avenel in 1243,
but the name was carried on by younger sons of earlier generations (see George
Chalmers, *Caledonia*, 3 vols (London, 1807–24), 1.513–15: *CLA*, 1). Actually,
'the grave on which the stone is set contains the heart of an abbot, who, having no
wife, would impale no coat at all' (E. A. Greening Lamborn, 'Sir Walter Scott's
Heraldry', *Notes and Queries*, 190 (18 May 1946), 209).

16.9 arms party per pale coat of arms divided by a central vertical line.
16.27 Potowmack or Susquehana rivers in America on which early English colonies were established.
16.40–41 I resisted ... fled from me see James 4.7.
17.1–2 the Court of Exchequer court of law dealing with matters concerning public finance. In this case it would decide on whether what was found
belonged to the crown: according to Lord Stair, 'treasures hid in the earth,
whose proper owners cannot be known, are not his in whose ground they are
found, nor the finder's, but belong to the King' (*Institutes of the Law of Scotland*,
ed. David M. Walker (Edinburgh and Glasgow, 1981), 2.1.5).
17.7–8 the three Kings of Cologne the alleged bones of the three Magi
or Wise Men which were deposited in Cologne Cathedral in the 12th century.
18.9 de'il hae me the devil take me. A common phrase in several languages.
18.19 dark lantern lantern with a slide or arrangement for concealing the
light.
18.21–22 which they doubtless trusted ... doomsday see Lewis Theo-
bald, *The Fatal Secret* (London, 1735), 5.1.233–34. Quoted in John Bower,
Description of the Abbeys of Melrose and Old Melrose, with their Traditions (Kelso,
1813), 63: *CLA*, 6.
18.33–36 an ancient Border-knight ... magic power Scott's Magnum
note (18.1xxiii) identifies the allusion to *LLM*, in which the border knight Sir
William Deloraine recovers a magic book from the tomb in Melrose Abbey of
the wizard Michael Scott, a legendary figure deriving from the mathematician,
physician, and translator of Aristotle of that name (*c.* 1175–*c.* 1234). A skeleton
found in a stone coffin in the Abbey in 1812 was said to be that of Michael Scott
(see Bower, *Description*, 62).
18.37 de trop in the groupe the contemporary fashion for picturesque art
ruled upon the grouping of subjects. Scott indicates that three subjects would be
too many, though in fact odd numbers were recommended as more picturesque
than even groups.
18.43 picked free probably 'picked clean'.
19.7 hail ... quarters it's all mine; no half or quarter shares. The term
halvers was a children's exclamation to claim a half share, and though the whole
phrase sounds proverbial the only similar instance known is in *The Antiquary*,
EEWN 3, 193.9–10, cited in Cheviot, 259.
19.19 Mattocks the sexton is named after a *mattock*, a tool used for breaking
up hard ground. .
19.32 My certes, no no indeed!
19.35 west-country whig frae Kilmarnock the term *Whig* was originally
a nickname for the supporters of the National Covenant of 1638 but came to be
applied in England to those who *c.* 1679 opposed the succession of James to the
throne because he was a Roman Catholic. At the Revolution of 1688, when
James was deposed, the word was used of those who favoured the Protestant

succession, and thus it became the name of the dominant political party of the 18th century. As used here 'whig' here carries its reference to the Covenanters (see note to 26.3–5), who were particularly strong in SW Scotland and were persecuted in the reigns of Charles II (1660–85) and James VII and II (1685–88) for their support of the National Covenant and Presbyterianism. But by the middle of the 18th century their religious views were considered to be outmoded, and their ostentatiously strict piety hypocritical; the joke here is that the horse-couper (horse-dealer), who had a proverbial reputation for dishonesty, is outdone only by a Covenanter. Kilmarnock is 33 km SW of Glasgow.

20.1   **mair by token**   the more so [because].

20.8   **up the water**   W up the Tweed valley.

20.18–19   **Saint Francis ... graves**   *Romeo and Juliet*, 5.3.121–21.

22.24–25   **Monastery of Saint Mary**   founded in 1136, the Abbey was dedicated to the Virgin Mary ten years later. See Historical Note, 438–39.

22.31–32   **as the man says ... read to you**   the allusion has not been traced.

22.35   **corrector ... of the press**   proof-reader in a printing house.

22.38   **Since the trees ... king**   see Walter Pope, *Moral and Political Fables* (London, 1698), 71–72: Fable 76, 'The Trees and the Thorn'.

22.41   **the great annual fair**   Melrose had an ancient spring fair known as the Kier-Thursday, or Scarce-Thursday (Maundy Thursday) Fair.

23.1   **Jedidiah Cleishbotham**   the fictional school-master who 'sells' to the publishers a number of Scott's novels in the various series of *Tales of My Landlord*. Jedidiah ('beloved of the Lord') is the name given to Solomon in 2 Samuel 12.25. Cleishbotham means 'flog bottom'.

23.16–17   **prize-money ... drum head**   prize-money was awarded by the navy for the taking of enemy ships, the money being sometimes apportioned to the crew on the deck of a ship in port. The drum head is the circular, revolving section of the capstan, the device used for winching the anchor-chain, on which the money would be placed.

23.28   **John Ballantyne**   (1774–1821) close friend of Scott, Scott's publisher 1809–13, and a younger brother of James, Scott's printer. John acted as literary agent in the publication of *The Monastery*: see Textual Essay, 355–64.

24.15   **terra incognita**   *Latin* unknown region.

24.22   **private book-cases**   often a euphemism for collections of pornography.

24.26   **turkey slippers**   carpet slippers made from heavy woven Turkish fabric.

24.32   **Watt of Birmingham**   James Watt (1736–1819), the Scottish engineer who patented the steam engine in 1769. In 1774 he moved from Greenock to Birmingham, where in the following year he entered into partnership with Matthew Boulton at the Soho Works.

25.2   **whether in body or in spirit**   compare 2 Corinthians 12.2.

25.3   **Northern Lights**   James Watt made a number of visits to his native Scotland in his later years. Henry Brougham describes Watt's being in Edinburgh early in 1805 when 'he was a constant attendant at our Friday club, and in all our private circles, and was the life of them all' (Henry Brougham, *Lives of Men of Letters and Science who flourished in the time of George III*, 2 vols (London, 1845–46), 1.383). In his obituary of Watt, Francis Jeffrey makes reference to another visit in 1817 when Watt received hospitality from many Edinburgh notables. Celebrating Watt's manifold talents and equable temperament, Jeffrey comments: 'His friends in this part of the country never saw him more full of intellectual vigour and colloquial animation,—never more delightful or more instructive,—than in his last visit to Scotland in autumn 1817' (reprinted in James Patrick Muirhead, *The Life of James Watt* (London, 1858), 529). The only recorded meeting of Watt and Scott (in the company of other well-known Edinburgh figures) was in December 1814: Watt mentions this in a letter to his son (James Patrick Muirhead, *The Origin and Progress of the Mechanical Inventions of James Watt*, 3 vols (London, 1854), 2.360). The term 'Northern Lights' is here used as a general one for Scottish intellectuals, although Scott had also used it to refer to the Edinburgh literati, punning on the Commissioners for the Northern Lights (i.e. lighthouses) whose inspection tour he joined in 1814: 'I dont mean the Edinburgh Reviewers but the bonâ fide commissioners for the Beacons' (*Letters*, 3.477: 28 July 1814, to J. B. S. Morritt).

25.15 Afrite in Islamic mythology, a huge winged creature made of smoke which makes frequent appearances in popular retellings of Eastern tales. The afrite is discussed in *Tales of the East* (1.xlii n), whose editor Henry William Weber had worked as a research assistant for Scott.

25.16 the rod of the prophet ... desert during the exile of the Israelites, Moses struck a rock from which water sprang (Numbers 20.11).

25.17–18 that time and tide ... man proverbial: Ray, 162; *ODEP*, 822.

25.18–19 that wind ... Xerxes himself Xerxes I, King of Persia 486–465 BC, built a bridge across the Hellespont to invade Greece. It was said that when a storm blew up and destroyed the bridge he gave orders for the sea to be whipped.

25.21 cloudy machinery an image derived from scenic props used in the theatre.

25.36 Cadmus reputed to have introduced a written alphabet to Greece.

25.40–42 the national adage ... wind said no not identified.

26.3–5 Claverse ... covenanters John Balfour of Kinloch (d. 1688) was a leader of the Covenanters (supporters, in the reigns of Charles II (1660–85) and James VII and II (1685–88), of the National Covenant of 1638, a manifesto for the establishment of Presbyterianism as the principal religion in Scotland). He appears as Burley in *The Tale of Old Mortality* (1816), which also features the best-known among the Covenanters' persecutors, John Grahame of Claverhouse (c. 1649–89; created Viscount Dundee in 1688), popularly known as Claverse.

26.18–24 Ne sit ... fiction too the 'paraphrase' is a free composition, probably by Scott himself, taking as its point of departure the opening of Horace's Ode 2.4, whose Latin may be translated: 'No need to blush, Phocian Xanthias, because you love a slave girl. Achilles was aroused by his fair-skinned Briseis.' There was scholarly debate as to whether Xanthias was a real person or a fiction himself. Scott is probably also recalling his reference to phantom authors at the conclusion of *A Legend of the Wars of Montrose* (EEWN 7b, 183.3–4 and explanatory note on 259–60).

26.32–33 an old Highland gentleman called Ossian the supposed 3rd-century Gaelic poet whose works were 'translated' by James Macpherson (1736–96) and published 1760–63. The authenticity of the Ossian texts was challenged and Macpherson was asked to produce a manuscript. An enquiry in 1805 concluded that, while the Ossian poems were genuine stories in circulation in the Highlands, there was no single source for any of Macpherson's works.

26.33 a monk of Bristol named Rowley a fictitious 15th-century Bristol monk and poet, invented by Thomas Chatterton (1752–70). Chatterton forged manuscripts for Rowley's work, but the fraud was exposed.

26.44 The Persian Letters a satirical portrait of French society seen through the eyes of two Persian travellers, by Charles-Louis Montesquieu (1689–1755), published in French in 1721 (at Amsterdam, and in an enlarged version at Cologne) and first translated into English by John Ozell in 1722.

26.44 The Citizen of the World a collection of letters to and from a fictitious Chinese philosopher living in London, published by Oliver Goldsmith in 1762.

27.2 Purchas...Hackluyt Richard Hakluyt (*c.* 1552–1616) compiled, edited, and published contemporaneous accounts of English sea-voyages and exploration. His work was continued by Samuel Purchas (*c.* 1575–1626).

27.4 Sindbad the adventurous sailor featuring in the *Arabian Nights' Entertainments*, a collection of Arabic stories popularised in French and English translations in the 18th century, and included in *Tales of the East*, 1.68–87.

27.4 Aboulfouaris an adventurous traveller, analogous to Sindbad, who features in 'The Adventures of Aboulfouaris, surnamed the Great Voyager': *Tales of the East*, 2.469–96.

27.4 Robinson Crusoe a shipwrecked sailor, the titular hero of Daniel Defoe's novel of 1719, who also appeared in numerous imitations throughout the 18th century.

27.5–6 Captain Greenland...Baffin's Bay the years immediately prior to the publication of *The Monastery* saw an upsurge in interest in finding the north-west passage, a northerly connection between the Atlantic and Pacific oceans. Baffin Bay off the N coast of Canada was named after the 17th-century arctic explorer William Baffin (d. 1622). The fictional explorers are the heroes of *The Adventures of Capt. Greenland*, probably by William Goodall, 3 vols (London, 1752) and R[obert] P[altock]'s imaginary sea voyage *The Life and Adventures of Peter Wilkins a Cornish Man*, 2 vols (London, 1751).

27.11 MacDuff's peculiarity in *Macbeth*, 5.8.12–16, Macduff is said to be not born of woman because he was delivered by Caesarean section.

27.13–14 Maria Edgeworth...England the Irish novelist Maria Edgeworth (1767–1849) was known as 'the mother of the novel'.

27.17 Cid Hamet Benengeli see note to 28.41–29.6.

27.17–18 the short-faced president...club the Spectator Club was a group of imaginary characters whose meetings were reported in the weekly essays of *The Spectator*, a periodical founded by Richard Steele in 1711. In No. 17 (20 March 1711) Steele complains about his face: 'I am a little unhappy in the Mold of my Face, which is not quite so long as it is broad.' He adds: 'I have been often put out of Countenance by the shortness of my Face, and was formerly at great Pains in concealing it by wearing a Periwigg with an high Foretop, and letting my Beard grow.'

27.18 poor Ben Silton a friend of the fictional editor in [Henry Mackenzie], *The Man of Feeling* (London, 1771) who also appears as a character in the novel.

27.37–39 the most interesting...snuff unbound sheets of printed books would be used for such purposes as this. Entire volumes could be so disposed of when a work had not sold well, but in the case of Scott's works the waste would consist of a small number of sheets which were for a variety of reasons surplus to requirements.

27.42 Les Voyages Imaginaires a French collection of imaginary voyages in 36 volumes, edited by Charles Garnier, published at Amsterdam and Paris in 1787–89 (*CLA*, 45–46). It included translations of a number of English texts including *Robinson Crusoe* and *Peter Wilkins*.

27.42 History of Automathes John Kirkby, *The Capacity and Extent of the Human Understanding Exemplified in the Extraordinary Case of Automathes* (London, 1745). This is the story of a shipwrecked young nobleman who educates himself: it is substantially based on the anonymous *The History of Autonous* (London, 1736). Kirkby's version, together with *Peter Wilkins* (see note to 27.5–6), featured in a collection of *Popular Romances* published by John Ballantyne and Co. in 1812 with an introduction by Henry William Weber (see note to 25.15).

27.43 Adventures of a Guinea the subtitle of [Charles Johnson], *Chrysal*, 2 vols (London, 1760), a satire narrated by the guinea of the title as it passes through various stages of society.

27.43 Adventures of an Atom [Tobias Smollett], *The History and Adventures of an Atom* (London, 1749 [for 1769]), a satire narrated by the Atom of the title.

28.3–4 cabalistic manuscripts...Agrippa the term *Cabbala* originally referred to Jewish oral traditions not contained in the Hebrew Bible, but came to be applied to the study of magic. Heinrich Cornelius Agrippa, or Agrippa von Nettesheim (1486–1535), was the author of *De occulta philosophia* (Antwerp, 1531), which explains the world in terms of cabalistic analyses of Hebrew letters.

28.4–5 the door open...come in see Robert Southey, 'Cornelius Agrippa: A Ballad, of a Young Man that would Read Unlawful Books, and How he was Punished' (1799), line 28. The ballad ends with a 'moral': 'Henceforth let all young men take heed/ How in a Conjuror's books they read.'

28.7–8 From my research...I read compare Erasmus Darwin, *The Botanic Garden*, 2 parts (London, 1789–91), 1.395–96: 'Bright o'er the floor the scatter'd fragments blaz'd,/ And Gods retreating trembled as they gaz'd.'

28.9–10 the Magician in the Persian Tales in 'The History of Avicene' (included in *The Persian Letters* (see note to 26.44) and *Tales of the East*, 2.452–57) the protagonist spends twelve months trapped in a cavern where he gains arcane powers from reading magic books. On his release he is mistaken for a wicked sorcerer and escapes execution in a flying chariot.

28.18–19 O, Athenians...praise! the allusion has not been traced.

28.41–29.6 Cid Hamet Benengeli...chastised Cid Hamet Ben Engeli is the Arab writer to whom Miguel de Cervantes Saavedra attributes the story of *Don Quixote de la Mancha*; the book's anonymous narrator finds Cid Hamet's manuscript in the market place in Toledo and has it translated by a Spanish-speaking Moor (Part 1, Ch. 9). The first part of *Don Quixote* was published in 1605. In 1614 Alonso Fernández de Avellaneda (probably a pseudonym) published a second part, passing it off as the 'genuine' continuation of the book. This in turn led Cervantes to write a Part 2 of his own, published in 1615, in which he dismisses the fake Part 2 of Avellaneda.

28.42 to play the Turk to act in a cruel or tyrannical manner.

29.6–7 Knights of the Straw knights without substance. See Samuel Butler, *Hudibras*, Part 1 (1663), 2.1056. Scott's form of the phrase is probably influenced by 'Don Quixote de la Mancha'.

29.7–9 a sly old Scotsman...bite you Scott later related this anecdote, making clear it refers to the notoriously malleable James VI and I, but not identifying the 'sly old Scotsman', in the second series of *Tales of a Grandfather* (originally published in 1828 (dated 1829); reprinted in *Prose Works*, 23.243–44).

29.10 amende honorable *French* public apology or reparation.

29.17–22 Jedidiah Cleishbotham...identity the Author refers to advertisements for a spurious novel in his own series *Tales of my Landlord* which appeared in the *Morning Chronicle* in 1819. See note to 23.1, and Textual Essay, 360–61.

29.19 take little by gain little from.

29.21 gentlemen of the long robe i.e. advocates.

29.23–24 sleeping partner...copartnery *copartner* is the Scottish legal term for a partnership and a *sleeping partner* takes no part in its management. The *firm* is the name of the copartnery.

29.26–29 a crime...felony a legal joke: counterfeiting a signature, in Scotland called 'forgery', was a capital crime (a *felony*), whereas literary forgery is merely a civil wrong giving rise to an action of damages only if the copyright in the literary property is infringed. Thus it is a crime to counterfeit a signature (an autograph in one sense) but not to copy someone else's literary property.

29.38　Gandercleugh　the fictional village in which Jedidiah Cleishbotham is schoolmaster. In Scots, *cleugh* is a gorge or ravine; hence, most obviously, 'goose-hollow'.

29.39–40　a Cameronian clergyman　a minister of the strict Reformed Presbyterian Church, which followed the doctrines of Richard Cameron (d. 1680), a noted Covenanter.

29.40　in extremis　*Latin* at the point of death.

29.41–42　to bring down ... the bonnets of Bonny Dundee　the *Mountain-folks* were the Covenanters who, excluded from their churches, worshipped in the hills. The phrase 'the bonnets of Bonny Dundee' comes from the traditional song 'Jockey's Escape from Dundee' (included in Thomas d'Urfey's *Wit and Mirth; or, Pills to Purge Melancholy*, 6 vols (London, 1719–20), 5.17–19), but Scott had already written an alternative version which appears in *Rob Roy* (1817), 2.218.21–24. Bonny Dundee is John Grahame of Claverhouse: see note to 26.3–5.

30.11–12　We have ... torch　see John Bunyan, *The Holy War* (1682), 'To the Reader', lines 159–60.

30.18–20　Mr John Ballantyne ... publisher　for John Ballantyne's part in the quarrels surrounding the publication of *The Monastery* see Essay on the Text, 360–61. Trinity Grove was John's Edinburgh home near the Firth of Forth.

30.21　irritable genus　*Latin* 'irritabile genus' (irritable tribe [of poets]): see Horace, *Epistles*, 2.2.102.

31.4–14　motto　not identified: probably by Scott.

31.9–10　yonder Harlot ... cup of gold　the whore of Babylon, depicted in Revelation 17.4 as 'having a golden cup in her hand full of abominations and filthiness of her fornication'. She was commonly identified by Reformation Protestants with the Catholic Church, here represented by Rome and its seven hills.

31.11–13　kind Sir Roger ... thunder　in *The Spectator* for 14 July 1711 Joseph Addison tells how the fictitious eccentric country Justice of the Peace Sir Roger de Coverley is puzzled by allegations of witchcraft against Moll White: these include activities involving a broomstaff and a cat.

31.17–19　The learned Chalmers ... stream　in his *Caledonia*, 3 vols (London, 1807–24), a topographical and philological survey of Scotland, George Chalmers notes (1.21, 2.899) that the name of the river Quair, from which Traquhair near Peebles derives, comes from the Gaelic term *car* or *char* meaning 'crooked' or 'bending', and (2.946) that this refers to 'the winding course of the stream': *CLA*, 1. (Modern scholars derive the name rather from a Celtic root meaning 'the clear one' or 'the green one'.) No place called Caquhair has been traced: it may be that Scott is thinking of Cathair, which as Chalmers notes (1.28) means 'fortress'.

31.22–28　founded by the first David ... Crown　David I (reigned 1124–53) founded and endowed many Scottish monasteries, including the neighbouring Border abbeys of Melrose, Jedburgh, and Kelso. His successor James I is reported to have made this remark by Hector Boece, *The History and Chronicles of Scotland*, trans. John Bellenden, [ed. Thomas Maitland], 2 vols (Edinburgh, 1821), 2.300: *CLA*, 4. It was popularised by its inclusion in David Lindsay, *Ane Satire of the Thrie Estaitis* (*c.* 1552), lines 2976–77.

31.32–32.2　His possessions in Northumberland ... Standard　a Scottish army led by David I was defeated by the English near Northallerton in North Yorkshire on 22 August 1138.

32.2　Teviotdale　see note to 6.30.

32.9   a ... Goshen   an oasis, after the fertile land allotted to the Israelites in Egypt: e.g. Genesis 45.10.

32.13–14   the union of the crowns   the monarchies of England and Scotland were combined in 1603 when James VI, King of Scots, succeeded Queen Elizabeth of England as James I, although the two countries maintained separate parliaments until 1707.

32.39   quit-rent   a small rent paid by a free-holder in lieu of services which might be required of them.

33.9   skiey influences   *Measure for Measure*, 3.1.9.

33.22   Snatchers   thieves, particularly associated by Scott with Border cattle-raiders: see *LLM*, 4.4.

33.26–27   the Zetland Archipelago   the Shetland islands. Scott visited Orkney and Shetland in 1814: see Lockhart, 3.161.

34.11   salmon ... Lent   the consumption of meat was prohibited by the Church during Lent (the penitential season preceding Easter), but fish could be eaten.

34.16   a buck of season   a male deer in the hunting season when game is at its fattest. Compare *The Merry Wives of Windsor*, 3.3.139–40.

34.20   moss-troopers   an anachronistic term from the 17th century to describe the lawless Borderers; it derives from their gathering together in troops and crossing the mosses or boggy country.

34.20–21   a start and owerloup   said of a flock of sheep which when startled leap over the nearest fence; hence an encroachment on a neighbour's property.

34.25–26   the "gude king's deer"   a common ballad phrase: killing deer was the legal preserve of the king and the nobility.

35.7   deadly feuds   a feature of Border history defined by Scott in his essay on 'Border Antiquities' (55) as 'private warfare, which was usually carried on with the most ferocious animosity on both sides'. See also *Minstrelsy*, 1.121–22.

35.9–10   the fatal wars ... Mary's reign   the infant Mary came to the throne in 1542. English incursions into Scotland inflicted much damage in the Borders, particularly in the years 1544 and 1545. See Historical Note, 435.

35.11–12   the English, now a Protestant people   Henry VIII, King of England 1509–47, had an uneasy relationship with the papacy and presided over the dissolution of the monasteries, but it was only on the accession of his son Edward VI (reigned 1547–53) that Protestantism became official ecclesiastical policy in England.

35.14   the peace of 1550   the English garrisons were withdrawn from Scotland in 1549 and a peace treaty between Scotland and England was finally signed on 10 June 1551.

35.28–34   motto   manuscript revisions suggest that this motto is of Scott's own composition.

35.30   fell Alecto   Alecto was one of the Furies (for whom see note to 202.21–22). See *2 Henry IV*, 5.5.37.

36.18   summer shealing   a hut on the pasture to which livestock would be moved during the summer.

37.4–13   sublime or beautiful ... Glendearg   *sublime* and *beautiful* were terms used in the aesthetic appreciation and representation of landscape, dating from the late 17th century. Sublime landscapes were wild, vast, and awe-inspiring, beautiful ones softer and soothing. The picturesque, a later addition which was often satirised, could be applied to most landscapes but especially those which were varied or irregular: 'the picturesque, whose characteristics are intricacy and variety, is equally adapted to the grandest, and to the gayest scenery' (Uvedale Price, *An Essay on the Picturesque, As Compared with the Sublime and the Beautiful*, new enlarged edn, 2 vols (London, 1796;

Hereford, 1798), 1.100: compare *CLA*, 10). These terms were applied to landscape from the 17th century, but became popular with the growth of tourism in the 18th. By the time Scott was writing, the proliferation of guidebooks and Tours, as well as the opening up of Scotland as a site for tourists, had made landscape-appreciation commonplace. In *Saint Ronan's Well* (1824), the village of Saint Ronan's is described thus: 'The situation had something in it so romantic, that it provoked the pencil of every passing tourist' (EEWN 16, 1.26–27).

37.19–20 Another glen . . . circumstances no references have been found to such a glen.

37.26 Brown Man of the Moors a supernatural being similar in several respects to the Brownie (commonly associated with the Borders), but more malevolent in character.

37.34 Corri-nan-shian a corruption of the Gaelic 'Coire nan Sìthean' meaning 'Hollow of the Fairy Knolls'.

38.22–25 family of Glendonwyne . . . Otterbourne at the Battle of Otterburn in Northumberland (1388) James, 2nd Earl of Douglas (born *c.* 1358, succeeded in 1384) defeated Henry Percy ('Hotspur', 1364–1403), son of the Earl of Northumberland, but he died before victory was assured. The events are recorded in a ballad included in *Minstrelsy*, 1.276–301. Glendonwyne was the name of an ancient family in the Western Borders (see Robert Douglas, *The Baronage of Scotland* (Edinburgh, 1798), 233). In a letter of 1818 Scott writes of 'the fine old family of Glendonwyne which is so ancient as to have figured at Otterburne' (*Letters*, 5.223: to the Duke of Buccleuch).

38.36–37 the Battle of Pinkie the catastrophic defeat of the Scots by the English in 1547. See Historical Note, 435.

38.39–40 the union . . . Henry VIII the reference is to the so-called 'rough wooing': English attempts to secure the marriage between Mary and Edward, son of Henry VIII, backed up by military incursion into Scotland. See Historical Note, 435.

38.40–39.2 The Monks . . . obliviscaris this episode is recorded in William Patten, *The Expedicion into Scotlãde, of the most Woorthely Fortunate Prince, Edward, Duke of Soomerset* (London, 1548), k.viii. Patten's *Expedicion* was reprinted in William Dalyell, *Fragments of Scotish History* (Edinburgh, 1798), where the episode occurs at p. 73: *CLA*, 4.

39.22 The Protector, Somerset Edward Seymour (*c.* 1506–52), created Duke of Somerset in 1547, led the English army at the Battle of Pinkie. He was Protector of England (1547–49) during part of the minority of Edward VI.

39.23 the ancient Castle of Roxburgh after the Battle of Pinkie in 1547, the English, under the Duke of Somerset, established a garrison in Roxburgh Castle which they repaired for the purpose.

39.24 take assurance receive a guarantee, under terms of peace, that they would not be attacked.

39.31 beyond Forth N across the Firth of Forth into Fife.

39.35 Stawarth Bolton Bolton is a town in Lancashire.

40.21 sarsenet chidings sarsenet was a soft, silky fabric; *hence* a very mild telling-off.

40.24 red cross the red cross of St George, patron saint of England.

41.29 go down decline.

41.30 white-head having fair hair, but possibly also 'white-headed' meaning favoured child (*ODEP*, 884–85).

41.30–31 ride a cock-horse nursery term for a child playing at riding.

42.15–16 those who have . . . cares compare the proverb 'Children are certain cares, but uncertain comforts': Ray, 4; *ODEP*, 120.

42.18 'drive a prey' from make a cattle-raid upon.

42.35–39　**motto**　see 'Auld Maitland', lines 32–35, in *Minstrelsy*, 1.232–75. The ballad first appeared in this collection.

43.8　**Eskdale**　a district in E Dumfriesshire.

43.21–22　**war of detail**　war fought by the engagement of small sections of an army one after the other.

44.7　**not a cloot left of the hail hirsel**　not a hoof left of the whole herd.

44.8　**Grizzy and Crombie**　traditional Scottish names for cows.

44.19　**make a fend**　look after ourselves.

44.28　**cast up**　turn up.

44.32　**even . . . to seeking**　demean . . . by suggesting she should seek.

44.34　**wish her to it**　wish it on her.

44.40–41　**the worst bush better than no beild**　referring to the proverb 'a bad bush is better than the open field': Ray, 75; *ODEP*, 25.

45.2　**white seam**　plain needlework.

45.8　**a thought of time**　a short moment.

45.12–13　**busk up**　get ready.

45.14　**Whisht wi'**　be quiet about; silence.

45.17　**Come awa**　let's go.

45.18　**Scots mile**　a Scottish mile was 1.8 km, or nearly one-eighth longer than the English mile.

45.18　**moss and ling**　bog and moor: a common pairing as 'moss and moor' (e.g. *The Black Dwarf*, EEWN 4a, 76.16–17). The phrase 'moss and ling' is found in Margaret Cavendish, Duchess of Newcastle, *The Presence: A Comedy* (London, 1668), 96 (supplementary scene).

45.24　**Shagram**　perhaps from the Irish 'shaughraun': a vagabond.

45.29　**lang-bow**　the English army destroyed the Scots at the Battle of Pinkie by the use of the longbow, for the Scottish army 'consisted almost intirely of infantry, whose chief weapon was a long spear, and for that reason their files were very deep, and their ranks close' (William Robertson, *The History of Scotland. During the reigns of Queen Mary and of King James VI. Till His Accession to the Crown of England*, 3rd edn, 2 vols (London, 1760), 1.102: *CLA*, 4).

45.37　**win to**　reach.

45.37　**the girth-gate**　the 'sanctuary road', followed by pilgrims between Melrose Abbey and Soutra, 27 km SE of Edinburgh, by way of Allen Water, traditionally Scott's Glendearg. The road was protected by the laws of ecclesiastical sanctuary.

45.39　**good neighbours**　the use of euphemisms for the fairies was a common folk superstition.

45.42　**the last day of October**　Mary's birthday on Halloween gives her the power to see spirits: 'It was believed, that children born on All Saints Eve were in after life patronised by the good neighbours, and endowed with the peculiar faculty of "seeing sichts"' (Chambers, 265n).

46.21　**win across**　get safely over.

46.22　**on the tap of**　right above.

47.7　**yon gate**　that way.

47.13　**for it**　*probably* 'for all I care', *but perhaps* 'in that direction'.

47.28　**Tell your beads**　count your prayers on the beads of your rosary.

48.2–3　**the last pledge of Avenel**　the term can be applied to a child as a hostage given to fortune, but in the Borders a *pledge* was literally a hostage used as security for loans or unpaid fines.

48.6　**bought and sold**　done business.

48.20–24　**motto**　see William Collins, 'Ode to Fear' (1747 [for 1746]), lines 58–59, 62–63.

48.27　**a reign of minority**　Mary came to the throne as an infant, and her minority reign lasted from 1542 to 1561, giving rise to a power struggle for the regency. See Historical Note, 435.

48.35　a male fief　an estate that can only be inherited by male heirs.

48.36–38　The ancient philosopher … legions　the meeting of a philosopher and a ruler, in which the philosopher always comes off the better, is a standard topos in ancient literature. The best-known version of the story (referred to 22 times by ancient authors) concerns a supposed meeting in the 4th century BC between Diogenes of Sinope and Alexander the Great. When the latter was marching with his army through Greece, he encountered Diogenes and asked the famous philosopher if there was anything he could do for him, whereupon Diogenes simply replied that he would be grateful if he would stand to one side and not keep the sun off him.

49.37　high holiday　solemn religious festival.

49.43–50.1　the Queen Regent (Mary of Guise)　Mary of Guise (1515–60), the mother of Mary I, Queen of Scots, Regent from 1554 to her death. See Historical Note, 435.

50.26　pulling the thread from her distaff　Elspet is spinning with a spindle and distaff. The *spindle* was a hooked rod which was made to revolve and to draw the fibres into thread; the *distaff* was a cleft stick about a metre long on which the flax was wound.

50.29　the modern crane　in the 19th century a crane was an upright revolving axle with a horizontal arm for suspending a pot over a fire.

51.9–10　the knowledge … personal danger　an act of 1543 had made it lawful to read the Bible in English. The idea that Catholic bishops had ruled reading of the vernacular Bible to be a capital crime was in fact a rumour circulated by Protestants. See also Historical Note, 436.

51.14　behoved needs to　had to; must.

51.40　misleard loons　badly brought-up rascals: here a term of affectionate rebuke.

51.41　yon gate　in that manner.

52.3　May ne'er be in my fingers　may I have no power in my fingers.

52.34–35　a beautiful hawk … its head　in his introduction to Berners (21) Haslewood writes of 'Hawks, heretofore the pride of royalty, the insignia of nobility'.

53.11–12　Be good to and preserve us　'God' is understood.

53.16　tods keep their ain holes clean　proverbial: James Kelly, *A Complete Collection of Scotish Proverbs Explained and made Intelligible to the English Reader* (London, 1721), 320: *CLA*, 169.

53.19　out o' gate　out of the way; not present.

53.24　wi' bell and book　excommunication by bell, book, and candle was marked by the ringing of a bell, the closing of a book, and the snuffing out of a candle. The phrase is proverbial: see Ray, 184 and *ODEP*, 44.

53.27　Saint Andrew's cross　St Andrew is the patron saint of Scotland. His cross is the X-shaped saltire.

53.30–31　the wedding of the Prince and our Queen　see note to 38.39–40.

54.6　have no skill of　know nothing about.

54.14　time about　in turn; one after another.

54.31　cellarer　the cellarer 'had the care of every thing relating to the food of the Monks, and vessels of the cellar, kitchen, and refectory' (Fosbrooke, 177).

54.35–36　to winnow my three weights o' naething　a Halloween tradition for divining one's future lover: the act of winnowing corn to separate it from the chaff is mimed three times, after which the apparition appears. Compare Robert Burns, 'To *winn three wechts o' naething*', 'Halloween' (1786), line 182 and note. A *weight* or *wecht* is a winnowing-sieve.

55.1–2 Cupid's shaft Cupid, the Roman god of love, is depicted shooting arrows into people to cause them to fall in love.

55.5 the grey-goose wing according to Joseph Strutt, *The Sports and Pastimes of the People of England* (London, 1801), 47, the wing-feathers of the grey goose are 'preferable to any others for the pluming of an arrow': *CLA*, 154. The phrase also occurs in ballads: see *Ivanhoe*, EEWN 8, 547.

55.13–14 Robin Hood . . . Lindsay's ballats ballads featuring the legendary outlaw Robin Hood were circulated in print from the 16th century. Sir David Lindsay (1490–1555) wrote anti-clerical verses which quickly entered into popular circulation.

55.16 ghaists and gyre carlines ghosts and witches. Compare Alexander Montgomerie (1545?–98), 'The Flyting between Mongomerie and Polwart', line 681: 'Leve boigillis, brouneis, gyr carlingis, & ghaistis', quoted (with different spelling) in *Minstrelsy*, 1.153.

55.25 of a constancy incessantly.

55.29 All-Hallow day All Saints Day, 1 November.

55.42 wadna be to seek in would not need to ask about.

56.5–6 ordinary saunts . . . Saunt Anthony, Saunt Cuthbert there are two possible St Anthonys: St Anthony of Padua (1195–1231) was a popular saint because of his reputation for miracles; a less likely alternative is the hermit St Anthony of Egypt (*c.* 251–326), celebrated as an early founder of monasticism. St Cuthbert (d. 687) was a local saint, probably born in the neighbourhood of Melrose where he was a monk for part of his life. His legend is recounted in *Marmion* (1808), 2.14–18.

56.8 the White Maiden of Avenel see Historical Note, 437.

56.11 haly be his cast may his lot be in Heaven.

56.13–14 make nae better fend for them provide for them no better.

56.16–17 to the boot of that into the bargain.

56.17 mind o' recall.

56.21 Our Lady and Saint Paul Melrose Abbey was dedicated to the Virgin Mary, and the N transept contained chapels dedicated to St Peter and St Paul respectively.

56.23 Candlemas 2 February, one of the four Scottish quarter days.

56.27 hap up . . . ower low make up the fire with a little piece of turf laid on the embers to keep it burning for a long time, before it gets too low.

57.2–9 motto by Scott; but compare John Milton, 'Lycidas' (1638), lines 113–29 and 'L'Allegro' (composed *c.* 1631, published 1645), lines 85–86.

57.29 the last consolations the last rites administered to the dying.

57.30 the Sacristan the officer in charge of keeping sacred vessels and other preparations for monastic services. 'He distributed the candles for the offices; took care of all burials; washed the chalices twice a week, or oftener, as necessary; and the corporals [cloths for wrapping the host] before Easter, or when expedient' (Fosbrooke, 186).

58.8–9 It is our duty . . . the widow see especially James 1.27: 'Pure religion . . . is this, to visit the fatherless and widows in their affliction.'

58.18–19 Benedictines . . . beggarly friars the Benedictine monks are distinguished from the orders of mendicant friars (Franciscans, Dominicans, Carmelites, Augustinians), who would make lengthy excursions from their friaries for apostolic work, especially preaching.

58.19–20 we may not desert . . . grievous unto us the phrase calls upon the frequent biblical image of God's servants as workers in a vineyard.

59.14–15 what avails . . . heresy? see Matthew 23.25–26.

59.23–24 a canker-worm in the rose-garland of the Spouse the image of the Church as the bride of Christ is a common one; the picture as a whole here recalls the poem 'The Coronet' by Andrew Marvell (1621–78).

59.26   kept house with   lived with.

59.29–30   they fly about like the pestilence by noon-day   see Psalm 91.6.

60.20   a daughter of Eve   a woman.

60.36–38   rendered into the vulgar tongue ... lay person   see note to 51.9–10.

60.43–61.2   even thus ... Death by Sin   see Romans 5.12: eating the fruit of the tree of the knowledge of good and evil was the first sin, making mankind subject to mortality (see Genesis 2.17).

61.8   the Word slayeth   see 2 Corinthians 3.6.

61.17   the Holy Father of Christendom   the Pope.

61.24–27   rectors, curates ... world   'secular clergy', unlike the 'regular clergy' of religious orders, are bound by no vows and may own property. The term would include *rectors* and *curates*, clergy working in parishes: Scott probably does not intend a precise distinction.

61.26   the seculum or age   'seculum' is the Latin for 'age'.

61.27–28   the mendicant friars ... uncrossed   for mendicant friars see note to 58.18–19. The various orders were distinguished by the colour of their habits: the Black Friars are the Dominican order; the Franciscans adopted brown robes in the 15th century but continued to be known as Grey Friars. 'Crossed' or 'crutched' friars were a minor order who wore a cross on their habits.

61.29–30   Monks Benedictine ... Cistercian   the Cistercian order of Benedictines was founded at Cîteaux in Burgundy in 1098. In 1115 Saint Bernard (1090–1153, canonised in 1174) established a house at nearby Clairvaux and continued to promote the order's emphasis on a more simple form of monastic life.

61.33–35   it hath produced ... Scotland   the inclusion of 'popes' (none of whom had been Scottish) makes clear the absurdity of the claim.

62.21–27   the Tweed ... streams   the River Tweed has unusually high banks and in the early 19th century was prone to sudden flooding: 'the many other streams that empty themselves into the Tweed, come raving down from the mountains and from the lakes, and, with their united volume, raise that river to an alarming height in the space of a few hours' (William Scrope, *Days and Nights of Salmon Fishing in the Tweed* (London, 1843), 146).

62.30   the Enemy   the Devil.

62.40–41   of the many fair bridges ... existed   at the time in which the novel is set the bridge W of Melrose was the only one across the Tweed except for that at Peebles upstream (1465–70). According to a Public Act of 1764, before that date 'there were only two bridges over Tweed [Kelso, Melrose] ... of any real utility, all the rest being either aukwardly placed or incommodiously constructed': *An Inventory of the Ancient and Historical Monuments of Roxburghshire* (Edinburgh, 1956), 50. From 1764 onwards the systematic improvement of roads in the Borders led to the construction of such fine bridges as that at Leaderfoot, a little downstream from Melrose (1776–80), and Kelso (1800–03, replacing one of 1754 swept away in 1797).

62.42–43   a bridge ... the curious   according to Thomas Pennant, fragments of a bridge fitting Scott's description could be found at Bridgend near Melrose, although the bridge itself had been demolished in 1772: Thomas Pennant, *A Tour in Scotland; MDCCLXIX and A Tour in Scotland, and Voyage to the Hebrides; MDCCLXXII*, 3 vols (1771–76, repr. London, 1790), 3.267: *CLA*, 4. In the Magnum (18.72) Scott quotes a description of the remains of this bridge in Alexander Gordon's *Itinerarium Septentrionale [Account of a Northern Journey]: or, a Journey Thro' most of the Counties of Scotland and those in the North of England* (London, 1726), 165–66 and plate LXIV, Fig. 1 (facing p. 166): *CLA*, 11.

64.7 **riding the water** fording the river on horseback.

64.28 **a...squire of dames** a ladies' man, originally a character in Edmund Spenser's *The Faerie Queene* (1590, 1596), 3.7.51: *CLA*, 42, 187, 209.

64.42-43 **the Lowland tongue** English, or Scots, as opposed to the Gaelic spoken in the Highlands.

66.2 **the vesper hour** the canonical hours are times of the day prescribed for the reciting of designated prayers. Vespers were said around 4 p.m. (Fosbrooke, 55).

66.10 **The Kelpy** a water-horse or malevolent water-spirit who could assume human form to lure humans to their doom. Kelpies lived in deep pools in rivers and would leap up behind passing riders.

66.16 **A man of mean or a man of might** standard phrases meaning a wealthy man or a warrior: see e.g. the ballad 'Willie o' Winsbury', in David Herd's manuscripts, lines 13–14, 17–18, in *The English and Scottish Popular Ballads*, ed. Francis James Child, 5 vols (Boston and New York, 1882–98), 2.400 (Child, 100B).

66.46 **Berwick** Berwick-upon-Tweed, a town on the E coast at the border between England and Scotland where the Tweed joins the sea; an English borough after its final capture from Scotland in 1482.

67.7-13 **motto** not identified: probably by Scott, alluding to the parable of the tares (Matthew 13.24–30, 36–43).

67.31-32 **purple Abbot** see Alexander Pope, *The Dunciad* (1728–43), 4.301: 'Where slumber Abbots, purple as their wines'.

68.2 **the Privy Council** the Privy Council advised the Scottish monarch and formed the executive of the realm.

68.2 **the Primate of Scotland** the Archbishop of St Andrews from 1546 to 1571, who at the time of the novel's action was John Hamilton (b. 1512), although Scott also associates this character with Hamilton's predecessor Cardinal Beaton (for whom see note to 88.41–89.3). See Essay on the Text, 371.

68.3 **the Queen Mother** Mary of Guise: see note to 49.43–50.1.

68.13 **a man of parts** a man of varied education and skills.

68.34 **a life-rent lease** the right to the possession and use of property only during his life.

69.15-16 **his house...the Monastery** the Abbot's Hall, probably with his private chambers above, was built in 1246 near the mill-stream, separate from the main buildings. Scott is probably influenced by John Bower, *Description of the Abbeys of Melrose and Old Melrose* (Kelso, 1813), 44: 'In the end of the north nave [i.e. north transept] are the remains of the abbot's house, which joins to the church with a Saxon door which leads into it with a stair, the remains of which are still to be seen' (this is actually the night-stair used by the monks coming from their dormitory).

69.27 **Dundrennan** a Cistercian Abbey on the Solway coast, SW Scotland; it was founded in 1142, probably by David I.

69.36-37 **the Abbey of Aberbrothock** the Abbey of Arbroath on the E coast of Scotland, a Tironensian foundation dating from 1178.

70.14 **half-sacked** a favourite metaphor of Scott's envisaging the eating of food as a military onslaught.

70.22-24 **A fiery soul...clay** John Dryden, 'Absalom and Achitophel', Part 1 (1681) lines 156–58.

70.37-38 **For the stomach's sake...the text** see 1 Timothy 5.23.

70.43 **an English pint** 0.57 litres; about a third of an old Scots pint.

71.10 **those be they...upside down** see Acts 17.6.

71.15-16 **a man under command...under him** see Matthew 8.9 and Luke 7.8.

71.19 **the Riding-burn** the stream has not been identified.

71.23–24 your vassals are obliged ... their lands this would be the case since Melrose Abbey was a regality expecting the normal feudal obligations from its tenants.

71.30 Baron of Meigallot a fictional title perhaps inspired by two localities near Melrose: Meigle Hill and Meggat Water.

71.35 the Chartulary of the House the charter, and the persons named in it, appear to be imaginary. No record to this effect is to be found in the collection of such documents published by the Bannatyne Club as *Liber Sancte Marie de Melros*, 2 vols (Edinburgh, 1837).

71.39 the Abbot Ailford the figure is imaginary.

71.41 Saint Bridget's Even 31 January; the feast of the Irish St Bridget (d. *c.* 525) is 1 February: it was almost universally observed in the middle ages.

72.11 put on set to make regular journeys.

72.12 compound the claim come to terms about the payment.

72.31–33 the spiritual sword ... the temporal sword a reference to John 18.10–11 where Peter severs the ear of Malchus and is told by Jesus 'Put up thy sword into the sheath'. From this (and also from Luke 22.38) papal apologists developed the doctrine of two swords—the sheathed sword (representing the spiritual rule of the Pope), and the drawn sword, also Peter's sword, but wielded by secular princes according to the will of the Pope. The theory was developed in *De consideratione* (*c.* 1148) by Bernard of Clairvaux, the founder of the Cistercian order of Benedictines.

72.41 Sancta Maria *Latin* Holy Mary!

72.42 perished from the way Psalm 2.12.

73.11–14 motto see *Macbeth*, 5.3.42, 44–45.

73.35 Hob a diminutive of 'Robert': a generic name for a rustic or clown.

74.4 his wits have gone a bell-wavering his mind is wandering: a reference to sheep following a 'bell-wether', a sheep with a bell around its neck which leads the flock.

74.13 vino gravatus *Latin* from 'gravatis omnibus vina somnoque' (Livy, 25.24.6: 'all of them weighed down with wine and sleep').

74.34–35 Satan ... his hand alluding to the trials of Job: Job 1.11.

75.26–27 what say the Decretals? ... debent a *decretal* is a papal decree containing an authoritative decision on some point of doctrine or ecclesiastical law. The Latin means: 'Crimes ought to be exposed to view until they are punished, but disgraceful acts ought to be kept hidden.' The precise source has not been traced.

76.28–29 magazine of artillery building where munitions are stored.

76.43–77.1 any spirit, black, white, or grey compare *Macbeth*, 4.1.44.

77.21 I am but a lost priest compare *The Tempest*, 4.1.202: 'Thou wert but a lost monster'.

77.35–36 the seven penitentiary psalms Psalms 6, 32, 38, 51, 102, 130, and 143: sombre texts recited on Fridays during Lent.

77.36 scourge and hair-cloth self-flagellation and the wearing of coarse undershirts were means of doing penance.

77.43 the syren tune syrens were mythical creatures whose song could lure sailors to their doom.

78.6–7 their possession ... his death a grant of land could contain a 'clause of return', by which the feu would, in the absence of male heirs, revert to the superior.

78.15 Pentecost i.e. Whitsunday: either the Christian feast day celebrated on the 50th day after Easter, or 15 May, one of the four Scottish 'terms', traditional days for the paying of rents.

78.20–23 motto not identified: probably by Scott. The 'fatal Fisher' is the

Devil, who contends with the Christian 'fishers of men' of Matthew 4.19 and Mark 1.17.

79.36 tell his beads see note to 47.28.

80.7 wear over live through.

80.12 a clean shrift full absolution.

80.33 Saint Waldave St Waldeve or Waltheof (d. 1159), a step-son of David I, Abbot of Melrose Abbey from 1148 to 1159.

80.42 Saint Cuthbert see note to 56.5–6.

81.26 upon nettles on tenterhooks.

81.29 to boot into the bargain.

81.34 to her hand without exertion on her part.

81.34–35 without costing her either pains or pence no other occurrence of this saying has been found.

81.37–39 red thread ... witch-elm popular charms for warding off witchcraft. See Joseph Train, *Strains of the Mountain Muse* (Edinburgh, 1814), 163: *CLA*, 165).

81.41 Be here! 'God' is understood.

82.3 Happer the Scots form of *hopper*: a receiver in the form of an inverted pyramid or cone through which grain passes into the mill.

82.3–4 as weel as the beggar knows his dish proverbial: Ray, 199; *ODEP*, 41. The *dish* is an alms bowl.

82.4 canty quean [Elizabeth Grant, 1745–1814], 'Roy's Wife of Alldivaloch', line 9, in *The Scots Musical Museum*, no. 342: Vol. 4 (1792), 352.

82.33 the water the neighbourhood (of the Tweed valley).

82.42 at whiles sometimes; now and then.

83.27 the fisher of souls see note to 78.20–23.

83.28 ambition and vain glory the factors which led to Satan's own fall from heaven.

83.32–33 the church must not break or bruise ... possible perhaps suggested by Isaiah 40.1–2 and 42.3.

84.19–20 as it fell, so it lies proverbial, ultimately from Ecclesiastes 11.3: Ray, 231; *ODEP*, 505.

84.35–37 the first sentiment ... unavoidable most notably, Martin Luther (1483–1546) began by urging reform within the Roman Catholic Church from 1515 onwards; he was excommunicated in 1521 by Pope Leo X who had eventually come to realise the implications of Luther's ideas. In Scotland, between 1540 and 1560 when the Scottish Parliament finally broke with Rome, reform had proceeded gradually rather than with any dramatic disruption, the papacy being largely ignored in the process.

85.2 suffer for a time i.e. in Purgatory.

85.7–8 the godly foundation—our blessed Patroness Melrose Abbey, and the Virgin Mary to whom it was dedicated.

85.13 erroneous prayers Protestants do not pray for the dead, believing that their salvation or damnation is determined at death.

86.7 the tree of Knowledge of Good and Evil see Genesis 2.9.

86.32–36 motto see 'John Upland', lines 36–39, in the Bannatyne Manuscript, a collection of verse made by the Edinburgh merchant George Bannatyne (1545–1608): *The Bannatyne Manuscript Written in Tyme of Pest 1568*, ed. W. Tod Ritchie, 4 vols (Edinburgh and London, 1928–34), 2.247–49. For the further quotation on p. 87 see lines 7–13 of the poem.

86.37–87.1 The Scottish laws ... Jack-men see e.g. Ch. 9 of the Act of 14 November 1524, which states that all lords (especially in Liddesdale and upon the Border) must be responsible that their male tenants keep good rule as far as is expedient: *The Acts of the Parliaments of Scotland*, 2 (1814), 286.

87.37 in saultfat in the salt-vat; salted away; disposed of.

88.13 horse-meat and men's meat food for men and horses.

88.28 Ave and Credo *Latin* respectively, the first words of the Latin prayer 'Ave Maria' ('Hail Mary') and the Nicene Creed, 'Credo in unum Deum' ('I believe in one God').

88.33–34 the Lord James drowned . . . black pool at Jeddart Lord James Stewart (see Historical Note, 435–36) headed forceful attempts to impose order in the Borders. The burgh court at Jeddart, an alternative name for Jedburgh (Jedworth, Jedward), was the principal centre for trying offences within Scotland. Although hanging was the usual punishment, drownings also took place in the River Jed. Scott gives an account of this practice in 'Border Antiquities', 109.

88.41–89.3 the Primate . . . set him hard Scott is here thinking of Cardinal Beaton, Archbishop of St Andrews from 1539, who, historically, died before the events of the novel. After a number of plots against him, David Beaton was killed in 1546 by a group of conspirators including Norman Leslie (d. 1554), son of the Earl of Rothes, who was Sheriff of Fife from 1541, and who had a personal grudge against him. Beaton was hard pressed or beset ('set hard') before being finally murdered. The *Governor* is Moray, the leader of the Lords of the Congregation (for whom see Historical Note, 434).

89.4 quit the slot give up the chase: *slot* is the track or scent.

90.40 as old as the hills proverbial: *ODEP*, 588.

91.5–12 Saint George . . . Saint Michael . . . Saint John . . . Saint Mary Magdalen these are illustrations from the lives of Saints: St George, according to popular legend, slew a dragon; St Michael the Archangel is traditionally the opponent of Satan (see Revelation, 12.7); John the Baptist was often depicted with a lamb to signify his designation of Christ as the 'Lamb of God' (John 1.29); Mary Magdalen was identified with the woman 'sinner' of Luke 7.37 and often represented in the act of weeping for her sins.

91.28–29 paint them . . . blazon them with gold medieval scribes used pigments and gold leaf in the construction of elaborately decorated capital letters.

92.7–9 the spirit . . . nearer home the most spectacular examples of such depredations took place following John Knox's sermon against idolatry preached in St John's Church, Perth, on 11 May 1559. They extended as far south as Edinburgh and Linlithgow.

92.13 benedicite *Latin* bless you.

92.42 a statute passed in the year 1455 see Ch. 8 of the Act of 4 August 1455: *The Acts of the Parliaments of Scotland*, 2 (1814), 43.

92.43–46 The community of Aberbrothwick . . . exhausted the source of this anecdote has not been traced.

93.1 neither bush nor brake compare *A Midsummer Night's Dream*, 3.1.97.

94.1 travel the world . . . night-mare the term 'mare' is a variant of a Germanic word meaning 'spirit' and has no relation to horses. The nightmare was a succubus believed to produce bad dreams by sitting on the chests of sleepers.

94.3 crook of the glen bend in the valley.

94.9 Cabalists and Rosicrucians for *Cabalists* see note to 28.3–4. *Rosicrucians* were a secret world-wide brotherhood dating from the 16th century which claimed to possess esoteric knowledge handed down from ancient sources.

94.13–14 Cornelius Agrippa, Paracelsus for Cornelius Agrippa see note to 28.3–4. Philippus von Hohenheim (*c.* 1493–1541), known as Paracelsus, was a Swiss physician who experimented with alchemy, the search to transform base metals into gold: he was reputed to be a founder of Rosicrucianism (see note to 94.9).

94.17   the gates of hell...against me   see Matthew 16.18.

94.28–29   the words of solemn exorcism...Rome   the rite 'De exorcizando obsessis à dæmonio' (for exorcising those possessed by an evil spirit) can be found in the Roman ritual as codified under Paul V (Pope 1605–21), *Rituale Romanum* (Antwerp, 1625), 316–46. An elaborate series of adjurations to the evil spirit invoking the merits and power of Christ, and including appropriate passages from the Bible, centres in the words (325): 'Recede ergo in nomine Patris, & Filij, & Spiritus sancti, da locum Spiritui sancto, per hoc signum Crucis IESU Christi Domini nostri' (Be gone, therefore, in the name of the Father, Son, and Holy Spirit; give place to the Holy Spirit, by this sign of the cross of our Lord Jesus Christ).

95.16   won upon   prevailed upon.

95.23   betwixt wind and water   compare the proverbial expression 'to shoot between wind and water' (*ODEP*, 892).

95.23   Scots miles   see note to 45.18.

95.25–26   distilled waters   distilled spirits.

97.10–11   hale and fear   whole and in health: a Scots phrase dating from the 12th century.

97.11–12   Te Deum laudamus   'We praise thee O God', the first words of a Latin canticle.

97.12   the blood of thy servants...sight   see Psalm 72.14.

97.21   double ale   ale of double the normal strength.

97.25–28   motto   apparently not by Thomas Dekker (1570?–1632). Probably by Scott: the phrase 'Heaven's high name' occurs in John Dryden, *The Hind and the Panther* (1687), 3.972.

97.31–32   chimney-corner   the chimney is the whole fireplace.

98.11   Flodden   on 9 September 1513 the Scots under James IV were defeated by the English on the Northumbrian side of the Border, the King, 9 earls, and 14 greater lords being among the slain who were said by the English (probably with some exaggeration) to amount to half of the 20,000-strong army.

98.13   Saint Giles   St Giles (d. *c.* 710) was the patron saint of the city of Edinburgh.

98.14   Monance   St Monans, a town in Fife.

98.15–16   one Wiseheart, a gospeller   George Wishart (*c.* 1513–46), a Protestant preacher, burned at St Andrews by Cardinal Beaton.

98.24   the Gallow-hill   situated S of the market square.

98.24   peep of light   first light.

98.26–27   feed the crows...at Carlisle   Carlisle was the judicial centre on the English side of the Border and hangings were common there.

99.21   Aberbrothock   see note to 69.36–37.

99.24–25   spirit of another sort   see *A Midsummer Night's Dream*, 3.2.388.

99.35–36   the black pool of Jedwood   see note to 88.33–34.

99.37   the sack and the fork   the sack used for drowning felons, and the fork of the gallows.

99.40   the proverb, 'Never Friar forgot feud'   this is the only example given of this proverb in *ODEP*, 288; see also Cheviot, 263.

100.3   the glittering earth   Henry Hart Milman, *Samor, Lord of the Bright City* (London, 1818), 9.242. In the churchyard at Melrose Abbey there is a headstone dated 1761 with an inscription beginning: 'The earth goeth on the earth glistring like gold.'

100.10   coat of proof   armour tested for impenetrability.

100.12   fall at feud   be suddenly drawn into a feud.

100.14–15   Julian the Apostate   Flavius Claudius Julianus (332–63), Roman Emperor 361–63, who publicly converted from Christianity to paganism.

100.32   bring these stray sheep ... fold   see especially Jesus's words in John 10.16: 'other sheep I have, which are not of this fold: them also I must bring ... and there shall be one fold, and one shepherd'.

100.33   the sword of Saint Peter   see note to 72.31–33.

100.35   strangling and burning   burning at the stake was a method of punishment for heresy; the more fortunate victims were strangled first.

100.39–40   a thought   slightly.

100.41   the field of Pinkie   see note to 38.36–37.

101.4   buff-coat   thick overcoat made of leather.

101.12   try conclusions   engage in a trial of skill.

101.13   Saint Mary's well   a well dedicated to the Virgin Mary. No specific well has been identified.

101.18   Oremus   introductory word, or bidding, to Latin prayers: 'Let us pray.'

101.21   strong thief   flagrantly guilty thief.

101.27   A cast of their office, and a cast of mine   to give somebody a cast of one's office is proverbial: Ray, 204; *ODEP*, 106. The baillie takes up and plays on the word *office* ('position') from Christie's speech.

101.30–31   wrangling betwixt justice and iniquity   compare *Measure for Measure*, 2.1.165: 'Which is the wiser here, Justice or Iniquity?'

101.42   Save a thief from the gallows   the proverb continues: 'and he'll be the first shall cut your throat' (Ray, 161; *ODEP*, 700).

102.4–5   Abbot Ingelram's days   this imaginary abbot's name may have been suggested by Ingeram, Bishop of Glasgow, who died in 1174: see the Bannatyne Club edition of *Chronica de Mailros* (Edinburgh, 1835), 86.

102.7   paid tithe   paid a tenth of the value.

102.8   something lightly come by   i.e. stolen.

102.14   he was a merry man   see *Romeo and Juliet*, 1.3.41.

102.14–15   the spoilers of the Egyptians   see Exodus 3.22 where the Israelites are commanded to 'spoil the Egyptians'.

102.15   John the Armstrang   Johnnie Armstrong, a famous Border outlaw and the subject of a ballad included by Scott in *Minstrelsy*, 1.330–62.

102.16–17   hemp was ... heckled   hemp, the material from which ropes for hanging were made, was prepared with a tool called a 'heckle', used for separating out the fibres.

102.26   Lanercost Abbey   Lanercost Priory, founded *c.* 1166 for Augustinian canons, is in N Cumbria, 17 km E of Carlisle.

102.28   clean naught   completely worthless.

102.28–29   proper men   men who are the best of their kind.

102.30   It skills not   there is no point.

102.33   lauds   morning prayer, usually said after matins around 3 a.m. (Fosbrooke, 53).

102.35   benedicite   *Latin* bless you.

102.39   Gratias agimus ... reverendissime   *Latin* thank you very much, reverend master.

103.16   virtue is its own reward   proverbial: *ODEP*, 861.

103.29   ex cathedra   *Latin* in an official capacity.

103.40   Which our deference and humility   that deference and humility of ours.

103.41   in some sort   to some extent.

104.23–24   the sacrament, as his church call it, of confession   Roman Catholicism recognises seven sacraments, of which confession is one. Protestants recognise as sacraments only Baptism and the Lord's Supper.

104.30–31   I should have spread my mantle over the frailties   alluding to Shem and Japheth covering the nakedness of their drunken father Noah: Genesis 9.23.

104.33 **but what** but that.

105.11 **supererogation** the performance of good deeds beyond what God commands.

105.19 **a stricken hour** a full hour, indicated by the striking of the clock.

105.42 **votive obedience** obedience to monastic vows.

105.43 **the philosophical discipline of the schools** theology and philosophy as taught in medieval universities.

106.8–16 **motto** not identified: probably by Scott.

108.7 **prop and pillar** a standard phrase.

108.23–24 **bespeaking for their master … market** alluding to the custom whereby a lord could claim for himself goods from a market held on his land before it opened to the public.

108.26 **the great Fisher of souls** the Devil: see note to 78.20–23.

108.32–33 **ignorant as the beasts which perish** see Psalm 49.20.

108.40–41 **an old proverb … wisest men** see *Canterbury Tales*, 'The Reeve's Tale', 1(A), 4054. For Queen Elizabeth's use of the proverb see *ODEP*, 126. It is also recorded by Ray, 88 and 307.

109.24–25 **the Laird of Hunter's-hope** apparently imaginary.

110.37 **from Yule to Michaelmass** *literally* from Christmas to St Michael's Day, 29 September.

112.16 **a man of lith and limb** a man strong in his joints and limbs: 'lith and limb' is a standard phrase.

112.17–18 **a painted shadow** compare Thomas Middleton, *The Wisedome of Solomon Paraphrased* (London, 1597), 13.18.3: 'They see the painted shadow of suppose.'

112.36–38 **I guess … exceedingly** Samuel Taylor Coleridge, 'Christabel' (composed 1797–1801, published 1816), 1.66–68.

113.4–11 **motto** not identified: probably by Scott.

114.2 **Araby** Arabia.

116.1–2 **Many a fathom … to sleep** echoing Prospero in *The Tempest*, 5.1.54–57.

118.45–46 **Not to us … Adam's race** i.e. spirits can have no share in the divine redemptive process. Scott is perhaps recalling 1 Peter 1.12: 'which things the angels desire to look into'.

119.18–21 **It fann'd … welcoming** see Samuel Taylor Coleridge, 'The Rime of the Ancyent Marinere' (1798), lines 461–64.

119.24 **hovering on the gale** see [James Thomson and David Mallett], *Alfred: A Masque* (London, 1740), 29 (Act 2, Scene 3): 'Light-hovering in the gale'.

120.9–13 **motto** 'Christis Kirk on the Grene', lines 181–84. This poem was formerly ascribed to James I, King of Scots 1406–37 (see Scott's note on 122), but it is now believed to be the work of an unknown author, possibly as late as 1500–10.

120.27 **tup's-head and trotters, the haggis** boiled head and feet of a young male sheep; sheep's stomach stuffed with its offal and other ingredients.

120.30 **Happer** see note to 82.3.

120.39 **abstracted multures** *multures* are the grain due to a miller taken out of the grain sent to be ground at a mill. As Scott explains, tenants would be bound to a particular mill by 'thirlage'. *Abstracted multures* are due to the miller if the feuar takes his or her grain to a different mill.

120.40 **barony or regality** in Scotland a *barony* was any large freehold estate or manor and did not necessarily belong to a baron; a *regality* was land held under a grant from the monarch.

121.2 thirlage of invecta et illata duty payable on grain brought into a place thirled to a particular mill, but not grown there.

121.3–4 I talk not without book I speak from authority.

121.42–43 his proverbial golden thumb alluding to the proverb 'An honest miller has a golden thumb' (Ray, 136; *ODEP*, 532). Millers were commonly suspected of dishonesty in weighing corn.

122.6 a life of "spur, spear, and snafle" the phrase denotes the Border life of fighting on horseback; compare Michael Drayton, *Poly-Olbion* (1613–22), 23.277–78: 'The lands that over *Ouze* to *Berwicke* foorth doe beare,/ Have for their Blazon had the *Snaffle, Spurre, and Speare*.'

122.7–8 the loop of an inch-cord i.e. hanging.

122.40–46 The miller ... his head *Canterbury Tales*, 'General Prologue', I(A), 545–51. The phrase 'for the nones' means 'for the purpose'.

123.6 coat of proof armour tested for impenetrability.

123.12–14 the old proverb ... bleid Cheviot (113) recognises this as proverbial.

123.19 her airy castle building castles in the air is proverbial (Ray, 180; *ODEP*, 107).

123.28 Johnie Broxmouth's Broxmouth is near Dunbar in the East March.

123.31–33 the milk-maid ... founded in Aesop's fable, a milkmaid is so preoccupied with thoughts of what she will buy with the proceeds of her milk that she accidentally drops the pail and spills the milk.

124.3 blessed be his cast may his lot be in Heaven.

124.20–21 a true widow *true* is here used in the sense 'honest'.

124.25 Andra Ferrara Andrea Ferrara, an Italian swordsmith of the late 16th century whose weapons were much esteemed in Scotland. The name became a byword for any sword of high quality.

124.26 a thing of mine office a matter of my professional responsibility.

124.27 reason good with good cause.

124.29–30 I live by my mill ... wife 'The Miller of Dee', in *Ancient and Modern Scottish Songs, Heroic Ballads, etc.*, ed. David Herd, 2nd edn, 2 vols (Edinburgh, 1776), 2.185–86, lines 9–10: *CLA*, 171.

124.40–41 In the old translation ... our Saviour 'It has been asserted that there is an English translation of the Bible, in which, at the beginning of the Epistle to the Romans, was read, "Paul, a *knave* of Jesus Christ." The assertion came originally from one Benjamin Farley, a quaker or seeker; but no such book has ever been seen': Robert Nares, *Glossary* (London, 1822), 271.

125.2 used and wont according to use and custom.

125.10 gay and goodly Edmund Spenser, *The Faerie Queene* (1589, 1596), 4.2.29: *CLA*, 42, 187, 209.

125.24 the shape of an Hebe referring to the Greek goddess of youth and spring, but also alluding to her role as cup-bearer to the other gods; *hence* with a stereotypical waitress's or bar-maid's figure. See *The Abbot*, EEWN 10, 79.8, where Hebe is contrasted with a Sylph.

125.26 might go further and fare worse proverbial: James Kelly, *A Complete Collection of Scotish Proverbs Explained and made Intelligible to the English Reader* (London, 1721), 368: *CLA*, 16.

125.31–32 from the snood ... single-soled shoes i.e. from top to bottom. A *snood* was a covering for the hair. *Single-soled shoes* were 'a sort of brogues, with a single thin sole; the purchaser himself performing the further operation of sewing on another of thick leather' (*Minstrelsy*, 3.391).

126.7 the sad rout at Pinkie-cleuch see note to 38.36–37.

126.14–15 made two pairs of legs ... hands proverbial: Cheviot, 245.

126.17–18 a pricker ... good a *pricker* was a light, mobile mounted soldier (from 'to prick', or spur). In the *Minstrelsy* Scott explains: 'the habits of the Borderers fitted them particularly to distinguish themselves as light cavalry; and hence the name of *prickers*... so frequently applied to them' (1.130). To leave 'while the play is good' is proverbial: see *ODEP*, 453.

126.22   bide the bang   endure hard knocks.

126.26   no fear of him   no need to worry about him.

126.35–36   as broken a ship ... land   proverbial: Ray, 282; *ODEP*, 723.

127.2   music   *hunting* the baying of hounds.

127.4–8   Morebattle ... Eckford ... Cessford ... Hounam Cross these all refer to villages or hamlets E of Jedburgh: Hownam is overlooked by the hill Hownam Law (450m), but no reference has been found to a cross there.

127.13–15   the proud Percy ... Fowberry   in 1528 the newly-appointed English Warden-general Henry Percy intercepted a Scottish raid and hanged fourteen men at Alnwick in the English Eastern March. The nearby Fowberry was sacked by the Scots in 1524 and 1532. The phrase *some gate* means 'some way'.

127.18–19   holiday-terms of hawk and hound   hunting had a specialised language, here characterised as sportive terms befitting a holiday.

127.25–26   the proverb of MacFarlane's geese   in the Magnum (18.184) Scott attributes this saying to James VI and I who, when visiting the MacFarlane family, was amused by the geese 'pursuing each other on the Loch' but found the one brought to the table to be 'tough and ill fed'.

127.36   the blood of Bruce   Robert Bruce (1274–1329), King of Scots 1306–29, a national hero who eventually expelled the invading English in 1314.

128.2–11   motto   not identified: probably by Scott. See John Fletcher, *Rule and Wife and Have a Wife* (produced 1624, published 1640), 4.1.204: 'Green goose you are now in sippets.'

130.38–39   laid down with silver lace   with silver lace applied to the surface.

132.8   old True-penny   traditional name for a mole; *hence* someone underground or below: see *Hamlet*, 1.5.150.

132.18   turnspit boy   boy employed to turn the spit on which meat was cooked over a fire, a lowly position.

132.26   Hout tout   nonsense!

132.26   keep a calm sough   proverbial, meaning 'to keep quiet': *ODEP*, 416.

132.26–27   better to fleech a fool than fight with him   proverbial: *ODEP*, 53. See also Allan Ramsay, *A Collection of Scots Proverbs* (1737), in *The Works of Allan Ramsay*, 6 vols, Vol. 5, ed. Alexander M. Kinghorn and Alexander Law (Edinburgh and London: Scottish Text Society, 1972), 71. The term *fleech* means 'flatter', 'cajole'.

132.39   with little din   without much disturbance.

134.2–3   the beggar ... Turks   an allusion to the legendary ferocity of Turkish soldiers.

134.21–24   the "only rare poet ... without snatching"   for John Lyly (1554?–1606), the author of prose romances, see Historical Note, 437. Scott derives the first part of the description from the title-page of Edward Blount's edition of Lyly's *Sixe Courtly Comedies* (London, 1632): 'the onely Rare Poet of that Time, The Witie, Comicall, *Facetiously-quicke and* unparalelld: John Lilly': *CLA*, 217. The form of adverb and adjective reversal introduced by Scott here was a common Elizabethan rhetorical device. The second part of the description comes from Blount's dedicatory epistle to *Endimion* in the same edition: 'For this Poet, sat at the *Sunnes* Table: *Apollo* gaue him a wreath of his owne *Bayes*; without snatching.'

134.29 parler Euphuisme *French* to speak Euphuistically.

135.25–26 as the words … "a lad for a lady's viewing" Scott's source has not been traced.

136.5 toll dish dish for measuring the toll of grain due to the miller.

136.17–18 Venus delighteth but in the language of Mercury see Lyly, 2.122: '*Venus* delyghteth to heare none but *Mercury*.' Lyly notes that Venus and Mercury were the parents of Hermaphroditus (as recounted in Ovid's *Metamorphoses* (*c.* AD 2–8), 4.285).

136.18–19 Bucephalus … Alexander Alexander the Great (Alexander III of Macedonia, 356–323 BC) broke in the apparently untameable horse Bucephalus, after which it would bear no other rider. The phrase is in Lyly, 2.107.

136.19 no one can sound … Orpheus in Greek myth Orpheus was in fact given a lyre by Apollo. Scott has misremembered Lyly's phrase 'none can sounde *Mercurius* pipe but *Orpheus*': Lyly, 2.107.

136.24 Pretty and quaint compare 'Pretty and apt': *Love's Labours Lost*, 1.2.18.

136.25 all-to-be unparalleled this form of adjective-construction, continued in this paragraph and throughout Sir Piercie's speeches, is probably modelled on the character Fastidius Briske in Ben Jonson's *Every Man Out of his Humour* (1599). Compare 'the most-to-be-admired lady in the world' (4.8.51).

136.35 Prudoe Castle near Hexham in Northumberland, the castle was one of a number belonging to the Percy family.

136.41 a small quarto volume a small square book.

137.1–2 hogs … pearls proverbial: Matthew 7.6; *ODEP*, 617.

137.23–24 a lippy of bran … a bushel o' them a *lippie* was a small measurement of grain: half a gallon, or 2.27 litres. A *bushel* was a much larger measurement: about 8 gallons (36 litres) of dry or wet goods.

137.25 under his worship's favour with his permission.

137.26–27 the race of Morham … near Berwick Scott may be confusing Morham, in East Lothian, with Norham, a town with a dangerous ford crossing the Tweed near Berwick: *race* may mean either 'river current' or 'raid', 'charge'.

137.28 a gad's length a *gad* was a wooden slat about 3 metres long used for directing corn to the scythe or binder.

137.33 a true son of Mars see Robert Burns, 'Love and Liberty—A Cantata' (composed 1785–86; published 1799 as *The Jolly Beggars; or, Tatter-demallions, A Cantata*), line 29. Mars was the Roman god of war.

137.38 old Hunsdon, and Henry Carey these were the same person historically: Henry Carey (*c.* 1526–96), 1st Baron Hunsdon 1559–96, who was Warden of the English East March from 1568. Two of his sons, John (*c.* 1556–1617, 3rd Baron from 1603) and Robert (?1560–1639), both became English March Wardens. Lord Hunsdon would not have been particularly old in the 1550s, but his father William died in 1529 and had no Border connection. See Historical Note, 436.

137.40 Bayard originally the name of a magic horse given to Renaud by Charlemagne in French medieval romance.

137.40–41 a man should ride … Tynedale 'A Border saying, as Discretion is the better part of valour' (Cheviot, 18).

138.1–2 precious stone … toad alluding to the belief that the toad carried a jewel of medicinal value in its head. Compare Lyly, 1.202: 'The foule Toade hath a fayre stoane in his head.'

138.13–14 all are not black who dig coals see Lyly, 2.89.

138.20–21 Scorn not the bush that bields you no other record of this proverb has been found: *bields* means 'shelters'.

139.10–15 Mungo Murray ... buck's-horn alluding to the folk beliefs that people falling asleep on fairy sites could be transported to fairy land, and that a wound inflicted by deer-horn would not heal. For the latter, see also *The Bride of Lammermoor*, EEWN 7a, 81.8–9 and explanatory note on 355 there.

139.20 her eye "in a fine frenzy rolling" *A Midsummer Night's Dream*, 5.1.12.

139.37 Hout ay indeed; to be sure.

140.36 trope or figure metaphor or figure of speech.

140.42 like Desdemona to Othello's see *Othello*, 1.3.128–68, where Othello recounts how Desdemona fell in love with him as he told the story of his adventurous life.

141.4–7 motto not identified: probably by Scott.

141.12–14 the national ballad ... mist see 'The Gaberlunzie Man', in *Ancient and Modern Scottish Songs, Heroic Ballads, etc.*, ed. David Herd, 2nd edn, 2 vols (Edinburgh, 1776), 2.49–51, lines 37–38: *CLA*, 171.

142.33–143.29 the soul of harmony ... nut-brown see John Milton, 'L'Allegro' (composed *c.* 1631, published 1645), lines 144, 100.

144.35–37 Elizabeth of England ... his Inspiration presumably inventions of Sir Piercie: Sidney was not on favourable terms with the Queen of England.

145.23 the King of Scotland, did he live James V died in 1542.

145.36–38 In Every Man out of his Humour ... Resolution see Ben Jonson, *Every Man Out of his Humour* (1599), 3.6 and 4.5, especially 4.5.66–70.

145.38–44 What is more to the point ... good?" see Ben Jonson, *Cynthias Revels* (first published in 1601 under its eventual sub-title *The Fountaine of Selfe-Love*), 2.2.

145.44–45 I think there is some remnant ... lodges examples of (to outsiders) bizarre Masonic names can be found in Stephen Knight, *The Brotherhood: The Secret World of the Freemasons* (London, 1983), 38–39.

146.10 so unsavoury a simile see *1 Henry IV*, 1.2.77: 'Thou hast the most unsavoury similes.'

146.13 Kitchener and Refectioner the kitchener's main duty was to arrange for the monastery to be supplied with provisions. The refectioner was chiefly concerned with the eating arrangements (Fosbrooke, 182–83, 199–201).

146.22 Kamschatka a Siberian peninsula; *figuratively* an extreme and isolated place.

146.29 to his beard to his face; openly.

147.21 the foul fiend the devil.

147.25 come aloft the command to a performing animal to appear on stage.

147.36–37 a Bilboa blade the finest swords came from Bilbao in Spain.

147.43 finely holped up in a real fix: an ironic use of a phrase meaning 'well helped over an obstacle'.

148.41–42 took "entire and aefauld part with her" no source for this phrase has been found.

148.43 mortreux, blanc-manger a thick soup, and creamed fowl with eggs, rice, almonds and sugar: delicacies perfected by the Cook in Chaucer's *Canterbury Tales*, 'General Prologue', I (A), 384, 387.

149.5–6 strewed with fresh rushes rushes were used as floor-covering.

149.24 to piaffe, to caracole, to passage these are all movements of the horse in *haute école* or dressage, a form of advanced horsemanship inaugurated in Italy in the late 16th century and popularised in France throughout the 17th; the specific meaning of the terms may be found in the glossary.

149.33 Deo gratias *Latin* thanks be to God.

150.6–12 motto Ben Jonson, *The Magnetick Lady; or, Humour Reconciled* (performed 1632; published 1640), 1.6.4–9.

150.18–20 Nimrod . . . against man Nimrod is 'the mighty hunter' in Genesis 10.9. Although this is the only reference to Nimrod in the Bible, the name came to stand for any tyrant.

151.4 Benedicite *Latin* bless you.

151.6 Saint Jude a 1st-century apostle and martyr.

151.7 pass over spend.

151.8–9 the stone couch of Saint Pacomius St Pachomius (*c.* 290–346), the traditional founder of Christian monasticism in Egypt, was said never to have lain down, but rested by sitting on a stone.

151.13 in some sort to some extent.

151.20 the good fight 1 Timothy 6.12; 2 Timothy 4.7.

151.27 matins morning prayer, usually said around 3 a.m. (Fosbrooke, 53).

151.39–40 Richard Cœur-de-Lion . . . carbonadoed this story about the exploits of Richard II ('Richard the Lion-heart') is related in the Middle English romance *Richard Cœur de Lion*, known by Scott in an excerpted and paraphrased version by George Ellis in his *Specimens of Early English Metrical Romances*, 3 vols (London, 1805), 2.180–279: *CLA*, 105. Scott later reprinted Ellis's version as an appendix to the Introduction to the Magnum *The Talisman* (38.xvi–xx).

152.14 no whit not at all.

152.26 turn-broche turn-spit: see note to 132.18.

152.37 a hart of grease a deer in prime condition to be killed: see 'Robin Hood and the Curtall Fryer', in *Robin Hood: A Collection of All the Ancient Poems, Songs, and Ballads, now Extant*, ed. Joseph Ritson, 2 vols (London, 1795), 58–65, line 11: *CLA*, 174.

153.2–3 frater ad succurendum *Latin* an assisting brother.

153.6–7 the weapons of the spirit see Ephesians 6.13–17.

153.22–23 stone-walls . . . have ears proverbial: *ODEP*, 864.

153.33–36 Dixit Abbas . . . concilia the lines are accurately quoted from an anonymous dog-Latin poem on the drinking habits of the Abbot and Prior of Gloucester. The Abbot of St Mary's evidently misses its satire. The passage quoted means: 'The Abbot said to the prior: "You are a man of good habits, because you always give me good advice."' For Fosbrooke's translation see Fosbrooke, 154.

153.41 Intravit in secretis nostris *Latin* he has become privy to our secrets.

154.15 viol-de-gamba the *viol da gamba* was an early type of 'cello, also played by Fastidius Briske in Ben Jonson's *Every Man Out of his Humour* (1599).

156.3 this present Earl of Northumberland Thomas Percy (1528–72), 7th Earl from 1557.

156.16 the choice . . . age see *Julius Caesar*, 3.1.164.

156.39 rem acu *Latin* 'rem acu tetegisti': you have touched it with a needle, i.e. hit the nail on the head.

156.42 flat-capp'd citizens hats with a flattened crown were fashionable for citizens of London in the 16th and 17th centuries.

157.11 Genoa velvet in the mid-16th century the centres of velvet production were Genoa and Venice in Italy.

157.12 Bonamico of Milan probably imaginary: *bon amico* is Italian for 'good friend'.

157.15 Alnwick see note to 127.13–15.

157.16–17 Northallerton a town in Yorkshire.

157.17 Henry Vaughan probably imaginary.

157.28–29 Sir Lancelot and Sir Tristrem knights associated with King Arthur. Both appear prominently in *Le Morte Darthur* by Sir Thomas Malory (d. 1471).

158.7 the hospitable gods *Ovid's Metamorphosis*, trans. G[eorge] S[andys] (London, 1626), 5.65, 8.783.

158.16–17 danced the salvage man at the Gray's-Inn mumming mummery was an early form of the masques performed at Inns of Court in the 16th and 17th centuries. The Salvage (or savage) man was an ancient character usually dressed in green foliage and originally representing fertility.

159.10 sad-coloured riding-suit dark riding costume.

159.10–11 falling bands see note to 276.13.

159.14–15 Where the treasure is ... also Matthew 6.21.

159.31 Rowland Yorke, Stukely both are adventurers. Rowland Yorke, duellist and mercenary, is described in William Camden, *The History or Annals of England, during the whole Life and Reign of Elizabeth late Queen Thereof* (first published in Latin 1615, 1627; in English 1630), in *A Complete History of England*, [ed. John Hughes and White Kennet], 3 vols (London, 1706), 2.361–676 (540): *CLA*, 249. Thomas Stukely (1525?–78) was said to be a natural son of Henry VIII; he also appears as a character in George Peele, *The Battell of Alcazar* (London, 1594) and is chronicled in Thomas Evans, *Old Ballads, Historical and Narrative, with Some of Modern Date*, 2 vols (London, 1777), 2.103–09: compare *CLA*, 172.

160.11–12 the one part French, the other part English see Historical Note, 435.

160.13 a prize-fighting stage a stage for boxing matches.

160.15 Benedicite *Latin* bless you.

161.24–29 motto the lines are not in James Duff, *A Collection of Poems, Songs, &c., Chiefly Scottish* (Perth, 1816). They may be Scott's own, alluding to *Canterbury Tales*, 'The Wife of Bath's Tale': 'As thikke as motes in the sonne-beem' (III (D), 868).

161.36–37 the butt ... against alluding to shooting at a target in archery.

162.12 the Brocksburn head *Brocksburn* means 'badger's stream'.

162.20 vain conceit foolish notion.

162.38 at the volley at random; without consideration.

163.1 in some sort to some extent.

163.21 as broken ... to land proverbial: see note to 126.35–36.

163.26 seen of seen by; made evident by.

163.38 five hundred punds of Scots money the Scots pound was worth one-twelfth of the English pound.

163.39 Pittenweem a royal burgh in Fife.

164.3 a hart of grease ... in full season *hunting* a fat stag, ready for killing. See note to 152.37.

164.17 They that ettle ... some rounds compare the proverbs 'He who would climb the ladder must begin at the bottom' (*ODEP*, 127) and 'Step after step the ladder is ascended' (Ray, 20; *ODEP*, 773).

164.18 They that mint ... a sleeve of it proverbial: *ODEP*, 483.

166.13–16 those faces ... arrest them laudanum, a tincture of opium, was widely used as a pain-killer and narcotic in the early 19th century although the dangers of its hallucinogenic properties were recognised.

168.1 Ulric the name derives from the Norman French form of the Old English *Wulfric*.

168.5–6 her date of life/ Hath co-existence with her life-span is the same as.

168.18 the champion of the Jews Samson, whose strength depended on the length of his hair: see Judges Ch. 16.

169.33–41 motto 'Adam Bell, Clym of the Clough, and William of Cloudesly' in Percy, 1.129–60, Part 3, lines 261–68.

170.14 puffed out filled with soft material as if inflated.

170.14 the newest block the latest fashion.

170.36 ciprus cypress: a name given to several valuable fabrics originally imported from Cyprus including satin and cloth-of-gold.

171.9 the Benedicite the first word (meaning 'May God bless you') of a set of Latin responses said as grace before a meal.

171.11 It is Friday so meat cannot be eaten. Fosbrooke in fact says of the Cistercians (113): 'neither do they eat of fat or flesh except in case of sickness'.

171.14–15 viatoribus licitum est—you know the canon the Latin phrase means 'it is permitted to travellers'. A *canon* is an ecclesiastical regulation, but no precise source has been found for the phrase.

171.17 the Confiteor the *Confiteor* (so called from the first word, *confiteor*, 'I confess') is a general confession in Latin of sins.

171.21 da mixtus *Latin* give [us] the mixture [of wine and water].

171.27 virtue is its own reward proverbial: *ODEP*, 861.

171.30 the Abbey of Dundrennan see note to 69.27.

171.32–33 da mihi vinum quæso, et merum sit *Latin* give me some wine, I beg, and let it be pure.

171.34–35 caritas or penitentia a *caritas* was an allowance of wine 'Given on Festivals, Anniversaries, &c. to remind the Monks of benefits received' or a more general dietary treat (Fosbrooke, 58, 357); a *penitentia* was an act of penance.

172.9–10 one swallow make a summer alluding to the proverb 'one swallow does not make a summer': *ODEP*, 791; compare Ray, 143.

173.23–24 the forest … David hunting rights in a royal forest could be granted by the King; David I (reigned 1124–53) was well-known for his generosity to the Church (see note to 31.22–28).

173.33–34 Pentecost see note to 78.15.

173.35 Candlemas see note to 56.23.

173.36–42 An hogshead of ale … Our Lady's meadow Martinmas, 11 November, is one of the four Scottish quarter days. Halbert's remuneration in kind includes ale brewed at normal and double strength and the right to graze two cows and a horse on Monastery land.

174.3 quæ nunc præscribere longum *Latin* which it would take too long to enumerate at present.

175.6 in some sort to some extent.

175.7 under reverence of with due respect to.

175.12 upon the upshot in the end; at last.

176.2–10 motto not identified: probably by Scott.

176.33–34 skyey influences see note to 33.9.

178.43 Donatus a primer for teaching Latin written by the 4th-century Roman grammarian Aelius Donatus and in use in Europe until the Renaissance.

178.43–179.1 Promptuarium Parvulorum *Latin* Children's Handbook (or Repository): a Latin-English dictionary used as a teaching text from the 15th century.

180.34 end it or mend it proverbial: *ODEP*, 525.

180.41 seldom doeth a good hawk come out of a kite's egg proverbial: *ODEP*, 431.

181.39 freaks of humour strange moods.

183.12 open … on *hunting* begin to cry loudly when in pursuit of.

183.27–28 to lay your judgment … at fault *hunting* hounds are said to be 'at fault' when they lose the scent.

183.32 in some sort to some extent.

184.4–5 a buck of the first head a male deer with its first full-grown antlers (compare *Love's Labours Lost*, 4.2.9).

184.27 discipulus impiger atque strenuus *Latin* a diligent and strenuous student.

184.41 Fosbrooke for Thomas Dudley Fosbrooke (1770–1842), English antiquarian, see headnote, 441, and also Historical Note, 437.

185.14–19 motto see Francis Beaumont and John Fletcher, *Love's Pilgrimage* (performed *c.* 1615; published 1647), 5.4.158–64.

186.30 use no terms of quarter to *give quarter* is to spare the life of an enemy who is at one's mercy.

187.3–4 too high a flight . . . checked at *hawking* a falcon leaves the pursuit of its proper prey to *check at* another bird that has crossed its path.

187.24 bear a smooth face give nothing away.

187.26 try conclusions engage in a trial of skill: *Hamlet*, 3.4.195.

187.41–42 mortal arbitrement deciding the dispute by the death of one party.

188.10 viol-de-gambo see note to 154.15.

188.11–16 the inimitable Astrophel . . . Countess of Pembroke Sir Philip Sidney (1554–86) adopted the name Astrophel ('star-lover') to write the sonnet sequence *Astrophel and Stella* (published 1591). Mary Sidney (1561–1621), Countess of Pembroke, was Sir Philip's younger sister, for whom he wrote his *Arcadia* (written *c.* 1577–80; published 1590), a pastoral prose romance with interspersed poems: compare *CLA*, 101. Parthenope was a siren in Greek mythology.

188.30–36 What tongue . . . must end these lines appear in Zelmane's song in Book 2 of Sidney's *Arcadia*: *The Countess of Pembroke's Arcadia*, ed. Ernest A. Baker (London, 1907), 180, 182.

189.20 brown hackles artificial fishing flies made from the neck-feathers of certain birds.

189.35–36 take . . . in fee a heritable office was held *in fee* on condition of paying feudal homage to the granter of the office.

190.3 Morpheus the Greek god of dreams.

190.6–9 Ah rest . . . exile the source has not been identified.

190.42 humourous as winter *2 Henry IV*, 4.4.34.

190.42–43 The vulgar word humour-some according to *OED* the first recorded appearance of the word is dated 1656 ('humoursomeness' 1653): it is used by Samuel Richardson in 1742 and by Thomas De Quincey in 1823.

192.40–41 the Pater and Credo *Latin* respectively, the first words of the Lord's Prayer beginning 'Pater noster' ('Our father'), and the Nicene Creed, 'Credo in unum Deum' ('I believe in one God').

193.34–36 warrant from holy Scripture . . . demons most notably in the temptation of Jesus in the wilderness: Luke 4.1–13.

194.13–14 Pride . . . falling proverbially, the reverse is asserted: Ray, 148; *ODEP*, 647.

194.20–24 motto not identified: probably by Scott, echoing *2 Henry IV*, 3.2.270: 'He is not his craft's master.'

196.38–39 Phœbus . . . car in Greek mythology the sun god, Phoebus, was believed to drive a fiery chariot across the heavens.

197.7 Phidelé a poetic name, meaning 'faithful'.

197.7 Felicia (also Feliciana): a poetic name, meaning 'happy' or 'fortunate'.

197.24 in some sort to some extent.

197.27 duello a common Elizabethan form of 'duel'.

198.15 at whiles occasionally.

198.34–35 telling . . . disposed of after hanging, the body of the criminal was sometimes beheaded and divided into quarters.

198.43　Vincentio Saviolo　Italian swordsman and author of *Vincentio Saviolo His Practise: In two Bookes. The first intreating of the use of the Rapier and Dagger. The second, of Honor and Honorable Quarrels* (London, 1595): *CLA*, 119.

199.24　place of vantage　position likely to give superiority in a contest.

200.2　coming off　leaving the field of combat.

200.10　privy armour　armour worn beneath ordinary dress.

200.18–20　match at ballon ... Oxford　Sir Piercie gives a very rosy account of relations between Sidney and his great rival Edward de Vere (1550–1604), 17th Earl of Oxford 1562–1604. Sir Piercie is perhaps thinking of a famous incident in September 1579 when Sidney and Oxford narrowly avoided a duel after falling out over the use of a tennis (*ballon*) court.

200.24　Urania　the Greek muse of astronomy.

200.28–29　Zephyr ... Sirocco　*Zephyr* was the personification of the West Wind in Roman mythology; the *Sirocco* is a warm, humid wind over S Europe.

201.1–2　the beatific vision　the sight of God.

201.23–24　the stoccata ... Italian masters of defence　in the art of defence (fencing) in the 15th and 16th centuries, Italian masters were the most sought-after teachers, and their manuals, such as those by Giacomo di Grassi and Vincentio Saviolo (see note to 198.43), were widely studied.

202.21–22　three furies ... shears　in Greek mythology the Furies were goddesses of vengeance who dwelt in the underworld. They are here confused with the Greek Fates: Clotho, who spun the thread of human life; Lachesis, who drew it off; and Atropos, who cut it short.

203.2–10　motto　not identified: probably by Scott.

203.28–29　falcon-gentle　according to Juliana Berners, the 'fawkon gentyll' was appropriate for a prince: Berners, cv verso.

203.34　close breeches conforming　matching, close-fitting breeches (although Scott may have in mind 'closed breeches', which are voluminous breeches tied below the knee and more in keeping with Sir Peircie's flamboyant dress-sense).

203.41　Claridiana　see Ben Jonson, *Cynthia's Revels* (1601), 3.5.29.

204.40　hell and all her furies　see note to 202.21–22.

205.26　middle air　mid-air.

205.30　stooping from her wheel　a falcon stoops when it descends rapidly with wings nearly closed.

206.22–23　a howling wilderness　see Deuteronomy 32.10.

207.5　the works of darkness　see Romans 13.12 and Ephesians 5.11.

207.6　By its fruits is the tree known　proverbial: Matthew 7.18–20; Ray, 9; *ODEP*, 837.

207.27　a clod of the valley　Job 21.33.

207.41–208.1　Swear not at all ... nay nay　see Matthew 5.34–37.

208.13–14　Wilverton　there are several English villages called Wo(o)lverton.

208.14–15　the great Piercie of Northumberland　see note to 156.3.

208.18–19　a forlorn hope　in the 16th century, a body of soldiers detailed to begin an attack.

209.16–20　motto　not identified: probably by Scott.

209.30–31　it has been said that sorrow must speak or die　see *Macbeth*, 4.3.209–10.

209.39–40　I have sent this man ... unshrieved　someone dying without taking communion or receiving absolution would be in danger of being sent to hell for having much to answer for at the final reckoning. Compare *Hamlet*, 1.5.77–79.

209.41–210.1　thou hast defaced God's image　see Genesis 1.26–27.

210.5 **balm in Gilead** Jeremiah 8.22, 46.11.

210.9 **cut him off ... in his sins** kill him before he can make confession.

210.15–16 **I have no money ... Holy Land** Halbert adverts to the acts of paying for requiem masses to be said for the soul of the departed, and of making a penitential pilgrimage to Jerusalem.

210.19–23 **It is not for the soul ... departed spirit** see note to 85.13.

210.23 **Where the tree has fallen, it must lie** proverbial: see note to 84.19–20.

210.28–29 **under whose banner ... soldier** see 2 Timothy 2.3.

210.31–32 **the Archbishop ... Twa-pennie Faith** John Hamilton, Archbishop of St Andrews 1546–71, was associated with 'Hamilton's Catechism' (a simple exposition of the Ten Commandments, the Creed, and the Lord's Prayer) which was approved by the council of the Catholic Church in Scotland in 1552. The 'Twopenny Faith' was the popular name of a cheap two-page pamphlet of 1559 properly entitled 'A Godly Exhortation' which explained the Mass. Both texts represented attempts to popularise Catholicism in the face of Reform.

211.6 **the powers of this world** see Ephesians 6.12.

211.13 **Knox's name** John Knox (c. 1513–72) was the principal figure in the Scottish Reformation.

211.16 **of a surety** certainly.

211.41–212.2 **like the barren fig-tree ... the root** the fig-tree is proverbially barren because leaves appear after fruit, so that an apparently flourishing tree bears no fruit. Jesus curses the tree for its lack of fruit in Matthew 21.19. For the phrase 'the axe is laid to the root' see Matthew 3.10 and Luke 3.9.

212.10 **quaking bog** quagmire.

212.27–28 **to bait your hook with fair discourse** the concept is proverbial: *ODEP*, 27.

212.28 **angels of light** see 2 Corinthians 11.14: 'Satan himself is transformed into an angel of light.'

212.31–32 **being instant out of season** see 2 Timothy 4.2.

212.33–34 **rescued, like a brand from the burning** see Zechariah 3.2: 'is not this a brand plucked out of the fire?'

213.16–17 **wild ... romantic ... sublime** see note to 37.4–13.

214.20–23 **motto** unidentified: probably by Scott.

215.4 **Lapis offensionis et petra scandali** Romans 9.33 in the Vulgate: a stumbling stone and rock of offence.

215.5–7 **We may say ... heart** James V is reputed to have made this comment about the castle of Lochwood (Dumfriesshire), the seat of the Johnstone family (*Minstrelsy*, 1.127).

215.30 **the straight and narrow way** see Matthew 7.14.

215.43 **the Black Rood** this ebony crucifix, containing an alleged fragment of the true cross, was especially venerated by Margaret, Queen of Scots (c. 1046–93). In 1346 it was captured during an invasion of England by David II (King of Scots 1329–71) and remained in Durham Cathedral until the Reformation, when it disappeared.

216.22 **Saint Barnaby** St Barnabas' Day, 11 June, was reckoned the longest day by the Julian Calendar operative in Great Britain until the adoption of the Gregorian Calendar in 1752.

216.23 **betwixt Millburn Plain and Netherby** localities in Cumberland, the English county adjoining Scotland on the W border.

217.42–43 **an ancient English family ... field argent** this information was communicated in a letter to Scott by Robert Surtees of Mainsford, antiquarian and prankster, together with one of his own inventions to be included as a traditional ballad in the *Minstrelsy*. He claimed to have discovered the ghostly crest in a manuscript insertion in a book from the library of a Mr Gill, attorney-general to the Bishop Durham. Surtees writes: 'I am tempted to add here a heraldic bearing inserted by Mr. Gill, in Gwillim's [John Gwillim's] Heraldry, now in my hands. "He beareth per pale or and arg. a spectre passant [walking], shrouded sable, by the name of Michael Newton, of Beverly, Esq. in Yorkshire;" probably the only attempt ever recorded to describe an unembodied spirit in Heraldry': G. Taylor, 'Memoir of Robert Surtees, Esq.', 17 (bound (correctly) in Vol. 4, or (sometimes) in Vol. 1, of Robert Surtees, *The History and Antiquities of the County Palatine of Durham*, 4 vols (1816–40)).

217.36–37   the devil is not so black as he is painted   proverbial: *ODEP*, 182.

218.6   Spanish plumes   feathers worn in the Spanish style.

218.8–9   those tall ... Salvator Rosa   Italian painter (1615–73), noted for his wild landscapes featuring soldiers or bandits.

219.2–5   the circumstance ... present shape   ballad phrases denoting pregnancy: see, for example, 'My girdle of gold that was too longe/ Is now too short for mee./ ... My gowne of greene it is too straighte;/ Before, it was too wide': 'Child Waters' in Percy, 3.59, lines 7–8, 11–12.

220.26–27   the Lord Warden   see Historical Note, 436.

220.36   our hounds are turn-spits and trindle-tails   i.e. they are worthless dogs. Dogs in tread-wheels were used to turn the spit, and 'trindle tailes' are listed in Berners as a lowly breed between with 'Dunghyll dogges' and 'pryck eryd currys' (e.ij verso).

220.41–42   In the kindly language ... singles   Berners differentiates between 'talons', which are claws at the back of the foot, and 'sengles' at the front (a.iiij verso).

222.31   greener days   days of youthful naivety.

222.37   some ejected monk of a suppressed convent   the dissolution of monasteries and expulsion of monks was a feature of the English rather than the Scottish Reformation; in Scotland, monks were allowed to die out in the course of time, as was the case at Melrose.

222.39–42   some pilgrim ... a dozen   the reference is to two major objects of pilgrimage. Santiago de Compostela in NW Spain is the traditional burial place of James the Apostle. The Holy House in Loreto, near Ancona in Italy, is alleged to have been inhabited by the Virgin Mary at the time of the Annunciation by an angel of her forthcoming motherhood, and to have been miraculously transported by angels from Nazareth to Dalmatia (W Croatia) in 1291 and thence to Loreto in 1295, after a stop in a laurel grove (whence its name) in 1294. Julian refers to the practice of selling relics of saints and indulgences, bringing remission of the temporal penalty for sin.

223.4   Simmie and his brother   referring to the anonymous poem 'Sym and his Bruder' in the Bannatyne Manuscript (for which, see note to 86.32–36): *The Bannatyne Manuscript Written in Tyme of Pest 1568*, ed. W. Tod Ritchie, 4 vols (Edinburgh and London, 1928–34), 3.39–43.

223.7–8   clouted coat, scrip, and scallop-shells   the traditional clothes of a pilgrim were a patched and mended coat, and a bag or wallet. The scallop-shell is the badge of St James which could be purchased in the form of a lead badge at the shrine of Santiago de Compostela in NW Spain: returning pilgrims would wear several of these on the brim of the hat (Fosbrooke, 423, 469).

223.19   gray groat   a proverbially worthless coin: see *ODEP*, 339.

223.27   broken man   *Scots Law* outlaw.

224.19–20   the new doctrine ... Congregation   the Protestant faith, although Julian may be referring to the anti-Catholic 'First Band' or bond, signed in December 1557 by a group of nobles who became the Lords of the Congregation. See Historical Note, 434.

224.26–29 No more masses ... marriages of this list the Reformation abolished only masses, corpse-gifts, penances, and private confessions to a priest.

224.36 turn the world upside down see Acts 17.6.

225.23–24 motto Oliver Goldsmith, *The Vicar of Wakefield* (1766), Ch. 24, in *Collected Works of Oliver Goldsmith*, ed. Arthur Friedman, 5 vols (Oxford, 1966), 4.136.

225.32–33 we rend our hearts, and not our garments see Joel 2.13.

225.36 a cast of thy office see note to 101.27.

226.25 handfasted in 'Border Antiquities' (93) Scott explains this practice: 'a loving couple, too impatient to wait the tardy arrival of this priest, consented to live as man and wife in the interim'.

226.29 inland clowns of Fife and Lothian 'The Borders had ... little reason to regard the inland Scots [i.e. those living at a distance from the English border] as their fellow-subjects ... the men of the Borders had little attachment to the monarchs, whom they termed, in derision, the kings of Fife and Lothian' (*Minstrelsy*, 1.115–16).

227.9 to have a fool in hand to have a fool to deal with: see *Twelfth Night*, 1.3.60–61.

227.10–11 Harry Tudor ... Kate after the Pope refused to grant an annulment of the marriage between Henry VIII and Catherine of Aragon, Henry VIII had his marriage to his second wife, Anne Boleyn, authorised by the reforming Archbishop of Canterbury, Thomas Cranmer, in 1533.

228.38 inland men of Fife and Lothian see note to 226.29.

229.9–10 whether I am to hide the light ... forth see Matthew 5.14–16.

229.11–12 I say to thee ... woman John the Baptist forbade the union of Herod Antipas and Herodias, the wife of Herod's brother: Matthew 14.1–12.

230.9 the ancient air of "Blue Bonnets over the Border" Scott's song was suggested by 'March! March! Pinks of election', found with the early-18th-century tune 'Leslie's March' in James Hogg, *The Jacobite Relics of Scotland*, 2 vols (Edinburgh 1819–21), 1.5–7. This tune, altered by R. A. Smith in 1824 to fit Scott's words, became known as 'Blue Bonnets over the Border': A. W. Inglis, 'Appendix 3: Regimental Music', in J. C. Leask and H. M. McCance, *The Regimental Records of the Royal Scots* (Dublin, 1915), 705–25 (717). The poem 'Lesly's March' which it originally accompanied can be found in *Minstrelsy*, 2.194–203.

230.38 Serjeant Kite a character in George Farquhar's play *The Recruiting Officer* (1706).

230.44–45 give the key a double turn to drive the bolt deeper into the staple.

231.31–35 This pitch ... demanded for Scott's account of the chivalric system see 'An Essay on Chivalry', in *Prose Works*, 6.10–11.

233.37 alighted on struck.

235.5–9 motto *Comedy of Errors*, 5.1.269–72. Circe is an enchantress in the *Odyssey* who changes men into pigs by a magic potion.

235.20–21 thy wits are harrying bird's nests proverbial: Ray, 216; *ODEP*, 905.

235.22 lying leaguer residing.

235.27–28 Hotspur ... Malcolm's time 'Hotspur' (see note to 38.22–25) was so nicknamed by the Scots because of his ability to patrol large expanses of the Borders. The family, Earls of Northumberland from 1377, was founded by William de Percy (1030?–96). Elspeth probably refers to Malcolm III (reigned 1057–93), although the Percy family were not associated with Northumberland until Henry de Percy (*c.* 1272–1315) purchased lands there.

235.28 sate in our skirts pressed hard upon us.

235.29 keep a weel-scrapeit tongue in his head watch what he says.

236.4 a belted baron a belt distinguished the rank of earl, but the term *belted* was widely used to indicate other ranks.

236.8–9 gaed a blink . . . gaed a gliff stepped out for a moment.

236.20–21 the head of a knowe the top of a little hill.

236.22 the Shaw a patch of wooded ground and a common place-name, perhaps suggested by a farm of that name in nearby Liddesdale: someone called 'Hab of the Schawis' is named in 'Maitland's Complaynt, aganis the Thievis of Liddisdail' (*Minstrelsy*, 1.189).

236.26 wastel cake probably an invention of Scott, presumably the same as wastel bread (see Glossary).

236.34 Wight Wallace . . . Good King Robert William Wallace (*c.* 1270–1305) led the opposition against the attempt of Edward I to annex Scotland. For Robert the Bruce see note to 127.36.

236.34–35 pock-puddings . . . bloody crowns the English got nothing but hard knocks and bloody heads. A *pock-* or *poke-pudding* signified the perceived gluttony of the English.

239.29 an earth-born Titan in Greek mythology the Titans were a race of giants born of Gaea (the Earth).

240.2 Chevy-Chace the Battle of Otterburn: see note to 38.22–25.

244.2–8 motto not identified: probably by Scott.

244.34–35 deals with Sathanas trades with Satan. This form of the name is used in the Wyclif version of the Bible and in Chaucer's *Canterbury Tales* (e.g. in 'The Miller's Tale', 1 (A), 3750).

245.3 downright passes vertical strokes with a sword.

246.11 holiday phrases see note to 127.18–19.

246.39 Feliciana see note to 197.7.

246.40 Vincentio Saviolo see note to 198.43.

247.7 the Queen's pageant in Southwark on 2 July 1559 Queen Elizabeth was entertained with a muster at Greenwich by the City of London, and the previous day 1400 men at arms marched 'over London Bridge unto the duke of Suffolk's park in Southwark; where they all mustered before the lord mayor and lay abroad in St. George's Fields all that night' before moving to Greenwich: John Nichols, *The Progresses, and public Processions, of Queen Elizabeth*, 3 vols (London, 1788–1805), 1.41–42 ('The Queen on the Thames—&c, 1559').

247.13 the British Court probably a mistake for the 'English' court: the Scottish and English crowns were not united until 1603: see note to 32.13–14.

247.13–15 more fancifully . . . quaint for this construction see note to 134.21–24.

247.39–42 the alacrity . . . fall-off compare Ben Jonson, *Cynthia's Revels* (1601), 4.5.83–84.

248.34 the peep of dawn first light.

249.4 voice potential voice of authority.

249.7 frampler and wrangler brawler and trouble-maker: *The Monastery*'s 'frampler', a variant on 'frapler', is the only instance in the *Oxford English Dictionary*.

249.33 the temporal and spiritual sword see note to 72.31–33.

249.34–35 Alnwick or Warkworth the castle of Alnwick in the English Eastern March was from 1309 the principal seat of the Percy family. Nearby Warkworth Castle belonged to the Percys from 1332.

250.30 Vengeance . . . requite it Romans 12.19.

250.31 deadly feud see note to 35.7.

250.36–42 On the Eastern Border . . . Bells these were all long-standing feuds between historical Border families.

252.31–35 **he felt . . . all mankind** derived from the fable in the *Agamemnon* of Aeschylus (525–456 BC), 717–36.

253.33–41 **If the government of Scotland . . . many Catholics** in addition to the Percies, other prominent Catholic families in N England were the Nevilles (the Earls of Westmorland) and the Cliffords (the Earls of Cumberland).

254.22 **her beautiful, her brave** see John Hume's tragedy *Douglas* (1756), 5.1.283.

255.5–11 **motto** *The Two Noble Kinsmen*, 2.6.2–17.

256.23–24 **make wild work** wreak havoc.

256.34 **a rude brangler** *brangling* or *baughling* was the Border practice of vilifying someone who had broken an agreement or failed to honour a debt. Because it was so provocative it was banned in 1563. See 'Border Antiquities', 129.

257.10 **Holyrood** the Royal palace in Edinburgh.

257.17 **I preach . . . in vain** George Crabbe, 'The Parish Register' (1807), Part 2, line 130.

257.35 **deadly feud** see note to 35.7.

258.32 **the last extremity of hazard** the most dangerous position, when most is at stake.

259.26 **Molendinar** of the mill.

259.30 **Dan of the Howlet-hirst** someone of this name is mentioned in the ballad 'The Fray of Suport': see *Minstrelsy*, 1.163.

259.31 **Adie of Aikenshaw** apparently an invention of Scott's, the surname meaning 'Oakwood'.

259.40 **Sir John Foster or Lord Hunsdon** Sir John Forster (1520?–1602), a notable English Border skirmisher, was knighted in 1547 and appointed Warden of the English Middle Marches in 1560. See Historical Note, 436. For Lord Hunsdon see note to 137.38.

260.1–2 **the Baker's nymph of Raphael d'Urbino** 'La Fornarina' (The Baker's Daughter), by Raphael (Raffaello Sanzio of Urbino, 1483–1520), is a portrait of his mistress, said to have been the daughter of a Roman baker.

261.23 **distaff and spindle** see note to 50.26.

261.36 **suited the word with the action** see *Hamlet*, 3.2.16.

262.7 **awaked watch** kept watch.

262.24 **fiend ane** not anyone.

262.29 **Mysie Dorts** from *dorty* meaning 'bad-tempered' or 'sulky'. Compare Allan Ramsay, *The Gentle Shepherd* (1725), 1.1.125: 'Then fare ye well, Meg Dorts, and e'en's ye like [just as you like]'.

263.4 **locked and double-locked** see note to 230.44–45.

263.19 **the milky mothers of the herd** John Dryden, *Cleomenes* (1692), 3.1.48.

264.2–6 **motto** *The Two Noble Kinsmen*, 2.6.18–21.

264.37 **Woe worth the hour** a curse upon the hour.

265.5 **a squire of dames** see note to 64.28.

266.10–11 **They did not "chase the humble maidens of the plain"** the phrase may have been suggested by a poem well known to Scott and an important source for *Kenilworth* (1821), William Julius Mickle's 'Cumnor Hall', from Thomas Evans's collection *Old Ballads*, 4 vols (London, 1784), 4.130–35. Stanzas 16 and 17 begin respectively 'Why didst thou praise my humble charmes' and 'The village maidens of the plaine'.

266.17 **first-rate beauty** 17th-century term for an attractive woman of fashion, who would sit in a box, the most expensive part of a theatre.

266.19 **in the pit** in the cheap area of seating in front of the stage in a theatre.

266.21   Beau Fielding   Robert 'Beau' Fielding (1651–1712), a leader of fashionable 'men about town' in the Restoration period. Scott's source for this anecdote has not been found.

266.25   en cavalier   *French* in a cavalier manner.

266.33–34   Queen Bess's age   the age of Elizabeth I.

266.34–35   wore...brass on their foreheads   displayed effrontery.

266.36–38   the very gentle perfect Knight...maid   see *Canterbury Tales*, 'General Prologue', 1(A), 69 and 72.

267.32   en croupe   *French* sitting behind the saddle on the horse's rump.

268.33   Kirktown   town or village in which the parish church stands.

268.36   causa scientiæ, to use a lawyer's phrase   the Latin phrase means 'cause of knowledge' and is used to discriminate between a witness's first-hand knowledge and that gained from a third party.

269.23   Langhope   i.e. Longhope: *either* fictitious, *or* a farm in the Scottish Borders, in Berwickshire on the Eastern March, called Langhope-Birks.

269.24   the Tasker's park near Cripplecross   a *tasker* is a piece-worker, especially a thresher. Cripplecross is apparently imaginary.

269.25   Lot's wife   Lot's wife was turned into a pillar of salt when she looked back on the cities of Sodom and Gomorrah: Genesis Ch. 19.

269.28   Mellerstane   Mellerstain, a hamlet in Berwickshire in the Scottish Borders.

269.41–43   Froissart...Northumberland   Jean Froissart (1337–*c*.1410), whose *Chronicles* Scott admired, writes (2.523): 'the kynge... made a dynner to the Englyssh knightes, and caused sir Thomas Percy to sytte at his borde, and called hym cosyn, by reason of the Northumberlandes blode': *Sir John Froissart's Chronicles of England, France, Spain, Portugal, Scotland, Brittany, Flanders, and the Adjoining Countries*, trans. John Bourchier, Lord Berners, 2 vols (1523–25; repr. London, 1812), 2.523: *CLA*, 29.

270.18   In fine   in short.

270.22–24   sweet engaging Grace...waiter's place   Thomas Parnell, 'Anacreontick' (1714), lines 10–12, in *Collected Poems*, ed. Claude Rawson and F. P. Locke (Newark, Delaware, 1989), 115.

271.13–14   Vincent Saviolo   see note to 198.43.

272.21–22   Cast my reckoning   make up my bill.

272.43–273.1   the three Cranes of the Vintry   a London hostelry in Upper Thames Street, so called from the three cranes on the neighbouring Vintry wharf used for lifting casks of wine. See also Essay on the Text, 386.

273.20–21   Ariadne...labyrinth   in Greek legend Ariadne helped Theseus escape from the labyrinth of the Minotaur by giving him a clue or ball of thread.

273.24   fourteen hands high   a hand is 4 inches (10 cm), so this is a large pony or a small horse.

274.17   Gled's-Nest   i.e. 'kite's nest'.

274.24   to boot   into the bargain.

276.13   the superiority...ruff   the *falling band* was a soft unstiffened collar draped over the shoulders of the doublet or gown; it was white, of lace or lace-edged cambric silk, and was tied at the throat. It did not supplant the ruff, with its high neckline closely encircling the throat, until the early 17th century.

277.2–6   motto   not identified: probably by Scott; 'the ranks that fell' are the angels who fell from heaven with Lucifer.

277.12   dogmata   dogmas.

278.36–37   the Living Dead...the Dead Alive   compare Dryden 'A Song for St. Cecilia's Day' (1687), line 62: 'The Dead shall live, the Living die.'

278.39   The Word, the Law, the Path   for Protestants the Bible is the Word of God, enshrining the divine law, and directing the believer in the path of eternal life.

279.20–21   grey hairs dishevelled . . . sybil   the *sibyl*, a female prophet in Greek legend, was traditionally depicted as a wild old woman.

280.8–9   the Jeddart tolbooth   the Jedburgh town gaol.

281.10   I will never . . . forsake thee   Hebrews 13.5.

281.11-12   Call upon me . . . deliver thee   Psalm 50.15.

281.16–17   its "still small voice"   1 Kings 19.12.

282.10–11   put the pinch nearer the staple   Edward is trying to have the *staple*, a holder for the bolt of the door, levered off with an iron bar, or *pinch*.

282.14–15   the captain of the Castle of Lochmaben   the keeper of Lochmaben Castle (accented on the second syllable, pronounced as 'may') in Annandale, SW Scotland, was called the Captain: see *Minstrelsy*, 1.368. Christie may be referring to Sir John Maxwell (1512?–83) Warden of the Scottish Western March in 1552–53 and again from 1561, who held the castle at various times.

282.24   there go two words to that bargain   there are two sides to that question.

282.25   What the foul fiend   what the devil.

282.33   a bedlam business   a matter of madness or confusion.

283.15   Robin of Redcastle   probably imaginary: there is no Redcastle in the Borders.

283.29   takes the bent   flies away.

283.32   sic like   that sort of; such.

284.2–6   motto   not identified: probably by Scott.

284.14–15   the tongue of the trump   the main thing or most important person (*ODEP*, 487).

284.34   have turned the world upside down   Acts 17.6.

284.40   the preaching of Knox   for the most spectacular example of Knox's preaching see note to 92.7–9.

285.2–3   since the art of printing   printing from woodblocks first appeared in Europe in the 14th century and a system of moveable type was invented by Johannes Gutenberg *c*. 1450 in Mainz, Germany.

285.3–4   lain floating . . . Leviathan   in Jewish mythology *Leviathan* is a sea-serpent, but the term is often used, as here, to refer to a whale. Scott is recalling John Milton, *Paradise Lost* (1667), 1.196–201.

285.12–14   still the hierarchy . . . asserting them   this is an accurate description of the legal situation at the time of the novel's action.

285.22–24   Earls of Northumberland . . . tenth of Elizabeth   in 1569, the tenth year of Elizabeth's reign, Thomas Percy (see note to 156.3) and Charles Nevill (1543–1601), 6th Earl of Westmorland 1563–71, led a rebellion whose object was to free Queen Mary and restore Catholicism to England. Scott describes this insurrection in *Minstrelsy*, 1.91.

285.33–35   The matter had been considered . . . the south   most prominent among the nobility in the north of Scotland who maintained their Roman Catholic allegiance was the Aberdeenshire-based George Gordon (1513–62), who succeeded as 4th Earl of Huntly in 1528.

285.36–37   the doom of heresy   the penalty for heresy was usually excommunication and burning at the stake.

285.41–42   the inquisitorial power in Spain   inquisitions were papal judiciaries to combat heresy, but the Spanish Inquisition, noted for its extreme use of torture and execution, was ceded to the Spanish crown by Pope Sixtus IV in 1478.

286.6–8   wield the thunder . . . terror   Jupiter (the Greek Zeus), king of the Classical gods, is generally depicted in art as holding a thunderbolt.

286.20–21   Lord James Stewart...Moray   James Stewart (*c.* 1531–70), illegitimate son of James V, became Earl of Moray in 1562. See Historical Note, 435.

286.40–41   a low quit-rent   see note to 32.39.

287.10   sword of Saint Paul...keys of Saint Peter   St Paul was usually depicted with the sword of his martyrdom, and Peter was often represented holding the keys of heaven (Matthew 16.19).

287.13   Pereat iste!   *Latin* let him die! Compare Christopher Marlowe, *Edward II*, 5.5.25.

288.3   a foreign university   many Scottish Protestants studied at Lutheran and Calvinist universities in Germany and Switzerland. Scott may be thinking of Geneva, which is close to Mont Blanc (see 289.4), and which was strongly associated with John Knox.

288.9   William Allan   the Sub-Prior's original name may be taken from that of William Allen (1532–94), the English cardinal who founded the seminary for English-speaking Catholics eventually located at Douai (see note to 13.2–4) and supervised the Douai translation of the Bible into English.

288.21   do nothing in hate but all in honour   see *Othello*, 5.2.298.

289.4   Mount Blanc   at 4807m the highest mountain in the Alps.

289.11   the shepherd...the universal fold   see John 10.16 and note to 100.32.

289.15–16   those fiends...prayer   see Matthew 17.21 and Mark 9.29.

289.16   not many wise...chosen   compare 1 Corinthians 1.26.

289.19–20   as the Greeks of old...wisdom   see 1 Corinthians 1.23.

289.23–24   the Councils...Church   in the Roman Catholic Church a *Council* is a meeting of bishops and other leaders called by the Pope to determine matters of doctrine and discipline; the Fathers of the Church are the eminent Christian teachers of the early centuries whose writings remained as a court of appeal for their successors.

289.34–35   that profitable purgatory...the keys   the Roman Catholic doctrine that souls in purgatory may be aided by almsgiving and the purchase of indulgences (as well as by prayer) was denied by Protestants.

289.41   ultima ratio Romæ   *Latin* the last resort of Rome.

290.19–20   'O gran bonta...diversa'   *Italian* O, the great generosity of the knights of old / They were enemies, they were of different faiths. See Ludovico Ariosto, *Orlando Furioso* (1532), 1.169–70 (stanza 22). The correct form of the lines ('Oh gran bontà de' cavalieri antiqui! / Eran rivali, eran di fe diversi') is given in *Parnaso Italiano*, 56 vols (Venice, 1748–91), 18.8: *CLA*, 55.

290.24   Buchanan   George Buchanan (1506–82), one of the leading Scottish Protestant reformers and campaigner against Catholicism. He was an eminent scholar, and author of four plays, an important work of political theory justifying the deposition of Mary Queen of Scots (*De juri regni apud Scotos*, 1578), and a history of Scotland.

290.25   Beza   Théodore Bèze (1519–1605), a Swiss theologian highly regarded by Scottish Protestants, who succeeded Calvin as the leader of the Geneva-based Reformation; he was a noted Latin poet.

290.37–38   rescue or no rescue...country   the phrase was used to invoke a code of honour obliging prisoners to keep to their word not to abscond even if rescued by their friends. See *Sir John Froissart's Chronicles of England, France, Spain, Portugal, Scotland, Brittany, Flanders, and the Adjoining Countries*, trans. John Bourchier, Lord Berners, 2 vols (1523–25; repr. London, 1812), 1.537: 'yelde you my prisoner, rescue or no rescue, or els ye are but deed': *CLA*, 29. Compare *Ivanhoe*, EEWN 8, note to 264.26–27.

291.16–17   Woe unto me if I preach not the Gospel   see 1 Corinthians 9.16. The Protestant preacher George Wishart is reported to have said: 'I have read in the Acts of the Apostles, that it is not lawfull to desist frome the preaching of the Gospell for the threats and minasses of men' (David Calderwood, *History of the Kirk of Scotland*, 8 vols (Edinburgh, 1842–49) 1.206).

291.29–30 in a prison . . . house see Acts 16.29–34.

292.27–35 motto see 'The Cruel Lady of the Mountains', lines 17–24, in *English Minstrelsy*, ed. Walter Scott, 2 vols (Edinburgh, 1810), 1.224–26.

293.37–38 a cabalistical spell see note to 28.3–4.

294.11–13 His holy Word . . . wild-fire compare Psalm 119.105, and see also John Dryden, *Religio Laici* (1682), 1–10.

294.32–42 the child of the widow . . . revixit two incidents are confused here. In 1 Kings 17.9–24 Elijah (from Tishbe in Gilead) restores to life a widow's son in the city of Zarephath. In 2 Kings Ch. 4 he similarly restores the dead son of a woman in Shunem who reproached him with having promised that she should bear the child: 'Did I desire a son of my lord? did I not say, Do not deceive me?' It was in Zarapheth, not Shunem, that Elijah asked God to 'let this child's soul come into him again' (1 Kings 17.21). The following verse is that quoted from the Vulgate: 'And the Lord heard the voice of Elijah, and the soul of the child came into him again, and he revived.'

295.1 shrouded in a tabernacle of clay for *tabernacle* as the mortal human body see 2 Corinthians 5.1, 4 and 2 Peter 1.13–14.

295.20 Saint Benedict see note to 13.1.

297.14–15 to be a stumbling-block in my paths see Romans 14.13.

297.17–19 the first murtherer . . . sacrifice Cain murdered his brother Abel out of jealousy because God preferred Abel's sacrifice: Genesis Ch. 4.

300.17–19 thou shalt aid . . . profane the Sub-Prior alludes to an incident when the Ark of the Covenant, which housed the tablets of the law given to Moses by God, was being transported by ox-cart: 'And when they came to Nachon's threshingfloor, Uzzah put forth his hand to the ark of God, and took hold of it; for the oxen shook it. And the anger of the Lord was kindled against Uzzah; and God smote him there for his error; and there he died by the ark of God' (2 Samuel 6.6–7; compare 1 Chronicles 13.9–10).

300.34–39 motto not identified: probably by Scott.

301.13 At open doors dogs come in proverbial: Ray, 279; *ODEP*, 599.

301.16 pith and wind toughness and endurance.

301.31 a fountain sealed Song of Solomon 4.12.

302.5 sowing his tares among the wheat see Matthew 13.24–30, 36–43.

302.12–13 his soul rescued . . . net see Psalm 124.7.

302.38 a brand from the burning see Zechariah 3.2.

302.40 the Rock of Ages from the Authorised Version's marginal note to Isaiah 26.4; the AV text itself reads 'everlasting strength'. The phrase is best known from the hymn 'Rock of Ages, cleft for me' by A. M. Toplady (1740–78).

303.2–5 that Rock on which Saint Peter founded his church . . . paronamasia the much-disputed 'text' is Matthew 16.18 where Jesus says to Simon Peter that he will build his Church on 'this rock'. Roman Catholics take this to mean that the Church was founded on Peter—whom Jesus called Cephas (*Aramaic* stone: John 1.42, corresponding to Greek 'Petros')—and his successors as Bishops of Rome or Popes. Protestants often take the rock to refer to Peter's faith and always deny papal claims to be Peter's successors. The Sub-Prior is elaborating on the original gospel *paronamasia* or play on words.

304.11 Go to come, come!

304.38–39 my neck . . . quarters i.e. he would have been hanged (with an allusion to the quartering of executed criminals: see note to 198.34–35).

304.40–41 Merse . . . Forest to-boot strictly speaking, *the Merse* is the plain occupying the S of Berwickshire and the E part of Roxburghshire in the Scottish Borders, but it was often synonymous with Berwickshire. For Teviotdale see note to 6.30. The phrase 'take the Forest to boot' means 'and Ettrick Forest [i.e. most of former Selkirkshire] into the bargain'.

305.11–12   take the air ... take the earth   i.e. if the Sub-Prior exorcises the devils so that they fly away, Christie will ensure that all human enemies are dead and buried.

306.9   Lords of Congregation   for the Lords of the Congregation see Historical Note, 434.

306.12   a round body of cavalry   a mounted troop of considerable numbers.

306.25–26   Lord Semple ... Kennedies   Robert Sempill (c. 1505–72) succeeded as 3rd Lord Sempill in 1548; his family seat was Castle-Semple, Lochwinnoch, Lanarkshire. Kennedy was the family name of the Earls of Cassillis; the 3rd Earl, Gilbert Kennedy (1517–58), succeeded to the title in 1527. The families were supporters of the pro-French and pro-English factions respectively.

306.28–31   From Wigton ... Kennedie   the Kennedy family owned land in former Wigtownshire in SW Scotland; the River Cree marked the county boundary. In Magnum (19.259) this rhyme is changed so as to conform essentially with the version appearing in Chambers, 165.

306.40   Newport   a town in Fife.

306.41   broke the wand of peace   in Scots law the *wand of peace* was a baton carried by a king's messenger as a symbol of his office and broken by him as a protest if he was resisted in the exercise of his duties.

307.11–13   promised him ... Avenel   i.e. Julian's obligation to contribute to the Church one sheaf in ten would not be rigorously enforced. The phrase 'in case' means 'if'.

307.16   old Gilbert of Cranberry-moor   character and place are both apparently imaginary.

307.18   dispone upon   dispose of.

308.4   comes to a point   decides.

308.26–27   the field of Pinkie-cleugh   see note to 38.36–37.

308.40   Flodden-field   see note to 98.11.

309.2–10   motto   not identified: probably by Scott.

310.5–6   the indulgentiæ—the gratias—the biberes—the weekly mess of boiled almonds   *indulgentiæ* were concessions in general; a *gratia* was a special dispensation; a *biber* was a time when alcoholic drink might be consumed; the boiled almonds are a reference to an allowance made to the monks of Melrose by Robert Bruce (King of Scots 1306–29) mentioned in the 'Carta de Pitancia Centum Librarum' (charter concerning a donation of £100) which Scott quotes in the Magnum (19.281–82).

310.12–13   that curious screen ... north-eastern wind   the surviving inside walls of the cloisters, on the N of the abbey church, have finely-carved blind arcadings attached to the exterior walls of the north aisle and the west face of the north transept: these were completed before the end of the 15th century. Shortly after writing *The Monastery* Scott was to erect a free-standing screen, decorated in imitation of the cloisters, to divide the courtyard from the garden at Abbotsford (*Letters*, 6.323: [1821], to James Skene; 8.112: 29 October 1823, to Daniel Terry).

310.14   holy Machabee ... voluntatem Dei   *Latin* the city is taken by the will of God (2 Maccabeus 12.16, in the Apocrypha). The quotation refers to the capture of Caspis without the use of any engine of war.

310.28   Hexham   a town near the Border in central Northumberland.

310.28   Sir John Foster   see note to 259.40.

310.32 Semple and the Kennedies see note to 306.25–26.

310.34–36 the Earl of Cassilis...Moray the Earls of Cassillis had interests in Crossraguel Abbey (founded 1244) in Ayrshire, SW Scotland; Quintin Kennedy (1520–64), younger brother of the 3rd Earl, was its Abbot from 1547. James Stewart took the title Earl of Moray in 1562.

310.37 Principes...Dominum *Latin* the princes have conspired together against the Lord: Psalm 2.2 in the Vulgate.

310.40 the Primate of Scotland see note to 68.2.

311.12 bell, book, and candle see note to 53.24.

311.14–16 Judas Maccabeus...Nicanors...Holofernes...head in a basket referring to stories from the Apocrypha. Nicanor was a Syrian general slain by the Jewish hero Judas Maccabeus: see 1 Maccabees Ch. 7. Holofernes was an Assyrian captain decapitated by Judith: see Judith Ch. 13.

311.22 Hexhamshire at the time of the novel's action Hexhamshire denoted a regality (territory granted by the crown) around the town of Hexham on both sides of the Tyne. It belonged to the See of York, but in 1572 it became crown property and part of the county of Northumberland. (Nowadays the term is used for a small area of country S of Hexham.)

311.27 Petrus Eremita Peter the Hermit (*c.* 1050–1115) led a party of civilians across Europe to Constantinople on the First Crusade in 1096. Most were killed by the Turks.

311.30 a man of Belial a generalised term for a wicked man in the Bible; see, for example, 2 Samuel 16.7: 'Come out, come out thou bloody man and thou man of Belial.'

312.18–19 suit and service attendance at the baronial court, and personal service, due to a feudal superior.

312.19 the Baron of Meigallot see note to 71.30.

313.5–6 when Benedict the Thirteenth was deposed Benedict was Antipope at Avignon from 1394 during the Great Schism of the Catholic Church when there were two rival papacies. He was deposed by the Council of Pisa in 1409, a decision confirmed by the Council of Constance in 1417 after which his last adherents (including the Church in Scotland) left him.

315.12 of name of distinction.

315.29–30 as ever cock fought on Shrove-tide-even cock-fighting was traditionally associated with Shrove Tuesday, though the practice is not recorded as having spread from England (where it had been popular since the 14th century) to Scotland until 1685. Scott's anglicisation of 'Fastern's Even' (Shrove Tuesday) is misleading.

316.1 the Lothian firth the Firth of Forth, separating Lothian from Fife to the N.

316.7 We of the spear and snafle see note to 122.6.

316.22 break no scurril jests compare *Troilus and Cressida*, 1.3.148.

316.33 Eckie of Cannobie Eckie is a diminutive of Hector; Cannobie, or Canonbie, is a village in Eskdale, SE Dumfriesshire.

316.33–34 the curve of the cawker a *cawker*, or *calkin*, is the turned-down end of a horseshoe which keeps the horse's heel from touching the ground.

317.6–10 motto 'Gil Morrice', in *Scotish Songs in Two Volumes*, ed. Joseph Ritson, 2 vols (London, 1794), 2.157–65, lines 53–56: *CLA*, 174.

318.4–5 some tuilzie in Ayrshire Ayrshire in SW Scotland was governed by the Catholic Earls of Cassillis and Eglinton. In 1563 there was an attempt to revive Catholic worship by the public celebration of Mass, protected by Kennedy lairds, but Scott is not necessarily referring to any particular historical event.

318.19 Ill hearing makes ill rehearsing proverbial: Cheviot, 201.

318.38 nae farther gane no later than that.

318.39–40   to teach the cat the way to the kirn   proverbial: *ODEP*, 805.

319.27–29   the strong waters . . . rarely used   Scotch whisky did not become widely used in the Lowlands until the 18th century.

319.30–31   the braes of Doune . . . the Laird of Buchanan   the Buchanan family seat is situated between Loch Lomond and Drymen, Stirlingshire. The 'braes of Doune' probably refers here to the environs of Doune hill on the W side of the loch.

319.33   Anti-christ   the antichrist of the New Testament (e.g. 1 John 2.18, 22) was often seen by Protestants as prophetic of the papacy.

320.3   the bastard of Morton   an illegitimate son of James Douglas (*c.* 1516–81), 4th Earl of Morton from *c.* 1550. Morton was Regent from 1572–78, defeating Mary's remaining supporters, but in 1581 he was executed for his alleged complicity in Darnley's murder. He had four illegitimate sons. The one referred to here is most likely Archibald (the second) or William (the fourth).

320.8   lads of the laird's belt   i.e. it is as though they were the laird's swords. The phrase has not been located elsewhere.

320.14   there were all the moan made   any complaints would soon be over.

320.35   enfans perdus   *French* literally 'lost children'. See also 'Border Antiquities', 70, where Scott defines this term as referring to retainers left to hold out a tower while the laird escaped.

321.43–322.10   But he abused . . . offences   throughout his career Moray sought to strengthen first the reforming faction in parliament, and then his own hold on the Regency, by seeking ties with England. Following the enforced abdication of Queen Mary in 1567, Moray, her half-brother, became Regent and presided over her imprisonment at Lochleven Castle (an episode which forms part of the plot of *The Abbot*). Mary's escape to England led to a conference representing herself, Moray, and Elizabeth I in 1568, the result of which was Moray's formally accusing her of the murder of her first husband, Lord Darnley. He received a loan of £5000 from Elizabeth and partial recognition of his government. Moray was murdered in 1570 by James Hamilton of Bothwellhaugh, with the foreknowledge of the Archbishop of St Andrews.

322.38   dark-red eye-brows   contemporaneous portraits show Moray with red hair.

323.7–9   The law both of God and of man . . . succeed   in canon law, which was accepted as binding by the secular courts, a declaration of intention to marry, followed by intercourse, was accepted as a valid marriage, though an irregular one.

323.14   say on   tell (freely).

323.29–30   Anti-Christ   see note to 319.33.

323.31   the death of a traitor   hanging, drawing, and quartering.

323.34–35   Let him go down . . . into Tophet   Baal, originally a Tyrian deity, is depicted as a rival god in the Old Testament. Tophet was a place beside Jerusalem where the ashes of sacrifices or images of false gods were cast: see Jeremiah 19.5–6. Later it became a rubbish-dump, with perpetual bonfires, and symbolic of hell.

323.38   the Earl's own mother   Margaret Erskine (*c.* 1510–72), the mistress of James V.

324.34–37   Moses . . . Benaiah . . . the sand   Benaiah acted as a hit-man for Solomon: see 1 Kings 2.25–34. Moses killed an Egyptian who had struck one of his fellow-Hebrews: Exodus 2.11–12.

325.14–18   motto   see 'The Field of Battle', lines 1–4, by Thomas Penrose (1742–79), in his *Poems* (London, 1781), 77.

325.37   Goshen   see note to 32.9.

326.31   Cardinal Beatoun   see note to 88.41–89.3.

326.34 **Pope Julius** Julius II (1443–1513, Pope from 1503) conducted wars to restore the temporal power of the papacy.

327.11–12 **fight dog . . . archer** variants on the proverb 'Fight dog, fight bear': Ray, 190; *ODEP*, 256.

327.23–24 **to the saddle . . . away** two of the five principal military trumpet-calls were 'Boot and Saddle' and 'Horse and Away'.

327.39 **bloody with spurring . . . haste** *Richard II*, 2.3.58.

328.36–37 **Saint Andrew's cross** see note to 53.27.

329.10–12 **War and terror . . . behind them** see 325.14–18 and note.

330.39–40 **ye were constant . . . fray** compare *1 Henry IV*, 4.2.77–78: 'To the latter end of a fray and the beginning of a feast/ Fits a dull fighter and a keen guest.' Proverbial: Ray, 106; *ODEP*, 52.

331.3–4 **ta'en the basnet** taken the steel helmet; joined the army.

331.17 **the cry of Saint George for England** a battle-cry invoking the patron saint of England.

331.26 **is your dream out?** have you come to your senses?

332.35 **the Privy Council** see note to 68.2.

334.12 **Sir George Heron of Chipchase** Sir George (d. 1575), Deputy Warden of the English Middle March, was killed at the Raid of the Reidswire. See Historical Note, 436 and *Minstrelsy*, 2.33n.

334.21 **under assurance** under protection.

334.41 **Commissioners . . . Border** border commissioners from England and Scotland met periodically from 1248 until 1597 to draw up or emend the laws governing the Borders. Morton, however, seems to refer to the Wardens who presided over actual trials.

336.17 **his own birth** see note to 323.38.

336.19–20 **The Earl of Morton . . . his amours** Morton's profligacy was well known: his wife became insane, and thereafter he 'loosed the rains to others, and begat three naturall Children' (David Hume of Godscroft, *The History of the Houses of Douglas and Angus* (1644, repr. Edinburgh, 1648), 278: *CLA*, 3). In *The Abbot*, EEWN 10, 345.2–3, Morton's wife is called Alice, but this name is apparently imaginary.

336.28–29 **motto** *King John*, 3.1.1.

336.38 **fight the good fight** 1 Timothy 6.12.

336.40 **Let us assume . . . faith** compare Romans 13.12.

337.5–7 **arriving at the vineyard . . . morning** see Matthew 20.1–16.

337.29–31 **even as you may have marked the heron . . . wing** 'the heron . . . has formidable claws, and, above all, a most frightful dagger of a beak. With this he stabs; but the great danger is not as generally supposed, and as Sir Walter Scott represented, from a thrust in the air, but on the ground, when the hawks, having let go to save themselves from the shock of the fall, "make in" to kill the quary' (Gage Earle Freeman and Francis Henry Salvin, *Falconry: Its Claims, History and Practice* (London, 1859), 141).

338.39–40 **Kyrie-Eleison, and Salve Regina** 'Kyrie eleison' (*Greek* Lord, have mercy) and 'Salve Regina' (*Latin* Hail [Holy] Queen) are the first words of liturgical prayers to God and the Virgin Mary respectively.

338.40 **our blood temperate and cold** see *1 Henry IV*, 1.3.1.

339.9 **the horns of the altar** the altar in the Jewish Temple had horn-like projections at the corners: see Exodus, 27.1–2.

339.33 **will-worship** worship according to one's own fancy, without divine authority: see Colossians 2.23.

340.6–7 **Heaven hath smitten . . . flock** see Zechariah 13.7, Matthew 26.31, and Mark 14.27.

340.13 **the Rock of Peter** see note to 303.2–5.

340.22 **Negatur, Gulielme Allan** *Latin* I deny it, William Allan.

340.34–36 I have not given … my charge   see John 10.1–4.

341.26–27 the Philistines   a war-like people hostile to the Israelites in Biblical times.

342.1–2 Fernieherst and his clan   the Ferniehursts were a branch of the Kerr family and often occupied the position of Warden of the Western March. The head of the family at the time was Sir Thomas Ker (d. 1586), an opponent of the Earl of Moray: he had succeeded his father, Sir John, in 1562.

342.5–11 The arms of Scotland … base birth   as an illegitimate son of James V, James Stewart bore the royal coat of arms, a lion rampant in a double *tressure* (border), with a black ribbon (*bend*) running diagonally from top left to bottom right to indicate his bastardy. When he became Earl of Moray, an honour originally bestowed by King Robert I in 1312 or 1314 on Thomas Randolph (d. 1332), the lion occupied the top left and bottom right quarters of his arms (still properly with the ribbon traversing both quarters), and the Moray arms of three cushions within a double tressure the top right and bottom left quarters.

342.27 the tents of wickedness   Psalm 84.10.

343.15 put over   endured.

343.42–344.1 distinguished … Scotland   the market cross in Melrose bears the royal arms of Scotland and the date 1645, but the cross's design is of the 16th century. It apparently replaced one in front of the abbey gatehouse.

344.2–3 an immensely large oak-tree … Druids   the oak tree was sacred to Druids (for whom see note to 12.5–6). There is no such tree in drawings of the Melrose Market Place between *c.* 1814 and 1832: *Fair Melrose* (Melrose Historical Association, 1989), 5–6.

344.5–10 the Bentang-tree … Mamre   according to Mungo Park's *Travels in the Interior Districts of Africa in 1795–6–7* (London, 1799), 22, the *Bentang* was not a tree but a large stage made of interwoven cane upon which public affairs were transacted: *CLA*, 236. In his *The Natural History of Selbourne* Gilbert White gives an account of an oak tree in the village square or 'Plestor': 'this venerable tree … was the delight of old and young, and a place of much resort in summer evenings; when the former sat in grave debate, while the latter frolicked and danced before them' (*The Works, in Natural History, of the late Rev. Gilbert White*, 2 vols (London, 1802), 1.9: compare *CLA*, 300). In Genesis 18.1–8 Abraham provides three supernatural figures with food as they rest under a tree.

344.33 De profundis clamavi   *Latin* Out of the depths have I cried [unto thee O Lord]: Psalm 130.1 in the Vulgate.

345.14–15 match-making and giving in marriage   compare Matthew 24.38.

345.24 young Bennygask   apparently fictitious.

346.2–4 Hay was but a rustic … the herald   the Hay family traced their descent to the Battle of Luncarty in Perthshire in 990. According to tradition, the peasant Hay and his sons led the Scots to victory over the Danes using as weapons the yokes from their oxen. The yoke was adopted in the family's arms as 'the instrument of their victory': Thomas Pennant, *A Tour in Scotland; MDCCLXIX and A Tour in Scotland, and Voyage to the Hebrides; MDCCLXXII*, 3 vols (1771–76, repr. London, 1790), 3.71–72: *CLA*, 4.

346.10–12 In the earliest … as now   various members of the Douglas family have been given the title Black Douglas and the name is used to distinguish the senior branch of the family from the Red Douglasses, the Earls of Arran. The 'original' Black Douglas was said to be Sholto Douglas who won a victory for King Solvathius against the Lord of the Isles *c.* 770 and was presented to the King with the words 'Behold yonder black, gray man': David Hume of Godscroft, *The History of the Houses of Douglas and Angus* (1644, repr. Edinburgh, 1648), 3: *CLA*, 3.

346.17 the humble Alanus Dapifer   the Latin title of 'dapifer', or cup-bearer to the king, was later dignified to 'Steward' or 'Stewart'. The original holder of this office, Walter FitzAlan (d. *c.* 1093), was created 'dapifer' by Malcolm III. He was succeeded in turn by his son Alan (d. *c.* 1153) and grandson Walter (1147–77), who was the first to be called 'Seneschallus *vel Dapifer Regis Scotiæ*' (Steward or Cup-bearer to the King of Scotland [David I]). This Walter was succeeded by his son Alan (d. 1204). The first Stewart monarch (1371–90) was Robert II; born in 1316, he became Steward in 1328; on his coronation in 1371 his eldest son became '*Stewart of Scotland*'. See Andrew Stuart, *Genealogical History of the Stewarts* (London, 1798), 1–9, 39: *CLA*, 3; and George Chalmers, *Caledonia*, 3 vols (London, 1807–23), 2.243: *CLA*, 1.

347.3–5   Morton...mind   see note to 336.19–20.

347.17   pull down....rooks   John Knox was reported to have said that '*the sure way to banish the Rookes, was to pull down their nests*': John Spotswood, *The History of the Church of Scotland* (London, 1655), 175: compare *CLA*, 13.

347.30–31   Peter the Hermit   see note to 311.27.

347.35   drawing his fang-teeth   a reference to pulling the venom-bearing teeth of snakes to render them harmless.

347.36   lay him under contribution   exact a levy from him; make him a tributary.

348.29   Lupus in fabula   *Latin* the wolf in the fable. The Abbot gives the plot of the first of Aesop's fables of the wolf and the lamb.

349.12   make wild work   wreak havoc.

349.17   the Knight of Wilverton   see note to 208.13–14.

349.21–22   If there be yet spirit...elsewhere   the imprecise chronology of *The Monastery* makes if difficult to tell what, if anything, Scott intends by this, but the Scottish parliament was not fully bound to Protestantism until the 'Reformation Parliament' of August 1560 which accepted the Reformed Confession of Faith, abrogated papal authority, and forbade the celebration of mass.

349.25   rescue or no rescue   see note to 290.37–38.

349.41   old Cross-stitch of Holderness   person and place are apparently imaginary.

350.1   cutters   with a play on the two meanings 'tailors' and 'reckless desperadoes'.

350.3–4   a-kin...blanket   descended from an illegitimate union.

351.7   make a composition   draw up a treaty of the terms of surrender specifying a sum of money to be paid by the losing party in a settlement.

351.34   the pride...a fa'   alluding to the proverb 'Pride goes before a fall': see Ray, 148, 302 and *ODEP*, 647.

352.19   act as her father   by giving her away in marriage.

354.7–8   the dates...histories   see Historical Note, 434.

354.10–14   Mr Laurence Templeton...summer   Laurence Templeton is the fictional narrator of *Ivanhoe*. In that novel the Saxon lord Athelstane is named as a descendant of the childless King Edward the Confessor, and in the opening chapter the peasant Gurth feeds his swine on beech mast and acorns although it is stated to be summer.

354.18–20   Captain Absolute's advice...necessary   Richard Brinsley Sheridan, *The Rivals* (1775), 2.1.32.

GLOSSARY

This selective glossary defines single words; phrases are treated in the Explanatory Notes. It covers archaic and dialect terms, and occurrences of familiar words in senses that are likely to be strange to the modern reader. For each word (or clearly distinguishable sense) glossed, up to four occurrences are noted; when a word occurs more than four times in the novel, only the first instance is given, followed by 'etc.' Orthographical variants of single words are listed together, usually with the most common use first. Often the most economical and effective way of defining a word is to refer the reader to the appropriate explanatory note.

a' all 7.39 etc.

abide await 182.37, 185.27, 192.7

a'gad O God! 147.41, 147.43

a's all is 236.7

abbot-elect person proposed to take over as head of abbey 314.32

abbot-expectant person expected to take over as head of abbey 314.9

abune above 55.43

abused worn out, consumed by use 34.13

abutment lateral support 63.1, 63.6, 63.11

accompt account 331.13

accoutrements clothes and trappings 223.42

adamant *poetic* hardest iron or steel 117.10

adieu *French* goodbye 30.13, 30.22, 42.17, 303.32

admire be surprised 24.9

ae one 53.26

aefauld simple-hearted, single-minded 148.41

afflictive distressing, painful 188.18

aff off 9.22, 304.4

afrite see note to 25.15

agape open mouthed 73.3, 269.14

ain own 9.28 etc.

alang along 304.9

alb white tunic worn by clerics during religious ceremonies 182.34, 309.31, 337.17, 343.34

amang among 19.23

an', an if 9.19 etc.

an' and 272.6

ance once 9.19, 55.31

ancient former, long-standing 289.41, 289.42

anciently from old times 251.37; in old times 255.21

ane one 3.32 etc.

anent about 7.22, 54.27

antiphonar book with responses to be sung alternately by two choirs or voices during worship 311.13

apothegm pithy maxim 277.12

arcadia ideal region of rural contentment 270.7

architrave see note to 7.25

argent *heraldry* silver or white 217.43

argute shrewd (especially in small matters) 274.21

ark see note to 300.18

arriage service by horses due by a tenant to his landlord 13.39, 125.1

artificially with special art or skill 184.5

ashen made of ash wood 98.2

aspect position of heavenly bodies as affecting the earth 168.33, 168.40

assay attempt 188.24

assoil, assoilzie absolve from sin 54.35, 172.25

assurance for 39.24 etc. see note to 39.24

attaint touch or hit in tilting 155.2, 155.40

auld old 9.10 etc.

avaunt be off! 192.18

aver beast of burden 125.40, 125.43, 307.26

avisement advice 67.12

awa away 45.17, 45.17, 54.42, 237.4

aweel well 54.18 etc.

awfu' fearful, very great, remarkable 280.7

awn own 47.13, 124.15

ay yes 19.38 etc.

aye always 54.37 etc.

babble *hunting* (of a hound) give unnecessary or excessive voice 183.11

back mount, ride 221.22

back-friend backer 284.26

back-parlour sitting room at the back of the house 9.21

back-plate plate of armour for the back 321.6

baffle confound, foil 155.10

bailie, baillie magistrate 5.14 etc.

bairn child 55.11 etc.

baith both 44.19, 45.15, 52.3, 54.37

baldric belt worn diagonally across chest for sword 158.14

ballat ballad 55.14

ballon tennis 200.18

bane bone 18.5, 44.31

bang drubbing, defeat 126.22

ban curse 42.31

bannock round flat thickish cake of barley, pease, or flour baked on girdle 95.38

barley-scone scone of barley-meal 85.40

barley-bread bread of barley-meal 85.24

barony for 11.42 etc. see note to 120.40

barret-cap small flat cap 40.24

bartizan overhanging battlemented turret projecting from a tower 237.6, 263.9

basket-hilt curved basket-shaped hilt 131.19

basnet small light steel headpiece 331.4 (see note)

bauld bold 54.37

bay *verb* bark 127.1, 146.7, 222.13

bay *noun* laurel 134.24

be by 9.43

beacon-grate metal grid covering a beacon 175.16

bead-roll list of persons to be especially prayed for 149.31

beads rosary beads 47.28 etc.

bear coarse variety of barley 33.3

beard *noun* moustache 131.14

beard *verb* oppose openly with daring or effrontery 165.1 etc.

beau-ideal *French* charming conception, height of beauty 122.14

beaver hat of beaver's fur 173.13

bedlam fit for a mad-house 282.33

bedral beadle, church-officer 9.42

beeves oxen, cattle 72.30, 102.25, 221.38, 225.13

begrutten tear-stained, lamenting 86.14, 86.41

behove see note to 51.14

beild shelter 44.41

bell-wavering see note to 74.4

belly-god glutton 239.38

belly-timber food, provisions 147.43

ben advanced in honour 126.34

bend see note to 342.10

benedicite *Latin* bless you 92.13 etc.

Benedictine belonging to religious order founded by St Benedict 13.24 etc.

benison blessing 131.27, 261.33

bent see note to 283.29

beshrew curse 102.25, 225.27, 305.7, 306.5

besognio soldier, worthless fellow 154.10

besom broom 339.22

bespeak ask for 149.31, 278.32; claim in advance 108.23; tell of 189.30; indicate 298.32

bewildered lost (in a pathless place) 146.19, 208.3

biber (plural -es) for 310.6 and 310.26 see note to 310.6

bicker move quickly and noisily 94.4

bide reside, stay 89.38 etc.

bield shelter, protect 138.20

bigg hardy variety of barley 33.42

bilboa see note to 147.37

binn receptacle for holding corn, meal, and other foodstuffs 310.17

bird-bolt blunt-headed arrow used for shooting birds 164.10, 177.8

bird-piece weapon for shooting birds 248.11

birn burnt mark on animals to denote ownership 87.36

bit denotes triviality 9.6

black-jack black leather jug 97.21;

weapon with weighted head and pliable shaft used for bludgeoning 102.12

blanc-manger see note to 148.43

blank-verse verse without rhyme 165.35

blazonries armorial bearings, heraldic devices 342.3

bleid blood 123.14

blench evade, turn aside 195.21

blink *noun* very short distance 236.9

blink *verb* shine unsteadily or dimly 187.22

block shape, style 170.14

bluff good-naturedly blunt, rough and hearty 8.36, 227.10

board table 50.17 etc.

board-end table-end 225.15

bodin provided, equipped 307.29

bodkin long pin or sharp instrument for making holes in cloth 169.11, 181.28, 183.7, 185.6

bodle Scots copper coin of the smallest value 4.22

body person 52.26, 81.35

body-servant personal servant 163.29

body-squire personal squire 164.27

bogle ghost 55.11, 304.1

boll measure of grain equivalent to six imperial bushels (218.2 litres) 13.37 etc.

bolt *verb* sift 82.41, 121.39, 134.36, 352.13,

bolt *noun* arrow of the shorter and stouter kind 166.38

bondsman man in bondage, serf 36.1, 241.14, 241.25

bonnet-piece gold coin of James V of Scotland 211.27

bootless useless, to no purpose 166.1

Borderer one who dwells near the border of Scotland and England 35.5 etc.

Border-knight knight of the Border region 18.33

Border-laird small land owner of the Border region 53.17

Border-pricker light mobile soldier from the Border region 157.26

Border-rider horseman of the Border region 53.27, 122.7, 164.34

Border-warden governor or keeper of the Border region 312.11

Bourdeaux wine made in Bordeaux,

claret 69.22, 70.15, 270.12

bower-woman chamber-woman, waiting-woman 43.34, 56.34, 236.40

brace pair 109.26

brae steep slope, hill-side 36.34, 319.30, 352.43

brake clump of bushes 93.1, 112.26, 165.17

brand sword 87.15, 163.24, 183.19; burning torch 212.33, 302.38

brangler brawler 256.34 (see note)

braveries splendid clothes 156.34

braw excellent, fine 54.16, 56.16

breast-lace corsage lacing to which ladies attached a small silk bag for money 54.25

breathed exercised, in good wind 327.25

bridge-ward keeper of a bridge 63.20, 72.4, 95.31, 95.40

brief-dated short-lived 114.25

brig, brigg bridge 9.13, 64.9, 64.12, 317.6

broach *verb* pierce for the purpose of drawing liquor 85.25

broach *noun* spit for roasting meat upon 235.20, 237.5

broad-cloth fine double-width black cloth used for men's garments 159.18

brochan thin porridge 111.5

brog prick, prod 44.10

brogue rude shoe of untanned hide 112.21

broken *Scots Law* outlawed, living the life of an outlaw 223.27

buckler small round shield 87.15, 122.38, 163.24, 230.25

buckram linen or cotton fabric 222.33

bucolical pertaining to herdsmen or shepherds 263.18

budget contents of bag or wallet, collection of stock 222.39, 222.41

buff stout leather 218.5, 218.12

buff-belt belt made of buff-leather 158.1

buff-coat stiff coat of buff-leather 101.4, 322.20

bug-bear object of dread, bane 68.24

buist mark of ownership on sheep or cattle 29.26, 29.44, 216.26

bull-baiting action of baiting a bull

with dogs 332.4

bull-rush tall rush growing near water 99.6

bull-segs bull castrated when fully grown, foul thick-necked ox 51.41

burnie small burn or stream 94.4

burr rough seed-pod or flower-head of a plant 77.13

busk see note to 45.12

buskin leather half-boot reaching to calf or knee 12.21, 165.14, 174.1, 177.11

buttery place for storing ale and provisions 102.37, 105.13, 153.3

byre cow-shed 44.9, 62.23, 262.35

byre-woman woman who looks after cows 262.25, 262.26

cabalist for 27.29 and 94.9 see note to 28.3

cabalistic for 28.3 and 293.38 see note to 28.3

cairn pile of stones built as landmark on hill (often in memory of the dead) 12.5, 47.30

caitiff despicable wretch or villain 220.31

callant lad, fellow 140.7, 140.12, 237.6

caller fresh 237.5, 237.7

callet lewd woman, strumpet 228.4

cam came 122.42

Candlemas for 56.23 and 173.35 see note to 56.23

canker-worm caterpillar that destroys buds and leaves 59.23

canna cannot 45.16, 56.4

canny skilful, sagacious 301.17

canon ecclesiastical regulation 171.15, 309.4

canticle little song 77.22; hymn 320.38

cantrip spell or charm 52.21, 54.33

canty cheerful, lively 82.4

canzonette short song or lyric 244.39, 271.1

car chariot 196.39

caracole half-turn or wheel by horseman 149.23

carbonadoed scored across and broiled or grilled 151.40

caritas for 171.34 and 310.27 see note to 171.34

carl, carle fellow 122.40, 216.25, 283.33; man of low birth, 162.41

carline witch 55.16; woman 56.32

carnal unsanctified, worldly 96.24 etc.

carriage service of carrying, or payment in lieu, due by tenant to landlord or feudal superior 13.39, 125.1

case state 159.3

casque military head-piece 111.3, 153.6, 319.37

cast see note to 124.3

castellan governor of castle 342.34

casting *falconry* anything given to a hawk to cleanse and purge its stomach 220.19

cate choice dainty 85.42, 236.29

cauld cold 19.23 etc.

caution security, pledge 284.19

cawker see note to 316.34

cellarer for 54.31 etc. see note to 54.31

censer vessel in which incense is burnt 343.25

certes assuredly, by my faith 19.32 etc.

chain-work metal rings intertwined to make net-work for armour 204.3

chalder for 13.37, 13.37, and 13.38 see note to 13.37

chalish chalice 18.8

chapter meeting of members of monastic order 104.16 etc.

charier more carefully, more cautiously 273.3

chartulary volume containing charters relating to a monastery 71.35

chary careful 225.10

chase to put to flight 27.20

chased engraved in relief 238.30

cheerer cheering drink 9.7

chimera wild fancy 79.9

chimley fireplace 20.4

chimney-nook chimney-corner, hearth 122.34, 154.14, 283.31

chirurgeon surgeon 347.11

church-feuars vassal or tenant connected to the Church 33.27

churl countryman, man, man without rank, serf 74.12 etc.

cicatrize heal, skin over 243.11

cicerone see note to 7.19

ciprus see note to 170.36

Cistercian see note to 61.30

clachan village 304.12

claiths, claithes clothes, 9.8, 320.10

clap, clapper contrivance for making grain move down mill-stones

127.12, 136.5

clecking brood 55.7

clerk scholar, one who can read and write 108.41, 126.33

clerkly scholarly 169.24

cleuch, cleugh narrow gorge or chasm with high rocky sides 43.18 etc.

cloak-pins peg for hanging a cloak on 125.5

clod-breaking loutish, peasant-like 187.20

clod-treading loutish, peasant-like 246.40

cloot hoof 44.7

cloth-yard ruler with which cloth was measured 45.32, 122.7

clouted patched 223.7

cock-horse anything on which a child rides for play 41.31

cock-laird small proprietor who cultivates his own land 56.33

coeval of the same generation 25.36, 26.3

coil row, stir 241.13

coin change physical properties by heavy pressure 210.22, 309.5

collop slice of meat 8.27, 9.5, 10.14, 10.42

commons[1] daily fare 145.18, 173.25

commons[2] common people 338.13

compeer companion, someone of equal rank 121.16, 154.8

compound settle (a matter) by payment 72.12, 312.21

conclave private or closed ecclesiastical assembly 67.7

confiteor see note to 171.17

conforming matching 203.34

conneeve connive 18.9

considerate careful 247.12

considerately carefully 247.13

constancy see note to 55.25

contribution see note to 347.36

contumacious rebellious, stubborn 47.1

convent-bred educated in convent or nunnery 45.1

convocate call or summon together 348.25, 348.31

co-ordinate of the same order 20.43

cope sleeveless hooded vestment 309.31, 337.17

copy-hold estate held by a kind of tenure relating to a manor 144.42

coquinarius *Latin* cook 172.6

coranto type of French dance 154.11

corpse-gift *probably* funeral donation 224.27

corslet piece of body-armour 41.36, 328.37

cot small house, cottage 167.12

couch lower to the position for attack 97.27 etc.

couldna could not 53.23, 95.37, 280.6

countenance composure 145.38; moral support 205.23

counter part of animal's breast lying between shoulders and under neck 65.21

countercharge see note to 16.6

countermarch march back in the opposite direction 42.12

counter-poise weight which balances another to maintain equilibrium 63.10

courser large powerful horse 149.22

couvre-chef, couvrechef linen square to cover woman's head 219.1, 318.39

covenanter see note to 26.5

coverlid uppermost covering of bed, quilt 190.13

cow-boy boy who tends cows 246.41

cowl monk's hooded garment 71.21 etc.

coxcomb conceited, showy person 134.8 etc.

crack *noun* conversation, news 10.2

crack *verb* boast 126.21

crane see note to 50.29

crave demand, need 67.12 etc.

credo creed 192.41

crest tuft on animal's head 252.34

crib appropriate a small part of anything 6.37

cricket-stool low wooden stool 237.11

cripple hobble 106.15

cromlech prehistoric structure with large stone resting horizontally on three or more upright stones 12.5

crook hook in a chimney for pot or kettle 50.28

crosier staff or crook of bishop or abbot 309.5, 309.17, 313.9

crost crossed 353.39

croupe rump or hind-quarters of a beast 106.14

crow bar of iron 282.11

crown coin worth 5s (£0.25) 274.13, 324.28, 324.31

cruize small iron lamp with handle for burning oil or tallow 254.21

crupper horse's rump 65.5, 269.9

cuddie donkey, ass 123.11

cuirass piece of armour consisting of breast plate and back plate 157.11, 321.6

cumbered troubled 320.12

cummer woman 54.22; female companion 82.5, 82.9

cur low-bred dog 222.13

curate see note to 61.25

curator *Scots Law* guardian of minor after age of tutelage 4.7

curb chain or strap passing under lower jaw of horse 308.13

curch linen square to cover head 140.40, 219.1

cushat ring-dove, wood-pigeon 109.31

cushion *heraldry* pillow-like device 342.6

custom rent, tax 312.36

cutter see note to 350.1

cuttie-stool low wooden stool (usually with three legs) 54.23

cut-work elaborate openwork embroidery or appliqué work 159.10, 159.18

cymbalum *Latin* bell, gong 171.30

d'ye do you 9.6

daffin, daffing *noun* frolic, merry-making, folly, stupidity 52.1, 272.27

dalesman inhabitant of a dale 299.15

dam-dike wall confining water in dam 264.16

darg work 45.9

de'il, deil devil 9.36 etc.

dead-set fixed 44.22

deal act 61.3, 61.11

decore decorate 201.6

decretal see note to 75.26

deer's-hair species of small rush 292.40

deevil devil 8.25, 9.13

defile narrow pass between mountains 204.39

delict offence 239.7

deliverly clever 163.23

dependence quarrel or affair of honour awaiting settlement 202.13, 202.17, 202.33

deputy-ranger deputy forest keeper 172.3

derogate fall away 187.20, 187.21

desuetude state of disuse 33.25

devote condemn 231.42, 288.34; oblige by a vow 285.35

dexter *heraldry* right 16.5

didna did not 55.22

dinna do not 10.17 etc.

dint stroke, blow 122.7

disparage dishonour 39.11

distaff for 50.26, 261.23, and 327.2 see note to 50.26

distrain levy a tax on (often by way of selling chattels, particularly for rent arrears) 160.3

dogmata dogmas 277.12

dole portion given out in charity 173.40, 178.15

Donatus see note to 178.43

donjon tower or innermost keep of a castle 214.31

dool sorrow, suffering 66.11

doom judgement, sentence 285.37

double *adjective* for 97.21 and 173.36 see note to 97.21

double *noun* evasive turn 214.16

double-piled having a pile or nap of double closeness 170.35, 201.8

douce sedate, respectable 140.10

downa do not 11.9

down-bye in the neighbourhood 125.41

downer lower 224.37

drabbing prostitution 320.42

dram small drink 19.35

dram-drinker tippler 24.20

draw-brig draw-bridge 9.10

drone non-worker, lazy idler 224.18

drum head see note to 23.17

dry-march boundary line not formed by a river or water 71.19

dry-nurse man charged with looking after another (especially one who instructs a superior in his duties) 68.20, 68.21

ducat gold coin of varying value 210.22

dudgeon kind of wood used for handles of inferior knives 177.10

duello a duel 197.27 (see note)

dulse edible form of sea-weed 27.35

dune done 55.41, 56.17

durance stout durable cloth 101.7

e'e eye 19.33
e'en evening 10.18
e'en just, even 6.31 etc.
e'er ever 125.40
eard bury 20.6
easement comfort 152.5, 160.35
ee-lid eye-lid 44.16
een eyes 123.1
effeir appertain 307.29
eke also 122.41
elbow-chair chair with elbows
    54.10, 151.2
elder former, ancient 193.43
election choice 297.43
elementary elemental 205.36
elysium place or state of ideal or per-
    fect happiness 147.8, 197.8
emboscata ambush 199.24
embrazure opening in parapet to
    allow gun to be fired through it
    181.22
empiric impostor (particularly in
    medical arts) 29.28
emulous imitative 175.22
endoctrinate instruct 180.25
eneugh enough 9.41, 45.14, 304.4
enow enough 139.18 etc.
enthralled held in thrall or bondage
    121.4
erst at an earlier time 97.27
escaramouche skirmish 337.26
essay put to the proof, test 204.20;
    attempt, try 77.12, 254.30
estramazone slashing cut 245.9
ettle aim 164.17
euphuism type of high-flown diction
    and style originating in the late 16th
    century 136.10, 136.33, 137.35,
    268.26
Euphuisme see note to 134.29
euphuist imitator of style of expres-
    sion known as euphuism 136.24
    etc.
even demean, put on a level 44.32
evidents Scots Law documentary
    proof, title-deed 71.33
exchequer see note to 17.2
excise overcharge 20.10
exordium opening of a discourse
    154.28
fa verb fall 3.32
fa noun fall 351.34
fabliau see note to 12.26
factor agent 108.22
faculty profession 151.17

faggot bundle of sticks 261.21,
    294.19
fain adjective willing 306.24
fain adverb gladly, with pleasure
    55.28 etc.
falchion sword 329.19, 339.2
falconet light type of gun 173.2
falcon-gentle female of peregrine
    falcon 203.28
fall-off, falling-off withdrawal
    247.42, 248.19
fane temple 201.4
farthing quarter of a penny 3.23,
    69.43
fasheous troublesome 235.21,
    235.23
fasherie trouble, fuss 53.17, 236.1,
    283.38
fastness stronghold, fortress 39.27,
    215.6
fause false 280.7
favoured looking 54.19
faye faith, assurance 169.38
fear see note to 97.11
fee see note to 189.36
fell fierce, cruel 35.30
fence¹ defence 117.36
fence² sword-fighting 198.12 etc.
fencible capable of being defended
    89.37; capable of making defence
    312.18
fend see notes to 44.19 and 56.14
feu feudal tenure of land by which
    tenant pays grain or money in place
    of military service 32.27, 122.31
feuar one who holds land under feu
    32.41 etc.
feu-duty annual rent paid by a vassal
    to his superior for tenure of lands
    held in feu 259.37, 304.14
fie, fye exclamation of disgust 40.21
    54.22, 54.22, 151.4
fief estate held on condition of hom-
    age and service to a superior 38.28
    etc.
field heraldry surface of an escut-
    cheon or shield, or of one of the
    divisions in the shield 217.43
fire set alight 42.37
firlot measure of dry goods equal to
    quarter of a boll (9.09 litres)
    172.32
flamm kind of custard or cheese-
    cake, or dish made from eggs, but-
    ter, and cheese 152.22

fleech flatter, cajole 132.27

flesh-fly fly which deposits its eggs in dead flesh 290.29

flighering flickering 44.15

flood water 48.22

fly-boat small boat 271.26

fool kind of custard (often mixed with fruit) 9.5, 10.14, 10.42

forbye besides 10.1 etc.

foregather gather together 9.19

fore-spent worn out already 206.32

fork gallows 99.37

former chisel 6.38

fortalice small fort 35.17 etc.

fosse grave 199.30

fou drunk 9.43

foul miry, muddy 271.36

frae from 19.35 etc.

frampler brawler 249.7

freebooter one who goes about seeking plunder 102.6, 139.36, 241.15

free-stone fine-grained easily-cut sandstone or limestone 217.10

frighted frightened 81.6

frisk frolic 147.26

frith thin scrubby wood 87.14

frock monk's long outer garment 98.4, 100.9

fulsome offensive, disgusting 320.36

fund, fand found 19.4, 20.3

fundations foundations 9.11

fury see note to 202.21

furs furze bush 86.34

gabble talk inarticulately 134.2

gad see note to 137.28

gae go 8.31 etc.

gainsay contradict 249.23

gallant fellow 54.16 etc.

galliard lively dance in triple time 136.15, 154.12, 198.10; air to which galliard was danced 258.21

gally-gaskins, galligaskins wide hose or breeches 158.8 etc.

gambado large leather boot secured by clasps 10.28 (see note)

game-cock cock bred and trained for fighting 302.43

gamut whole scale of notes recognised by a musician 137.18

gane gone 55.20

gang verb go 56.6, 237.4

gang noun right of pasturing 173.42

gar make 9.31, 86.24

garner store-house for corn 40.10

gat got 20.6, 236.35

gate, gait way, road 47.7 etc.

gathering see note to 56.27

gaul claw, scrape 139.13

gay very 86.25

gear possessions, wealth, equipment 53.29 etc.

gelding castrated animal (particularly a horse) 89.39, 283.15

gew-gaw pretty thing of no value, bauble 165.1

ghaist ghost 55.16, 238.13

ghostly spiritual 57.26

gie give 45.8

gilding golden surface 218.17

gill narrow stream or brook 127.8

girdle circular plate of iron suspended over fire on which cakes are baked or toasted 236.29

girth-gate see note to 45.37

gled kite, bird of prey 220.5, 220.18, 274.17

glegg nimble 301.14

gliff short distance 236.9

gloze comment on, interpret, gloss 61.21

gnar thick-set fellow 122.44

gombado bound or spring of a horse 184.35

good-man, goodman, gudeman husband 34.15, 44.32, 53.30

good-wife wife 34.9

gorget piece of armour for throat 41.36, 330.14, 330.21

Goshen for 32.9 and 325.37 see note to 32.9

gospeller one who preaches the gospel, in particular a 16th-century Protestant 98.16, 227.9

goss-hawk goshawk, large short-winged hawk 218.29

gossip familiar acquaintance 41.20, 64.2, 235.18, 304.19

goupen as much as can be held in two hands, a perquisite allowed to a miller's servant 124.27, 124.43

grace-cup nightcap 102.36

gratia (plural -as) see note to 310.6

green young, inexperienced 222.31

greenly simply 282.10

greensward-ring ring of grassy turf 139.11

greet cry 126.23

grey-beard large earthenware jug or jar 95.38

grey-goose-shaft arrow 123.5

gridiron cooking utensil of bars of iron in a frame used for broiling meat or fish over fire 127.32

griesly horrible, terrifying 190.38

grieve manager on a farm 5.11

grips close struggle 301.17

grist corn to be ground 121.15 etc.

grit great 55.42, 56.1, 56.1

groat a coin worth around four pennies (1.5p) 183.16, 223.19, 229.7

gross-fed coarse, inferior 187.23

grot grotto 165.40

grunds grounds 95.37

gude good 14.3 etc.

guerdon *noun* reward, recompense 267.40, 272.16, 279.1

guerdon *verb* reward 311.33

guesten be entertained as guest, lodge 235.30, 318.3

guinea English gold coin worth 21*s.* (£1.05) 6.7, 27.43

guissard masquerader 25.8

gull *noun* person easily tricked 227.13, 325.4

gull *verb* deceive 227.15

gyre weird, repulsive 55.16

gyve shackle 229.2

ha', hae have 9.36, 137.30

ha' hall 51.41, 55.43

hack-but early kind of portable firearm 173.1, 283.32

hackle see note to 189.20

hae have 9.36 etc.

haena haven't 9.19

haggis see note to 120.27

hags marshy piece of ground in moor 212.11

hail, haill whole 19.7 (see note), 44.7, 55.24, 56.9

halberdier soldier with weapon combining spear and battleaxe, civic guard 100.39, 101.32

hale free from injury 97.10

half-bound see note to 7.1

halidome holy place 38.35 etc.

haly holy 56.11

hame home 236.11, 272.3

handfast, hand-fast agree to probationary period of cohabitation before marriage 226.25 etc.

handfasting, hand-fasting act of agreement to cohabitation before marriage 226.35, 322.33

hap see note to 56.27

happer cone-shaped device for feeding corn into a mill 127.13

harbour shelter 115.16

harquebusier soldier armed with early type of portable gun 333.19

hashed cut into small pieces and reheated with gravy 7.29

hasna hasn't 304.3

hatched ornamented with engraved lines to imply shading 157.40

hatchment lines with which hilt of a sword is ornamented 218.17

haud hold 45.36, 53.22, 54.16

hauteur haughtiness 175.40

havena haven't 56.1

having possession 244.5

havings (good) manners 88.3

head-court meeting of freeholders of county held three times a year 5.9

heather-ale ale made from heather 229.40

heather-blitter snipe 55.34

heavy swollen above normal height 63.40

heckle see note to 102.17

hectic wasting 147.26

hempie mischievous unruly young person 54.13, 236.24

henchman, hench-man follower or attendant 130.36 etc.

heritor landowner, proprietor 9.16

hersel herself 56.33

het hot 42.36

heuch precipice 327.18

hidalgo Spanish nobleman of lowest class 29.12

hie hasten 7.43, 152.11, 299.43, 328.15

high-blood of noble blood 122.33

high-mall sheltered walk serving as fashionable promenade 5.23

himsel himself 53.11, 55.23

hind household servant 39.16, 50.23

hinder posterior 236.3

hirsel herd, flock of farm animals 44.7, 230.22

ho la exclamation to attract attention 226.3

hoar venerable, ancient 18.13

hoar-frost frost feathering objects with white 74.22

hob-nailed rustic, boorish 197.11

hodiernal present-day 136.12

hogshead large cask for liquor 173.36, 309.7

hold fortress 215.37

holiday-term sportive term befitting holiday 127.18

hollow halloo 204.37

holly-brake clump of holly bushes 165.17

holp see note to 147.43

holy-rood cross 44.14

horary hourly 150.8

horse-couper horse-dealer 19.33

horse-meat food for horses 88.13

horse-trick joke, trick 261.43

hose stocking, legging 75.8 etc.

hospitium *Latin* hospice, lodging 153.20

host army 126.16 etc.

hosting military expedition 126.11

house-dame wife 226.10

housewife-skep housekeeping 123.27

housing ornamental cloth cover for horse 184.33

hout-tout strong negative 53.15

howkit dug 20.6

howling dreary 206.23

humourous, humorous subject to fancies or whims 190.19, 190.42, 190.42, 336.3

humoursome fanciful 190.43

hussar soldier of light cavalry regiment 6.3, 6.38

hussar-cloak cloak worn by hussar 206.1

hustle hurry 5.41

I'se I will 8.31 etc.

ilk name, family 56.34, 127.40; each 81.38

imbrocata pass or thrust in fencing 201.23, 271.13

impeach accusation 235.5

imprecation oath 228.13

incartata foot movement in fencing where a turn is made 201.24

inch-cord cord an inch in thickness 122.8

incommodities discomfort 151.32

indented *heraldry* having a series of similar notches 16.6

indulgentia (plural -ae) for 184.18 and 310.5 see note to 310.5

infer involve 161.12

in-field, infield farmland near the homestead 33.1, 34.5, 121.20, 214.36

influence power exercised over

humanity by heavenly bodies 115.19, 167.43, 168.31, 168.41

ingenuous noble in mind, straightforward 177.24, 177.39, 242.10

ingine intellect 147.35, 333.36

instant pressing 212.32

inland *noun* part of country distant from the border 343.14

inland *adjective* distant from the border 226.29, 228.38

innovation revolution 15.14

interjected interpolated 307.14

intown land lying near farmhouse 121.2

iota very small part 314.5

ither other 55.21, 55.30, 55.32

itsel' itself 10.13

jack foot-soldier's sleeveless tunic (sometimes made of iron) 87.1, 130.38

jack-an-ape tame ape or monkey 254.13

jack-boot strong leather boot 218.4, 321.7

jack-man attendant or retainer kept by nobleman or landowner 86.40, etc

jackoo monkey, ape 29.8, 29.9

jerkin close fitting jacket or short coat 130.37 etc.

jess *falconry* short strap of leather or silk fastened round legs of hawk 218.30, 220.14, 229.25

joe sweetheart 54.29

joint-stool stool made of parts fitted together 145.17

jointure joint right of tenancy 57.41

justice-air sitting of the Scottish supreme court when on circuit 198.34

kale meal, dinner 14.3

keeking-glass looking-glass 130.40

keepit kept 55.43

kelpy, kelpie for 66.10, 66.19, and 77.5 see note to 66.10

ken know 7.22 etc.

ken-speckle, kenspeckle easily recognised, conspicuous 87.36, 87.44, 316.32

kiln building with furnace for drying grain and hops 74.2

kirk church 20.4 etc.

kirk-feuar tenant of Church land 163.35

kirk-folk church-goers 53.16

kirk-town village or hamlet in which the church is 268.33

kirk-vassal tenant of Church land 44.33, 164.32

kirn churn 318.40

kirtle woman's gown 82.19, 125.11, 125.17, 148.38

kist chest 141.12

kitchener see note to 146.13

knabe *German* boy, lad 124.39

knave boy or lad employed in service 124.17, 124.38, 124.40, 127.4

knaveship, knave-ship quantity of meal or corn payable to miller's servant 82.31, 124.41

knight-errant knight in medieval romances wandering in search of adventures 232.3

knowe small hill 236.21

kyte stomach 304.27

laird landed proprietor 5.6 etc.

laith loath, reluctant 272.36

lamp stride, prance 304.25

lang long 20.3 etc.

lang-bow long-bow 45.29

lang-cale borecole with less wrinkly leaves and of a more purplish colour than the ordinary variety 34.10

langsyne a long time ago 52.28

lap spring to one's seat 53.14; leap 140.8

lauds see note to 102.33

lawing reckoning 272.28

lay trim, embroider 45.2

lay-baron non-Church baron 121.7

leach leech, physician 76.34, 203.37

leach-craft art of healing 206.30

leaguer see note to 235.22

leddy, leddie lady 44.15 etc.

lee *noun* lie 9.40

lee *verb* lie 272.27

lenten appropriate to Lent, meagre 157.37

leviathan see note to 285.4

levin-bolt lightning-bolt 41.28

liege *adjective* loyal, faithful 172.27 etc.

liege *noun* one to whom loyalty is due 245.37

liege-lord, liege lord lord to whom feudal service is due 186.19, 240.19, 274.10

lieutenancy-meetings see note to 5.8

life-rent see note to 68.34

light-handed nimble-handed, deft 53.18

limmar scoundrel 223.19

ling heather 45.18

linstock staff with forked head to hold lighted match 145.29, 181.23

lippy measurement of grain weighing about 1.75 pounds (0.794 kg) 137.2

Lisbon see note to 11.1

list wish, desire 99.27 etc.

lith joint 112.16

lock small quantity 124.27, 124.42

lone single 81.41 etc.

loon lad, chap 44.26, 51.40; scoundrel, rogue 132.16, 305.9

loop-hole narrow opening in wall to admit light and air or for passage of missiles 64.7, 233.12

lord-priest priest with baronial authority 133.11

luckie form of address for elderly woman 8.29

lucubration product of nocturnal study, literary work showing careful elaboration 11.16

magazine armament 76.28

magnetic attractive, seductive 150.12

mail, maill travelling bag, wallet 148.10, etc.

mair more 7.22 etc.

maist most 9.37, 53.14

maister master 44.13

mak make 55.22

malaper impudent 183.29, 282.7, 316.17

man-at-arms soldier 71.22, 153.9

manege art of horsemanship 149.21

march border 250.37, 274.27, 315.25

march-treason border-treason 12.2

mark gold or silver worth 13s. 4d. Scots 52.25, 173.35, 174.25, 180.20

marry exclamation of surprise, indignation, or asseveration 102.3 etc.

mart ox or cow fattened for slaughter 34.8, 87.34

Martlemas see note to 173.36

masterfu' *Scots Law* using violence and threats 53.14

matins, mattins morning performance 197.9; for 151.27 see note

mattock tool for breaking up hard

ground 199.20, 283.24, 292.39

maun must 54.12 etc.

May-game merrymaking and sports associated with 1 May 136.15

mazer-dish bowl or drinking-cup often richly carved and ornamented 309.13

meal-girnel granary 225.12

mean low quality 66.16

meat feed 127.35

meed reward 314.4

melder quantity of meal ground at a time 82.41, 269.23

menseful neat, decorous 261.32

meridian mid-day rest 184.16

merk see **mark**

mess portion of food 57.7, 173.40, 310.6; company of persons eating together 230.1

mete measure 294.7, 294.10

mew cage for hawks 220.18

mickle, muckle much 7.39 etc.

middle-ward middle body of army 320.37

mien appearance, bearing 57.13, 67.19, 144.43, 178.3

mill-dues dues payable by tenants of estate to estate miller for grinding corn 124.19

mill-knave lad belonging or apprenticed to mill 124.32

mill-post post on which windmill was supported 137.15

mill-service certain tasks in connection with a mill laid on tenants of estate as part of their rent 125.2

min' mind 54.36

mind remember 56.17, 163.24; look after 280.6

minority rule by person under age 48.27

mint address 140.9; aspire 164.18, 164.42

misericord indulgence 184.18; apartment in which monastic indulgences were permitted 184.41

misgive fail to function 54.36

misleard unmannerly 51.40; misguided 223.3

mis-proud, misproud wrongly proud, arrogant 320.32, 349.42

mist missed 141.14

molendinar of or concerning a mill 259.26, 264.41, 338.31

mony many 20.4 etc.

moor-cock male of red grouse 55.34

mortal long and tedious 280.14

mortreux thick soup 148.43

moss marsh, bog 45.18 etc.

moss-hagg marshy hollow or pit in moor where peats have been dug 320.10

moss-trooper lawless borderer 34.20, etc.

mot must 67.1, 87.17

mows laughing matter 120.10

mud-eel young of lamprey 77.6

mug-ewe female of breed of sheep having face entirely covered with wool 9.9

mullion vertical bar dividing parts of window 7.25

multure toll consisting of grain or flour paid to owner of mill for privilege of having corn ground at it 82.31 etc.

mumming masquerade 158.17, 274.12

murrain pestilence 132.4

murrey-coloured purple-red, mulberry 157.10, 170.35, 247.3

murther murder 100.20, 239.7

murtherer murderer 238.37, 238.43, 297.17

muse wonder 243.23

mysel, mysell myself 44.18, 54.42

n'as was not 122.45

n'old would not 122.45

na no 8.29, 19.7, 19.7

nae no 9.30 etc.

naebody nobody 9.41

naething nothing 53.15 etc.

naig horse 19.34

nane none 53.20, 54.29

natheless nevertheless 41.39, 156.22, 259.25

naught wicked, evil 102.28; worthless, good for nothing 220.32

negatur *Latin* I deny it 340.22

negus punch made from sherry or port 11.1

neist next 10.16, 64.9

nicker neigh 307.30

niggard scanty 161.38

night-crow bird which crows in night (said to be of evil omen) 77.5

no not 8.25 etc

noble gold coin worth 6*s.* 8*d.* (33.3p) or 10*s.* (50p) 102.19, 102.21

noited knock 120.12

nombles inward parts of animal used for food 164.23

non-age early stage, youth 188.12

nones¹ see note to 122.40

nones² monastic service said about 3 p.m. 171.30

novice probationer in religious house 102.35 etc.

o' of 8.31 etc.

oat-bread bread made of oat-meal 319.19

obloquy abuse, slander 289.38

obnubilate overcloud, obscure 239.3

occult secret, mysterious 94.14

od in the name of God 19.41

ony any 7.22 etc.

onything anything 81.8, 81.33

or before 56.27

orderly-book book kept for entry of general or regimental orders 15.32

oremus see note to 101.18

orgulous proud, haughty 198.25

orisons prayers 292.34

out-field, outfield outlying land of farm 33.7, 33.10, 33.13, 121.21

out-lying making its lair outside a park or enclosure 164.2

outrecuidance self-conceit, arrogance 198.24

out-scourer scout, advanced lookout 319.39

out-shot *adjective* projecting 131.38

outshot *noun* extension, portion of building projecting beyond the usual line 255.17

ower over 19.35 etc.

owerloup leap across, trespass 34.21

pale bounds, jurisdiction 15.26, 345.12

palfrenier groom 320.41

palfrey saddle-horse, *especially* small saddle-horse for ladies 137.17 etc.

pallet straw-bed, mattress 161.39, 190.27, 259.1

pardoner person licensed to sell papal pardons or indulgences 222.41

parler speak, talk 134.29

paronamasia play on words, pun 303.5

party see note to 16.9

pass *noun* passage 95.18

pass *verb* make 346.36

passage move sideways 149.23

passant *heraldry* walking and looking towards the right 217.42

Pater see note to 192.40

pater-noster Lord's Prayer 294.30

patienza *Italian* patience 147.29

patrimony estate of a church or religious body 32.20 etc.

pattle small spade with long handle chiefly used to remove earth from plough 108.2

pavin grave and stately dance 198.10

pearlins, pearling lace trimming 45.12, 52.33

peat-hagg broken ground where peat has been dug 319.40

peck measure for dry goods equivalent to two gallons (9.09 litres) 87.38, 270.30

pedder-coffe pedlar 317.40

peel-house small tower or fortified dwelling 33.32

pelf money, riches 176.3

pellucid transparent, translucent 112.6

pend vaulted gateway or passage 20.2

pen-fold fold for penning sheep or cattle 171.4

penitentia for 171.35 see note

Pentecost festival of the Holy Spirit observed seven weeks after Easter 78.15, 173.33

peony-rose dark red rose 122.12

petticoat skirt, garment descending from bodice 262.33

piaffe advance the diagonally opposite legs of a horse in a showy way, strut 149.23

pinch iron lever, crow-bar 282.11

pinion wing 190.2

pink flower of excellence 147.2, 170.25

pinner woman's close-fitting cap 45.12

pip disease of poultry 90.2

pistolet pistol 319.16

pitch degree, exalted level 231.31

pith energy, vigour 301.16

pix, pyx vessel in which the host (consecrated bread) is preserved 18.8, 343.24

place fortress 42.32

plaid long piece of woollen cloth 151.1

plash bend down, weave between 65.34

plenary complete, entire, having full authority 21.3

pleugh-pettle long-handled tool used to remove earth from plough 126.39

plough-share pointed blade of plough 228.39

plover lap-wing 217.29

plump band 320.2

pock-pudding steamed pudding 236.34

poignet hilt of dagger 157.39

point indicate 225.19

point-de-vice to the point of perfection 247.26

points lace or cord used to tie bodice or to lace hose to doublet 161.18, 161.40

poldroon piece of shoulder-armour 321.7

poltroonery cowardice, laziness 299.21

pontage toll paid for use of bridge 63.23

porphyry a hard red rock 19.11, 20.31

port to carry a weapon diagonally across the body 333.19

portioner *Scots Law* owner of small piece of land 54.26, 269.23

post-horse horse kept at inn for travellers or post-riders 12.18 (see note)

potential possessing power 249.4

pot-hook curved stroke in writing, scrawl 28.2

pottinger apothecary 152.23

pouncet-box small box with perforated lid for holding perfumes 238.29

pow head 120.12

practise scheme, play tricks 239.39, 286.29

praeterite past tense 338.1

praetermit overlook, omit 244.32, 247.36

precatory 149.30 entreating

preceptor teacher, instructor 251.15

prejudicate prejudice 246.32

preparative preparation 10.40

presence, presence-chamber room where royalty or other high dignitary receives guests 248.1, 332.28

prick thrust, stab 126.17, 235.26; spur on 126.17, 137.38, 137.39

primate archbishop 68.2 etc.

prime *adjective* choice, first-rate 18.43

prime *noun* monastic service at 6 a.m. or sunrise 184.18, 184.40

prink preen 220.1

profession promise 214.11

prolixities length of discourse 188.42

proof of tested power of resistance 110.10, 123.6

proper belonging to oneself or itself 76.14 etc.

Protector see note to 39.22

prove test 117.37 etc.

prune preen 220.1

psalmody psalm-singing 77.42

psalter portion of the psalms 77.14; book containing the psalms 216.43, 305.10

pshaw expression of denial 40.21; exclamation expressing contempt, impatience, or disgust 89.34, 194.20

puir poor 44.13, 44.18

pund pound 163.38

punto-reverso, punto reverso back-handed thrust 201.23, 271.13

pursuivant junior heraldic officer 332.37 etc.

pyet chattering 137.22

quaestionarius (plural -ii) *Latin* church official granting indulgences on the gift of alms 223.42

quaff drink 95.35, 309.7

quality rank, social standing 137.8; people of good social position 20.7

quarter *heraldry* divide a shield into four portions 342.6

quarters four parts of a human body each containing a limb 198.35, 304.39

quean girl 82.4, 125.39, 228.25, 334.28

quene queen 169.37

quit-rent small amount of rent paid by freeholder in place of services due by him 32.39, 286.41

quiz make fun of 6.26

race see note to 137.26

rade rode 53.20

ranger forest keeper 127.20, 178.1, 179.15, 179.20

rank formidable, wild 139.18

rape rope 254.28

rapine plunder 164.33

rate scold, drive away 332.35

raze erase, obliterate 11.22, 73.11

receipt office for receiving tax or rent 312.36

reclaim *falconry* come back when called 220.15

rector see note to 61.24

rede counsel 259.42

rees rice 128.7

refectioner see note to 146.13

regality see note to 120.40

regent one who rules in place of another 49.43

relict widow 56.28

relish make pleasant to the taste, add flavour to 10.17; gratify 34.11; taste 151.38

rental-mail money due for rent 304.14

reveille morning wake-up signal to soldiers 6.15

revestry vestry; place in a church where clothes, records, and precious goods are kept 161.15

rhenish wine from the Rhine region 171.24

rickle ramshackle collection 127.14

riddance deliverance 101.7

ridge raised or rounded strip of arable land 33.4

riding-wand switch or whip used in riding 92.25

rifler *falconry* hawk which catches its prey only by the feathers 220.36

rin run 237.6

rock distaff, cleft stick on which flax was wound during spinning 27.2, 53.24

roisterer riotous fellow, rude or noisy reveller 136.14, 197.15

rokelay short cloak 318.31

Roman Roman Catholic 19.36 etc.

rood[1] cross 77 32, 215.43, 312.9

rood[2] measure of land corresponding to square pole or perch (5.03 metres) 285.4

rose-noble gold coin of the 15th and 16th centuries of varying value 272.41

round *noun* part of a building which is circular in shape 60.9; rung 164.17

round *verb* whisper 313.7

rout bellow 44.9

rude of little education or experience 94.33

rudesby insolent unmannerly fellow 146.6

ruff small freshwater fish of the perch family 128.7

ruffling swaggering 159.31

rullion shoe made of undressed hide 273.29

rum-toddy drink made of rum, hot water, and sugar 9.7

russet coarse homespun 177.6

rustical *adjective* countrified 136.13 etc.

rustical *noun* countryman, rustic 181.9

rydere horseman 169.36

sable *heraldry* black 217.42

sack white wine from Spain and the Canaries 228.42

sackless innocent 94.32, 94.32

sacristan officer in charge of keeping sacred vessels 58.1 etc.

sad-coloured dull, neutral-tinted 9.8, 159.11

sae so 7.39 etc.

saft soft 55.24, 263.3

sain to cross oneself as a blessing 67.1, 85.41, 93.19

sair sore, very 54.36 etc.

saker form of cannon 173.2

salvage savage 158.16

sandal any kind of low shoe 204.35, 204.37, 273.30

saraband music for slow and stately Spanish dance in triple time 258.22

sarsenet see note to 40.21

satinetta imitation of satin woven in silk or silk and cotton 201.8

saul soul 19.33

saultfat salt-vat 87.37

saumon salmon 8.41, 9.13

saunt saint 19.23 etc.

saw sow 124.14

say cloth of fine texture sometimes partly of silk, sometimes entirely of wool 318.30, 318.38

scabellum (plural -a) *Latin* low stool 151.5

scald heat to point just below boiling 50.27

scallop-shell see note to 223.8

scapulary cloak cloak covering shoulders 67.17 etc.

scathe harm, damage 276.25

scathed destroyed by fire or lightning 64.23

scaur precipitous bank, ridge of hill 37.19, 62.18

scholastic academic, pedantic 289.9

scholiast one who writes explanatory notes upon an author (particularly commentaries on Classical texts) 289.13

school university 289.27

Scotticé *Latin* in Scots 36.33

scrip small bag or wallet carried by pilgrim 91.9 etc.

scullion-boy young servant of the lowest rank performing menial tasks in kitchen 160.1

scurril scurrilous 316.22

sea-mew common gull 262.40

secret coat of mail concealed under one's usual dress 218.13

sectary adherent of heretical sect 210.38

secular living in the world and not in monastic seclusion 61.25

seculum *Latin* age, generation 61.26

self-opinion, self opinion conceit, exaggerated sense of one's own merits 103.42, 105.6, 302.21

self-sufficient self-conceited 183.6

sell self 9.20

sepulture burial 199.33, 207.19

sequels small quantity of meal or money in lieu given by tenants to miller's assistants for their services 124.44, 125.1

seraglio harem 35.23

serge durable woollen fabric 206.1

shady dark or affording shade 128.42

shame be ashamed 28.40

shape cut out or fashion clothing 352.3

shaw thicket, copse 236.22

shealing remote hut or rude shelter used by shepherds during summer grazing 36.18

shell-work crocheted shell patterns 45.2

shieling-hill, sheiling-hill knoll or piece of rising ground on which husked grain could be winnowed by the wind 276.21, 276.28, 276.39

shift provide for one's own safety and livelihood 53.17 etc.

shingly stoney 216.12, 319.4

shoon shoes 75.8

short-gown dress with very short skirt worn by women engaged in housework 262.33

shot-window casement 130.29, 130.41

show-scene beauty-spot 37.8

shrift confession to priest 59.11, 80.12

shrive hear confession 77.38, 80.9, 80.10; confess (oneself) 194.6

Shrove-tide-even period of merry-making leading up to Shrove Tuesday 315.29

sic such 44.30 etc.

sigil occult sign believed to have magical powers 161.27

similitudes similes 138.6 etc.

single *noun falconry* middle or outer claw on foot of hawk or falcon 220.13, 220.42

single *adjective* weak 173.36

single-soled see note to 125.31

single-stick fighting or fencing with stick provided with guard 30.19

singult sob 265.18

sinister *heraldry* left 16.7

sippet small piece of toasted or fried bread served with meat for dipping in gravy 128.8

skelp gallop vigorously to and fro 53.28

skiey pertaining to the sky 33.9

skirl scream, screech 280.5

skill avail, help 102.30, 272.21

slaked moistened 319.20

slashed having vertical slits to show a contrasting lining 131.15 etc.

sleuth-dog *hunting* species of hound for pursuing game or tracking fugitives 316.2

slops wide baggy breeches or hose 158.14

slot *hunting* track or scent of animal 89.4

slouched of soft material and hanging over face 205.43, 218.6

slough apparel 170.25

snaffle simple form of bridle-bit 122.6, 316.7

snatcher thief, robber 33.22

snood ribbon or band for confining the hair (particularly worn by young unmarried women) 123.3, 125.14, 125.31

so ho call to draw attention 220.17, 228.25, 331.26

so la call to draw attention 220.13, 220.13

soh gently, softly 149.28

solecism incongruity, inconsistency 273.16, 354.11

sorne exact free board and lodgings by force or threats 92.24, 92.41, 294.28

sough see note to 132.26

soupirail *French* air hole or vent 232.38

southron English, Englishman 41.26 etc.

spars particles of crystalline mineral 116.33

sparry consisting of crystalline minerals 116.45

spauld shoulder 86.33, 87.21

speer ask 9.9

spence room where victuals and liquor are kept 40.9 etc.

spindle simple wooden rod used in spinning by hand 261.23

spirituality ecclesiastics as a body 286.3

splenetic ill-humoured 31.28

splent metal armour plate 86.33, 87.21

springald youth 125.42, 172.10, 225.16

spring-lock common form of lock in which a spring presses the bolt outwards 24.25

spur-gall chafe horse with spur when riding 224.26

spurrowel *heraldry* mullet, figure of a star 16.7

spurtle sword 3.33

spur-whang spur-strap 327.22

stack-yard farm yard 143.14

stancheon upright bar 232.24, 232.41

stand suit 9.8; piece of furniture on which to stand articles 69.20

standing-cup cup having foot or base on which to stand 309.13, 315.18

stane stone 18.43, 19.5, 19.23, 20.4

staple rod of iron driven into post as keeper for bolt or hook 282.11, 282.18

start leap 34.21

stays corset 161.41

steek stitch 320.10

steel-bonnet hat made of steel 218.5

steel-cuirass breast and back plate made of steel 154.2

steer, stir trouble, disturb 44.27, 45.34

stick *noun* spear 9.12

stick *verb* stop 82.42, 160.27

stir see **steer**

stirring active 324.21

stirrup-cup parting-cup drunk on horseback 273.2

stoccata thrust or stab with pointed weapon 201.23, 202.30, 247.1, 271.13

stock tree-trunk 119.38

stocking livestock 53.32

stone-eater conjuror who pretends to swallow stones 25.8

stoup drinking vessel 69.22 etc.

straik blow 236.35

strait pressing condition 322.28

straitly tightly 291.40

streamer the Aurora Borealis 167.40

stricken see note to 105.19

stripling youth 164.14

strop strip of leather or wood used to sharpen a razor 147.35

strophe verse, stanza 189.21, 270.43

study meditate, take thought 219.18, 308.7

subscription-collection books in library supported by subscription 6.40

subsist remain in existence 339.30

sucken lands within jurisdiction of mill 121.4, 122.23

suckener tenant of district under jurisdiction of mill 124.44

suit see note to 312.18

suld should 9.12, 54.33

sumpter-mule mule for bearing luggage 146.14

supererogation good works beyond what God commands or requires 105.11

suspiration sigh 154.4

swankie smart active fellow 161.10, 175.1, 221.31, 324.37

sward turf 163.43

swarf swoon 54.41

swingeing huge, immense 124.25

sybil female prophet 279.21

syncope failure of heart resulting in unconsciousness 203.23

syne ago 19.39, 82.5

tack tenure 307.12

tangle sea-weed 27.35

tap top 46.22

tare vetch, weed growing in corn-fields 67.9, 302.5

tarn small mountain lake having no tributaries 213.9

tasker one paid by piece-rate, particularly for threshing corn 80.31, 80.39, 269.24, 274.19

task-work oppressive or burdensome work 291.27

tauld told 272.36

teind-sheave, tiend sheave sheaves paid in support of the Church 307.12, 310.34

tell for 47.28 etc. see note to 47.28

tell'd told 54.27

temporal belonging to the secular rather than ecclesiastical sphere 13.31 etc.

tenement body as the abode of the soul 70.24

tent-bed bed with canopy 5.38

terrific terrifying 192.5

tester canopy over bed 5.38

thane Scottish lord 11.42

themsels, themsells themselves 56.8, 236.13

thick very dark 20.3

thief-like disreputable 272.6

thirl jurisdiction covered by particular mill 124.37

thirlage *Scots Law* condition of servitude whereby tenants were bound to restrict their custom to a particular mill 121.2, 121.5, 124.38

thought little bit 45.8

thraldom bondage, duty 121.5

thraw twist, turn 254.28

threep contend, argue 55.2

through-stane horizontal gravestone 19.42

tike dog 54.19

tilbury light open two-wheeled carriage 16.37

tilt-yard enclosed space for tournaments 154.7 etc.

tirl strip 320.10

tissue rich cloth interwoven with gold and silver 201.7

tithe payment of one-tenth of one's earnings or goods to the Church 102.7, 102.9, 102.14, 224.27

tocher goods for a marriage portion 54.25, 122.35

tod fox 53.16

tod's-tail fox's tail 127.19

tokening sign 236.20

toll-house house where dues are collected 289.33

tourney tournament 156.41, 201.6

tower tour 9.21, 9.21

town-herd herdsman belonging to the town 33.20

traffick negotiate 156.30; deal 208.17

train line of gunpowder laid to light charge 156.26

transmew change, transmute 170.25

travail bodily or mental labour 151.16

trencher flat piece of wood on which meat was served and cut up 59.16, etc.

tressure *heraldry* narrow band 342.5

trindle-tail low-bred dog with curly tail 220.36

trow believe 10.15 etc.

truckle low bed on castors 230.42

true-penny honest fellow 132.8

trump Jew's harp 284.15

trumpery trash 254.12

trunk-hose short breeches 131.16

trunk-mail trunk, baggage 147.41, 254.8

truss tie laces fastening hose to doublet 161.18, 161.42

trustee-meetings see note to 5.8

tuilzie skirmish, fight 318.5

tup ram 44.36

tup's-head ram's head 120.27

tup's-horn ram's horn 319.24

turkey see note to 24.26

turn-broche boy whose duty was to turn spit 152.26

turnspit boy whose duty was to turn spit 132.18

turtle turtle-dove 167.8

twa two 9.18, 9.22, 19.38, 45.16

twain two 239.25, 241.11

twalscore two hundred and forty 9.11

twa-pennie twopenny 210.32

tyro beginner, new recruit 198.24

umquhile late 57.31, 124.2, 318.13

unchancy ill-omened, ill-fated 81.36

unco awful, great 301.12

unction earnestness, appreciation 276.11

un-houseled not having the Euchar-
ist administered 209.40

unrig strip of clothes 158.9

unshrieved without having confessed 209.40

uphaud guarantee, vouch for 9.24,
10.13

used see note to 125.2

usquebaugh whisky 319.27

van foremost division of military or
other force 106.10, 320.27, 332.17,
344.25

van-guard, vanguard foremost division of army 320.18, 320.28,
331.23

vassail vessels (especially of silver
and gold) 150.32

vassal one holding land from another
in a relationship of homage and
obedience 32.32 etc.

venia (plural **-æ**) *Latin* pardon, permission 310.19

venue bout or turn in fencing 202.13

veshell vessel 18.9

vesper for 66.2, 67.14, and 69.6 see
note to 66.2

vesper-service evensong 70.35

vestiarius person in charge of ecclesiastical clothes, valuables etc.
160.1

vestments garments 158.20, 203.31

via exclamation urging action
201.15; exclamation urging departure 349.16

viand food, provisions 151.41,
152.17

villagio villain, scoundrel 137.12 etc.

viol-de-gamba, viol-de-gambo
stringed instrument held between
the legs 154.15, 188.10, 188.24,
189.3

virtuoso learned person, scholar 9.8
etc.

visit punish, requite 120.24, 208.24

vivers food, provisions 152.30

vulgar common or usual language
60.36, 76.14

Vulgate Latin version of the Bible
made by St Jerome 294.40

wad would 3.32 etc.

wadna wouldn't 9.40 etc.

waeter water 9.11

wafer light thin crisp cake often eaten
with wine 152.21

wake festival 128.30, 246.42

wand whip, stick 81.38; rod, sceptre
306.41

ware cautious 127.17

wark work 54.42, 236.13, 127.35,
304.26

warld world 55.7, 254.41

warp threads extended lengthwise in
the loom 118.1

warse worse, less 19.1

warst worst 150.33

wasna wasn't 54.13 etc.

wassail, wassell revelling 222.23,
227.25

wastel, wastel bread, wassel-bread
bread or cake made of finest flour
121.40 etc.

waur worse 53.42, 237.2

wax grow 7.40 etc.

way-faring travelling, journeying
216.28

weal wealth, welfare 72.1 etc.

wean child 55.35

wear see note to 80.7

weary troublesome, vexatious 238.13

wee small, little 45.16, 53.17, 56.27,
81.4

weed garment 117.31

weel well 9.41 etc.

weel-favoured attractive, good-
looking 54.20, 54.24

weel-scrapeit see note to 235.29

weights for 54.36 and 54.38 see note
to 54.36

weis show 55.35

well-a-day exclamation of lamentation 80.5

welt frill, fringe, border 276.11

wem injury 98.3, 247.2

wend betake oneself 127.11

wester travel westward 169.8

westlandways to the western counties of Scotland 318.4

wha who 53.22, 54.33, 126.34,
235.22

whae who 54.35

whare where 52.26, 236.6

wheel spinning wheel 53.24

whiffling insignificant, trifling
164.36

whig see note to 19.35

whiles sometimes 55.20; times
82.42, 198.15

whilk which 9.21 etc.

whinger dagger, sword 254.27

whirry hurry 20.8

whisht be quiet 44.14, 45.14

whit bit 40.12, 40.12, 268.21; in the slightest degree 152.14

Whitsuntide festival of the Holy Spirit observed seven weeks after Easter 81.7

wi' with 9.22 etc.

wicket small door or gate 282.12

wierded fated, destined 168.9, 168.49

wile coax 86.11

will-worship see note to 339.33

win succeed in making one's way 45.37, 46.21

wind get the wind of 316.2

winna won't 19.32, 272.27

winnow expose grain to the wind so that the chaff is blown away 54.35, 54.38, 276.38, 294.7

wist knew 156.11

wit knowledge, learning 60.41

witch-elm witch-hazel, Scots elm 81.39

without outside 50.22 etc.

woe see note to 264.37

wold would 122.43

wonderfu' wonderful 140.11

wont custom 125.2

woof threads that cross from side to side of a web 118.1

worship honour 136.34 etc.

worshipful honourable 155.38 etc.

worth see note to 264.37

wot know 58.24 etc.

woxen swollen 61.41

wrang wrong 236.7

wrang-doing transgression 54.36

wrangler quarrelsome person 249.7

wrang-suffering ill-luck 54.37

wrest twist 210.11; deflect from the true meaning 289.25; pluck 306.20

yammer yell, howl 55.24; utter cries of lamentation 56.9

yarn-clew ball of knitting wool 300.35

yaud old worn-out horse 164.24, 164.43

ye you 9.6 etc.

yeoman-pricker mounted attendant at hunt 164.6, 172.3

yester-e'en yesterday evening 318.38

yett gate 301.12

yon yonder 35.28

youngling young man, 216.19

yoursel, yoursel' yourself 9.42, 55.30

zone girdle 353.26